THE DREAM COLLECTOR

BOOK I
"SABRINE & SIGMUND FREUD"

R.W. MEEK

HISTORIUM BOOKS

First Edition published by Historium Press

Images by Shutterstock, Imagine, & Public Domain
Cover designed by White Rabbit Arts

Cover: *Woman with a Green Parasol*
Claude Monet, 1886

Visit R.w. Meek's website at
www.ronmeekauthor.com

Library of Congress Cataloging-in-Publication Data on file

Hardcover ISBN: 978-1-962465-13-7
Paperback ISBN: 978-1-962465-14-4
E-Book ISBN: 978-1-962465-15-1

Historium Press, an imprint of
The Historical Fiction Company
Macon, GA / New York, NY
2023

for pamela

This is the truth

This is not the truth

This is the holy truth

PARIS, 1899

Dearest Bijou,

Quelle surprise! Dr. Sigmund sends us a postcard from Innsbruck where he vacations.

His important news: the book he has worked on for five long years is finished! *The Interpretation of Dreams* will be published, propitiously, in time for our next century. I look forward to reading it. He has analyzed the dreams of a great number of patients and I am more than certain that his interpretive findings will further the cause of the new science, psychology.

I do wonder, were the dreams I collected and sent to him included... perhaps disguised?

To think, he left Paris, and us, so long ago. I remember well when he first arrived at the Salpêtrière Hospital, the youthful Dr. Sigmund Freud, handsomely bearded, overly ambitious, and speaking atrocious French.

Our Psychoanalyst (for that is now his title) hopes for your continued good health. I know he would be pleased, as I, that your perseverance to work in the field of science has come to fruition. Your position as laboratory assistant, if I adequately grasp the research involved, seems a dawning to amazing possibilities. The pursuit of Nature's observable mysteries and to conquer them is a laudable goal—my ambition once, when I first came to Paris, before art found her way with me. Perhaps Art and Science are angels who dance, *pas de deux*, upon the same pin.

At this very moment, outside the gallery window, the early revelers begin to pass in greater numbers, crowding toward the Champs-Elysée to celebrate the New Year. Business is slow. Be that as it may, the paintings are my favourite company.

Do I continue to write? you ask. Yes, the occasional article for an obscure art journal, those who think I have some recondite insight into the art of Cezanne, Gauguin, and Vincent. Yes, I know you gently urge that I chronicle the year that brought all of them into our lives. 1886 was clearly the year of beginnings, of trans-formation. *Annus Mirabilis*.

But is there not inherent danger in resurrecting the past? The intricacies of our relationships, the regrets so unwanted? Hiding the heart can sometimes be the most suitable way to survive; then again, a certain Psychoanalyst once told me that memories can be the mortar which prevents us from crumbling.

Let me ponder the idea of taking up the pen.

Now please, take time from your demanding schedule and communicate. Let us have a flurry of letters between us. I'm so glad that you will be bringing in the new century quietly at the home of your employer. What a remarkable scientist she has become.

Your devoted sister,
Julie

P.S. I imagine the story, our story, might begin with an artist, a white-bearded artist in the rain.

Chapter 1

We're living in a bad season, in a vitiated atmosphere, with the century coming to an end and everything in process of demolition... How can anybody expect to be healthy? The nerves go to pieces, general neurosis sets in, and art begins to totter.

"The Masterpiece"
Émile Zola, 1886

RAIN

A Paris sky maddened with rain poured down in sheaves, pounding and flooding the streets, keeping the elderly artist rooted at the intersection, hesitant to cross. Parisians everywhere were running, holding onto their hats against the winds, darting for shelter, while Camille Pissarro braced his ageing legs as best he could, his hoary beard billowing like a tattered sail.

Fierce and unholy weather, he thought grimly, *the kind that unhorns bulls and defrocks priests. Sure to last the day and impede my progress through the city.*

Place de l'Europe was a frenzy of confusion: horse drawn omnibuses and taxi carriages recklessly galloped back and forth, sloshing up mud and manure while hordes of criss-crossing umbrellas dodged traffic. Pissarro had no umbrella, the workman's cap he wore was quite soaked and the cold travelled straight to his old bones. He dug through pockets with hope of finding spare change for an omnibus, but the five-centime coin he felt would not even put him on the upper deck.

A most unpleasant situation, he thought, *to tramp through winter rain from morning till night, weak from fatigue, from dealer to dealer, begging them to take one picture.*

"Begging, most unpleasant," he muttered to a passing umbrella then twisted to inspect his backpack, hoping the tarpaulin cover Gauguin sold him last year would protect the new landscape, and the damnable fans his wife insisted he paint for the bourgeoisie.

With a sigh and a curse, he forged across the cobblestone lake. *Damn every picture dealer! Nothing more than middlemen, ravenous wolves, who feed off the talents of the creators. And because of the new direction I take, no one even dares take a canvas on consignment, not even my supposed mentor, Durand-Ruel! I spit on capitalism!* The artist shook his fist at the sky. *Let a farmer give me four cabbages and a sack of potatoes for my picture, that would be honest commerce!*

Clutching at his cap, he focused on avoiding the splatter of passing carriages and not having them run him over. *An absurd situation, here I am, a man past fifty, husband and father of six, trotting like an old circus horse from dealer to dealer, toting my pictures and pretty-painted fans, just to scrape up enough money to return home to Eragny, pay the rent, keep the creditors at bay and get back to the real business of painting.*

Reaching the safety of the sidewalk, he realised he had an urgent need to relieve his bladder. He hurried down a narrow street, looked around, and satisfied no one would observe him urinate, he unbuttoned his fly. The artist in Camille Pissarro took to studying his stream, the arc of faded gold that splayed the wall and splashed upon tattered posters, leaving in its wake rising vapours in fugitive lustres of his favourite greys. The poster he aimed at displayed dancing can-can girls and through the mist of evaporating colours, he imagined the kick-up flounce of their petticoats and knickers could be captured in scumbled whites, their bright orange bouffants tempered with the powdery saffron he newly discovered at Tanguy's paint shop. *And yes!* came the exciting idea, *Let me brush into the rising steam delicate shades of violet, subtle half-tones—that's the key to the success of this painting!*

A feeling, a premonition, made him turn. At the far end of the narrow street someone was approaching, shielded behind a huge umbrella. When the stranger drew near, the umbrella rose, their eyes met. Pissarro's male member still splaying the wall, he tipped his cap to a young, dark bearded man. "I ask, Monsieur, can an old Don Quixote lower his lance in midstream?"

The bearded man, whose eyes were keen, laughed without losing his stride. "My favourite novel."

So Pissarro thought he heard as the gentleman passed, a German sounding French: *Mon roman plus favourite.*

He smiled to himself. *Happy are those who find inspiration in the most awkward situations. The secret lies in knowing how to interpret.*

The artist wagged away a few remaining drops, rebuttoned his fly, and wondered where he could escape the rain. Theo van Gogh's gallery, he remembered, was not too far. A chance to get dry and visit the only picture dealer he respected raised his spirits.

* * *

Pissarro peered through the first gargantuan O of BOUSSOD & VALADON lettered on the window. Not a single customer to be seen. The manager Theo van Gogh sat motionless on a gallery sofa, absolutely motionless, as though fallen into an unhappy trance.

Pissarro entered, shaking the rain from his cap, bellowing, "Armageddon weather it is! Soon people will be rowing boats down the Champs Elysée."

Startled, the young picture dealer jumped from the sofa—"Why, Father Pissarro! You are streaming wet!" He rushed to assist the artist in removing the tarpaulin covered backpack, guessing a protected canvas lay underneath.

"My feet are certainly soaked!" grumbled Pissarro.

"Come, we will make you comfortable."

Pissarro let himself be taken to an armchair of plush velvet and plopped down. "May I take off my clodhoppers?"

"Certainly! What about a warm cocoa? Or may I offer you a thimbleful of cognac?"

"Any herbal tea?"

Theo promptly disappeared into the gallery's kitchen alcove, calling out from behind the curtain. "Fate is on your side! Only yesterday Dr. Rivet gave me a new tea concoction, guaranteed to increase blood circulation."

"Rivet, good man, good homeopath. He shows us our duty, keep the fluids circulating." Pissarro pondered the holes in his stocking feet. *More darning for my wife*, he thought. *The dear woman has enough of the children's clothes to mend.*

When Theo set two steaming cups of Rivet's remedy on a small table between them, Pissarro took interest in the steam curling from the cups. *How to lock the sinewy, shredding grey into a stable design? How to link the pale tones of Monsieur Theo's hand reaching for the cup? An intermediary hue needed to hold fast this fugitive scene.*

The painting's creation interrupted. "What forces Father Pissarro out in such dreadful weather?"

Watching the cup put to near colourless lips; *will mauve work for such delicate lips?* "Monsieur Theo, might the time be ripe to smuggle another painting into Boussod & Valadon?"

Sipping tea, Pissarro kept his focus on several toes which peeked from the holes of his sock—*does my suggestion embarrass him?*

Theo smiled his sympathy, aware of the artist's penurious situation. "Getting my bosses to showcase progressive art is an unending battle. On rare occasions, I'm granted permission to put a new Impressionist painting in the mezzanine, as none can be displayed on the ground floor. They consider the colours too outrageous for respectable tastes."

"But you have managed to sell a painting of mine?" noted Pissarro.

Neither cared to mention the two years of patience in finding an interested buyer. Theo set down his cup. "Please, do show me your latest creation."

Encouraged, the artist unbuckled the large knapsack, brought out the stretched canvas and unwrapped the tarpaulin. A country scene more luminous than anything he had ever painted. Central, a farm girl, a reddish kerchief covering her head, held a shepherd's crook and leaned against a fence. A distant village of white stone houses were enlivened with tiled roofs a marvellous, bright red. He liked in particular how the rows of cabbages sparkled in the sunlight. A remarkable achievement, he thought, to create the entire scene from an assemblage of coloured dots.

Theo murmured, "Astonishing, almost blinding—is this the method Seurat employs?"

Proudly, in his stocking feet, he propped the painting on a chair. "Yes, the dot! I wanted to infuse my compositions with a deeper sense of design and structure. The dot's the answer, the purity and simplicity of the coloured dot!"

Theo picked up the tarpaulin left on the floor. "The avant garde journalist, Felix Fénéon, has coined a word for the technique, Neo-Impressionism."

Pissarro shrugged. "Neo-Impressionism, Divisionism, Pointillism, whatever `ism' is necessary to set me apart from my old colleagues."

As Theo took to folding the tarpaulin, Pissarro hoped the gesture of tidiness meant the painting would be accepted for the mezzanine. "Quite a departure from your previous work," noted the gallery manager, "a radical departure."

"I'm finished with the brushwork we Impressionists started. Now, in their hands, it's become too loose, too fluffy, too romantic."

Theo, a circumspect man, knew of whose hands he spoke, but made no mention of Renoir or Monet.

"The time has come for another leap," said Pissarro. "And I gladly admit, yes, proclaim! I've learned this new optical technique from the younger lads, Seurat and Signac." He picked up the painting and found an easel for it. "Step back, Monsieur Theo, allow your eye to fuse the dots. Don't you think it has more purity and light than my previous paintings?"

"Purity and very bright light, most assuredly."

Pissarro frowned, pushed his hands into his trouser pockets "I will be frank, Monsieur Theo, just yesterday I visited Durand-Ruel at his gallery. The man refuses to take my new work. It gives him a headache. 'Too many dots and not enough articulation,' he says. 'Your farm girl, Pissarro, has no real body, she cannot be felt.' Felt! Blazes, the man has a wife he can wrap his hands around and feel to his heart's content. I asked for twenty francs on credit, but he won't part with a sou. Can you believe it?"

Theo van Gogh was astonished. "But Durand-Ruel has pioneered your work and the other Impressionists."

"He has been my primary dealer, but now the man has nothing but criticism for the new path I dare to take. He complains, 'Nature is not as exaggerated as you now represent.' He actually scolds me, 'Pissarro, the poetry in your canvases has vanished.' What Durand-Ruel prefers is the wispy brush, romantic Impressionism, the man is wedded to it." Finding a small sofa, the great bulk of him collapsed. "All of this is so tragic, so tiring."

Theo went to refill their cups, grimly certain that his superiors, especially Etienne Boussod, would forbid such a brightly scalding painting to be placed anywhere in the gallery.

Pissarro took the offered cup, gulping down the tea, feeling renewed, "Give me your critique," he gently demanded, "for I trust your judgement."

Not his habit to speak at length about art to anyone, Theo sipped the tea and reflected. "Regardless of your new Pointillist method, your work still emits extraordinary calm, evokes a mysterious sense of life. Of all the Impressionists, it is Camille Pissarro who never fails to interlock the elements of a composition into a harmonious design. You bring, as always, peacefulness in the cultivated fields, and the hint of infinity in your horizon. This, as with all of your paintings, leaves me feeling comforted."

"Ah, my friend, you see like a poet. I'm humbled by your praise."

"Unfortunately..." Theo set the painting carefully beside the artist's knapsack, "it is far too original for my employers to comprehend. They will not let me show such a dazzling landscape, not even in the mezzanine where I'm allowed a modicum of modernity. The vigour of your pointillist brush work will be unappreciated and only baffle them. I'm truly sorry."

Pained, unable to look at the old artist, he took up the task of covering the painting with the tarpaulin.

Pissarro broke the awkward silence, "I understand. Yes, my friend, I understand only too well."   He set to putting on his boots with regret that his stocking feet were not dry.

Theo anxiously looked at the growing darkness outside, the rumbling of far-off thunder, a far worse storm approaching. "Oh, will this damnable rain ever stop?" he wondered aloud. "It's so depressing."

Pissarro began to see how thin and undernourished his friend appeared. *Much too fragile, the poor fellow, if he steps out in this kind of weather, the wind will surely blow him down rue Montmartre like a leaf. Needs a country wife's cooking to give him some heft. Inquire of his brother, that usually cheers him up.* "How is Monsieur Vincent progressing?"

"He studies at the Antwerp Academy of Art, works harder than the devil."

"I shall be very curious to see his art."

Theo shook his head. "He's not ready. Vincent still needs time to develop, to absorb and assimilate what he thinks is necessary from the Northern painters."

Pissarro, lacing his boots, murmured, "Ah, Rembrandt and the old way of chiaroscuro."

"He knows nothing of Impressionism, of coloured shadow," admitted Theo, "let alone your Neo-Impressionist work."

"Then Paris, should Monsieur Vincent come, will be a great awakening. And don't forget, I'm always willing to aid beginning artists in any way I can."

"How well I know that!" Theo brightened. "Father Pissarro's generous spirit is known to everyone. When my brother's work reveals more promise, I hope to receive your advice."

Finished lacing his boots, Pissarro stood, only to feel a wave of vertigo; he waited for the spinning room to stop, wishing he could afford holistic advice from Rivet. *But five centimes won't get me anywhere close to a consultation.* When the surroundings fell back into place, he walked carefully. By the door, he took note of a painting wrapped for delivery. "What's this, good news?" The title on the wrapping read, '*Hillside Poppies, Impression.*' "Have you sold one of Claude Monet's paintings?"

Theo handed the old painter his damp cap. "I'm sending it on a contingency basis to Dr. Jean-Martin Charcot. Hopefully, the doctor will find Monet's poppies attractive."

"What, the same Dr. Charcot who directs all the neurological experiments at the Salpêtrière Hospital, who enthrals the Paris intelligentsia with his stage demonstrations?"

"The very same."

"I've heard he hypnotizes the women who inhabit his asylum, the hysterics, and makes them perform all manner of wonderments for his audiences."

"I cannot attest to what he does on stage, but I've heard that science expects much from this re-discovered power to hypnotize."

"In his hands, an astounding power, apparently," conceded Pissarro.

"Imagine, influencing people through sheer willpower." Theo looked almost worried. "Where will this century, so quickly coming to a close, take us?"

"We shall hope that science," Pissarro grunted, as though he had no hope, "takes our superstitious society forward."

"Dr. Charcot is considered very progressive and does much to promote humane conditions for women who must be institutionalized."

"It boggles the imagination," Pissarro wrung a few drops of water from his cap, "all those damaged minds, together, at the Salpêtrière. More than five thousand women, they say, live there."

"He treats them very humanely," Theo again noted, "and has instituted many progressive measures. Within the Salpêtrière confines, the women can work outdoors, tend to vegetable gardens, fruit orchards, and the like."

Pissarro placed his cap squarely on his head, looked down at the wrapped Monet. "I gather your Charcot is progressive enough to risk purchasing an Impressionist painting?"

"Well... not exactly," Theo van Gogh demurred. "He has an art advisor with an open mind to the modern, who hopes to pry the good doctor from his traditional taste in art." Theo shrugged. He was accustomed to clients without taste. "Let's wait for his appreciation of our Monet."

"This art advisor... perhaps... can be shown a few landscapes of mine?"

"At the first opportunity! We still have your superb '*Peasants Gathering Apples*' upstairs in the mezzanine."

"In my old, worn-out Impressionist style," grumbled Pissarro, "but it will suffice as a first sale." His hand on the door latch, he thought to ask, "Just who is this fellow who lays claim to being Jean-Martin Charcot's advisor? Monsieur who?"

"Not a Monsieur," Theo corrected, "but a Mademoiselle."

"All the better!" declared Pissarro. "Women are more receptive to embracing new styles, be they fashion or art."

"Her name is Julie Forette and she appears quite receptive to Impressionism."

"Ah, a good omen, the name Julie, the same as my dear, long-suffering wife. Your Mademoiselle certainly shows her keen eye by choosing a Monet."

"Actually, she came to the gallery in search of art by Cezanne."

Pissarro's eyes narrowed. "Now, that is interesting."

Theo looked glum. "I had to confess to her that I possessed no Cezannes. Can you imagine Boussod or Valadon letting me show his work? If your paintings remain difficult for them, a landscape by Cezanne would be impossible for them to understand."

"The Sphinx certainly follows his own path."

"Have you seen him lately?"

Pissarro hesitated to reveal anything. Cezanne's bizarre note had been delivered to him this morning.

The gallerist observed Pissarro's discomfort. "I ask only for the young Montmartre artists who keep popping in, dead-set on finding their new hero. Students from Cormon's literally camp out at Tanguy's paint shop, where his work appears in the window, waiting for him."

"Cezanne, believe me, would be extremely unnerved to learn that he has such a fervent following."

"But where on earth does he hide?" Theo wondered aloud.

Pissarro could only contemplate the rain, giving his long, straggled beard a tug. "You know how secretive Paul likes to be. He gives his address to no one." Cezanne's note in his breast pocket felt like a pressing weight against his heart. "Between you and me, sometimes I think that our Paul is... well... not quite balanced."

"Whoever pursues art is a little touched."

"True, true..." He could only agree as he turned his attention toward the flooding streets, an unhappy prospect. While adjusting his backpack, Theo brought him an umbrella—

"Left here a long time ago."

Pissarro stepped outside, opened the umbrella, and wondered why Theo closely followed... until he felt the money, twenty francs, pressed into his hand.

"Monsieur Theo, no, you needn't, no, really..."

He ignored the artist's protest. "You must consider it an advance."

"Of course!" Pissarro pulled him under the umbrella. "Those apple pickers in the mezzanine are bound to find a new home soon."

"I'm sure. The painting would look wonderful in anyone's home."

Awkward under the umbrella, both men listened to the steady drumming of rain. *No words to suit this damn generosity*, thought Pissarro. *Best to get on with the business of trying to sell this painting yoked to my back.*

"Now Monsieur Theo, you will catch your drowning death out here."

Urging his benefactor back inside the gallery, Pissarro hurried off toward rue Lepic, the next gallery stop, determined to convince the dealer

Petit of his painting's worth. *Persistence, that's the ticket! Hold your ground, old fellow; keep prodding all of them, lest they forget you altogether.*

He tucked the twenty francs deep inside his breast pocket, next to Cezanne's troublesome, nearly incomprehensible note. Tomorrow he must get to the bottom of it all. *But this rain, pouring, relentless, will it ever stop?*

Chapter 2

We must not overlook the influence of memories, most from childhood, which have been suppressed or have remained unconscious...

The Interpretation of Dreams
Sigmund Freud

JULIE'S MEMORY

Father, a bibliophile, shepherded Bijou and I and not our brother to books. He brought them back from the far corners of his sea travels. Our house, crammed among other run-down houses along a shoddy street near the port of Marseilles, thus boasted a worldly library. Before my sister and I could even read the books or reach to the top shelves we fell under their spell, fully seduced and enchanted by the mystery of their undecipherable print. Our older brother, Justin, abhorred books, never getting near the library. He couldn't stand "the stink" of them, he said. My sister and I, when too young to know that schools existed, easily learned to read. We read and read and read.

* * *

My sister, at age twelve, developed a passion for ancient Egypt, which occurred after our father inundated the library with books on Egyptology. Her fervor for things Egyptian was soon followed by a fierce resolve to master hieroglyphics. Our local bookseller in Marseilles, who had many dealings with Father, happened to be part Egyptian and part Indian. Monsieur Prasadaba gladly assisted my sister in her pursuit. I could only marvel at how quickly, almost effortlessly, she accomplished her goal. She spelled out all the names of the family in hieroglyphs.

One day, after poring over the Egyptology books for months on end, she marched into our room, plopped down on the bed we shared, and announced, "You, Julie, lived a former life in Lower Egypt."

Millenniums past, I had been—she deduced heaven knows how—a scribe. Possibly—she was not yet certain—I was once reincarnated as the "Scribe Heti." Lending legitimacy to her hypothesis, she thrust a picture book before me, showing the scribe, a look of gentle wisdom chiseled and captured in his face, seated cross-legged with a blank tablet across his knees, poised to write, aeons ago, the first word of his king's history. She tapped her finger on scribe Heti's shoulder, as though to urge the image to speak and confirm her intuition.

"Julie, you must see the physical resemblance, despite the difference in sex, his and your narrow waist branching up to square-like shoulders, then the same prominent cheek bones. Of course, your breasts are a little larger." She had me laughing and blushing. We were adolescents. She educated me further, "When our souls reincarnate, we can choose to be either male or female."

She pointed to another picture in her book. The beak-face Thoth, she said, was the god of letters, and my personal god.

Playfully pushing her back onto the bed, I chided her for yet another flight of fancy and left to help our mother in the courtyard. Mother washed laundry for others and I was her assistant.

Later that day my sister strolled into the courtyard to keep me company while I scrubbed clothes clean on the washboard, delegated to do the petticoats and undergarments.

She sat down between the iron tubs to share another discovery. "Julie, the letter J is the hieroglyph for snake."

Perturbed, perhaps a little anxious, I asked, "What does that portend for me?"

She enjoyed explaining what she learned: "The snake, according to ancient Egyptian cosmology, is the seeker of knowledge."

With my arm I wiped off sweat and huffed, "The snake is a slimy creature who crawls in the muck." It displeased me, that my first initial meant snake.

Undeterred, she continued, "Sister Celeste says that snakes, prior to being punished, pranced in Eden."

My sister attended a Catholic School, ruled by nuns ordained in the Order of the Sacred Heart. As older sister, I was ordained to stay home to labor beside mother in her laundry business.

"Snakes pranced? Oh, really now!" Scoffing at her belief in the nuns' fabricated nonsense.

"It was the snake's primal ability," she stated quite seriously, "to stay erect."

"I get it." I made no attempt to hide my sarcasm. "As punishment for tempting Eve to eat the apple, the snake slithers instead of dancing."

"Prancing," she corrected.

"Poor snake."

She nodded solemnly. "Yes, for imparting too much knowledge, too soon."

At age twelve, did my sister speak so perspicaciously? Were the words 'imparting knowledge' and 'primal ability' part of her vocabulary? Or does adoration for one's sister enhance such memories?

But the idea she planted—Julie, the ancient scribe—began to work its way into my consciousness. I would leaf casually through the Egyptology books, in plentiful supply, and catch myself admiring the many Egyptian gods who bore the fanciful heads of falcons, crocodiles, and baboons; but Thoth, ibis-headed, was the god who mesmerized me. Sometimes he held in his hands the tongue and heart of Ra, the sun god. More often, Thoth stood, feathered stylus in hand, poised to write on his tablet. Within the pantheon of Egyptian gods, Thoth seemed very important. He was the record keeper for the deities, especially the mighty Ra.

The notion that I, Julie Forette, bereft of formal schooling, could be a scribe embarrassed me, yet like the obsessed lover who cannot restrain from touching her beloved, I could not stop from caressing the idea that I might be destined to write, to chronicle like Thoth.

Chapter 3

**I, carried on the wings of two leaves of coca,
went flying through the spaces of 77,438 worlds,
each more splendid than the one before.**

Paolo Mantegazza, neurologist,
1859

MORE RAIN

I

Keen to conduct the experiment, Sigmund Freud brought out the newly purchased Burq dynamometer. The French merchant had shamelessly overcharged him for the instrument, but he had become accustomed to the mercenary character of Parisian shopkeepers when it came to foreigners.

In the centre of the dynamometer box a large glass dial made it easy to read the compression strength, so he gripped the spring-metal clamp and squeezed. Exerting all his strength, he managed to raise the dial to reach 34 kilograms of pressure which he logged in his notebook.

The next step in the experiment was to pour out half a glass of burgundy. He then chose the .07-gram packet of crystallized cocaine Parke-Davis supplied for testing, having advised the American company to send him their purest grade, that is, if they hoped to successfully compete with their pharmaceutical rival, Merck. He noted that their hydrochloride crystals dissolved exceedingly well with the wine.

Settling into an armchair, badly worn, he surveyed the shabbiness of his furnished room, the hideous floral wallpaper was beginning to peel, hanging in coils, and last night he was certain that he heard mice scuttling from one place to another, but cheap lodgings were a necessity if he wished to economize on the 300 gulden travel grant awarded him by the Vienna General Hospital. Sigmund wanted to stay as long as possible in Paris. The Salpêtrière Hospital and Asylum had so much to teach an ambitious pathologist.

He took the first sip, as would the connoisseur, letting the cocaine infused wine linger and roll over his tongue—swallowing, he felt the strong alkaloids peppering his throat.

"Prelude... prelude..." he murmured with a smile, waiting.

When a wonderful warmth radiated through his chest, he grew eager for the full effect and finished the remaining mixture in one greedy gulp, closing his eyes to savour cocaine's steady progress through his bloodstream, distributing the coca leaf's magic power. Soon he felt inside his head a tremendous, pulsating heat where billions of neurons must be lighting and firing. He gripped the arms of the chair—it came, an explosive rush of lucidity! Then bliss!

The extraordinary sensation of lucid bliss. He saw, he heard, he understood... *the nature of all that is!* Quickly jotting in the notebook:

The rain strikes the window, each pellet upon the pane I distinguish, I count them 1, 2, 3, 500 to 1,000, 7,001

He stopped to laugh at mathematics. *What need I of additions, subtractions, divisions when one gains a glimpse of totality!* A thunderclap rattled the hotel window—*Zeus claps and booms into the room,* he laughed again, *and we gods collude!*

"My word, my word!" Sigmund slapped his thighs. "Such extraordinary joy!"

Far too exuberant for inaction, he jumped up and stalked the room to acclimate himself to the new-found energy.

The dynamometer! Rushing, seizing the copper clamp, he pressed his super strength into the measuring device, the red needle jiggled, fighting back. He squeezed harder, inculcating more strength, until the needle began its reluctant ascent, the arrowhead arcing to 36, 37, to 39! A new gain! Five more kilograms of pressure! The results, indisputable!

The Parke-Davis people in Detroit, Michigan will be pleased. In the boardroom the American entrepreneurs will stand and applaud. Yes indeed, Mr. Freud's findings prove cocaine increases muscular strength.

The Olympian gods applauded as well with more rumbling thunder. He donned his frock coat, top hat, and ran out the door—only more adventures awaited him at the lecture hall!

* * *

Umbrella aloft, he hurried across Paris to the Salpêtrière. Happily fighting the wind-driven rain, he deduced if the effects of Parke-Davis's cocaine held strong for more than four hours, he could publicize the benefit for the company and finally be financially rewarded for his two years of research with the drug.

Down the length of the narrow alley a white-bearded old man was urinating the walls with liquid gold. Wearing the rumpled clothing of a tramp, the good fellow tipped his cap to him: "Don Quixote has his lance, Monsieur, but so too Sancho Panza, and we find relief where we can."

Euphoric, Sigmund tipped his hat and he thought he heard old Sancho say, 'There will be more bliss, much more.' *Il y aura plus de bonheur, beaucoup plus!*

At the corner of *Boulevard de l'Hopital*, far ahead of schedule for Dr. Charcot's lecture, he stood content under the umbrella and gazed admiringly at the enormity of the Salpêtrière. Behind the walls he knew that there was a city, a complex of streets, shops, houses, teaching hospitals, outpatient clinics and numerous laboratories conducting neurological research. The greater part of Salpêtrière were the resident wards which housed well over five thousand patients, all women.

The fellowship allowed him to study here for two months. His first week, so far, had been spent either in the pathology laboratories or in the medical library. He hoped soon to meet Salpêtrière's Director, Dr. Jean-Martin Charcot, who was considered by all neurologists in Europe and America as the leader and pioneer in the science of neurology.

"Meet him I will," he said under his breath, for it was Sigmund's chief reason for obtaining the internship.

Checking his pocket watch, he decided to present himself early for the Friday lecture. *The great man might very well take notice of me in the front row.* The umbrella held high, he jumped the puddles across the boulevard with the ease of an athlete, and among the many arched entrances along the immense brick façade, he quickly found the Mazarin gate which led to the lecture hall.

II

A yellow placard placed on an artist's easel announced the morning program:

The Mystery of Hysteria

A Demonstration

by

Dr. J.M. Charcot

Shaking off the rain, Sigmund deposited his hat and umbrella with the cloak attendant and proceeded directly into the amphitheatre. The hour not yet nine, he found to his amazement a tightly packed audience numbering in the hundreds, a noisy din, every visible seat occupied. There were clusters of distinguished physicians and eminent professors, some of whom Sigmund recognized from the laboratories, and legions of boisterous medical students. Most of the amphitheatre, however, had been taken over by the elite of Paris, gentlemen elegantly attired and row upon ascending row of women in fluttering, feathered hats, everyone gaily chatting, laughing. Here, Sigmund observed, were the wealthy, the influential and the intellectually curious, all cognizant of Dr. Charcot's radical experiments with his patients, all expecting another of his neurological miracles to unfold.

Sigmund stirred himself to climb the stairs, searching for a vacant seat, and found fellow interns in the last row who made room for him on their bench, so he too joined in the eager wait for their renowned Director to appear.

At the simple tinkle of a bell, all fell dutifully silent. Behind Sigmund, hand-cranked machinery ignited a limelight onto the stage curtains. People hunched forward, the swaying of feathered hats grew still, and not a person dared make a sound.

From a side wing he marched across the stage, sixty-one-year-old Jean-Martin Charcot, attired in a black, high collared cape. Reaching centre stage, he confronted them, clearly a man of self-assurance, and undid the tassels of the cape with deliberate ceremony, a signal for an assistant to run on stage and quickly carry it off.

The doctor's hair was dark, silver-streaked, and fell long behind his ears. He was plump, well-fed, thought Sigmund, and surprisingly short.

Yet what the newspapers said was true, he bore an uncanny resemblance to Napoleon, possessing the same brooding brow, the same aquiline nose, and in his bearing something inherently regal.

Raising his hand, as an emperor might, a whoosh of bright light enveloped him. He looked severe, lips grimly pressed, as though to give stern warning to everyone: 'This morning shall be dedicated to the pursuit of scientific knowledge with no room, none whatsoever, for the faint-of-heart.'

While the audience waited, perhaps imagining themselves brave-hearted, he refused to utter a single word, offering nothing but the legendary power of his hypnotic stare. Once assured that every single person remained captive, a gradual sadness settled into his eyes. 'I have endured, as each here, much suffering in life,' the tired, grey eyes seemed to say. 'Knowing too well the purgatories into which we mortals sometimes plunge.'

Jean-Martin Charcot then whispered one question: "What is hysteria?"

The theatre fell so quiet that Sigmund heard the steady hiss of the gas lamps and the unrelenting rain striking the cathedral windows. People shifted uneasily, their wooden seats creaking. Charcot walked to the side wing, pulled a gold tasselled rope, and the curtains parted. On stage, illuminated by intense spotlights, were two seated men, obviously patients, secured to the arms of chairs by leather straps, both men squinting and blinking wildly into the glare.

Charcot came behind them to place a paternal hand on each of their shoulders. Sigmund, still benefiting from the heightened effect of cocaine, saw a religious tableau, a Godhead trinity, or was it Christ flanked by two crucified thieves?

"I ask again!" his fierce challenge rang out. "What is hysteria?" When satisfied that no one possessed the medical wisdom to answer, he smiled. "A daunting question, yes, worthy of the Sphinx."

Sigmund noticed two rows below him, a woman singularly hatless, busy writing. He leaned forward, puzzled that her notebook seemed filled with nonsensical markings.

Charcot spoke: "Greek in origin, the word *hysterikos* means uterus."

The word, in English, appeared on the woman's page:

uterus

Loose auburn strands escaping from her upturned hair, near the nape of an elegant neck, delighted Sigmund.

"Thus the myth persists that hysterikos, the heightened state of emotional instability we call hysteria, is peculiar to the female sex. However, I give fair warning that after today's demonstration" —he patted both men's shoulders—"you will acquire the habit of speaking of hysteria without linking your thoughts to the uterus and the female sex."

Leaving the men, Charcot paced the stage, hands behind back, pacing as though he needed to harness his daring ideas. A journalist once described the doctor's restless energy: "Like our little Corsican general reborn, he struts the stage, brow furrowed, weighing his military options. We, devoted troops. cry out encouragement: 'Jean-Martin Charcot! Our Napoleon of the Neurosis! We follow thee to battle!'"

Charcot returned to the captured patients. He approached the elderly man, a scrawny fellow whose protruding wisps of side hair give him a clownish aspect. He noticeably trembled, his legs especially shook. Sigmund diagnosed a neurological disorder. *In all likelihood a chorea from a lesion near the medulla oblongata.*

Charcot questioned him, "How fare thee this morning, Monsieur Gugère?"

His entire body commenced to shake more violently. "My full name, beg your pardon, is Jean-Martin Gugère." His knees were continuously bobbing, his feet uncontrollably stamping the floor. "The very same baptismal name as Monsieur himself, Jean-Martin!"

"Why, *c'est vrai!* " A true fact," declared the doctor. "So how are you, Monsieur Jean-Martin?"

"As best as one can expect, Monsieur Jean-Martin."

Ripples of laughter ran through the amphitheatre.

"Yes-yes, a little humour is medicinal balm for the soul," Charcot conceded. "Now, Jean-Martin Number Two—which is what we will call you, to liberate our audience from confusion—why don't you stop your shaking?"

"Alas, Jean-Martin One, I cannot. Such shakes are now my burden since the cholera attack last winter. The good doctors say a lesion of the nerves is my sickness."

"So! You are afflicted with the convulsive disorder known as chorea or, as we commonly say, St. Vitus' dance."

"*Bien sûr,* Jean-Martin One, it is my misfortune."

Charcot approached the other strapped-in patient, a young man who might have been twenty or twenty-one, his left arm and hand grotesquely crooked. "Your name, Monsieur, and explain your malady."

Apparent to everyone, a side of the young man's face sagged, causing him extreme difficulty to speak. "M..ma.. my name is H..He..Hen-ri. And I ca.a.n't mo.o.ve an.y.thing on-the-left-side of..of..my body, ss..ssir."

"And why is that?"

"S.s.s.since...the fall."

"Explain yourself better."

Henri struggled and stammered through his story. "Hap..hap..pen cup..ple weeks ago..." A railway worker at the St. Lazarre Station, he slipped from a cross-beam, falling onto the rails below: "Twen-tee me-me-meters, sir."

Sigmund had seen such debilitating cases of hemiplegia at the Vienna Hospital. He watched with increasing curiosity as Charcot signalled an assistant to unfasten the restraining straps of both patients.

"Perhaps, a question preys upon some minds in the audience? 'But Dr. Charcot, aren't these patients bound because they are dangerous?' No-no, not in the least. Our restraints exist solely to protect them from falling and injuring themselves."

Politely, he invited Henri to stand. Not a few spectators winced as the young man struggled to push himself from the chair, his left leg grossly bowed and his foot twisted inward, but the hemiplegic persisted until he stood.

"Lift your right arm," commanded Charcot. Henri raised the arm high in the air, beaming his pride to the audience. "Now, young man, raise the left arm."

Henri frowned. "Ca-a--n't do-o it, s-s-sir."

Charcot seized and raised the twisted hand for all to absorb the deformity—less a hand than a claw. When let go, the arm resumed its crooked position. He gave Henri a strangely cold smile before turning to the audience. "Many of you saw this same young man at last Friday's lecture, just days after his fall. I told you then the importance of treating these contractures as soon as they appear; but we have made an exception to our own rule—waiting a full week without the slightest intervention. 'But Dr. Charcot!' you protest 'How in good conscience can you wait and allow this young man's deforming contracture to worsen? Are you some sort of monster?'"

Charcot straightened, his manner knowing, and came to the edge of the stage, as though prepared to face any accuser. "You," he wagged an admonishing finger and Sigmund in the last row felt certain that Charcot had singled him out. "Must learn to distinguish which disorders are neurological in origin and which are produced by—yes—hysteria! 'But Dr. Charcot!' you still object. 'Hysteria is a woman's disease and plagues only them.' I reply: 'Let your eyes, today, become the dispassionate lens of the photo-camera!'"

Two assistants clad in surgical aprons marched on stage, one to set up a folding chair for the doctor, the other to hand him a cloth-covered mallet and a disc-shaped gong. Charcot sat facing his patients. "Look nowhere else," he gave the stern command, "but into my eyes—and listen."

Three times he loudly struck the gong, an exquisitely orchestrated scene that enthralled Sigmund. As the vibrating rings slowly subsided, Charcot's soothing voice entered. Their eyelids were growing heavier, heavier, and heavier. Jean-Martin II closed his eyes first, his head dropped, and young Henri soon followed, both in a deep sleep.

He hypnotizes in mere minutes! Charcot's famed technique was what urged Sigmund to Paris, to the Salpêtrière. The Director stretched out his arms as if to prove he had no tricks up his sleeves, asking the audience with mock alarm, "But how are we to be certain that these gentlemen are hypnotized? 'Maybe' you are tempted to say, 'we are witnesses to a clever hoax and old Charcot is nothing but a charlatan.'"

Strolling confidently down the proscenium, he leaned toward a woman in the front row. "Madame, may I say, What a magnificent chapeau!" The hat was preposterously large, bedecked with artificial flowers, stirring Charcot to a shower of compliments. "Such an attractive array of anemones and hardy chrysanthemums, all in delightful bloom. Perchance, one hat pin is planted in your garden to borrow? Or more apropos to my purpose, perhaps two?"

Blushing with pleasure, the lady took from her hat two pearl-tipped pins. Charcot raised them high, one in each hand, for all to see. Sigmund thought them sufficiently long to be lethal.

Charcot returned to the slumbering patients, whose heads remained bowed, and issued a new command, "Open your eyes, gentlemen, and extend your right hands, palms up! Keep them absolutely steady and you will each now receive a shiny gold Louis!" Whereupon he gripped the wrist of Jean-Martin II and without hesitation plunged hat pin into palm. Breathless gasps sounded throughout the amphitheatre as half of the pin emerged from the other side of the hand. "Now, dear fellow," Charcot counseled, "don't spend your gold Louis all in one day."

Jean-Martin II gazed at his pierced hand, a silly grin on his face, as though he had received a delightful gift. Sigmund observed that the old man no longer trembled, his affliction seemingly forgotten.

Gingerly, Charcot moved to the semi-paralytic Henri, took his right palm, and repeated the violence, a quick thrust, and the pin passed clean through until stopped by the pearl tip.

Neither man exhibited the least hint of pain. When instructed to display their gold coins, both proudly extended pierced hands. Charcot swiftly withdrew one pin then the other.

An assistant reappearing brought out a silk pin cushion for Charcot to insert the hat pins, the theatrical performance that so many came to see. He went to each of his hypnotized subjects and held up their hand—"Behold! Believe your eyes! No blood."

How could such a phenomenon be anatomically possible? Sigmund wondered. *How would Charcot explain?*

"What we have engendered in these men is a condition of consciousness I have named the hypnoid state—a discreet, morbid state where sensory stimuli, no matter their nature or degree, can be completely altered through suggestion. Cold felt as heat, say, or heat experienced as cold. Additionally, as you witnessed for yourselves, pain, no matter how severe, can be commuted to pleasure. Perception, topsy-turvy, *n'est-ce pas?*" Charcot then spoke with greater gravity. "Gentlemen, colleagues, and ladies—we have entered a neurological netherworld where the traditional rules of anatomical stimulus no longer apply."

He leaned into young Henri's ear with a gentle instruction to close his eyes. "Dear Henri, you now are feeling the many, many knots in your limbs untying themselves, loosening... the stiff crookedness of your arm and hand are returning to normal, the twisted tightness of your foot is no more; no more." Charcot stepped back. "Henri, you are whole; renewed; eager for action!" Loudly he commanded: "Walk to me! Eyes open, lad, and walk!" Charcot took small steps back. "Walk!"

Such a command confounded Sigmund, seemed cruel. *Why, the boy is paralyzed, Dr. Charcot, pure and simple, incurable.*

Henri opened his eyes. Slowly he rose, his first steps toward Charcot cautious. The realization suddenly came to Henri—"Merciful God!"

He now walked as any normal man! The audience and Sigmund were amazed witnesses. Henri's grotesque contractures had completely vanished. Henri had been cured!

A cursory nod from Charcot prompted the assistant to extract the hat pins from the cushion and put them gently in Henri's healed hand. As though a conductor, Charcot gestured for the lady with the enormous flowered hat to rise.

"Henri," came his hypnotic suggestion, "the rightful owner of gold coins stands in the front row, please repay her, then return."

Obedient, Henri relinquished the hat pins, "They be a tidy sum, Madame, but they be yours." Bowing courteously, he walked somewhat mechanically back to his place.

"Without going to Lourdes our young man may well have been cured of hemiplegia!"

Charcot smiled satisfied and turned his attention to Jean-Martin II. The poor fellow stood trembling more violently than ever. One heard Charcot's lulling, sing-song voice: "Oh Jean-Martin II, is it not cold in here? So cold, everywhere, so cold.... feel the snow falling... cold white snow falling on you, white snow falling all over you, your eyelids, your lips, your face, falling, tingling... cold crystals of snow upon your arms, your legs, cold crystals sinking into the veins of your skin, into your blood, thicker and thicker, ice crystals, colder and colder. No longer, Jean-Martin II, do you shake, no longer do your limbs tremble... icy snow stills all suffering, all is still... open your eyes." He opened his eyes to Charcot's hand raised as though to strike him down—"Jean-Martin II! Be still! Here and now, be still!"

People from the audience exclaimed: "Unbelievable!" "Incredible!"

A man afflicted with severe palsy standing straight, still, as firm as a tree, the man responsible unable to hide the pleasure of his success. "No, you are not a witness to miracles; I am not God; I am but a man who, as you can see"—he patted his plump belly—"has a fondness for food. No, my friends, what has transpired can be rationally explained."

Sigmund listened closely.

"True, this man's palsy—what simple folk call St. Vitus' Dance—occurred after a severe bout of cholera. And our railworker, Henri, developed hemiplegia after a fall. But these abnormalities were, in actuality, the result of brain trauma. Let me elucidate: now, could Henri's fall, which authorities measured less than fifteen feet, result in the serious neurological damage he displayed? Could such a minor fall, with trifling bruises and abrasions, cause grievous injury to the nervous system? Possible, yes, but I would not affirm it. As for Jean-Martin II, can cholera cause an uncontrollable palsy? I find no record in medical science of this being the case.

"Another factor then must be considered which would produce these neurological anomalies. And that is the emotional terror which the trauma engenders, which found expression in Jean-Martin's chorea and in Henri's hemiplegia. This condition, peculiar to both men, I have named, 'Hysteric Traumatism.'"

Sigmund was exhilarated. Like the Biblical Adam, he bestows names to the unnamed. *Such a man can only be described, a genius!* He then observed Charcot whispered to each of his cured patients and turned to the audience:

"Gentlemen, colleagues, ladies! The demonstration proceeds! Let us de-hypnotize our subjects completely." His single handclap awakened both to full consciousness. "Jean-Martin II, Henri—observe yourselves!"

Wordlessly amazed, both men found their afflictions had vanished. The old man, beside himself with emotion, cried out: "You are like Christ!"

Charcot walked away to the left of stage. He allowed himself to chuckle as the young medical students, grouped in the upper tiers of the amphitheatre, began stamping their feet.

It was a rowdy appreciation for their hero and his mind-defying demonstration. Hurrahs! and Bravos! sprang from everywhere. The uproar mounted until the maestro lowered his hands to orchestrate them to silence —

"No-no, remember my earlier statement, I am not the Almighty..." His smile was wistful. "I am only too human. We might say, if we lived in Medieval France, that I have exorcized devils from these men; but we live in modern times; if I'm not mistaken, 1886."

Then, unexpectedly, he turned to his cured patients and suddenly clapped, deliberately, three times. Who dared believe or comprehend the spectacle now presented? Jean-Martin II, crumbling to the floor, gave out a piteous cry, "I'm paralyzed!"

It was irrefutable to everyone. The left side of Jean-Martin had contracted and warped into the identical deformity once possessed by the young Henri. The old man's leg was crooked and his arm now frozen into a primordial claw, similar to hemiplegia. Charcot then clapped four times and produced more strangeness. Young Henri was overtaken by a paroxysm of violent tremors. All too bizarre! Each manifested the original neurological malady of the other!

"If I'm not mistaken, an exchange of devils appears to have taken place."

Charcot's ironic tone caused unpleasant murmuring through the lecture hall. He held up his hands to pacify the growing anger—"No cause for alarm, ladies and gentlemen, as these switched afflictions are neither permanent nor organic in nature. "Hypnotic suggestion, whispered in their ears, perhaps unnoticed, produced our reversals. So to prove the inherent pathology of the hypnoid state. Rest assured, a double handclap shall return Henri and Jean-Martin II to their curative states. Only first, let me address those who are aligned with science, especially my Salpêtrière interns—the work of neurological anatomy is far from complete. Consider the events of today's demonstration and weigh them well. Is this not the time in history, the propitious now, 1886, to pursue, no matter how deeply hidden within the nervous system, the origins of this pernicious disease, hysteria?"

A few rows below Sigmund, the hatless woman, head bowed, remained totally absorbed in writing. He saw in her elegant script:

now 1886

When the double-clap resounded, the hypnoid subjects were released from their neurological maladies—as the master hypnotist promised. The two men gaped at each other, at themselves, once again completely cured, the curtains closing on their helpless confusion.

Medical theatre, the spectators had no doubts, but theatre at its best! No one left on stage, how to respond to the scientific miracles witnessed except with thunderous applause. Many stood, tirelessly clapping, shouting, a clamorous fusillade of more hurrahs! and bravos! from every quarter of the amphitheatre, a near deafening uproar, even the more dignified joined in the tribute, proclaiming that Jean-Martin Charcot was leading France, like Pasteur, like Bonaparte, to new glory!

Amidst the pandemonium, the curtains ruffled, and Charcot reappeared. He stepped with alacrity toward the ovation, offering his signature gesture, a curt bow, measured steps backwards, gathering the curtains around him like a garment, and gone! He had disappeared as would a magician. Sigmund Freud remained in his seat, moored...

Chapter 4

I am almost worried;
no adventure of any kind
comes my way.

Sigmund Freud

MEETING SIGMUND FREUD

Customarily, I was the last person to leave Charcot's lectures. An empty theatre gave the opportunity to proofread my notes. So it came as a surprise, as I was leaving, the notes secure in my purse, to observe someone far up in the last row. A gentleman, still seated, motionless, who had either fallen asleep, or worse. For occasionally during Dr. Charcot's hypnosis demonstrations a member of the audience unwittingly entered a light hypnogogic state.

Concerned, I called loudly, *"Monsieur! Monsieur! Reveillez-vous!"*

His failure to respond worried me more. A past incident came to mind, a white-haired gentleman I found after a Friday lecture, slumped in his seat, ashen, head down, spittle bubbling from his mouth. I tried to revive him, but he had succumbed to an anuretic stroke.

Now I hurried half-way up the stairs and called again, "Monsieur, wake up!"

Slowly, as though emerging from a deep reverie, he regained awareness. The gas lamps, long ago dimmed, gave him little light to see me with my questioning look. The only sound, the rain peppering the vaulted windows. He made an attempt to rise, but seemed unable to find the strength. Such fatigue struck me as odd since he seemed close to my age, no more than thirty.

Embarrassed, he waved a hand to dismiss any concern. I studied him. He possessed a fine, well clipped beard, richly brown, dark. I found beards attractive, especially a full beard that did not obscure the mouth or cheek bones. His hair was also dark, parted, with a touch of pomade vanity. A handsome gentleman.

I adjusted my hair comb, fallen loose. *"J'ai pensé que monsieur etait mort."*

He replied in stilted French: *"Parlez vous l'allemagne ou l'anglais?"*

"I thought you were dead."

"Dead?"

"A stroke, heart failure, a brain rupture. Such events occur."

"No; I'm not dead," he replied, "but the few precious ideas I brought with me to Paris are hemorrhaging severely."

Our conversation proceeded in English. "You speak like a doctor," I said.

"A neuropathologist; but after what I witnessed on the stage today, an unsettled neuropathologist, for I presumed to know hemiplegia and chorea when I see them, but since when do neurological diseases submit to hypnotic commands?"

He garnered my sympathy straightaway, his struggle to understand the profound strides Charcot was making in neurology. "Your diagnoses are not entirely incorrect. What you witnessed may be considered variants, but not directly caused by physical trauma or infectious lesions. Dr. Charcot has categorized them as hysterical diseases."

He reflected. "If not caused by physical trauma or infection, then by what?"

I playfully quoted my employer. "That is a question worthy of the Sphinx. Dr. Charcot's quest is to find the answer to the riddle of hysteria."

He looked at me with more interest. "Is Mademoiselle a doctor?"

I shook my head, almost smiling. How easy to assume another identity if one displayed a smattering of knowledge. "You are new to Paris?"

"Six weeks new and my French is atrocious. What a welcome relief that you speak English."

"Are you on holiday?"

"No, I'm here to study under Dr. Charcot. An internship at his hospital."

I said nothing. *Why not tell him that I am Dr. Jean-Martin Charcot's personal stenographer? What stops me?* I only smiled, turned away, and began walking back down the stairs. He aroused some curiosity in me.

"May I introduce myself?" he called out.

"Practice your French!" I called back.

He jumped up from the seat. *"Je m'apelle Sigmund Freud."*

Ah, regrettable, a Prussian accent, I thought. Dr. Charcot, who still fought the Franco-Prussian War, loathed Germans.

"It's probably best that we speak English," I said.

He hurried down the stairs, defending himself, "I do understand French and can read it well enough."

"So, you only suffer from motor aphasia."

"Your medical knowledge escapes again. Can one be sure that Mademoiselle is not a physician?"

"I must be going."

"Wait, don't go."

He was handsome. And earnest. My hesitation encouraged him.

"That's an interesting pendant you wear," he noted. "Egyptian, isn't it?"

I touched the amulet, the winged eye. A piece of superstition I was almost inclined to discuss. Instead, I wished him good luck, *"Bonne chance aux Salpêtrière, Monsieur le docteur Freud."*

I headed for the exit, he followed. The lobby was deserted. Even the cloakroom attendant had disappeared. "Don't you think what happened today was extraordinary?" the new intern asked.

"When and if you get to know Dr. Charcot, you will find every day with him extraordinary."

"I've already concluded that he's a genius. Nothing shall keep me from his demonstrations or lectures. I have but one goal, to learn as much as I can from him."

"Our Professor is a holy magnet to those in the medical profession who are spirited adventurers."

The remark emboldened him. "Before I leave the Salpêtrière, I must understand the underlying mechanism of hypnotism."

We walked together to the cloak room. Our things had been left on the counter, arranged orderly, umbrella and umbrella, hat and hat, cape and coat. The dish for tips we both ignored.

As I put on the cape, he again focused on the jewelled eye tied about my neck. Most considered it a quaint piece of costumed jewellery, a trifle I oddly chose to wear.

"The sacred eye of Horus," he ventured.

"Your knowledge of Egyptian iconography is impressive."

"The only art that attracts me is ancient."

"Perhaps living in Paris will change that."

The relentless sound of rain outside made us dally.

He put on his coat, not his top hat, and ventured another observation, "The demonstration must have held some interest for you since you were busily taking notes."

"Were you spying, Dr. Freud?"

"If so, I learned little from the odd runes you make. Is it some arcane form of hieroglyphics?"

"A short-hand I devised."

"Yet occasionally," he noted, "a legible word emerged from the runes. As though you had a need to communicate what in Dr. Charcot's discourse was significant."

"Oh, it's just a peculiarity that I do without thinking."

"Then I would hypothesize that those words bubble up from another strata of thinking."

Sigmund Freud kept intriguing me. *And eyes nicely brown.*

I put on my hat. The distant bell of Saint Louis Chapel rang through the rain, a solemn bass tone to remind Salpêtrière's devout of midday prayers, reminding me that today's lecture notes had to be reshaped for Dr. Charcot's perusal before his hospital rounds.

We stepped outside, under the portico, neither of us quite ready to brave the downpour. "Have you been assigned to any particular laboratory yet?" I asked.

"I now assist in the outpatient clinic, Charcot works there on Tuesdays, but unfortunately my day is Wednesday. The long range plan is to do research work in Pathology. I soon better find out where the laboratory is located." He looked out at Salpêtrière's maze of streets, the plethora of buildings. "I've heard they have a horse trolley to speed you about."

Amused, I thought of Artemis, the trolley horse, who would not speed anyone about unless there was the promise of carrots at the end of the line.

"I need to go." I opened my umbrella.

"Must we remain strangers?" he asked.

"I would hypothesize," I replied, "that we will soon meet again."

I knew the remark had a tinge of mystery.

Chapter 5

Midway upon the journey of our life, I found myself within a forest dark, for the straightforward pathway had been lost.

The Divine Comedy
Dante

THE SLEEP WALKER

I

I have forgotten the name of the philosopher who made the observation that most human beings sleepwalk through life. I suppose the philosopher meant that we never allow ourselves to become fully cognizant of our surroundings. The buzzing of thoughts and seesawing of feelings get in the way.

* * *

At age sixteen, I was brought home at dawn by a Marseilles policeman who discovered me in my night dress, asleep on the steps of *Église Saint-Michel*. Apparently, I walked the three miles to the Church of St. Michael the Archangel while in a deep sleep. Following this strange night were more nights where I meandered through the house, not fully awake, until my watchful mother caught hold of me and put me back to bed. For a full week the sleepwalking continued then stopped as suddenly as it began. Father was quick to make one of his medical diagnoses.

Considering himself a self-taught physician, he assured the family that my short-lived "somnambulation" was due to a flare-up of "brain fever."

For me, the sleep walking episodes stirred interest into what I might be dreaming at night. I decided to write down any dreams I remembered, and a ripe opportunity, I thought, to launch my career as a scribe.

But I came to a sobering discovery. The dreams were wretched. Most, if not all, are of being lost. Bleak, haze-ridden scenes where I find myself in unfamiliar, unwelcoming parts of a city, in search of someone or something, as though I am the apocryphal *Wandering Jew*, penitent and ashamed, harbouring some sort of vague hope... of making amends? Or to rectify a misunderstanding? Or a wrongdoing? Nothing is ever explicit or distinct in the dreams. I wander interminably through sinister neighbourhoods, streets and alleyways that reek of loneliness, and no one in this hazy dream world lonelier than me. There are times when I peer into open doorways, aware that they are brothels. *What does an adolescent girl search for in brothels?*

And whoever inhabit my mournful dreams stay friendless, people who stand indistinct in shadowy places, who wear obscure smiles, who offer only mockery or heartless indifference. The dreams have no joy. No spirited story to tell. If, by chance, a story exists, it stubbornly eludes me. I wake up from these hapless dreams with my brain in a fog and pounding headaches that last the day. I gave up recording them.

* * *

The desire to write still lingered; I resisted, reminding myself, how naive the idea that I, essentially a scrub woman's assistant, could record any of life's meanings.

A series of family disasters kept me more than emotionally occupied, rounded out adolescence, a sudden desertion by one parent, followed by the sudden death of the other. But whatever unexpected reversals of fortune came, what mattered most was the proper care of my sister, to keep her from harm's way, for surely no one else seemed fit for the task.

My sister, spirited, impossibly imaginative, brimful of dreams, was the only person I knew to love. I, and no one else, called her Bijou. Like a precious jewel, she sparkled. And dazzled my heart. One day, together, we would escape the confines of the Marseilles harbour.

II

Before Father vanished, he left a legacy, he created our library, filling it with nearly as many books as a Paris book shop, and instilled in his two daughters a passion for reading. Three voracious readers we were, in silent collusion, poring over books, Father smoking rum cured cheroots and taking judicious sips of cognac whenever the time came to turn the next page.

Our older brother Justin, who was Mother's favourite, mocked us for reading so much. He and Mother derisively called the library the "Pickle Room" since that was where our brains supposedly got "pickled." In truth and fact, the room was once a storehouse for pickles. Our late grandmother worked in a pickle bottling factory near the Marseilles harbour. She brought home free jars of pickles almost daily and shelved them in what was now our library. When Justin passed by us reading, he never missed the chance to smirk and hold his nose at his imagined smell of pickles. Justin simply smelled the leather-bound books and ink filled pages, not the brine of pickles. What really repulsed my older brother was the invigorating drift of knowledge.

Ours was a rotating library, continuously renewed with fresh books, supplied by a Marseilles bookseller, the kindly Monsieur Prasadaba, in exchange for the rare tomes Father brought back from his sea voyages. I remember Bijou speeding through the nine-volume "Description of Egypt" put together by scholars who accompanied Napoleon on his Egyptian conquest. Also, Father came in possession of the entire writings of Jean-Francois Champollion who broke open, thanks to the Rosetta Stone, the Hieroglyphic code. All of which helped my sister become a self-taught Egyptologist.

The decipherable power of the Rosetta Stone intrigued me. How for millenniums the strange hieroglyphs painted on Egyptian tomb walls were considered unreadable, a mystery buried with the Pharaohs, until the Rosetta Stone supplied the code, and inserted meaning to what seemed only fanciful imaginings. I kept wondering if dreams, whether laughable, weird or lunatic, could be deciphered. What if dreams were, like hieroglyphics, nothing less than pictograms, a parade of symbols that, when gathered together, told hidden stories? Suppose the scenes in dreams, which appeared disconnected, vague and absurd, were quite rational—if you had a Rosetta Stone to interpret them.

So my new experiment came to be: collecting dreams. Not my own, which were too depressing, but those of others. From the outset, the project was not viewed favourably. Father thought it both suspicious and odd. Mother reacted angrily, her typical reaction to anything she did not understand. Her anger, I came to realize, concealed her fears of which were many. She slept fitfully, the blame on Father's snoring, and often left the bedroom, sitting up nights, sometimes sewing or sometimes trying to steal a few hours of rest on a small sofa in Justin's room. As no one else in the family had ever heard Father snore, I now wonder what night-time dreams my mother may have feared?

"You listen to me," she scolded, "no more of this dream rubbish. What you want to learn and practice is getting the customers' wash brighter, cleaner."

I thought to allay my father's suspicions by persuading him with reason: "The impulse to collect is not that unusual," I said, "some collect stamps, old coins, ancient maps, pressed flowers, butterflies—I choose to collect dreams."

"Juliette, dreams are..." he set down Dante's *Inferno*, pouring himself another glass of cognac, "...insubstantial." He lit another cheroot. "So much like Chinese fireworks, they burst into the night, and die. Besides," he concluded, picking up his book again, "I can never remember a damn one."

I had no use for being called Juliette by my father, as though I were a doomed character in a Shakespeare tragedy. Mother accorded me her own mocking sobriquet whenever she thought I strayed beyond my station in life. "Once and for all, *la Comtesse*, I have no time for dreams and neither should you. There's real and honest work to be done!"

Behind our house was the communal yard where mother had established her laundry business, a substantial scattering of tubs and a make-shift hutch where she did the ironing. I foraged for dreams, while washing and hanging clothes, among the neighbours who loitered or passed through.

What needed to be done, I decided, was to collect the most vivid dreams, to ask for the one that he or she could not forget. My sister sometimes watched me draw arrows, arcs, equal signs throughout a dream I transcribed. She said nothing, her long silences becoming more frequent.

I stayed focused, intent on connecting scenes, peculiarities, characters, actions, to perhaps find a hidden truth about someone. The dreamer whom I excluded from my scientific experiment, who I did not ask to participate, was Bijou.

Chapter 6

Martha, the sister of him who was dead, said to Him, "Lord, by this time there is a stench, for he has been dead four days."

Jesus said to her, "Did I not say to you that if you would believe you would see..."

And he who had died came out bound hand and foot with graveclothes, and his face was wrapped with a cloth.

Jesus said to them, "Loose him, and let him go."

John 11: 39-44

The Charcot Castle

I arrived in Paris a year before Sigmund Freud. We both came to seek out the same man—Jean-Martin Charcot. But I had no travel grant to Charcot's research hospital, like Sigmund Freud, so I had to find another way to enter the world of science.

Uninvited, I walked through the palatial gate and straight to the door of the doctor's house. It was a cold, wintry evening and I rehearsed an introduction one more time: *'Dr. Charcot, I come as an admirer of your beneficent work with the neurologically impaired women at the Salpêtrière...' (No! Too pretentious). 'Professor Charcot, your quest to find the origins of neurological diseases is held in high esteem all over France...' (Quest? A touch too romantic). 'Dr. Charcot, the experimental research you conduct at the Salpêtrière Hospital is closely observed by neurologists all over Europe and America...' (too grandiose).*

The door knocker, I observed, was in the form of an upright bear, open mouthed and baring teeth. *To warn away the uninvited*, I thought, *the unsolicited job seekers such as myself.* But here I was, on the rue de St. Faubourg, the most fashionable part of the city, in front of a mansion, more a castle. *And here I stay.* I peered up at the many windows, at the two turrets on either end. Might he, like a wizard or magus, work in one of them?

I lifted the bear knocker which was made of iron and heavy in my hand. In a moment he himself might come to the door. I needed to speak persuasively: *'Dr. Charcot, my skill as a verbatim recordist is unrivalled. Let me assure you, if given the opportunity to work at your hospital, I can duplicate your spoken words with...' (to the point before he shuts the door in my face) unerring accuracy.'*

The black, menacing bear gripped an hourglass in its paw. Lifting the bear, the sand granules gathered at the top of the hourglass, and when I slammed it down, the sand rushed to the bottom—as though to demonstrate the speed of time, moments passing, best intentions crumbling, my own courage like sand ebbing away; I thought to run down the path and hurried out the gate. *No! Seize this chance!*

I hammered at the door: sand gained, sand lost. I made such a determined noise, yet no one inside stirred. Later I learned that the great man sequestered himself at night in his library, a ritual which brooked no disturbance, for there Charcot laboured until the early hours of morning to draw out his thoughts and theories.

The door calmly opened to a young woman who stared with interest. She was perhaps twenty, attractive auburn hair in folds, her dress high-buttoned and austere in black. The flowered printed sash, awkwardly tied around her waist, seemed a hasty afterthought. Before I could speak, another woman made an almost magical appearance, popping over the young woman's shoulder. She was older, in her fifties, short, and stood on tiptoes to peer at me with the same open curiosity. The two were unmistakably mother and daughter, possessing the same rounded faces and short stature. Madame Charcot and daughter Jeanne, as time would reveal.

Madame Charcot was a remarkable pleasure, her tiny eyes twinkled, and her hair belonged to another century, powdered white like royalty, finely frizzed to form a ghostly halo.

Yet how strange and provocative I must have appeared, wearing the hooded cloak my father claimed came from 16th century Spain.

"How can we help you, dear?" she asked.

Hurriedly I proceeded, declaring my admiration for Dr. Charcot, his exploratory work with hypnotism and hysteria, and a rushed litany of his many medical achievements, until finally stating my goal—"I seek employment."

Both Jeanne and Madame Charcot exchanged quizzical looks, presumably wondering what on earth to do with me.

"My name is Julie Forette," I added. "Since my arrival in Paris, I have attended each and every one of Dr. Charcot's Friday Lectures." To prove the claim, from inside my cloak I pulled out a folio. "Here is a transcribed copy of his lecture on hystero-epilepsy which I recorded verbatim this week at the Salpêtrière. If you would kindly show the transcription to the Professor so that he can assess my proficiency." Neither mother nor daughter chose to take the folio. Instead, Madame Charcot inquired if I happened to be from Marseilles, for she detected the southern accent I had not yet erased.

Nodding 'yes' seemed to sanction my sanity for they graciously invited me inside. Jeanne Charcot, unable to take her eyes off me, plainly found her new guest an amusing wonder. From the vestibule, they escorted me into an antechamber so spacious it could have served as a village train station. The floors of Carrera marble gleamed bluish white and towering palms rose from huge porcelain urns. Our journey continued, mother and daughter on either side of me, toward an undeclared destination. We next passed through a ballroom where I visualized a full orchestra playing to hundreds of waltzing couples. The rooms then decreased in size, smaller and smaller, unlit rooms too dark to see clearly. Madame Charcot gently took my hand and became my diminutive guide until Jeanne opened a door to what I will always remember as a demi-paradise, a cosy sitting room, warmed by a small fireplace, and dreamily illuminated by table lamps of burnished copper. An oriental carpet, thickly woven, felt as though I were stepping across grass. Exotic flowers bloomed in a variety of Japanese vases and Chinese urns. A scattering of silk, tasselled pillows decorated the chairs and sofa. Gilt-framed paintings hung on the walls. The room struck me as designed by women for women, a feminine haven of charm and comfort.

At the far side of the room, a candlelit table had been set with an assortment of foods. After taking my cloak, Madame Charcot had me sit, or rather sink into a deeply cushioned chair. I looked over at the festive table setting. "Have I come at an inopportune moment?"

Jeanne Charcot, quick to find irony, let out a laugh.

"From time to time, dear," Madame Charcot volunteered in her gentle manner, "Jeanne and I devise *les petites soirees*, with themes. Tonight, we celebrate *La Bohemia*."

Jeanne went to inspect the various dishes spread out on the table. "Let's see what Marcel and Janine have prepared. There's herring, codfish cakes, knockwurst, pumpernickel, mustards, pickles, various condiments, and..." She held up a tall, dark brown bottle in each hand. "German bock! But..." One bottle she raised higher for a closer inspection. "This one half consumed before your arrival."

Madame Charcot hid a laugh into her scarf. I could guess the scarf, long flowing and gaudily coloured, might fit into their Bohemian theme. Madame chided her daughter, "Have we mislaid our manners, Jeanne, not to offer Mademoiselle Forette refreshments?"

"But Mother, she comes on a mission." Jeanne had stationed herself near the fire, having lost interest in the refreshments. She waved a hand toward the gilt-frame painting above the mantle, the singular masculine presence, the image of Jean-Martin Charcot who radiated the same commanding stare he displayed in his demonstrations. I wondered if he could hypnotize me as easily as the patients he brought on stage. The artist seated him in a throne-like chair, robed in the deep scarlet of academia. Charcot appeared nothing less than regal, a patrician nose and a brooding,

Napoleonic brow. The peculiar line of his mouth made his expression almost cruel.

Jeanne noticed my fascination. "Father is quite imposing, even in paint." A whiff of sarcasm in her tone or was it pride, or both?

Madame Charcot expressed simple admiration. "The portrait was executed by the great Tofano." (I had never heard of him.) "I'm so glad I insisted," she addressed her daughter, "that your father wear his Legion of Honour pin, for see how accurately the artist renders it."

Jeanne agreed. "A nice touch, a spot of blood, over his heart."

An unwanted memory came of the single keepsake our mother brought with her from Ireland, the Sacred Heart of Jesus, a morbid relic from her Catholic upbringing. She nailed it above the bed my sister and I shared, a red heart made of iron, the only piece of art she ever allowed, as nothing else could mar the walls of our house except the plump, tortured Jesus heart, entwined with thorns and exuding seven drops of blood. *Arriving in Paris, no wonder I was ravenous for art.*

The other paintings the Charcot women had hung were where I wanted to linger, but they brought me to stand closer to the portrait, praising what they considered the great Tofano's realism, the slavish attention to extraneous detail which represented a style I could no longer tolerate—not after spending all my spare time in Paris galleries.

Daughter Jeanne disarmed me. "How would you appraise the artist's technique?" Her voice sounded mischievous.

The artist Tofano was to my eye a hack, a product of the state-sponsored art found at the Salon, and the painting with its ersatz background of Roman columns was typical commissioned rubbish.

How could I formulate a diplomatic response to artificiality? The suave brushwork and studio colouring bored me beyond measure. But Madame Charcot thought to give me more to consider. "Isn't the background cleverly metaphorical? Tofano builds solid Roman columns to impart a certain sense of dignity, and deeper in the background, do you see the scene from the Bible?" Madame Charcot was helping me see what I had overlooked, an artistic device of inserting a painting within a painting. "Tofano told us he wished to pay homage to another great artist..." She looked at me questioningly.

Both Charcot women, shrewder than I imagined, were exploring what I might know about art. "Andrea Mantegna," I replied.

Madame was pleased. "Yes, dear, yes. *Lazarus Resurrected.*"

Jeanne Charcot, arms firmly folded, wanted her question answered. The artist's technique.

"A studied likeness of your father," I noted.

Jeanne released me from further discomfort by pouring out beer into three steins. "Let us drink to verisimilitude!"

We drank bock, sat, nibbled on codfish cakes while I absorbed the other paintings which glowed in the reflected firelight. It was an impressive collection, works by masters I had only seen at the Louvre, paintings by Frans Hals, Jan Steen, and a dry point etching by Goya. "How enchanting to have made of this room a private museum," I observed.

Jeanne laughed. "Why, the entire house is a museum!"

"In more ways than one," added Madame Charcot.

Jeanne explained Madame's cryptic comment. "Mother alludes to the various diseased brains and deformed limbs that Father likes to collect in his formaldehyde jars."

The Delacroix drawings I suddenly saw hanging in an obscure corner made me jump to my feet, compelled to examine them more closely.

Madame Charcot apologized, "I am afraid that they are only preliminary sketches on paper... nothing finished."

I could not hide my excitement. "But how privileged to peer into his process!" I could see Delacroix's scribbled notations for the future placement of colours.

"Are you an artist?" inquired Madame Charcot.

"That vocation is for others of a more imaginative disposition. I am a transcriber, a verbatim recordist."

"Which explains your presence here tonight," said Jeanne. She liked to show that I remained the focus of her attention.

"Yes!" I answered. "Wanting more than anything to work for your esteemed father."

Madame Charcot grew thoughtful, "I do believe his words need to be recorded for posterity."

Jeanne raised her rounded eyebrows which reminded me of calipers. "Tut-tut, Mother! Surely, not every word worthy of verbatim recording?"

I took issue, "There is no parallel in medicine today to Dr. Charcot's bold exploration into the nature of hysteria."

"Are you truly a stenographer interested in my husband's scientific endeavours?" Madame Charcot looked dubious, and perhaps disappointed.

"Yes, Madame."

"Mother is an artist," Jeanne clarified.

"A craftsperson," Madame corrected. "I work predominantly with stained glass, sometimes costumed jewellery, bracelets, trinkets and such. But Mademoiselle Forette," she looked at me questioningly, "art, not science, seems your forte."

I wasn't sure how to respond. Science was my lodestar. All that I had read, before coming to Paris, pointed to science as the path I should take. Yet here tonight, the wonderful Charcot women had drawn from me an altogether different love.

Jeanne eagerly refilled my stein. I soon confessed to frequent visits to the Louvre and certain galleries in Montmartre which offered intriguingly new styles of painting. 'Were they acquainted with the Impressionist painters?' I asked.

"Are they considered a school, like the Barbizon School?" asked Madame Charcot.

"They do band together for periodic exhibitions, all of which occurred before I came to Paris. I hope one day soon they will organize another show."

"Corot was of the Barbizon School. We once had a Corot," she remarked somewhat wistfully, "purchased by my own dear, departed father."

I replied, "The Impressionists, so I've been told, have been strongly influenced by plein-air painters, like Corot."

"I remember the painting well," she said fondly. "An idyllic landscape, the tints were golden, very light, with a certain softening as though he had given a delicate smear to the whole thing."

"What happened to it?" I asked.

Jeanne answered, "Too smeary for Father; he sold it."

Madame came to her husband's defence. "You know your father, he prefers the canonical in art and distrusts the contemporary."

An odd stance, I thought, for the Director of the Salpêtrière. It was Charcot who had embraced the most progressive ideas for his asylum, transforming the Salpêtrière into a laboratory for neurological understanding.

"Maybe the time has arrived," said Jeanne, showing a little of the devil in her eyes, "for Father to change his views of art."

I liked these two women who drew me into discussing art far into the late hours. I reflected much later on the absolute oddity of how events unfurled, how I became that evening an adopted member of the Charcot household, not because of an aptitude for dictation nor my interest in neurological hysteria, but because the kind women appreciated and supported my new-found enthusiasm for art. They assured me at the door that although I had not met the man I wanted to work for, arrangements would be made tomorrow for an interview, at a more decent hour.

Cheerfully they waved good night as I made my way to the front gate, unable to resist glancing back at the house. They said that Charcot was working in his library and I saw one window with a lamp still burning. Charcot's vast collection of books reputedly rivalled the library of ancient Alexandria. My goal was to one day gain access to those books.

Closing the gate, more of their farewells sailed down to me. *"Jusqu'matin, Mademoiselle Forette, jusqua'matin!"* Tomorrow morning! *Yes, an appointment tomorrow morning, standing before Jean-Martin Charcot!*

Wrapping my cape closer, I walked briskly to stave off the night's cold. Montmartre and my rented room was some distance from the prosperous houses on rue Faubourg. A swirl of images from the evening kept me company. Charcot's portrait appeared—I felt the weight of his gaze, unaccountably mournful, and then the Mantegna painting of a stunned Lazarus, bound in graveclothes, who rises at the Lord's command, no longer dead.

That very night, in a dream, two black-clad nuns came to my door. They said they were mother and daughter who had taken vows together, sworn to the allegiance of Jesus the Saviour. They brought terrible news that my sister had died four days ago, but not to worry, if I hurried to the Church of St. Michael the Archangel, she would be on view before the burial. Greatly distressed, I reached the church to find her in an opened sepulchre. The mother and daughter nuns were there with a man they claimed was Jesus Christ. The nuns praised the peaceful beauty of my sister, laid out so purely in morning white, that they thought it would be a shame to wake her from such a deep sleep. The man beside them looked nothing like the pictures I had seen of Jesus Christ. He was dressed, similar to a conservative Parisian notary, in a plain, thread worn suit. He wore extremely thick eyeglasses, his hair pomaded and severely parted in the middle, which hung untidily over his ears. I said, "You're not Jesus Christ." The nuns each placed a hand over their Sacred Heart medals to swear he was the one, true saviour, only "cleverly disguised." Jesus Christ apologized for his mundane appearance, but the spectacles were now a necessity for the extensive reading he has done on all manner of subjects, including hypnosis. He then began to beckon my sister with his hand, and she rose up in the sepulchre, eyes closed. The nuns, mother and daughter, were ready with tortoise hair brushes, and reverently began brushing my sister's long hair.

The dream ended.

Chapter 7

It rains in my heart
As it rains upon the city
What is this langueur
That falls into my heart?

Il pleure dans mon coeur
Comme il pleut sur la ville
Quelle est cette langueur
Qui penetre mon coeur?

Paul Verlaine

IN ATHENS, WAITING FOR CEZANNE

*W*hen will this wicked, unwanted rain end? Pissarro wondered, sitting grimly alone, the sole customer in the New Athens Café. *Yes, who else but an old fool like me would dare brave such ungodly weather?*

The wind's fury was hurling the rain in sheets against the window. The morning outside had turned strangely dark. He tried to discern the traffic of the street, but everything was shimmering, the carriages rushing and sloshing down the rue Faubourg like phantom shadows. Pissarro signaled the waiter for another coffee. And waited for Cezanne.

Heaving a sigh, he took out the crumpled note, and tried once more to decipher its meaning. His old comrade's tone greatly concerned him.

Who in this cesspool of thieves and harlots called Paris can I count on? Camille Pissarro??? Please meet me, as in days of yore, at New Athens. I am in a state of cerebral unrest, most serious. A vipress has her fangs in my heart. No, wait! I am being unjust to this honourable woman. It is my own vile lusts which have placed me in this hell. Oh, I must sort out this preposterous affair! I will explain everything when I see you. Do not, I repeat, do not mention to a living soul that I am presently in Paris. I have enemies.

Paul Cezanne

Pissarro shook his head in dismay. *Certainly our Paul grows stranger and more neurotic with each passing year. Can it be, as Zola claims in his damnable novel, that we live in an unhealthy age, ridden with neuroses, teetering on the brink of self-destruction?*

Waiting for Cezanne, he reflected upon their relationship, going back many years, trying to remember a beginning. *Perhaps the brisk autumn morning, yes, when our beards were not grey, the year 1861—dragging my fellow artist, Oller, by the coat sleeve to the Academie Suisse. 'You must see some figure drawings done by a curious Provencal, but be forewarned, they're ridiculed by everyone at the Academy, except Monet. Oller replies, 'Well, if Claude gives the nod, the stuff is worth a gander.'"*

Cezanne's nudes were a wonderment to us: strange, brawny, bulbous shaped women and men, soaring through clouds, figures less drawn than forged by turbulent, curving strokes. What this rather wilful artist had was the audacity to dredge into the dark, fertile muck of things and pulled up muscular Adams and Eves unflatteringly swollen with appetite.

Pissarro remembered.

I brought him here, at the New Athens. We ate vermicelli, the cheapest food on the menu, and handsomely finished off a bottle together. No, I didn't utter the irksome word, genius, but I spoke plainly: 'You can make of things something solid.' But I suggested he rid his work of the romance, the melodrama. 'Leave that sort of thing for literature,' I told him. Only the stubborn, thick-bearded Provencal told me in no uncertain terms where to go, and it wasn't heaven!

In due time my advice took root, Paul discarded the romance, the turbulence, and left behind his muscular Titans.

Invited him to Pontoise... when was that? Had to be after the Prussian war, 1872. We roamed the countryside together, paintboxes hitched to our backs, set up easels whenever we excitedly found it—it, the visual sensation, a freshness in the arrangement of forms, colour and light. Oftentimes almost drunk on the sensation but sober enough to pin it down.

Some still say it's impossible to distinguish who is Pissarro and who is Cezanne in the Pontoise paintings. Maybe he did borrow portions of my technique, maybe I did have something to do with his development. Mais quelle différence? Who cares? Good painters learn from other good painters. That's the truth of the matter.

So Pissarro ruminated and waited.

Lightening cracked and flared menacingly across the sky. Would this awful weather keep Paul Cezanne away? The waiter, a rather tall, lantern-jawed fellow, showed sympathy for his only customer, bringing Pissarro another fresh cup of coffee and the newspaper.

Unfortunately, he brought the *Gil Blas* with the latest installment of Zola's traitorous novel. A column from Chapter V had been inserted on the front page to entice the reader. Reluctantly, Pissarro read:

The rift among the Impressionists was there, though barely visible as yet, which would soon crack apart the old sworn friendships... and one day would shatter them in a thousand pieces.

Slanderous remarks! He slammed the marble table, coffee spilled across the page. "We will prove Zola's thousand pieces the outrageous lie it is!" he cried out to the baffled waiter who came to wipe up the spilled coffee.

Now Theo van Gogh's suggestion makes perfect sense, he thought. Bring all the Impressionists together again for another show. Yes! An event long overdue. Which was bound to stimulate new interest in everyone's work. He imagined crowds queuing for blocks to see the Eighth Show.

The waiter gathered up the soaked newspaper. "I will bring Monsieur another copy."

"Bring me an honest paper, *The Intransigent*; or half-way honest, *Le Figaro*."

"I shall check the rack, Monsieur."

Pissarro, suddenly curious. "What are those two silly things which protrude from your apron pocket?"

"Ah, Monsieur," the waiter brought them out, "these are my little friends." He put one on each of his long, bony fingers. Brightly coloured, cloth puppets, nonsensical creatures they were, with tiny buttons for eyes and fennel seeds for toothy smiles.

"My hobby, Monsieur, finger puppets. I make them for my children and sell a few to customers."

"Why, they are positively delightful!" Pissarro was full of admiration. "You are an artist, my friend. What a wonderful gift for my Coco, she's eight."

"Which would Monsieur like?" He wiggled the creatures. "The green *Crockothump* or the orange *Kangaclop*? Three sou apiece."

"I think Coco would like Crockothump best, what with all his scary teeth; not that she wouldn't appreciate the little pouch you've sewn for Kangaclop," chuckled Pissarro, counting out three pennies. His omnibus fare. *Well, to walk in the rain can cause me no serious harm*, he decided. *And the storm may very well travel south if the wind shifts toward Vincennes.* He pushed a finger into Crockothump. The cloth puppet resembled a crocodile with the absurd addition of an American turkey tuft. *Coco will laugh. Ah, and our Minette, our nine-year-old Minette would have laughed too. What a curse, scarlet fever.*

The waiter, satisfied with his sale, ambled off, returning with another issue of *Gil Blas*. "The only paper to be had, Monsieur. The storm has prevented the other papers from arriving."

Pissarro resigned himself to more distortions:

In his blind fury Claude Lantier was about to put his fist through his canvas... quivering with wrath... glaring at the picture, his eyes

burning with the unspeakable torture of his impotence. His hands had refused once more to produce anything clear or life-like…

"Claude Lantier be damned!" he shouted out his anger again. The waiter thought it best to stay behind the counter, re-clean glasses, and pretend to understand his customer. "All of Paris will know the character is Cezanne," Pissarro spoke across the room. "This Lantier is flimsy camouflage. How can Émile Zola insult his childhood friend?" asked the distraught Pissarro. "To describe the great Paul Cezanne as a failed, impotent painter is a monumental injustice!" He continued to rant to the waiter, "Why, among the good painters, Cezanne must be considered the most advanced. We all wait expectantly for him to take art to a new plateau. Yes, we're all waiting…" his voice trailed to silence.

"Waiting for Cezanne," murmured the waiter in sympathy.

* * *

Heedless of the hard pouring rain, Cezanne watched through the window. *If, if I focus complete attention on Pissarro, might I be able to read the man's mind? She manages to get into my own head. How? Psychology, she names it, the solution for the next century. When the mind will be mapped. There are conscious and subconscious zones, she claims. She… she, she!*

Try as he might, Cezanne could not banish the woman from his thoughts. On route to *New Athens* the wind had swept away his cap, his few wisps of hair blew wildly, but Cezanne stood rooted, impervious to the raging storm, and worried. Was his old comrade sitting in the café but another enemy? He scrutinized him, hunched over an unfurled newspaper—there in the window Cezanne's own morose reflection melded with the rivulets of rain, the two of them, two ageing artists, misguided dreamers, overlapping in the same composition, bearded, weather-beaten faces splintering with every drop of rain that trickled down the windowpane. He yearned to paint the sensation, to solidify the shifting shapes, to carve geometry into the fleeting images, make from nature's ephemera something lasting. *I'll paint Pissarro's beard a white stone slab, the newspaper's whiteness I'll shape into a solid, blank rectangle. Ha! The Menu du Jour soaped onto the window, push its lettering though space and chisel new front page headlines—*

Bouillabaisse, 2 francs

* * *

Pissarro forced through the chapter then realized Zola's Achilles heel. *He has no inkling of art's new directions. He lives smugly in decades past. I'm unquestionably his other fictional character, Gagnière, an artist whose "weakness for technical experiments" leaves him without a future. But his most miserable interpretation is reserved for Cezanne, a distorted Cezanne, the artist doomed to fail:*

The usual story, Lantier worked himself out in one magnificent burst of genius; after that, nothing would come and he was unable to finish what he had started.

His impotence returned.

The waiter touched his coat sleeve, nodding toward the drenched figure on the other side of the rain-streaked window. A shockingly eerie sight, Paul Cezanne alone in the midst of a rainstorm. A mute, doleful apparition.

He shouted through the glass, "Have you lost your senses, man!" He rushed outside to lead his fellow artist into the shelter of the café.

Placed in a chair, Cezanne seemed to awaken, and glared. "By all that's sacred, do you swear that no one knows of our meeting here? Do you swear?"

Pissarro, quite unable to hide his irritation. "I followed the instructions in your letter."

"There are people out there," Cezanne stared forlornly into the rain shrouded darkness, "trying to track me down."

Accustomed to Paul's infamous bouts of suspicion, Pissarro chose silence.

Cezanne took sudden notice of the waiter. "You! Desist from your goggle-eyed staring as if a madman were in your midst! Can you not comprehend that I am Cezanne the painter! Bring wine immediately! The cheap house stuff will suffice." Pissarro remained patient until surprised by Cezanne's worrisome laugh, close to hysterical, pointing to their trickling reflections. "Take a close look! Two bald-headed, heavy-bearded fools who have been scratching paint on canvas for over twenty years without a soul giving a damn about our work! No one has the slightest understanding of what you or I seek to achieve!"

"Monet and Renoir are starting to sell well," Pissarro responded. "Our turn will come."

"I refuse to have their names discussed in my presence! The ever-so-cunning Monet and the Jew-hating Renoir. Yes, these two have learned to weasel their way into the good graces of the bourgeoisie!"

Pissarro found it hard to believe his ears. "Paul, they are among your greatest admirers, two of your most loyal supporters."

He was not listening. "If we tramped through this city today with our paintings, went into every gallery, every pawn shop, stopped every passerby, what would we sell? Not a single canvas, I tell you. We are failures. Can you deny it?"

Pissarro discreetly placed the *Gil Blas* on an empty chair. *That's all his fragile mind needs right now, to read that his dearest friend slanders him in instalments.*

Cezanne was occupied with sundry suspicions—*This waiter sets down the wine bottle, I see, in a contemptuous manner. Intrigue is under foot. That voodoo doll on Pissarro's finger, what part does it play?*

Pissarro, observing the furtive glances, removed the finger puppet and placed it in his pocket. "Paul, how can you pronounce us failures? We've been true to ourselves, we've stuck to our guns, we've held on to what is essential in our hearts, the only thing that matters, is to take up a damn paint brush and render the sensations."

"The reason I'm here..." Cezanne began haltingly, "is that I crave your advice. There's a woman who has me under her thumb."

"Hortense?"

"Who?" Cezanne looked baffled.

"Hortense Fiquet."

"Who?" repeated Cezanne.

Pissarro shrugged. Hortense Fiquet, the woman no one was supposed to know existed, Cezanne's mistress for nearly fifteen years, the secret Paul had to keep from his father or lose his monthly allowance. He regretted mentioning Hortense.

"This woman is someone else... a woman of science... But she's..." he turned pale, his hands gripped the edges of the table as if he would pick it up at any moment and hurl it across the room, "she's making a monkey out of me!"

"Calm down," Pissarro gently insisted. "Start from the beginning."

Cezanne gave a rambling story which revolved around a mysterious woman whom he accidentally knocked onto the sidewalk. "I was exiting one of the brothels which rim the *Place de Pigalle*."

"A brothel?"

"Yes, I **pay** for it—I know it's a dirty business," he muttered. "But how else to cope with things, with... my passions... pent up..."

Pissarro guided him back to the event. "The woman? The woman you knocked to the ground?"

"Finished with my business, coming out the door, in a hurry to make myself scarce in that neighbourhood, I slammed into her. Knocked her off her feet, right to the ground, on to the filthy sidewalk."

He paused. The rumbling of distant thunder seemed to signal something ominous still to come. Pissarro tasted the wine, sour on his tongue, and set it down.

"I made profuse apologies," Cezanne continued, "introduced myself, 'Paul Cezanne, the painter!' said I. Such a smile she gave, while brushing the dirt from her frock, a smile that lingered. 'I believe,' she said, 'no lasting injury has occurred.' Yes, those were her words, 'no lasting injury.' But she gently demanded recompense, 'Could we share a cup of coffee'?"

"A rather aggressive female," remarked Pissarro.

"I confess, I thought her a tart. She suggested the café Voltaire."

"Yes, at the *place de l'Odeon*. Interesting choice." Pissarro was well aware of a group which met there Monday nights, headed by the critic Félix Fénéon, to read poetry and discuss literature.

"I'll be frank, Pissarro, I'm very skittish around females."

"That is a fact," nodded Pissarro.

"But somehow this woman puts me at ease. What came to pass was our decision to meet again at the same café, for I discovered her knowledge of art was considerable, more than considerable." He leaned across the table. "Pissarro, can you believe, she has seen my paintings in Tanguy's shop window? And admires them!" He nervously turned his wine glass round and round. "After the next meeting, I found the courage to ask if she would pose for me. At first, she was reluctant. But as I've said, she being a devotee of art and science, imbued with modern ideas, I convinced her."

"Undoubtedly," Pissarro allowed himself a bit of satire, "your charm won the day."

"At my studio, she agreed to pose nude."

"My, my!"

Cezanne looked mournful. "Lustful ideas overtook me."

Or the woman's lust, the story veering in different directions. Pissarro found it difficult to make sense out of Paul's increasingly confused narrative, the absurd remarks. "Syphilis either sends us to the madhouse or kills us outright— yes, that's how love stories end."

What was one to make of this quixotic man? Cezanne stared vacantly at his untouched glass until he broke a long silence, "I have a son."

"You and I are accustomed to minding our own affairs," answered Pissarro.

"He's fourteen, maybe fifteen, I think. I have trouble with his birth year."

Glumly Pissarro focused on pouring a little more of the bad wine into his glass. "You must keep him well hidden."

"I don't see the boy as often as I should..." He shook his head, twisting his glass, tears in his eyes. "Countless sins mar my soul... I have nightmares of burning in hell for all eternity."

"Better to focus on the here and now," said Pissarro.

Again, the troubled man was not listening. "You, Camille Pissarro will surely go to heaven; I will be driven by devils and their pitchforks to a different fate."

"Get a grip on yourself, man!"

"Her painting is not finished; it will take a long time. She has promised to return to my studio. I'm unaccustomed to this kind of lust."

"Listen, can you accept advice?"

"Yes, by heaven, yes!"

"Desire... when it arrives, signals the moment to act. Far too soon, my friend, such urges evaporate."

"I will express myself in writing, something poetic; she believes in the power of poetry. I once wrote poetry, in my youth, when I thought I scribbled as well as Zola."

Pissarro changed the subject. "Here is what I want you to dwell upon —another exhibition. All of the Impressionists banding together again, like the old days. Did we not hatch our first show here, at this very table?" His hands patted the marble. "Time to give birth to another one and more marvellous."

"You shall be escorted to the heavens by winged angels, I am certain of it, Pissarro. And if you die first, will you communicate? I shall attend séances."

"I communicate through my art. Listen, a different kind of show," pressed the artist. "Theo van Gogh put the idea in my head. Let's bring in the young painters—Signac, Seurat. Such a show will allow us to intermingle our ideas with theirs."

"Just to contemplate touching her... makes me feverish. Then I start to smell the stink of brimstone. Last week a copy of Dante's Divine Comedy fell from her purse."

"If she's Catholic, she may spray you with holy water." Pissarro rose to escape the situation, only to feel dizzy... the wine or the crazy conversation, or worse, his blood pressure. *Dr. Gachet takes the train up from Auvers on Tuesdays to see patients. He will examine me in exchange for a painting.*

"Another Impressionist Show?" Cezanne looked up questioningly. "Seven seems enough."

"We include the young artists with talent. Be assured, Paul, every last one of them admires your work. They are the youth who realize that you travel toward a different reality in art. For them, you are the vanguard for the next century."

"They want to steal my ideas."

Pissarro angrily put on his cap. He must leave in spite of the storm outside. *Get to dealer Alphonse Portier, climb the rue Lepic hill, climb the rickety steps to the second floor of his apartment where he runs his business.*

"She will pose, if there's recompense," remarked Cezanne.

"Ah, so it's money she wants." Pissarro thought how an unlucky encounter can be enough to ruin a fellow.

"Money? Were it only that!" bellowed Cezanne. "For I would pay any amount she asked!"

"What does she want?"

"A dream."

"I beg your pardon?"

"She collects dreams."

"And you say she's a woman of science?"

The confused man had no answer.

"Paul, I must be going, there is a dealer I need to see."

"I would rather give her a bundle of francs than any dream of mine," he grumbled.

"*Salut*, old comrade." Pissarro turned away.

"If an ounce of sense is left in my head," muttered Cezanne, "I should return to Provence. Paint mountains, not breasts."

* * *

Pissarro caught again in the rain without an umbrella, he trudged down the puddled rue Blanche. *Portier's an amateur dealer, but he has a fondness for the bold. We might discuss a special arrangement with my Pointillist paintings.*

"Stop! Wait!" Cezanne stood hatless in the downpour. Both painters, faces wet, beards dripping like faucets, walked toward each other. Cezanne began reluctantly, "My mother asks that I come home. And evaluate my father. She thinks he's not well in the head, going about the estate day and night, burying pennies, two at a time."

Alarmed, Pissarro remembered the father a prosperous banker. "For love and grief, Paul, return at once! Find him a doctor. A consultation is necessary."

"Is there a cure for miserliness?"

Pissarro ignored the sarcasm. "With age, minds can flounder. Any parent may, at times, lose their bearings."

"I'm terrified to leave. She might well walk out of my life. I shall be devastated. A painting is taking shape. Between us, a painting exists."

"You can still communicate. Pen letters to each other."

"My father opens all my mail, and she refuses to give me her address. She suggests our correspondence pass through an intermediary."

"An intermediary?"

"Which you can be. As you do in your paintings, the subtle intermediary hues to diminish distance between two distinct tones."

Pissarro wished to be somewhere dry again. "But Paris is not my home. I come, maybe sell a painting, a few gouache fans, then return to Eragny and Julie."

"Julie?"

Cezanne inexplicably suspicious again, Pissarro steered him to what he hoped was their shared reality. "Julie, my wife. You do remember my wife?" One could read the man's struggle to sort through memories.

"Yes, yes, yes." Cezanne wiping the rain from his face. "She brought us picnic lunches wherever we set up our easels."

"Yes, she **and** Hortense."

"My mind has been playing tricks, forgive me. Maybe I've reached a second childhood. Maybe I'll help my father bury pennies."

"Paul, I'm really ill-suited to assist in your present love life."

An alternate solution suddenly came to Cezanne. "Someone in Paris with a fixed abode is who I must have. "Émile. Yes, Émile! Besides, he writes about such conundrums, he knows women."

The idea startled Pissarro. *Can he be totally ignorant of what so many in Paris have discerned? Zola's betrayal.*

"Maybe," began Pissarro, lamely, "I could meet with her when I am here in the city."

But Cezanne now felt certain. "No, Zola is the ideal man for the mission. I shall visit him immediately."

Pissarro wished to dissuade him, but Cezanne turned without a good-bye, setting off in the opposite direction, marching through ankle-deep puddles, soon lost in the swallowing rain.

Chapter 8

After all, there are many things which one has to keep secret from other people but of which one makes no secret to oneself...

Sigmund Freud

Charcot's Scribe

I

Led into the library by the servant, I had scarce time to absorb the grandeur of my surroundings for the man sat behind a mammoth desk —which seemed a mile away—beckoning me with his fingers. *Stay focused*, I reminded myself. *He holds Julie Forette's future in his hands.* Each step I took was muffled by the Turkish carpets. How I yearned to examine the walls of books I passed.

When reaching two armchairs still quite a distance from him I waited, but he gave no further directions; instead, he leisurely swivelled, no longer looking at me, as though quite alone. The armchairs were very different, one severe and plain with spindly legs, the other richly upholstered with floral patterns, flying birds and blue peacocks worthy of a Florentine palace. I chose the palatial chair then waited and watched him guardedly, swivelling left and right. His smooth-shaven profile, the patrician forehead and aquiline nose, could have been embossed on a Roman coin. *When will he speak?*

Patience, I decided, would be my ally. And silence. But when peering deeper into the room, I grew apprehensive—the bear again, he loomed, no longer in the guise of door knocker, but monstrously large and more menacing, grafted into a stained-glass panel that hung from the ceiling by heavy chains. He stood twice my height on hind legs, and in his taloned paw he still gripped an hourglass of sand.

I tried to keep my focus on the man, *the man who brings me to Paris*, while farther behind him the bear hovered mid-air, as if the gate keeper. The swivelling stopped, but still he chose not to speak. I sat attentive and straight, resolved to show no timidity. He then began watching me with amused curiosity. The silence, the stained-glass bear and the stained-glass French doors (which led to the gardens) gave the library an ecclesiastical air. We might have been in a church. The Church of Dr. Jean-Martin Charcot. His gaze grew more serious.

I shall be the one person, I promised myself, who dares lock into the stare of the eminent hypnotist. He gave in to a slight smile. "Does Mademoiselle worry," he finally spoke, "that I shall be able to read her thoughts?"

"I have read that Dr. Charcot has an eye which can penetrate a person's mind and open an entire life."

He raised his eyebrows, responding in a soft voice, "This is what you have read?"

"Many articles, yes," I admitted... *perhaps too quickly.*

"How is it possible," he feigned bewilderment, "that I could have such magical powers?"

"I'm not a believer in magic." I rose higher in the chair, determined not to cower in his presence.

"Am I to extrapolate that Mademoiselle gives no countenance to a higher power?"

"I bestow my belief to the power of science."

"Splendid-splendid!" He tapped together fingertips. *Tiny applause?* "That is to your credit, Mademoiselle Forette, plus the fact that you were raised by a father with medical knowledge."

The surprise on my face delighted him. I had been very careful, since my arrival in Paris, not to share a shred of information with anyone regarding my family history.

He pressed his advantage. "And your father, if I am not mistaken, was a doctor... or, at minimum, an apothecary in Marseilles."

"But how could you possibly...?"

A curt wave of his hand signalled silence. He had more to reveal. "Mademoiselle herself is quite learned. A woman of exception, armed with a working knowledge of Latin, additionally endowed with a connoisseur's appreciation of art, and burdened with an antipathy toward animals not of a gentle nature." He settled back in his chair. "Possibly, this is a page from your life."

I tried to maintain composure. "A page you have read, Dr. Charcot, with a high degree of accuracy." The mantra in my mind: *You will not be cowed by him; you will not be cowed by him.*

He rocked in the chair, completely relaxed, wondering aloud, "Is Mademoiselle baffled by my insights? Perhaps alarmed?" His eyes, coldly luminous, sharply focused, made me think of a bird of prey who, when ready, could easily swoop down. *Will he snatch at a vulnerable flaw to ruin any chance of becoming his personal recordist?* Worrying me more, he boasted, "Before our interview terminates, I may very well turn another page or two of your life."

"You provoke my interest in understanding how you seemingly enter into one's mind, read memories, thoughts."

"Mademoiselle Forette," he placed his hands (small, delicate hands) flat upon open journals and books, "I do not read thoughts, I read the bodily signals that reveal thoughts. When entering the library, a choice awaited you: two chairs arranged, equidistant. You put yourself in the decorative chair, an aesthetic choice. As you sat, I observed you catching sight of the bear, the image instilled both repulsion and attraction."

Charcot gleaned a portion of truth. The bear's ferocious and massive aspect, his hungry ring of teeth, the deadly curve of talons so prepared to tear at flesh, made me feel threatened. Yet aversion gave way to the sheer beauty of stained glass, the coloured shards pieced together to create him. The eyes as deeply red as rubies, the cobalt blue that described his fur, the hourglass he gripped a dazzling glow of amber.

"While you loathed and admired my bear," he continued with his analysis, "the rapid flickering of your pupils left no doubt that you were reading the Latin lettering. I asked myself, how does a woman, particularly a woman whose accent stems from a less refined part of Marseilles, learn Latin, a language generally reserved for gentlemen entering medicine or science? A father, most likely, who perhaps failed to complete his studies, limiting his career opportunities, but wished to pass his knowledge on to a daughter with more potential."

He was amazingly perceptive. I had to be his scribe. Wanting to please him, I read aloud the gold lettering which encircled the bear's head —"*Tempus et hora.*"

Charcot pointed skyward in oratory fashion. "Time and the hour! The motto, Mademoiselle Forette, by which I live—one must seize the moment!"

He seemed (there was no other word) exultant. Perhaps the demonstration of his perceptive powers had bolstered his elation. He left his desk, came mysteriously behind me, gripped the finials of the chair and leaned toward my ear. A clock somewhere in the house chimed ten, like a church bell. He whispered. I felt cool breath on my neck.

"Look at him now!" he urged. Rays of midmorning light entered from a highly placed window. He seemed to know the exact time when the shards of coloured glass forming the bear would shine to new brilliance. The bear's eyes ignited like two burning flames. "In triumph, he seizes time!" exclaimed Charcot. "The bear is my coat of arms, the family crest we proudly display. And the message he delivers is the secret to my success." Charcot came around to face me, half sitting on the front of the desk, "The secret? Each moment, if observed severely, holds an opportunity." He studied me again. I believe I was in a state of awe.

When he signalled me to rise, step closer, I noticed the slight cast in his left eye. I had a disorienting sense of being observed from two viewpoints. *Is this a clue*, I thought, *to his easy ability to hypnotize anyone he chooses? An optical anomaly that works to his advantage? What chance have I to escape a gaze that will perceive too much of me? I had secrets to keep.*

He spoke with smiling satisfaction. "I know what needs to be known about Mademoiselle Forette—her essence. On a winter's night she seized the hourglass to knock loudly on Jean-Martin Charcot's door." He nodded approvingly. "Showing her mettle."

He strolled to the door and pulled the bell cord for the servant. Only then did he make his pronouncement: "Consider yourself Salpêtrière's new recordist!"

One declarative sentence secured me a post to the greatest research hospital in Europe. I felt triumphant. And relief. He penetrated no further into my past. No more had been unearthed.

Dr. Charcot placed restrictions on the first months of employment. I would not accompany him on his rounds at the Salpêtrière, particularly amidst the bedlam of the mental wards, until certain that I could perform my duties with the objectivity necessary. He deemed it prudent to test my stenographic skills under the less tumultuous environment at his Saint Germain residence, the 'Charcot Castle' where he maintained a private practice. Here the wealthy patients came from all parts of the globe to benefit from a Charcot consultation.

His private patients, whether they were aristocrats or ministers of state, might very well wait for days in various antechambers for the privilege of a consultation. Neither affluence, class nor personal power held sway at the Charcot Castle. The order of admittance was almost whimsical, dependent on assistants who sought out cases which offered the most puzzlement, as the unspoken goal among the staff was to challenge the doctor's diagnostic acumen.

"The interns especially hope to outfox the fox," he chuckled, beginning to share confidences with me, "but it never happens."

The staff, however, was expected to adhere to certain formalities, as Charcot had a penchant for a hierarchical environment. The patient was brought into the consulting room by an intern who then found an unobtrusive place beside one or two assistants where they waited for further instructions. Patients were forbidden the company and support of spouses, an injunction which occasionally caused a wife to protest (husbands dutifully accepted the ban). The patient who finally entered the inner sanctum—the wealthier, the more grateful—found a sombre Dr. Charcot stationed behind an expansive desk of polished mahogany. He stayed behind the desk throughout the proceedings. A *Chief du Clinique*, having examined the patient beforehand, read a short clinical summary. At the beginning of my probationary period, the *Chief du Clinique* was Dr. Pierre Marie Janet, considered one of Charcot's most brilliant assistants, a doctor who went on to make several important neurological discoveries. Pierre Janet respectfully called his superior, Professor Charcot, as indeed Charcot was a faculty professor at the Paris University of Medicine.

Janet compensated for his balding head with a full, block shaped beard. He had formerly been Charcot's private secretary, a role I aspired to gain, which perhaps he sensed, so he derived devilish pleasure in reading his summaries at top speed in hopes of exposing errors in my dictation—which never happened.

When finished reading the patient's symptoms, he placed the summary on Charcot's desk. Janet's habit was to insert a terse personal opinion, in Latin, at the bottom of the summary. No one but Charcot knew that I read Latin and was well versed in several other languages.

My privileged seat, as Charcot's scribe, was close behind him, so I became a witness to the many extraordinary examples of his diagnostic genius. Oftentimes one detail, overlooked by others, became his key to bring a well-hidden disease to light. One of the first cases I transcribed gave proof to Charcot's power of observation.

A young judge, freshly appointed to the *Palais du Justice*, entered the consult room with an air of indifference. He wore crisp cuffs, an expensive silk cravat, and a light camel coloured suit jacket, cut short in the current fashion. Janet recited the summary of physical complaints: small scabs inexplicably formed across the top of the patient's left hand, disappeared after seven or eight days, only to make their scurrilous re-appearance several weeks later.

The young judge interjected, "Thank Jove, it's not my writing hand, so I have no trouble rendering decisions." Janet dryly continued, citing no other complaints other than "erectile difficulties." Again, the patient intervened. "On the rare occasion," he specified, giving a twist to a dandified moustache.

Charcot listened almost with disinterest. I moved the summary page closer to the doctor. He gave a cursory glance at Janet's addendum: *coniectura neque probare possunt.* 'Have hunch; cannot yet prove.' It was nothing less than a challenge to Charcot's diagnostic skills.

Curiously, he engaged the patient in a rather irrelevant discussion regarding France's current political climate: the meteoric rise of General Boulanger, the nationalistic clamour for a military leader who would stand up to Bismarck, etc.

As they both seemed to have similar nationalistic views, Charcot leaned forward, "Invade before..."

"You are invaded!" the patient raised a stern fist to complete the thought. I suspected Charcot was merely testing his mental alacrity.

"Yes!" agreed Charcot with an approving smile. "Seize the moment, as

I often say." He then turned very serious. "So, we must lay siege to these physical embarrassments of yours. I shall prescribe a salve of mercury and eucalyptus for your skin condition. And prior to your... bedroom adventures, let's prescribe a calmative powder dissolved in a half glass of gin for you, and your wife."

After the patient was dismissed with assurances that his situation would improve, Charcot turned to Janet. "The unfortunate fellow will die of an enlarged heart within two years. Spell out the diagnosis to him when he returns, as surely he will."

"Then it is acromegaly?" Janet arched his brows. "Mmm, the symptoms pointed in that direction, but I lacked confirming evidence."

"Acromegaly, without a doubt."

Later I learned acromegaly to be a rare, puzzling disorder which caused grotesque enlargements of various parts of the body, resulting in premature death.

Janet asked, "How did you become certain of his disease, Professor?"

Charcot turned to me. "Mademoiselle Forette, give me one word to describe the patient's demeanour and appearance."

"Fastidious."

"Yes. Also an intelligent and militant man. So the question naturally arises: Why does such a person appear in public with untied shoelaces?"

To a room full of confused faces, Charcot patiently explained, "Obviously, his feet were expanding and he no longer could tie his shoes. More importantly, I noticed the young husband no longer wore his wedding ring because of enlarged fingers." He looked at Janet. "Find the insidious lesion which causes this misery, Pierre, and you will increase the fame of Salpêtrière."

III

After Charcot rendered a diagnosis, typically with astonishing celerity, the patient paid the consultation fee to an assistant. Charcot's rule was not to touch money in the presence of patients—and, oddly, except on a rare occasion, would he touch the patient. The moment the patient left, however, the doctor derived a distinct pleasure in putting the bills in discreet piles which multiplied throughout the day.

Among my ever-increasing duties was to fasten hot water bottles to the doctor's chair whenever he felt inconvenienced by low back pain, but the more exhilarating assignment was to carry the accumulated fees to *le banc Rothschild* near the Bourse, the four to five hundred francs hidden in Madame Charcot's knitting bag.

Charcot's particular genius came to fore the day a patient, a prosperous American from Louisiana, was escorted in for examination. Suspected of having tabes dorsalis, an insidious neural degeneration of the dorsal column, he had the room's rapt attention, as everyone wished the opportunity to expand their understanding of American English. He was a cotton merchant who had taken an ocean liner in the company of an elderly Negro servant, determined to get from Jean-Martin Charcot the real "low down" (as he phrased it) on his condition. A jovial man of wide girth, he showed up snugly fitted in a cream coloured, Panama suit. His servant, a white-haired Negro, was elegantly liveried in a black suit and filagreed silks. As the Negro sat in dignified silence, I wondered if as a youth he had been a plantation slave, wearing ragged clothes and picking cotton.

That afternoon the clinical summary was read by a new member of Charcot's inner staff, Joseph Babinski, a young doctor just a year out of the Paris Medical College, already considered a Charcot "favourite." An extremely tall, moustachioed man, of fair complexion, he was devoted to the "Maestro" in every way. Babinski captured my interest because he had been appointed, as if by sword on shoulder, Charcot's personal assistant and happened to be, as I, of Polish descent. I had hopes of speaking with him in the native language of my father, but Babinski refused to engage in any conversation whatsoever. I found him reserved, not particularly

67

cold, just very private.

Charcot listened with evident pleasure to Babinski's case summary as he spoke in a sonorous tenor. The cotton merchant was plagued with a list of shifting symptoms, ranging from urinary incontinence to a burning tongue. During the recitation of complaints, Charcot never took his eagle eyes off the patient.

Suddenly, unexpectedly, Charcot addressed me, "Mademoiselle Forette, put down your dictation pad, walk to the window, and keep your back turned."

Babinski, two interns, and I exchanged puzzled looks before I followed instructions. Back turned, I listened to Charcot's congenial banter with the cotton merchant. "Is not Mademoiselle's hair a lovely colour? Auburn, I would say, a tad bit reddish. Stand up, Monsieur, and come closer to observe. Yes, a little closer. And her hair so nicely arranged, swept up by combs which are most interesting. Mademoiselle says her father brought them back from Egypt, supposedly ancient artefacts. Perhaps yes. I should have them evaluated at the Louvre antiquities department if I were her."

"A-a-h don't know much about combs, sir," drawled the merchant. "But a-a-h know Egyptian cotton, mighty fine threads. Length, you see, makes the difference."

"Length, yes!" answered Charcot with a slam on the desk. "I do wonder about the length of Mademoiselle's hair. Now, if I were to remove the combs, her hair would cascade down, yes? But how far?"

This foolishness, I had to remind myself, must have a purpose.

"Now Monsieur-from-Louisiana, focus your complete attention on those ancient combs, for you must remember where they are positioned. Come, come, do as you're told," insisted Charcot since the American gave out an embarrassed grunt, not one to follow nonsensical instructions. "I shall remove the combs and you, Monsieur-from-Louisianna, must help Mademoiselle replace them in their proper position."

Bewildered, the American focused on the hair combs, Charcot later confided, "As though his cotton crop depended upon it." Then came the command: "Sir, shut your eyes!"

The cotton merchant closed his eyes and instantaneously collapsed onto the floor.

"The man has tabes dorsalis!" declared Charcot.

I turned to see the liveried Negro help bring the dazed merchant to his feet.

"Take your master out into the antechamber," Charcot ordered, "and wait for further instructions."

The staff was subsequently enlightened by Charcot. "When the lower spine reaches significant degeneration, one loses the ability to feel one's position in space. But!" He wagged a finger at Babinski as if his new assistant should have known. "Some patients afflicted with tabes dorsalis learn, without conscious awareness, to keep their balance by relying on visual cues. To unmask this trick," he explained, "something ingenuous must be staged to distract the man from his unconscious reliance on objects in space, thus, when least expected, I ordered him to shut his eyes. Instead of Mademoiselle Forette's lovely auburn hair falling down, our Louisiana merchant fell—I may add, with quite a loud thud, befitting his weight."

Babinski was overcome with awe. "This compensatory symptom you expose will enable us to make a proper diagnosis."

Charcot shook his head. "Would that I could take credit for the discovery, but that dogged German, Romberg, observed the symptom and published his findings before me. But let's not be discouraged, the Salpêtrière shall discover more signs to pinpoint this particular spinal degeneration."

"Of course, Maestro, another sign or reflex!" proclaimed Babinski. He and other staff members of the inner circle, including Pierre Janet and Giles de la Tourette, had no greater ambition than to find a tell-tale sign for a neurological disease and have it named in their honour.

* * *

I learned that the talent behind Charcot's rapid diagnoses was to either see a key detail or to synthesize numerous observations into a paradigm. I, as the rest of the medical world, had nothing but reverence for Charcot's fabled 'Eye.' He exceeded all the expectations I brought with me to Paris. I became convinced he was but a step away from tearing off the mask of the most enigmatic of neurological diseases, hysteria.

There were paradoxes in Charcot's behaviour that I found disconcerting. The cold and distant tone he used to address his patients especially perplexed me. One such incident, concerning another American patient, made a deep and lasting impression on me. The American came all the way from New York City seeking from Charcot a cure. Word had spread that the gentleman was a renowned publisher.

After Dr. Pierre Janet read out the medical report, he handed me the page. Before giving it to Charcot, I read Janet's personal comment, penned in Latin at the bottom:

omnia praeter mortem corrigi possunt

all but death can be corrected

The American entered with peculiar calm. There was an unassuming sophistication in his manner. He found a suitable seat then placed his Homburg on an empty chair next to him. The American let his gaze pass by every man in the room before he settled on me. Apparently, Charcot's reputation had little effect on him.

"I'm here at the bequest of my wife," he remarked. In his eyes I saw something world-wearied, yet I judged him as a man who had learned to accept situations and people as they were.

Earlier, Charcot alerted me to the gentleman's eminence as the publisher of Ralph Waldo Emerson, knowing I was a fervent admirer of the American essayist. Charcot also forewarned that the publisher had come with his wife's thin hope of a cancer cure.

Charcot wasted no time, giving his blunt diagnosis: the cancer had expanded too far in the subventricular region of the brain. The corrosive damage meant impending death. He was shockingly specific: "I predict, before autumn."

Hearing the death sentence, the publisher reflected, "Well, to reach the season of autumn in the Adirondacks–which is where we live—shall be an unexpected pleasure. I will be a falling leaf among many."

Charcot shrugged. *"L'imprevu est toujours possible."*

The unexpected is always possible—I kept my head down as I translated Charcot's half-hearted attempt to condole the patient. The American smiled. He pulled money from a wallet, proffered a sizeable amount of American dollars to Charcot who, of course, pretended not to see. Janet intervened and took the consultation fee.

After the publisher closed the door behind him, I saw that he had forgotten his grey felt Homburg; I grabbed the hat and ran after him. Halfway down the corridor he stopped at the sound of my echoing footsteps. I was politely thanked for the retrieval of the Homburg.

I asked, "Did you know Mr. Emerson, personally?"

"I stood before him but one time, at his funeral in Concord, although I knew him well by his words."

We smiled kindly at each other. I wished to offer him sympathy for his condition, but overt sentimentality had no place in Charcot's House of

Science. He turned away.

"Cut these words and they would bleed," I called out, "they are vascular and alive."

He stopped again, surprised—"So you know your Emerson."

I felt awkward at my attempt to establish our affinity.

He donned his Homburg and rewarded me with another quote: "'When it is dark enough, you can see the stars.'"

As I returned to the consulting room, a thought came: *Unforeseen calamity either shatters one's psyche or strengthens it.*

Dr. Charcot was stacking the American dollars into a distinct green pile among the faded hues of the francs. "Eureka!" he announced, his smile extremely broad. "Now it's apparent why one calls them greenbacks."

Hunched over and concentrating on building towers of banknotes, he suddenly winced. I was familiar with the crease in the centre of his brow which indicated a surge of lumbar discomfort—my signal to retrieve the hot water bottle.

He was the god of Science and I worshipped him for his masterful identification of disease. Yet Dr. Jean-Martin Charcot could not tolerate the least scintilla of physical pain.

Chapter 9

**We learn geology the morning after the earthquake,
on ghastly diagrams of cloven mountains,
upheaved plains, and the dry bed of the sea.**

Ralph Waldo Emerson

Words Collide or Dance

Charcot, during our first meeting, ingeniously put together a credible portrait of my family background. Deciphering behaviour to glean facts from one's past was his unparalleled talent. But he had missed much.

My father was not a physician, although he pretended to be one. He used to hire himself out to those sailing companies too miserly to hire a genuine ship's doctor. Father's medical training came solely from the books he read. When not gambling away his money or frequenting the brothels, my father pored over books. He read not to be entertained, but to learn.

My sister and I gained our deepest education through his books, the sailor bag of books he brought home from his world-wide voyages. The three of us spent hours and hours in our "Pickle Room" library which was also crammed with medical and nautical paraphernalia. Father facilitated our education by teaching us a method of rapid reading. We learned to scan pages quickly, extracting their inherent idea from first and last sentences in paragraphs. For what use are words, Father asked, if they do not serve an idea? Read aggressively, he advised.

When Father's friend, Monsieur Prasadaba, the Marseilles bookseller, observed my method of reading, flipping and snapping pages in rapid succession, he expressed disappointment. Taking off his gold-rimmed glasses, he reproached me for becoming "a most unholy reader."

But the goal, Father said, was to reach the heart of the idea, the core, the philosophical construct latent in the text. All the little words, *touts les petits mots*, will either awkwardly collide or eloquently dance to a theme.

Father, the bibliophile, the pretend physician, immigrated to France from Krakow, Poland when he was a young man. My mother was born in a small village in Ireland called Killaloe. She came to Marseilles with her parents who fled the terrible Potato Famine. She was only two-years-old. How Father and Mother met remained an untold story. Margaret, my mother, cared little for memories and so never discussed the past. She had but one ruling concern in life: all and everything around her must be immaculately clean. The laundry business suited her perfectly—washing, scrubbing and cleaning a compulsion. A religion. We wore clothes and slept in bedding washed daily. The sheets (and our undergarments) might on occasion still be damp from a fresh wash, but never soiled or dirty. All spotlessly white. Some in the neighbourhood, mostly girls my age, who would be lucky to bathe once a month, mocked me, said I smelled of soap.

Mother's need to protect herself from grime and life's debris meant the house contained nothing deemed superfluous. No photographs or pictures were on display. Nothing should ever mar or blemish the walls in any room. Her one exception was the Sacred Heart, a Catholic keepsake from Ireland, a holy icon for her, which approximated the size of an actual heart. Cast in iron, the red heart, surrounded with faux gold rays, was nailed above our bed, not centered, but on the side where Bijou slept.

Mother had another peculiarity—which I thought our family's shame. She could not read. Not a word. When I repeatedly offered to teach her, she refused. Such eccentricities and family differences put all of us in erratic orbits to each other.

Yet, if our family constellation had a pattern, a leitmotif, it was abandonment. Father set the pattern in motion. The way in which he abandoned us was both—can these words be linked together?—subtle and brutal. The subtlety of Father's desertion showed itself in increments, monthly voyages to Mediterranean ports, then yearly excursions to more remote lands, then—just when I reached adolescence, and Bijou puberty—Father's last voyage extended indefinitely. He had, cleverly it seemed, erased himself, as a teacher erases an unneeded sentence from the blackboard.

Mother left more suddenly, a violent cerebral haemorrhage. My brother Justin found her insensate on the floor, her eyes open wide and blood trickling from both ears. Death, with irony, claimed her in the one place she practically never ventured, the Pickle Library, staring with uncomprehending horror at the titles on the spines that filled the shelves. Justin sought me in the courtyard, amidst the fire-heated barrels, where I tended to the wash. Wordlessly he escorted me as far as the library doorway. Like a circumspect stranger, he would go no farther. I rushed to mother who lay motionless. Having absorbed a modicum of father's medical knowledge, I pressed the carotid artery for a pulse. There was none. Only the quickly coagulated blood on the sides of her face, and mother's familiar smell of soap and lye. I turned in despair to Justin, but he was gone. I found him later in Mother's bed, my twenty-year-old brother, curled in a foetal position.

Justin soon managed his own flight, leaving Marseilles without a word or a good-bye. Reputedly, he went to try his luck in Australia, refuge for thieves and felons. No one ever, as far as I could discern, missed Justin.

Chapter 10

Dear Monsieur Sezanne (sic),

I begin by wishing you good day and at the same time to inform you of my straits; imagine, my dolt of a landlord has just sent me a notice of eviction for the six months advance rent I owe him according to our lease, but since I find myself unable to pay him I am writing to you, my dear Monsieur Sezanne and am begging you to exert every effort to send me a payment on your bill...

In the hope that you will be kind enough to accede to my request, please accept in advance my thanks and believe, dear Sir, your devoted servant.

Julien Tanguy

(Dictated to daughter)

THE PAINTER'S PAINTER

I

It is difficult and awkward to explain my affair with the painter Paul Cezanne. A touch of willful delusion on my part. I was drawn to the mystery of him.

It began in Montmartre when searching for paintings that might please the Charcot family. I was on the narrow rue Clauzel in front of an inconspicuous paint shop. Displayed in the window a rather odd pairing of paintings caught my attention. What brave-hearted merchant, I mused, would dare exhibit such a disparate coupling of genres—a nude and a still life. Perhaps the shop owner had hopes that at least one of the offered fruits might lure a customer. The nude I found extraordinarily hideous, her flesh trowelled in cement grey, a body cobbled together as if by a street paver. The still life, however, would not let me leave. A bowl of fruit, *c'est tout*, nothing more than oranges, lemons, and apples, but so solidly painted as to seem imperishable. The fruit, piled in a ceramic bowl, rested upon a precariously tilted table and appeared quite ready to roll riotously from out of the canvas, yet everything on the tilted table somehow remained locked into place. My new passion, after several months of living in Paris, was Impressionism, but this painting gave me none of Impressionism's éclat. There was no blur of motion, no dissolvement of form, no bravura flurry of brush strokes, yet the *facture*, the brushwork, enthralled me. I ransacked my mind, searching for the word to convey how the artist used his brush. *Construction, he constructs*, I decided.

The bell above the shop door tinkled when a kindly looking gentleman stepped out, peering over a pair of spectacles perched at the end of a bulbous nose. I had been caught standing awe struck in front of the painting. "I see that Mademoiselle has discovered the Sphinx."

"The Sphinx?"

"Paul Cezanne, the greatest living painter in France!"

"I have never heard of him."

The man removed and placed his spectacles in his breast pocket. "So far, he is known only among the elect, those with intense understanding of painting technique. Most often, other painters."

I returned the gentleman's smile, eager to learn more. "Then he is a painter's painter."

"Mademoiselle is most perceptive," he happily noted. "Which painting captures your fancy, his early or later work?"

"He painted both?" I was surprised. I found the boulder- like shapes that formed the nude too turbulent.

"The still-life is most recent," he said.

"That is my preference."

"Would you be interested in purchasing it?" he inquired hopefully. "I am the shopkeeper," he added, managing to button a tight-fitting jacket of rough blue cloth.

"Well, not for myself..." explaining my role of appraising new art for my employers, the Charcot family.

"So, you are their art muse," he decided.

"That is a most flattering way of putting it."

So began my friendship with the benevolent Julien Tanguy. He was a short, thickset, elderly man, with a grizzled beard and large beaming eyes of dark blue. Inviting me into his shop, he soon admitted that the paintings he displayed in his shop window were not his principal means of livelihood. He was a craftsman, an expert grinder of paints which he sold to artists. I came to learn that the Impressionists bought their colours from no one else, for Julien Tanguy's mixes were superior to all others. The Impressionists also could count on Tanguy to extend their credit when money was tight.

He invited me to a chair and brought over the Cezanne still-life. Putting his metal spectacles back on, he sat beside me, the canvas on his lap, his stubby fingers grazed lightly over the brightly coloured fruit. "Does not the brush work intrigue Mademoiselle?" asked the paint-maker.

"Yes, it does."

"He has re-thought the Impressionist stroke," he said. "Instead of Impressionism's flickering commas, the Sphinx offers geometric mystery."

Julien Tanguy, I soon discovered, had an unwavering reverence for Cezanne's work. We eventually came to an agreement that I would take the still life on contingency, with the hope that I might convince Dr. Charcot to purchase it. After Tanguy happily wrapped the canvas, he showed me to the door.

Concerned, I asked, "Shouldn't we design a contract and affix our signatures?"

"I trust Mademoiselle," he replied.

"But Monsieur Tanguy," I gently protested, "that makes poor business sense."

He looked downcast. Had I offended him?

"Mademoiselle, the truth is that I never learned my ABCs," came his admission. "I had to earn my bread early in life; began as a plasterer. It is my youngest daughter who writes for me when necessary. She's receiving the proper education I never had," he added proudly.

"A signed contract between friends is not necessary, Monsieur Tanguy."

He smiled. "I agree."

A simple, uneducated man, who could not write, Tanguy nonetheless loved and appreciated art more wisely than most.

II

Whenever I found time from my stenographic duties, I visited the paintmaker's shop, eager to benefit from Tanguy's wisdom in the sphere of art. And my other motive, wanting to learn more about Paul Cezanne. And possibly meet the artist.

Julien Tanguy talked rapturously of the Impressionists who were, in his decided opinion, the vanguard soldiers of "new art." Courageous fellows who were "of the people," he emphasized. They set their easels wherever necessary, in humble village markets, atop hotel balconies, down in the railway stations, everywhere to catch the hubbub of modern life. "They show our busy boulevards, bridges, factories, and the steam engine trains at St. Lazarre. What's around them, Mademoiselle Forette, for they are dedicated to depicting real folk who must earn their bread and butter, our working citizenry who sometimes gain a few hours of pleasure in the Sunday parks and outdoor cafés."

A committed socialist, Tanguy peppered his views of the Impressionists with his own political beliefs. He was, for the most part, extremely mild-mannered, polite, even deferential, but could work himself into a socialist lather when espousing his convictions—freedom, equality and fraternity! After the disastrous war with Germany, Tanguy confided with pride that he had promptly joined the Communard to rid France of emperors and give the people equality. The Communards' defeat cost him two years of life in prison.

Tanguy sometimes called the special group of artists he admired, "chromo-luminists" for they had removed certain lugubrious colours from their palette. "They're finished with those dark tobacco juice pictures you see in the bourgeois, state-run Salon."

The commitment he had made to Impressionist colour became evident when one afternoon a customer entered the shop, asking to "have a gander" at what paints the owner had available. The man stood rather confidently in knee high boots of polished leather and wore a wide brim, cloche hat at a rakish angle. I took him for a prosperous artist. Tanguy tookout several drawers of paint tubes in organized rows, gazing down at

80

them with all the fond love of a parent for his beloved children. He squeezed smidgens onto a make-shift palette, a rich spectrum of chromo-luminist colours he silently invited the customer to admire.

"But where is black?" asked the man in the soft cloche hat.

"Monsieur!" Tanguy looked offended. "You'll not find that odious colour among my tubes, neither lamp black nor bitumen."

"But I need black for my chiaroscuro," insisted the customer.

"Black is an illusion, Monsieur, it does not exist, not even in the darkest shadows." Tanguy showed him several tubes which he thought were appropriate substitutes.

"But I must have my bitumen," the artist complained.

Replacing the tubes carefully into their allotted row, sliding drawers back in their slots, Tanguy came from behind the counter and gently took the customer by the arm. "Let me show you the door, Monsieur."

After the astonished customer was escorted from the shop, my paintmaker friend said, "Obviously the man has not truly looked at a shadow which takes in the colours that surround it. This is science. All of my chromo-luminists, long ago, tossed their tubes of black in the rubbish bin."

Occasionally I had moments of uncertainty—might this new passion for art be something frivolous, a pursuit to lead me astray, subtract from a devotion to science? My very purpose for coming to Paris was to embrace science in the guise of Charcot. Science, above all else, would be the means to rid the world of its ills and Tanguy's social inequalities, so how comforting it became to hear him speak of art and science in the same breath.

He held out a tube of paint. "Here we have the scientific breakthrough of the century, putting paint in a tube, letting our artists escape from their studios, giving them precious freedom; thus, with the tube, we progress."

"Also, chemists and their chemistry enhance your pigments," I hurriedly added, eager to keep science in the picture.

That day, before leaving the paint shop, I spoke the thought as though unimportant. "It might be interesting to make the acquaintance of Paul Cezanne."

Tanguy laughed with good-hearted mirth, as if what I wanted was too fanciful to consider. "No one ever secures a meeting with Cezanne. One only waits for a rare appearance. My shop has two or three students who regularly pop in, the clever ones from Cormon's art school, who hang around and wait, hoping the Sphinx will unexpectedly pay a visit and—ha! —explain his technique."

"Then I, as well, shall accustom myself to waiting for the unexpected."

"That's a smart way of putting it, Mademoiselle Forette."

The Cezanne affair was, in a manner of speaking, just waiting around the corner.

III

A marital squabble was embarrassingly evident when I quietly entered the rue Clauzel shop. Behind the counter a contrite Tanguy was enduring the glare of his wife. My first impression of Madame Tanguy was that she looked as thin as a stick and seemed twice as hard. She gave Tanguy one final, withering glare before she stormed through the beaded curtains into their private domicile. The angry clatter of the curtain beads lingered until a distraught Tanguy became aware of my presence. His spirits suddenly lifted, he approached gingerly, dressed as though for a special occasion, his Sunday jacket tightly buttoned to barely contain his bulk. Tanguy's bristled hair had been combed flat and freshly parted. He brought with him the piney scent of a barber's aftershave.

"They were here!" he exclaimed. "You just missed them!"

"Who?" I asked.

He beamed. "The three kings."

I looked around the shop for evidence of missed royalty. There were three chairs, rather comically mismatched, arranged in a horseshoe around a painting propped on an easel. I recognized the Cezanne, a house perched amidst blue, mountainous pines, on my wish list to show the Charcot family.

Tanguy knew my intent. "It's been sold, Mademoiselle Forette, to one of the kings, the artist supreme, Claude Oscar Monet. Imagine, he will take *le Chateau Noir* to his home in Giverny."

Monet! What bad luck to have missed him.

Claude Monet, the artist whom the Montmartre gallerists mentioned first when discussing Impressionism. "Who were the other kings?" I was keen to know.

"Messieurs Edgar Degas and Auguste Renoir."

Speechless, I stared at the three empty chairs. I was always on the lookout for a Degas painting or pastel in the galleries, adoring his ballerinas, and had recently seen a surprising work at Durand-Ruel's, a remarkable composition, giving a less than elegant, bird's eye view of a dancer adjusting her slipper. And to see a voluptuous nude by Renoir, whenever good fortune came my way, was a tingled thrill.

Tanguy patted the arm of a shabbily worn upholstered chair. "Renoir chose the most comfortable. He was the first to sit." Tanguy enjoyed describing the details. "He took off his floppy straw hat, stretched out his long, bony legs in front of him and rested his arms right here." He looked reverently at the armchair as though a sacred relic. "Monsieur Renoir," he reflected, "such elegant hands."

I encouraged a full account, not a single detail should be excluded. Tanguy was delighted to describe the momentous occasion.

"Degas chose the middle chair; but being the finicky sort, dusted it off with his initialed handkerchief."

I sat down in Degas' chair, ready for more of Tanguy's fabulous experience.

"Monet graciously accepted the last chair," said Tanguy. "I worried for him. See?" He shook the chair. "One of the legs is a little wobbly." The paintmaker suddenly stopped his story when he heard the faint clicking of the beaded curtains. An uneasy silence reigned until a woman's voice, more like a crackle, muttered, "Idiot husband!" and a door that led to the family quarters slammed shut. Tanguy shrugged and resumed. He was such an excellent story teller, giving insights into the painters' personalities that the scene easily came to life.

* * *

For Tanguy, it was as if distinguished leaders from the Communard had seated themselves in his humble shop. He dared not utter a word. Renoir spoke first.

"So, Père Tanguy, have you found a market for his work?"

(All the artists called him Père Tanguy for he treated their paintings with fatherly care.) Taking a respectful step back, he clasped his hands. "Alas, Monsieur Renoir, he remains a painter's painter." (Ha! I laughed to myself that he had borrowed my phrase.) His stage play continued, speaking all the parts: "Gentlemen," he addressed the three Impressionists, " I can say that Paul Signac, a young artist of much promise, purchased a Cezanne landscape... but that was a year ago come July. Of course, the more progressive students at Cormon's atelier are enthralled by his technique, but what money can they spare? Then... there is Monsieur Paul Gauguin. He seriously speculates and owns several."

Degas laughed. "Ha! Gauguin, the Fox! Does he have future plans to make a killing in the art market with his Cezannes?"

Renoir, who refused to take his gaze from the painting, shook his head. "The Fox will suffer a long wait before the marketplace accepts, let alone fathoms, this mysterious style."

Tanguy could tell that the window light troubled Degas' sensitive eyes. "May I move your chair, Monsieur Degas?"

"No need, standing will do me good." He rose and patted the paintmaker's shoulder. "I do congratulate you, Père Tanguy, for your courage. Even our dealers, Durand-Ruel and the like, find such..." he pointed his walking cane at the painting, "too radical."

"Oh, Monsieur Degas! I could not compare myself to such a distinguished art dealer as Durand-Ruel. I'm only a paintmaker who takes pleasure in offering my window to those artists who have not yet achieved your stature. Yet someday," Tanguy looked fondly at the painting, "Monsieur Cezanne will sell as well as the masters in the Louvre."

"What does he call this landscape?" asked Degas.

"Le Chateau Noir," answered Tanguy.

Moving closer to the landscape, Degas expressed irritation. "The house hasn't a damn drop of black!"

"Ah Messieurs!" Tanguy shrugged in bewilderment. "Who can say what is in his mind? He baffles all who meet him."

Renoir jumped up and approached the painting. "If I could rope the Sphinx to a chair, I'd ask how he gets such vibrancy in his blues?"

"There is much blue in the painting," noted Tanguy with caution. He saw that Renoir clearly coveted the painting.

The artist peered closer, his neck stretched forward, reminding Tanguy of a whooping crane. "A blue sky, a blue roof, even the branches and leaves of the pine tree are infused with blue," remarked Renoir.

"The buyer could," suggested Tanguy delicately, "retitle it *Le Chateau en Bleu*?"

"Such translucence in the colour," murmured Renoir, almost in rapture.

Tanguy felt a surge of hope: *Perhaps Renoir will make a reasonable bid. My wife watches through the beaded curtains. The rent on the shop is past due.* But Renoir turned silent and sullen. *He regrets his enthusiastic outburst*, thought Tanguy. *Renoir doesn't want to show his cards.*

Tanguy spoke, "No one but Cezanne demands that I grind his paints to the finest consistency."

"What one must admire," noted Degas, "is the quiet dynamism of the composition, a blending of forms that both recede and rush forward—yet everything, be it branch, leaf, cloud, remains in equilibrium."

"Monsieur Degas is so right." Tanguy lost himself in his love for the painting. "Looking at his compositions, my heart races faster."

Degas paced. "Gentlemen, it's obvious that we all wish to possess *le Chateau Noir* which has no black, so let's get down to business." Degas took on his official tone and Tanguy lost all hope for a genuine auction. "I'm sure Père Tanguy will be more than satisfied with a fair, flat price of a hundred francs."

Degas looked sternly at him. "Fetch three straws and trim them to varying lengths."

Tanguy rushed through the back rooms, into the yard where Madame Tanguy was feeding several hens. Ignoring his wife's suspicious glare, he found straw from a hen's nest and hurried back. As instructed, he gave Degas three straws snipped in different lengths.

Degas showed Renoir and a silent Monet just the even tips sticking out from his fist. "The solution to our dilemma is that each draws," he ordered with his business voice. "Long straw takes home the painting for a hundred francs."

The unhappy Tanguy caught sight of his wife peering through the beaded curtains. She shook a threatening finger. He could almost hear her rebuke: *Again the dolt has failed, he should have insisted that they bid on the painting.* The beads rattled, she disappeared, and he thought glumly, *My ear will be sorely pinched before this day passes.*

Renoir came forward to pull out the first straw. "Plain to see mine is shortest," he complained. "Lady Fortune has turned her buttocks to me."

Degas drew a longer straw, but Monet came forward to draw the longest. He turned to Tanguy, dug into his pocket, pressed a hundred francs into the paintmaker's hand, and since his arrival uttered his first words, a query: "Does he do water?"

"He depicts water rarely," Tanguy responded, grateful to receive any money for a Cezanne painting. "But mountains, as you know, many mountains from his beloved Provence, and a portrait now and then, for those who dare sit a hundred hours. And fruit, many apples and pears pose in patience for his unique brush stroke."

Monet reflected further, "I wonder how his brush stroke would do water?"

"Like shards of coloured glass, I suppose," Renoir ruminated as he chewed on the piece of straw. "Well, Degas and I need not worry that Cezanne will compete with our nudes, for who would pose for someone possessed of such volatile moods."

"Ah, messieurs!" Tanguy lamented. "If only he were more sociable.

Why, only yesterday he passed by the window without a glance at my display of his paintings."

"In Paris, is he?" Monet expressed surprise. (I, too.)

"Surely Père Tanguy saw a ghost," joked Renoir.

"If a ghost, Messieurs, I ran after it; but when I reached him, grabbed his shoulder, you would not believe the look of terror on his face, as if I, Tanguy, had the touch of a leper."

"Ah, his fear of being touched still plagues him," noted Renoir with a disappointing shake of the head.

Degas took interest. "This must be what they call a phobia."

Tanguy further lamented, "And he scolded me in a most virulent manner for spying on him. Me! Old Tanguy! Can you imagine? I who give him all the paints he wants on credit."

"He is a victim of too much self-doubt," remarked Monet sadly. "He needs to be encouraged, Tanguy, his spirits need to be lifted. Let him know how much we admire what he's doing with his brush stroke, for it is less a stroke than a geometric plane. Do your best, Tanguy, to let him know that he is a genius."

"I will remind him that there are those who believe in him, Monsieur Monet, I will!" promised the paintmaker.

"Please ship the canvas to my home in Giverny," said Monet.

"Where will you place *le Chateau Noir*?" asked Degas.

"I think above my bed, to contemplate before sleep."

* * *

After a farewell look at what was now Monet's painting, I thanked my friend for describing his momentous day so colourfully and sharing what the three Impressionists had divulged. I had much to absorb. Cezanne's painted chateau, set high in the forest of pines, was certainly not black, the facade a luminous, sunbaked ochre and cathedral windows which reflected the blue sky. As Degas had observed, the leaves, twisting branches, clouds and sky blended without losing their forms. And the myriad of forms did rush forward even as they receded. The artist found a way to express the dynamic energy of nature. No matter how volatile his character, he found equilibrium in his art. My desire to meet Cezanne deepened.

Chapter 11

1886

My dear Professor,

As for the past two months I have been fascinated by your eloquence and immensely interested by the subject with which you deal in a masterly manner, it has occurred to me to offer you my services for the translation into German of the third volume of your 'Lessons' ...

Your completely devoted,

Dr. Sigm. Freud

1886

My Dearest Marty,

(His library) is as large as the whole of our future home, a room worthy of the magic palace he dwells in.

Sigmund Freud

(Letter to fiancée,

Martha Bernays)

LE RÊVE

I

Sigmund Freud stood on the corner of Boulevard St. Germain and rue St. Dominique, peering at Charcot's palatial house through Madame Richetti's opera glasses. She stood beside him, rummaging inside the confection bag for her second pastry, offering him historical information. "The house was erected in the early 18th century as a hotel for French aristocracy." Finding a sugar powdered bun, Madame Richetti added, "The *dottore* has transformed it into a medieval castle and neurological clinic."

He adjusted the makeshift spy glasses for a panoramic view. The length of the queue forming at Charcot's front gate amazed him —scores of patients willing to wait in the early chilled hours of morning. And they were not typical patients, Sigmund observed, but a procession of dignitaries and millionaires from the capitals of Europe and America, waiting with silent patience for their appointed hour.

Madame Richetti exchanged the bag of pastries for her turn with the opera glasses, deftly adjusting the lens for a closer look. Madame Richetti, married to an Italian neurologist, Sigmund's colleague at the teaching clinic, was a middle-aged woman of great bulk. Wrapped in a heavy sable coat whose collar hid a double chin, she wore a hunter's cap which sprouted an arched pheasant wing. Madame Richetti, his new found ally, was fond of extravagant feathers and furs. He noticed on her upper lip a bristle of sugar powder as though she had acquired a white moustache.

The queue stretched to the far end of the block, some patients leaned precariously on canes and others were shaking with a variety of palsies. Not a few were accompanied by personal nurses. A pasha wearing a white turban was being carried on a litter.

Madame Richetti, an emotional Italian, expressed her softhearted sympathy, "Oh, *Sigmundo*. Such a *spettacolo tragico*! Here are dukes, barons and sultans, cursed no less than the poor unfortunates at the Salpêtrière."

He chose a cinnamon coated pasty, trying to forget that he would soon need to summon courage in order to cross the street and keep his appointment. "*Dio mio!*" Madame Richetti continued to lament. "I see men over there who must be captains of industry, yet they meekly wait like quivering beggars!"

She handed back the opera glasses to reclaim the pastry bag. (Both he and Madame Richetti shared a sweet tooth.) It was thanks to Madame's warm relationship with the Charcot family that he had secured a private appointment with Dr. Charcot. She had also helped him artfully compose a letter with the suggestion that he translate Charcot's lectures into German.

Sigmund's ambition, as a new intern, was to gain a more personal relationship with the Director of the Salpêtrière Hospital. The letter now in Charcot's hand, his great opportunity had arrived!

The queue of disabled patients continued to sadden Madame Richetti, the third powdered bun further whitening her moustache. "*Dio mio!* So many of them shake like leaves ruled by unseen winds. What *malattia neurologica* afflicts them?"

He explained, "Much of the uncontrollable trembling you see presents as Parkinson's disease."

But she had no use for medical terminology, preferring lyrical descriptions. "Though they be Midases, still they suffer from a Pandora's box of maladies."

He pondered the attractive pastry with caramelized swirls, but a growing nervousness settled in his stomach. Would Charcot consider him an upstart possessed of too much ambition and too little experience? He listened to Madame Richetti wax more poetical—

"All in a dutiful line waiting for the gates of their salvation to open, driven by one desire, to be examined by the near divine healer Jean-Martin Charcot, all harbouring one consuming hope, to obtain his magic cure! *La cura magica!* Thus they will wait under the sun, moon and stars to find relief, a release from their trembling and crippling hells." She gripped his arm. "Don't you see, my handsome but insolvent young man, that such sufferers are willing to pay a king's ransom for a cure. This I tell you, as I repeatedly remind my husband Giovanni, a king's ransom! You in your Viennese home, Giovanni in our Firenze, a medical practice in neurology, the surest road to prosperity!"

He checked his pocket watch, realizing that the momentous hour had arrived. Madame Richetti, the dear woman, adjusted his tie. The white powder on her upper lip reminded him of cocaine—which he wished he had taken this morning.

"Il coraggio!" Courage she called out as he crossed Boulevard St. Germain. "And remember my caution!"

Hurriedly he passed the queue, patients eyeing him with wonder and admiration as he freely entered the gate. "Be prepared, Sigmundo," he remembered Madame Richetti's cautionary words, "do not lose your bearing. The man is brilliant, but eccentric—as anyone must be who keeps a Congolese monkey faithfully at his side. The two of them, man and monkey, have been rumoured to often embrace each other with tender affection. It's been said, though I shall not swear to the veracity of the fact, that the monkey," Madame added in a more ominous tone, as though what she would say next had a certain significance, "is named *Napoleon*."

Feeling alarmingly giddy, he banged the bear and hourglass knocker with idiotic fury. The door opened quickly and he faced, not the Congolese monkey, but Charcot's chief clinician, Dr. Gilles de la Tourette.

La Tourette, a privileged member of Charcot's inner circle, glared. His face was long and sallow with eyes deeply sunk into dark sockets. Unforgiving eyes. Tourette towering over him, resembled a praying mantis. *I'm being escorted by a huge insect but I must appear reasonably calm.* Sigmund was led into the centre of a grand foyer, directly beneath an enormous chandelier.

"Remain here pursuant to further instructions, Herr Freudstein."

"Freud, Dr. Freud."

"Your card?"

If only I could afford such a luxury. What money he saved from the stipend went to his mother and sisters, Rosa and Anna. "My card? At the printers, as we speak."

"I will inform the professor of your presence."

Left alone, his anxiety mounted, his suspicions multiplied. The crystal chandelier would come crashing down upon him, a release lever pulled by la Tourette. He felt and saw himself a supplicant in the Medici palace, waiting for a favourable audience with the prince. The floor, of Carrara marble, gleamed spotlessly. Behind him a wide, marble stairway, guarded by twin caryatids, led to regions he would never reach. The caryatids were full-breasted, twice Sigmund's height, and bore huge candelabra upon their muscular shoulders. He could only marvel before such a display of grandeur.

He had heard that Charcot's wealth had been gained through a propitious marriage to a wealthy widow. How much of a dowry could he reasonably expect from his fiancée's family? *Not much, as long as that shiftless brother of Marty's continues to make fishy investments.*

From the far side of the foyer yet another of Charcot's personal assistants appeared. He recognized the quick-witted Georges Guinon walking with his customary alacrity across the polished floors. Guinon's meticulously combed beard and hair, arranged in two admirable bays, glistened with French pomade. He called out in the loudest voice. "Herr Freud! Our young Prussian doctor abides with us mere weeks and—*voila* —secures a private audience with our *Patron*." As always, Guinon was affable, sarcastic, and cynical. He placed an arm through Sigmund's as though the two of them were co-conspirators in some undisclosed plot. "Admit to me, Herr Freud!" He reeked of lavender cologne. "Was that not a splendidly diseased brain I secured for you yesterday? A near perfect representation of gross sensory aphasia, yes?" Guinon played many unusual roles at the Salpêtrière, not least supplying the pathology department with cadavers and miscellaneous organs.

Sigmund expressed his appreciation: "The right hemisphere was quite riddled with lesions."

"Yes, a regular Swiss cheese," Guinon chuckled.

Propitious to let him think we are allies. "I must express my gratitude, Dr. Guinon, the cadavers you bring..."

Guinon interrupted, "As to these children's brains you request..." *Why does he maintain his conspiratorial tone?* Sigmund wondered with some irritation. Guinon lowered his voice, "You do understand... the children, who suffer from your speciality, are more difficult to procure? Rest assured, however, my contacts are everywhere," he wiggled his fingers like tentacles "assiduously scouring Paris, from Montparnasse to Montmartre."

"Dr. Guinon, I will be satisfied with whatever the fates bring to the Morgue."

"Oh, let us leave nothing to chance! After all, neurological paralysis in children is your area of expertise and you must be allowed the opportunity to pursue your research. But what intrigues me, Herr Freud, is how you find the time to pursue other interests? For example, this magnanimous offer of yours to translate our professor's lectures into German, eh?"

"Do I have too much ambition?"

"Did the lean and hungry Cassius have too much ambition?"

"I come to praise Caesar."

"Such erudite wit," laughed Guinon, escorting Sigmund from the foyer. "I told Tourette only recently that Herr Freud has what I would characterize as winsome bravado. And to have such praiseworthy characteristics coupled with youth!"

"I am already twenty-nine... but still really at sea."

"Consider the good Christ, did he not begin his ministry at age thirty? Let me speak in all candor." His arm locked more firmly into Sigmund's, Guinon slowed their pace. "While our *Patron* might consent to your translating his work for the Germans, one has to wonder if the Boche are worth the effort, for we do not find it easy to forget the war of 1870—the boom of cannon fire still echoes in my ears."

Guinon's head, almost perfectly round, is uncannily similar to a cannon ball. Putting aside the thought, Sigmund reminded him, "I was twelve at the time."

"No one holds you responsible, Herr Freud... per se." Guinon led him through a maze of passageways, their footsteps muffled by exquisite millefleurs carpets, passing a surprising number of alcoves, decorated with church windows, and each furnished, to Sigmund's astonishment, with a prayer stool. Guinon had no trouble breaking into his thoughts. "The prayer stools baffle you, yes? Why, you wonder, would Professor Jean-Martin Charcot, avowed Republican, one of France's most renowned atheists, the man who swept all the old nuns out of Salpêtrière to replace them with lay nurses, why would such a man, devoid of superstition, collect religious artefacts, particularly prayer stools?" Guinon shrugged. "I only know it's his obsession; although wouldn't you agree that this paraphernalia imparts a certain medieval charm to *le Patron*'s palatial abode? Ah, here we are!"

Directed into a vast room of shadows, Sigmund was oddly abandoned.

II

Alone, adjusting his vision to the shadowy dark, he found himself at the threshold of an immense library. Nothing could have prepared him for the magnificence.

Dearest Marty, I stand in Jean Martin Charcot's library! Alone! Here, where the great neurologist conceived his many brilliant ideas!

He would recall the interior precisely for Marty as he took careful steps into a room more spacious than his entire apartment in Vienna. The French doors, which accessed a garden, were inlaid with a mosaic of coloured shards throbbing with varying intensities.

My dear fiancée, I believe the stained glass doors demarcate the room, divide the library into two distinct hemispheres, as if to duplicate the brain's binary functions.

The right half of the room was clearly devoted to visual pleasure, the wall tapestries surely dated to the Renaissance and gold-framed paintings he suspected were done by Dutch masters. But the left region of the library drew him—where Dr. Charcot's scientific interests dominated. The many glass cabinets were stocked with a variety of medical curiosities, some displayed as though jewelled treasures, a group of ancient surgical instruments, torturous looking saws, pincers, pliers and bone-handled scalpels resting upon silk cushions. He passed between a row of cabinets displaying nothing but spines, animal, human, each grossly deformed by disease. When he came to a cul de sac, he saw the most amazing display: upon a pedestal a small glass box, lined in black velvet, inside a tiny skeleton, delicate blanched bones, as if a religious relic, shaped into a perfect S.

A marvelous, exquisite sea horse! Dr. Charcot, how admirable, gives proof to the inherent beauty of the spine's curvature.

Sigmund had more to explore in the analytical hemisphere of Charcot's library, the bookcases made of elegant rosewood which covered entire walls, their shelves filled with innumerable books, topics that ranged from science, medicine, history, to literature. He walked by master writers: Shakespeare, Racine, Daudet, Zola. But what thrilled him most was to discover an antique edition, in Spanish, of *Don Quixote*! He touched its leather-ribbed spine with reverence, the novel he held in the highest esteem, and suddenly recalled his encounter with the hefty, old fellow urinating in the alley, who tipped his cap like Sancho Panza to Don

94

Quixote. Now it seemed more a cocaine dream.

Somewhere chimes rang nine times, a clock alerting him to his appointed hour. Almost on cue, the great man himself entered the library at the ninth ring. *Jean-Martin Charcot!*

The Director of Salpêtrière proceeded toward him—Sigmund's heart skipped. He recognized his own letter that Charcot gripped, but what dark thing did the doctor cradle?

Coal black, the Congolese monkey! The creature, sighting Sigmund, bared its teeth and emitted a hideous, high-pitched screech. He drew back in fear, aware an infectious bite from a monkey to be more deadly than that of a rabid dog. The monkey's screeching, screeching, screeching caused him to retreat farther.

Charcot gave the monkey a sharp rap on its head. "Supreme rudeness!" he scolded. "Now be polite to our guest." He started to set the monkey down.

Terror-stricken, Sigmund pleaded, "Please, don't release him! Hold him!"

Charcot set the monkey down. *Does he not know a drop of saliva from a rabid monkey proves fatal?* The creature screeching louder raced toward him. Frantically he sought shelter behind a chair, but suddenly the monkey changed course and scampered agilely up a spiral staircase to another tier of the library. The monkey pressed its face between banister posts which were carved into gargoyles and with its grotesque companions stared down watchfully.

I've fallen into the worst of nightmares. In a moment I shall collapse from nervous exhaustion. All is lost!

"Dr. Freud." The professor proffered a smile. "I do apologize for my little friend's antic behaviour."

Sigmund saw no sympathy, no sympathy in the smile. He felt his position weakened, his opportunity lost, doomed for obscurity at the Salpêtrière as his idol took a seat behind a large mahogany desk. Charcot assumed a very dry manner.

"An unfortunate fact, Dr. Freud, the dear creature has observed so many of my high-strung patients that he himself has caught the illness."

Sigmund worried. *Am I now considered high-strung?*

"Please, Dr. Freud, find yourself a chair."

He took the closest chair, another medieval artefact, the arms hewed into taloned griffins. Uncomfortably seated, he then noticed, deeper into the library, the mammoth glass panel hanging from the ceiling, the huge, upright, stained-glass bear, its mouth open in a silent roar. Sigmund struggled to maintain a semblance of composure… the menacing bear, Charcot's steady scrutiny. He yearned for a tenth of a gram of cocaine to restore confidence, untie his tongue.

Jean Martin Charcot's presence was so powerful, he emanated such force of character that Sigmund wished to move his chair farther back.

"As the Italians say, *finalmente*! We meet, finally!" grunted Charcot.

Seeking to regain credibility, he feigned nonchalance, "Does the monkey have a name?"

Charcot's eyes widened with surprise. "How devilishly interesting that you are the first person, ever, to ask that question. Bravo, Sigmund, bravo! But…" He put two fingers to sensuous lips. "May I call you, Sigmund?"

"It would be the highest honour, Dr. Charcot."

"Sigmund, the monkey indeed has a name—*le Rêve*."

Dream—feeling adrift with waves of unease lapping around him, he began to observe the man from a great distance. Strange impulses welled, to snigger like a schoolboy, to jump up and bow with reverence, absurdly imagining the man before him Napoleon disguised as Charcot! No, no, Madame Richetti said that the monkey was Napoleon. *Hold on, Sigmund, find your bearings, too many trivial details, random connections, flooding the mind, everything fighting for significance.*

He toyed with reading glasses, the emperor, tapping them on the desk, relentlessly tapping. "Pierre Janet informs me that you are the young doctor who discovered the use of gold chloride for staining nerve tissue."

A hundred ways to respond, all scrambling to reach his lips. A dream, Professor Charcot, a dream, but the monkey is the dream. "Yes," he managed to say, deathly afraid to mention that his discovery had, in fact, emerged from a dream, that the day before his discovery he had clumsily broken the gold ring Marty had given him, and that night dreamt of gold, of utilizing gold chloride to better examine nerve tissue. Dreams abound. The dream of the white-bearded sage in an alley, the hoary old man urinating liquid gold against the wall…

He had to focus, he shifted his gaze up. The monkey, scratching its genitals, still watched.

Charcot's voice: "Your discovery offered my hospital staff a temporary spark of jubilation; but alas, further experiments degenerated into mixed results. It seems for microscopic examinations in France, simple spirits of alcohol prove superior for tissue fixation."

"Dr. Charcot… my letter…"

"Yes-yes, your letter… offering to translate my Tuesday Lessons for the Germans." More eyeglass tapping.

"Professor, may I lay bare my thoughts and feelings?"

"By all means."

"I've read all of your lectures on hysteria. Your discoveries have been for me... shattering. I can no longer think of neurological disorders in quite the same way as I did before coming to Paris. Your Friday lectures, which I never fail to attend, are not only incisive, they are exquisite! I leave, awestruck. To discriminate hysterical illnesses from other somatic diseases, to eradicate *in situ* a hysterical paralysis and then re-induce it! I leave your lectures with the same feeling I had when I first walked out of Notre Dame, overwhelmed by the sense of depth, magnitude. And then to demonstrate that hysteria is a condition peculiar to both women and men! Then there is the astounding experimental nature of your work with hypnosis. Dr. Charcot, you..." he leaned forward, he had gained control over his anxiety, his own hysteria, "open new doors."

Charcot listened appreciatively. "Yes, a glamorous tool, hypnosis, to capture the interest of my audience. And which placates," he tapped his heart, relinquished a small smile, "the artist who resides in me."

"You've opened a very new door," Sigmund repeated. "Your experiments with hysteria are ground breaking." The moment arrived to press his case. "But not yet accessible to the greater German medical community."

"Hmm, the Germans... the Germans." The tone conveyed scepticism.

"Dr. Charcot, what a privilege, if only to play some small part in translating your brilliant lectures to them."

Charcot's countenance darkened. "Your German doctors and their abstract theorizing! That's their problem. When, if ever, will the Boche learn," he went on with scorn, "that visual observation is what advances science? Dare they admit, Herr Sigmund, that when it comes to clinical observation, it is the French who dominate!"

"I come to Paris and the Salpêtrière, the beacon of scientific progress, to learn from one Frenchman, Dr. Jean-Martin Charcot."

Somewhat mollified, Charcot grew thoughtful. "Perhaps we French are too obsessed with wreaking vengeance upon Germany."

"An understandable prejudice," he was quick to admit.

"The next war with Germany," the doctor predicted, "will be most ferocious."

"I adhere neither to Germany nor Austria," he found himself saying.

"Not a German or a dedicated Austrian? Then how shall we label you?"

"I am a Jew."

Charcot fell silent, choosing to look at things on his desk and not Sigmund, absentmindedly spreading papers about. The glint of a blade caught his attention, Sigmund's attention. Charcot picked up the letter opener, tapping the flat of the blade upon an open palm, a steady, rhythmic tapping. "Prejudice... yes, prejudice can fester within the psyche of a country, like gangrene, eh?" His smile and thoughts seemed only for himself. "Or is prejudice more like a boil upon the derriere which need only be..." he pushed the point of the blade into a pile of papers. "... lanced."

A new look startled Sigmund, aware for the first time of the slight inward cast in Charcot's left eye, a distinct physical anomaly, as if the left eye expressed no emotion while the other showed mild amusement, yet in an instant, the disconcerting defect strangely vanished.

Does he control his vision by sheer will power?

Charcot grew cheerful. "I'm sure a perceptive, resourceful young man, such as yourself, will find the means to escape whatever wrath results from our country's neuroses." He gave up toying with the letter opener and rose with a genial laugh. "Let the only meaningful treaty we shall respect be good science."

A knock at the door caused him to sit again. Giles de la Tourette, mournful, entered, handing Charcot a sealed envelope then, without a word, left. The envelope, sealed with a noticeably thick layer of red wax, seemed to disturb Charcot, his lips compressed and a vein of tension came to the side of his forehead, but quickly recovering, he rose to shake Sigmund's hand. "I have made my decision—the Tuesday lessons of the past year are yours to translate for the German people."

Elated, Sigmund was barely aware of being escorted to the door. Charcot wagged a finger at him. "You I want at tomorrow's Tuesday lesson. Our princess takes the stage, a medical case which will arouse, if I'm not mistaken, your deepest interest."

Before he could express gratitude, his benefactor's covert glance at the desk showed his urgency to be alone... with the letter. "Guinon, my sentinel, is out there somewhere, to direct you to the front gate."

Walking down the corridor as lightly as he could ever remember, honoured to be invited to a Tuesday demonstration, Sigmund felt confident that he had manoeuvred closer to Charcot's inner circle. Guinon emerged, from somewhere, coming forward with a smile he mistrusted.

"Success, assuredly, written on your face," Guinon remarked "Let me be the first to offer congratulations." He clicked his heels in military fashion and gave a sharp salute.

Ignore the mockery, Sigmund. "Thank you, Dr. Guinon."

Gladly he followed his rival's brisk pace through another maze of corridors. At the front door they paused. "If you climb any more rungs on the ladder, Herr Freud, I may lose sight of you."

"I'm sure there are many ladders in Charcot's mansion."

Chapter 12

Their faces looked a little older too, a little more worn; but there was something else besides; he felt they were growing apart, he could see they were really strangers to one another...

"The Masterpiece"
Émile Zola, 1886

THE GO-BETWEEN

"Does Monsieur desire coffee?"

Cezanne, in a haze of remembering his last encounter with her, looked up at the waiter. "What?"

"Un café, Monsieur?"

Cezanne began to see that the man bore a suspicious resemblance to a distant cousin, a poor relative owing a debt to his father's bank. Had this cousin been enlisted by his father to work in the *New Athens Café* as a spy?

"Coffee? Yes, you charlatan! No! Wait! Bring me pen and paper, and another glass of wine."

The waiter thought it much too early in the morning to be drinking wine, cheap wine at that, but one must serve the foolish as well as the wise.

Cezanne wrote:

My Dear Lady,

Since your kiss, my heart that I deemed a lump of dank coal, has at last ignited, but into a conflagration I know not how to regulate. What little brain matter left me is in a fever.

I drink to quench the lust which...

Cezanne crossed out everything and began again:

Dear Mademoiselle J,

Since you allowed me to kiss you, I have been agitated by a profound unrest...

Finally finishing something half-baked, he stuffed the letter into a pocket, now to be deposited with Émile Zola, their agreed upon go-between, as the mysterious Julie refused to give him her address. He slammed down several coins. "No tips for spies!" he called out before leaving the café.

Hurrying across the city to Émile's bourgeois house on the rue de Boulogne, he passed billboard columns pasted with lurid posters advertising Émile's forthcoming book.

How queer, he thought, *to have your childhood chum reach such a pinnacle of fame. Most of Europe scooping up his novels before the ink dried. No question, Émile Zola has made himself into a mighty success—just as he once vowed to do.*

Ah, so many years ago, when they were school mates in Provence and near inseparable, when they shared their dreams and ambitions, when a scrawny fourteen-year old Émile shouted into the Gardanne valley, "You and I, Paul. We will go to Paris, that fancy dressed whore, and we will conquer her!"

"Rape her if need be," the equally determined Paul responded.

They took off their rucksacks, lay on the grass, and gazed up at the Provence sky, imagining their futures in the passing clouds.

"You will be a famous painter," Émile assured him, "and I will become France's most renowned writer."

Why not? he thought then. *Everything is possible when you're young and clever lads, and so very, very talented.*

Paul Cezanne hurried through the Bois de Boulogne, deserted in winter, wrapped his scarf tighter to ward off the cold. A grey sky hinted of snow. He ignored a heavily rouged trollop standing at an unlit lamp post and passed by her wan smile.

* * *

Émile Zola at his desk, on the respectable side of town, gazed out at the same bleak, February sky, nostalgic for a moment twenty-five years ago: running up the stairs to Paul's studio, trembling with excitement as he opened the door, the pure joy they felt to see each other, hugging strongly, friends, now in Paris together! Sitting and smoking countless pipes in the unheated studio; or bundled in hats and scarves, tramping through countless Paris parks; talking, endlessly talking, never running out of things to say, Paul giving ardent lectures on art, poetry, even thrift when his pockets were usually empty. And finishing their days when Paul forced him into a café to share a beer. More often than not, Zola came up with money for his friend, 50, 60 francs, whatever he could afford. What did it matter? he used to think. We were going to conquer Paris! And stubbornly we pursued our original paths. Working so damnably hard. Oh, we had great hopes for each other.

Zola turned from the window, from the past. The door knocker downstairs rapped repeatedly. He grimaced—all had changed.

* * *

Cezanne at the handsome oak door, cap in hand, practised patience, waiting for Zola's maid to make her hateful appearance. As expected, the maid Marta opened the door with a look to make less brave hearted men quake. The keeper of the gate looked daggers at him, adding disgust at his mud-caked boots, the signal to scrape them clean on the shoe peg spiked into the wall beside the door. The wench would not allow him to enter the master's house until he complied. *Is it the razor sharpness of her nose or the straggled hairs on her upper lip, he wondered, which kept her in a perpetual foul mood? Better she be a man, grow out the damn moustache, become an Argentinean gaucho and learn to guard her post with a horse whip.* He scrapped just one shoe on the iron peg with lazy disdain and passed by his taskmaster.

Once upon a time he enjoyed his visits to the Zola house. Émile's companionship, his encouragement meaning so much; but literary fame changed him. For a while Cezanne attempted to accommodate the new situation. He frequented Zola's so called literary Salons until it became downright unbearable to hear him and his writer colleagues prattle on about the number of copies printed of their last book. It was just too distressing to watch his friend grow stupid with the rest of them. But today, he reminded himself, *Émile, he's still my best friend; we're still Provencals from the south; and by God, he's willingly taken on the job of being the go-between. Why, dammit, wouldn't she give up her address? Most of life just smells too fishy.*

Entering the great writer's study, he found Émile comfortably ensconced behind a desk large enough for five writers. He had on his head a silly Turkish hat, cone-shaped, complete with a gold tassel. Fancy department store cologne saturated the air.

"Look at him!" Zola called out in a lighthearted fashion. Rising slowly, he removed his pince-nez, treading across the elegant carpet in Oriental slippers (*which matches his ridiculous fez*). He laughed, "When this man visits he inevitably brings the red clay of Provence on his boot soles! I warn you, Madame Zola will be mad as a hatter."

The writer choosing to remain at arm's length pondered Cezanne's dry-caked boots. Both men took a moment to observe the mud tracks across the carpet.

Cezanne grunted out the words stuck in his throat. "My apologies to Madame Zola."

He remembered when Madame Zola was simply Gabby, a country dimwit he and his family had introduced to Émile. At their wedding, he stood as an official witness.

Inexplicably, Émile put the gold tassel on the other side of the Turkish fez before declaring, "You must! Must stay for dinner, yes? We will have the cook make our favourite bouillabaisse, a salad as well, accompanied by a light Burgundy from the cask in my cellar... not too tart. It will be a peasant's meal," he assured him with a broad smile. "Like days of yore, remember? Every Thursday night you came. The old gang, Pissarro, Monet, talking art, literature and probably too much starry-eyed nonsense."

Cezanne tried hard to manage a smile which he imagined looked more like the grimace of a gargoyle. "The two of us used to do a lot of talking," he was able to say.

Émile slapped his forehead. "Ach! I just remembered today is the cook's night off. Some other night then?"

"Some other night, yes." Cezanne could not bring himself to stare directly into Émile's eyes.

The writer inquired, his look serious. "Paul, you are reading my chapters as they come out each week in the *Gil Blas*, aren't you?"

"Haven't read a word. But I see the damn posters slapped on every billboard column in the city, with that woman wearing next to nothing and looking horrified at that fellow hanging from a rafter with a noose around his neck."

"Engineered by my publisher——an integral part of the selling business."

"Well, I'm not going to read it piecemeal," Cezanne grumbled. "Why should I? When the author never fails to send me a free copy. I can wait. Your last book, *Germinal*, very good that one, those coal-face miners brought tears to my eyes."

"And what of your masterpiece, Paul?" The writer looked worried. "How is it progressing?"

My masterpiece? wondered Cezanne, perplexed and silent. *What the hell is he now exaggerating? I'm not out to make a masterpiece. Just decent paintings, one stroke of colour at a time.*

"The... blue landscape?" Zola inquired further. "The one you carry from town to town?"

Cezanne shrugged. "That one I stabbed multiple times with a palette knife and tossed into the fire. A well-earned death."

"Paul, Paul," the writer looked as though he were heart-broken. "You worked on that painting for two whole years."

"A failed experiment. As soon as you consign your failures to the ashes, the mind is empty for a fresh impression."

"Mmm..." Émile Zola looked skeptical; he had observed the tragic pattern: *Paul works, Paul reworks, then the painting is reworked into a bloody mess.*

A smile repressed, the writer knew that his current novel followed a line of truth. His main character's fatal flaw, like a Greek tragedy, belonged to Paul as well, an inability to bring a sense of completion to one's work, and so it would always be for both, a path toward futility.

Paul and my character Claude Lantier are artistically impotent.

Scanning the walls, Cezanne wondered, *None of the paintings I've given him over the years are in sight, why is that? At least 'The Black Clock with Lemon' had some merit, didn't it? Maybe he keeps all of them in the privacy of his bedroom? Anyway, the time for beating around the bush has ended*—"Has my lady friend left me any letters?" He didn't like the smile his question evoked. Didn't like it all.

"Paul, tell me truly?" Émile's voice sounded syrupy. "Are you fond of how the light skims over her satin-smooth breasts, her amber-coloured hips... her downy loins?"

"Be careful," warned Cezanne, "you walk upon thin ice."

Émile laughed as he went to a sidetable. "Don't be cross, that's just literature!" He opened the drawer of the *Louis Quatorze* table, handing Cezanne the letter. Facing each other in silence, there was no more to say. Even though they could dredge through thirty years of close memories, neither man found a single one to reunite them.

The writer spoke with weary resignation. "I imagine you also have a letter to deposit?"

The artist took out his letter and placed it in the open drawer. Émile closed the drawer. "Ah, the benefits of my *Louis Quatorze* letter box. No postage required. Nothing else required but to maintain our friendship and..." He shifted the fez tassel back to the other side, "accept the woman's visits."

He pulled the bell cord to summon the maid. Cezanne could not wait to escape. The witch Marta appeared and gladly led him to the door.

Outside, he tore open the envelope; he read glumly—more damnable literature.

Dear M. Cezanne,

I have learned that you and M. Zola are the same age, 47.
And childhood friends. That is commendable—more, it is an immeasurable blessing to have a life-long relationship with a like-minded soul.

Although I confess, in appearance and manner, you two seem completely different. He is refined, a forehead broad and clean, a beard well-trimmed, and a nose delicately scooped. You, rough looking, a beard as thick as wire brush, and your nose Semitic, directed downward, flared at the tip as if you were always fuming.

Clothes wise, M. Zola's suits are impeccably tailored while you march about in a weather-beaten jacket and baggy pants, describing yourself to me, a common workman—who happens to paint. And who wants me to be his model.

I think I'm not your type, not Rubenesque enough.. However, I am ready to abandon all my misgivings and become your much too thin model for a day if you, M. Cezanne, risk granting me one request. A dream. It may seem preposterous, a dream, but it is my preposterous request. We can discuss this further through your (reluctant) go-between.

Sincerely,
J.F.

Chapter 13

I think I am in hell therefore I am

A Season in Hell

Arthur Rimbaud

SABRINE

Dismayed when entering the hospital theatre, Sigmund realized he should have heeded Guinon's warning: 'Come early, my ambitious intern. His Lessons fill quickly.' A room of thirty odd chairs, ascending in six rows, were all covetously occupied by staff and very distinguished appearing personages. He then noticed a hand shoot up from the back row. Georges Guinon was cheerfully waving and pointing to the vacant seat beside him.

Hurrying to the seat, he patiently listened as Guinon playfully chastised him, "Tut-tut, my tardy intern, try as I might to save two in the front row, I was summarily sentenced to this airier region."

"A privilege to be here, particularly alongside Dr. Charcot's most able assistant."

In a pretend pantomime of being out of sorts, Guinon fussed with the perfume laden handkerchief in his breast pocket, arranging it one way then another. "While a more profuse apology is warranted, I shall settle for the well-deserved compliment. However, when you find yourself in Dr. la Tourette's company, be sure to lather your compliments more thickly."

"I don't see him in the audience."

"Oh, he will appear soon enough," said Guinon.

Sigmund searched until Guinon became suspicious. "Who are you really looking for?" .

Apparently, nothing escapes his watchful eye. "A woman," he admitted, "whom I met at last Friday's lecture."

"Describe her," insisted Guinon; he relished intrigue.

"A hatless woman with upswept hair; we exchanged a few words."

"Surely this woman has other distinguishing features?"

Very well, Guinon. "Copper coloured hair, held up by marvellous clasps I believe were genuine Egyptian antiques. She was taking notes, unusual hieroglyphic jottings."

Guinon showed genuine surprise. "So, you have made the acquaintance of Mademoiselle Forette and yet..." a doubting finger went to his lips, "you are not aware of her esteemed position at the Salpêtrière?" His eyes narrowed. "But surely you know, for such a person might prove advantageous to Sigmund Freud, the climber of ladders. Yes, a valuable connection, another rung for you to grab."

"Come Guinon, enough of your ladder metaphors, who is she?"

"The woman who catches every word Charcot casts, be they pearls or stones, as Mademoiselle Forette is Salpêtrière's recordist. Only today," Guinon produced a pad and pencil from inside his jacket, "it is I who will record Charcot's gems. Yes, here at the Salpêtrière we often play musical chairs. As Charcot's former secretary, such tasks once fell upon my shoulders; of course, my notes are not spectacularly verbatim, like Mademoiselle Forette's."

Sigmund noticed custodians entering the theatre, closing window curtains, dimming wall lamps. He asked Guinon, "Why isn't she recording today's Tuesday Lesson?"

"Mademoiselle, I'm told, is under the weather." His smile, all of Guinon's smiles, carried an undercurrent of irony.

"Nothing serious, I hope."

"One supposes a woman's issue." He patted his abdomen. "Cycles to confront, et cetera."

Behind them a spotlight generator began to hum, Guinon confiding, "Today Charcot treats us to a special patient. Some call her the Princess of Salpêtrière."

Before Sigmund could inquire further, the Director himself entered to confront the audience with his regal silence, Jean-Martin Charcot expecting nothing less than devoted attention. A select group of spectators had been invited today, a cadre of esteemed professors from the Sorbonne, high ranking political figures, and well-regarded journalists from the leading newspapers. Sigmund observed that each and every attendee, no matter how pre-eminent or illustrious, waited with eager anticipation for the master of hypnotism to present his Tuesday Lesson.

The theatre was now crammed full. There was standing room only in the semi-darkness, the side walls lined mostly with interns. A nervous cough from someone prompted Charcot to begin:

"Today, like Oedipus, we go to the Sphinx to boldly confront the enigma of hysteria."

A spot of light, coin size, struck the red rosette pinned on Charcot's lapel, his Legion of Honour ribbon. The light, after paying due respect to Charcot's rosette, dropped like a coin to the floor, meandering, seemingly in search of an uncertain target—a surprise when the light enlarged and changed colour, a diaphanous blue.

Guinon whispered, "Very pyrotechnical lighting, the accomplishment of Charcot's son." He nudged Sigmund toward a group of young men standing in a far back corner. "Jean's the doctor with arms crossed, a modern spirit, knowledgeable in all manner of theatrics."

The blue circle of light, energized, took on the life of a whimsical butterfly, performing loops and fanciful arabesques until settling upon the stage floor. Another circle, deeply red, appeared and superimposed over the blue circle, a fusion of colour took place, a pleasing shade of violet, which delighted the audience. The newly created circle of colour rested upon a trap door, an oubliette.

Guinon was very amused. "Dreamful becomes my best description, worthy of the Paris Opera, which is probably where Jean Charcot would prefer to work."

The trap door, glaringly lit in violet, swung open on hinges—out climbed Giles de la Tourette, Charcot's chief clinician, and from this pool of violet a young woman emerged, dressed quaintly in a ribbon-laced blouse and billowing skirt, she followed by another of Charcot's personal assistants, Dr. Joseph Babinski.

The spectacle of three people emerging from the stage floor entranced everyone. Sigmund had heard the rumour of an underground tunnel connected to the ward housing Salpêtrière's hysterics. *The Figaro* newspaper referred, tongue in cheek, to this special ward of women as *La Salle des Étoiles*. Charcot's Room of Stars. Regularly the star hysterics were brought to the theatre to demonstrate particular aspects of their volatile illness, Grand Hysteria. Residents Blanche Whitman, Augustine Gleizes and Justine Etchevery were extremely popular with the press and public.

"Today we are privileged," announced Charcot in a triumphant tone, rocking on his heels, "to have with us a long-time patient and Salpêtrière resident, Mademoiselle Sabrine."

A contagion of knowing whispers swept through the audience as Guinon hurriedly summarized for Sigmund the unusual case of Sabrine Weiss. She was brought to the Salpêtrière at age fifteen, said to be suffering from hallucinations and amnesia. Dr. Charcot subsequently discovered that his young patient possessed a disease altogether different, a form of Grand Hysteria called Hystero-Epilepsy.

"Salpêtrière has been her home for five years," said Guinon.

Another spotlight enveloped the twenty-year-old in an aura of gold. Sigmund gazed, wonder-struck, as her beauty was almost shocking. Her two escorts seemed to knowingly step back from the young woman's radiance. She looked out, the centre of everyone's attention, with an innocent eagerness. She had a pleasantly round face with a sprinkling of youthful freckles. Sigmund thought her eyes as green as jade. Could she be Irish, he wondered, for her crowning glory was bright, red hair. It was parted, Christ-like, and fell in abundant waves around her shoulders. Perhaps enhanced by the stage lights, her billowed hair seemed aflame.

Whatever the origin of her blood, she was for Sigmund the last person in Paris to suspect of suffering from a neurological disorder.

"And how are you today, Sabrine?" asked Charcot.

Looking happily curious at the audience, she answered, "I feel..." then paused with such innocent consideration that people began to smile. One could easily tell that she had admirers comfortably familiar with her behaviour. So Sabrine took her time to answer as to how she might be feeling, then with a burst of emotion, she said, "WONDERFUL!"

Charcot went on, "In the best of spirits, are we?"

"But awfully hungry!" she confided. "I might be as hungry as Charcot's bear... but I'm hungrier than that. I think I'm as hungry as a dragon. Shall I eat..." she put a demure finger to her cheek, "... my dragon tail? Flap my wings to China? Or lay an egg?"

Guinon clapped with positive glee while a great many in the audience readily laughed at her answers. Sitting nearby a grey haired, mutton-whiskered gentleman in a well-tailored suit spoke under his breath, "Don't fly away from us, Sabrine, not just yet."

"She's more than clever," Guinon remarked, "I would wager a fresh corpse that Mademoiselle received an education of considerable breadth before appearing at Salpêtrière's gate."

"Would you be so kind," Charcot asked his patient, "as to allow Dr. Babinski to escort you to the examining table?"

She behaved as though a school girl wanting to prove her obedience, and with a grave expression followed Babinski.

"A half-decade of observation," Charcot addressed his audience, "has enabled me to specifically diagnose our Sabrine as a hystero-epileptic."

Sigmund leaned closer, not wanting to miss a word. He had heard much about the new neurological disease discovered at the Salpêtrière hospital, a disease most of his teachers in Vienna could not quite fathom. Charcot rolled down a chart. "Gentlemen, let me elucidate." The chart displayed two life-size drawings of the female body, an anterior and posterior view, both riddled with dark circles. "I have succeeded, after many years, in mapping all known hysterogenic zones of the female hysteric." Sigmund quickly memorized the number of circles, four on the back, thirteen on the front of the body. Charcot looked out, and Sigmund wondered if the great neurologist had caught a glimpse of him in the back row? "Some of you wear puzzled faces," Charcot observed, "asking yourself, hysterogenic zones? Hystero-Epileptics? What in the sacred name of science is Professor Charcot talking about? Yes, new words, new terms for you, but soon to be written in the book of science."

Guinon laconically scribbled a line or two. Sigmund seriously doubted if the notes would compare favourably to those Mademoiselle Forette might transcribe.

Charcot picked up a pointer to indicate certain circles on the female torsos. "In Sabrine's case, she has a hysterogenic zone here, close to the coccyx." He then pointed to certain circles on the front torso. "A hysterogenic zone here, under her left breast, very near the heart. Another at the navel, and two sensitive points in the ovarian region." Handing over the pointer to the ever near la Tourette, he advanced to centre stage. "Sabrine Weiss," he explained, "is what I have classified as an ovarian type. Among hysterics several other classifications exist which can be enumerated at future lessons." He signalled Babinski to have Sabrine lie face down on the examining table. "Bear in mind," Charcot reminded the audience, "that when one attempts a scientific demonstration with animals before a large group, the results often differ from those seen in the laboratory; I therefore caution you of a similar possibility today, although..." he looked steadily at his recumbent patient. "I am practically certain of the outcome."

He nodded to Babinski who pressed the palm of his hand above the patient's coccyx. Nothing happened.

This caused Charcot to pace back and forth, thoughtful, hands in trouser pockets. "I will not feign surprise if success eludes me today. Women, after all, are not machinery." He then mumbled something to la Tourette who left the stage. A moment later Tourette and a white-haired nurse carried out a mattress. Charcot explained, "The physical position most amenable for a demonstration of hystero-epilepsy requires the patient to be stretched out horizontally on the floor, or if possible, a mattress." Tourette and Babinski, leading the compliant Sabrine to the mattress, were instructed to help her lie face up, Babinski given the order to press the left ovarian zone. Again, no response. The patient's eyes were shut tight. "Press, Dr. Babinski, press hard!"

Making a tight fist, Babinski pressed the lower zone. Her head rose slightly as if in protest then snapped back, a violent thud causing gasps of alarm through the theatre.

Jubilant, Charcot cried out in a voice excitedly high-pitched, "The hystero-attack has been triggered!" He waved away his assistants and circled Sabrine with an urgent need to observe her from various angles. "She has lost consciousness, her breathing weakens, mouth agape, and see, her neck begins to swell. Now, yes, a moderate oscillation of limbs. Here is Phase One, gentlemen, the Epileptoid Phase, a benign mimicking of epilepsy."

Astonishing everyone, Sabrine's next violent act was to arch her back into a crescent moon which caused Charcot to nimbly step back. "Phase Two has begun! The sensation here, described by more than one patient, becomes a pure white bolt of lightning."

Guinon muttered under his breath while copying down Charcot's words. "Who, pray tell, experiences a lightning bolt, much less pure and white, then lives to boast, eh?"

Sigmund had to ignore Guinon's sceptical remarks. He would observe through the filter of his own intelligence as Charcot narrated the ongoing attack, continuing to circle Sabrine. "This very acrobatic posture I place under the rubric of Clownism, the beginning of Phase Two. A phase which sometimes stuns the patient's brain to the point of befuddlement." Sabrine groaned, her pelvis thrusting upward, her body strained and fixed in an agonizing arc. *"L'arc du Ciel!"* Charcot called out. "The Rainbow pose! When pain can bore through the spine's cavity like a fire-heated rod of steel."

A scream escaped from the girl which reverberated through the theatre, a scream so unearthly that murmurings of unrest were heard everywhere. Even the imperturbable Guinon showed concern.

Charcot's voice stayed high-pitched with delight. "We witness an exquisite, textbook example of Phase Two!" He rushed to a blackboard, picked up a piece of chalk and waved it toward Sabrine, "Emotional vocalizations now solidify the Clownism Phase," then wrote:

Phase I: Epileptoid

(Mimics epileptic shaking)

Phase II: Clownism

(Simulates contortions and acrobatics of circus performers)

Sabrine's scream prolonged to an animal like howl. Sigmund thought he heard, "Sn-a-a-ke!"

Charcot assured the audience. "Wait but a moment! Phase Three now unfolds—passionate outbursts, often hallucinatory conversations."

Sabrine seemed to beg for mercy from an unseen torturer. She then passed from the rainbow arc into a much more horrible contortion, folding into herself as if wanting to disappear, every limb twisting inward. For Sigmund it seemed *foetus-like*.

"Be prepared for the single limb deformity," Charcot announced, "which I consider a sub-contracture to Phase Three. There!"

Sigmund watched her right hand thrust skyward, bizarrely bent, a frozen claw, a gesture he very much hoped was defiance of her neurological suffering. She then began to stir, her limbs seemed to unravel, slacken. Then she shouted what he thought sounded like 'Blood!' before shifting into yet another contortion, her entire body stiffened and her arms shot out and froze.

"The Crucifixion pose," said Charcot and wrote:

Phase III: Attitudes of Passion

(e.g. Terror, Torment, Amorous Supplication & Ecstasy)

"In Sabrine's case," he added, "the Crucifixion can be torment or ecstasy or a mixture of both. This pose can persist to an insufferable length of time until the final phase decides to rule."

He nodded to his assistants who lifted their charge, still completely rigid, and placed her back on the examining table. "No amount of force will make her limbs bend," said Charcot. "But..." he looked carefully at the audience, "I see frustration entering your faces. You do not wish to see our Sabrine helplessly frozen. So, in this particular instance..." he approached the table, "intervention seems appropriate. I shall compress the ovarian zone." For the first time Charcot touched the patient, firmly pressing down on her abdomen until—to everyone's relief—the rigidity began to subside. "What we prove is that Sabrine is an authentic ovarian hystero-epileptic. Apply this type of pressure on a real epileptic and no relief will be forthcoming. But bear in mind, Sabrine's attack remains in remission only as long as I am prepared to administer firm abdominal compression. If I relent"—Charcot stepped back. "The attack re-commences!"

She shot up in a seated position and shouted, "Father, I am so frightened! Take me home!"

Charcot went to the black board and scribbled, **Phase IV: Delirium.** "Here the patient hallucinates. She may exhibit great fear or great joy, wholly dependent upon the images her fevered mind conjures."

Sabrine cried out, "The white ray blinds and scorches!"

"Her delirious vocalizations will eventually elide into a normal state of consciousness." Again, he turned to the blackboard. "Let us summarize and emphasize: the four phases of a hystero-epileptic attack succeed each other with mechanical regularity." He underlined:

<u>**Epileptoid**</u>

<u>**Clownism**</u>

<u>**Attitudes of Passion**</u>

<u>**Delirium**</u>

He looked kindly at Sabrine. "She now sleeps and will eventually awaken, without a single memory of what has occurred."

Two nurses came out with a canvas litter which they dexterously unfolded. Babinski carried Sabrine in his arms and rather tenderly (thought Sigmund) laid her upon the litter. The nurses, lifting with seasoned strength, took Sabrine away.

How will he make scientific sense of her hallucinatory behavior? Sigmund wondered.

Charcot came forward and took time to scan the faces of his spectators. He seemed to acknowledge his son, Jean, with an enigmatic smile before going back to the blackboard and writing:

Hystero-Epilepsy Exists!

"And can any of you here today," he asked them, "after witnessing the destructive power of this disease, doubt its existence? Who will dare argue against the evidence? I have clearly demonstrated that hystero-epilepsy can be segregated into discrete and predictable phases. So, we must ignore those who deny my discovery. What prompts their slanderous articles, whether ignorance or jealousy I will let history decide. For now, our duty as guardians of Salpêtrière's unfortunates is to find where in the brain this insidious disease instigates its tragic mischief. But for now its mysterious origin remains with the Sphinx." Charcot gazed and Sigmund hoped he, his German translator, might be noticed.

"Who knows?" Charcot asked with a small smile. "Perhaps one of you young interns, in your research at Salpêtrière, might someday find..."

He left the sentence unfinished, as though the thought carried too much sentimentality. Charcot's professorial tone returned, "Next Tuesday's Lesson will refocus on the science of hypnotism." He ended with a cursory bow. *"Merci."*

* * *

After vigorous applause, the stage lights fell dark to allow Charcot his dramatic disappearance.

The time has arrived, Sigmund realized, *to re-examine what to believe and what not to believe. But this much is fact, I wish to do something important with my life. Might I attach myself in some manner to this man's bold experiments?*

While attendants re-opened curtains and reset the theatre's gas lamps, he and Guinon stayed seated, watching the audience disperse in animated groups, all excited to exchange views regarding the novel disease Charcot had demonstrated.

"Your opinion?" Sigmund curiously asked his companion.

For a moment Guinon inhaled into his breast pocket handkerchief as if needing its flowery scent. *"La Grande Hystérie*, that is the generic name Charcot bestows upon the illness. Which verily runs rampant through our Salpêtrière. Sabrine, more than most, can demonstrate its many tragic subsets."

"So, these four phases have subsets?"

"Most assuredly." Guinon stood. "Let me offer a tour of our art gallery."

He led Sigmund slowly down the stairs, time enough to study the engravings and photographs upon the walls: all Salpêtrière women, captured by the artist's pen, or caught by the camera, displaying a particular phase of a hysterical attack.

Guinon stopped. "Here is a definite favourite of mine, an aquatint, which superbly renders a hystero-epileptic contracture." The small brass plaque read 'Rainbow Arc.' "Recognize her?" Clad in a closely clinging hospital gown, her back dramatically arched, giving an evocative view of a well-formed body, she was unquestionably Sabrine Weiss. "Drawn and tinted by the well-known André Brouillet."

"But isn't this contracture somewhat *exaggerated*?" Sabrine posed in a severe, yet perfect arc, her red hair dangled in rippling waves, artistically

116

rendered like the snakes of a Medusa.

"Its only flaw, I venture to say, is Brouillet not finding the correct tint to match the deep crimson of Sabrine's hair; but overall... a certain voluptuous grace one has to admire."

"But nothing in this picture," Sigmund observed, "shows the pain and anguish we witnessed today."

Guinon's ironic smile, his mask, held tight. "The artist, yes, does help us forget her pain. Art, after all, exists to please the eye. Brouillet presently works on a larger, more finished painting of Sabrine with Dr. Charcot, including a select audience to duplicate a Tuesday Demonstration of hystero-epilepsy. Many of us harbour a secret hope to be part of his painted audience, ready to pose, if necessary. Those who have been fortunate to visit the artist's studio and observe the painting's progress, say it is turning into a masterpiece."

Sigmund offered a cigar. "Are the true epileptics mixed in wards with the hystero-epileptics?"

Guinon gladly accepted the cigar. "Oh no, the hystero-epileptics have their special ward in the East wing of the Pinel Building, as Charcot prefers his star attractions to live together, although they are awarded a fair amount of freedom, wandering about, and like the deserving stars they are, invite themselves into the various research departments." Guinon waited for his cigar to be lit. "The doctors welcome the diversion." Both soon puffed with contentment. "Although in the case of Augustine, Augustine Gleizes, another star hysteric, it might be more practical to keep her under lock and key, especially after curfew. She is found too often outside at night, sitting on a bench, naked as you please, in the most frigid weather, her chemise folded beside her, waiting for the Salpêtrière trolley to take her to the city proper so that she can enjoy the Trocadero circus. Of course, our horse trolley only makes stops inside the complex, nor does it run at night. But this is Augustine's peccadillo. Our maestro allows her much latitude. She is, as the newspapers say, a crowd pleaser at the public demonstrations." He took Sigmund by the elbow. "Come, I'll show you what authenticates her speciality."

Sigmund first thought the photograph a theatrical trick, a visual joke devised by a playful staff. Guinon exhaled a stream of smoke at the photograph. "Augustine, hypnotized."

A pair of cane chairs faced away from each other, her body suspended between them, her head resting atop the back of one chair, her feet resting upon the edge of the other chair, Augustine rigidly stretched between them. Sigmund saw no visible support beneath her, as though she were afloat. He was confounded by the physical impossibility. "How can she maintain such a position without buckling?"

Guinon took pleasure in re-lighting Sigmund's extinguished cigar. "Dr. Bourneville, our enterprising neurologist, calls the condition, 'muscular hyper-excitability.'"

He explained to Sigmund the elaborate procedure to induce Augustine's extreme state of rigidity. "First, she's placed in a lethargic trance by Charcot, her head then gently positioned atop one chair top as Bourneville kneads the muscles of her back, thighs and legs, until stiffness occurs, then Bourneville and Charcot lift her feet onto the second chair. Our marvellous Augustine can stay an inflexible object for hours at a time. At her last performance," Guinon proudly noted, "a weight of eighty-eight pounds was placed upon her stomach without causing the least bit of difficulty, the body would not yield, would not bend."

"Why does she wear the cap and apron of a nurse?"

"Some of our long-term residents perform various nursing duties at the Salpêtrière, earning minimal salaries. Augustine takes naïve pride in wearing her uniform at demonstrations. I've been told that her next appearance will guarantee full coverage by the newspapers, as Charcot plans, once she is rigidly established between the chairs, to ask for a volunteer to participate in the demonstration, someone preferably stout."

"To do what?"

"To sit on her stomach."

Sigmund's cigar went out again. "Is that not a shade..."

"Undignified?" He relit Sigmund's neglected cigar. "You must understand that our Director needs to garner the public's interest which, in turn, convinces government authorities to keep the state's purse strings open for continued neurological research. Such spectacles of modest showmanship are done only in the best interests of the Hospital." He waved his cigar at the contorted poses along the theatre walls. "For without Salpêtrière, where would such troubled women go?"

"I have much to learn."

"Indeed you do, Herr Freud." Guinon blew a stream of smoke directly over his shoulder.

Sigmund frowned. "I must get to the pathology lab."

Guinon followed down the stairs. "Yes, your autopsies." At the doorway Guinon held his arm. "Wanting the little ones."

"As you're well aware, Guinon, my area of research is infantile paralysis."

"What I'm saying, Herr Freud, you do present Salpêtrière with a challenge. Although death occurs frequently among six thousand women, our corpses tend to be... well, to put it another way, some of the women are old enough to think they remembered having kissed Napoleon's hand when he marched triumphantly into Paris."

Guinon, a master of directing smoke, sent a stream past his ear. *The last cigar he shall receive from me.* "Indeed, I'm becoming aware of Salpêtrière's limitations."

Guinon's mask, the smile. "Nonetheless, I shall remain vigilant in procuring the corpses of the little ones. In truth, baby corpses are fished and netted out of the Seine every day."

"Is that a French phenomenon?"

"I know not the statistics for the Danube."

Looking quite satisfied that he wielded his satire well, Guinon put the notebook in a side pocket.

"Guinon, tell me, were you actually able to record all that was said today?"

"I'm not a verbatim recorder like Mademoiselle Forette, but I get the gist."

"Do you record the patient's remarks?"

"Why on earth write down all those oddities that come from a state of delirium. Distillation is the hallmark of my dictation."

The two parted. For Sigmund there were more questions than answers.

Chapter 14

**"I'll be your slave, I'll exist only for your pleasure...
Do you hear? I love you, I love you, I love you!"**

Claude Lantier in
The Masterpiece
Émile Zola, 1886

THE BROKEN SEAL

I

Fate interceded. We collided on rue Caumartin. A near brutal collision which left me half-kneeling on the sidewalk. Paul Cezanne stood stunned, literally helpless, while I hoped to get back on my feet with a modicum of grace. I was near certain who peered timidly at me. Profusely apologetic, he invited me to the nearby *la Taverne Olympia* "for a restorative, a lemon tea perhaps" so that we both could "regain our equilibrium." Thus we met—I had found the shy, elusive, irascible Cezanne!

Beyond my expectation, he willingly engaged in conversation. Hesitant at first, he became more at ease when discovering I was also from the south of France. In his mind, this connected us in a special way. Also the keen interest I had in art ("modern art" I specified) made him comfortable. And so we continued to meet daily at the same tavern, at the same time. Cezanne insisted, superstitiously or obsessively, that we establish regularity in our tea-time, Tuesdays, when the tavern was practically empty, save for a few regular customers who sidled to the marble bar for their late afternoon absinthe. Our arrangement coincided perfectly with the schedule I maintained at the Salpêtrière. Tuesdays I only had to transcribe Charcot's morning lessons in the clinical theatre, given the remainder of the day to polish the notes. At the *Taverne Olympia* the chief topic was art. Cezanne appreciated my relatively new found passion. A full year of fruitful conversations with Père Tanguy and gallerist, Theo van Gogh, gave me a reasonable education in Impressionism. Monsieur Cezanne, however, preferred to discuss the artists from prior centuries, among his favourites he had the highest praise for Nicolas Poussin and Paul Rubens whose styles, I initially thought, were diametrically different. But I was content to listen, hungry for his insights into any artist he admired. "Go to the Louvre, more often than not," he advised.

"Which paintings would you urge me to look at?" I asked.

"If there were a fire, I'd carry out on my back *Marie de Medicis Disembarking at Marseilles*."

For the better part of the week I found time to stand before the epic scene by Rubens, hoping to see what Cezanne saw. The style was Baroque, the painting emphasized movement, colour, drama, and sensuality. A dignified queen disembarks, but all attention falls to the harbour's churning waters where mighty sea gods and sirens, all splendidly naked, muscular and voluptuous, comport themselves with lusty ebullience.

When I looked at Poussin's paintings, the innumerable Holy Families, they were characterized by clarity, logic, and compositional order. Perhaps Cezanne's ambition for his work was to integrate the disparate temperaments of Nicolas Poussin and Peter Paul Rubens. Later I realized, when my understanding of art ripened, that the commonality between the artists Cezanne admired was in their magnificent handling of colour, exploiting colour's varied richness.

"My mother so loved the Marie de Medici painting that she christened me 'Paul' after Rubens," he blurted one afternoon. "I guess she saw herself in the painting, the queen coming to rule Marseilles and France." He regretted the slip, revealing personal information, and turned sullen. (Our switch to red Dubonnets increased the chances of slips.) But any direct questions regarding his family irritated him. His mother, father, and two sisters, Rose and Marie, lived in Aix-en-Provence, residing on a thirty-seven-acre estate they called *Jas de Bouffan*. Home of the Winds.

Still sullen for revealing something about his mother, he muttered that he had to get back to his studio.

"Is your studio far from here?" I longed to see more of his paintings.

My inquiry clearly alarmed him. He waved a hand in a nebulous direction. "Some street out there." In a rush he paid the waiter, gained my promise to meet him next week, then quickly retreated.

No one could ever precisely locate Cezanne, not even his Impressionist colleagues, for he was a most secretive man. Apparently he moved from studio to studio, the address dispensed to no one. One could only predict his ritualistic return to the family home in Aix-En-Provence. There he spent his days painting the mountains and countryside he loved.

Our collision on rue Caumartin, I shall admit, was scarcely an accident. Père Tanguy's informative tip that a Cormon art student had spotted the elusive artist on several occasions having an afternoon coffee at the *Taverne Olympia* put me on his scent, kept me stationed at the tavern on my free afternoons from stenographic duties, watching from the tavern window. He was easily recognizable, dodging street traffic, cursing carriage drivers, and wearing a round brim, yellow sun hat that one saw only on farmers from the countryside in Provence. He looked nothing like a Parisian, his brown beard too thick, and a broad, strong countenance tanned by many days in the sun. I ran out of the tavern for the collision.

Yet for all of my determination, diligence and planning, I failed to keep the next scheduled appointment due to transcribing duties for Dr. Charcot. When I arrived the following week, Cezanne was beside himself with anxiety. He insisted that we must find the means to correspond when unforeseen events occurred. Only Cezanne had no desire to divulge his address. And for my own reasons, I refused to give him mine. The plan for a go-between to exchange our correspondence was hatched by Cezanne. When necessary, we would communicate through an intermediary, his dear friend, Émile Zola.

A certain thrill ran through me at the prospect of someday meeting the famous author. Sooner than expected, an event precipitated the need for the illustrious go-between. Cezanne's father required his immediate presence in Aix-en-Provence to discuss "financial matters."

"In matters of business," grumbled Cezanne, "the old man's a cut-throat."

Initially, I so looked forward to meeting Émile Zola, perhaps the most popular novelist in France. I had read the entire Rougon-Macquart series, following the trials and tribulations of the respective families. Zola was the first French writer to make a serious attempt at describing the psychological temperaments of his characters. He eschewed the romance novel and sought to depict the modern environment we all lived in. Zola's characters actually lived less than ideal lives. Certainly I related to the washerwomen who toiled and scrubbed amidst the hot, swirling, suffocating steam of laundries.

The literary journals credited him for forging a new school of literature —dubbed 'Naturalism.' And like everyone else in Paris with even a passing interest in art, I rushed to a newspaper kiosk when the latest instalment of Zola's new book made its appearance in *Gil Blas*. Reportedly a *roman à clef*, describing the Impressionists, the rumour circulated that the novel's protagonist was based upon Paul Cezanne.

What might I learn about Cezanne's art from Zola? Cezanne admitted that he and Zola had been boyhood friends in Aix-en-Provence. I was all eagerness when knocking on the door of Zola's apartments on rue de Boulogne. A hope I harboured was to see the paintings Cezanne said he had given his friend over the years. By now I had developed a slight obsession for Cezanne's art. I think because there was the hint of science in his work, as though he sought and struggled to express the underlying structure of things. The idea that art might be able to meld with science appealed to my temperament.

A middle-aged woman, primly uniformed in jet black with a white cap and lace collar, came to the door. Marta, the surly maid. Stone silent, she allowed me inside, but no farther than the vestibule. I waited a quarter of an hour before she returned, taking me as far as the open doorway of the master's spacious study. He sat, easily recognizable, behind a desk grander than Dr. Charcot's. On one occasion, at Charcot's Friday lecture, he sat a mere row from me. Zola was part of the literary intelligentsia who admired Charcot's scientific work, particularly in the area of heredity.

Today, the author was informally dressed in a silk morning jacket with a busy, Oriental pattern. Squarely on his head, a red fez with a gold tassel completed the picture of a Turkish pasha. To observe me better, he put on his pince-nez. I made the mistake of taking several steps inside only to have the maid bar my progress, her look reminding me of a mean finch quite prepared to peck. I waited for the situation to resolve itself. She hurried to her master's desk for the envelope he handed her, then promptly came back to show me the front door. Given the envelope in a brusque fashion, I found myself once more on rue de Boulogne.

My Dear Lady,

I still seek a way to express the confusion of feelings that I carry. Might you, with your gift for peeking around the corners of people's minds, help make sense of them?

I'm here in our native Provence, the light harsh that sometimes I must squint my eyes to paint, yet so vibrant that the sensations I receive are enchanted. Here I get closer to understanding the essence of colour. I do believe God invites us to meet Him in the living universe of colour. Am I mad?

Regrettably, the weather has been hatefully hot these past days, preventing me from painting outdoors. Also violent headaches assail me each and every evening. My remaining solace is the reading of great literature.

Tell Émile I'm re-reading his La Joie de Vivre, the twelfth in his Rougon-Macquart series, a sentimental favourite of mine. The Joy of Life! Isn't that what we all strive for? I suppose I'm quite attached to the heroine, Pauline, left an orphan at the tender age of ten. Yet, she finds optimism in spite of the dreadful people who enter her life. Pauline fights and overcomes the jealousy and possessiveness that destroy others in her family. Pauline shows her indefatigable love for everyone by releasing even her fiancée from his commitment so he can marry Louise, daughter of a rich banker, who gives birth to a stillborn baby, but dear Pauline saves the baby's life by breathing air into his lungs, a baby christened Paul who survives healthy and strong. See? Hope for one Paul is hope for another.

I cannot yet leave, so please continue to receive my correspondence through Émile—a blessing that the man finds a willingness in his heart to assist in love's growth.

Remaining your servant,
Paul Cezanne

I put the letter in my purse. Zola, a blessing? Or a curse? Experience has tried to teach me that first impressions are not necessarily to be trusted.

The rude condescension he seemingly displayed may have been a go-between's discretion. I reasoned that a successful, prolific author, like Émile Zola, grounded by discipline, needed to focus on the business of completing his novel, not waste valuable time concerning himself with the liaisons of others, especially one mired in ambiguity.

On the next occasion at the Zola residence, the sour-faced Marta again made me wait amidst umbrellas and fur-collared coats hanging in the vestibule, again a quarter of an hour until she brought me to the doorway of the master novelist. At his desk, he gave what I could only interpret as a sneer before swivelling to gaze out the window. His efficient maid retrieved another Cezanne letter from the desk. Both irritated and bored with his behaviour, I curtsied to Zola's back, bowing my sardonic way out. I put the letter in my dress pocket, then impetuously closed the sliding door of his study with the loudest bang possible. Émile Zola was one of a select few for whom I developed an aversion.

I broke open the letter's seal. Cezanne praised my "feminine patience" for enduring our "unorthodox arrangement." Unhappily, he had to extend his stay in Aix-en-Provence, but pleaded that I return to "Dear Émile's" for next week's letter and begged for mine in return. "As I'm so grateful for your undreamed interest in my art," he concluded, "I'm sure that Émile will be happy to show you his art collection, including my immature efforts. He has a superb Manet, an artist whom you should familiarize yourself with and not devote all your attention to the Impressionists. Oh, how Manet's *Olympia* inspired all of us! Like a firecracker up our behinds (pardon my expression)."

III

The following week I was at Zola's door. The maid displaying her customary haughtiness, allowed me inside, only on this occasion she wasn't wearing her uniform. I saw almost a different person, no maid's cap, no lace collar, instead an ankle length dress, black, severe, yet elegant. She had her black hair pulled back into a meticulously arranged bun and might have passed for the lady of the house. Nonetheless, she stuck to the condescending ritual and I was instructed to wait in the claustrophobic vestibule.

In time she escorted me to Zola's doorway. Again, I was expected to stand quiet and still, like a servant—I marched inside. Marta quickly caught my arm; I wrenched free; she hissed, *"Putain!"*

Called a whore took me by surprise. The word stung.

"Marta," he intervened, "let her be."

Regal behind the desk, he dismissed his seething maid. I received his formidable silence, his weighted gaze, as though I had been soundly judged and found wanting. Whatever unfavourable opinion the great writer had formed was no concern of mine. He swivelled laconically in his chair. Apparently Émile Zola had no intention of offering me a seat. "So, where did the Mademoiselle and Paul meet?"

Let him speculate. I'm not painting a picture to defend myself. "It's difficult to remember precisely where we met."

"Paul does, on occasion, frequent the streets around *Place Maubert*."

Aware of the area he called in his novels the gutter streets of debasement, I seriously wondered if he thought me a prostitute? I was tempted to laugh, but waited for what would follow. I looked around for Cezanne's paintings, but there were none, no pictures at all, only bookcases where in gilt lettering his titles were prominently displayed— *L'Assommoir, Nana, Germinal*— any of which I could easily discuss. Zola and Cezanne, in certain respects, had both become modern experimenters within their chosen vocations. But I held my thoughts.

Suddenly, he began addressing me in a writerly fashion, inanely in third person. "She grips her purse tightly. Does it, perchance, contain a love letter she has laboured to compose? And now she waits, in humble silence, for what she can only hope is a similar letter from her new-found *amoretto*. Who knows? His missive might contain a few generous ten-franc notes."

He pushed a sealed envelope dismissively across the desk. What hope of an amicable interchange with a writer of undisputed talent crumbled. *At best, Émile Zola considers me a tart.*

"This situation goes beyond my comprehension." Zola tilted his head back, preferring to address the rococo ceiling where winged cupids were shooting darts pell-mell at fleeing nudes. "Why, when Paul flees Paris, doesn't he send his correspondence *poste restante* so she can pick it up at a post office?"

I was tired of being addressed in third person, tired of standing. Still he continued his one-sided dialogue with the dart shooting putti above. "Ah, but *poste restante* requires Paul's return address and our Paul is a very secretive man. Does she know," he narrowed his gaze toward me. "that our Paul, plagued by many fears, has certain secrets to hide?"

"As do we all, so let's not waste each other's time—the letter, Monsieur Zola?"

Which he patted. "Yes, her *raison d'être*, so to speak. And does she expect her go-between to rise courteously and hand it to her?"

His smiling stare came uncomfortably close to a leer. I decided on tact, searching the room for a scrap of beauty, something to shift the unsavoury moment. *Why are there no Cezanne paintings?* It remained a puzzlement.

I found a needed distraction atop a side table, an open case displaying a highly polished clarinet.

"Do you play?" I asked.

He had been put off-guard. "Not well, any more. One must practice."

I picked up the shiny black clarinet and brought it to him. "Play a tune, something jaunty, Monsieur Zola."

His smile made it certain that he thought me an impudent tart. He rose and returned the clarinet to its case.

"How sad," I was regaining confidence, "to behold a musical instrument no longer played." He waited, cautious, curious—sensing my words were turning subtle. "Monsieur Cezanne mentioned that the two of you played in the school band. He, the cornet. You, the clarinet."

Surrendering to nostalgia, he laughed. "Paul the braying horn, I the delicate woodwind."

Would the recall of memories be our path to a truce? "Aptly said, Monsieur Zola. There are glaring differences between the two of you. Zola the refined man of letters, Cezanne the rough-hewn painter."

He lifted out the clarinet, his noticeably feminine hands fingered the keys. "We were so proud of our musical prowess," he admitted.

"And one particular night you both decided to serenade a local beauty with your instruments."

"He told you that?" Much surprised, he carefully replaced the clarinet, snapped the case shut, and looked at me with new interest. "And did he tell you how we were rewarded for our romantic bravado?"

"Your reward? Yes, a bucket of water the beauty's father doused on your heads."

"We were fifteen, so young!" Shaking his head in disbelief, he sat back behind the desk, staring into space as if at projected memories. "How do twenty-five years pass so quickly?" Nostalgia softened his tone until my presence, a woman he did not trust, brought back the condescending smile. "And you, so much younger than Paul, than me, how can you understand such passages of time? How?" His look turned strange, cruel. I felt uneasy. He murmured, "Youth, a delicious obscenity…for men our age." He motioned to a chair, but closer to him than I cared to be.

I stood behind my assigned chair, wanting a barrier. "He spoke of your days together as young boys. The childhoods of great men hold great fascination for me." The remark caught him completely off-guard; I pursued the advantage, no matter the recklessness. "The schoolboys despised you, called you, 'Émile the weedy, bespectacled smarty-pants— so Paul remembers—and the word was put out that you were to be ostracized. But Paul refused, he made the decision to become your friend —as a consequence, he received a thorough thrashing from the ruffians... because of his loyalty to you."

"I never heard that story," he said, affecting an air of boredom. He slid the envelope forward, ensuring that it fell, at my feet. I picked it up, the postmark not from Aix-en-Provence where Cezanne said he would be, but from the village of La Roche-Guyon. It was sealed with pomegranate-colour wax, but I detected the tampering, a thin coating of a slightly different colour, an inept concealment of the broken seal.

He reads our correspondence then re-seals!

As I turned to leave, Zola's manner changed. "You must be eager to read his missive, so please, use my study for as long as you need," he spoke in a conciliatory tone. "Simply pull the bell cord," he proceeded to the door, "and Marta will show you out."

When he disappeared, I sat near the desk and broke the seal, that is to say, I re-broke the seal.

My Dear Lady,
We encountered and you permitted my brutish advances—from that moment I have been greatly agitated. I must see you again and beg of

you to model for a painting. Whatever remuneration you think appropriate I will pay. Enclosed is my new Paris address to which I will return in a fortnight. No one knows the location of this studio, for too many fools and charlatans seek to steal the secrets of my painting technique.

Say you shall relieve my profound unrest and become my model. There is the long length of your legs which culminate at your high hips that must be captured. And your secret parts... forgive me, my lady, see how you have quickly taught me to be ravenous!

Ach! How apparent that the thick-headed workman from Provence that I am lacks subtlety. But I entreat you! Do not hold my rough manner against me.

Come the 14th, I beg of you; I will remain all day in the studio, by the 3rd story window, and if necessary, all night.

Yours in fidelity,
Paul

His hysterical tone was a concern, sounding sadly, eerily, too uncomfortably similar to the artist in Zola's new novel. *How will the novel end?*

I seriously wondered what outcome Zola planned for his artist, Claude Lantier? A pile of folios lay on the desk. I leaned forward, to the cover page:

The Masterpiece

(Last Chapter Draft)

A thrill ran through me. Zola's denouement! But before I could ever turn a page, a courteous rap made me bolt upright; I froze, not daring to turn, listening to the door slide open then, after an interminable minute, close with a muffled thud.

I soon sensed his presence, Zola hovering somewhere in the study, alarmed when his hands fell flat onto my shoulders. I mechanically put the letter in my purse, remaining calm, still not turning. He inquired, the weight of his hands purposely gentle: "Glad tidings from Paul?" I said nothing. "And shall I take your missive for him?"

I stiffened, alert to the syrupy seduction in his voice. "Nothing today." The first lie of many to come.

"Then... shall I see you again soon?" His hands slipped from my shoulders, down my arms, as though measuring me.

"Perhaps," I answered.

He gave a slight squeeze and I listened unhappily to his: ***"Yes, I would like that."***

What Zola's advances aroused was my singular contempt. His lecherous behaviour showed the depth of his friendship for Cezanne.

"Monsieur Émile... perhaps a private, a very personal tête à tête is warranted," I suggested while slipping from his grip. I rose, proceeded to the door, slid it open.

He said, "Believe this, at a moment's notice, my wife and maid can be sent packing to our Medan home for a weekend visit."

"That might be more appropriate," I said. "I shall be in touch, Monsieur Émile."

Chapter 15

**In my last severe depression I took coca again
and a small dose lifted me in a wonderful fashion...**

Sigmund Freud

In His Prime

I

Taking scissors to beard, Sigmund scrupulously trimmed his new French cut for Charcot's after dinner soiree. Stepping back he appraised himself in the full-length mirror. The evening suit, rented from the nearby pawn shop, afforded him a certain smartness. Still he wondered, could he reasonably consider himself a handsome man?

Marty assures me of the fact; but will worldly and flighty French women agree with a naïve girl from Wandsbek? Oh, damn it all! My task tonight is simply to present myself intelligently.

But Sigmund, events might unfold unfavourably. A graceless misstep to undermine all of your efforts to gain success with Dr. Charcot. His vicious monkey jumps from its hidden lair, leaps upon you, bites your ear! Makes Sigmund Freud the laughing stock of the soiree!

He took a harder look at the image in the mirror... *there is the depressing question of your nose. Too Semitic? Oh, come now! Get a grip on yourself. Marty adores the nose in the mirror. Your little princess finds it masculine, like the prow of a boat, she said. But what kind of boat? A strong Viking vessel that ploughed the Nordic waves? Or a humdrum tug boat in her Hamburg harbour?*

He rummaged desperately in his toilette case for tweezers and pinched out several offending nose hairs. Now, at the very least, he had a respectable nose and proceeded to the the dresser, choosing Parke-Davis's stronger hydrochloride cocaine paste over Merck's. At the mirror, he dipped his cocaine brush into Parke's jar and painted the turbinate bones inside each nostril. Deeply inhaling, the sudden exhilaration was measureless! He laughed. None of his anxieties withstood the euphoria which roared through his system. The urbane gentleman in the mirror spoke wittily—"Monsieur Freud, may I say, there's more to the nose than meets the eye! *Le nez plus de l'oeil.* And Monsieur le docteur, let me assure you that at twenty-nine years of age, you are in your physical and intellectual prime. So let the cocaine phantasmagoria unfold!"

Donning coat, scarf, top hat, Sigmund stepped confidently into the Paris night. *Yes, I'm certain to be a veritable French chatterbox at Charcot's soiree!*

Only in retrospect, after the mishap, his stupid carelessness, would he wonder why, before dashing out the door, he had made the decision to slip into his pocket the Parke-Davis injection kit? He rarely administered subcutaneous injections.

II

Sigmund happily entered a glittering palace! The plenitude of brightly candle-lit chandeliers cast a festive glow as he strolled with new-found grace amidst gayly chatting groups, a smile for everyone, expecting at any moment his encounter with Jean-Martin Charcot. He and the great man would grasp wrists, like Roman nobles, exchange insights, revel in triple-entendres, and by party's end reach profound conclusions. Leaders, together, in the field of neurology.

I shall name my first-born after him, he shall be called Jean; no, too French. Martin!

So his thoughts raced and expanded as he meandered, delighted by the elegance of the guests who surrounded him. The French women provocative in low cut gowns were particularly admirable. *My!* How animated their gestures, their deep-throated laughing, the elegant turning of swan-like necks, the swishing of satin skirts, the sparkle of jewels on their white powdered bosoms, the distinct click of the pearls that dangle from their lobes. *Which I wish to nibble upon.*

Growing more adventurous, he left the ballroom for further exploration. Boldly he entered the billiards room to confront the rumour that Charcot's black monkey often cavorted here, the creature fond of sitting Hindoo style on the billiard table, they said, rolling the balls in some clever fashion. He was now fully prepared to battle the monkey, if it dared appear, to the death, a black death.

Instead, a pair of grey-whiskered gentlemen, smoking cigars, played a leisurely game at the table. Sigmund savoured the acuity of his senses as he listened to the solid knocks of ivory balls, hearing their muffled roll across the green baize to planned destinies. He could hear, see, smell, and extrapolate like no one else! To gaze deeply at the ivory balls brought him to the ivory tusks of elephants, their long noses swaying, sniffing and smelling. *The mighty nose!* He breathed in deeply, knowing he smelled as keenly as the elephant, spurring his return to the ballroom, to be near the women, to breathe in their secret, hidden scents, offering his total attention as he passed among them:

A playful curl she brushes from her forehead, young and coquettish, she smells freshly of cinnamon; her companion, wiser, emits savoury cardamom, deep throated laughter, tilting her head welcomingly back, her nostrils dark sensual openings of arousal.

Every observed gesture brought Sigmund voluptuous pleasure, a feast of sensuality that belonged only to him.

Then surprised when his name was joyfully called—"Sigmundo! Oh, Sigmundo!"

From afar Madame Richetti smiled broadly, waving her little hand laden with opulent rings. He gladly approached. In Madame Richetti's circle a slim-waisted woman looked vaguely familiar, opposite her a large, rotund man possessed a round head with a mass of ink black curls, both engaged in an animated discussion, the man sometimes gesticulating with dramatic hand flourishes. Sigmund drew closer to the conversation, their Italian sounding so musical the notes might well be dancing in the air above them.

How wonderfully mysterious yet perfectly natural for the slim-waisted woman speaking Italian to be Mademoiselle Forette—who looked extremely elegant. Bare shouldered in a light strawberry coloured dress which might have looked flamboyant on another woman, she wore no jewellery, neither necklace, earrings (nor Egyptian pendants), as though unaccustomed to glittering social gatherings. Mademoiselle Forette's auburn hair was pulled back from her face into a plainly knotted coil.

Madame Richetti rushed to him with an affectionate embrace, the soft folds of her fat pleasantly pressing upon him while he inhaled her delicious, sugared bun scent. He need do nothing else but luxuriate in Madame Richetti's protective warmth.

"Young man, young man," she breathed huskily into his ear, her sweet breath tickled. She stepped back—releasing him much too soon. "You must be officially congratulated! Appointed by *il dottore* to be his German translator!" She was filled with motherly pride. "I have been informed of the good news by Julietta." She turned approvingly to Mademoiselle Forette. "To think, Julietta, you and *Sigmundo* will be working in tandem. A *duetto*! I'm so glad!"

"*Un duetto?*" The rotund man raised bushy eyebrows in a querulous manner before offering Mademoiselle Forette a supercilious smile. "*Why, Si! Il violencello per la signorina!* The cello for Mademoiselle." And added mockingly, "*Per il signore scelgo l'ottavino.*" For the monsieur I chose the piccolo."

Julie Forette stayed silent, a glass of champagne in hand, smoothing back the side of her hair. Richetti happily clarified. "Dear Sigmundo, our Julietta is responsible for organizing the French edition of Dr. Charcot's lectures. It was **she** who actually gave me the idea that someone should be employed to do a German translation. You are in her debt, Sigmundo."

"Without your help in composing the letter, Madame Richetti, I would not have succeeded, for you softened the brittleness of my words."

Giving the compliment, he found himself locked into a stare with Mademoiselle Forette... *Julie... Julietta.*

An avuncular hand suddenly slapped his back—"Dr. Freud!"

He turned to face Jacob Knapp, the ophthalmologist from New York whom he had recently met at the Salpêtrière eye clinic.

"Dr. Knapp!" he gave a strong American handshake and wondered if his prodigious strength might break Knapp's tarsal bones.

Introductions were politely exchanged in the newly formed circle. The man of gargantuan girth was an Italian painter named Émile Tofano who wasted little time in his boast of being Dr. Charcot's favourite artist. He had painted *il dottore's* portrait.

"An undeniable claim to fame," volunteered Julie Forette, peering over the champagne glass she sipped, clearly unimpressed.

The chandelier light sparkled in Dr. Knapp's eye glasses. Clean-shaven, confident, he smiled. "Another person here must also claim the mantle of fame! Dr. Sigmund Freud!"

Émile Tofano looked warily at Sigmund. Dr. Knapp lifted two champagnes off the tray of a passing servant, offering a glass to Madame Richetti.

"No more bubbly for me," she waved it away with tiny ringed fingers, "or I shall be quite tiddly; but do tell us, *Signore*, what achievement does Sigmundo hide from us?"

"This man—" Knapp handed Sigmund the champagne, "is the discoverer of cocaine!"

Sigmund drained the glass. He wished for another to quench the persistent thirst. When cocaine courses through your system, he could tell them, it desiccates the mouth. "Dr. Knapp exaggerates."

"Come now, don't be modest," Knapp protested. "You certainly are famous in America for introducing us to the many magical properties of the drug."

He was fighting the urge to buckle over with laughter and wouldn't they all join him if they knew his cocaine research had been inspired by an American article? *Restrain yourself, Sigmund, Sigismund, Sigmundo.* "Let's give credit to the Peruvians," he said, "who were first to chew the coca plant and experience its invigorating effects."

"Humility be damned, Doctor Freud. As a result of your pioneering treatise *'On Coca'* and your research into the numbing properties of cocaine, ophthalmologists throughout our thirty-eight States of America now have a God-saving anaesthetic for the eye."

"Dr. Knapp, I must correct you—the research on cocaine's numbing properties as applied to the eye was conducted by other colleagues at the Vienna Clinic, not I."

Not I, not I—Drs. Ornstein, Schrab and Koller outwitted me.

"But you started the ball rolling," said Knapp. "You gave your colleagues the idea, Doctor."

"Perhaps," he conceded, exchanging his glass as another liveried servant appeared with more champagne. A sip of alcohol mingling with the cocaine soon made him forget his resentment. He began to feel extraordinarily magnanimous. "Albeit, the attribution is now theirs."

Auf Wiedersehen to the glory, the fame, the financial advantages. Auf Wiedersehen. Auf Wiedersehen. He drank.

"I, nonetheless, give Dr. Freud a *merci beaucoup*," smiled the American opthamologist. "Now I can perform cataract operations on my patients with absolutely no pain involved."

"I can assure **you**, Dr. Knapp," he replied, "that cocaine anaesthetisation is merely an ancillary benefit."

"I can assure you," Dr. Knapp looked irritated, "that the alleviation of pain is not a minor benefit."

"I meant no offence, Jacob." he used the doctor's first name. *My father's name is Jacob.* "As a matter of fact, I myself assisted in administering cocaine to my father's eye for a successful operation in relieving his glaucoma, so I know the importance of the discovery." *It just isn't **my** discovery, Dr. Knapp.*

Julie Forette's voice came to him in the softest undertone, "How rare to have an opportunity to cure one's own father."

"Yes-yes, but I tell all of you," he had to insist, "that still greater benefits wait to be derived from the cocaine formula."

"Oh, Sigmundo, please forgive me, while this all sounds truly fascinating," Madame Richetti gave him a rueful smile. "I fear I've strayed from my husband far too long. Giovanni shall begin to conjure all sorts of jealousies. I left the dear man somewhere out there amidst the crowd to search for Dr. Charcot and Madame Charcot. We wish to interest them in a trip to Venice."

Sigmund gallantly kissed Madame Richetti's hand, her gold rings felt cold on his lips. *Can this be a significant property of gold? I could this very evening begin research into the relative temperature of metals. Slip into Dr. Charcot's library and research the project. He will discover me there, deep in intellectual thought.* "Give my hellos to Dr. Richetti," he said to her, "and Dr. Charcot."

"We shall all meet later, I'm sure," she waved her good-bye.

Julie Forette brought him back to the topic. "Is it true that the drug heightens mental and physical vigour?"

He saw in her eyes a deep curiosity. "Most certainly, Mademoiselle!"

The artist Tofano interjected, "I have heard that it is addictive."

"Nonsense!" he snapped. *Why, this man resembles a barrel and should be rolled off to a distant corner.*

He let Jacob Knapp extol on several other of his publications on coca while he took in the singularity of Julie Forette, the interesting details, the nicely formed lips, the clean line of her nose, the pit marks of childhood smallpox upon her upper cheeks, the steady rise and fall of her bosom where two beauty marks nestled, like small drops of chocolate. She sipped her champagne quickly, nervously, while he exchanged their empty glasses for more.

"How does one take or administer cocaine?" she asked between sips.

Her interest encouraged him. "No other drug, Mademoiselle, has so many different modes of application, all of them more or less effective. It can be injected intravenously into any vein of the body, imbibed as a tonic, smoked in cigarettes, thrust into the nose with a brush, rubbed into the gums and even..." he concluded, "inserted into the anus."

Tofano expressed his displeasure with a swelling chest. *He not only resembles a barrel but an empty one. Devoid of perspicacity.* "Isn't this discussion," the Italian suggested, "reaching a dangerous level of distaste?"

The man's moustache, he decided, must be the thinnest moustache in existence. *I will precisely measure its width, compare the meager specimen with the other moustaches at the soiree, make a chart of all the moustaches in ascending breadth and lengths, and publish the results in an American journal, becoming truly famous.*

Julie Forette derailed the train of absurdities—"Signore Tofano obviously does not keep company with doctors who are obliged to speak frankly."

"In America," Knapp contributed, "the nasal cavity remains the preferred site of application."

"Each method has its followers," added Sigmund. "And surely others will be discovered."

Tofano looked at his pocket watch with a great show of weariness. "I must abandon this conversation. Professor Charcot awaits my opinion," he added with an air of importance, "on a new painting he ponders purchasing."

"Let no one here keep you from advancing the weight of your opinion," she said. Sigmund saw the glint of irony in the green of her eyes. The painter, the critic, the thin moustache, the prodigious belly, bowed, turned and swaggered away. She seemed happy to turn her full attention toward Sigmund and Dr. Knapp. "Well gentlemen, shall we all escape the French language and speak English?"

The men laughed. He admitted, "Speaking French with a German accent is not the best passport for acquiring French friends."

"It does appear," Knapp observed with a furrowed brow, "that the Prussian-Franco war remains an open wound for the French."

"Fifteen years, a rather intolerable stretch of time to keep a wound open," he replied.

"Many lost sons and fathers," Knapp cast an apologetic eye at Mademoiselle Forette.

She laughed, "You misdirect your compassion. My father was not among the bravely fallen. His sudden departure from France to distant shores might have been interpreted by some as suspiciously unpatriotic."

Dr. Knapp seemed much relieved to catch sight of a colleague. "Why, there's Alphonse Grenière at the hors d'oeuvre table. French ophthalmologist, cataracts his speciality! Must discuss my new version of the ophthalmotrope with him." With quick apologies he left Sigmund and Julie Forette alone.

"I missed you at last Tuesday's Lesson," he ventured. She only shrugged. He wondered if someone responsible for Charcot's French publications belonged to his inner circle? "I find a demonstration by him akin to a carefully constructed piece of music," he wanted her to know.

"You are perceptive, Dr. Freud. Most have no idea how scrupulously the maestro prepares for the spontaneous."

"I am convinced that he is making medical history with his use of hypnotism."

"He does seem to be taking neurology to a turning point. But what about Dr. Sigmund Freud?" she gave him a searching look. "What are your intentions?"

"Honourable, one hopes."

She fell silent, nervously brushing a stray strand of hair from her forehead, avoiding his gaze.

He tried to apologize, "I meant my remark to be more wit than innuendo."

She then pursued, "What are your ***professional*** intentions?"

"I conduct research in the pathology laboratory at the Salpêtrière. I am a neuropathologist."

"What specifically do you do?" she persisted.

His mouth dry from cocaine, a servant thankfully approached and he grabbed another glass. *Let her hear the truth, the essence...*

"I dissect the dead brains of children, preferably fresh."

"I only wish, Dr. Freud," she answered in a tone as dry as his mouth, "that I could be so easily shocked."

He drained his glass. "I suppose my phrasing was a test of sorts. More often, the nature of my research produces a chilling effect. Apparently, you perceive differently."

"My father..." she hesitated... "shared with me his keen interest in medicine, including the more sobering aspects of surgery."

He wanted more knowledge regarding her father but sensed it an awkward subject to pursue.

"I gather your research," she continued, "your search..." she clarified, "is to find causes for neurological disorders."

"Yes, specifically paralysis in children."

Another grey-haired servant appeared to silently tempt them with another tray of endless champagne. Both declined. She asked him with utmost seriousness, "But do you have a precise methodology? A foreseeable goal?"

He laughed with delight, suddenly desiring to explore the hidden regions of her neck, to push back her stray hair and smell her skin, to playfully bite.... "Your questions, Mademoiselle Forette, seek nothing less than to sum up my professional life."

She gave up what might have been a smile. At least her lips drifted into a slight curve. "Then shall we lighten the topic of conversation?"

"I go where you lead?"

"How have you been utilizing your leisure time in Paris?"

"So as to practice my French I attend the theatre, mostly Molière comedies, find the cheapest loges, mind you, high up in the clouds, shameful pigeonholes really, but it costs me only one franc." He had the urge to share personal aspects about himself. He missed his fiancée, his mother and sisters. *I will turn in this rented evening suit a day early, send the extra money to Mother.* "You see... I am here on a stipend."

"One does not need much money in Paris to find adventure."

He turned and looked out admiringly at the room crowded with clusters of elegantly attired guests. "There is adventure surrounding me. One gathers that not a few here are celebrities of some sort."

"Come! Let's eavesdrop on some of them!"

Unexpectedly she grabbed his hand, passing quickly from the room into a corridor. Uncertain as to where she would take him, he felt the oddest thrill in being led, compliant, as though he were the woman, the roles of gender switched.

Julie Forette obviously possessed a familiarity with Charcot's palatial house as he lost track of the turns they made in a labyrinth of corridors. *She must*, he thought, *be a member of Charcot's inner circle.* He began to notice that certain rooms they passed were occupied with small gatherings of men engaged in lively discussions.

She explained, "Over time, certain rooms gain reputations for particular topics of debate. Where subjects, purportedly, are examined in noteworthy depth."

Julie Forette's sarcasm was not lost on him; he stopped at the doorway of one of the noteworthy discussions and discreetly peered inside. "Who is that gentleman?"

A distinguished group were seated in a comfortable conclave of armchairs, listening to a man who had stationed himself in front of a warm glowing fire. He wore a Turkish fez squarely on his head, had an impeccably neat beard, and clearly enjoyed holding court. He took with good humour the questions hurled at him.

"What is the truth to the claim," came the query from his audience, "that this current novel of yours is a *roman à clef*?"

"Any art worth its salt and vinegar must appropriate reality. But let me assure you, gentlemen, that the Paris I depict in *The Masterpiece* is the stuff of illusion." He paused to remove his ribboned pince-nez and stare thoughtfully up at the ceiling. "Or do I mean to say, allusion?"

Amid the laughter, guffaws and foot stomping, someone shouted, "Cleverly he begs the question!"

"Gentlemen, if you must look for real people in my new book, why then look for me! I have vivisected myself into so many pieces that a surgeon would be envious." He took a drag from a cigarette encased in an amber holder and blew smoke over them. "Read astutely," he advised, "and you will find my precious parts in each and every character."

Sigmund felt Julie Forette pulling him back from the doorway. She did not want to be seen. He whispered to her, "Is that who I think it is?"

"None other than the literary raja of Paris, crowned, if not turbaned, to inform us of our city's seedier aspects." Speaking under her breath, her contempt was unmistakable and startling to him. Stranger still, as they stayed hidden in the shadows of the corridor, the crowned raja seemed to sense their presence. Placing the pince-nez further up the bridge of his nose, he looked questioningly in their direction. Julie Forette recoiled and clung to his arm, as though for protection. "I feel the taint of his gaze." She pulled him away. "Come, Dr. Freud, there are more interesting rooms to visit. And someone whom you truly wish to encounter."

He deduced a troubled relationship between this woman and the famous author. *But to think, she actually knows Émile Zola!* He revelled in his new found situation, a night of nights, where he was in the throes of discovery!

At headfirst speed down corridors, turning left, turning right, Julie Forette led and brought him to a halt at another opened door. A finger to her lips signalled him not to utter a sound. He peeked inside to recognize the distinctly barrel shape of Tofano and the round rug of dark curls atop his head. The conceited Italian helped form a semi-circle of four who stood around a painting propped on an easel. Sigmund caught his breath, in the huddled group he saw the patrician profile of Dr. Charcot. The others were unfamiliar: a man with bushy side whiskers in the English style, and a plump young woman standing akimbo, dressed in severe black, and wearing ankle high shoes usually worn by hospital nurses.

Julie Forette lowered her voice to a conspiratorial whisper, "The young woman is Charcot's daughter. The man with the muttonchops is Albert Wolff, a stuffed shirt who writes art fodder for *Le Figaro*." She tugged at his sleeve, pulling him from the doorway. For a reason unknown he was expected to stay hidden. Such new capriciousness coupled with the slyness of her behaviour concerned him. His courage, engendered by the cocaine, had completely vanished. He fretted as to why on earth were their backs now pressed against the wall, why was this woman transforming him into an eavesdropper? Together they listened.

"The artist simply bewilders me," sighed Albert Wolff. "Now some younger critics, like Félix Fénéon, look upon him as a naturalist, but nothing could look less natural than this agitated hallucination which is before us."

Charcot emitted a chuckle. "The landscape certainly appears to be an ungentlemanly slap in the face of Lady Nature."

"Landscape!" exclaimed Tofano with great indignation. "*Professoré*, you are much too kind. I implore to your practicality, waste no money on such nonsense."

Again, Albert Wolff could be heard sighing with an air of feigned despair. "Basically, the artist, Claude Monet, is nothing but a dreamer."

Julie Forette's eyes closed, a private smile on her face, seemingly seeing the painting in her mind, murmured to herself, "But what gorgeous dreams he creates!"

Sigmund felt miserably at sea. He no longer thought that he was being guided by a sensible person. The situation, once invitingly extemporaneous, now had changed into something aberrant. He had a desperate desire for more cocaine to keep his uncertainty at bay.

"Gentlemen," said Charcot, "perhaps we judge the painting too harshly. One looks at the knitted brow of my daughter, Jeanne, and we are told that she is... a little miffed."

"Perhaps, yes perhaps we are too hasty in our judgement," agreed Wolff. "Let me move closer."

"Caution, Monsieur Wolff," warned Tofano with mock fear, "do not fall into the artist's hallucination."

Wolff cleared his throat for a new pronouncement. "Well, now that I look more closely, Monet does appear to show some species of vegetation. But I agree with Tofano, a landscape glimpsed by a man hallucinating!"

Sigmund heard through the male laughter the voice of Jeanne Charcot, putting forth a defence, "Sirs, don't you see the grass carpeted with multicoloured flowers? And the path leading down from the hillock beautifully strewn with poppies?"

"A path of poppies!" scoffed the Italian painter. "I see a viscous torrent of currant jelly!"

Amidst more laughter, even an eavesdropper could sympathize with Jeanne Charcot's defeated silence.

"Monet, a man of talent," acknowledged Wolff, who seemed accustomed to having his critiques accepted as gospel, "but he has strayed too far from shore; he drowns his abilities in a totally incomprehensible form of art. What a pity," he sighed yet again to finalize the opinion.

"But Father!" Jeanne Charcot objected. "Monsieur Burty, your writer friend at *la Republique Francaise* has patiently explained Monet. He is an Impressionist."

"Impressionist?" queried a baffled Tofano.

"Yes, Impressionistic," answered Jeanne Charcot, "in the sense that he and the painters from his school render not the landscape as an accurate photograph but offer us the quickened visual sensation."

Wolff spoke sternly, "Monet and his Impressionist gang are hooligans of art who have abandoned the discipline of rendering reality."

Sigmund became panic stricken to see Mademoiselle Forette leave the safety of the wall and stand brazenly at the doorway. No one had yet taken notice of her, so Sigmund dared a momentary glance inside: Tofano, behaving strangely, trotted frantically around the room, in a desperate search for something. Sigmund thought of a man on a sinking ship in need of a life preserver. When Tofano found an empty soup tureen on a side table, he rushed to the painting and held the tureen beneath the canvas.

"What in blazes are you doing, man?" demanded Charcot.

"But *Professoré*, as you can see, the current jelly is about to spill out of the painting!"

Charcot chuckled at the fat man's tomfoolery. "Come now, Jeanne says they are poppies, but perhaps a little too smeared to be easily recognized as such."

"I think Monet would benefit from a few more art lessons, a classical teacher, like Gérome or Ingres, who could instruct him in the art of accurate detail," remarked Wolff.

"*Professoré*," Tofano's raised his hands in dramatic exasperation, "What diagnosis do you give this dreadful mishmash of distortion? Or better still, what diagnosis of the man who paints colours not found on our planet? If this is grass," he pointed to a portion of the canvas, inviting Charcot to inspect, "why does he make it peculiarly blue and purple?"

Charcot drew near, only to shake his head and express bewilderment. "His tonality is strange; implausible, really. He permeates the air with far too much violet."

"Drenched in violet," added Wolff.

At the out-patient clinic," Charcot went on, "I have examined not a few with nerve anomalies along the optic nerve, restricting or altering their impression of certain colours."

Tofano saw an opening for more ridicule. "I have the answer, *Professoré*! Your French artist suffers from *violetto-mania*!" His joke of a medical diagnosis brought silence. Tofano's smile dropped.

"These Impressionists renounce all sense of reality," was all that Wolff could utter.

Sigmund thought to save Julie Forette from the social indiscretion he suspected her soon to commit—pull the woman back; but fear of being caught as her imprudent accomplice far exceeded his desire to help. He had lost the capacity to take any action. And Mademoiselle Forette, apparently unable to tolerate the ridicule heaped upon the painting, walked inside, fuming.

Sigmund abandoned, he pressed himself cowardly against the corridor wall. The only hope he harboured was to escape his ridiculous predicament before someone discovered him.

"With all due respect, Monsieur Wolff," Julie Forette remarked, seemingly astonishing everyone to silence, "what the Impressionist painters renounce is false perception—the fallacy of painted lines not found in nature, the fallacy of shadows that conservative painters claim to resemble brown sauces. An Impressionist seeks a deeper reality, he dares to perceive through his emotional temperament. What can be more real than one's personal feelings?"

Sigmund mustered some courage to peek inside again. He found Julie Forette directing Charcot to move back from the much maligned painting. "Dr. Charcot, standing too close makes the novice viewer insensitive to the effects of Monsieur Monet's separate brushstrokes. From afar is where this painting must be judged. See!" she pointed out when Charcot stood next to her. "The ragged surface strokes combine and dance to new life." The others joined to study the painting from a distance while she attempted to justify the painting. "Monsieur Claude Monet does not trace the contours of objects with painted lines, but rather with colours. He wants you to receive a more intense impression of nature."

"Monet makes me see the freshness of nature," Jeanne Charcot volunteered.

"I still see nothing but agitation," Tofano complained. "If you ask me, the painting may be injurious to the nerves."

She ignored Tofano. "Motion of the moment, Dr. Charcot, is what is captured. See how the clouds in the rising horizon pursue each other across the sky."

"And a thousand poppies rippling in the wind," daughter Jeanne added.

"There is movement," admitted Charcot. "Perhaps too much."

"It's kinetic, immediate, it's modern," put in Julie Forette.

"It gives me a headache," declared the annoyed Tofano.

Sigmund fumbled for the handkerchief in his pocket, wiping away the perspiration beading his forehead. What possible right did this woman have to intrude on a private discussion and very likely incur Dr. Charcot's wrath?

Wolff called her to task, "Where, Mademoiselle, are the details you claim are in the landscape? They escape my eye. All I see is vagueness," he argued.

"Light and the artist's memory define the forms. It is a personal vision," she stated.

"Are not personal visions, *Professoré*," inquired Tofano with a great show of seriousness, "the bane of the females at your asylum which keep them forever confined?"

The remark, predictably, plunged the room into another silence. All knew that Charcot deemed the residents of Salpêtrière his sole purview. Charcot's female wards were not to be frivolously inserted into discussions.

"Father," began Jeanne Charcot, eager to escape the awkwardness and aid in revealing the painting's worth. "Monsieur Burty says that the Impressionists are scientists of light."

"Scientists?" Charcot sounded incredulous. "How so, Jeanne?"

"I'm not..." she faltered, "quite sure."

Julie Forette intervened, "Because the Impressionists prove what Science promulgates, that pure light is composed of a spectrum of colours. The Impressionists utilize the concept by separating the colours and letting your eye fuse them into light."

"But aren't the colours a little too high-keyed?" wondered Charcot. "Especially the reds."

"They may seem jarring at first," she answered, "because we are accustomed to colours being mixed and modified by traditional artists... like Signore Tofano, for instance. Claude Monet and the other Impressionists break the long-standing taboo by putting colour in its pure form onto the canvas. That is what makes their work so innovative."

"Taboos exist for a reason, Mademoiselle!" huffed Tofano. He looked gravely at her. "Established to save us from excess."

"I'd rather view a painting that can elevate my perception than one that bores me to tears," she countered. "We are not Italians who are content to drink wine that smells of tar; we are French happy to drink champagne. Unlike Italians with cheeses that stick to the roof of the mouth, we are French who eat Brie that runs!"

Sigmund now realized that her capricious behaviour had turned to arrogance. *Does she even remember that I've been left neglected in the hallway? To walk in now, uninvited, is out of the question.* Besides, he knew nothing about modern art.

Charcot's voice had reached a note of irritability—"This discussion is rapidly losing focus."

Sigmund worried that at any moment this Forette woman might be asked to leave the party along with the fool who was eavesdropping in the corridor. He heard the intervening voice of Charcot's daughter—

"Father, perhaps we should view other Impressionist artists for comparison. I've heard Mademoiselle Forette speak of a Paul Cezanne."

Julie Forette replied, her tone emphatic. "The Charcot household should be patient with Monet. Take time, Dr. Charcot, to absorb his innovations before advancing to Cezanne."

She dares to instruct Charcot, a known art connoisseur—really unbelievable! Sigmund's anxiety mounted. How much longer could he remain an interloper in the hallway while this woman might very well be spoiling his dream of entering Charcot's inner circle? *Should I declare my presence? No! Absolutely not! Far too many unknown variables to confront. The wise choice is to seek an escape route.*

He slunk away.

Chapter 16

I'm still working, with difficulty,
but at last something is coming.
It's important, I think, feelings being
at the bottom of what I'm doing...

Paul Cezanne

BEARD TO BEARD

I

I agreed to take my clothes off under certain conditions. First, Cezanne would give me a dream. What I wanted was the dream that no one forgets. The dream that defies the gravity of common sense, escapes propriety, and trespasses past the boundaries of morality. The dream which opens a door to the most improbable fantasies and desires. I had a theory I hoped to prove—Cezanne's chosen dream would be the lodestar to explain what led the artist along his path.

The second condition was that I would not pose in a recumbent position. I deemed Cezanne too innovative to follow the worn-out pattern of the compliant nude.

Lastly, the more elaborate condition, I had to observe his painting method. Cezanne said that he could, through a series of mirrors, set at proper angles, fix it so that everything was visible to me. I would have a view of his palette, the colours he chose, and also a glimpse over his shoulder to watch how his brushstroke was applied.

"Your desire to understand the construction of painting," he admitted, "is impressive."

At the appointed hour I came to rue Val-de-Grace and Cezanne's nondescript building in a district dominated by cloth merchants. His top floor studio comprised one large room with a minimum of furnishings which were utilitarian and of solid woods. A modest amount of light filtered down from the skylight. The place was in reasonable order, cleanly swept, with many canvases tantalizingly propped to face the wall. What caught my attention was a wooden platform, conspicuously raised three feet, which must be waiting for the model. Happily, I saw that he had complied with my request for mirrors, a well thought out arrangement, where anyone from the platform would be able to see him paint.

Our conversation began awkwardly, neither of us accustomed to idle or small talk. He busied himself with lining up brushes on a small table beside his easel. I approached.

Picking up a brush, I wanted to show off my knowledge. "Sable hair. But the others?"

"Hogs-hair... pole-cat." He spoke so gruff and low I could barely hear him. This was our first time truly alone.

I unpinned my hat, looked around for where I would eventually hang the rest of my clothes, and noticed a canary in a spacious, gilded cage, the bird hopping about and tweeting a pleasant song. Cezanne followed me to the cage.

"Are blue canaries rare?" I asked.

He pushed a little crust of bread between the thin wires of the cage. The blue bird fluttered excitedly, flying straight to the treat he held, pecking away crumbs in mid-air. "Not so rare. The greens are harder to find."

I pushed a finger in between the bars to see if the bird would perch, but only succeeded in agitating the bird, causing it to flutter in frantic circles.

"Canaries are not finger perch birds," he said. "They don't like to be touched."

We fell silent. I had the advantage of having heard from Père Tanguy of Cezanne's phobia—his dread of being touched by anyone. At our café meetings, I had once touched the sleeve of his jacket only to see him involuntarily recoil. Phobias had a fascination for me, Cezanne's in particular.

"Doesn't your blue canary get lonely?" I asked.

"They are solitary birds, not sociable at all. And they sing more freely, especially the males, when they are by themselves."

Flapping my hat against my leg, fidgety, I still wondered where and when I should remove my clothing.

"Does your canary have a name?" I asked.

"No."

"I'd call the bird, Blue."

He responded with a knowing laugh, "The bird is not at all blue, he appears so because his white colour blends with an underlying pigment of brown."

Studying the canary, now at rest on a perch high up in the cage, he still looked pale blue to me. "Can your eye," I wondered aloud, "actually separate the blended colours?"

"Such is God's gift to a real artist, for his eye exists only for colours and the bright delight they give." He spoke of his visual gift without a trace of vanity. And surprised me with his belief: "Colours emanate from the Great Being whose thoughts they are."

While he spoke fervently of colours as "God's glories" I could only puzzle as to why he did not welcome human touch as another of God's gifts? I left him to roam the studio, taking in all the penny reproductions pinned on the walls, which were mostly full-bodied nudes, male and female, by his favourite artist Paul Rubens. On a dresser top I saw a nicely arranged bouquet of white irises and ruby tinged primroses—but the petals I touched turned out to be nothing but raffia paper.

"I paint slow." He stood morosely beside me. "Slow. Causing my mother and sisters to think it best I have flowers that don't rot." He fingered several petals, forcing a laugh. "Let them bask too long in direct sunlight and even these pretty strumpets will fade."

I shrugged. "Nothing is incorruptible, I suppose."

A comment he pondered before bringing me back to our purpose. "Are you ready to model?"

I cast an uncertain look at the big bottomed women surrounding us, nodding: "Clearly Paul Rubens and Paul Cezanne favour a particular body type. Perhaps you might want to reconsider..." I was tall, wide-shouldered, but otherwise slim bodied.

"Mademoiselle, it is you that I want to reconstruct in colour and light," he reassured me. "No one else."

Calmly I began to undo the top button of my dress, resolute not to exhibit any prudery. He shook his head, sullen and uncomfortable with my boldness, and nodded toward a folding screen in the corner of the room. Without more ado, I went behind the screen, finding just a washstand, a travelling chest, and a bench bed covered with a single woollen blanket. There were two pegs on the wall where a bowler hat and pair of trousers hung. I removed my clothes, placing each article over the screen—dress, petticoat, corset, stockings—then marched naked, barefooted, across the studio, going up three steps to the makeshift stage which directly abutted a floor to ceiling window, offering a vertiginous view, as it had no balcony, of his Paris neighbourhood. If someone in the far off apartment buildings possessed opera glasses, he or she might be able to see me.

I immediately assumed a professional air, offering a pose that I knew he had never seen before in his Rubens' paintings, flat-footed, legs spread apart, casually interlacing the fingers of my hands so as to cover my sex.

For several minutes he remained silent, occupying himself with stirring a mixture in a tin with his palette knife before asking, "So are you going to keep your hands over... what is it the sailors call it in Marseilles?"

"Beard."

"Yes, beard."

I dropped my hands to my sides. "Is it not now evident, Monsieur Cezanne," I said, standing exposed to his gaze, "that I do not have the body you need?"

"I look at your body no differently," he took pains to clarify as he applied what seemed a white pigment to his canvas, "than a landscape or a still-life. Keep the pose, it's suitable for you. And re-twine your hands."

I resumed my original pose. How it felt, to be stripped of my clothes, standing naked before him, is difficult to describe. A tangled rush of emotions passed through me, foremost an awful flash of shame when I admitted to myself that, just like any prostitute, I was bargaining with my body—the recompense, instead of money, was knowledge. The allure of his originality as an artist and a personality drove me to want to understand both. My nakedness seemed a small price to pay to gain entrance to his thinking. What I also began to feel was a sense of freedom, a delicious taste of rebellion, for I was not only discarding my clothes but, as well, the conventions of a restrictive society. Then a special thrill passed through me like nothing I had ever experienced. To suddenly realize that my entire body was being offered, taken over by a unique consciousness intent on extracting every shade, every tone of comeliness.

Because of the mirrors, I had a voyeur's view over his shoulder. I could tell that he was preparing the canvas to control the absorbency of his oil paints. It was called priming or sizing the canvas. Typically, artists brushed on a coat of rabbit glue. "You're not using rabbit glue?" I asked.

"No, white lead—now shush and let me work without interruptions."

Suddenly I saw that Cezanne's technique was exactly as Zola had described in a recent chapter—*'all that the artist Claude Lantier did by way of priming was to lay on with the knife a coat of white lead; he refused to size it, as he wished it to remain absorbent since that made for...'*

"Light yet solid painting," I quoted the novel aloud, "is that why you use white lead?"

"That's the short answer, yes; now be quiet."

Then the rumours were true, Claude Lantier was modelled after him—I had the proof! And to learn how Zola would treat his Cezanne in fiction took on more importance. The draft of the last chapter, was it still on the author's desk? The tête a tête I had offhandedly suggested now seemed tempting, but the loathing I had for the man overruled the thought.

Instead, I tilted my head to the side for a better view of Cezanne working, his cleverly arranged mirrors gave me three different viewpoints.

"Yes, keep that slight tilt," he urged, "it gives you an air of insouciance."

He worked—all three mirrored views of him—very slowly, each stroke painstakingly considered before being applied. I counted eighteen separate colours loaded on his palette. After he chose a colour and finally made a stroke, he stopped, carefully wiped the brush clean with turpentine, and began the process of pondering which colour would best follow. This was how he worked on the painting of me through the entire day. Each stroke, each patch of colour had to rightly express what he felt within himself, had to be justified, and he showed his anxiousness, not wanting the next stroke to possibly ruin everything. But the stroke, when it came after laboured thought, was surprisingly quick and dexterous, from right to left, always right to left. Then he again stopped as if finished, sitting on his stool, washing the sable brush clean in a pewter cup of turpentine, pondering again, growing hunchbacked, his neck sinking into his shoulders, all tension, completely consumed with where the next stroke would go. Such deliberation caused him to perspire and his feral smell filled the room.

When we were finished for the day, I hurriedly dressed behind the screen and ran back to look at the canvas. Although distorted, he had managed to compose what might have been my ear, and a supple arc of blue that gave the vague promise of being someone's neck. I chose not to comment. Optimistically I had expected a rough draft of my body by day's end, but here were random patches of colour. Then to further disappoint, he asked if I might help relieve his tension after toiling on "the portrait" for near five hours.

I took a moment to compose myself—"How?"

"Checkers."

"Checkers?"

"A game of checkers," he said. My surprise made him grumble, "Can't tolerate the machinations of chess."

So he carefully covered the easel with a swath a duck cloth, brought out the board and pieces, and we sat on the bench bed and played. After four games, evenly tied, I had to leave. He gave no good-bye kiss as he sometimes awkwardly did at Taverne Olympia when his beard and lips merely brushed against my cheek. Paul Cezanne fabulously innocent with women, or so I thought for a time.

Standing naked on the raised platform, flat-footed, legs slightly apart, my hair piled high, I offered Cezanne what he now referred to as 'The Eiffel Tower' pose. I presumed he was being satiric, yet I found myself feeling flattered, that his image of me, all legs and narrow hips, compared favourably to the pylons and iron scaffolding of the soon-to-be erected tower. As though, I too were uniquely modern, part of a new generation.

While he painted, I managed the semblance of a conversation, taking the form of questions and Cezanne's terse replies or occasional grunts.

"Are you reading, like the rest us, Zola's *Masterpiece*?" I asked, keeping watch through the mirrors on how he applied his colours in parallel patches.

"Nope. So, you consider the novel a masterpiece already?"

"No, that's just the title. Which explains the raison d'être of the protagonist, the artist Claude Lantier and his all-consuming desire to create a masterpiece."

"Romantic hogwash. Émile should know better."

"I would think, based on his other novels, that he seeks to be authentic. When will you start reading his conception of an artist?" I looked out the window at a bright, cloudless sky, hoping to hide my apprehension, concern. As the chapters appeared serially each week in *Le Figaro*, the artist-hero Lantier was becoming a less than flattering figure.

He dipped his brush into turpentine, wiping it clean. "After Émile's properly edited and removed the drivel for the published version, then I'll read." His tone clear that the topic was closed.

I refocused on the several mirrors, beginning to grasp how he employed his colours systematically, from dark cool tones toward lighter, warmer hues. He was building from the shaded contours of my left breast toward an illuminated centre. The closer his brushwork moved toward the areola of my breast, toward my nipple, the more transparent the strokes. I began to imagine the breast as another of his exquisitely coloured layered apples. Perhaps Cezanne also. Yet what an extraordinary length of time it took for him to place his mid-tones onto the nipple precisely where he wished. And still no right breast, nothing but raw canvas where it should have been by now. I realized that I might be standing naked on the platform for many more hours. Many more sessions. I believe he sensed my concern and stepped out from behind the painting.

"In order to paint your body well..." he stopped, a struggle to find the words.

"Yes, what about my body?"

He took steps closer to the platform; I stood above him. "Your body," he answered, "is a landscape. In order to paint it well, I first need to discover its geological structure."

"Am I just a landscape? Truly, just a landscape, Monsieur Paul Cezanne?" I felt the devilishness in my voice. Naked and looming above him.

"To me, yes." He brought a full length mirror for me to see myself. "Everywhere a contour line surrounds a colour, holding it prisoner, and I want to free that colour. Don't you see the infinite number of blues, ochers, pinks within your flesh!" His temper flaring. "And each patch of colour I apply must encapsulate the light particular to you, and also the kind of shadow your skin reflects. Thus my responsibility," he spoke with fierce conviction, "my God-given duty to accurately record these sensations."

Would any other man ever observe me with Cezanne's intensity? I took pleasure in my discipline, maintaining the spread-eagle pose for him. He fiddled and readjusted a platform mirror so as to show another area of the canvas. "Regard how the breast reaches its ultimate point of equilibrium and colour saturation... one false stroke and I lose everything! I cannot permit the landscape of your body to slip from my reach; I must make the transient colours permanent..."

Unlacing hands, letting my arms drop, I chose to no longer hide any part of me. His descriptions stirred in me an erotic curiosity to explore my own body. I cupped my breasts and closed my eyes for a moment; when I squeezed, I dared to catch his reaction, in his eyes the flicker of alarm. I looked questioningly... *Do I behave badly? So-so badly?*

Nervously he fiddled more with the mirrors, causing a shaving mirror to detach from his intricate apparatus and fall at my feet. We both could observe, from its novel angle, the cleft of my vagina. I stayed still. After days of showing myself in maiden grace, here was an extraordinary view. And I wondered, my heart pounding, what the artist, breaths away, saw?

"Mademoiselle...?"

"Go ahead," I quietly urged. "Go ahead," I whispered again, losing all sense of propriety.

His hands gripped my hips. I closed my eyes. I knew he had the strength to lift me from the platform if he chose. Instead, his calloused hands slid slightly down, only to press deeper into the flesh of my thighs. It was as though I were being branded. Wanting him closer, I took hold of his bearded face, a mistake, a touch he couldn't tolerate. He grabbed my wrists to keep me passive.

"I have an ugly mug," he complained, his voice thick.

"Yes, you do!" I laughed, more as if in delirium, letting him burrow his face into my belly. I wanted this lewdness, this unknown sensation. I both craved and feared to have him taste me. When his mouth nuzzled and searched, I let myself say, "Beard to beard."

Welcoming Cezanne's lips, his tongued kisses below, I felt the thrill of abandonment.

III

At our next session I quietly resumed the Eiffel Tower Pose. Occasionally I glanced out the large picture window at the distant apartment buildings, wondering if someone might have witnessed the brazen behaviour of a naked woman and a fully dressed, bearded man? Would he or she have been appalled at the woman's surrender to lust? Examining my own conscience, I had no regret for our sensual encounter. I was glad for the experience. Cunnilingus I had read about, but no boy or man had ever attempted it with me. Perhaps artists, who painted nude women in various positions for days on end, were more inclined to experiment. I felt freer.

And so I resumed watching him paint his sensations.

The patches of colour, placed here and there, might conceivably evolve into a recognizable image, but as the day progressed, the painted me remained disappointingly fragmented. The shape of a head came into being but, eerily, without features.

Mid-afternoon we briefly stopped for a peasant's lunch of bread, cheese, sausage and wine. I took advantage of my release from the confines of the platform to inspect the canvases turned against the wall— shocked. Not one could be viewed as completed, some barely started, all in desperate need of more articulation. I stepped back and gazed at unfinished rooftops, windows without walls, a tangle of branches which had neither trunks nor roots for support. The dominating view was a wasteland of misbegotten beginnings.

"Yes, I'm slow to bring anything to fruition... which makes me unhappy." He turned the canvases, one by one, to the wall. "Let's not be distracted by abortions."

But I learned his pessimism easily misled. Cezanne never truly abandoned his creations. In the course of time he resumed work on each and all of the paintings, re-arranged them, reconfigured, until satisfied he had unified the composition... his art was continuous exploration.

I gained more insight into his process when, back on the posing platform, I observed him gazing intently with his brush, mid-air. Assuming his pause was a free moment, I broke pose to scratch away an imagined mite frolicking in the hollow of my back.

"Damn you, woman!" He startled me with his anger. "You just made me lose the brush stroke gaining vigour in my head!"

159

I became exasperated. "Offer some verbal justification for me to wait for the brush stroke inside your head or I'm finished for the day!"

"All right, all right!" He put down his palette and paint brush. "Watch!" He held his hands apart, fingers spread wide, then slowly brought them together until they were interlocked. "This is what I seek. The hands must come together this way, unimpeded, if one hand is too high, too low, all is ruined." He kept his hands tightly clenched. "See! Not a single link can be slack in the composition, nothing escapes, neither light nor the emotion I put into it. And so, on this canvas all the scattered brush strokes must advance at the same time and if they do not meet, do not interlock, the painting is… a disaster. Worse than a train wreck."

"As if, I suppose, the future Eiffel Tower collapsed because of improper riveting."

"Far worse, my dear, far worse."

I resumed the pose and eventually the imprisoned stroke found its position upon my breast, a reddish ochre with sunlit warmth, reminiscent of rooftops in Provence. In the mirror, a well-formed breast, apple fresh, had come to life. The exciting paradox! Through transparent layers of light-filled colour he constructed something solid. Somehow his meticulously brushed-in colours slowly revealed a fire-like essence.

I'm being seen by not just an artist but a metaphysicist.

As the day progressed, when more shadow than light entered the studio, he declared he could go no further. As I was about to step down to dress, he blurted: "I must leave Paris for a time."

"But my portrait?" was the first selfish question from my mouth. I wanted, I yearned to discover what diaphanous geometry he would make of me. Convinced that Paul Cezanne would produce something outrageously modern.

"It remains a work in progress," he replied.

"So be it." Resigned to the abrupt news, I thought to step down from the platform.

"Must you dress?" he asked.

Past pleasures tingling through me, I hesitated. A desire or greed rose of possibly more pleasure. I had to collect these emotions and sat on the nearby stool, but already feeling the wetness between my legs. Cezanne hoisted himself to the platform; I stood quickly, perhaps to leave, but his lips found my nipple, and I stood still and content, the kisses that wanted to drink up every part of my breast.

Passion welled, I took his face and pressed him harder to me. My hands, my touch made him recoil. Bewildered, I watched a man helpless, pale, frightened with sweat beading his forehead. The most terrible moment for us, awkwardness and the bewilderment, followed by irritation, knowing we had somehow lost each other.

I left, running to hide behind the dressing screen. I heard a crashing sound, a stool thrown and perhaps breaking. The canary chirped frantically, hearing its wings flapping against the cage, seeking an escape. I dressed quickly, but lacked courage to come from behind the screen.

Should I reconsider and undress for him? Let Paul Cezanne, whatever the neurosis, take me as he will?

My heart was thumping in hollow uncertainty. I sat on the bench bed, still hidden, far too miserable to make a decision. He roamed, judging by his errant footsteps, around the studio. A food tin opened, a cracker snapping, the clink of the cage door opening, Cezanne feeding the blue canary.

Inspiration struck. *Checkers.*

A game to soothe his nerves. I rummaged through his seaman's chest and found the checkers board and arranged the pieces. Pushing aside the divider screen, I sat on the bunk bed and focused on the game board. I announced, loud enough for him to hear. "I'm choosing black."

He found his seat across from me. "Black is my colour," he insisted.

"Then I go first."

We played several games, having time to regain a semblance of calm, so the question that occupied my mind was:

How does he find his way to kiss with such passion and yet unable to tolerate touch?

It was as though my hands sent shocks of electricity though him. What laws of logic did phobias follow? I had my own.

The red checker reached his king's row, forcing him to king me. "Paul, have I mentioned that I'm deathly afraid of being lost? An unusual phobia of mine."

"All phobias are unusual," he muttered.

"A horrid ordeal for me when first arriving in Paris." I skirted my new king forward; he focused on the board; I admitted more, "For a while, I went nowhere unless the destination was precisely mapped out." From inside my handbag, I showed him my map. "I carry it wherever I go... to be safe."

"Better safe than sorry."

"That's a cliché."

"There are many people out there who consider me a cliché."

I considered the board strategy, realizing the red king was able to leapfrog and scoop up most of his black checkers. I looked at him and smiled kindly. "Out there in Paris, more than a few consider Paul Cezanne a genius."

"Do geniuses get preferential treatment?" he asked.

"Sometimes— but not today." The red king decimated what pieces he had left on the board. I gave him another look that I hoped he could interpret, that said, *Don't worry. We will keep our phobias under lock and key, but let time, our mutual trust, get at the heart of things.*

"My dearest lady...?" he hesitated, his look sheepish. "Can we still correspond through Émile?"

To keep Zola as our go-between remained a loathsome strategy. Our last encounter, the broken seal, his salacious intentions, gave me the resolve to never to step inside his house again. "Paul," I took the leap, "our letters can come directly to each other. I shall tell you where I live."

Expecting his delight, Cezanne frowned. "My lady, I think it best to maintain the arrangement. Why disrupt what works well? Émile's discretion is to be trusted."

"The melodrama of a go-between is not to my liking." I stated flatly. "Let's just not correspond."

He panicked. "I need to stay in touch with you!" He then turned shamefaced. "You see... my mail is monitored by my father. Shrewdly monitored. The bastard wields so much influence in our town that even post office officials are subservient to his demands. He becomes privy to what I send; and the mail I receive, he opens beforehand. Except my correspondence with Zola whom father intensely dislikes; to read a single word only infuriates him."

"Why does he not like Zola?" I asked.

Cezanne surprised me with the truth. "Long ago, Émile convinced my mother that I should be a painter. Father never forgave him for that."

"But why does your father open any of your mail? Why?"

"Since I'm given a monthly allowance, the blockhead says that affords him certain parental rights." I looked at Cezanne, astounded. "I know, I know," he grumbled, "I'm forty-seven years old and my father treats me like an errant child. If the money weren't so important to my life as a painter, I'd tell him where to go, a downward direction."

"Paul, I'm afraid I can't..."

He pleaded in his courtly fashion. "My dear lady, you've changed my life! Please show compassion for my aberrant family situation. Please write until we can be together again."

"But..."

"You think me a genius, right? You alone!"

"Not just me, so do your Impressionist colleagues and Père Tanguy."

He was not listening. "There's still your portrait to finish. And my great ideas to share with you. And the dream I promised."

I looked down at the board, sliding red and black pieces pell-mell. "Yes, there is all that."

"And so much more! The exploration we have begun... with each other. Don't you agree?"

I said nothing. In spite of the enticements, I worried for us, that we were being too gullible, too anxious to delude ourselves—and the word, love, deliberately unspoken. In that moment, the thought was certain: *I do not love him.*

But what of tomorrow? The future brings promise of change. Winter finds April.

I put on my cape, hat, and was followed to the door. "That left breast still needs a great deal of modulating," he said with utmost seriousness, "before I can attempt the right."

I never heard 'modulating' mention before. He found his way of making me extremely curious. "What does modulation mean?"

"I can't speak about the process now; I need to be certain I can trust you."

"Paul, will you ever finish my portrait?"

"Allow me a little more time to discover the geological structure of you."

"You've said that before. In reality, Paul, I'm not a landscape, I'm flesh and blood."

"There is earth's history in every one of us, my lady, dating from the day when two atoms met, when two whirlwinds entwined, when two chemicals danced and joined together. And the history is in every one of my finished paintings. Let Émile show you my beginning work. You will understand me better." The workings of Cezanne's mind was near intoxicating. He pleaded yet again, "Please send me letters through Émile. I'll tell him to expect you next Friday."

"Well, maybe he'll let me see the ending of his new book," I half-joked.

"There you go! And I'll give you my autographed copy when our High Prince hands it over to me."

The only way I would risk seeing Zola again, I thought after I left Cezanne's studio, was to have complete control of the situation. I would have to devise a special plan for Émile Zola.

Chapter 17

**At the Salpêtrière we are not inclined
to cavil at a sedative that works.**

Jean-Martin Charcot

TOUR OF THE TEMPLE OF SCIENCE

I

Dear Mademoiselle Forette,

You are quite correct, what was found seemingly abandoned on the floor of the corridor belongs to this negligent doctor. Thank goodness you placed the pouch under your protective care. Upon mental reconstruction, it had to have fallen from my handkerchief pocket. Certainly in and of itself the objet trouvé (containing needle and syringe) bears neither a positive nor negative connotation; nonetheless, I thoroughly appreciate the discretion you have displayed in this matter.

As part and parcel of a physician's repertoire one cannot consider such, unusual, although slipping from my person appears to indicate a carelessness not typically on the list of Sigmund Freud's 'transgressions'.

Having offered the above clarification, I still think an expanded explanation is in order. As you rightly intimate (again with admirable discretion) that the contents in the syringe, if a powerful opiate, would have served no one well if retrieved by the wrong hands. However, the solution is not morphine, dear Mademoiselle Forette, for I know only too well the danger of such an opiate, having watched my closest friend become addicted to the scourge that is morphine; no, in fact, the hypodermic contains hydrochloride cocaine.

May we arrange a 'face-to-face' to discuss the situation in toto? All goes back to my paper, On Cocoa, to which Dr. Knapp alluded at the Charcot soiree.

> Thank you again.
> Sincerest regards,
> S. Freud

II

Unsure as to how I should respond, I kept his letter locked in the drawer of the escritoire which the Charcot women had generously gifted. Dr. Freud's request for a "face-to-face" occurred, but not as he might have imagined.

* * *

Dr. Charcot tipped his tall stovepipe in polite recognition of those who encircled him in the courtyard. Twelve of Salpêtrière's new interns, including Sigmund Freud, most eager for the morning tour. I stood at the fringe, notebook in hand, while Dr. Freud stole side glances, unsure as to what my presence signified.

"These gates," Charcot pointed his walking stick toward the entrance, "opened as a shelter for homeless women in 1657."

My stenographic duties thus began:

Shelter for homeless women

"From the 17th Century and forward," Dr. Charcot continued, "our asylum has maintained an estimable history of coming to the aid of the female sex, and we will never waiver from our mission as long as I am Director. It remains my solemn vow that our ladies in physical and mental need shall always find a safe haven behind these walls—safe, Messieurs! be they the aged, the destitute,or the chronically ill—safe from mocking eyes and hardened hearts."

Under his spell yet again, I so wished there was a way to show on paper the conviction in his voice:

safe Messieurs!

from mocking eyes and hardened hearts

The hospital tours, no matter how many I transcribed, kept me in state of high expectation. Accompanying Dr. Charcot, one learned to anticipate the unexpected, for he never failed to pull, as it were, revelations from his sleeve.

He stretched out his arms to encompass his beloved Salpêtrière. "As

166

you can see, we are a veritable city. We have our own streets, sidewalks, street lamps, and shops. Merchants establish prosperous businesses here and offer a variety of goods from wine to tobacco. We house well over five thousand patients, many of whom are employed, as our goal is to be self-sustaining. We have one hundred or so structures which include a post office, two churches, and a firehouse with a fire-fighting team that is, as the Americans say, crackerjack." He smiled with pride. "And much more, so follow me."

The walking tour began. I remained a respectable distance behind the group, having no trouble in hearing Charcot's stentorian voice. I also preferred being in the back for the freedom to observe the reactions of the fledgling interns who were, in essence, strangers touring a strange land. I was particularly keen on observing the discoverer of cocaine, Dr. Freud.

"Stay close to your old guide," warned Charcot, "or you could very well find yourselves lost in our labyrinth of narrow streets, courtyards and gardens. However," he allowed himself a wry smile, "if you do lose your way, panic not." He pointed his cane to the dome of *Le Chapelle Saint-Louis*, the gold painted cross agleam in the morning sun. "Our magnificent church, constructed in 1680, serves as a lodestar, and can be reached by trolley. Yes, indeed!" he boasted. "Salpêtrière has urban transportation in the form of the horse trolley."

I smiled to myself. *Artemis*, Salpêtrière's horse of many faithful years, was a grey-white mare we all loved, but clopped along at a pace hardly equal to a brisk walk.

The interns, unsurprisingly, grew aware of the women wandering the grounds. While dressed no differently than women outside the confines of the asylum, the interns had trouble ignoring their eccentricities. Either sitting on benches, standing solitary in the gardens, or walking to and fro with no apparent direction, the female residents were a collection of vacant faces and cryptic gesturing. One observed the quivering hands, the twitching eyes, the moving lips speaking inaudibly, the furious scratching of tangled hair; a congregation of compulsive behaviours.

An anxious question rose from the group—"Dr. Charcot, do we need to take any precautions?"

"Rest assured, young man, while our citizens are granted a certain amount of latitude— after all, this is their city— any patient encountered outdoors may be deemed harmless. The more you acquaint yourself to the Salpêtrière, the more you will appreciate the many engaged in productive activity, their tending to flower and vegetable gardens, the sewing and mending which is necessary for a large institution, their positions as laundry workers, cooks, and nursing aides—all duly compensated; are they not, Dr. Tourette?" He addressed his chief assistant who dutifully nodded.

"Are there no violent patients?" another intern queried.

Whether from compassion or resignation, Charcot heaved a deep sigh. "Yes, there are *les isolees*." I transcribed,

the isolated ones

"Who are confined for general safety, but more for their own protection."

I looked up at the barred windows on the top floor of the Pinel Building; Freud's eyes followed, no doubt guessing who lived behind the bars.

"Come," Charcot led everyone onward, "you must see our kitchens—we have two buildings where patients, for the most part, run the operation. He stopped before two low-roof buildings where the smells of cooking swept over us. "Yes, two buildings which stretch for an entire block!" he declared, brimming with pride. "After all, we do have six thousand mouths to feed. Ah, sometimes ..." a sudden softening came to his voice "...they seem to me, injured birds, fragile, broken-winged, forced from nests, hungry for nourishment." His melancholy lingered until his gaze rested upon Sigmund Freud. "Dr. Freud," he turned completely cheerful (such mercurial shifts often confused people) "will you lead us to the autopsy laboratories, for if I'm not mistaken..." he smiled knowingly, "... that is where you spend most of your time."

So ours became a march toward the pathology building, Charcot's steps jaunty, keeping Freud by his side, my odd thought that they looked like a father and son on an outing. Charcot's special interest in the new doctor from Vienna was apparent to everyone, especially the ever watchful Tourette.

Charcot's tone was now solemn as he stationed himself in front of the Pathology Building. "I'm sure Dr. Freud understands the extreme importance of Salpêtrière's autopsies."

Dr. Tourette hurriedly signaled me, scratching in the air with his invisible pen: *Mademoiselle best be transcribing our Director's every word.*

I well knew the importance of the autopsy, the culmination of Charcot's celebrated 'anatamo-clinical' method, his two-prong approach to understanding neurological diseases. First, clinically observe the symptomatic behaviour of the neurologically impaired patients during the years of their internment, assemble the data in personal dossiers, then promptly at death, dissect to search for the causative pathology.

Charcot waxed philosophical. "Let me ask all of you, would Christianity survive without the doctrine of resurrection?" His stern gaze riveted the group and no one knew how to respond. "I dare say, no! So too, at the Salpêtrière we cannot progress without the body's *scientific* resurrection. Our dead illuminate the correlations between physical and symptomatic. Our fiercely devoted pathologists—I count Dr. Freud among them— play a crucial role in untiringly seeking out the somatic lesions which cause our resident women so much... so much suffering."

Often after heralding the importance of the anatamo-clinical method, Charcot turned truculent, compelled to rail against the investigative methods of other countries, especially Germany. "Others outside of France actually question," he searched for foreign faces, "our empirical paradigm of observation and dissection, who foolishly replace our pragmatic approach with theory and abstractions. I speak in particular of the German medical establishment," he grunted, "always so eager to generalize disease, for they have not the living laboratory which is Salpêtrière! We are not just a hospital applying bandages to the maimed nor an asylum anaesthetizing those out of control. No! We are scientists of observation!"

The fire burning in Charcot's eyes shamed all to reflective silence. Until a voice, a cheerful Italian accent, asked (Italian doctors flocked to the Salpêtrière), "*Professore*, how is your hospital staff divided?"

Charcot removed his stovepipe hat for the handkerchief inside, wiped his brow and considered: "At the moment, those numbers escape my memory."

I eagerly spoke, "Dr. Charcot, those numbers were enunciated by you at last Thursday's tour." Scanning my notes, I ignored Dr. Tourette's disapproving frown. "Support staff," I read, "consists of 700 nursing assistants, 85 doctors..." Murmurs of admiration came from the group. "While interns—excluding those being initiated today—are numbered at 43."

Charcot chuckled, "Mademoiselle Forette's ability to decipher those hieroglyphics she scribbles never fails to impress."

His praise made my heart beat faster; I struggled not to look foolishly proud. How many years at home in Marseilles had I practised to master my stenographic technique?

Suddenly the Director looked up at the sky (and so we looked). He seemed to query the heavens with a frown. "What have we here?" he held out his palm.

Rain like gentle pins began to fall on our upturned faces. Dr. Tourette opened an umbrella and with admirable dexterity held it over the maestro. The rain came down lightly at first, allowing Charcot to continue. "Salpêtrière is rather like a custodial village, a working institution where we take our various enterprises quite seriously—especially farming."

"At present," la Tourette volunteered with marked pride as he kept the umbrella over Charcot's head, "we are experimenting with America's Idaho potato."

"Like everything in America," came the maestro's chuckle, "I'm sure it will be big, but perhaps lacking in subtle taste."

The raindrops became large dollops and splashed upon my transcription page. No one was prepared to acknowledge the steadily increasing rain until Charcot launched into an awkward trot toward a nearby building, Tourette with the umbrella in faithful pursuit. The rest of us dashed after them, laughing at the unusual turn of events. Freud had his chance to run beside me. "Hope you received my letter of gratitude."

"Yes, Dr. Freud, yes indeed!" I huffed out between breaths.

He stopped me at the steps as the group followed Charcot inside. "And?"

"And we're getting wet," I answered, but knew he wanted more. "Well, you've piqued my interest in your paper on cocaine."

"Good! Stay here" He ran up the steps, retrieved the umbrella la Tourette abandoned on the portico, and held it over us. "Now when and where can I see you again?"

"Well, Dr. Charcot suggests a meeting between we three," I said—his face blanched. "Oh, don't be alarmed. He knows nothing of your *objet trouvé*. The maestro thinks that I may be of assistance with your translation work."

Visibly relieved his cocaine filled syringe stayed our secret, he scratched his bearded chin, thoughtful, "Destiny appears quite capable of weaving us together."

The rain drummed pleasantly on our shared umbrella. "Shall we enter and catch up with the group?" I asked. Freud raised the umbrella higher to read the engraving upon the lintel.

La Clinique du Recherche Experimental

III

Never, based upon my experience, had Charcot taken a tour group into the experimental research clinic. The architectural façade was quite impressive, styled in the Doric Greek manner, including fluted columns. I was curious as to what experiments took place inside.

Entering the vestibule, Freud and I found everyone brushing the rain from their frock coats, excited, expectant and cheerful—until Charcot made his grave announcement:

"Make no mistake, *mes amis*, here you will be moving through a vast emporium of human suffering."

An admonition which wiped away all smiles. Charcot turned on his heels, carried his cane over his shoulder, and marched down a corridor that seemed to have no end. Hurriedly we all followed to catch his words:

"In the civilized world the Salpêtrière has become the epicenter of research into nervous disorders. It is a beacon and Mecca to the best and brightest of Europe's neurologists." He pointed his cane forward. "Before you, the longest corridor in the Salpêtrière, leading to our departments of experimental research. If I am not mistaken," he showed a small smile, "departments that will provoke your utmost reflection."

The first door we entered brought us to stunned confusion; instantly engulfed in dense swirls of mist, we became lost to each other. Charcot, as well, disappeared into a thick miasma of steam. The disembodied voice of our leader called out a warning: "Do not wander, stay close!"

Everyone invisible, immersed in a white fog, our ears were filled with the strident shouts and shrill screams of unseen women. It was such a frightful cacophony of tortured shrieks that my heart chilled. I imagined myself in a vaporous netherworld where bands of spectral harpies were in dreadful flight.

Through the rolling clouds came Charcot's assurance: "Be patient."

I strained to see. There were vague shapes ghostly walking and as the white veils began to lift, the steam shredding, they became Salpêtrière's nursing assistants, male and female. We were in an enormous room, a hippodrome, amidst a vast scattering of iron tubs. Charcot emerged, distinct in the dark suit and chimney hat, as though etched in ink upon vellum.

"Salpêtrière's Hydrotherapy Department!" he thundered.

171

Submerged in the hundreds of tubs were women, glisteningly naked, madly screaming or struggling to escape the waters, but burly male attendants forcibly held them down. Some in the tubs simply wept or whimpered, some behaved like playful children, slapping the water and jabbering gentle nonsense.

I waited with Freud and every other intern for Charcot to make sense of the chaos spread before us—"You witness patients in the throes of hysterical attacks, brought to our Hydrotherapy Department in the hopes of alleviating their sufferings." He took in the pandemonium of women shouting, splashing and protesting with an air of benign acceptance.

I put my pencil to the dampened page, to follow as best I could.

"The myriad neural agitations that assail the body can and do bring their havoc to the mind. This we know. Our charge here in hydrotherapy is to re-balance the body's circulation, a pacification process, if you will, to return stasis to the cerebral pathways." His scientific rationale helped to check my mounting anxiety. "What proves most effective are alternating applications of hot and cold water."

I channelled what remained of my unease into documenting the operational procedure of the Hydrotherapy Department: a continuous supply of hot water came from fire-heated cauldrons, carried bucket after bucket by a procession of untiring male attendants, handed to female attendants tasked with dousing the women with the heated water. Everyone seemed suitably clothed for their tasks, the women attendants wearing black-netted snoods to protect their hair, the men vulcanized aprons and rimless caps. The alternate of cold water came from hoses wielded by the men, utilizing a pumping system borrowed from Salpêtrière's Fire Department.

Charcot detached an industrial size thermometer from the rim of a tub and handed it to Freud to inspect. "Lowering, raising temperatures in incremental stages necessitates the proper device to gauge its effect upon the bathers."

The doe-eyed woman in the tub smiled at Freud, a placid smile. He reattached the thermometer. "Professor Charcot, is hydrotherapy confined just to temperature variations?"

The maestro stamped his cane in approval of the question. "Hah! Dr. Freud's mind seeks more than one modality—and so he should! And so does Salpêtrière! Into a certain number of tubs we pour varying amounts of sulphur salts followed by a course of electrostatic jolts. We correlate the shock intensities with thermal degrees to ascertain what hysterias are alleviated or aggravated. Thus, clinical data is amassed and scrutinized through the years."

A shudder ran through me. The sea of women in tubs was a perverted reminder of the courtyard of tubs at home in Marseilles where I mindlessly toiled at scrubbing clothes for my mother's clients. I, too, experienced temperature extremes. Fancy colour garments demanded water as cold as ice, the whites I scrubbed in water that scalded. My brother Justin for mischievous fun once threw a flailing lobster into one of the tubs, proving it would boil red in minutes. The endless scrubbing, the biting sting of potash and lye soaps never left one's hands.

What if I had gained no stenographic skills? Where in Salpêtrière would I have found employment? Here? Assigned to the Hydrotherapy Department!

A nightmarish thought best swept from my mind; I waited for more dictation, more words of science, only to realize that I was alone! Charcot and the tour had gone! I was alone in a room of shrieks and pleas for mercy.

Running for the door, and running down the corridor after the group, straining to hear the words he conferred, words that seemed to flutter in the air, pieces of truth, and I must assemble them on paper:

"At Salpêtrière, we are burdened with one desire, to alleviate suffering, and no methodology will be judged too unconventional."

Another door opened.

IV

"Above you..." skyward he waved what many surely deemed his sorcerer's wand. "... a special group of unfortunates."

(Like Thoth, the dutiful scribe my little sister predicted I would become, the truth needed to be recorded, no matter the imbedded sorrow.)

"Above you," he spoke, "are outpatients who suffer from cervical and spinal neuralgias. Thus, you are witness to another experimental methodology, the utilization of the suspension bar, the purpose of which is to stretch the full length of the spinal column for relief."

All eyes looked up. How difficult to believe! How was one to comprehend the aerial spectacle above! We waited, anxious for a scientific explanation as to why men, still in their frock coats, and women, attired in fashionable dresses, were suspended in mid-air? Why did they hang, entrapped in head harnesses? Gently swaying like pendulums? Charcot rescued us from incredulity—

"Those who dangle from so high are unique outpatients, gentlemen *and* women, who courageously dare to undergo a new therapeutic modality." He regarded the swaying bodies with admiration. "Fortunately," he murmured, a confidential aside I knew not to transcribe, "they are in a financial position to pay for their treatment."

The head harnesses, secured by leather straps over the ears and under the chin, were attached to an overhead, horizontal bar, further controlled by a rope and pulley mechanism. The ropes were pulled ever so slowly by attendants standing underneath. The rope pullers, wearing sleeveless shirts, had enormous biceps. And slowly they raised and lowered the neuralgia-riddled outpatients to varying heights. It recalled to mind the graceful ascending and descending of fanciful animals as they turned on a carousel.

"The pulley process produces different degrees of tension," explained Charcot.

I could hear them moaning discreetly, such well-dressed gentlemen and women, enduring heaven knows what discomfort. Rhythmically they rose and descended in accordance to some singular formula learned by the muscled men below. At certain points in the course of treatment, the long-suffering patients were locked, albeit briefly, into stationary positions, the creaking pulleys stilled, while the harnessed bodies continued to sway, ever-so-gently.

On my laundry deliveries, I regularly passed the open shed of Marseilles' abattoir, where the carcasses hung like this, and sometimes swayed.

"Let us not forget"—thankfully the Marseilles memory and stink of blood dissolved as Charcot gave firm assurance—"that what we practised in all of our departments and laboratories is Science!" And then he shared his insight: "All is system and gradation."

Twelve grave interns nodded in agreement, perhaps still perplexed, yet eager to cast their allegiance to whatever rules of Science that Charcot had discovered. I too nodded, no less a convert, ready to accept the demands, oftentimes cruel, placed upon Science (which I most often capitalized).

Silently Charcot left, as another experimental department waited for us.

V

I pushed my way to the front of the group, convinced of his genius, a desire for closer proximity. He travelled the corridor, optimistic, confident, and clearly enjoyed the tour. He was not only conducting us through wondrous doors, I realized, but inviting all of us to open the doors, the compartments within our own minds.

His mind, both bold and inexhaustible!

I stole a glance at Freud as he, too, manoeuvred closer to Charcot, his desire equal to mine, wanting more knowledge.

The sign on the door indicated we were entering the 'Department of Electro-Therapy.' Dr. Tourette took solemn charge, signalling to an elderly man; he shuffled forward, struggling with severe palsy, his hands out in an odd manner, clenched, as though dependent on this gesture for balance. I felt immensely sad.

Freud silently mouthed the words to me: *Parkinson's disease.* I nodded in glum agreement.

Tourette guided the Parkinson man into a most peculiar chair from which protruded an adjustable rod, this connected to a metal helmet.

"Cure me," the patient whimpered to the one person he recognized, Dr. Charcot.

I lost focus. The unexpected plea made me unable to put pencil to pad. The old man's trembling, his utter frailty, momentarily swept away all my objectivity.

Charcot answered him, "Dear friend, I am not God; but I will do what I can."

Encouraged, I put the kindly promise to paper.

I am not God

But I will do

What I can

The electrode wires, a series of them in different colours, which ran from a generator box, were attached by Tourette to the trembling man's arms and legs. Charcot expatiated on the origins of the chair. "I make no secret that the idea of an electric-powered chair came to me, as do all my

176

important discoveries, by way of the eye." He pointed to the left eye, the eye with the subtle inward cast, the eye which escaped the interference of emotion. An all-knowing eye, as if divinely endowed. I touched the pendant hidden beneath the neckline of my bodice, the Eye of Ra.

"A true doctor," he asserted, "one who contributes to the progress of medicine, does so through observation. Thus, I observed that certain Parkinson's patients who came to the out-patient clinic after a carriage or train ride evidenced a marked decrease in tremor agitation. One need only interpolate that the stimulation caused by the vibrations of the vehicles bestowed nutritional benefits to the afflicted muscles. Thus! so I reasoned, 'Why not devise a vibration chair?' One to replicate the rhythmical movement of vehicular rides, yes?"

Tourette fitted the helmet over the trembling head. Charcot elaborated: "The helmet, a copper alloy, was made under the direction and supervision of Dr. Giles de la Tourette to whom I give deserved credit." Tourette allowed himself a curt bow of recognition. "His invention now the companion piece to my electrode chair."

Tourette, when certain that the proper wires were connected to the chair, proceeded to the generator machine.

Charcot went on, "Reports pour in from assistants of the invention's efficacy. discreet cases of neurasthenia and vertigo have been cured, as well as certain types of facial pain."

Tourette turned large knobs to specific currents of electricity. We watched, riveted. The patient tightly strapped in his chair were soon thrown into a state of vigorous vibration. The dials were ratcheted higher, the chair bounced violently. As the chair and distraught patient began migrating haphazardly across the floor, Freud pulled me back from harm's way

Charcot unable to suppress a chuckle. "'*Charcot's Dancing Chair.*' *Ha!* So dubbed last year by a witty batch of interns; but let's put wit aside." Tourette was signalled to disengage the electrical current, the chair came to a sudden halt. "Unbuckle the restraining straps. Let's see what harm or benefit we have caused our dear friend. But! Before we permit him to rise, let me remind our new interns of the precise nature of his tremor and gait."

A near preposterous change took place in Charcot's demeanour which I deemed unbelievable. Altering his posture in dramatic fashion, he hunched his shoulders, bent his knees slightly, and began a tottering, near drunken march across the length of the room, just as if he were a man with palsy. Anyone familiar with Parkinson's disease would have thought him genuinely afflicted, so accurately did he mimic the patient's symptoms.

Tourette, smiling for the first time, at least in my presence, pointed a finger to his eye, to say: *Charcot, and none other, has the photographic eye.*

Charcot extrapolated, "My successful wobble, shake and unsteadiness is the direct result of the ability to register without emotion, like the photo-camera, only what I see."

The Parkinson man released, cried out, "Blessed sir, I am cured!"

I watched the man's struggle for balance, putting arms stiffly at his side, and choosing to walk toward me. Still he trembled from head to toe, still he faltered, dragging his feet, but he walked; I saw that the severity of his palsy, to a modest degree, had diminished.

"Am I cured, sir?" he asked.

Charcot smiled his sympathy. "Not quite, old friend; perhaps some fine day..."

Chapter 18

**Colour is the place where our brain
and the universe meet.**

Paul Cezanne

Tryst Brightened in Yellow

To behold the mighty Zola unconscious on the sofa, his mouth unflatteringly agape, snoring as loud as you please, gave me more satisfaction than I thought possible. The red fez he was fond of wearing had slipped from his head and lay, slightly misshapen, on his shoulder; his beard showed a trickle of camomile tea which had dried and stained to an unpleasant yellow. I crudely fantasized—such was my antipathy toward him—that someone had urinated onto his face; but the only abuse he suffered was to be temporarily anaesthetized from the several milligrams of chloral hydrate I had slipped into his tea cup.

The apartment—at least for two hours—was now mine to search. He had dispatched his maid and wife to their country house in Medan—all part of Zola's plan to facilitate his seduction of me. Only my plan was now in play. I wanted to find the early paintings that Cezanne had given Zola, I wanted to see them so badly that I took the risk of drugging the most famous author in Paris. It was reckless behaviour that might put me in trouble, but such was my deepening interest in the artist's work. I also knew to find the draft of Zola's novel which I had previously glimpsed on his desk, determined to read the ending.

Before the soporific took effect (one easily obtains chloral hydrate at any apothecary shop) I forced myself to listen to Zola pontificate. He had inane opinions regarding Cezanne:

"Paul possesses the mind of a great painter, but he lacks the will to become such. Surely you are starting to see that he is a flawed artist, short of fulfilment." He paused to gauge my reaction, so I nodded, watching the drug's stupefying effect, the glaze clouding his eyes. "The slightest obstacle sends Paul into... in-to-o... des-pair-rr." He struggled for words. "He wo-o-rks so-o slo-o-ow." The tongue thickened. "And yu-uoo... swe-e-e-t gu-ur-l... are... just anoth-ther ob-sta-ca-al for him. But me-ee... that's differ-rent. Yo-o-o and me-e-e can..." The words slurred to meaninglessness. I took the cup as he suddenly slumped sideways, the fez toppled, and his limbs went limp.

I should have guessed where a philistine like Zola would have stored the paintings of a genius, but I wasted precious time combing through every room of the apartment. I finally found the Cezanne collection, near twenty canvases, by climbing a steep, narrow flight of stairs to the attic. The door stuck and I had to push hard to open it, surely entering a forgotten place, my footprints became sharply etched in the undisturbed dust as I made my way toward paintings leaning against the walls. Having them turned away, abandoned and neglected, seemed criminal.

I set to work, as though an experienced art thief, checking dates, lining the canvases up in chronology, and brushing away spider webs. All signed, Paul Cezanne, their quality far exceeded expectations. So often he disparaged his early works, grumbling that back then he relied more on passion and impasto. True, I now saw that he had thickly layered his paints with a palette knife, but I found them more revolutionary than the Courbet canvases once shown to me by the gallerist, Theo van Gogh, who claimed Courbet the master of the palette knife. But here was a bolder impasto. I was thrilled!

And startled, when deep within the attic's shadows, Cezanne stared— his youthful self, an unframed portrait propped in a corner. He stared aggressively, more handsome than I ever imagined. A mane of dark hair curled at the shoulders, the beard untamed, and eyes that had the fire of wild dreams. A Paul Cezanne for whom I might have dropped my shift to the floor with far less misgivings.

He had given brave battle to his image, a countenance smeared and scarred with raw sienna, the prominent forehead trowelled with luminous ginger, and a background burnished in deepest burgundy. Only an artist touched by the muse could lay down such passionate colours. What might I give to possess the self-portrait? How far to barter with the man downstairs?

The other paintings in the attic were executed with the same virile brushwork. Creations of a Paul Cezanne unknown. A daring romantic I might have loved. But now, at least, here was the opportunity to gain understanding of his beginnings, his evolution as an artist.

I calculated that Zola would remain unconscious, oblivious to any outside stimuli for another hour, sufficient to study Cezanne's early paintings one by one. By the time I happened upon the truly neglected treasure, the floor was well mapped with my shoe prints; the canvas was turned away, leaning near a window not completely closed, the verso badly mottled from seasons of rain blowing through the slightly open crack. Under the back cross-frame, an envelope had been inserted, extremely brittle, needing extra care to extract. The envelope was still sealed, bearing a postal date of 1866, addressed to Émile Zola.

Incredible! In my hands, at the point of crumbling, a twenty-year-old letter, never opened, affixed to a painting very much abandoned. A letter that deserved to be read—

To my dearest friend, Émile

I want you to have this painting. It's small, only a three-foot size picture, but I think the best I've done so far: my sister Rose, sitting in my father's armchair, reading to her doll; pretty much all done in a range of blue with a smattering of yellow. I thought to submit it to the Salon, but if you say you want it, I'll give it to you.

Your friend always,
Paul

Cezanne's plain-spoken generosity had obviously been unappreciated. I turned the canvas to see what he had painted and gasped, having to stifle a heartbreaking cry. A girl maybe ten or eleven, Cezanne's little sister, Rose, sat small in a large, grown-up armchair, a story book in her hands, reading to her doll in a doll chair, Rose pretending to be grown-up. I choked back tears as I beheld the tender age of make-believe, and fought back memories, when little sisters played with dolls or guardian angels or invisible friends, memories that threatened to overwhelm me; I focused on Cezanne's colouring.

Rose and her doll wore identical smocks of cornflower and cobalt blues. He conveyed light in the picture predominately with blue. He challenged my eye to delight in a myriad of blues— blue patterned in the armchair, the unexpected blue sprinkled in the hair of Rose's doll, and Cezanne's gentle stroke of blue across Rose's arm. He created a lively contrast of blue and orange, the warmth of orange subtlety powdered into the doll's little ladder-back chair. Then I saw the culminating colour, if such a term exists, just beneath Rose's blue smock—Cezanne conjured her dress by a mere slash of yellow. Never had I seen him use such a joyful yellow. A buoyant yellow, prompting the tears to trickle down my face. *But why do I cry for a colour? A stroke of yellow?*

Somehow, I felt that the colour signalled or stood for Rose's innocence, every little girl's innocence when, for a brief passage of time, they play with dolls and dance with angels, until the intrusion of human experience leave their marks. No one spared.

I allowed the tears, cried in an attic of dust, spider webs and desecrated kindness, where beauty done with a 'smattering' of yellow, however thoughtlessly disregarded, still glimmered.

Then I heard footsteps stumbling up the attic stairs. It was best to stand my ground and confront him here. He staggered through the doorway. Only rage could have kept him on his feet.

"Whore! What treachery are you up to?"

"I came to see your best friend's art."

I went to the door, tried pushing him aside to escape, but he caught my arm, screaming into my face. "You drugged me, you whore!"

I slapped him—then stunned when he returned the slap, hitting me so hard I heard ringing. The violence enacted on each other shamed us to silence.

Recovering composure, I walked down the stairs, Zola followed. When we reached the vestibule, he watched me put on my hat and cape. "Don't you think you owe me an explanation?"

"Working so persistently, so diligently, so faithfully on your novel, I thought you deserved a nap." I turned the door handle, prepared to leave, but I paused when he spoke one name—"Charcot."

He smiled, he relished my hesitancy. "Should not the professor be informed of his stenographer's criminal actions?"

"Do you think, do you believe that you have the power to have me dismissed?"

He shrugged at my angry outburst while closing the door to my escape. "Paris can be cruel to an unmarried woman without financial means."

Blackmail surely worked both ways. "And won't Madame Zola be fascinated to learn of our pre-arranged tryst?"

Like chess, Zola had been checked; but he found another smart move: "The novel has an ending." The tether hook to keep me from leaving. "Now, maybe..." he added in a sincere voice, "the last chapter requires some polishing; but the denouement. . . c'est fini and will be ready in a day or two for publication in the *Gil Blas*."

I wanted more than anything to learn the fate of his main character, Claude Lantier, who was Paul Cezanne thinly disguised.

Zola, self-satisfied, gauging me well, smiled and held out a hand for my cape and hat. I gave them up, offering no resistance; he led me leisurely into the study, pointing out red smudges on the fine Turkish carpet. "The mountain clay that Paul invariably brings from Provence."

Once comfortably and confidently settled behind the desk, adjusting the pince-nez on to the bridge of his nose, he gave the order to sit. "You shall enjoy the rare privilege of an author's reading. Sit, Mademoiselle, sit."

Upon the desk a modest pile of pages, held together by twine, which he untied… Chapter 12 elegantly hand-written on the top page, the ending for which his reading public craved.

He skimmed through pages. "Let me find the passages sufficiently polished."

Accustomed to reading before audiences, he gave distinct inflection and tone to characters whom I quickly grasped were part of a funeral cortège: "'No doubt about it, the man we're burying today is a dead man; dead in the fullest sense of the word!'"

Another character, the author Sandoz, a very poorly disguised stand-in for Zola, joined in the eulogy, "'There's one, at least, who was both logical and brave. He admitted his impotence and did away with himself.'"

Appalled, I jumped from the chair. "You have Cezanne committing suicide!"

"The fictional character," he corrected, "hangs himself as he can no longer muster the will to live."

I forced myself to sit down again. "Read me more about your fictional character, Lantier."

After cleaning some annoying speck from his glasses, he re-perched the pince-nez. "'His trouble was this,' he read in a cold voice, "'Lantier was not the man for his own artistic formula. By that I mean he hadn't quite the genius necessary to plant it on a firm foundation and impose it on the world in the form of some definitive work... And now what is there to see for all he's done? Nothing; nothing...'"

Nothing. Above our heads, in the attic, the marvellous impasto paintings. "So, suicide is this artist's only logical choice?" The novel read like sensational trash and I felt weary.

He clarified. "Convincing you and certain others of my artistic objectivity will be impossible, like persuading the towers of Notre-Dame to perform a quadrille." My visible unhappiness goaded him onward. "His jumping from the ladder blatantly a dramatic device; however, I take some pride in the description." He thumbed through a few pages. "Ah, here we are! 'And there he hung, in his shirt, barefooted, and an agonizing sight, his tongue blackened and his eyes bloodshot and starting from their sockets, still, motionless…his face turned toward the picture...'"

"Picture?"

"The unfinished masterpiece, the nude portrait which obsesses him and which he can't satisfactorily bring to life—the hoped-for masterpiece, hence, the title's irony."

Could he possibly know that I pose for Cezanne?

"Of course, the woman who provokes his mental breakdown is the fictional mistress, Christine."

He toys with me. "A woman causes Claude Lantier's downfall?"

"No, only provokes, the cause is hereditary."

"Because his brain is three grams short of grey matter."

"Ah, you have read my previous chapters closely. Yes, three grams, more or less. I think I will reiterate that in the ending." He picked up a pen and scribbled in the margins.

I rose to retrieve my cape and hat. "Good day, Monsieur Zola."

When I left the house and reached the sidewalk, he stood at the open door, speaking in an extremely loud voice. "Yours is not the only affair he hides from his father who happens to hold the purse strings." How base that I waited for his gossip, but I did. "No, no. Paul returns regularly to the family home not just to paint his Mount Saint-Victoire Mountain." Zola spoke in a light airy manner that could not hide his spite. "Her name is Hortense Fiquet, his mistress of fifteen years; and not to forget, their fourteen- year- old son, Paul Jr." That Cezanne was able to maintain a long-standing affair and have a fourteen year-old son genuinely surprised me. Then came more secrets. "And during those early years of his liaison when he habitually squandered his father's monthly allowance, I alone bailed him out so he could keep his Hortense in comfort! And send his son to school. Me, Zola!" he shouted.

Everyone has secrets came my weary thought. But for a friend to disclose them was abhorrent. "Has the distance between you and Paul Cezanne widened to this extent?" I managed to murmur.

He stiffened. "My conduct with Paul has never been anything but frank and blameless. I have loved him like a brother, always wishing his happiness, always trying to shore up his wavering courage."

"Your betrayal is unconscionable."

I walked away and he angrily followed me down rue Boulogne, oblivious to curious passers-by. "I tried above all to make a sensible man out of him—to put iron in his spine!" Zola unable to make me stop and respond, threw out a final remark: "The pity I have for Paul is deep— his destiny will be obscurity."

Not looking back, I laughed aloud at his preposterous ignorance. The renowned writer, Émile Zola, specialist of Parisian life, had no inkling of the exhilarating art now displayed in Montmartre's galleries, nor the slightest sense of his best friend's revolutionary eye—the eye, I believed, that saw into art's future. The paintings, waiting to be born, gestating within Cezanne's fertile mind, filled me with excitement.

Chapter 19

Thank God it's over, it had been dull to bursting, only that bit of cocaine kept me from it.

Sigmund Freud
Letter to fiancée, Martha Bernays
February 2, 1886

CAUGHT

I

*T*he entrance gate to Charcot's mansion locked! What the devil? Locked! How could...?

Sigmund in panic struggled to pull open the iron gate, shaking and rattling the bars, desperate to get in. Suddenly he felt a prisoner of the street, on the wrong side of freedom, denied access to all he deemed instrumental to his career.

What if? The thought terrified him. *What if I've been deliberately locked out! Arriving late, Monsieur Freud, a breach of etiquette too serious to ignore. But to exclude him from the dinner gala? Unreasonable punishment. Most unreasonable.*

And this disastrous situation, why? A tie! All because of a necktie! The damnable, eel-slippery tie! If he had not made the extravagant purchase, silk! He would have tied a proper knot at one go!

But there must be a means to get inside?

Then he saw on the ground, illuminated by the moon, a rock the ghostly colour and size of a human skull. His tool! He pried the rock free, aghast at the worms swarming beneath, worms frantic like him, burrowing into the earth to hide. *No, not me!* He lifted the rock above his head and bashed down at the latch, but without consequence. He came down harder and harder, yet the latch stubbornly resisted. Furiously, he pounded, pounded, would not stop! Even iron possesses finite strength, he told himself, pounding until the latch broke, snapped, gave way.

Sigmund ran up the grassy slope, the mansion distantly aglow, every window glittered with festive candles. He ran at a safe vector, not to be seen, worrying if he possessed sufficient courage to mingle with Charcot's guests—*as an equal, as an equal!*

Their laughter sailing through the night prompted him to take cover within a copse of pine and weeping willows, only unable to escape their laughing ridicule, what he imagined:

Sigmund Freud, trespasser, upstart, Jew! Hysteria ruled and corroded his thoughts. *Must I retreat?* His pounding heart seemed ready to explode. He yearned for more cocaine, fumbling frantically in pockets for the vial, the allotted mixture for tonight somewhere lost. A louder, Zeus like laugh rose above the soiree din, a burst of Charcot's scorn striking Sigmund.

He fainted, crumbling, his last memory the wetness of the grass.

Staring down the far length of the snowy-linen table, Julie couldn't take her eyes off the loathsome, black monkey; the creature fidgeted in a child's high-chair next to Charcot, craving his master's attention. Her disgust and hatred for the monkey was as deep as it was inexplicable. He was not a dainty monkey one saw leashed to organ grinders on street corners, not a Lilliput monkey who wore a tiny pillbox hat and held a saucer for centimes. He was a large, evil-looking monkey, as black as Lancashire coal. *Le Rêve*, his absurd name.

Julie thought, *le Rêve Noir* more appropriate. A black, foul-smelling dream she wanted no part of. The creature squirmed out of the high chair, jumping on to Charcot's shoulder, fastening himself like a malignant growth. Despite her revulsion, she could not look away. Charcot treated the monkey as if his child, taking fatherly delight in spooning him rice pudding, occasionally bestowing a kiss upon the sloping forehead.

More astonishing to Julie were the thirty dinner guests pretending a jet-black monkey that made obscene smacking noises with its lips was of no particular concern, the monkey's antics politely ignored, the elegantly attired guests focused on spearing salad leaves and accepting another glass of champagne from a servant. Periodically the monkey scrambled down the table to steal a dinner item: a napkin, a name card, a baguette from the bread basket, only to scamper back to his amused master who rewarded the theft with yet another paternal kiss.

Julie sometimes looked inquiringly at the Charcot women who sat closest to the black dream and its stench—*Dear Madame Charcot and Jeanne, can you not smell him?* But the women remained indifferent, gaily conversing.

The guests this evening, as at any Charcot soiree, comprised many Paris luminaries. Novelist Alexander Dumas *fils* sat directly across from Julie. He chatted with the art critic Philippe Burty. Whenever Dumas leaned toward Burty to whisper some witty remark, it sent Burty into a roar of laughter. Julie had made a special request of Madame Charcot to place her near the two men. She hoped to gain more knowledge in the realms of literature and art, only Philippe Burty categorically refused to discuss art. "If I express my insightful opinions tonight," he joshed to questioners, patting oyster juice from his grey beard, "who will then read my articles tomorrow?"

Dumas *fils* became an equal disappointment. The novelist deciding his evening's goal was to flirt shamelessly with her. At first she felt flattered that the author of *Lady of the Camellias* found her attractive, but stiffened when the writer's choice of words took on the whiff of lechery. Dumas *fils*, son of the more famous Alexander Dumas *père*, was a man of 62 with an exaggerated moustache. What remained of his hair, a kinky texture, stood out in unruly clumps. He seemed determined to outperform his promiscuous father and whisk home a female companion at evening's end. Yet Dumas *fils* became her blessing in disguise as he became a surprise ally, equally annoyed with the monkey's thievery, especially when the animal took her knife, grabbed his bread and steadfastly crouched between the two of them. A barb came from Dr. Guinon at the other end of the table. "Is our gourmand, perchance, looking for the paté!"

Amidst the laughter, Dumas and Julie were too close to the monkey's buttocks to be amused, unable to avoid the repulsive view, as its buttocks began to change hues—a flesh pink rising to bright rose and eventually deepening to a ruby red. Dumas angrily snatched back his bread which caused the monkey a fright and he raced back to his master's safe embrace.

Dumas spoke out mockingly, "Your monkey, *Chère Docteur*, appears to blush in a rather unexpected area of his anatomy."

"He blushes not from modesty, I assure you, Monsieur Dumas." Charcot was barely able to hide his mirth. "As nature, so far, has not seen fit to bestow the creature with modesty. Rather, you are witness to an interesting metabolic phenomenon."

A wit like Dumas recognized a humorous debate in the making. "Shall I rightly suspect that this rainbow display is indicative of his carnal desires?"

"So, indeed, is the case," replied Charcot, readily planting another kiss upon the monkey's head. "As to why nature chose this pragmatic site for such passionate expression remains an enigma of science."

"A prodigal display of colours," noted art critic Burty. "First orange, like the tropical fruit, then changing to a marvellous crimson our paint-grinders would fight each other to discover."

Jeanne Charcot expressed her disgust—"Appalling!"

"We should remember, dear Jeanne," Charcot patted his daughter's hand, "that what one sees as ugly or beautiful varies from eye to eye."

Madame Charcot signalled several of the servants, always lank and sober, to ladle out the asparagus consommé. Madame's novel idea tonight was to have all the servants dressed in Louis Quatorze attire which included periwigs, high knee hosiery and brightly brocaded jackets.

As cold consommé poured into Dumas' cup by a costumed servant, the author chose the moment to offer Julie another suggestive smile. She fiddled with Sigmund Freud's name card propped on the dinner plate next to hers, another prearranged seat, but the young doctor was late for his first dinner invitation. She hoped that this would not spoil his chance to translate the lectures and work with her.

"Now some advice," Charcot suddenly warned all at the table, "never laugh directly at a monkey. The simian cannot tolerate ridicule, as he is endowed with an extraordinarily sensitive nervous system. Any explosive noises can bring him to hysterics, and possible convulsions."

Not caring the least for the habits of monkeys, Julie picked up the soup spoon and in that moment happened to look out the window into the night, catching a glimpse of Sigmund Freud running like a crazed thief across the lawn, strangely, a silk tie dangled from his jacket pocket. She managed a pretend smile for Dumas and dipped the spoon into the consommé.

III

Amidst the guests lively table chatter, a servant whispered in Charcot's ear which prompted him to slip surreptitiously out the door, the monkey jumped from the highchair and followed. After a lengthy absence Charcot returned in the company of Sigmund Freud. The young doctor looked particularly handsome tonight, fitted smartly in evening dress, and his brown eyes piercingly bright. He had such an exhilarated air about him, causing Julie to wonder.

Charcot laughingly called for the table's attention. "Ladies, gentlemen —*regard!*"

All gawked, thoroughly astonished, wondering if they should be amused: Drs. Charcot and Freud began to behave—there were no other words to describe their antics—like hired clowns. The two men obviously had rehearsed their comedic skit: Charcot and Freud pulled at their stretch bowties in unison which produced a tittering among the women, as each man's tie was elastically attached. When the doctors let go of the ties, they snapped back in place and everyone burst into laughter.

"A hilarious coincidence!" bellowed Charcot above the laughter. "This evening both I and Dr. Freud found ourselves bedeviled by our silk ties, simply unable to tie the damnable things, so when Dr. Freud informed me that the reason for his tardiness was an uncooperative tie, I seized the opportunity to introduce our young, German doctor to French modernity."

"No, no, dear husband!" corrected Madame Charcot. "I should receive credit for introducing **you** to the prefabricated tie. But I think we have sufficiently embarrassed Dr. Freud. Go, young man, and take your place," she gently commanded. "You will find your name card toward the end of the table—and at least in time for dessert."

Julie watched him, the sureness of his step as he quickly absorbed the place names of the French luminaries he passed, his eyes brightly alert to everything. She had a strong suspicion that he had fortified himself with the drug he extolled.

For Sigmund, in his altered state of consciousness, it was a glide through a phantasmagoric dream where everything sparkled and glittered, the necklaces and diamond earrings of the lovely ladies he passed, the polished gleam of silverware down the length of the table, the pinpoints of light which danced in the crystal glasses of wine. Before him a sea of splendid shimmerings!

Finding his seat next to Julie Forette, he watched her slide all manner of delicacies near him: tiny dishes heaped with goose and chicken pâtés, miniature mountains of black, orange and red caviars. "But I feel as if I have already dined well!" he proclaimed across the table to no one in particular.

Dined on what? she wondered.

Charcot resumed the imperial seat and the black-furred jester climbed into the highchair. At such dinners, Charcot became the discerning Caesar who chose topics of conversation. "Consider this new book of Zola's, serialized in the *Gil Blas*—the hero, the artist...what is his name?"

"Claude Lantier," the name sprang from the other end of the table.

"Yes, Lantier; thank you, Julie."

Both Dumas and Sigmund had their eyes on her.

Charcot spoke to the novel's underlying theme: "Zola attempts to show how Lantier's bloodline, tainted, perpetuates certain degenerative characteristics. The artist's pathological and self-destructive behaviour stem from the branches of his family tree. What I, as a scientist, prefer to call the neurological tree."

Guinon smilingly addressed the doctor. "Surely Zola has researched your essays on heredity and relies on them."

My procurer of corpses is here, thought Sigmund, *how bright his oiled hair shines.*

"I'm convinced of the very fact!" la Tourette joined in the compliment. "The author is to be seen in regular attendance at your lectures."

"Yes, Giles, possibly my ideas have influenced him," Charcot nodded in agreement, "Monsieur Zola, on occasions, has interrogated me on this very subject."

A question came from art critic Burty. "Professor, is it your conclusion that neurological diseases, such as hysteria, are hereditary phenomena?"

"Most neurological diseases," Charcot affirmed, "are rooted in heredity."

Sigmund brimmed with delight. *To be here, here at Charcot's table where profound ideas and vigorous debate abound!* He watched their questions form, the *why* in Dumas's mind.

"Tell me," Dumas did demand, "why does this so-called hysteria infiltrate Paris and run rampant like a plague?"

Another guest was emboldened by Dumas' scepticism. "Yes, Doctor, tell us. Why such an epidemic?"

The black dream snatched the dish of pudding to spoon-feed himself, Charcot not in the least concerned. "Our clinical research identifies three provoking agents: physical environment, infection, and frayed emotions. Any one of which, if sufficiently severe, will trigger a neurological disorder."

"There!" proclaimed Dumas with a smile that presaged playfulness. "The proof is in the monkey's pudding! Venereal infection! Does that not suffice to explain our neurological epidemic, Professor Charcot? The growing proliferation of prostitution?"

An index finger tapping his lips was Charcot's preparatory gesture for a thoughtful response. Sigmund Freud and Julie Forette were more than attentive—"Syphilis, to be sure, will incite a neurological disease."

Madame Charcot spoke up. Her hair, frizzed and powdered, matched the colour of the periwigs her servants wore. "I read recently in the *Journal de Paris* that the police, this year alone, have raided 408 of the most notorious brasseries where waitresses, paid a token pittance, wait on tables in order to earn their living as prostitutes. Some unscrupulous owners even charge the poor women for the privilege."

"How much can a prostitute earn?" Burty asked Dumas who, all knew, had written a most famous novel about a prostitute.

The Italian artist Tofano leaned his huge bulk forward, asking plaintively, "Isn't this topic too *risqué* for mixed company?"

"Was *risqué*," Jeanne Charcot amended, "for now we live in a modern age. After all," she added with an air of certitude, "it is 1886."

"Working in a brothel of some distinction," Dumas noted, "a woman can easily earn fifty francs a day."

"An impressive sum," Charcot remarked. Julie calculated that three evenings in a brothel could earn a woman 150 francs, Julie's salary for a month. Charcot signalled a servant to replenish *le Rêve's* pudding bowl. "I had no idea the profession could be so lucrative," he said.

"While seamstresses must work a twelve-hour day," put in Jeanne Charcot, irritably, "to earn a paltry two francs. Which forces them to live in one-room flats in the worst areas of Paris?" She cast a stare that dared any man to contradict her. As Jeanne's custom, she dressed in severe black, shunning feminine frills.

Dumas countered, "All the more reason that our ladies of the night receive a valued sum for their special services." He looked questioningly around the table. "For what professions are open to women in this century of industry when they are given no opportunity for formal education?"

"With no education they become seamstresses," agreed Jeanne.

"And laundresses," said Julie.

"My point exactly!" said Dumas while the cleft of Julie's low-necked bodice became the new line of his focus.

"There is the sacred career of wifedom and motherhood," declared Tofano who ferociously sawed a knife into his second portion of beef brisket.

Jeanne confronted the Italian, "What is marriage but another form of slavery?"

Madame Charcot spoke pleadingly, "Perhaps, dear Jeanne, you stray too far?"

"My sentiments exactly, Madame!" put in Tofano who felt himself unjustly injured, taking solace in a moist forkful of brisket, wiping away the drippings from his little moustache with a napkin.

Dumas assured Madame Charcot that her daughter "has hit the mark." Under a twirled, bushy moustache one discerned a rather charming smile. "It is the smart, sensible woman who quickly learns that in our culture the power and money rests in the hands of men so, accordingly, she gives up her gentle hand in marriage."

Jeanne seemed stirred to feeling offended for all intelligent women. "Wives who choose abject obedience only reinforce the male sense of power."

Dumas, enjoying himself, angled to procure Jeanne his ally. "Indeed, Mademoiselle, one must wonder which role imparts to a woman the greater freedom, the chatteled wife? Or the prostitute handsomely paid?"

Madame Charcot, no fool, smiled kindly, "Our illustrious author, as is his mischievous custom, tries to incite our ire; but we married women will not take your bait, Monsieur Dumas."

Sigmund had to speak his insight. "I wonder if a woman enters such wretched employment from a deeper desire."

No one responded (or knew how to respond) to the strange remark. Jeanne gently queried the new voice at the table, "Deeper desire, Monsieur?"

"To debase herself," he said.

Dumas heatedly disagreed, "What desire a prostitute possesses can only arise from her ardour for money."

The brisket devoured, a satisfied Tofano injected his own novel ideas regarding desire. "For some, the career of prostitution arises from the love of their own body; hence, to choose such a degraded lifestyle is only a means to incite their megalomaniacal lusts."

Charcot reasserted his leadership. "You are speaking of nymphomania, itself a severe and degenerative form of hysteria." His eyes narrowed down the table to Sigmund. "Is that what you mean by debasement?"

Sigmund showed his cocaine confidence, "I mean to say, a woman might prostitute herself as a means of self-punishment."

Dumas was quick to deride. "What nonsense! Punishing oneself by means of pleasure? Hardly!" He signalled a waiter to refill his wine glass and Julie's.

Sigmund countered, "Have you not heard of masochism?" He held up his glass after the waiter poured Julie's. "For masochists, punishment, pain, debasement, are conduits to pleasure."

"How can that be?" asked Madame Charcot, looking distressed. Sigmund was delighted to address Charcot's wife, "I suspect the person believes, at some level of consciousness, that she, he, justifiably deserves punishment. The saint's reward, if you will."

"From my research, as a novelist and playwright," Dumas responded haughtily, "I've seen no prostitute behave as if she were receiving punishment. *Au contraire*."

"There's something to be said for on-site observation," chuckled Charcot.

Madame Charcot looked disapprovingly. "Please, dear."

"Clinical observation proves fruitful for the Salpêtrière," defended Charcot. "And so, too, for writers devoted to Naturalism, like Monsieur Dumas and Émile Zola, who use their eye to see what is around them."

"I do so look forward to Zola's chapters," said Madame Charcot, "and hope Claude Lantier can be a successful artist and..." she cast a look at her husband, "escape the degeneracy of his family tree."

Stroking the monkey's head, Charcot assumed a serious mien. "Understandably, my little duck finds difficulty in embracing the idea of fatality, yet it is an aspect one cannot ignore."

Discussions of heredity and fatality irritated Julie. Drumming her fingers on the table, she became impetuous. "Well, tomorrow we shall all learn more of Claude Lantier's preordained propensities. Zola has finished the final chapters."

When Julie threw out the news, excitement ran like an electrical current around the table and not a single person to imagine that Salpêtrière's recordist had been read the conclusion by the author himself.

 Charcot gave her a look of admiration. "As always, Mademoiselle Forette somehow becomes privy to the inner sanctum of writers and artists. Well then, tomorrow bright and early, I will procure my place in line at the kiosk like the rest of Paris to purchase the *Gil Blas*. However, one need not be a clairvoyant to predict an unhappy ending for our artist."

Julie remembered that tomorrow was promised to the real Claude

Lantier. How much longer would she stand naked for him? *When I have his dream, I must reevaluate our affair.* From the corner of her eye she watched Sigmund Freud plunge a spoon into the sugar bowl and consume a mouthful of crystals.

Charcot ruminated before making the announcement. "I make a confession to all of you. I, Jean-Martin Charcot, man of science, once gave serious consideration to becoming an artist."

"An artist! Is this true!" the fawning Tofano exclaimed. There might be more commissions in the wind if he held on to this thread and pulled further.

"Quite true." Charcot nodded solemnly. "As a young man I used to decorate my father's carriages. He, of sympathetic character, recognized a son's proclivity toward art and offered to support my education in the field. He lay before me the choice, Science or Art."

"Most extraordinary!" Tofano interjected, searching the faces of others for confirmation of this additional and wondrous talent of the Master.

"But I could foresee," Charcot said, a certain melancholy in his tone, "the inherent frustration in a life devoted to the vagaries of art."

Julie thought it poignant, this rare moment of nostalgia from Charcot, his grey speckled eyes showing regret for a path not taken. He then startled his guests by slapping down his hands upon the table, rattling the tableware. "By Jove! I will keep the memory, be it bitter-sweet, of once having an artist's eye!"

A heart-felt voice then took everyone by surprise. "But all know that Dr. Jean-Martin still possesses the artist's eye! And mercifully for mankind, he has offered science this eye!" Sigmund's effusive praise stirred Dr. Tourette to compete:

"Art's misfortune has become medicine's triumph!"

"Hear-hear!" Guinon joyfully shouted. He seized a spoon, tapping his glass, prompting everyone to follow suit. A cacophony of ringing filled the room.

Sigmund sprang to his feet. Julie discerned the flush of desire upon his face, his wish to be Charcot's boldest disciple. The wine steward, vigilant for spontaneous toasts, signalled servers to fill the champagne glasses. All eyes fell on the young doctor.

"I begin with my confession." The guests waited, no one more curious than Julie. "Because of you..." he raised a glass to Charcot... "what perceptions I've brought to Paris regarding neurological maladies have been demolished. You alone are categorizing, almost daily, hysteria's burgeoning symptoms."

Julie then rose. *"Cher Docteur,* if I may be permitted a few additional words."

Charcot was surprised and delighted. "By all means, Mademoiselle Forette, speak!"

"Chère Maitre, were the power mine, I would pin, beside your Legion of Honour ribbon, a special medal, *la medaille du courage,* as justice has returned to the female sex because of you. For you, sir, have demonstrated that hysteria is not the sole bane and province of women—rather, a disorder common to both sexes. This... **revelation** liberates the female from a judgement unfairly endured for centuries; henceforth, the search for a final cure can no longer remain focused upon—excuse my bluntness— the female anatomy." She clinked her glass to Sigmund's. "A salute to Dr. Charcot, the mighty annihilator of myth!"

Glasses were raised, a few perhaps dutifully. Tears watered the old man's eyes. "Sigmund, Julie... your eloquence... I am moved..."

Madame Charcot rescued the table from embarrassed silence. "Dear guests, forget not the dessert."

The costumed servers deftly placed fruit cups before each guest. After staring intently into his cup, Sigmund asked, "What magic occurs inside my fruit chalice, Mademoiselle Forette?" He looked positively mirthful. "Are there sets of mirrors which multiply the cherries, whips and sugarplums? For when I take one—*voila!"* he plopped a cherry into his mouth—you behold two are gone. Most peculiar."

"It is a French phenomenon," she said. "Our predilection toward illusion."

He laughed, so gaily.

IV

When Charcot rose with an air of finality, the Charcot women also rose, the unmistakable signal that dinner had ended. The guests were granted free license to wander, the Charcot custom of liberality. Groups of like-minded dispositions found their havens in the various adjoining rooms, able to lounge and converse.

Julie stopped art critic Burty. "I regret not having the opportunity to discover whatever opinion you may have regarding up and coming artists?"

Burty smiled politely. "Monet, of course, leads the pack; but if you want a bit of my insight, I think the next generation of artists would do well to look for fresh sources of inspiration, as the new quickly becomes the old."

"What sources have you in mind?" she asked with curiosity.

"Japan," he replied. "The art they produce is quite unique. Artists with open minds would be served well to see what they can learn from their woodblock prints. But please, no more discussions of art."

"I apologize." *Japan*, she repeated in her mind.

Madame Charcot came to them. "There you are, Monsieur Burty, to capture! What an immense honour if you would take a tiny peek at my stained-glass panels. My tiny studio is but a few corridors away. An old woman's pastime, arts and crafts, but counsel from an expert would be so very much appreciated."

Burty, ever the gentleman, bowed. "The pleasure would be all mine."

No sooner had they departed then Dumas *fils* and Sigmund Freud approached Julie.

Behaving not unlike determined suitors, Dumas lit his pipe, Sigmund a cigar. Then Jeanne Charcot came, clearly with a mission, sternly addressing Dumas: "As you are a man of letters, I strongly recommend that you increase your limited knowledge of prostitution." Dumas calmly puffed his pipe with the air of waiting for a storm to pass. "Read Flora Tristan's *Promenade in London*. Then in short order, you will learn of the horrors such women endure, and hopefully no longer treat the subject so lightheartedly. I will say no more."

They watched Jeanne march away in a huff. "The daughter of Dr. Charcot has spoken," quipped Dumas, "and if I'm to stay in the maestro's good graces, I shall comply."

The three began to idly stroll. Julie spoke without looking at Dumas. "Flora Tristan's social commentaries should be on everyone's reading list."

"But, of course," replied Dumas as he suddenly stopped a servant bearing a large urn of long-stemmed carnations.

"As I wish, above all else, to stay in Mademoiselle's good graces, let me bequeath a flower to her." Dumas gave her his gallant smile. "Which colour, Mademoiselle?" The bouquet was a mix of white and red. "Alas, they are not camellias."

The allusion to *Lady of Camellias* escaped no one. Dumas' heroine, the demi-mondaine Marguerite, wore a white camellia when available to her lover, a red camellia when inconvenienced by a menstrual period. Aware of the author's invitation, disguised as jest, she extracted a white carnation, broke half of the stem to shorten it, and inserted the flower into the button-hole of Sigmund's lapel. Sigmund was greatly amused. The servant smiled as well. Next, she plucked off a single, red petal, letting it fall at Dumas' feet.

Dumas puffed, bowed respectfully. "Mademoiselle expresses her inclinations with a literary flair I find admirable." He bowed again and tried his best at a graceful exit.

"He seeks better prospects, I suppose," Julie remarked as she leaned toward Sigmund's lapel to inhale the flower's scent.

Sigmund admitted, "Once, in another lifetime, another clime, I forbade my younger sister, Rosa, to read *Lady of the Camellias*. I remember wagging a paternal finger at her, coupled with the warning that such books were far too unsuitable for young ladies." He laughed at his past prudery.

"Would you offer the same caution today?"

He laughed again. "Mademoiselle Jeanne Charcot reminded us at dinner of the new age we live in—'It is, after all, 1886.'" As they walked, turned down a corridor, he reflected, "I think I shall present my sister Rosa with a copy."

"Perhaps we can persuade Alexander Dumas *fils* to autograph it."

"With this very flower pressed inside." He whiffed at the pleasant scent. Both thought how effortlessly their conversation flowed.

She then happened to notice his leather-soaked shoes, the evidence of his moonlit run. "Shall I guess the grass was wet?"

"I watched the dipping of your spoon into the soup at the precise moment I fainted."

How eager they were to understand each other.

"You looked ghastly pale. I hoped the cause simply moonlight."

"One of my attacks. They occur periodically."

"Do you know the cause?"

"Panic, completely irrational—until I find a rational cause."

"You made a dramatic recovery, it seems."

"Thanks to a bit of cocaine."

Before she could respond—as the matter of the hypodermic syringe still loomed—the couple were interrupted.

V

Charcot appeared and nimbly moved between them, locked his arms into theirs, and insisted on becoming their escort.

"This scribe of mine who rarely utters a word at the Salpêtrière, surprises me this evening with her flattering eloquence."

She focused on their footsteps, Sigmund Freud's soaked shoes, Charcot's, brightly polished. "Dr. Freud inspires," she replied, "or incites me to boldness."

Charcot's arms locked tighter. "Such gifted children! May I adopt both of you?"

She lightly protested, "But Dr. Charcot, you have a gifted son and daughter."

He ignored the remark and blithely chattered, "Dr. Freud, are you aware that Mademoiselle Forette not only records verbatim my lectures and edits them for publication, but performs other duties as well? I confide to you—and few others," he lowered his voice, "she is my procuress." He said no more. Julie knew that the remark was designed to intrigue Freud with its ambiguity. Reaching the library, he smiled, ready to complete the double entendre. "This adventuresome woman ventures, on my behalf, into the back streets of Montmartre, seeking to appease my visual appetite. Her latest procurements, however, are somewhat unusual."

"Impressionism," she clarified.

"And first impressions can be deceiving, *n'est-ce pas*?" Charcot was in an extremely cheerful mood. "But be that as it may, I maintain an open mind with regard to the experimental. Mademoiselle Forette knows that."

He released them and Julie met his smile. "To date, Dr. Charcot has not purchased a single, new painting. I fail as his procuress."

"No new paintings, you say? Ah, I think Mademoiselle is mistaken!" He could barely contain his glee. She thought of the plump cat who swallows the canary. He pushed open the door, walked straight toward an easel covered with black silk and planted himself beside it. Sigmund and Julie dutifully followed. They waited while Charcot obviously savoured the painting's concealment. When he thought that he had maximized the suspense, he grabbed hold of the funerary silk and pulled it off with one grandiloquent swoop—*"Voila!"*

Revealed was a near-to-life size canvas, the picture so large it actually sat upon two easels. While Freud reacted with admiration and awe, she

203

hoped to hide her deep disappointment. *No Monet*, she thought unhappily, none of Impressionism's sparkle she had so wished for Charcot and his family. She stepped back to take in the dolorous scene. The canvas measured at least 12 feet in length and 9 feet in height. The engraved plate at the bottom of the frame gave its title: *'A Clinical Lesson at the Salpêtrière'*.

Grouped tightly within the left side of the composition, a distinguished audience of doctors focused their attention toward the stage and Dr. Jean-Martin Charcot. Beside him, his star hysteric, Sabrine Weiss, depicted in a graceful swoon, caught just in time by Dr. Joseph Babinski.

"One of your Tuesday demonstrations has come to life!" said Freud, still in awe.

Charcot chuckled, "I do believe I read Dr. Freud's mind. 'If only I had been painted into the picture, eh?'"

Salpêtrière's chief staff members were included in the composition: Georges Guinon, Pierre Janet, Giles de la Tourette and more. Charcot continued to tease Freud, "Whose place would you usurp? Dr. Babinski who catches our Sabrine before she falls?"

"La Tourette's seat in front would be my preference," he found the boldness to say. "But has she fainted?"

"Goodness, no! Fainting is for the faint-hearted. Here I have hypnotized Sabrine who succumbs to the first stage of hypnosis, lethargy, a pathological state where she becomes intriguingly malleable; I can make her do virtually anything; tell her to pass a hand over a burning candle without even the hint of pain; give her soap, suggesting it's chocolate, and she will eat with ravenous pleasure. Why, I can order Sabrine to bark at an imaginary moon and she will comply willingly. The process still remains unclear, but I have given it a name. Autosuggestion."

Freud was unable to tear his gaze from the painting. "Here is a visual testament to the importance of your work with hysteria."

"Andre Brouillet, the artist, does seem to believe," Charcot enjoyed admitting, "that we are making medical history at the Salpêtrière. He insists that he be allowed to enter the painting for the Salon competition next year. And I extracted a promise that he make me many engraved copies if the honoured Salon accepts the painting."

"Surely it will, and I shall hope to someday possess an engraved copy!"

Silent, Julie struggled to mask her depression. Might Sigmund Freud's curative cocaine benefit her now? She just wanted to leave. Be alone. Be angry. Maybe cry. She didn't know.

Charcot looked questioningly at her, "We have yet to hear a critique from our art expert?"

"How could the Salon Jury not accept it?" she conceded. "As it's executed in the grand manner of the great historical paintings, the committee will grant their unanimous consent."

"But does the artist handle his medium well?" he asked.

How well could she feign objectivity? *Speak of the technical aspects.* "Brouillet creates interesting colour arrangements. The men predominant in black suits..." *Black, insidious black!* she wanted to shout, but remained the art expert, erudite and pretentious: "So the judicious use of bone white become quite effective."

Charcot went closer to follow where the white was highlighted. "Yes, in the surgical aprons of Drs. Londe and la Tourette."

Freud contributed, "Tourette with his white apron, leaning so far from his seat certainly distinguishes him from the other onlookers."

"Where Dr. Freud would like to be," Charcot still teased. "Actually, both doctors assisted with an emergency amputation that very morning. Thank goodness Brouillet did not include the blood on the aprons."

"There are also highlights of white," Freud noted, "in the nurse's uniform."

"Dear Nurse Botard, been with me for over twenty years."

"And Sabrine's blouse is white."

Charcot grumbled, "I wonder if the artist needed to lower her blouse so far below the shoulder." He shrugged. "But I do like the detail of her clenched fist."

Julie wanted to conclude, "You, Dr. Charcot, become the fulcrum of the composition, and cleverly situated between the tall, light-filled windows."

"So *'Clinical Lesson at Salpêtrière'* passes the test for painterly proficiency?" Charcot wanted certainty.

"No one will doubt the realistic detail," she assured him.

"I'm greatly relieved by your approval." Studying and scanning the painting one last time, he reflected, "Ah, the empty chair in the painting." He turned to Julie. "Which belongs to Mademoiselle Forette. Your absence was missed that day."

Charcot suddenly took Julie and Sigmund by the elbow and escorted them to the door. "Off you go," he smiled. "I think my young protégés have need of more stimulating entertainment. As for old Charcot, there are overlooked duties to which he must attend."

When Freud and Julie reached the end of the corridor, he asked, "What did he mean by the empty chair, your absence?"

"I ask to be excused from Tuesday Lessons when Sabrine Weiss is the subject."

"That explains why I didn't see you last Tuesday."

"Jeanne Charcot and I have found ourselves becoming quite fond of Sabrine. And sorry for her. Charcot does appear to use more showmanship when demonstrating her condition."

"I suppose it must be difficult to witness her hystero-epileptic attacks."

"They are purposely induced at the demonstrations—I know, to show the pathological link between the hypnoid state and hysteria, but still..." She shrugged, her smile tight. "I find her spontaneous attacks sufficiently horrifying."

"I begin to wonder if being hypnotized is something more than an alternate expression of hysteria."

"What do you mean?"

"Perhaps the hypnoid state reaches a deeper level of consciousness."

"Like cocaine?" she thought to ask.

"Yes, like cocaine," he answered.

Chapter 20

And I seriously request, knowing that you will concur, that we name our first born son after him (Jean-Martin Charcot).

Sigmund Freud to fiancée Martha Bernays

1886

THE LAST AUTOPSY

Scalpel poised, Sigmund took a moment to gaze at the infant on the table: she slept, so it seemed, a discomforting sleep, her tiny brows furrowed, her body tightly curled like a question mark. Sigmund had been assured by Guinon that the corpse was but a day old.

"Sudden, unexpected, and tragic." So Guinon characterized the death when he unwrapped her on the dissecting table. "The morgue's report indicates a series of rapid-fire seizures, verified by the mother who witnessed the event."

Watching Guinon expertly refold the burial shroud for future use, Sigmund thought it politic to express appreciation "for your efforts."

Guinon returned a slightly crooked smile. "When Herr Freud wants a cadaver that has succumbed to neurological trauma, Herr Freud gets his cadaver."

Sigmund took to sorting through the instrument tray. "I am in your debt." He hoped Guinon would make his exit.

"Not a very pretty blue," noted Guinon as he gazed at the baby's colouring. "Yet she was guaranteed fresh." He frowned. "I worry, have I been duped?"

"With cadavers of such negligible body mass and weight, the blood can deoxidize with extreme rapidity." Sigmund placed the curled body on the scale. "She weighs less than fifty grams."

"*Vraiment?* So she remains suitable for your surgical research?"

"Truly, quite suitable. Thank you again, Guinon."

"I will confess to ignoble thoughts..." *Ignoble thoughts? What will follow the devious smile?*

"Since we are, shall we say, rivals for the maestro's esteem, I thought of not giving you the slightest assistance."

"Come now, Guinon." He occupied himself with examining the crescent bone scalpel to escape Guinon's smile.

"Tut-tut! No need for denials, Herr Freud, for we can only hope there is enough space within Dr. Charcot's inner circle for both of us to dwell comfortably." Guinon in evening dress doffed his top hat. He reeked of perfume stronger than usual. "Well, I shall leave you two alone." He tucked in his white silk scarf. "I'm off to the Black Cat! Their new shadow play, 'The temptation of St. Antony' has Paris buzzing. The debate is whether the piece is spiritual, erotic, or psychological."

Guinon left.

Sigmund noted how the infant's hands were bunched into tiny fists as if to protest the lethal sharpness of the blade he held. Swiftly he made a vertical incision from the base of the neck up to the crown of the head, peeling back the cutaneous layers, applying Pallone clamps to expose the cranium. Deftly he severed the nerve endings and the oblongata stem to unhinge the brain. Cupping the organ, he took care in extricating it from mucous debris, lifting it slowly, hoping that none of the cranial nerves would crumble or break. He transferred the baby's brain onto the Latimer scale. In size it was no larger than a lemon, its weight gauged at twenty-one grams. He then returned his attention to dissecting more of the corpse, drawing parallel incisions down the length of the vertebrae to fully expose the spinal cord. In systematic fashion, as with hundreds of previous autopsies at the children's hospital in Vienna, he looked for possible bony spurs or fusions, but he found the spine free of abnormalities. The hope now was that the brain might show tissue deterioration. Placing the organ back on the table, he moved the gas lamp closer, using the Alrick pry-pick to perforate the edges of the medulla stem to a depth of two centimetres. His principal task this evening was to track the paths of the auditory and cranial nerves in search of lesions.

While examining one of the tiny cerebral arteries, a strong suspicion took possession of him, an uneasy feeling that he was no longer alone in the laboratory. Had Guinon returned? He heard noises, odd scraping sounds, a shuffling as though someone were dragging their feet. Or were the rats, notoriously plentiful, keeping him company? A muffled thud then came from someone who obviously bumped into something. He turned, scalpel in hand, calling out in the darkened laboratory with less authority than he would have liked: "Who's there?"

Far back, beyond the rows and shelves of pathology specimens, Charcot stepped out of hiding, wearing a smile that was oddly diffident. Before Sigmund could collect his thoughts, Charcot disappeared again, veering down one of many aisles, slowly perambulating it seemed, deliberately keeping a distance from him, all the while speaking loudly, even cheerfully: "Working arduously, and late I can see! And a fresh cadaver from the wily Guinon! How does that man get whatever diseased body we ask for? A wink and a nod from the authorities, I suppose." Charcot began fondly touching chemical bottles on the shelves, inspecting labels, picking up and examining various surgical instruments—actions he performed lackadaisically, slowly drawing nearer. Sigmund stood enrapt. When Charcot reached the dissecting table, he sniffed the air and laughed —"Formaldehyde! Such an invigorating fragrance! I dare say, it was my eau de cologne for a good many years!" Dapperly dressed, his coat draped over his shoulders as though prepared to attend a ball, he faced Sigmund with an amiable smile. The portly Charcot took in another deep breath of the pungent preservatives which filled the room then swept his hand toward the countless jars occupying the shelves, the array of organs, from testicles to hearts, all perfectly preserved and floating in alcohol—he sighed, "Regrettably, long-long ago I stopped conducting postmortems... at Madame Charcot's bequest. My dear little duck, for that is what I affectionately call her, detested the smells I brought home from the pathology laboratory." The silver-grey haired Charcot at last gave himself over to gazing at Sigmund's surgical handiwork. "I'm reminded of the unopened ferns which appear in my garden during spring—only this little one will never unfurl." He shrugged, as one accustomed to life's cruelties. Turning his full attention to Sigmund, who remained silently uncomfortable, Charcot asked in a kind voice, "Have you dreams of one day having a family?"

It seemed a father's gentle invitation to speak freely of intimate matters. "I plan to marry when I return to Germany, which is where my fiancée lives; then, if Providence allows—yes, by all means, children."

"A great responsibility, children." Charcot nodded solemnly, then came a peculiar question, "Having met my daughter and my son, tell me, frankly, who most resembles me?"

Charcot's earnest expression required an answer. "Your daughter Jeanne, I think, bears many of your features."

"If I am not mistaken, much more than physical resemblance. My daughter, born with spunk, shows an avid interest in medicine, a passion I cannot find in my son, Jean."

"He appears most competent in his medical duties at the Salpêtrière," Sigmund thought best to add. "We have done rounds together in the wards. Certainly Jean-Baptiste attends all of your Tuesday Lessons, sometimes seated not far from me."

"Jean plays his role well, but he lacks the true heart of a physician. I forced him to earn his medical degree, gave him no choice, that's the tyrant I am. My defense? A parent's hope and expectation that the son will walk in his father's shoes and take even greater strides." Charcot shook his head, sadly. "Such fatherly dreams will not come to fruition. And so the two of us pretend all is well in the Garden of Salpêtrière. Our masquerade." Reaching, Charcot took the scalpel gently from Sigmund's hand. Inexplicably, he placed it in a side pocket of his top coat. The Director of Salpêtrière turned his attention to the dissecting table—"How admirably you cut! The posterior opening at the skull... like a door. Inside, her brain," he strangely concluded, "a child's ball that has rolled out." With a forefinger, he nudged the brain on the table, and Sigmund would have sworn he was trying to roll it, but the dangled cranial nerves made this impossible. Charcot wrinkled his forehead, suddenly troubled. "What, specifically, do you seek in this most mysterious organ?"

"Lesions which might correlate to epilepsy. She died from unaccountable seizures."

"Ah, Sigmund, I have precious memories of a thousand evenings, conducting postmortems such as these."

"With glorious results; historical discoveries," added Sigmund, "to have successfully identified the lesions which correlate to tabes dorsalis, multiple sclerosis and amyotrophic lateral sclerosis, to name but a few."

"Which you have accurately named, having done your scholarly homework on me." Charcot smiled, clearly pleased. "Would that my son were so attentive, would that he were here, instead of you, labouring through the late hours. More than likely, he is now at some bohemian haunt, the vile Black Cat, or some such café where they play with shadow puppets and recite witty poems to ridicule the prestige of France."

"Youth is a time for rebellion," he said, wondering if he could still consider himself young.

"Be that as it may." Charcot no longer showed concern, tapping a finger upon the brain, occupied with a new thought. "My discoveries, yes, assure me an honoured reputation as an anatomist—but accomplishments from the past no longer matter. The greatest achievement will be to find hysteria's true origin, and cure it! Where in this organ," he asked, almost plaintively, "are the lesions which trigger the hysterical attacks one witnesses daily at the Salpêtrière?"

"The cure will be found," he hoped to comfort his mentor, "and it will be your crowning discovery!"

Charcot looked severe. "Do you really think, Sigmund, the lesions for hysteria will be located in the brains of the dead?" His own question agitated him and he began circling the infant curled on the table. "What if the lesions are dynamic, not localized, not at all fixed in a specific area of the brain? What if we have a chemical process on our hands which leaves no visible scars?" He stopped, lowering his voice to a theatrical whisper, looking down at the eviscerated infant. "Perhaps the scars are only to be found within the soul? And where, pray tell, does the soul reside? If such a thing exists." He smiled sadly. "But we know Jean-Martin Charcot is not a believer in the mystic. Jean-Martin is the atheist, the ogre, who swept all of the nuns out of the Salpêtrière." He let his fingers lightly trace the furrows of the brain. "Yet, why does the infamous atheist allow crucifixes to return to the walls, eh?" He came closer to Sigmund who was forced to confront the disconcerting eye, the cast which gave Charcot, at will, disparate emotions. The choice seemed either Charcot's compassion or haughty disdain. "Why do the crosses of the Holy Saviour return? Because the plurality of our patients believe in their significance. I understand all too well that until the day arrives when all suffering can be alleviated by Science, one must permit, in the interim, less scientific ways for suffering to be endured."

Charcot's silver-grey hair fell behind his ears and over his collar in a slightly unruly fashion; he seemed, as he placed a compassionate hand on Sigmund's shoulder, less the renowned neurologist and more a poor country curate whose only aspiration—to save souls from suffering— eluded him. "Tell me, my boy, what are your plans as a doctor?" he asked.

"A book," Sigmund admitted.

"A book, you say?" the still dark eyebrows arched sceptically. "Regarding what topic?"

"The anatomy of the brain."

Charcot picked up the brain, held it out. "Picking apart the brains of these dead, little ones." He rotated the brain. "Does any particular area catch your fancy?"

"Presently, aided by a colleague, I'm engaged in tracing the path of the auditory nerve, attempting to correlate functionality and ..."

"Do you not comprehend?" he interrupted. "The geography of this organ and the rest of the human body has been almost entirely mapped! Anatomical research, *c'est presque complet!* Practically finished!" He grew agitated again. "*Ecoutez-moi bien!* Listen carefully! The anatomical framework for pinpointing organic diseases has been established. Of course, I played no small part in this endeavour. But is your choice to rummage in the dead brains of children like this?" He brought the brain closer to Sigmund's face. "To perhaps find, like your venerable Professor Charcot, another culpable lesion?" He held the brain higher, aloft, the cranial nerves dangled like snakes.

He never leaves the stage, thought Sigmund

"Relinquish this mundane research to those of lesser ability. We at the Salpêtrière need gifted doctors like yourself to explore the clinical frontiers." Charcot's power to persuade kept him speechless. "There must be one who dares to study more deeply the behavioural aspects, to make assessments while the brain still functions, to intervene while the patient still lives!" *What does he want of me?* he wondered. "If Guinon could somehow bring us a living brain! And not waste another moment with this dead lump of tissue!"

The strangest incident took place, so unexpected, so out of character for Charcot that Sigmund would never forget. Charcot's nostrils flared, quivered with anger, and his face twitched spasmodically. Sigmund knew that the great man had lost control of his temper. He threw the brain against the wall. The hurled force caused the brain to splatter, much like over-ripened fruit. Seizing Sigmund's shoulders, Charcot's theatrics mesmerized. Sigmund felt giddy, he worried he might faint in Charcot's arms. The urgent charge was whispered in his ear—"Abandon autopsies!"

Perplexed, anxious, on guard, Sigmund whispered back. "What would you have me do?"

"Now you ask the right question." Charcot released him, stepped back. "No more dissections." The doctor walked to what remained of the brain which had slid from the wall to the floor. He stared grimly at the gelatinous remnants. Sigmund came, removing his surgical apron, and covered the desecration.

"I want you to observe behaviour," said Charcot. "The hysteric's behaviour. So let's give you a fitting title, say, chief assistant clinician, sufficient to ward off unnecessary interference from staff." The plans, conceptions and ambitions Sigmund brought to Paris were demolished. "I have a patient for you, a most interesting young woman. Conduct an examination of her," he summarily ordered. Sigmund hurried in his mind to sift through the complex web Charcot wove. A new position, a special assignment, he had to craft a response, but suddenly he was gathered into his mentor's arms, an inexplicable embrace, and more whispering. "A rigorous examination, a comprehensive report; record emotional responses, the particular mannerisms a chronic hysteric manifests. I consider no detail unimportant."

Released from the strength of Charcot's embrace, a dark wave of depression gathered force, waiting to engulf him. "Yes... whatever you deem necessary for the task," he managed to reply. "I consider it an honour to be entrusted with such behavioural research."

"She is our princess. *La princess des hysteriques*!"

Sabrine Weiss, none other, he realized, the woman of the rainbow arc, who faints in Babinski's arms.

"A preliminary meeting, tomorrow," Charcot concluded, "the three of us, an introduction, at my residence."

In the French fashion, Sigmund received the double kiss before Charcot draped his overcoat closer around his shoulders and headed toward the door, shouting out his final directive: "Remember this, if you remember anything, the age of the neuroses has come upon us! And so has the time for a cure!"

Chapter 21

When the work of interpretation has been completed, we perceive that a dream is the fulfilment of a wish.

Sigmund Freud

CEZANNE'S DREAM

I

Upon Cezanne's return from Provence, I said nothing to him about the Zola episode, and doubted if the famous author would care to make it known. The painting sessions resumed, only Cezanne continued to procrastinate in giving up his dream (the singular dream, I repeatedly reminded him, that we find impossible to forget). Only after I threatened to step down from the platform, retrieve my clothes, and end my career as a model did he relent. He described the dream while he painted, insisting that I continue to pose. But during our lunch break, while he cooked his rice and mutton over the coal stove, I sat in the alcove of one of the studio windows, a sheet wrapped around me, and diligently transcribed the dream before details faded.

Not looking at me, stirring the pot, he asked, "Will you give it a title?"

"I beg your pardon?"

"Like a poem or a painting."

I never thought to entitle his dream, any dream. "Do you have something in mind?"

He dished out his favourite rice and mutton into a glutinous mound. I learned to bring fruit for myself. He sat on the edge of the platform, a tin plate on his lap, but seemingly not hungry. "'Broken,' sums it all up," he said.

The brutal murder in his dream made me venture a guess. "Because the pawnbroker's skull is broken?"

He shook his head, stuffing a forkful of food in his mouth, washing it down with wine. "Because the dreamer is broken."

* * *

My 'Dream Book' is quite full, but here is the first dream I recorded in Paris.

"Broken"

Cezanne scoured the back streets of Montmartre in search of a pawn shop, desperate for money to buy colours and more canvas. At the end of a disreputable street, the shop came into view. The trademark of three globes hung above the entrance. The copper globes were badly dented and misshapen. Cezanne suspected that young hooligans enjoyed throwing stones at them. Nervously he scanned the neighbourhood where such thugs might jump out from anywhere and rob him of the painting he carried. Clutching the still-life more tightly under his arm, he stepped inside.

Behind the counter an elderly pawnbroker waited with folded arms, glaring at him. Cezanne tried hard to recollect where he had seen the pawnbroker before, but he could retrieve no memories. For some idiotic reason, the pawnbroker wore a black bowler hat tilted at a rakish angle, as though he thought it made him look younger. The hat's tilted brim, just at the line of the eyebrow, irritated Cezanne. Infuriated him!

Why does the old fool wear the hat in such a ludicrous manner? he asked himself. *The man's a buffoon! A foolish embarrassment to whatever family he can claim.*

Everywhere in the shop Cezanne was aghast to see bowler hats. There seemed little space for anything else. The rounded, black hats crammed the shelves, hung on pegs that covered the walls, and were stacked in piles on the floor.

Where were objects of value? Pawned wedding rings, gifted pocket watches from fifty years of service, or at the very least a set of dueling pistols with ivory handles?

He saw nothing of worth in the shop except round bowler hats, tall towers of bowler hats that reminded him of American skyscrapers. Everywhere hats! They hung on strings from the ceiling like black fruit. He was surrounded by a pestilence of black hats!

A cunning character, the pawnbroker pretended not to notice the painting he placed on the counter. Cezanne swiped aside hats to make room for his still-life. He trembled with rage he could barely control. The pawnbroker wrinkled his nose.

He smells my desperation. I'm at his mercy. It's unbearable! I will show my indifference to his money. I will show my pride.

"There's the work, Monsieur, judge as you will. It speaks for me."

The pawnbroker smirked. "But does it sing?"

"I do not bring you a songbird, Monsieur."

Oh, how the rage mounts within me!

The pawnbroker re-folded his arms against his chest and warned, "Understand, here a transaction is business only. Nothing more, nothing less. Business. Now what value has this thing, this scribble scrabble Monsieur Paul brings me."

How does he know my name? I must not become confused. I will set him straight! "This is art, you fool, which I've laboured over for fourteen years."

Why, why do I give him a guarded secret?

The pawnbroker screwed his face into a false resemblance of sadness. He slowly shook his head, heaved a sigh of pity. "Fourteen years is a long time, Monsieur Whoever-You-Are—a long time."

"You know my name is Paul! Paul Cezanne!"

The pawnbroker, behaving clownish, grabbed a hat to shield his face from Cezanne's spit and anger.

I must calm down, behave reasonably, gain the pawnbroker's respect. "My mother named me after Paul Rubens."

Tilting back his hat, the pawnbroker gave him a mocking grin, "Is that a fact, Sonny Boy?" Then he looked dubious. "But I shall neither attest nor disclaim this business of names."

"Just look at the painting," said Cezanne wearily.

"What in good earth's name is this supposed to be?" The pawnbroker looked perplexed and scratched, not his head, but the rounded crown of the bowler.

Refusing to acknowledge the display of buffoonery, Cezanne's contempt for the moneylender mounted—"A village idiot can see this is a still-life, a work of art."

"Well, I'll be the father of a monkey!" The amazed pawnbroker again scratched the crown of his hat. "Sonny boy, here's the question on the pawnshop floor: Is there still any life left in it, eh?"

A huge magnifying glass in hand, he scrutinized the painting, shaking his head in disapproval. "Nope, wouldn't offer you a sou for this crap, not a sou."

"I am Paul Cezanne!" he shrieked, furious, for now he remembered the old man. He had signed pledges with him many times before.

I'm in his pocket, he thought glumly.

"Not a sou for this," repeated the pawnbroker, tapping the rim of the magnifying glass on the canvas. "Just look at all the unpainted patches." He tap-tapped. "It's not finished! Not by any stretch of imagination. Heed my advice, Pauley boy, and inject some oomph into it! Then we'll talk cash, we'll talk moolah, we'll talk francs or..." he chuckled again, "at least a few centimes."

Cezanne lost all patience. "Take the painting! As a gift! I'm fed up with you! What need have I of your filthy lucre?"

"Pauley boy, I'm not interested in your offer, hats be my trade. My bread, my butter, my raspberry jam. Now, let's get down to brass tacks. May I interest you in a gentleman's hat? The ladies admire the English derby."

Waiting for his temper to cool, wanting to be utmost deliberative in his actions, he slowly found his way around the counter, removed one of the bowlers from a wall peg, picked up his maligned canvas and—smashed it through the peg!

The old man, gleeful, clapped at the act of desecration. "Splendid, Paulie! You've finally managed to put a round peg into a square hole!"

"What do you imply?"

The pawnbroker shrugged. "When the shoe fits, wear it, then surely the heel will follow the sole."

The bowler hat in Cezanne's hand was unbelievably heavy. Was it made of iron? He let the hat fall, landing upon the floor with a tremulous clang, a loud ringing which sounded like a church bell.

The old pawnbroker shook an angry fist. "Leave my bowlers alone, if you please! Such hats shall be my fortune, sir—hats!"

"Hats?"

"Hats with oomph, cast in iron, shall protect the brain from rust." He cocked a thumb at the hat on his head with triumph.

Cezanne drew menacingly close. "Hats?"

"Not bats, Monsieur Rubens, but hats! Hats in the belfry!" laughed the old man.

Very slowly, Cezanne removed the old man's bowler, also made of iron, even the brim was skilfully forged in iron. *Heavier than the skillet I used to cook cheap vermicelli.*

The old man read his thoughts and taunted, "Vermin in a cello is that what you wish, Paulie boy?"

"Rice and vermicelli are all I can ever afford."

"I can sell you vermin in a cello for 10 francs 4. Now return my hat at once or, or!" Again he showed his threatening fist.

Cezanne raised the bowler high in both hands, turned it upside down and, unable to tolerate the clownish behaviour a moment more, slammed down the hat crown upon the old fool's head. The force of the blow caused the pawnbroker to totter, dazed, knees buckling and sinking. Cezanne raised the hat again. Mustering all of his human strength, he brought down his iron-weighted weapon; he pounded, pounded and pounded, in a fury, unable to stop, until the pawnbroker's head cracked. He saw and heard it crack, like a walnut—a deep, dark fissure appeared in the middle of the pawnbroker's skull.

From the cleaved skull, to Cezanne's astonishment, came a volcanic eruption, a towering fountain of precious gemstones, pouring out with no sign of subsiding. He stepped back, at first terrified, until he saw how wondrously it became a rainbow arc of multi-coloured jewels —rubies, sapphires, emeralds raining down like glittering hailstones, pattering the floor, scattering everywhere in the shop, rushing in rivers to every corner, a fast rising tide that soon covered the pawnbroker, his victim buried in a treasure of colour. Cezanne stood knee deep in translucent gems, his joy boundless, as though he waded in a lake of unimagined colours, a mosaic of warm ambers, vernal greens and unfathomable blues.

A dream only to be conjured in the mind of an artist. Yet I wondered, why so steeped in violence? After dutifully resuming my pose, the spread-eagle and interlaced hands, I waited for the right moment to ask how he felt about the dream. He kept hidden behind the canvas, applying a stroke or two, spending more time cleaning the paintbrush and pondering the next colour. The mirrors reflected he still laboured on a patch that might be my right breast. Would the portrait ever be finished? Was I to become the female character in Zola's novel who posed day after day for Claude Lantier's unattainable masterpiece?

He interrupted my thoughts when completing a stroke that seemed to please him. "Now that you have the damn dream, what will you do with it?"

"Understand it."

"There's nothing to understand, dreams are meaningless absurdities."

"Dreams are thoughts."

"No, dreams are pictures," he retorted.

"More accurate, they're scenes from a play," I countered, "and you wrote the script for your actors."

"You're fidgeting too much, be as still as possible," he ordered.

"I'm not a still-life." Remembering the still life in his dream took an improbable fourteen years to complete.

"I understand the dream," he said.

"Really?"

"I was getting something off my chest."

"Off your chest?"

"My anger about taking so much time to finish paintings, I get it out of my system in the dream."

"By hammering someone over the head with an iron hat?"

"Please re-fold your hands..."

I laced them over my 'beard'—now the unspoken word in our love ritual which took place after each modelling session, our 'beard-to-beard' method to attain physical satisfaction. I to stand on the dais, an armless Venus, forbidden to touch while he performed cunnilingus.

"Pawnbrokers and their ilk are scum," he unexpectedly complained, swirling his favourite oxtail brush into a small pool of Prussian blue. "Pawnbrokers, stockbrokers, bankers—money, money, money, that's all they think about. No heart, no soul. Every blasted one of them deserves a sound thrashing."

Does he unconsciously give out clues to the dream's meaning? I waited for more to escape until a quirk of fate made me sneeze, the pose came undone, and wherever his train of thinking was heading became derailed.

"Enough!" The session ended abruptly. He stayed busy, placing used brushes in glasses of turpentine then arranging them in a seemingly mystical semi-circle.

Now I waited for the sexual approach, having since discovered his physique appealed to me. When he half undressed it turned into a surprisingly erotic experience. I fantasied Paul Cezanne, his barrel, hair-matted chest and muscular limbs, as my ageing satyr still full of masculine vigour.

He went down, our ritual, thirsting so ferociously for the taste of me that I felt myself his mountain spring. He remained relentless, holding my wrists, burying his mouth and tongue inside me until I reached the zenith of love—never allowed the initiative to touch or kiss.

Afterwards that day, behind the partition screen, I dressed slowly, reflecting on our relationship, admitting that having my wrists firmly bound in his iron-clad grip was part of what excited me, as if his prisoner of love; but now I began to feel and think differently. The repetitiveness of the act gave the relationship an aura of aberrancy. Paul Cezanne's phobic fear of human touch saddened me. I wondered whether I really wanted to remain within such strictures of physical intimacy?

When I emerged from behind the screen, he was fully dressed, no longer the satyr, but ill-fitted in a mud brown, corduroy jacket and baggy pants the colour of sawdust. Once more the workman painter. He was feeding the new canary a bread crumb. The one I christened "Blue" had died in its cage, he said of unknown causes. I thought, *most likely, claustrophobic exhaustion.* I had no heart to name the new canary.

"Why not let your canary fly occasionally around the studio," I suggested. "His wings might need exercise."

"The cage is extremely spacious.".

"Then let him out for a taste of freedom."

He detected my irritation. "The cage, for a tamed canary, is a home, not a prison. The cage becomes a safeguard from a hostile, danger-ridden world. Allowing the bird out for supposed freedom or exercise is akin to throwing a child off a steamship for a little swim in the rough Atlantic—it will, at best, be a terrifying experience."

Duly educated, I went to examine the progress of my portrait: a smattering of transparent planes that were evolving, I believed, toward the construction of a body. The warmth of his ochres about the abdomen area created a contrast to cooler blues of perhaps my pudenda. The careful, meticulous blending of tonal contrasts gave me an inkling of why he spent much of his time wrestling with each brushstroke.

As I prepared to leave, he noticed my forgotten hat, newly purchased, my own lively colour contrasts of crushed maroon velvet and yellow raffia primroses. He held it for a moment. "It's very light."

Not like the pawnbroker's iron hat.

I puzzled over his unbridled hostility toward a pawnbroker, whom he called, "a money-lender." Putting on my hat, I dared one more dream question. "Do you personally know any pawnbrokers, stockbrokers or bankers?"

"I once knew a stockbroker until he thought himself a painter and left the Bourse. And my father, in fact, is a banker—a money-lender."

At the door, after absorbing the fact, I heard him ask, so soft, "A game of checkers?"

"Not today, Paul."

Chapter 22

I saw in his hand a long spear of gold, and at the iron's point there seemed to be a little fire. He appeared to me to be thrusting it at times into my heart... The pain was so great, that it made me moan; and yet so surpassing was the sweetness of this excessive pain, that I could not wish to be rid of it.

St. Teresa of Avila
Autobiography, 1580

OUR PRINCESS

Midnight must seem to you, Sigmund, an extremely odd hour for a medical consultation, but I find the night offers fewer distractions." Charcot stood by a darkened window of the library. "Our patient will be here shortly. My private carriage is transporting her from the Salpêtrière." The doctor moved the curtains almost surreptitiously as he peered out. "Paris sleeps for a few hours and forgets," he murmured sadly, "but our city within a city, the Salpêtrière—never!"

Sigmund, uncomfortable in the medieval chair of taloned griffins, watched: Charcot's eyes sometimes burned with terrible memories. "When assuming the directorship of the asylum, I took nighttime strolls through the courtyards, listening. The cries, shrieks and howls might be mistaken for animals of the night but for the fact that that I walked amidst an asylum of mentally disturbed women, hundreds upon hundreds , and I thought, 'What tormenting dreams must fill their restless nights!'"

The desk lamp cast a meagre rim of light, yet Sigmund saw the photographic plates. His mentor sat down and fanned out the plates like a deck of cards. "Because of Dr. Londe's remarkable chrono-photographic camera, a spontaneous record of a classic attack of Grande Hysteria." Sigmund recognized the person in all the pictures. "The camera's rotating disc of nine lenses can capture an equal number of hysterical contortions." Charcot pushed forward a photo-plate.

She was depicted, locked in the rainbow contortion, the soles of her feet and the crown of her head pressed into twisted bed sheets, her mid-torso thrust upward into a torturous arc.

Charcot came to stand behind him. "Look at more," he urged.

In the next picture Sabrine Weiss sat cross-legged on a dormitory bed. Her hospital gown, with a ribboned sash tied snug around her waist, resembled a toga. She gave a wide-eyed and welcomed smile for the camera's eye, for the viewer.

"Extraordinarily photogenic, isn't she?" *Yes*, Sigmund had to agree, *a Grecian muse*. "And damnably seductive," Charcot added. "Not a few of my interns have schoolboy crushes on her. Of course, she encourages such silliness. Sabrine, as with most hysterics, can be very flirtatious. Now examine this pose," Charcot pointing over his shoulder, "a variation of the *Attitude Passionnel* which is Phase..."

"Phase Three of the classic attack," Sigmund interjected, having perused Charcot's volumes on hysteria day and night, hoping his efforts would be recognized.

"Exactly!" Charcot was pleased with him. "The phase which introduces highly emotional attitudes, visions, conversations with invisible interlocutors. Really, all manner of hallucinations. Here you can see that she experiences some sort of auditory hallucination."

There was no difficulty in interpreting the theatrical pose: Sabrine sat, hand cupped behind an ear, to show the camera's eye that she was hearing something in the air wonderfully pleasant. There were many more poses, many more highly emotional states to which Charcot assigned specific titles. "Here, she teases."

Playfully Sabrine pointed a scolding finger at them, her eyebrow raised for a naughty wink, as though the three were partners in a clandestine moment.

Another of her melodramatic poses was labelled 'Amorous Supplication'—her hands reverently crossed over her breast to obviously express a great ardour in her heart. *For whom? For what?*

Sigmund wondered as Charcot's hand dropped upon his shoulder. "A cigarette, my boy?" Politely he declined, "Yes-yes, of course, of course!" His shoulder vigorously patted. "I recall, you favour cigars. Be assured when next you visit, a box of South America's best will be here. But for now..." Charcot went to the liquor cabinet. "We will share a cognac!"

Sigmund pondered one interesting pose after another until a photograph startled him. "My word!"

Charcot brought two filled glasses. "Ah, yes! What do you think she experiences in this hallucinated state?"

Sabrine's arms were outstretched, her face showed unmistakable anguish. "It seems... a crucifixion." He was handed the needed cognac.

"Agreed! And I have labelled it so, *le Crucifiement*! Sabrine, more than my other hysterics, gravitates toward this torturous pose." Charcot took the photograph and gave him another. "This pose often follows— unequivocally ecstasy!"

"*L'extase*." Sigmund repeated in French.

Her hands fervently clasped, her head thrown back, Sabrine rolled her eyes as though toward a heavenly vision. Logically, one might say the saint's pose, only he detected the sensual aspect, a coarse satisfaction in how her lips parted, her body slackened.

Charcot focused on the religious aspect. "Her heightened state brings precisely to mind Bernini's sculpture of Saint Theresa of Avila. You must go and see it in the Church of Santa Maria at Rome. Yes, St. Teresa's ecstasy, the moment she is pierced by the archangel's golden spear."

"Amazing, Dr. Charcot, to find so many different emotional states encompassed within a single attack."

"*Sabrine est nôtre princesse des hysteriques.* She demonstrates more variations than any other hystero-epileptic in the wards. She is the paradigm from which I diagnose the disease in others."

The warming, pleasant effects of the cognac had Sigmund sorting through the photographs with greater leisure; he started to savour them as if paintings—until one particular pose troubled him. She was photographed curled into a corner of the bed, her back pressed against the wall, and her head thrust forward with a swollen and distended neck, barring teeth like a vicious animal. It was frightening to behold someone less than human. He gulped what remained of the drink.

"She threatens," Charcot explained. "I call this attitude, *Le Menace.*"

Before Sigmund could respond with a reasonable question, whispering sounds outside the door of the library caused him to turn. He heard quick retreating footsteps, watched the door latch click open and instinctively recoiled at her sudden appearance. She wore a white smock identical to the photograph in his trembling hands and he braced himself for whatever menace she might express.

The princess of the hysterics walked forward, wearing a most natural smile, presenting such uncommon composure and confidence that he could not believe that this woman had spent the past five years of her life confined in an institution for the diseased and insane.

When she offered her hand, specifically to him, he tried to assure himself that she must be in the state Charcot labelled, *l'État Normal.* Sigmund searched for any sign of abnormality. What might be considered unusual were the coloured ribbons ostentatiously braided throughout her hair and the wide scarlet sash tied around her waist. She had the same coloured ribbon sewn into the hem of her hospital smock, but the colourful additions simply lent her a charming air, as though a travelling troubadour or a gypsy. She exuded health, a fair complexion, rounded cheeks, and a smidgeon of freckles around a nicely formed nose. Most striking was the billowing hair, richly red, gorgeous. He thought of rose-hip jam.

The only suspicious signs of ill health were dark rings under her eyes. And the cold, clammy feel of her hand. The first words she uttered, with a sibyl's wisdom and a gentle smile, shattered any ambitions he had of remaining reserved and objective.

"Your eyes are dark chestnut, wintry beautiful, the same colour as the horse who took my breath away a December morning, cantering riderless through snow in the Bois de Boulogne." Her eyelids closed for brief seconds, as if to absorb a personal epiphany; he saw the reddish colour in her soft eyelashes before the eyes re-opened, green and knowing, like a mysterious cat.

A flicker of self-doubt came to him, unwelcomed—that the knowledge he had earned through his life was brittle, breakable, unreliable.

"A snow flake!" her voice rose high in awe. "One, two, seven!" She seemed to be seeing them in a vision until her voice, so melodic, lowered in disappointment: "My feet are bare in the crystal cold."

He looked down at her feet, clad in slippers, while a suspicious Charcot peeped through the curtains to verify that no snow had fallen.

Putting a hand to her mouth to stifle a giggle, she then arched an eyebrow at Charcot, warning or perhaps teasing him. "Words I will bake, munch, and swallow; and no one will be the wiser."

"Sabrine, Sabrine!" Charcot happily cried out as he trotted to her with quick, little steps. "What a supreme delight!" His merriment seemed needlessly feigned. "Drs. Babinski and la Tourette have delivered you safely."

Where, wondered Sigmund, *are his favoured assistants? Why their stealthy retreat? Do they object to Sabrine being placed in my care?*

She suddenly addressed Charcot with haughtiness. "As you see, I have accepted your gracious invitation." She then turned to Sigmund and voiced her concern. "He speaks, but rarely do I catch the words, for they fly from his lips like escaping blackbirds from a pie and flutter to freedom." She gazed wide-eyed around the library. "Oh, how easy it is to lose one's brain in such surroundings! But where are the other guests?"

"Guests?" queried a confused Charcot.

"Why, for the masked ball!" And before she could be stopped, Sabrine rushed through the library, blowing out each and every gas lamp until the room plunged into total darkness.

A door slammed and Sigmund heard Charcot's troubled voice: "Our patient, it seems, has foolishly wandered off." His face soon re-appeared behind the candelabra he lit. "I will fetch the doctors and conduct a thorough search of the house."

"May I be of assistance?"

"Best to remain here." Charcot handed him the candelabra, its three candles gave scant light. "There's devilry in that girl," Charcot complained and quickly left.

Alone in an immense room of thick shadows and hiding places, he prudently explored. The flickering light of three candles soon dwindled to one, yet the light was sufficient to find her. Oddly, she faced a corner in the library, as though a school child sentenced there for misbehaviour.

"Mademoiselle?"

She spun lightly, blithely, like a dancer, a sequinned mask held by a stick, covered her eyes and nose. He watched transfixed. The smile she gave was disturbing, the mask making her smile almost fiendish, and her eyes now only slits behind the mask.

She spoke gaily, "I know someone who collects dreams. But no one knows that I, too, collect."

He stayed calm, wary, curious. "Dreams as well?"

"Oh, no-no-no! What I collect are fears."

Suddenly she ran off, light-footed and quick as a deer, disappearing into greater darkness.

He held the candelabra high, the light too feeble to penetrate far. She hid herself well. "Mademoiselle, please show yourself—I would like to learn more about your interest in collecting fears."

Her voice came from everywhere. "Then, Monsieur, give me a fear."

"At this moment, I have fear of the darkness which makes me unable to see you."

"No! No! You must give me your greatest fear!" Her voice continued to bound everywhere around him. "But be truthful or I will abandon you."

"What frightens me most..." he wavered then found himself admitting, "is the possibility, quite remote, of being inflicted with Broca's Syndrome."

"What is that?"

"Please come closer, make yourself visible."

Cautiously she moved into his ring of candlelight, waiting for him to explain. Her hair rippled over her shoulders, a deep scarlet colour that seemed to burn in the flame light.

"A disease of the mind," he explained his dreaded fear, "which paralyses cognitive functions."

"There are paralytics at the Salpêtrière; and many club-footed dancers; but nothing stops them from attending the annual ball."

He now could see the silver and purple glitter clustering at the edges of the mask, *forming dragonfly wings*, he thought. "Won't you put down your mask?" he gently suggested.

"Why? There will only be another mask beneath. Tell me more about Broca's Syndrome."

Should he honestly answer? "What often happens with those afflicted is that, tragically, one begins to mistakenly use one word for another."

"When one says crucify instead of beautify."

"Yes. And when the aphasia progresses, speech soon becomes too jumbled, too entangled to understand—one loses the ability to communicate."

"When thoughts fail to properly emerge from here?" her forefinger pressed into the side of her temple.

"Yes, sadly, yes."

She clutched her throat, speaking in a choked voice: "When words no longer have the strength to make sense?"

"Yes," he said.

Still she held up the mask by the stick. A darkly absurd thought skittered through his mind—what if she were not Sabrine Weiss? What if Charcot and the staff were playing mischief with him and had brought in another patient? And this mask business was nothing but an elaborate ruse, concocted to make sport of him.

Or to uncover whatever my weakness might be.

"Your fear is a terrible one," she remarked. "Most terrible for anyone who wishes to dwell in the realm of words. To have such a disease might lead one to feel that life was no longer worth the effort. But thank you," she added in a sincere voice, "for your fear."

He moved the candelabra closer, her broad forehead signalled a woman of intelligence. And now this woman, whoever she was, knew his paramount fear. As a docent, Sigmund had seen patients at the Meyerbank Clinic in Vienna with severe subcortical lesions, incapable of coherent speech, making a cruel mockery of human intellect.

"What will you do with my fear?" he inquired.

"The fears of others help me feel less alone in this world."

"Do you have a special fear?" he decided to ask.

"I have no fears, so it's my duty to take them away from others."

She stepped out of his rim of light, skipping away. He could not shake the thought that she was behaving like a mischievous schoolgirl. As best he could, he followed her with the one trembling, tallow candle.

"I want to dance!" she announced loudly.

And so she did, making gentle turns and playful leaps, delighting in being the centre of attention. Sigmund had never found the temerity to engage in dancing, but he easily guessed its pleasure as he followed her with the candlelight. Keeping her mask in place, she performed pirouettes and self-assured spins before concluding with a charming bow.

She dropped the mask—Sabrine and no other. The candle's flame flickered in the green of her eyes. "On special occasions the young doctors allow us to have costumed balls," she said. "The hypnotized are not supposed to remember them, but we do."

Pounding at the library door prompted her to quickly whisper: "Shall we meet again to share more secrets?"

The commotion outside grew louder. "Someone has locked it from the inside! Find another key, another key!"

As the door flew open, Sigmund eagerly conceded to her, "We can meet again, Mademoiselle, if you like."

Drs. Babinski and la Tourette rushed to seize her, Charcot grumpily following. She made no effort to resist. The doctor was completely out of sorts, wearing neither jacket nor tie, his celluloid collar unbuttoned, angrily ordering the assistants to take her back to the asylum.

Under escort, she managed to mischievously raise the mask and turned to Sigmund. "A pleasure, perhaps, to make your acquaintance."

When the door closed behind them, Charcot summoned a wry smile. "I dare say, a dramatic introduction to Sabrine." He had brought in a very bright gas lamp and set it on the desk. "Of course, our princess has never been to the Bois de Boulogne, much less encountered a riderless horse cantering across the snow."

Chapter 23

I was admitted to the circle of his personal acquaintances, and from that time forward I took a full part in all that went on at the Clinic.

Sigmund Freud

SHE IS VERY SPECIAL

*U*nusual, I thought, *for Dr. Charcot to linger in the library, as though he had nothing but time on his hands.* He seemed content to occasionally smile his approval as Sigmund Freud and I pored over our respective translations. In our corner workspace, we tried our best to ignore his presence, comparing texts of Charcot's lectures and discussing how certain words might best be translated to German. Our shared wish, I'm sure, was the opportunity to be alone, to speak privately.

Charcot, instead, sank deeply into a nearby armchair. "What you are compiling, Sigmund, will become Volume III of my Tuesday Lessons. Your German doctors, however, shall not have the good fortune to benefit from my previous volumes on hysteria."

Freud was quick to respond, "Volume III will suffice as a revelation for them."

"All based on clinical observation, I must emphasize," said Charcot haughtily. "Not un-demonstrable, Germanic theorems." I so wished he might remember more pressing duties and leave. There were issues to discuss with Freud. The first was to learn more about cocaine.

Unexpectedly, the wish was granted—commotion outside the library caught his ear. The hallway reverberated with shouts and running steps.

"Father, help!" Jeanne Charcot's voice sounded an alarm; she appeared in the doorway, looking extremely dishevelled. "Father, you must come at once! Your monkey, *Le Rêve*, has gone berserk in the billiards room!"

Charcot jumped angrily from the chair. "What are you saying? *Le Rêve*, disturbed? Undoubtedly someone has taunted or teased him!"

"Hurry!" pleaded Jeanne.

Grumbling, her father strode out the door. We could hear him ranting down the hall: "Doesn't anyone understand that monkeys are the most sensitive of creatures?"

Jeanne chose not to follow him. She remained in the doorway. Her dishevelled appearance was rather comical to behold. Her hair was in utter disarray and several of her blouse buttons had come undone. "I should think the only sensitive thing about that foul smelling monkey," she muttered under her breath, "is his *derrière*." Jeanne's exasperation with the monkey was apparent. "It's all I can do to stop myself from kidnapping the loathsome creature and depositing him in some faraway zoo."

"Darling Jeanne," I rushed to embrace her, "you have offered what we needed most, comedic relief." I tactfully re-buttoned the stiffly starched blouse, turned her around and rearranged her wildly tousled hair.

Pretending not to care that I was putting her back in order, she gave Freud a stern look over her shoulder. "Why does he gawk at me with amusement?"

I laughingly said, "Probably because you bear an uncanny resemblance to your father."

"Yes, I know," she harrumphed, "short and stout."

"Jeanne, what I meant was that both you and your father are strongly opinionated."

Freud stepped forward. "Mademoiselle Charcot, my amusement was in imagining a monkey out of control with billiard balls."

"Remind me to tell you what Victor Hugo says about imagination; that is, if and when..." she entered without taking her eyes off of him, "we come to know each other better."

The mischievous glint in Jeanne's eye similarly matched Freud's artful answer. "I might be familiar with the quote."

Jeanne's delightfully round face became a mask of innocent concern. "Do you think me wicked, Doctor Freud?"

The glance she shot at me asked for permission to flirt. I replied with a very slow blink. *Why not, dear Jeanne, why not?*

Alert to our little feminine exchange, Freud became more amused. "Wicked? Why, yes, I'm sure you both are—to the core."

Imagination (I remembered the quote) *is intelligence with an erection. So that's settled*, I thought, *we were all devotees of the naughty Victor Hugo.*

Our drawing room drama proceeded with prescribed irony. Jeanne declared in a shocked voice, "Oh Julie, you have heard for yourself! Dr. Freud has penetrated our hearts, found us out, the shameless hussies we are, so there's nothing left but to discard all pretence."

She initiated a commanding strut around the library, picking up objects randomly, an elephant head ink jar, a feathered quill, a set of wooden teeth Charcot used as a paperweight; she scrutinized each, as if her father's objects had to pass some mysterious inspection before replacing them. Typical for Jeanne, she dressed solely in black and white, her chosen uniform, crisp white blouses and black, ankle-length skirts of English wool. I once delicately suggested long skirts possibly made her appear shorter, but Jeanne eschewed what she considered feminine frills, insisting on practical attire; thus, we watched her thump about the room in thick-soled shoes of black.

"Ah-ha!" rang out a cry of triumph when she spotted a full decanter of brandy in a glass cabinet. And knowing exactly where to find the key—inside the broken skull of an Indian water buffalo—she unlocked the cabinet, seized the bottle and scooped up three glasses. Expertly for a twenty-year-old, she poured out two neatly even drinks, handing them to us before plopping down into the very armchair her father had recently vacated. Bottle and glass in hand, she heaved an exaggerated sigh before I received her severe gaze. "So!" She filled her glass. "Shall we discuss Dr. Freud's *objêt trouvé?*"

I hurriedly explained to the startled Freud, "It was Jeanne who found your..."

He interrupted, "Then I owe equal gratitude to Mademoiselle Jeanne."

Head bowed, she stared down into her brandy, pretending not to hear. I suspected she deliberately enjoyed showing off the magnificent folds of her rearranged hair. She sipped before responding, a new honey-like tone in her voice, "Naturally, I was concerned... to find it on the floor just outside Father's library."

"Thank you again."

"Dr. Freud, you losing a hypodermic syringe and me finding it, was.... what's the phrase I seek, Julie?

"An intriguing caprice of fate."

Freud's expression turned grave. "Mademoiselle Charcot, a full explanation is owed to you."

"I did worry," she went on to repeat much of what I wrote in the letter to Freud, "that the remnants in the syringe might be an opiate, and I did not want such things to find their way into the wrong hands." She then held out the red Moroccan case. "Our Julie has since explained that the residue is liquid cocaine."

He took the offered leather case and opened it, the syringe and hypodermic inside. "And enclosed in such a handsome case which I cannot accept."

"Which you must accept, we insist! Regard it as a Paris memento." Jeanne looked at me. "Our advisor on all things artistic carefully chose the red colour." She took a more generous sip. "Although I thought black more suitable."

He put the Moroccan case into his pocket. "I thank you both for your generosity... and discretion."

Jeanne concentrated on refilling our empty glasses (we all seemed quite thirsty), refilling precisely to the rims. "The American, Benjamin Franklin says, 'Three can keep a secret if two are dead.' Jeanne's eyes widened—a gesture I had to admire—and practically bore into him. "But rest assured, you are with two women where discretion rules."

"Dr. Freud has written a well-regarded monograph on cocaine," I said.

"The coca plant," he clarified.

"I would like to read it," said Jeanne.

"Unfortunately, I failed to bring a copy with me to Paris."

"Perhaps you could give us a précis?" she suggested.

He set down his glass, considered, then took another drink. "Coca is largely cultivated in Bolivia and Peru, amongst the Indian tribes who chew the leaf in order to make themselves resistant to privation and fatigue. In earlier times coca was used in burial ceremonies."

"Really?" Jeanne encouraged him.

He nodded, taking another sip. "Participants masticated the leaves then stuffed them into the mouths of the dead, a rite which secured for their fallen comrades a clement voyage through the perilous regions of the underworld." He turned to me. "The effecting ingredient is the alkaloid, cocaine. When the South American Indians macerate the coca leaves with ash of chenopodium quinoa it liberates the alkaloid."

"How does one procure it in France?" I asked.

"Two pharmaceutical companies, Merck and Parke-Davis, produce and offer cocaine in its pure alkaloid state, and in combinations with muriatic acid or hydrobromic acid. Serendipitously," he swished about his remaining brandy, smiled wryly, and finished off the glass, "cocaine crystals dissolve extremely well in alcohol. Most recently, I secured an arrangement with Merck Pharmaceuticals to receive the drug at moderate costs as the company is sympathetic to my efforts of furthering the cause of science."

"What drew you to study the drug?" I asked.

"Reading of its therapeutic properties in American medical journals, I became intrigued, for it seemed further experiments were warranted. I quickly discovered that cocaine's fundamental effect is to increase the physical capacity of the body for a prescribed period of time and to hold strength in reserve to meet further demands when circumstances deem necessary."

"It could be helpful in wartime," Jeanne mused.

"Or in situations like mountain climbing and arduous expeditions; but notwithstanding its marvellous restorative and anaesthetic properties, I am convinced...." he leaned forward toward Jeanne... "convinced that undiscovered benefits can be derived from the drug. Perhaps the drug can be effective in alleviating nervous exhaustion, particularly in relieving many of the neurasthenic symptoms we encounter at the Salpêtrière."

"The drug interests me," I said. "Leaving aside its empowering effects on human strength and stamina, cocaine appears to produce some sort of shock to the cranial nerve system. Do you really suggest it might be used as a therapeutic agent for nervous conditions?"

"Most definitely! I have been employing it as a therapeutic experiment in the hope of curing my friend from his morphine addiction. Cocaine mercifully relieves the dreadful nervous exhaustion and depression which incurs following the withdrawal of morphine."

I finished off my brandy. "Possibly cocaine experiments could be conducted at the Salpêtrière in the treatment of those women who suffer most miserably from dementia." We looked closely at each other for a moment. "To think that cocaine might burst through the fog that debilitate so many of the minds at the asylum."

"I'm much encouraged by Mademoiselle Forette's attentiveness to the potential benefits of cocaine. According to Inca legend, Manco Capac, Son of the Sun-God, presented the coca leaf to man as a celestial gift, to provide courage to the faint-hearted, and offering the unhappy an opportunity to forget their miseries."

Jeanne looked concerned, if not troubled. "Goodness, Dr. Freud, your praise for the drug and its potential seem almost boundless."

I came to his defence. "As a scientist of neurology, Dr. Freud's eagerness to explore cocaine's possibilities is understandable. And," I added, "laudable."

She frowned, uneasy about my openness to the drug, and rose to return the decanter to the cabinet. There would be no refills. "We should all be cautious," said Jeanne, locking the cabinet door and dropping the key back into the water buffalo skull, "of a substance which modifies normal thinking and behaviour."

I stated plainly, "To be placed in such an altered state of consciousness is what truly arouses my interest." *What is hysteria if not an altered state?* If I dared ingest the drug to self-observe cocaine's heightened effects, I began thinking, would I step closer in understanding extreme mental states which women at the Salpêtrière experienced? *What Sabrine Weiss experiences.* "Dr. Freud," I informed Jeanne, "was in attendance at your father's Tuesday Demonstration."

"So, you saw Sabrine?" she inquired.

"Most remarkable." He seemed careful not to say more.

"According to Dr. Charcot's general classification," I said, "she typifies Grand Hysteria."

"Speaking for Julie, and myself as well," Jeanne joined in, "Sabrine is very special to us."

"She is a special person," he replied, nothing more. I could tell he waited for where we might take the discussion. Sigmund Freud, I learned, dissected every word directed at him.

Jeanne went on. "We are happy to report that in recent months, Sabrine gains more awareness of her surroundings. We accompany her on walks within the confines of the Salpêtrière and keep her abreast of current events."

He nodded. "That sounds encouraging."

I hurried the conversation. "We would like to see Sabrine have living quarters apart from the ward that houses the hysterics. An opportunity to develop... a modicum of independence."

Jeanne added, "Julie thinks that the hysterics in the ward influence each other too much... something psychological."

Deep interest showed in his eyes, but again he responded carefully. "There could be psychological reinforcement amongst the women... possibly."

"We just have to persuade my father," said Jeanne, "of a more liberal arrangement for Sabrine."

"Only you, Jeanne," I stressed, "can convince your father."

She invariably tried to downplay any influence she might have with her father. Jeanne's flirtation with Freud resumed. "Father finds you a remarkable intellect, the special intern who most likely will advance neurology."

"To enter his sphere of influence is all I desire."

Suddenly we heard activity in the hall. Jeanne walked briskly to the doorway to listen. I leaned closer into Freud's ear, speaking low. "Jeanne and I are pleased that you will be personally attending to Sabrine." He waited, sensing I had something else to say.

"Father is coming!" Jeanne stepped out into the corridor and disappeared.

I hurried, not wanting to share the next thought with either Jeanne or her father. "At some near point in time, Charcot will reclaim Sabrine from you." I looked squarely into Freud's eyes so that he would not fail to grasp the import of my warning. "One hopes that you would find her case sufficiently challenging to protest."

He showed discomfort. "I can only follow..."

Charcot entered, the monkey comfortably nestled under his jacket, eager to show that his pet had recovered from whatever trauma had been inflicted upon him. Just the monkey's shrewd eyes and flattened nostrils were visible. Charcot beamed a smile: "So my busy bees, the translations are correlating well?"

I replied, buoyantly, "Dr. Freud elucidates even my text!"

"Yes, it can be helpful at times, having a different eye."

Chapter 24

You wouldn't believe how difficult it is for me to make certain collectors, who are friends of the Impressionists, to understand how precious Cezanne's qualities are. I suppose centuries will pass before these are appreciated.

Camille Pissarro

As for me, I should remain alone, the double-dealing of mankind is such that I can't get over it...

Paul Cezanne

THE COLLECTOR

Our affair was over. I had reached the limits of desire for Paul Cezanne. But before severing the relationship, I granted him one last meeting. I had an ethical obligation to return the gifts: his cherished Zola novels and the paintings.

We were to meet at the New Athens Café, once the gathering place of the Impressionists, their early years, when Cezanne was more open and less suspicious. My heart sank when I reached the café and spotted him through the window, at a table. the first customer of the morning, offering a smile that made me feel queasy, a fixed and timid smile I knew came from desperation. He waved happily, the man who normally kept a stronghold on all tender emotions, waved as though to prove that he could muster a friendly gesture. I thought, *Keep walking, pretend you do not see him waving and waving.* I so much wanted to avoid the awkward situation waiting for the two of us. It was a miserable feeling, to see Cezanne, an artist of immense dedication and talent, having lost his bearings, reduced to confusion as to why he was being forsaken.

I entered the café and approached, burdened with the memory of having stood gladly naked before him, offering myself. Clumsily I carried the wrapped paintings and portmanteau of books. A young waiter, seeing my struggle, took my parcels and followed me. Cezanne half-rose, he clutched the sides of the table and seemed incapable of any other action. An angry Cezanne could have easily thrown the solid marble table across the room. I remembered his strength, lifting me onto the platform of mirrors as though a weightless feather, when I happily surrendered to his coarse handling, his rough-hewn hands around my waist, his mouth pressed upon my vagina. Somehow finding the composure to sit, I directed the waiter to place the parcels on the floor beside me. Cezanne sat down, meek and humble. Am I to forget him unleashing my dormant passions, giving me license to moan like someone sweetly wounded, giving me freedom to shout out sailor obscenities?

The paintings stayed near my leg while I pushed over the heavy portmanteau of books; he bent, peered inside, and brought out a Zola novel, puzzled. "But surely you want to keep this treasure?" I said nothing.

Irritated, he slapped down the yellow bound *Germinal*. "Look!" He opened the first page. "Autographed! Dedicated to me!"

I answered softly (keeping him ignorant of Zola's sordid and failed attempt at seduction), "Yes, autographed… as all are." *When will he read the newest novel and learn of Zola's ultimate betrayal? I* took out the other novels, one by one, to be sure none were missing.

Moodily, he stared at the two stacks on the table, all autographed by his famous friend, his best friend since boyhood. He mused, "They must be valuable."

"Collector's items, for sure, Paul."

"Well, you're a collector, aren't you?"

I ignored the petulance in his voice. "A collector of dreams," I replied.

"Yes... dreams..." His pensive stare had me guessing the thoughts: *Will the dream she finagled from me cause trouble down the road? Cause me harm? Did I reveal too much of myself?* "You could, if ever down on your luck, pawn the books." He still wanted to convince me of their value. "Bankers, like my father, call it reserve collateral."

I managed a wan smile and put them back into the bag. "Someday you might miss these mementos."

"Someday I may miss Émile Zola—but this I gravely doubt, as he now shares my father's longstanding opinion: Paul Cezanne, the so-called artist, has not a shred of talent." He saw my surprise. "Yes, I've finally read what Paris has read, other artists have read, you have read, and absorbed." In his eyes were shimmerings of tears, too deep to fall.

I must help. "Paul, one could argue that Émile Zola was first to encourage you to be an artist. If not for him, you might have ended up a lawyer, or a banker like your father. So perhaps you should forgive his current lapse in understanding."

"Forgive the man who writes in his puke-filled novel that I'm a botched painter? How does he sum me up? 'A man who is just two grams short of gray matter.' Now he's turned scientist, I suppose, a neurologist like your boss who herds all the hereditary failures like me into his asylum."

"Forget his novel. You're right, it's rubbish. Maybe your friendship with him is not worth saving."

Judgement escaped, and I regretted the harshness. What right had I to weigh the friendships of others? Thoth's duty, my strict duty, Bijou said after our father left us, was to record the deeds, free of judgement.

"My dearest lady, if... might you..." He reached for my hands, I pulled back. The waiter brought coffees. Absentmindedly, I began dropping sugar cubes into the cup, watching them splash...

Suddenly, without warning, he slammed down on the table, the coffee cups rattling. "I insist upon one thing! You keep the paintings! Keep the damn things!"

"I couldn't." The three paintings, which I had taken care to wrap and tie in butcher's paper, were still leaning against my leg.

"If you don't take the bloody things, I'll rip them to shreds or just hurl all of them into the Seine."

He was capable of such a sacrilege, and I was so tempted to accept them. My heart, in fact, began pounding at the very idea of having Cezanne's paintings forever on my walls. "What if I admit," I dared not look at him, "that I have imagined keeping one."

"Then choose. Which one?" He was very curious.

"The view of your mountains in Provence." I did not hesitate.

"Mount Saint Victoire—why that particular one?"

He was tempting me to detail the masterful colouring, the unique blend of brush strokes, but to launch into a passionate exploration of its many merits, extolling his talent, was just how our affair began.

"Why Mount St. Victoire?" he probed.

"I would feel a sense of loss to live without it."

He laughed gruffly. "Well, bless you! That's the best damn reason to own a painting."

"All three are masterpieces."

"Then I will submit the others to the Salon."

"A ludicrous idea! Which you should know."

He replied, affronted. "I beg to differ,"

Unfortunately, he still clung to hopes from his youth, still unable to fathom that those who joined the Salon jury were dunces who wore their collars too tightly to ever see through to his genius, who would never in a hundred years consider his work worthy for their Salon Show. But what was there to gain by arguing with Cezanne, attempting to convince a genius he wasted precious time by kowtowing to his inferiors, those far beneath his talent? I just wanted to leave, escape, but gave him one last chance to rethink his generosity. "Paul, are you absolutely sure that you want Mount St. Victoire to be mine?"

"I said, it's yours! Yours! Yours!" The angry insistence bade me to silence. He reached down, somehow guessing which was Mt. Saint Victoire, and began tearing away the wrapping with a fury. I feared for the safety of the painting. Gazing at the landscape, he murmured, "Mount Saint Victoire will be at the end of every road I travel, always in my horizon. The mountain is my bride. No one can take her from me."

I rose, ready to leave without the painting, but I extended my hand in friendship, to say good-bye. Did I hope for a final, tender clasp from the man who feared the touch of most human beings? His sudden grip felt as if my hand had been caught in a vice. He pulled me back into the chair.

"Your flesh is cold, like a corpse," he spat out before releasing his hold. I hoped the situation would not deteriorate further. "Everyone accuses me of having too many secrets," he said in a bitter undertone. *Will the other woman, Hortense, and his school age son now step from the shadows?* He smiled, no, he grimaced. "Oh, the only important secret I've kept hidden from Mademoiselle Julie is my desire to experience a great love, yes, thinking you might be that woman, you." I rose from the chair while he stared into a cold coffee. "Shame," he muttered, "seems to have lost its power over me."

"I must go." Certain in my heart that I would now choose my own path and remain free of any man's grasp.

"I will pay you," he said without looking up.

"Foolish man."

"Take the painting."

Picking up the canvas, I exited the café, not once looking back. Out on the sidewalk there was the pleasure of bright morning sunlight. *New beginnings*, I thought, and with a masterpiece locked under my arm, I crossed the Place Pigalle. The square was already busy with women who had come to earn what they could for the day, the prostitutes, of course, who favoured the Place Pigalle to ply their trade, but the would-be models were out as well, attired in folk dresses to attract the artists; most of them Italian immigrants from the less prosperous country villages in the North. I, too, an immigrant, a laundress from Marseilles; a Parisian model; a recorder of untamed dreams. The women sitting on the rim of the plaza fountain watched my jaunty walk and we exchanged friendly smiles. Ours a sisterhood.

Heading toward Boulevard de Clichy, the gift of *Mount St. Victoire* now in my possession, I experienced a rush of exhilaration. *The laundress who once washed other people's clothes was now a collector of art!*

Chapter 25

The remedy has also been recommended as an aphrodisiac, and Dr. Freud has undoubtedly observed sexual excitation occur after the use of cocaine.

> von E. Merck
> October 1884

The Cocaine Experiment

Cocaine insinuated itself into all that transpired between Freud and myself during his stay in Paris. From the outset the drug's mind-expanding potential became apparent, especially its power to propel us into richly layered discussions. Not once did we suffer an injurious experience, nor was there any law to prohibit its use. I remember sometimes passing the Mariani Distillery at 41 Boulevard Haussmann where they produced their popular Mariani Wine infused with cocaine's base, cocoa. The dosages Freud prepared were most often a twentieth of a gram, dissolved in wine.

Our first cocaine experiment took place when he invited me to his new lodgings at the Hotel de Bresil. He had recently moved from a one room flat in the Latin Quarter, admitting that the new hotel on Rue de Goff increased his monthly costs a hundred francs, but included board and a modest sitting room to receive guests. I arrived on a cold January night.

Politely taking my cloak, he invited me to a badly worn settee from a bygone era. I sat, hugging myself for the chill in the room. Apologizing, he went to a coal bucket and tossed a few lumps into a small corner stove. "I hoard the stuff, for economy's sake, to hopefully prolong my stay in Paris."

When he sat in the only chair, our staring match began, as though we were preparing for a weighty debate. Soon growing uncomfortable with the solemnity, I looked around at anything which would reveal his interests. The sitting room, sparsely furnished, showed a writing table, a jar of pencils, a cigar butt in an ash tray and a manuscript with the handwritten title, *Draft II*

."A work in progress?" I asked. He followed my inquiring gaze.

"An effort," he acknowledged, "to map the route system of the acoustic nerve. I expect a third revision might make it suitable for publication."

I continued to look around, very surprised that the adjoining room had no door, neither a curtain nor a screen, the four-poster bed in plain sight. *I could walk ten steps and be there* was my idle thought. I noticed above the bed a framed embroidered panel.

I was a little curious. "A fondness for crochet?"

Again, he followed my gaze. "A gift from my fiancée."

I rose, wanting a closer look, but careful not to step beyond the threshold to where he slept. The embroidery panel had been elegantly woven with one sentence.

EN CAS DE DOUTE ABSTIENS TOI

'When In Doubt, Abstain' was my translation. I had to ask, or taunt, "Is it a philosophical observation or a moral admonition?"

He chuckled while searching his pockets for a match to light a cigar. "I suppose," he said, "there are multiple meanings stitched into it."

I thought it best to return to the decorum of the Sitting Room where I happened to notice a framed photograph on a side table. "Is this your fiancée?" On strange impulse, I handed it to him.

He looked at the sepia coloured photograph with a certain warmth and affection. "This is my Martha, but I call her Marty. Her physique is quite harmonious, don't you think?"

He gave me a taunting look of his own so I followed the risqué tone. "The dress accentuates her form to splendid advantage." His firm buxom fiancée appeared far younger than me. "How long have you been engaged?"

He invited me back to the settee and replaced his Marty on the side table. "I ruefully confess that we approach our fourth year."

"Such a long, long time."

His brow knitted, a moment of irritation I almost missed, then he gave a stoic response, "A man must secure his profession and get his financial house in order."

"Nonetheless, so frustrating... for both of you... to be apart." I concentrated on taking off my gloves, finger by finger. The room was becoming warmer.

"We correspond almost daily," he boasted. "My little princess informs me that my last missive brings our total to nine hundred."

"Quite impressive."

Little princess. Nine hundred letters.

We lapsed into silence. I found myself brooding. Yes, such fortunate people existed, those who made loving commitments to one another. Cezanne and I fell into a less fortunate category. Our final good-bye haunted me. The despair in Cezanne's eyes. And my callous decision to end our affair in a public café—a terribly cruel mistake... misdeed. I, the cause of another's disillusionment.

I began to feel that something worrying lurked in the dismal apartment. A dark, deep, unwanted depression—outside of me and trying to get inside. Freud's silence told me that he sensed my growing agitation. I struggled for an explanation that would not brand me a neurasthenic. "Dr. Freud, I shall tell you... lately my nerves have been a little strained."

He nodded sympathetically. "Those of us who work at the Salpêtrière, amidst such volatile minds, cannot avoid being prey to some degree of neurasthenia."

We were leading to the reason for my presence in a bachelor's apartment. Cocaine. Sigmund Freud was an astute reader of others intentions; he presented a small apothecary packet. *"Un cadeau pour vous."* The gift, in his open hand. He knew I had come to experiment. Sitting beside me, he showed the contents inside the packet. "A mixture from Parke Davis, an American company that is competing with Merck for my endorsement." Amused by his advantageous situation with the pharmaceutical companies, he waved the opened packet under my nose. "Take note of its rich aroma."

Unable to detect any odour, I politely nodded.

"Observe its colour." He sprinkled some granules into my hand. "Pure white, no tinge of yellow whatsoever. More soluble as well. This batch is much, much superior to Merck's."

"More white, more pure?" My mind went to linen, bed sheets, undergarments.

"In this instance, yes."

I brushed the granules from my hand back into the packet. "Are you suggesting that we experiment together with the drug?"

Had we known each other better, we might have laughed at the disingenuous question.

"It's not dangerous, I assure you," he said, wanting me to be comfortable.

"How am I supposed to take it?"

"Serendipitously, cocaine crystals mix readily with alcohol."

"Do you take the drug regularly?" I asked, almost certain he did.

"It is a powerful and useful stimulant."

"You do not strike me as a man who needs to be artificially stimulated."

"I have much work to accomplish at the hospital before my tenure expires," he emphasized. "Besides, there is nothing artificial about cocaine. My working hypothesis is that the drug has a regulatory effect on the body's systems, thereby permitting a more natural state to exist."

"A heightened state."

"If the latent power of one's mind and body is unleashed, I would consider the resultant state most natural."

I was buying time before the inevitable occurred, asking, "Besides mental and physical stimulation, does cocaine offer you other benefits?"

He pondered the packet in his hand. "I believe, at the Charcot soiree, I made a candid admission to Mademoiselle. I suffer periodically from anxiety... even bouts of depression—cocaine dispels them all."

The packet he held now had my solemn attention.

His bright, brown, shrewd eyes fastened upon me. "I suspect you also know that I am, by nature, an adventurer."

"This will, I suppose, lead to an adventure."

"There are moments..." he looked serious, a little severe, "when we confront opportunities which can change the tenor of our lives."

"What do you propose to use as a solvent?" I asked.

He looked over to a wall shelf where a bottle of Amontillado and two glasses waited, like props in a play. "Sherry will suffice," he said.

To show my resolution, I retrieved the bottle and glasses. I wanted him to look at me as no less an adventurer. While he emptied the powdery contents of the packet equally into the glasses, I poured in the dark brown sherry.

We stood facing each other. What I think we observed made us smile: the mutual glint of daring. I raised my glass. "Is a toast in order?"

"Taste of it and live!" he exclaimed.

Greedily Freud swallowed every last drop of the brownish mixture. And I drank, what now seemed our holy beverage—waiting for the adventure to occur. The first change was near instantaneous, a numbing of my mouth and lips. *Nothing to cause alarm*, I thought, until a feeling of giddiness overwhelmed me. Suddenly unsteady on my feet, I backed into the settee and rather ungracefully lay down, with the glass still in my hand. He quickly found a cushion for my head.

I managed a smile. "Please don't be alarmed. I need a little more blood to flow to my brain."

He leaned over me, watchful.

Ever so slowly, a pleasant feeling of mild heat began to pervade my entire body. A smile came to my lips, for in equal measure I felt relief, contentment, and strength. I sat up. It became imperative to set down the sherry glass, carefully, as not to give in to the impulse to test my new found strength and crush the glass to bits and pieces; then I closed my eyes, certain that I approached, unimpeded, the shores of bliss, at first content to warmly sail to the region, and then able to thrillingly soar!

"What is your reaction to the drug?" he asked excitedly.

"I find myself..." I opened my eyes and decided to hurry over to a mirror on the wall. My pupils were extremely dilated, like dark discs, gleaming wildly bright. I searched for the exact words to describe the feeling. "I find myself transcendentally stimulated!"

His laughter sounded like the heralding of a bright trumpet. "The drug clarifies the mind," he eagerly informed. "Soon you will become aware of new bodily strength. You will probably ask for a Peruvian mountain to climb."

"The Butte of Montmartre will suffice."

His sweet, angelic, trumpet laughter interweaved with my cello-like chuckle.

I promenaded devil-may-care around the room, wanting to interpret the phenomenon taking place in my nervous system with scientific exactitude: "For me, the overriding pleasure consists of an increased consciousness of being alive, of knowing that I can think more keenly."

His musical laugh again vibrated through my entire body. He shouted his exaltation, "I feel as strong as a lion!"

I spun around, feeling the whoosh and swirl of my dress. He lavished me with praise. "There's levity in your eyes, eyes so violet I wish at this moment I were not betrothed."

"You wish recklessly."

"How can I not be reckless when your smile is so appealing?"

I laid my hands squarely on his shoulders. "Let us see who is the stronger," I announced with mock aggressiveness. "Dr. Sigmund Freud or a fiery, wild woman with cocaine in her body!" I pushed, he playfully resisted.

Overcome with great hilarity at behaving like schoolchildren, we fell into a laughing spell.

"I say, without inhibition, that if I were not in love already..." declared an ecstatic Freud, "I could be led into temptation with such a kindred spirit."

"Do not worry, Dr. Freud, I will not play Lady Lust to your tempted St. Antony. Besides, upon your return to Vienna, your fiancée will want to find you as you will certainly find her... untouched."

"You have misperceptions of me."

"Has Paris corrupted you already?"

"Paris is a fancy-dressed Sphinx, a puzzlement, where one finds mirrors everywhere, mirrored doors in cafés which lead to brothels, mirrored fruit dishes where one sees phantom plums."

"Is it difficult for you to distinguish between object and reflection?"

"Not at all."

"Then help me on with my cloak."

"What a marvellous purple!" he said admiringly, placing the cloak around my shoulders.

"*Aubergine*, Dr. Freud, *aubergine!*"

Freud donned his topcoat, snatched up a top hat and very willingly followed me out into the star-studded night.

"It is marvellous," I waxed poetical as we strolled briskly down the street (our silvery winter breath streamed great distances and astoundingly curled), "with one glass of cocaine wine I can rejoice in the splendid vigour of a newly discovered self, a higher self!"

Truly, it seemed as if all the avenues of the possible lay open; I felt as though the diversity of genius of which the human intellect is capable had descended upon me. All ideas I ever entertained, all the books and poems read, now tingled fresh and accessible inside my brain, like pulsating stars. If desired, I could speak in blank verse and Shakespearean beauty. Nothing was beyond my grasp.

Once inside our hailed carriage, Sigmund Freud peered out at the passing scene, the streams of attractive promenaders along the avenues, the crowds of onlookers in bundled scarves at cafe terraces, the aproned waiters busily serving one and all. He grinned. "And to think I feared a most uneventful evening!"

In our whirlwind escapade through nighttime Paris, what did we not do? I took Freud to a succession of cafés that I thought might satisfy his adventurous spirit, bohemian haunts, the Marengo and its rowdy artist crowd near the Tuileries Gardens, the Tambourine decorated with tambourine tables, and lastly the Black Cat where we were greeted by staff dressed in the green robes of the French Academy who escorted us to our table with exaggerated politeness, bestowing us with noble titles, all part of the cabaret's theatre of satire. We laughed hilariously at the cabaret performance mocking the French aristocracy.

After midnight, the cocaine spurred us out on the streets to the Café Voltaire where we engaged in a monumental game of chess, other players at chess tables stealing glances at the rapidity of our moves. I was guided by uncanny foresight, sliding pawns and bishops into complex formations for multitudinous manoeuvrers. "She's determined," someone whispered, "to protect the king."

The glorious king!

"Dr. Charcot," I remarked loudly, inviting heads to turn and listen to insight, while absconding with Freud's unguarded bishop, "has taken hypnotism out of the hands of charlatans and made of it a genuine tool of Science."

Freud was equally loud. "Hypnosis may very well be that mysterious borderland between the somatic and the psychosomatic." The ivory knights in his army jumped around the board with admirable bravado. "His lectures on the subject must be read by every neurologist in Vienna—and will be, when my German translation is finished."

The nearby players showed annoyance that we dared to break the taboo of chess silence. I, astounded by their incomprehension, telegraphed my thoughts. *Yes, we are chatterboxes, but of the highest intellectual magnitude.* Yes, I agreed with Freud, hypnosis had unlimited potential and noted how he under-utilized the powerful queen.

Thoughts, ideas, sensations and impressions connected in rapid fire. His knee and mine grazed intermittently under the table. Unlike Cezanne who played checkers to soothe frayed nerves, my chess companion strategised to win; our under-the-game-table-touches were meant to be savoured.

Several of my stalwart pawns surprised at being captured! We exchanged competitive smiles, the battlefield assessed, and sallied forth through the thick haze of Sigmund Freud's cigar smoke, his pieces decimated one by one, removed, until one knight attempted to brave off my relentless attack. Manoeuvring the queen, I discreetly pushed the king into an inescapable corner.

"The fatal error in my game," he puffed out his realization, "turns out to be a cavalier disregard for the queen's agility."

"She can be underplayed, she can be overplayed, and few strike the proper balance. Now, checkmate!" I slid my half-finished cream gateau to him, as compensation.

Gobbling away the gateau, he licked specks of cream from his fingers, certain that more of his desires would be met. "I know where I want to go next."

Our knees touching, not quite pressing, now an accustomed warmth, the café's customers had vanished, closing time long past, then his legs perceptibly shifted, and the loss of contact disappointed me. "Where? Where do you want to go?"

He puffed out a cloud through which he announced, "*Le Sacre Coeur.*"

The cocaine ceased to rush through my loins. "The Sacred Heart?"

"I'm told the architecture shall rival Notre Dame."

The Sisters of the Sacred Heart who tormented my sister scurried like roaches back into the past. "But the Basilica is still under construction," I said.

He escorted me outside. "All more reason to investigate."

III

The night sky was losing stars to the encroaching dawn. Some undefined reason made us hurry toward the church in Montmartre, he talking nonstop —cocaine loosened the tongue, the libido, the past.

Revealing personal aspects of one's life. "My friends, both doctors, have financially helped extend my stay in Paris," he said. "I depend dearly on them, Fleischl and Josef Breuer."

Dr. Fleischl-Marxow, he had mentioned in his first letter to me, the friend once addicted to morphine, now cured because of Freud's recommended cocaine. While unfamiliar with Dr. Josef Breuer, in time I would become very much aware of his importance.

"Fortunately," I said, "you will be reimbursed for your translation work."

"Which will allow me to continue sending a few extra gulden for my mother and sisters," he added proudly.

I made the mistake of asking if he were close to his family. Yes, he was, less so with his father, and predictably, he asked about my family.

"My parents are dead." *My mother, for sure.*

He fell respectfully silent as we hiked the hilly streets. I had no room for anyone's sympathy or grief, not tonight, not as we approached dawn. "But I have a sister whom I adore."

He questioned her whereabouts. Marseilles, I said, and hoped some day to bring her to Paris. If he probed for more details, I would give her the name, Alexandria. But he asked nothing else, eager to reach *Le Sacre Coeur*, marching with manly strides. I followed, looking up at the sky, the stars all gone, the moon dissolved; I fought the temptation to talk more about her, my sister, goddess of the moon.

"Why are you walking behind me?" he asked.

"Japanese women do so," I said. "I'm exploring how they might feel."

"Does this connect to those lacquered sticks you often wear in your hair?"

"They are just an artful way to sweep up the hair from my neck." *How might your lips, Sigmund Freud, feel upon the back of my neck?* "Japanese women," I quoted the line from a book I once read to learn about courtesans, "consider the neck an extremely erotic zone."

"We've reached the stairway to the summit!" he announced. Indeed, we stood at the bottom of the newly paved stairs. The ascent was steep.

"Onward then to the magnificent Basilica of the Sacred Heart!" I laughed, for what could we expect on the recently excavated site but construction tools and building materials? He began the climb up the many, many steps while making outrageous claims and assertions. He was gravity free. Each light-footed step, he brazenly declared, evoked a site on his fiancée's anatomy where he imagined to implant a kiss. So the luscious cocaine still pounded through our veins and we both conjured erotic zones. Sensibly, I kept my swelling passions to myself. Climbing, my long legs were an asset, swifter than his, and I challengingly passed him.

At the last step he managed to seize my arm. Held, I had no choice but to look directly into the eyes of a handsome man. We had been stimulating each other physically and intellectually through the evening. He moved closer. Was the aphrodisiac simply the cocaine or him? His proximity aroused me more. Freud's lips reached for mine, a breath away before he made the mistake of closing his eyes for the impending kiss. I turned my face away, removed his hand, and wandered toward a collection of large stone blocks which littered the site. The huge, smooth chiselled blocks were yet to be hoisted, as the foundation was still in an early stage.

He came to me contrite. "I hope to be forgiven."

I let him help me up on to one of the white limestone slabs. I sat, nervously rearranging my dress, pressing it down over and over to my thighs. "There's nothing to forgive."

I watched him and now knew what I wanted: the true aphrodisiac, the beautiful complexity of his mind, his deeply brown eyes that never seemed to stop searching for meaning. But the Cezanne affair taught a lesson, kept me alert—under no circumstance would I slip into an intimate liaison because of an attraction to adventurous thinking.

He awkwardly scrambled on to the stone block, sitting beside me. "You should understand, I sought only a kiss."

I answered with a small smile. "But we know there are many kinds of kisses; at least two hundred and thirty-five," I added with cryptic intent. "Any one of which might prove most troublesome."

"Well done!" he laughed, so able to catch the allusion. "You counted the precise number of steps to get here."

"All to be kisses for Martha." *Marty.*

Freud understood—our Platonic relationship discovered. We sat in silence while dawn cast a rosy hue over Paris.

As ruminative philosophers who might sit among fallen stones at the Parthenon, the new day awakened in us a desire to talk to each other, seriously, to plumb the nature of our reality.

So I told him that I collected dreams, and he listened closely.

"Not my own dreams," I emphasized, "only those of others... interesting people who have more interesting dreams than mine."

He suddenly took his forefinger to wipe away the remnants of the cream gateau from my upper lip and, like the kind brother I wanted, said the notion was laughable that I should consider myself uninteresting.

"Then I should clarify, I collect only the dreams of men and women I find extraordinary, who are, by their very nature, intense. Those who more often manifest behaviour others might deem … out of the ordinary."

"Your personal research project?"

"Yes, a scientific inquiry into the nature of dreams. What they might be able to tell me about a person's fears, desires, or even destiny. A worthwhile inquiry, don't you think? All in the name of science," I reiterated.

He stretched out on our stone block, his hands behind his head, a guise to imitate laziness, only I knew his mind was racing. "Call it by its proper name," he finally said, "psychology."

"I might be willing to share a recently recorded dream," I said.

"But you have a stipulation?"

"Your opinion as to the dream's significance."

"This particular dreamer, what makes him or her so extraordinary?" he asked.

"Aside from being a genius of a painter," I said, "he's neurasthenic, burdened with a phobia, a chilling fear of being touched."

Freud needed no further persuasion to hear the dream. When I reached the scene of Paul Cezanne bludgeoning the pawnbroker to death with an iron hat, he sat up, as though it came to life before him: multi-coloured jewels spewing from the pawnbroker's cracked skull.

"And all of this violence done to a pawnbroker whose only crime seems to be ignorance?" He sensed something suspicious.

I gave my interpretation. "The pawnbroker, I'm near certain, is a disguise for his father. A retired banker."

"The connection, yes, the nexus, as both professions deal with the loaning of money."

"Exactly."

"Surely his father must be a monster for the son to wish him dead?"

"I know next to nothing about his father."

"And to bludgeon your father to death with a hat? And one made of iron? Most peculiar." The dream threw him into deep reflection and a search through his pockets for a cigar. "No doubt the hat is a symbol for something."

"Which I haven't yet figured out," I admitted. "And the jewels ejaculating from the pawnbroker's skull."

"So you think every unusual detail a symbol?"

"The more out of place a detail, the more it belongs."

"And not just imaginative nonsense?" he sharply queried.

I held my ground. "The absurd is the cover for underlying sense—anyway, so goes my hypothesis."

Disgruntled at not finding another cigar, he tossed out an idea. "If odd details make sense, you better consider the number fourteen."

"Fourteen?"

"In the dream your painter friend has taken fourteen years to finish the painting he wants to pawn. The detail seems unnecessary and such a large number of years appears on the surface quite nonsensical."

I had overlooked the number fourteen. "Well," I reasoned, "this artist has a reputation for taking a long time to finish paintings."

But I found myself savouring the acute attention he gave to details, eager for more: "Other observations?"

He shook his head. "It would behoove you to learn more about the dreamer's life experiences in order to gain more insight."

There seemed little chance of that happening... so I thought.

When my companion edged off the stone block and landed on his feet, I squirmed to the edge to figure out if I could jump. He watched and I guessed he was deciding whether to take hold of my waist and lift me down. He walked away.

With less than grace I scrambled down the side of the stone block to join him. Southward we had a spectacular view of the city just as the sun, a blood-orange disc, began its ascent.

"Look!" I marvelled. "How the sun changes all the cream-coloured edifices to pink."

My enthusiasm for colour amused him. "Who will finally claim you, Mademoiselle Forette? Art or Science?"

"Shall we begin our descent?" I suggested.

"Well, it should be even easier going down."

"Not necessarily."

Chapter 26

**I know something about you already;
you had a father and a mother!**

Sigmund Freud

The Mermaid's Looking Glass

Sigmund opened the lid to a luxurious supply of South American cigars, touched by the great man's thoughtful gift. Inside he found a note—

My Dear Sigmund,

If I'm not mistaken, Wednesday's midnight encounter with Sabrine was an extraordinary experience for you, if only to judge by your determination and enthusiasm to involve yourself in this most difficult case.

You have my permission, indeed my blessing, to examine her as often as you deem necessary. The one caution (mentioned before): Sabrine Weiss can be extremely flirtatious. More than one Salpêtrière intern has been seduced by her eccentric charm.

However, the letter of recommendation received from your mentor, Dr. Josef Breuer, assures me that Sigmund Freud owns a maturity beyond his years. A knight, he says, who has promised himself to science.'

If so, let Sir Sigmund gird himself well in the knight's steely armour, to protect against the arrows of Sabrine's seductive glances.

J.M. Charcot

P.S. Take ownership of my consultation room for the remainder of your internship. My daughter Jeanne has already organized a shopping expedition with her mother to find suitable rugs that will somewhat palliate what the ladies brand as my "chamber of grotesqueries."

P.P.S. The cigars lay atop Sabrine's file.

Sigmund felt elated, and moved by Breuer's recommendation. Breuer, like a father, loaned him money, encouraged Paris. Choosing a cigar, sniffing its rich aroma, sitting back, he looked around his now personal consultation room, and conveniently located within the outpatient clinic.

He suspected the anatomical peculiarities and deformities Charcot collected and made into plaster casts, displayed everywhere, were what the ladies deemed grotesque. He viewed the diseased organs and malformed limbs worthy of scientific interest.

There was an almost lighthearted tone in Charcot's note, undoubtedly Charcot enjoying a bit of satiric humour; but Sigmund knew, nonetheless, that he was being entrusted with a seriously complex case.

He lit the cigar, opened the case file, and came to the first entry—

7/7/1880

Sabrine Weiss, age 15, enters the Salpêtrière

No coherent memory of her past

He read no further because the door swung open. Dr. Josef Babinski, without as much as a courtesy knock, stood silent and sullen. Before Sigmund could manage a response, Charcot's clinical assistant stepped aside to reveal his charge, the new patient, Salpêtrière's princess. Sigmund then observed a change in Babinski's expression when he turned to Sabrine, his look anxious, yet his expression replicated, remarkably, the tender concern he showed in the Brouillet painting. She smiled and he reluctantly left.

Sigmund stubbed out the cigar, rose, his chance to observe her in full daylight. She was dressed exactly as in the Brouillet painting, the same gypsy blouse trimmed in red lace and the same peasant skirt. Her hair billowed in unruly waves upon her shoulders and he took note of how a particular shaft of light from the window ignited the beautiful tresses into ribbony flames. She had a pale, freckled complexion that seemed both translucent and radiant. Her green eyes sparkled. The thought came.

Any man born with desire cannot deny her physical beauty. There is absolutely no woman in Paris more breathtaking.

He extended his hand.

"Enchanté, Monsieur. A gentle hand you have, and so too must be your heart—have we met?"

Is she merely teasing? "You don't remember me?"

She lowered her eyes.

Such long, beautiful, deeply red eyelashes.

She shrugged. "Perhaps we have met... although I shall not admit to the fact but to the possibility, as all our remembrances are malleable in fire." She looked inquisitively around the room. "I do smell burnt paper, or is it brimstone? There can be no doubt that Dr. Charcot has passed through this room today. Invariably, he leaves his imprint or should I say, imprimatur?"

She took away her hand. Which he regretted.

"If we haven't met," he began, "let me introduce myself. I am ..."

"The vivisector."

"I beg your pardon?"

"You are the Dr. Sigmund Freud who dissects the little ones. Drs. Babinski, Guinon and la Tourette, who are all very fond of me, reveal the secrets of the Salpêtrière when we play ring-around-the-rosy. All fall down we do." She looked at him searchingly. "Are the children's brains not innocent?"

How to explain to her?

"Do they cry when you cut?" she inquired.

The children are dead, he almost said in defence.

"I'm not a clinical surgeon," he replied. "I am a neuropathologist." *Which probably makes no sense to her.*

But her concerns moved swiftly elsewhere. "Are you one of the great council members of the Underworld? Some make rare visits to the Salpêtrière to watch the undead dance and vote their favourites."

He felt an urgent need to explain himself. "I'm here to further my research on the neurological diseases of children. Presently, I search for the lesions that cause infantile paralysis."

"Are you here to dissect my brain?"

"I do autopsies, I search..."

"For cures." She began circling him. "Which is why you have bravely chosen to pass through the portal and come to the Salpêtrière, my birthplace." Still she kept circling him. "Pay the other doctors no mind"— she smiled kindly—"they are lesser gods, without access to the deeper knowledge, and very jealous that the Great One has chosen you."

Awkwardly, he stepped through the invisible circle she was making, took a seat at the desk. He lit a new cigar to reclaim a sense of control. "What has he chosen me to do? The Great One?"

"To vivisect my condition."

Rapport with the patient, cultivate rapport, Breuer advised me. One need no other arsenal than two ears and an open mind.

"Sabrine..."

Her smile cut him short, a provocative smile, as though he had been caught passing a boundary, and she might whisper, 'Yes, let us become intimate. Please do call me by my first name.' He remembered Charcot's cautions regarding seduction.

She asked, "Shall I call you, Sigmund?"

He puffed clouds of calming smoke. "As you wish."

"No, I shall not! That would be far too bold of me; instead, I shall call you, Dr. Sigmund."

"As you wish." He enjoyed her pertness, her testing him. "But what if, in fair exchange, I call you Mademoiselle Sabrine?"

She fought back a giggle and suddenly walked away. Finding the skeleton on the L-bar, she put its arm around her shoulder, offering a winsome pose, and joked, "Birds of a feather? Well, not precisely, but two of a kind… eventually."

His laughter at her odd wit stirred her into a fit of giggling. For an absurd moment the two of them seemed the sanest of friends. She came back to gaze at the case file he had negligently left on the desk. "I haven't had the chance to read it and learn about Mademoiselle Sabrine's family history."

"I have no family history."

"But we all had a father and a mother—that's the beginning point."

"But I came to earth, a big egg, dropped by a big dragon into a bird's nest atop the church belfry of St. Louis, left to fend for myself and ultimately hatched by the summer sun—such a nice and splendid beginning, don't you think?"

"It's the place where we can begin."

"Do you think me fanciful?"

"Should I?"

"Dr. Charcot has named me 'fanciful.' He often scolds, 'Sabrine, you must focus on what is before your eyes, what you can touch and seize. To be cured, you must not play with the phantoms that flame up from your imagination.' I tell him in my sternest voice that even the most solid rocks are made up of invisible gases, that the world is but thickened light, our minds imprisoned electricity." Her rush of thoughts was mystifying and provocative. "What am I, then, to doctors of science? How substantial is this Sabrine?" she asked. "Do I come from a handful of atoms?" She returned to the skeleton and playfully rattled it. "To an arrangement of bones? She rapped the skull. "A deposit of thoughts? I ask Dr. Charcot, 'Am I the chooser of my atoms, of my thoughts?'"

He puffed the cigar, trying to calm his racing pulse, unsure as how he should react to her queer speculations. Was she an idiot savant? A mystic philosopher?

"And how does the doctor respond to your inquiries?" he managed to ask.

"The Sultan? Mmm..." She squinted to think. "The Sultan only frets, stamps a slippered foot, and asks, 'Who is smuggling books into the harem?' I tell him that all of the missing tomes of Alexandria have found shelves in the cobweb of my mind. The Sultan smiles, frowns, calls me flirtatious." Sabrine then looked at him with a mournful expression. "I'm very concerned, Dr. Sigmund."

"About what?"

"He soon might remove my navel. Erase the escape hatch."

The fragility of Sabrine's mind was all too apparent, yet he had no desire to hinder her flow of thoughts. So completely absorbed in the mystery of Sabrine Weiss, he continued to listen to her many outlandish observations. Time passed without notice. Her parade of moods entranced him.

She laughed, she cried, she sang cabaret songs her ward mates taught her. She folded her hands to pray for the babies in Limbo then announced her plan to rescue them. "Together with my Salpêtrière sisters we will grow our hair long and into braids and drop our braids over the walls into the darkness of the underworld and the babies of Limbo shall be pulled up to freedom. Then!" She walked restlessly and spun. "Strawberry jam for all!"

Sigmund remained a willing captive to her fabulous world. He smoked and took notes, not foreseeing the calamity which would end their session. Observing him writing, she asked for a pencil and paper of her own.

"I want to write a poem," she said.

Intrigued, he tore out a page and gave up his pencil.

She sat on the floor, bowed her head and became absorbed with writing. *What will she compose?* As time passed, he tried to see what she was writing, but her falling hair prevented any view.

She was eerily still. "Mademoiselle Sabrine?"

When she looked up, the colour had completely drained from her face. Alarmed, he beheld a changed woman, a Sabrine inexplicably in the grip of total fear. She jumped to her feet, trembling and very agitated, her hand tightly clenching the pencil, as if at any moment she might do something rash.

Stab him? Impossible! Would she dare? "Sabrine, give me the pencil."

She took several steps forward, unsteady, swaying, until she clutched at her abdomen, clearly in great pain. She uttered a loud cry, and as she collapsed, she tipped over a side table, a glass lamp smashing onto the floor and splintering into countless pieces.

Taken over by violent convulsions, Sabrine screamed as though invisible hallucinations assailed her. He rushed to her aid, desperately trying to restrain her frenzied thrashing, wanting to spare her from the splintered glass, but her strength seemed unconquerable. She flailed, squirmed, resisted, grabbed at him, ripping at his shirt, pulling at him until he lost balance and fell beside her in a sea of glass. Sabrine arced violently into the rainbow contortion, her feet and her head pressed into the floor. He struggled to roll over, feeling the pain of piercing glass.

Amidst the chaos, Babinski barged into the room, the spectacle of Sigmund crawling, seeking safety, Sabrine heaving in spasms. She gnashed her teeth, like someone demonically possessed. Babinski acted quickly, stuffed a handkerchief in Sabrine's mouth so that she would not bite her tongue. He angrily ordered Sigmund to pin down her shoulders. "She's in the clonic phase of the seizure! Restrain her, damn you!"

He seemed unable, watching her neck dangerously swell, her face turning bright crimson. Babinski pressed his palm down on her pelvic area, the force soon pushed Sabrine flat to the floor, but the moment he removed his hand, her entire body stiffened, one foot crossed the other, and her arms shot out as rigid as beams of wood. Muttering, Babinski sought the hysterogenic point along her rib cage, a precise area beneath her left breast and applied steady pressure. He showed himself persistent, pressing more and more forcefully until, at last, her body slackened and she closed her eyes in sleep.

Babinski opened her curled hand and took away the sharply pointed pencil. Both men rose, but Babinski towered over Sigmund, "Monsieur, you sink even below common sense."

Sigmund had no answer. The very able assistant went into the corridor, shouting for orderlies to bring a litter at once.

When Sabrine was eventually taken away, Babinski lingered, handing Sigmund the handkerchief used to keep Sabrine from biting her tongue. "Take it, Monsieur Freud, as there's a deep cut on your nose which requires attention... it might very well leave a scar."

There was little charity in his voice. When Babinski grabbed the case folder from the desk, Sigmund blocked his exit. A silent confrontation between the two men ensued before Sigmund shrugged and stepped aside to let him pass.

Patting his nose with the handkerchief, observing the dark drops of blood, he sat down, wretchedly fatigued and unable to bring the day's events into meaningful focus. He found that his thoughts were uncomfortably adrift. Only pain forced him to regard the glass splinters in his jacket sleeves which he picked out one by one.

What had precipitated Sabrine's attack? He looked down at the floor glittering with glass—there, the crumbled piece of paper, her poem. When he smoothed out the page, the poem, he saw that it was unfinished.

* * *

i have lost

my face

in the mermaid's looking glass

i have lost

my breast

under her seaside shell

i have lost...

Chapter 27

The reason why a work of genius is not easily admired from the first is that the man who has created it is extraordinary and few resemble him; but in time's due course his work will fertilize the minds capable of understanding it. Thus art flourishes, thank heaven!

Félix Fénéon

Meeting the Mother of Christ

I stood outside the offices of what I hoped was *la Revue Independante* as there was no numerical address to be found. It was spring, April, a pleasantly warm day, the sky was clear blue and the chestnut trees along *rue de la Chausee d'Antin* were in fresh bloom. For the occasion I wore a wide brim, flowered hat better to shield me from the afternoon sun and a brocaded frock of almond white.

The Independent Review was the most respected art and literature journal in all of Paris, yet looking at the battered, heavily scarred door, I procrastinated. *Am I foolish to come? Will I be permitted to meet Marie Christos?*

There was no other critic I admired more. She invariably penned the most fascinatingly styled reviews. Her critiques were crisp, to the point, and sprinkled with the driest of wit. Behind everything she wrote, she hinted of a scholarly bent. In some mysterious fashion, Marie Christos, my female Virgil, guided me to the right books and art exhibits. Whatever she recommended never failed to expand my knowledge.

Her intriguing name, Marie Christos, invited unending speculation. While there was the inescapable allusion to Mary, Mother of Christ, I supplied her with deliriously imaginative backgrounds—raised in a Catholic orphanage by fanatical nuns who were determined to make little Marie Christos one of their own, but Marie escaped to Paris, to literature and art. Or more melodramatic, her parents, religious zealots, leaders of fanatical cult, baptized her Marie Christos believing the child destined to become a saint, but again she escaped, always from suffocating circumstance, slipping from hands that would control her, to seek literary fame in Paris.

So here I stood, with my far-fetched imaginings, at the possible door to where she was employed, still procrastinating.

Oh, just go inside, Julie Forette, and introduce yourself to the woman!

Aside from Jeanne Charcot, I had no women friends in my life—which I considered a serious deficit. I wanted balance. While Jeanne brought to our friendship an admirable degree of wit and brashness, it remained a friendship cast in the shadow of her father. I also realized that even though Jeanne eagerly and willingly followed my interests in the pursuit of art, she had no independent grasp of art's transcendent power. The heart of the matter was the lack of depth in our relationship. I became watchful for a woman who might share more of my modern interests.

Then one particular review by Marie Christos appeared. She proclaimed that her "prayed for" translation of *Crime and Punishment* had just been published which she promptly read and declared it "a boldly delirious accomplishment." If one, two or five "perspicacious readers" might still exist in France, each was urged to buy or steal what she presciently called "the first psychological novel."

Crime and Punishment I quickly purchased, transforming my concept of the novel. To reach the last page I stayed up the entire night. The writer, Fyodor Dostoevsky, hurled me into the troubled mind and fevered thoughts of a young, penurious law student, Rodion Raskolnikov, who would have surely been diagnosed by Charcot as a hysteric. No prior novel prepared me for the deep exploration of the twists and turns of a conflicted psyche. What struck me in particular was Raskolnikov's horrid dream of a horse whipped to death, a symbolic foreshadowing of the violence he would perpetuate. For the Russian writer, dreams were there to reveal one's deepest desires. And it was an astute critic, a woman, who brought me to Dostoyevsky, to truly modern fiction—but now I was losing courage to introduce myself to her. I walked back and forth in front of the building, debating whether to impose on a busy, important, gifted critic.

Sheer impudence, I decided. Besides, it would not be prudent to enter a building without an address plate. The situation, however, changed when I observed an extremely tall gentleman approaching from the other end of the street. He wore a top hat of fine bombazine silk, gleaming in sunlight, and he walked with long, confident strides. Interestingly, he carried and held out a potted plant, a single red cyclamen, as if ready to bestow his flower to the first person he met.

The gentleman had a most unusual goatee, fastidiously tapered to a slight curl at the tip.

With a well-structured face and his long jaw line, he reminded me of America's eponymous icon, the long-limbed and goateed Uncle Sam. The gentleman was a dandified dresser, wearing a frock coat that was bright tan and pin-stripe trousers of grey and plum.

Reaching me, he offered not the cyclamen, but a slight bow. "May I be of assistance, Mademoiselle?"

His courtly manner put me at ease. "Can you tell, Monsieur, if I'm at the door of the *Independent Review*? The address is supposedly 23 rue Chausee d'Antin."

"Hmm, certainly there is neither number nor signage to indicate an ongoing enterprise, nor a decent door to suggest it is flourishing." His gloved hand traced initials carved on the door which I had not noticed. Roughly carved, it seemed to read:

J.C.

L.

M.C.

"I believe," the gentleman said, "I observe in your demeanour some serious intent. Perhaps Mademoiselle comes to demand payment for an outstanding bill from this journal or to register a complaint?"

"Neither. I wish to meet their journalist, Marie Christos."

He returned his gaze to the defaced door. "Are your initials, perchance, J.C.?"

"No."

"Hmm." Long, elegant fingers stroked the curled goatee as though he needed a moment to properly assess my intent. "Well... perhaps I can be of assistance." Opening the door with a key, he proceeded up the stairs, his cyclamen extended. It seemed I was to follow.

The offices of the *Independent Review* were not what I expected, nothing but a single room, carpetless, with little furniture. There were no visible employees, no printing press, only a desk and three folding chairs, their wooden backs oddly stamped, "War Office." On the wall I noticed a grouping of framed articles, the notoriously succinct, biting critiques which were the journal's trademark. I recognized several names, but nothing by Marie Christos. The gentleman removed the elegant silk top hat, showing hair scrupulously trimmed *en brosse*, and placed the hat on a war office chair. He pulled aside a thread-worn window curtain to centre his potted cyclamen on the sill. He then politely dusted off another war office chair with a handkerchief, inviting me to sit.

I waited for him to reveal his identity. He preferred the edge of the desk for a seat, one long leg nonchalantly dangling over the other. I noticed his two-toned shoes were tan and plum. He began to remind me of a daguerreotype I had once seen of the American president Abraham Lincoln, a younger Lincoln, but a similar countenance, gaunt, angular, and deeply etched. His austere features and thoughtful demeanour were at odds with his debonair attire. Somehow he gave me a comforting sense of a man of unalterable character.

"Let me introduce myself," he spoke in a sonorous voice, "Félix Fénéon, chosen pharaoh of The Independent Review." (Later I learned that Monsieur Fénéon was chief editor and performed most all other duties at the journal.) "Now, who among our illustrious critics did you say you wished to meet?" he asked.

"The woman on your staff who writes with such originality and perception—Marie Christos."

"Marie Christos?" He pondered my interest for a few minutes. His long reach enabled him to lean and readjust the flowerpot to (I supposed) a more aesthetic position. He heaved a sigh toward me. Did he regret the intrusion?

"I could return another day, if she is presently busy," I suggested, although wondering where in a single-desk office she might write?

He looked thoughtfully at the red cyclamen on the sill, as if contemplating another adjustment. "The person in question is no longer in our employ. A minor critic—we were forced to relieve Mademoiselle Christos of her position." He watched, first my disappointment, then my barely disguised anger. "This Mademoiselle Christos or Madame Christos —we at The Independent care little for such distinctions," he went on in a languid manner, "somehow expected financial compensation for that piece on Dostoevsky. Which any of our other luminaries could have knocked off before finishing a cigarette."

"How presumptuous of her," I remarked caustically, "wanting to be paid."

"Yes, and such a Christian name; we expected more altruism."

I began to wonder about this Félix Fénéon. Had I not read an article or two in the magazine signed by an 'f.f.'? Concise, insightful pieces which invariably expressed a tone of amused irony.

"Mother of Christ," I murmured, more to myself, beginning to see a bigger picture.

"My goodness! Are you a Papist?" His look of alarm could not be taken seriously. My lips drifted toward a smile. *What naiveté, Julie Forette, imagining a 'Marie Christos' existed?*

"A Roman Catholic are you?" he persisted.

"Only until I began to read, ergo, think." I replied, accepting the cigarette he offered.

Félix Fénéon, alias 'f.f.', inserted his cigarette into a long, amber mouthpiece, inviting me into dialogue. "Is there a particular aspect of Catholicism that disturbs you?"

Unusual questions from a relative stranger. But I took intellectual pleasure in answering. "First and foremost, the needless angst the Church instills regarding afterlife and judgement."

The memory of my mother's miserable death intruded. Justin, my brother, who served as Death's messenger, relayed mother's last fear when she collapsed on the library floor. *Will I be sentenced to hell?* she whispered to Justin as her brain matter probably crumbled, like stale cake.

"I expect death as I expect sleep," remarked Fénéon.

"In sleep there are dreams," I replied, "sometimes unpleasant."

"Death is a black lake with no dreams—no return." Fénéon's eyes were unreadable, his lips pursed around the cigarette holder, savouring languorous puffs.

"You are certainly no Christian," I said.

"I seek a spirituality which logically..." he drew in more smoke, "leads to total detachment."

"We are moving far afield," I said, wanting to match his emotional composure, but his thinking drew me in like the cigarette smoke he inhaled.

"Well then, Mademoiselle... Madame?" he waited for a name.

"Why make a distinction? I'm Julie Forette."

"Well then, Julie Forette, I'm sure in the very near future you will see pieces by Marie Christos in other journals more modern than ours. Writing about literature and art remain Marie's compulsion."

"Perhaps philosophy and religion are part of her repertoire as well?" I raised my eyebrows.

We exchanged a look sufficient unto itself. The silent acknowledgment that Félix Fénéon, f.f., and Marie Christos were a trinity of one. The female I sought for intellectual companionship had been singularly replaced by a male.

Yet, the wonder: a real friendship was launched and cemented all in the course of one spring afternoon. Félix Fénéon took a sincere interest in me. We shared his modest lunch of mineral water and a piece of Swiss cheese he divided into two. The surprising similarities in our views on literature and art led us from one topic to another. We agreed that Fyodor Mikhailovich Dostoevsky had no literary rivals in the realm of philosophy and psychology. Laughingly we settled the matter of Émile Zola's talent. Not much.

He admitted that he did the lion's share of the writing at the *Inde-*

pendent, regularly taking the newly written articles at night to the printers far outside Paris while his financiers stayed in the background.

Perhaps the most important information we learned about each other was our admiration for Cezanne, in agreement that his style was a radical departure from all other artists, even the most modern of the Impressionists, Claude Monet.

"Three pears on a cloth by Cezanne are so intrinsically real as to border on the mystical," he remarked. "Other still-life painters are as uninteresting as the Chamber of Deputies."

I chose not to mention my personal past with Paul.

Before our parting and promise to meet again, he disclosed his journalistic secret: because he wrote reviews for numerous magazines, he found it convenient to use pseudonyms, oftentimes female.

"We need more female critics, and we shall have more," he affirmed. "I'm just hurrying the process."

Dear Félix Fénéon (whom I was to henceforth call f.f., as his friends did) became my Hindoo sage of art. And while my quest for a woman friend came to naught that day, she merely waited in a different part of Paris. f.f. would eventually guide me to her. And my extra good fortune, she was August Renoir's favourite model.

Chapter 28

The lunatic, the lover, and the poet
Are of imagination all compact:
One sees more devils than vast hell can hold.

A Midsummer Night's Dream
William Shakespeare

ANOTHER POEM

I

Charcot settled on to the sofa, lighting a cigarette, preparing himself for another of her poems, the one Babinski found clutched in her hand at the Tuesday Demonstration. Unfolding the piece of paper, he felt the same sad weariness. The tangled thoughts still poured from her head.

> **Self-Scheherazade**
>
> **i weave and unweave words**
>
> **to seduce & subvert**
>
> **The Sultan**
>
> **i raise a parchment hand**
>
> **against daylight**
>
> **fight the ending**
>
> **implicit in every pattern**
>
> **of telling**

He leaned back, exhaling a billow of smoke, watching the silvery drift. As the poem offered nothing more, he let the cigarette burn through words...

> **seduce...**
>
> > **subvert...**
> >
> > > **fight...**

But what do you really fight against, dear child? The light of sanity?

Holding the page pock-marked with brown rings, he wondered what hope for a cure he could offer Sabrine Weiss. Soon to enter her sixth year at the Salpêtrière, she showed no tangible sign of improvement. Her hystero-epileptic attacks only increased in intensity, the repertoire of hysteric postures expanding (admittedly, much to the admiration of his audiences).

Bored with dissolving the words, he gave the page to the burning embers of the hearth, watching her ramblings flare into ash.

* * *

The pervasive smell of burnt paper was what Sigmund first noticed when he entered the library. He looked toward the desk. As promised, Sabrine's case file again waited for him. Making himself comfortable in Charcot's chair, he saw another box of fine South American cigars in front of him. He appreciated the doctor's dark humour, the match sticks nestled in a skeleton hand chosen for its misshapen fingers.

Degenerative arthritis, he diagnosed, lighting a cigar.

The chronicle of Sabrine Weiss' five years at the Salpêtrière now secured his full attention. The first page he had read before, namely, that Sabrine came to the Salpêtrière in 1880 with "no coherent memory of her past."

What followed were more than three hundred pages of clinical notations. He noticed that Charcot's initial impressions were succinct and peculiarly composed in a columnar style:

Sabrine Weiss, age 15

5' 7" in height

Strong for her age

Skin freckled

Birthmark on inside of left thigh

Fully matured breasts

Jewish blood

Sabrine's Jewish ancestry proved frustratingly vague. Brought to Salpêtrière by order of regional medical examiners with the diagnosis of "severely delusional," she was accompanied by an unnamed physician. The legal paperwork was turned over to Nurse Botard at the gates, along with Sabrine and no further history.

Within the first several weeks, the new patient evidenced:

Hallucinatory outbursts

With cyclical frequency

No further information was given as to the nature of the hallucinations nor what was meant by cyclical. A subsequent entry:

Often displays

a dreamy stupor.

The case file descriptions often bordered on the provocative:

An expansive intelligence

But capricious

By nature coquettish

One must be watchful

At age 16, after one year at the asylum, Sabrine Weiss experienced her first hystero-epileptic attack. Soon there followed comparisons to other hystero-epileptics:

During the clownism or acrobatic phase,

predisposed to the crucifixion and rainbow postures

More supple than Genevieve or Augustine

Reading for several hours, finishing many cigars, Sigmund was left with a very blurred picture of the asylum's most distinctive patient. If he could only find more substantive notes to lead him closer to an understanding of Sabrine's medical condition. Only two tantalizing entries:

Continues to converse

with her guardian spirits

And beside this entry, another lightly written in the margins, almost missed:

Another childish poem

Mermaids again

And no further details here to digest, he thought with increasing exasperation; however, he continued reading, alert for more notations in the margins. In the second year, Charcot became inspired toward experimental treatments. He subjected his young charge to both faradic and galvanic shocks until the head of the electrotherapy department, M. Vigouroux, apparently seeing no benefit, insisted that they be discontinued. Charcot replaced the electric treatments in the weeks that followed with "metallotherapy"—a modality unfamiliar to Sigmund—in which various metals were applied to Sabrine's "body surface." This treatment was soon replaced by immersions in a varying series of metallic solutions. When Charcot could effect no visible change in her mental status he discontinued the immersions, satisfied that "our Sabrine is such a healthy subject, having no muscular atrophy or degeneration, the metallic nutrition absorbed by the musculature is at best redundant."

At age 17, her third year at the asylum, she was given the definitive diagnosis of "Classic Hystero-Epilepsy." The neurological disorder was no longer in doubt, as the physical postures and emotional outbursts associated with the disease steadily increased. Charcot voiced his certainty in an 1883 entry:

Sabrine's latent hystero-epilepsy

now full-blown.

The rainbow arc, particularly pronounced

Scribbled in the margin: **even elegant**

By 1884, the year Sabrine turned 19, Charcot abandoned his terse columnar format to offer a more personal narrative.

Yesterday, Bastille Day. The staff organized a parade for the entertainment of the patients. Tricolor flags hung in abundance from the upper windows of Salpêtrière City. Our grey-haired ladies, surely imbued with memories of patriotic days past, especially enjoyed marching through the cobbled streets, circling the courtyards and gardens, waving tiny flags, blaring toy tin horns.

I permitted a modest ball in the evening for the staff and residents, allowing our princesses of hysteria to dress as festively as they wished for the occasion. Augustine, Blanche, Genevieve and Sabrine were quite imaginative with their attire. Sabrine in particular loves to attract the attention of the doctors. She takes great care with fixing her hair, arranging it sometimes in one way, sometimes in another, adorning her red tresses with all manner of brightly coloured ribbons.

He hoped for more of such spirited descriptions, but the remaining year and half of Sabrine's life at Salpêtrière were given over to clinical observations, for the most part regarding her bodily functions. The hospital doctors filled hundreds of pages detailing her breathing patterns, digestion, and arterial pulsations. What made him extremely puzzled was the obsessive attention given to her menstruation. Month upon month, year upon year, Charcot and staff made meticulous recordations of the onset, length, heaviness, as well as the colour of her menstrual blood. A plethora of diagrams were inserted in an attempt to correlate Sabrine's menses to the various phases of the moon.

While 38% of our female population exhibit menstruation at the appearance of the new moon, Sabrine's menses becomes particularly heavy during the phase of the full moon.

An entry dated October 1885, the month Sigmund arrived in Paris, summed up Sabrine's five years of confinement at the Salpêtrière.

No therapy thus far has proven effective. In accordance with our clinico-anatomic methodology, we shall continue with clinical observation until the Pathology Department can, in due course, perform a microscopic analysis of nerves and tissue.

Sigmund again recognized Charcot's handwriting in the margin:

The microscope—the final eye.

There appeared to be no coherent treatment plan for Sabrine Weiss unless one considered a death vigil as a plan. Snubbing out what was left of his cigar in the arthritic hand, he closed the file. No further insight could be gained from its contents.

He went over to have another look at the Brouillet painting—Tuesday's Clinical Lesson memorialized. The star patient, falling back in a hypnotic trance, as graceful as an archer's bow into Babinski's arms. Charcot standing a discreet distance from the patient makes no effort to catch her. But Babinski ever present, his hand settled close to Sabrine's breast. It annoyed him, how the clinical assistant seemed always nearby or just outside a door whenever she experienced an attack. Her dreamful swoon in the painting bore no resemblance to yesterday's attack. Her scream, worse than a wounded animal, came back to fill his ears, her terror-filled hallucinations, the tormenting serpents biting into her stomach.

II

Charcot's question boomed across the library—"Tell me! Has our star patient sufficiently exasperated you into fleeing the Salpêtrière?" He marched forward with his typical energy to stand beside Sigmund in gazing at the painting.

Once recovered from Charcot's unexpected appearance, he replied, "To the contrary."

Charcot stayed close, their shoulders touched. "Has not Brouillet rendered the scene in near photographic detail?"

Yes, Sigmund agreed that each person attending the Tuesday Lesson was clearly recognizable. *More details of Sabrine's past prior to the Salpêtrière is what I would prefer to see.* But he dared not speak ill of her case file.

"There's Philippe Burty," Charcot pointed out the grey bearded art critic whom Sigmund recognized from the dinner party. Standing by the back wall, Burty obscured part of the lithograph of Sabrine in her elegant rainbow arc. "There's my son, Jean, near the window."

Why do I never see his son Jean at any of the family's soirees?

"If I'm not mistaken..." Charcot put on eyeglasses, "what Brouillet fails to capture is a true physiognomy of Sabrine." He moved closer to the canvas. "Unaccountably, he neglects to bring out the rosy hue of her skin. And how could any artist be blind to the flaming red of her hair?"

The woman in the painting, Sigmund had to concur, was a pale imitation.

"What if you had been French born?" Charcot wondered aloud. "Or made the journey to Paris years sooner? Would you have been the one attending to Sabrine Weiss instead of Dr. Babinski?"

Uncanny, how he seems to read not only thoughts but my desires. "But, Dr. Charcot, I am attending to her now."

"And a severe abrasion on the nose, I see, to prove it."

He resisted the urge to touch the cut. A sliver of glass had penetrated the bridge of his nose when grappling with Sabrine over the seabed of glass. "It's nothing of consequence," he said.

Sabrine's painted image continued to hold them. "Try as I do," Charcot remarked, "I can find no features to distinguish her as Jewish."

He gently took Sigmund's elbow and escorted him to a sofa. The two took a seat together, facing the unlit hearth. Charcot reflected, "I suspect her roots lie closer to Ireland."

Sigmund took the risk and broached the subject, "I found next to nothing in the case folder with regard to her family history."

"Experience has taught me, Sigmund, that even if I had been furnished with a detailed history of her family tree, it would be suspect, and in all probability grossly erroneous. When it comes to family histories, each member paints a different picture. I have learned more of Sabrine from careful observation than any so-called family history."

Satisfied with his cogent justification for the lack of family history, Charcot kept his eyes half-shut for a moment as if to further persuade. "Regrettable," he removed his eye- glasses, "your disastrous results with Sabrine. Dr. Babinski informed me her of attack. Yet... the event gladdens me." Rising from the sofa, he went to the bell cord beside the hearth and gave it a deliberate tug.

Who might he be signalling? Surely not Babinski bringing them Sabrine?

Sigmund received a sympathetic smile. "Gladdens me, yes, because of your firsthand opportunity to observe the classic symptoms of Grand Hysteria."

A servant entered, went directly to the hearth, expertly arranged a pyramid of kindling and logs, ignited an impressive blaze, then left without uttering a word.

"Let us be comforted by the fire," said Charcot, "while you relate all that you observed in the attack."

He began his sober description. "Without warning she lost consciousness and collapsed to the floor."

A knowing nod came from the doctor. "The first phase of the hysterical crisis—go on, more details."

"Then a marked shuddering of her body turned into violent thrashing."

"Yes, as if palsied. I call it Clownism, the second phase of Grand Hysteria; but get to the pains, describe them accurately."

"She sobbed, claiming great suffering in her abdomen, that..." He looked questioningly at Charcot. "That serpents had penetrated her stomach."

"Yes-yes, all expected behaviour. Periodically she makes such hallucinatory complaints, then for days the poor child refuses to eat because she does not want to feed these painful beasts."

"As you know, Dr. Babinski arrived. He eventually subdued her convulsions by the application of pressure..."

"Yes-yes, to a relevant hystero-zone."

"Then she grew rigid, her arms outstretched as if she were nailed to the floor."

"The crucifixion posture," explained Charcot. "The one most difficult to alleviate."

"Soon thereafter Babinski took her away," he concluded, although tempted to add, *jealously so.*

In the hearth there was a pop, a red-hot ember jumped to the floor in front of them. Charcot found iron tongs, returning the escaped ember to the fire. "Of course, in her debilitated state, she had to be taken back to her home." Again he looked at Sigmund with marked sympathy. "And you, if I'm not mistaken, experienced a shock to your own nervous system. But nonetheless, instructive, yes? Now a time for a change, a new and different case to further instruct you in other types of grand hysteria."

Julie Forette's warning came straight to mind—*At some near point in time, he will reclaim Sabrine.* The doctor had to be dissuaded. Tactfully. "Am I too bold in asking permission to continue with the case?" He chose not to mention the promise in Charcot's note of no time limits.

"Too bold?" Charcot showed exaggerated surprise. "Why, that's precisely the attribute we encourage at Salpêtrière—boldness! How else to gain a greater understanding of our patients' neurological condition?" A hint of condescension in his tone was uncomfortable. He watched Charcot turn his attention to the fire, putting on a new log, asking, "Does not Sabrine's behaviour whet a neurologist's appetite? One simply wants to learn more about her. But we must not forget," the Director heaved a sigh and returned to the sofa, "that in due course Dr. Sigmund Freud will return to his fatherland while Jean-Martin Charcot remains at Salpêtrière entrusted with protecting his fragile birds, none more fragile than Sabrine." Both men fixed their gaze upon the crackling fire. "In all likelihood," came the dire prediction folded in the softness of his voice, "I shall be the one at her bedside death."

Charcot's anatomic-clinical method was sacrosanct, clinical observation of symptoms for a lifetime, then autopsy. Sigmund kept his focus on the coiling flames until he could find a way to respond. "There is the enigma of her ovarian pains."

"Yes, for her a particularly vexatious symptom," noted Charcot. "But each hysteric at the Salpêtrière, you will come to discover, suffers from a special stigmata. Ovarian pain is Sabrine's neurological cross."

"Have you found her pains to comport with neurological pathways?"

"The findings can be contradictory, thus I'm not prepared to adequately answer your question." Charcot then lapsed into a brooding silence; he seemed to be weighing what he would say next. "Certain members on my staff..." (both men seemed constrained not to look at each other, only at the fire) "are championing a possible solution to the abdominal pains."

"Solution?"

Charcot retrieved the poker, leaned forward to prod the logs. "A surgical procedure." The flames danced higher. Sigmund could not imagine what procedure the Salpêtrière had in mind. More prodding of the logs produced higher flames. "An oophorectomy," said Charcot.

"Removing her ovaries?"

"Yes. A total ovarian resection."

Careful not to frown, he ventured, "Might such a decision be... precipitous?"

Charcot smiled the sad, worldly smile belonging only to him. "One ponders long and hard upon such matters, Sigmund. The procedure has proven successful for many. With my own eyes I have seen it work; yes, controversy exists... opposing camps—even at the Salpêtrière."

"I should think ..."

"Please, Sigmund." The imperial hand was raised "Let's not engage in needless debate. I have postponed any decision, at least for the present."

Sigmund was not at all comfortable with the prospect of a radical surgical procedure looming like a Damocles sword over Sabrine Weiss. Escorted to the door, he stopped. "I nearly forgot to ask you, Dr. Charcot."

"What is it, my boy?"

"A notation I found in the margins of her case folder. A reference to her poetry?"

Charcot paused, again as though he were sorting out what he would and would not say. "Ah, her poems..." he nodded. "We have learned not to encourage Sabrine's penchant for poems, having found that such endeavours overexcite her and can precipitate the most virulent attacks."

Sigmund left with an uneasy suspicion of having received a censored response; yet how could he refute what had happened in his session with Sabrine—a poem followed by chaos.

Chapter 29

... the dream-thoughts can often only be discovered precisely in some transitory element of the dream which is quite overshadowed by more powerful images.

The Interpretations of Dreams
Sigmund Freud

Dreams Come True

I

Cezanne dared not believe such a change of fortune. He took out his handkerchief, wiped the beads of sweat from his forehead, and read the telegram again.

> **Paul, come home. Father dead.**
> **Jas de Bouffan is yours.**
> **All now your rightful inheritance. The bank as well.**
> **Mother and I wait for your return.**
> **Your sister, Marie**

Pissarro expressed his condolences. "It is the natural cycle, Paul, everyone must die." They sat in a remote corner of the New Athens Café. Pissarro watched Cezanne struggling with the full meaning of the telegram. "Dear friend, you have been given what every artist dreams—the wealth to freely follow your own path. This is the underlying reality of your new situation."

Yes! Cezanne realized his father's considerable wealth now belonged to him. *I am—yes! A free man!* No longer need he hide secrets from the old codger. The banker of Aix-en-Provence, holder of the purse strings, has drawn his last breath.

He read the telegram a third time, tossing it onto the table. Grunting, he understood. "Well, the nail has been hammered into the post."

"Never will you again need fear the shackles of poverty," said Pissarro, "and that's good news." He signalled the waiter for another coffee.

"It's an incontrovertible fact!" Cezanne slammed a hand down on the telegram. "The bald-pated buzzard is dead!" And quite unexpectedly, he roared with hysterical laughter that caused heads in the café to turn. Wiping the tears from his eyes, he eventually calmed down and confided to Pissarro, "My father was fond of warning me, 'You die with genius; you eat with money.' Yes, he reminded me over and over about my precarious future, *'On meurt avec du genie mais on mange avec de l'argent.'*"

"Ah Paul, not so untrue." reflected Pissarro, for today he still had many financial hoops to jump through. Soon leave, catch the number 9 omnibus to Deylabrette's, and convince the dealer to purchase, at the very least, another watercolour fan. He must sell something before daring to return home to his wife. Could he get an advance for his paintings in Durand-Ruel's gallery? There were his children, six mouths to feed, and a bundle of bills to pay.

Suddenly he felt his shoulders gripped, Cezanne's eyes ablaze. "Don't you see, Pissarro? Don't you see? My father dies with genius and now I live with money and eat the bread!"

Inverting the remark had its savage irony but seemed heartless to Pissarro. *Surely,* he thought, *my friend speaks from a deep well of grief. Surely in his own peculiar fashion, he has loved his father.*

"Pissarro, an important mission awaits you." A new sense of urgency came over him, scribbling an address on the back of the telegram. "Here, go to her, I beg you from my heart, tell her of my good fortune, of my sizeable inheritance."

Pissarro frowned. *This mysterious woman again who torments him.* "Is this a sound idea, Paul?"

"Ask her to reconsider the sincerity of my love. Make it clear, Pissarro, make it clear, she can have every last centime!" His high pitched voice trembled.

"What of your son?" Pissarro voiced his concern. "Where does the young lad fit into this situation? And what of your son's mother, Hortense, who has been faithful to you for these past fifteen years?

Cezanne brooded for a minute before glumly making the promise: "If this woman rejects the offer you bring, I shall resign myself to a married life with Hortense."

Pissarro looked at the address given him. *23 rue Molard* was not too far, but he stayed seated, uncertain as to the propriety of carrying out the request.

"I shall be here, tomorrow," said Cezanne, "at this same hour, waiting for my destiny to be decided."

Pissarro heaved a sigh and rose; he guessed loyalty to friends required such idiotic tasks. "Who shall I ask for at this address?"

Cezanne grabbed the telegram and wrote "Mademoiselle Forette" in florid script.

Many misgivings weighed upon Pissarro, but he would seek out the

Forette woman. As he turned to leave, Cezanne stopped him with a troubled look. "Ask her," he lowered his voice for fear of being heard by others, "about the dream she wrenched from me."

Dream?? Pissarro's job as messenger started to appear, at best, imprudent. Better suited for a Don Quixote. *I'm a man who has six children to raise and fans to sell.* "My friend, you confuse me. Ask her about what dream?"

"Inquire if the dream is my responsibility. Show her the telegram. She will comprehend. She lives at a very modest boarding house... within walking distance. Maybe I should wait for you here."

"I will come back tomorrow with Mademoiselle's answer," Pissarro said firmly. "Take time to think of the responsibility you owe Hortense and your son."

"If love is ephemeral, as I suspect," said Cezanne. "I shall soon return to Provence where I can at least seek in art something solid, geometrical... lasting."

Pissarro donned his cap and buttoned his jacket. "My friend, passion is ephemeral, not love and family."

Camille Pissarro made a considerable impression on me. Foremost, I was moved by what I can only call his gentility. As soon as I met him, I wanted to share my feelings with Bijou. I intended to begin writing to my sister, to tell her that Paris had both great artists and men of good character. *Which you will see for yourself when you rejoin me.*

Pissarro found me at Madame Dujardin's boarding house where I had begun to live soon after I started working at the Salpêtrière. The ever-solicitous Charcot women had recommended me to Madame Dujardin who held high standards of probity for her lodgers. I lived in a comfortably furnished room on the second floor where several nurses and attendants from the hospital also lodged.

The artist announced his presence with a hearty tug of the front doorbell. Peering through the curtains, Madame Dujardin judged him respectable and brought him to the communal sitting room, hurrying off to find me.

When I entered, he removed his cap and bowed. Startling was his beard, fleecy white and wonderfully enormous, it covered most of his shirtfront. We sat on opposite divans, a proper distance to evaluate the intentions of each other. He stated his mission in a straightforward manner and I gave him my answer, "Tell Paul, gently but plainly, 'No, thank you.' You see, Monsieur Pissarro, I have something more valuable than his entire inheritance, I have a Cezanne painting."

Embarrassed, he rose. "Mademoiselle, forgive me and Paul for our crude assumptions. It is obvious that your sensibility and intelligence far exceeds that of two weather-beaten artists." He heaved a sigh, "Dunces we be."

As he took out his peaked cap which he had stuffed in a side pocket, preparing to leave, I responded, "May I beg to differ. I've seen your work at Theo van Gogh's gallery. I consider it intelligently conceived and solidly, splendidly executed. And may I admit," I added, enjoying the surprise on his face. "Impressionism is inexorably becoming my passion. But with regard to Paul, would you mind chatting for a while?"

"Well, I..."

"You show yourself his trusted friend and it would be important to me if I could understand him better. Perhaps, by learning more about his father?"

Uncertain but much intrigued, he sat back down, his hefty weight had him sinking into the deep-cushioned divan. He put his old cabbie's hat beside him. "What I can share, Mademoiselle, is that Paul's father was a hardworking, responsible man who provided for his family."

"Who owned and ran a bank, I'm told."

"True, yes, but he started in life as a humble hatter's apprentice. In time, Louis-Auguste Cezanne went on to establish his own hattery business."

Hats! The absurd amount of hats in the dream now had new meaning. Very much excited, I listened to the story of Louis-Auguste Cezanne's progression from hatmaker to businessman to becoming a major exporter of felt hats.

"The business did so well," Pissarro informed me, "that the elder Cezanne went on to start up a bank in Provence."

I could see how Cezanne's unconscious mind easily linked hatter to banker to pawnbroker. In the dream the pawnbroker obsessed with hats had to be his father disguised. But was the dream created to express a son's murderous impulse toward his father?

"Did Monsieur Cezanne treat Paul... kindly?" I asked.

"It's not for me to say," answered Pissarro, "but in our bourgeois society how many fathers are comfortable with a son who wishes to be an artist? I'm sure that Louis-Auguste Cezanne felt dismayed and hoped that his son would seek a more practical career. I don't think he ever saw Paul as a full-grown adult. Yet until the very end, he supported him. A monthly allowance, I believe."

"So, a father who rose above his disappointment. A father who ..." I ventured, "cared."

"I believe," said Pissarro, "there is love in every family. How one expresses that love varies according to one's temperament. Yes..." the white-bearded, broad belly artist reflected. "A family is a tapestry, each member contributes to its design. Perhaps his father preferred tougher thread and more muted colours."

Tapestry. Tougher thread. I remembered something. The coarse army blanket that covered Cezanne's studio cot. We sat on it often to play checkers. He insisted the several holes in the blanket were bullet holes. I knew better, as they were only moth holes, but I asked him how the bullet holes came to be. 'My father bought it on the cheap from a war veteran, covered me with it when I contracted the measles.' He bent and put his nose close to the blanket. 'It still stinks of the measles. Yes, I convalesced under this blanket.' 'What's wrong, Paul?' I saw him no longer concentrating on the checkers game that he liked to win. 'My father gave me my first box of colours,' he confessed. 'when I was cooped up with the infection.' 'Your father gave you your first box of colours,' I repeated, noticing his watery eyes. 'I was eight then. He put the tin box on this blanket, on my lap. Back then he was in the ironmongery business and bought up a lot of packing cases from another itinerant ironmonger—where he discovered the tin box of colours.' 'Your father was your first muse,' I ventured, trying to be lighthearted that day. 'Maybe…' He still hadn't made his move on the board. 'Get better, Son,' he said, 'here's something to dawdle away your time.'"

Get better, Son. That day was the closest Cezanne ever came to tears.

Pissarro broke into my reverie. "Mademoiselle, I must ask the question which preys upon Paul's mind. Has the dream come true? Is he responsible? Of course, I have no idea what this is all about."

I knew what Cezanne meant—the guilt he felt about the dream. And now ready to take blame for his father's death. Unless I came up with the right answer. Pissarro waited for the answer.

The father's ironmongery business… iron hats and murder. But what of love? Might the yearning for love be encoded somewhere in the chain of symbols?

"First, a question, Monsieur Pissarro. Does Paul Cezanne have a son?" Zola had said as much.

He hesitated, picked up his cap, turning it round and round. "Yes, Paul Jr., who is fourteen-years-old. The boy and his mother, Hortense, are at the moment staying with Cezanne's mother and sister, at Jas de Bouffan in Provence. Waiting for Cezanne's return."

Of course! The number 14 in the dream now revealed meaning. Importance. The painting taking an improbable fourteen years is nothing but a ruse! What Cezanne says is that he, too, has a son. In his own convoluted manner, he sought to communicate, to reconciliate with his father.

"Tell Cezanne the dream has nothing to do with death, mayhem or murder." I spoke with all the authority I could muster. "Tell him to remember the tin of colours that came to his father by way of the ironmonger. Remind him of the many faceted colours which are in his work and akin to the jewels in his dream." I escorted the elderly artist to the door "Tell him the dream will always be coming true, the jewels always pouring from the original source, his father's love."

Perplexed, he shook his head. "Ironmonger… jewels? Hopefully, it will make sense to him. So, you are a Sibyl! A divinator of dreams," he remarked jovially.

"I collect a few... an idiosyncrasy." I gave a dismissive shrug.

"You seem interested in collecting paintings as well, for it has dawned on me that you are the same Mademoiselle Forette who seeks art for the renowned Professor Charcot. Did the Professor find the Monet to his liking? I happened to notice it at Monsieur Theo's gallery, all wrapped and ready to be delivered."

"Dr. Charcot's taste for art, unfortunately, does not extend to the moderns—such as yourself."

"Your employer is not alone with his limited appreciation of art."

"The public just needs a little prodding," I said. "Another Impressionist Show is long overdue, Monsieur Pissarro."

He reflected, "That idea appears to be gaining currency among the cognoscenti."

"Well organized, properly displayed, an Impressionist Show would be the most spectacular art event of the year," I said.

The venerable artist studied me for a moment before a twinkle came into his kind eyes. "Perhaps in the near future we can discuss this show you so confidently imagine."

"I'm at your beck and call."

"But after this Cezanne business is settled," he added, soberly.

"I know it is in Paul Cezanne's best interest that I stay out of his life."

"Good, good." Pleased with the statement, he prepared for the outdoors, adjusting his cap and pressing down on his beard so as to button his jacket. When he opened the door, he turned once more. "You are a perspicacious woman, Mademoiselle Forette, and it has been an honour to make your acquaintance. I confess, it worried me that you would be tempted to take advantage of Paul's new-found wealth. But that was worthless cynicism. In my humble opinion, for him to marry Hortense and raise his son in the country would offer Paul Cezanne the emotional stability he needs."

"I couldn't agree more."

Watching him happily walk away, I knew I had just met the artist who would become most dear to me.

Chapter 30

The key is to keep good company only with people who uplift you, whose presence calls forth your best.

Epictetus

Two Are Stronger Than One

I

Félix Fénéon and I sat on a banquette to study the painting. He said there was no need to distract ourselves with any other paintings in the museum today. We were at the Louvre where f.f. took me from time to time to deepen my education. His critiques were deliberately concise so as to encourage me to expand upon his few choice adjectives.

"Supple; fluid; emphatic," he said. I waited for more. His hands folded over the ferule of his cane, he leaned forward and rested his goateed chin onto those graceful hands of his, but regarding the Ingres painting without a hint of emotion. "Cruel in its perfection," became his final comment.

My turn came next to interpret Ingres' extraordinary painting of *Oedipus and the Sphinx*. Young, manly Oedipus stood fearless and naked (except for a token cloak) before the she-monster. I found the 'suppleness' and 'perfection' in the splendid body of Oedipus who, planting a firm foot on the cave boulder, points a confrontational finger at the Sphinx in her lair. Answering her riddle incorrectly will unleash the she-creatures' murderous wrath. The 'cruelty' f.f. mentioned is stamped upon the face of the Sphinx, her cave floor littered with the bones of those who failed to solve the riddle.

"Everything in the painting brings me to one terrible, suspenseful, suspended moment," I remarked.

"You are now educated in Ingres' cold fury for detail." f.f. rose and put his gloves back on. "School is finished for today."

"My employer, Jean-Martin Charcot, might possibly pay a handsome sum to have such a painting in his collection as he weaves the myth of the Sphinx and her riddle through almost all of his lectures."

When f.f. casually informed me, standing on the steps of the Louvre, that another version of the painting existed, in the hands of a private collector, I made sure the next day that Charcot became aware of the fact. His interest piqued, I was instructed to find the owner of the painting who, if offered a fair price, might be persuaded to sell.

Thrilled by the prospect of hunting down the second Oedipus and Sphinx, the first stop would be Theo van Gogh's gallery on rue Montmartre. f.f. suggested that the knowledgeable gallerist might know who owned the painting. Any work by the distinguished Jean-Auguste-Dominique Ingres, I realized, would cost Charcot a considerable sum. The standing arrangement we had was a ten percent commission on the purchase price of any artwork I found which met his approval. Such a commission would certainly earn me more than a year's salary as his recordist.

Increasingly excited about my imagined financial boon, I gave the coachman a generous tip when dropped off at the gallery. Theo van Gogh was surprised to see me as our last business venture had not turned out well. He had in good faith entrusted his Monet canvas to my care, holding hope for a sale, which unfortunately did not come to pass. Now here I came again—perhaps he wondered if I were on another fool's errand. His pale blue eyes gave me a sympathetic look.

I wasted no time—did he know the whereabouts of Ingres' second *Oedipus Confronting the Sphinx*? The young gallerist's knowledge of sales and purchases proved impressive. The Sphinx painting had been bought nine months ago at the Megère Auction by none other than Edgar Degas.

He led me into the gallery's main viewing room. Lining the burgundy damask walls were the gilt-framed paintings of well-established artists who would not stir controversy. The radical Impressionist works he kept on the mezzanine, discreetly out of sight. After I was invited to settle into one of the many plush velvet settees, I waited for more information.

"To forewarn the Mademoiselle," he gently cautioned, "Degas keeps his collection an extremely private affair and, unfortunately, I can offer no help as to how you or anyone might approach the unapproachable Degas." As I tried to take in the news, the quandary, that a leading and unapproachable Impressionist owned the painting, he invited me to stay for a cup of tea. "I'm experimenting with certain health producing teas. Won't take but a minute to fire up the kettle."

He disappeared inside a curtained, cubby-hole of a kitchen to boil the tea while we continued to converse. "Apparently not a few Impressionists are serious collectors," I called out loudly, remembering that three of them fought for a Cezanne painting at Père Tanguy's.

"Who knows paintings better than a painter," Theo joked. "But none is more serious in collecting art than Degas. I'm told he has accumulated several thousand works. Unlike the other Impressionists, Degas is a man of independent means."

"We should all be so fortunate."

Waiting for the tea, I happened to notice a letter half-stuck in the crevice of the settee. Pulling it out, I scanned it quickly. As was my gift or curse, I absorbed its essential content.

My dear Theo,

I have to tell you that I'm really hard pressed now—the five francs left from the 150 you sent this month was spent for canvases, plus my laundry which just came back. Now but a few centimes are left, so I urgently ask: For God's sake, don't put off corresponding, send me more money or a little, such as you have—and know that I'm starving, literally! The paint bills weighs on me like lead, and yet I must go forward!!! But you, to my despair, say: 'I have a very great deal to pay out to my own creditors, so you'll just have to manage until the end of the month.'

Am I less than your creditors? Who should wait, they or I???

When "Dear Theo" returned with a pot of tea on a tray, I handed him the letter (refolded so that he would not suspect anything.) "I found this."

"Oh, thank-you. A letter from my brother, Vincent."

A brother, I thought, *seemingly accustomed to receiving an allowance, and in dire need of more:*

As regards this month, I really ask you most kindly but absolutely that you manage to send at least another 50 francs. Let at least one of your creditors do without 50 francs (they can stand it, rest assured) but please not me, because EVEN THEN it will still be tough for me.

> **Regards and with a handshake**
> **Yours truly,**
> **Vincent**

We sipped tea. My own salary amounting to 200 francs a month showed Theo van Gogh to be quite generous to his brother. "I believe I can smell the jasmine."

"Yes!" He was enthusiastic about his teas. "A combination of red peony root, mulberry leaf and jasmine flower. My doctor, an avowed herbalist, says that it lowers blood pressure."

I nodded approvingly, "Pungent but delicious."

"My brother is an artist," he volunteered.

"A family of artists?"

"Three uncles who are in the picture selling business, but Vincent is the first Van Gogh with the courage and talent to create genuine art. I'm very proud of him, a chap who found his true vocation late in life." He rose with the letter, went to an étagère, opened a drawer, and put it with a packet of other letters. "I keep the letters in chronological order, this packet is from Antwerp." He now seemed eager to talk about his brother. I needed to get to f.f.'s office before he left for the day so as to receive advice on how to meet Degas. "My brother seriously took up painting at age thirty. Can you imagine?"

"How old is he now?" I asked.

"Thirty-Three."

I finished the tea. "Do you have any of his work in your gallery?"

"Not yet." He smiled, somewhat embarrassed. "But someday, when we have our own gallery together. That is our plan. He paints, I sell." Then Theo van Gogh's mind seemed to wander. "Two are stronger than one. That is what I believe," he added.

(His brother and I would meet under exceptional circumstances, on a train of all places, but that was a month away.) I thanked Theo for his help and went straight to the offices of *La Vogue*, the new magazine where f.f. now worked. I took the 50-centime omnibus, deciding that there would be no more extravagant taxi carriages until I actually earned a commission.

f.f. watered the cyclamen plant on the windowsill in his new office at *La Vogue*. *The Independent Review*, where we first met, had closed its doors due to financial difficulties. Avant- garde magazines, it seemed like mushrooms, were prone to short life spans, only to re-sprout when least expected. f.f. assured me that *The Independent Review* would someday mushroom to life again.

"My shoemaker has become accustomed to waiting for payment whenever I'm between magazines." He sat at his new desk, his feet up, showing off a pair of polished two-tone shoes. He reflected on my need to meet Edgar Degas, putting a cigarette into the amber holder, lighting up and taking long, soothing drags. "The way to Degas is through the young model Suzanne Valadon. She doesn't model for him, but has somehow gained easy entrance to his hearth and home."

Point blank, I asked, "Is she sleeping with him?"

He looked over at his cyclamen plant, rose and meticulously plucked off several dry leaves. "Who can say? Degas is a closed book in that area."

To find the Montmartre model, f.f. advised, "Start having *dejeuner* at the *Auberge du Clos*, a café on the avenue Trudaine which she frequents."

"How will I recognize her?"

"Alas, I have only seen her in a Renoir painting, naked and robust, bathing with other frolicking maidens who all, thanks to Renoir, look alike, but I'm told that her flamboyant attire when at the cafés would put a gypsy to shame."

* * *

How curious that I would meet the renowned Edgar Degas through a girl barely nineteen. Still more curious, that in spite of the significant difference in our ages, Suzanne Valadon and I would become fast friends, *les copains*, or as the Americans say, 'pals.'

She was at the *Auberge du Clos*, an enchanting picture to behold. She wore her thick auburn tresses tucked up under a flat straw brim, embellished with taffeta flowers, dyed the brightest orange. Her dress was striped in scarlet and cream with specially made lace and ribbon cuffs. I most admired the outlandish corsage, pinned to her bosom, which appeared to be a concoction of young turnips and radishes. She looked ever so much a Bohemian denizen of Montmartre.

I boldly went to her table after having watched her closely for the better part of an hour. She looked up with a pretty smile, closing her sketchbook, as I introduced myself. She had been making sketches of patrons in the busy café, drawings which she apparently did not want me to see.

"Are you an artist?" I asked, watching her place a handbag over the sketchbook.

"An artist? Cold blazes, no! Sure as heck wish I were. Nope, I just chicken-scratch."

"Then you do so with an artist's concentration. Perhaps there is a chicken scratch of me in your sketchbook?"

While sipping a coffee at my table I had purposefully offered a profile, as motionless as possible. A devious lure.

"Perhaps Mademoiselle herself is an artist?" her eyes drank me in, the darkest blue I'd ever seen, very close to violet.

"I neither draw nor paint," I answered, "But highly admire those who do. You could say I'm an art lover—if that doesn't sound too banal."

"No, not at all. Please, won't you join me? I've become quite bored."

Sitting down, I didn't want to disturb the little female pup asleep on the coat she had brazenly laid on the floor. The dog, a white Maltese, wore a string of turnips around its fluffy neck to match Suzanne's vegetable corsage. The young girl, it was easy to conclude, gladly invited attention to herself. She had an open smile and a round face which reminded me of my sister.

I had come to the café armed with information—thanks to f.f.—about Suzanne Valadon's background. Hers was a chequered career. And Suzanne herself would later give me tidbits of her adventures and misadventures. Forced to leave school at age eleven to help her mother make ends meet, she started selling vegetables at *Les Halles* while also working as a laundress, washing and delivering. At some juncture she apprenticed in a milliner's workshop, decorating hats, then gained the talent for making funeral wreaths. What fascinated me most in her Dickensian past was Suzanne's stint as a circus performer, able to both stand balanced upon the backs of cantering horses and swing gracefully upon the trapeze bars. f.f. mentioned her bad fall from the trapeze bar one evening at *le Cirque Mollier*, ending Suzanne Valadon's dream of a life in the circus and a return to doing laundry. She had a slight limp which she learned to hide well. So much experience for one so young, I thought, gazing at her across the café table.

She gave a familiar nod to the waiter—"Alphonse, two peppermint liqueurs, *s'il vous plait*." And lowered her voice to me, "When you order two, they pare down the cost to one franc each. We save eighty centimes."

A model extremely popular with the artists in Montmartre, Suzanne first caught the eye of Puvis de Chavannes when she was just shy of fifteen. Chavannes, a major artist, transformed a girl who delivered his laundry into a muse who lolled about in the sacred groves of his idyllic paintings.

She clinked the dainty glass of peppermint liquor to mine with a toast she wanted all the patrons in the café to hear: "Let love live free!"

"To art!" I clinked again. Friendly patrons smiled, raised up whatever glass or cup they held.

f.f. cautioned me beforehand about Suzanne, her inclination toward fabrication. 'She has a connoisseur's fondness for untruths' was his phrase. So I decided to put her veracity to the test. Revealing I was twenty-seven, hoping to find female friends my age, I asked, "How old are you Suzanne?"

"Twenty-six."

A fib the nineteen-year-old rattled off as easy as her name. But I persevered, thinking more of my truth might beget truth from Suzanne. Aware of her early life as a laundress, I shared a part of my own past. "Before settling in Paris I was a laundress."

Without any hint of acknowledgement, she smiled. "You don't say?"

I thought of those backwater girls who gladly enter the bohemian life in Paris, eschewing class distinctions, while pretending to be of better stock. For irony, I buttered more of my past. "Apprenticed to the best laundress in Marseilles." She raised her heavy eyebrows inquiringly until I added, "My mother."

She laughed. "Modelling is easier than those bygone days of washing someone else's dirty bloomers. And I love posing naked."

"You must have a body to envy," I remarked.

She let out a more raucous laugh. "I'll show it to you sometime and you be the judge."

Her almost greedy willingness to express her sensual feelings now made my subterfuge, at best, petty. If I really wanted to enlist her help in getting to Degas, then she should know the entire story. "Suzanne, this meeting has been no accident." I then confessed my plan, more my hope, to acquire the Sphinx painting for a client. "Degas owns a version and if I can convince him to sell... well, I stand to earn a sizeable commission."

She laughed so loud many at the Auberge stared with the hope of learning the joke. Even her Maltese pup, *Lop-Lop*, gave Suzanne a look of inquiry before nestling more comfortably in the folds of her mistress's coat.

She gave me a knowing eye. "So! You are less the art lover and more the businesswoman."

"But I do love art," I defended. "And to meet such an accomplished artist as Degas would be a privilege."

"I suppose this is where I fit into the scheme." Those beautiful, dark eyebrows of hers arched.

I could only look down at the table, play with the empty glass, and hope she wouldn't send me packing. She fished into her handbag to take out a packet of cigarettes. Watching Suzanne Valadon smoke a cigarette was a pleasurable experience, the knowing grace as her head dipped back, closing her eyes, parting her lips, gliding in the cigarette with two fingers, inhaling smoothly, and letting the smoke roll out through pursed lips.

"May I join you?" I asked.

She slid over the box, a brand I had not seen before: the large head of a solemn black cat was embossed on the packet; beneath the cat, it said 'Virginia Cigarettes, Matured Tobacco'. "They're packaged in England," she said. "I get them from Renoir who gets them from a source he refuses to reveal."

Renoir. I complimented her, lighting up a Black Cat. "Everyone agrees, 'Suzanne Valadon knows her way around.'"

She leaned down and inexplicably blew smoke at her dog. "Lop-Lop loves 'Black Cats,'" she said as the little Maltese jumped gingerly into my lap, gazing up with canine adoration, and waiting for more smoke.

Amidst the coiling and drifting plumes of smoke, Lop-Lop, Suzanne and I were almost ridiculously content. She ordered two more peppermint liqueurs, soon admitting that she wanted nothing more than to be a painter herself. "Started when I was nine, drawing pictures on the sidewalk with bits of stolen coal."

"How are you progressing?" I asked.

"Oh, I'm drawing like a maniac these days. Mind you, not to make beautiful pictures to be framed, but to do a good drawing, one or two, that capture an instant of life, and declares its intensity." She showed the sketch that she had done of me. "I was attracted to your face because the contours are already so firmly etched which allowed me to emphasize the line."

My cheekbones looked high and severe. I supposed they were. But she outlined my profile very thickly. "Drawn, like cloisonné," I remarked.

"Some of the students at Cormon's are experimenting with the technique. I would break a leg to study there; but it's out of the question. The boys would only persuade me to take my clothes off and pose for them."

"Couldn't you receive instructions from the artists for whom you pose?"

"They would just laugh in my face. And Renoir would laugh the loudest."

"And Degas?"

She eyed me more closely. "I thought about it." She dipped her little finger in the liqueur glass and sucked on it. "But so far, I haven't found the courage to broach the subject. He enjoys my visits because I regale him with the latest gossip."

Our desires, we soon realized, might very well coincide. Then and there at the *Auberge du Clos* we hatched a plan for both of us to achieve our aim.

Before parting, Suzanne insisted on paying my bill and telling a truth, "I'm nineteen. Hope you don't mind."

"It's best for you to meet him, as if by accident," Suzanne decided. "Now Degas is an opera nut, a season ticket holder, and I'm dead certain he'll attend the premier performance of *Sigurd*." The pure and simple plan was for me to bump into him during intermission. "Don't bump too hard," she joked, "for Monsieur Degas is a fragile sort."

I had nothing suitable to wear for such an elegant event, but Suzanne gave assurances we could "fancy ourselves up" for the occasion and "turn a few necks." She had inherited a wide assortment of clothes and costumes from the artists who dressed her in many imaginary guises. So coupled with Suzanne's tailoring skills from her time as a seamstress, she fitted me in an organdie dress of eye-catching stripes, the hem line trimmed in a full inch of fox fur, and my waist cinctured rather tightly with a black satin ribbon I thought too audaciously wide but which she insisted would accentuate a slender waist such as mine.

The fact was that Suzanne and I were markedly different in appearance. I loomed tall even in bare feet, with an angular figure I thought off-putting to men. Suzanne was blessed with what men called a strapping figure. Although barely five feet there was nothing diminutive about her. She had an innate robustness, a way of carrying herself with confidence. I came to call it her "tall confidence."

As women, we were needlessly critical of our own physical deficiencies. She thought her shoulders too rounded while mine she deemed magnificently broad. I praised her unblemished complexion while harbouring a lifelong regret for the tiny islands of pockmarks on my cheeks. I could not compliment her enough. "You possess perfect, ivory skin," I said, "from head to toe."

She thanked me with a toothy smile and admitted, "Renoir seems to think so."

A Renoir model, I thought, *an honour indeed!*

Preparing for our debut at the opera, I took charge of fixing our hair, sweeping Suzanne's dark brown hair upward with a modest pompadour and little sideburn curls. I piled my hair high and made deep folds with the use of several ancient Egyptian combs that belonged to my sister.

After almost a week of dress-up and making ourselves over, I did wonder if we were being too extravagant, too ostentatious, but Suzanne beside me in the mirror was always ready to remind, "It's all a lark!"

Repeatedly dressing and undressing before each other, we grew very familiar with each other's nakedness. At first I was somewhat flustered whenever she caught me gawking at her naked figure. It came as a surprise that a woman's thighs and buttocks could be so generously ample and still be firm. I guessed her training as a trapeze artist had earned Suzanne such muscular grace.

On the night of the opera, climbing the wide marble stairs to our loge seats, we felt wonderfully flamboyant, like two exotic princesses. Suzanne had made a corsage for herself out of fresh grapes. I settled for fake pearls. We both wore white, low-heeled shoes with sequinned stars pasted on the front. A gentleman friend of Suzanne's purchased our loge tickets and also donated a pair of opera glasses so that we could keep close watch on Degas's subscription loge on the opposite side of the packed theatre. During the entire performance Degas' loge remained disappointingly vacant. Days later we learned that he was vacationing in Naples.

The opera, my first, was an epic spectacle set in the 5th century with kings and Nordic heroes wearing impressive helmets crowned with dragon wings. The music meandered hour after hour, either lugubrious strings or horns blaring bombastic crescendos. We endured the tragic conclusion, Sigurd and Brunehilde atop a funeral pyre of lively paper flames, singing their lungs out. Soon their ascending sprits, made of more papier-mâché and wires, were pulled up by barely hidden stagehands.

We left, low-spirited, and decided to take a late night walk along the Seine to forget our missed opportunity. Still dressed like princesses, albeit with her greengrocer grapes and my fake pearls, we strolled in our star pasted slippers under a canopy of faraway, twinkling stars. We had no direction in mind. Breathing in the peacefulness of the night seemed to bring us closer together. There were thirty odd bridges along the Seine which connected the two banks of Paris. We passed beneath one bridge then another when, gradually and without effort, the secrets slipped from us. Perhaps the many days of exposing our naked bodies to one another paved the way to the nakedness of our personal lives.

I shared with Suzanne my ambition to meet all the Impressionists for I was so enamoured with their paintings. I told her of my bungled relationship with Cezanne, of my new, Platonic relationships with Sigmund Freud and Félix Fénéon. She shared what she knew of Degas, how he loved to study women, delighted in their company, be they tyro dancers in the opera or hardened harlots in the Paris brothels, enjoying whatever they had to say, and always quick to flatter them.

Now Renoir, she declared, was a curious contrast to Degas. Rennie's attitude to women was altogether different. (Rennie was what she called Renoir.) "Rennie depicts us at our seductive best, but gets not a bit of pleasure in conversing or listening to what we value."

"It would be an incredible experience to meet Renoir," I remarked.

"You shall, Julie. I'll introduce you to all my painter friends," she promised, "and sooner than later!"

The hours drifted like the river to our left. We let the important moments of our lives pass idly between us. Laughing at the disasters, mocking the hardships, we knew that we were two women who intended to survive, no matter the obstacles.

At the river's edge, Suzanne began picking up stones and skipping them across the water. She gave up the secret of a son, Maurice—"He's three and my mother takes more care of him than me. Hardly anyone knows I have a kid, the artists especially. Bad for my business, you understand." A bitterness crept into her voice. "There are my assigned roles to play for the painter boys." She laughed at the silliness. "And you can bet a sou they have no desire to paint their Suzanne as a damn Madonna."

She gave no hint as to the identity of Maurice's father, nor did I ask. She looked for flatter stones to increase the number of her skips. I picked up a stone, wanting to compete, threw it as hard as I could but the stone splashed once and sunk.

I gave up some truth about my sister. "She's not unlike some of the lost girls at the Salpêtrière where I work."

Suzanne stayed stooped on the shore, seemingly deciding which stone looked flattest. "How terrible it must be for you. Where is she?"

"She stays at the Charenton Asylum in Marseilles," I said. "I work at the Salpêtrière because of Dr. Charcot, to stay in his proximity, for he's the only doctor boldly experimenting to find a cure for illnesses like Grande Hysteria. When he finds the cure, as he will, I'll be there, then his success can be transferred to other asylums, to my sister, Alexandria." Hearing my own optimism, I wondered: *Do I try too hard to convince myself that all will turn out rosy? All the wrong, in the course of time, made right?*

"You'll be there when it happens, I'd bet a beer on it." She stood up, handing me a flat and smooth stone. "Try this one."

Skipping it again across the river's surface, I counted one more skip than hers. She and I walked farther along the shoreline until we reached the Pont Carousel. Underneath the bridge were empty bottles of all kinds, mostly discarded by drunks and opium addicts. We began to set sail to some in the water, watching how long they would float. Most invariably filled with water and sank, but two of the bottles, tipping slightly, trapping sufficient air, stayed buoyed, the current sending them down the Seine to points unknown. Proud of the successful launch, we agreed that our reward should be bottles filled with beer.

In our star sprinkled shoes we strode toward Montmartre, Suzanne declaring that she was desperate for: "Gay music! Guitars! And accordions, if you please!"

I hurried to keep up with her. A friendship, I thought, sealed with our secrets.

Chapter 31

Couldn't I find a good little wife, simple and quiet,
who understands my oddities of mind,
and with whom I might spend a modest working life!
Isn't that a lovely dream?

Edgar Degas

THE TERRIBLE DEGAS

I

Félix Fénéon steeped me in the work of Degas when learning that I might actually meet the artist. He took me to galleries where his pictures were on display. The consensus of the gallery dealers was that among the Impressionists, "Only Degas sells consistently."

We spent the most time at the Durand-Ruel Gallery on *rue des Petits Champs* which had an abundance of Degas' dancers to admire. I was drawn to the strangely beautiful colours he infused in his pastels. His ballerinas on stage, dreamily illuminated in gaseous light from unseen footlights, bowed and spun in muslin dresses which were a diaphanous blur of purple, plum, and pink pastels.

f.f. helped me see that Degas had the surest touch of modernity. His dancers were not idealized. Degas caught them in rehearsals, a spy to their prosaic moments, the not-so-graceful yawn, the smoothing of a wrinkled stocking, or a girl's ungainly bend to lace a slipper. Degas' viewpoints were also ingeniously unique. He had you peering up at the stage from the deep bowels of the orchestra pit or gazing down at the dancers from the airiest height of a box loge.

"Appreciate him," f.f. advised, "for his daring croppings. This artist has no qualms in slicing a woman in half if it gives a dynamic boost to a composition. Be on guard when you meet such a dissecting mind. I would prefer you in one whole piece."

Ha! f.f. the solemn jokester.

* * *

Suzanne Valadon and I stood before Degas's front door on rue Fontaine, she making last minute adjustments to her hat. Suzanne wore a wide, soft brim hat which she re-pinned precariously at the back of her head. She wanted to show off her hair which, parted at the middle, fell in lovely, auburn waves around her face. The felt bonnet she had created for me had a stiff curled brim with a trailing tail of tulle. I thought it too severe, something for a Victorian lady to wear when horseback riding. She saw me looking grim and nervous so she turned me around and tied the tail into a flower like bow. "He will like the combination of English prim and pretty ballerina tulle."

"Suzanne, please let me thank you beforehand for this opportunity. I only hope he won't consider me a bothersome nuisance." I was on edge, for Degas was known for his cantankerous nature. I was beginning to feel unsure as to my true motives for wanting this meeting.

Suzanne reassured me: "Monsieur Degas would never turn a woman away from his door."

But the very idea of me bartering with Edgar Degas for the purchase of an Ingres painting now seemed absurd. The goal of gaining a semblance of financial security no longer seemed a compelling reason to finagle my way into the house of such an eminent artist.

Before Suzanne could raise the door knocker, I had to ask, "Are you having 'relations' with him?"

Her dark blue eyes widened. "With Monsieur Degas?" She burst into laughter. "Heaven to purgatory, no! But what an interesting experience that might be! No, never! Not even the tiniest kiss. Monsieur Degas chooses to play the eunuch with all women, be they models or prostitutes; his way, I think, to keep us devoted to him. Safe to label him a confirmed bachelor and leave it at that." Raising the handle of the door knocker, she added cryptically, "And don't remove your gloves for awhile. It will add the needed mystery to your hands."

Before Suzanne could even bang down on the knocker, the door swung open, and we were confronted by a middle-aged man.

He had a trimmed, brownish beard, moustache and side whiskers speckled with gray. The receding hairline gave his forehead an intelligent prominence. The smile he offered seemed an experiment, a hope to look hospitable, and not the terrible Degas whose acidic barbs were known to bring people to despair.

He acknowledged my presence with a mild nod then stared sternly at Suzanne. "So, my imp, have you somehow managed to tear yourself away from Renoir to honour me with a visit?" It was a mock rebuke, for one could tell that he was glad to see her.

She regarded him with genuine affection and happily introduced me. "My newest, bestest friend, Julie Forette."

Politely nodding again, he turned to Suzanne, asking with some suspicion as he looked around her. "Now Suzanne, you haven't brought along that pesky dog of yours because I've warned you..." Degas did not tolerate dogs or cats.

"Lop-Lop stays with ma-ma," she reassured him.

"Splendid! Then we shall all luncheon at *la Maison Dorée!*"

His firm pronouncement delighted her. "Oh, the Dorée will be a scrumptious treat!"

He snatched a homburg from the foyer table and picked one of many walking sticks from a large Chinese urn. "Let our caravan begin!"

He urged us down the front steps and took a gentlemanly position on the far side of the sidewalk. I was finding it remarkable, being escorted to the most fashionable restaurant in the city by Edgar Degas, the most respected of the Impressionist painters.

Suzanne walked in a carefree manner, swinging her closed parasol, ignoring the admiring glances of the men who slowed as they passed. She kept looking up at the sky. "Oh, such a lovely day, Monsieur Degas, a sky so blue I yearn to swim in it and clouds so delicious I wish to devour them!"

"Save your appetite for the fried gudgeon at the Maison Dorée," quipped Degas. "It's decent enough."

She went on, undeterred, "One certainly understands why the Impressionists enjoy painting outdoors. Yet it makes me wonder, Monsieur Degas, why you seem to lack all desire to paint *en plein air*. Don't you think it advantageous to capture those scudding clouds?"

"No, I do not," he replied with gruff finality.

I noted the mushroom pallor of his skin, guessing he spent precious little time in sunlight, not then aware a serious eye condition made harsh sunlight painful for him to bear.

Suzanne, keeping to the custom of expressing her feelings, came to halt. "But this moment!" For effect she dropped her parasol to the sidewalk, as though a needless encumbrance, and lifted her arms in an embrace of the passing clouds. "It's inspirational! If I were an artist I should capture the clouds and sky before my spontaneous emotion faded into oblivion."

He walked faster, showing no sign of having heard, much less appreciated, her artistic opinions. I picked up and dusted off the pink parasol—Suzanne had crocheted the blue lace edge herself. Degas turned a corner and we ran to catch up.

Inside the Maison Dorée he told the maître d' exactly which table he wanted, then he had us placed in the direct light while he sat with his back to the window. "Now, Suzanne Valadon," he chided, "why do you insist on a chaperone?" He targeted a glance at me and arched an eyebrow at Suzanne. "Are you fearful that I will seduce you?"

She giggled. "*Au contraire*, Monsieur Degas, *au contraire*; there is no fear on this side of the table."

The flirtatious exchange was familiar fun for them. Throughout our afternoon luncheon, I detected their playful, underlying theme of 'Eunuch and Harem Slave Girl."

When a momentary lull came in their banter, I spoke: "Monsieur Degas, this meeting was my idea."

A half-truth, as Suzanne had brought her own agenda: a hope—if she gathered the courage—to declare her dream of becoming an artist. Degas, however, showed no interest in my reason for meeting him; he took charge of our menu: for the first course, sheep's trotters, followed by fried gudgeon, then choosing sausage with mashed potatoes, giving the Dorée credit for "admirable potatoes." He also ordered a side dish of gherkins, insisting the waiter bring them "in a garden pool of vinegar."

I was lunching, awe-struck, not only with a stellar artist but a grand gourmand.

While settling in with our aperitifs, three white Dubonnets, Degas chose to enlighten Suzanne on the questions she posed on the street. "Of inspiration, spontaneity, temperament, I know nothing," he said, strangely taking out a well pressed handkerchief from his breast pocket, placing it centre table, then, arousing more curiosity, crumpled the handkerchief and set it into a beam of light. We stared at what might have been a spontaneous sculpture.

He placed the crumpled handkerchief in the flat palm of his hand, observing from different angles. "Here is what I do when I want to draw a cloud."

Ah, I thought, *Suzanne's first lesson in painting just might have occurred.*

She realized as much, suddenly pleading her case: above all else she wanted to learn how to paint! Would he be willing to guide her, offer advice from time to time? Her impassioned plea concluded, she waited in trepidation for the response. I, too, waited. Would she receive a condescending *No*. Or worse, mockery?

He carefully refolded the handkerchief into his breast pocket. "Since I've revealed a painting secret of mine, I might impart a few more tidbits, at least as I perceive painting. The work I produce, Suzanne, is the result of reflection and laborious study–and yes, some sprinkling of imagination; but it has nothing to do with running over hill and dale, shirttails hanging out, trying to catch a fleeing cloud with a dripping paintbrush."

When the first course arrived, he was speaking of his early development, the important influence of the artist Jean-Auguste-Dominique Ingres. I perked up. He praised Ingres' superb draughtmanship.

Has the moment arrived to bring up Charcot's offer to purchase his Ingres painting?

But I put the question aside and decided to sup in silence. The trotters were served in a broth, so I removed a glove to pick up a spoon.

"Mademoiselle," he interrupted. "Please remove the other glove for I must study your hands." As I complied, he turned them one way then another. "Interesting, interesting." He concentrated on my hands for a full minute. "Now, eat your trotters."

When the gudgeon arrived, he spoke more of Ingres. "He was an artist who found hands so fascinating that he devoted an entire life to drawing them properly, down to fingernails!"

The meal proved to be a gourmet delight and Degas was much pleased to discover that I, too, shared his passion for well vinegared pickles.

When at last the bill arrived, he generously paid then asked Suzanne brusquely. "Now, are you ready for a real lesson?"

Her smile was wide. "You bet!"

As we all rose, I watched her deftly slip two of Maison Dorée's exotic oranges into her purse.

When Degas included me in his invitation to return to 19 Rue Fontaine, I could barely conceal my excitement. Yet, while walking back to his apartments, f.f.'s final advice haunted me: "Degas has no pressing need for money. The chances of him selling for profit are practically nil. But...stay attuned, alert, there is no better art collection in Paris than that amassed by Edgar Degas. He is a wise collector, and if you wish to be the same, get to see, by hook or crook, the treasures he keeps under lock and key on the third floor."

Degas' apartment was situated on the southern fringe of Montmartre where he occupied at great rental expense four entire floors. He took us directly to the second floor where he received visitors. Before he could even insert his key, a no-nonsense looking maid, he called Zoe, opened the door. We were shown into one of two sitting rooms, furnished in an old-fashioned, somewhat genteel style. The walls were densely hung with pictures, and there were glass cabinets filled with sculptures, displays of Japanese books, and piles of lithographs. It made what was a large room feel very cramped. I almost ran to the painting which held the prominent space above the mantle—the Ingres which I now suspected was worth a small fortune.

"A recent procurement," he said, proudly. "Oedipus confronts the dreaded Sphinx."

It, indeed, showed the crucial moment when Oedipus, after unknowingly having slain his father, faces the Sphinx and ponders her riddle. A wrong answer means certain death for Oedipus. The gruesome human bones littering the floor of the Sphinx's lair show the fate of those who failed to solve the riddle. Yet Oedipus, in the bloom of manhood, superbly naked, leans a foot upon a boulder and displays a lack of fear; he thrusts a scolding finger at her terrifying countenance, armed, he knows, with the correct answer. As I considered Oedipus's fate and future, the abominable marriage to his mother and the self-gouging of his eyes, the maid returned sullenly with tea, setting the service on a table in front of Suzanne who spoke admiringly of the naked Oedipus:

"The body is handsomely drawn. Such a muscular fellow would do well as a circus acrobat."

I decided to jump into the waters of art commerce. "Would you be willing to sell?" I asked Degas. "I have a buyer."

"Who might that be?" he asked with a look of amusement.

"My employer, Dr. Jean-Martin Charcot."

"Ah, the famous neurologist and hypnotist. At one of his Friday lectures, I watched him hypnotize a young woman. Quite interesting. To prove she was oblivious to pain, he borrowed a hat pin, pierced his subject's palm clean through; no blood whatsoever issued from the hand. Most remarkable."

"Mind over matter," noted Suzanne.

"How much is your employer willing to pay?" Degas asked.

"25,000 francs."

"Ah, he might be able to buy a Gérome or a Cabanal for that price, but an Ingres such as this? Hardly." Degas turned to Suzanne. "Ingres has taught me more about drawing than any other artist."

"Dr. Charcot might pay more," I said.

"A more appropriate price would be 50,000 francs. Would he pay such an amount?"

"He might be persuaded," I said, suddenly realizing that I could possibly earn a ten per cent commission of 5,000 francs. The money gained from such a transaction, I calculated quickly, would amount to nearly two years of service at the Salpêtrière. The prospect of such a financial boon had my heart racing.

"The painting is not for sale, at any price," he said abruptly.

f.f. was right, Degas cared little for the world of profit and loss. Had he been cruelly teasing me?

"I would not want the painting," volunteered Suzanne. "It makes me shudder. The Sphinx could easily tear his flesh to pieces as she has obviously done to others. Ugh! Do you see that skull and leg bone near the entrance to the cave?"

"Yet the proudly naked Oedipus shows no fear," Degas noted. "A crown and a kingship await him."

"Poor Oedipus," Suzanne remarked. "He will then unknowingly sleep with his own mother."

Degas sighed. "I admit that the scene evokes, with our foreknowledge, a certain dread... perhaps that's what holds me captive," added Degas. He put down his teacup, joined me in front of the Oedipus painting. "Not a day goes by that I do not spend a few minutes with my Ingres. What he depicts is a reminder of our own ignorance as to the workings of fate. There are tragedies, in one form or another, which inevitably wait in the wings for all of us."

Suzanne frowned. "Oh, Monsieur Degas, you're taking such a morbid turn."

Degas looked at her. "Such reminders of life's uncertainties keep us on our toes."

I wondered if Suzanne was remembering her own catastrophic fall from the trapeze bar which put an end to her circus career. And the slight limp she so well concealed.

She focused on bringing Degas back to the art of painting. "That far away town in the background gives the painting a wonderful sense of space and depth."

Degas eagerly agreed. "Yes, a tad of Leonardo's blue *sfumatto* in the far horizon."

Suzanne gazed with admiration. "Ah, what many rare paints and exquisite brushes one must need to execute such delicacy."

"Nonsense!" Degas responded, irritably. "Give me three old wooden paintbrushes and a can of green pea soup and I will have enough material to paint all the landscapes in the world! The only pre-requisite is..." he wagged a finger at her, similar to the way Oedipus pointed at the Sphinx, "concentration!"

"And talent!" added Suzanne.

"Concentration and ample reflection," he corrected her. "Come, let's begin our lesson," he said. "We will employ Mademoiselle Forette as our model. I want you to quietly observe her face, then you and I, without the presence of Mademoiselle Forette, shall go upstairs to my studio where you will draw her from memory."

"But you must first give me pencil and paper to make at least a rough sketch of her!" pleaded Suzanne.

"No." He remained adamant. "It's all very well to copy what you see, but far more instructive to draw Mademoiselle Forette from memory. What we want, Suzanne, is for your memory to collaborate with your imagination. We want to teach you to free yourself from the tyranny of mimicking nature. Come, you have looked at her long enough. Let us proceed to the fourth floor." He turned to me. "You will not be bored alone?"

"Certainly not—there is so much in your collection to gaze upon, and solitude frees me from the tyranny of others' opinions."

"If you wish more tea and Zoe's delicious raisin cakes, pull the bell cord. And..." he ended on a playful note, "I trust you will not abscond with my Oedipus?"

I answered him with a silent smile as he and Suzanne departed for their lesson.

It surprised me to see no works by the Impressionists, his closest colleagues. No Monets, no Renoirs, no Pissarros—at least none on view. The paintings displayed were primarily from the early and the mid-century, the artists now established in the public's eye as "Masters." Walking back and forth between the two visitor rooms, I began to perceive patterns. Degas selected the masters from whom the Impressionists had learned: the feathery blur of Corot, the heavy dollops of Courbet, the complementary colouring of Delacroix. Such paintings, I sighed, would fetch very high prices if he wished to sell to interested connoisseurs; only now, I knew that Degas had not the least concern for money, much less the desire to profit from his distinguished collection.

Having exhausted all of the artwork visible, I longed to see the 'treasures' that f.f. insisted occupied the third floor—more provocative art only a privileged few ever saw. My bane, imprudent curiosity, prompted me to investigate where Degas' protective maid spent her time when not needed. Passing through the kitchen quarters, I guessed her private room lay beyond a quaint, Italian tiled archway. Removing my shoes, I tiptoed to a door and listened. The sound of light snoring encouraged the belief that Mlle. Zoe was taking a cat nap.

Hurriedly I left and crept up the stairs to the third floor. Dismayed by the locked door, I guessed Degas had the key, and his Zoe probably a duplicate, but there might be a third, stored somewhere for emergency use. Judging by the keyhole, the key had to be large. In stockinged feet I hurried back downstairs, searching through cupboards, cabinets, drawers, and any containers large enough for the key. I had no luck until I noticed on the mantle, on either side of the Oedipus painting, silver matchstick cups. One had matchsticks protruding, one had none. I turned over the cup without matches and out came a cast-iron key.

Returning to the third floor, the key went in snugly, unlocked the door, and I found myself in a room crammed with hundreds and hundreds of paintings which decorated the walls and were perched upon a dense forest of easels. Degas' hidden collection! I took mental notes, examining them, methodically looking for elements attractive to a connoisseur—**the** connoisseur I kept telling myself that I would become. It was no surprise to find several superb Ingres paintings and several drawings Ingres made just of hands. There were many contemporary artists who were unfamiliar but showed merit. He also possessed a Tiepolo and a spellbinding El Greco of a saint writing at a silk covered desk which was a tour-de-force of texture. In much of the works Degas chose, he seemed to appreciate those who modelled textures through unique uses of light and dark. Then the shock came, the Cezannes! I found three undated landscapes, and one still life of apples from 1875. Degas collected Cezannes! Now I realized that Père Tanguy's rhapsodic claims for Cezanne were not exaggerations—the Impressionists sought his work. Cezanne was the painter's painter. I was more than pleased. Here was vindication that I too might have a perceptive eye, that it was not ruinous folly to pursue art——to collect. Elated, I allotted as much time as I dared with the three views of Cezanne's beloved Mt. St. Victoire mountain, bathed in different aspects of light, his mysterious blocks of stone that stored a kind of translucent fire. *My Mt. St. Victoire is equal to these,* I thought. *Ha! My connoisseur collection of one painting, so far.*

When it seemed unwise to stay a minute longer, I turned to leave, only to notice in a far corner a bathtub. Draped over the bevelled edge of the zinc tub was a frayed, woman's bathrobe, and farther behind, a dark panelled mahogany door. How did I know the door led to Degas' bedchamber?

I approached as far as the bathtub which was coated with a thin layer of dust, seemingly never have been filled with water—an artist's prop, I assumed. Picking up the robe, it was far too small for me. For a child, perhaps. Staring at the door, I considered the temptation to enter. If Degas' bedroom, what art might a masterful artist choose for his personal abode? The door latch, when I pressed down, proved to be unlocked.

Was I to commit a much more egregious breach of social etiquette? Enter and get caught? When would the maid awaken and find me missing? Suzanne once mentioned that two places were denied the maid Zoe's dust cloth and broom, the painting studio and Degas' bedchamber. I then heard voices faintly from the floor above. The painting lesson in Degas' studio was still in progress. Quickly I went inside and closed the door behind me.

Engulfed in darkness, nothing was visible, nothing, not even my own hand. I could not believe a room so dark. And the air! A thickness, stale, stagnant. I found it difficult to breathe. Trying to overcome a feeling of faintness, I stepped cautiously, putting out my hands, groping blindly in the dark until I ensnared myself into what must have been curtains. I struggled with the heavy folds and with much effort managed to pull the curtains aside. The material was thick damask, sewn into a double layer, effectively sealing out all light. The window, made of glass blocks usually installed for factories, made it impossible to open for fresh air, and what light that penetrated was scant. Slowly my eyes began to adapt to the semi-darkness, the dim outline of a bed. I sat on the edge. A bed to accommodate one person.

The room, by degrees, showed itself to be disappointingly drab. Walls, painted a moss green, matched the colour of the curtains. A lonely colour, monotonously repeated in the bed coverlet. The room was unbelievably devoid of any art but for one Japanese wood-block print, framed in ebony, above his bed. An erotic picture. Several scantily clothed courtesans lounged in a bathhouse.

I thought it extremely odd that Degas chose to keep his private sleeping quarters purposefully Spartan, unadorned, leaving the dazzling art collection outside. The sadness here was palpable.

What manner of nighttime dreams unfolded for him when he slept in this room? Would I dare, ever, to ask Degas for a dream?

Perched on the edge of his bed, an anxiety began to rise through me, a gradual feeling that I might not be alone in the dark gloom. Apprehensive, I peered more closely into the corners where the shadows fell thickest. Where, so it seemed, a figure eerily began to take shape. Was I seeing a girl?

She stood very still within the veil of shadows, but I was convinced a young girl—for whatever reason—hoped to remain unnoticed. Too shy? Or too afraid to emerge? A terrible suspicion took hold that I had discovered Degas' well-kept secret. The lonely man's paramour. He concealed her from the outside world, a shy creature, perhaps too young even for the Parisian brothels. A child. I began to ridiculously imagine that Degas had bartered for her, like a painting, taken her from a procuress' care. Remarkably, she appeared to be in costume.

"Hello..." I spoke out a warm greeting, rising slowly so as not to frightened her. "Won't you, please, come forward?"

My eyesight sharpened. She wore pink leggings and a flared skirt made of tulle—a ballerina hiding? Then I realized my utter foolishness. She was a Degas sculpture, near life-size, formed out of red wax.

I recognized her. Suzanne mentioned the notorious "Fourteen Year Old Dancer" which Degas had presented in the 6th Impressionist Show. His first sculpture to be publicly displayed, the critics declared it an unmitigated disaster. To render a young girl realistically and to clothe her in an authentic ballet costume was something no one had seen before. Everyone reacted with strange hostility.

I approached her. Here in a musty corner of his bachelor chamber was where Degas had posited his little ballerina. At least here, I guessed, he could keep her safe from further scorn and derision. I walked around her, admiring how Degas had sculpted her in such realistic detail. She stood as high as my bosom, her head lifted, her chin proudly jutting, with arms and entwined hands stretched behind her. Dressing a sculpture in an actual ballet costume was an audacious gesture on Degas' part. But the intervening years had taken their toll. Sadly, her pink stockings and linen bodice were now faded, having turned to a miserable gray.

I thought of the gray in Degas's beard, of people and things turning old. I wondered what emotions Degas, bereft of wife and children, experienced when he first dressed his fourteen-year-old? What were his feelings when he knelt to slip up the stockings and place the pink ballet slippers on her feet? And when he rose to wrap the green sash about her waist, and tie the ribbon around the ponytail of her hair, did he do so as a proud parent?

The pose his adolescent ballerina struck was pure effrontery, her shoulders thrown back and arms stretched behind her as she locked her hands, raising her head slightly, thrusting out that narrow chin in a gesture of spunk. He must have seen a plucky girl like this when he haunted the dance schools, she one of many determined to gain a dancing position at the Opera. The particular expression put into the girl's face began to affect me deeply. She showed an adolescent obstinacy. A mirror to my own adolescence in Marseilles. The anger and resolve to escape the narrow confines of a working-class life.

But it was so disheartening to see the dancer's costume deteriorating, the silk of the bodice wearing thin. And barely touching the tulle, it crumbled between my fingers. I began to feel blue and doubtful. Would my own hopes crumble like the dancer's tulle? Was it foolishness to think I could find work and dignity outside the confines of the Salpêtrière? That I would somehow immerse myself in the world of art and write about art as Fénéon suggested? And this burgeoning desire of mine to collect art, without financial resources, was it not pure madness?

A flash of light from the opening door suddenly blinded me.

III

A slender shadow, like an accusing spectre, stood outlined against the light. I felt caught, a violator, and fled from the ballerina, stumbling against the bed, sitting myself down, guilt ridden.

He came forward. "I see that you have found her."

Absent in Degas' voice was the wrath I expected to rain down. He merely sat beside me as if accustomed to audacious intruders.

"Marie was her name," he said.

How to frame an apology for the intrusion into the sanctum of another's bedroom? Impossible. Yet, Degas's matter-of-fact tone might be an invitation to pretend no transgression had been committed. I gambled, "Suzanne told me about your much maligned ballerina. I searched for articles written about the incident."

"Then you know my little gutter snipe did not receive a pretty welcome at the Exhibition on the boulevard des Capucines. I can still feel the wounds to this day. The critics were merciless."

"The sculpture is extraordinarily naturalistic."

"And they jeered at that very fact. 'Monsieur Degas has thrown away his talent,' was the unanimous judgement. 'How could he create such an odious female? Why, her body, they complained, has none of the grace of ancient Greece.' One critic went so far as to insist the loathsome creature should be mounted in a museum of zoology."

While he gazed gravely at the ballerina, I reminded him of a favourable critique, "Huysmans said, 'Here is the first attempt by any artist to do something really modern in sculpture.'"

"Unfortunately, all the others thought poor Degas had lost his wits."

Together we sat, not taking our eyes off of the fourteen-year-old dancer.

"Was she your first sculpture, Monsieur Degas?"

"The first in a public exhibition... most likely the last," he added wearily. Rising, Degas walked to his little Marie; he touched the ribbon in her hair, lost in thought.

"What was she like?" I asked.

"The real Marie?" He pondered the question then grunted, "Just one of the many 'student rats.' You know, those skinny kids who prowled the Opera House... pug-nosed ragamuffins, ambitious to escape the slums, carrying with them their dreams of pirouetting upon the stage... to bloom like a flower under the spotlights and become one of the darlings of ballet." Degas gave the faintest smile.

I saw the sadness latent in his grey eyes, borne of too much reflection. I risked another offence, "People say that Degas has no heart for women, that he paints only hardened harlots and faceless dancers."

I held my breath. He took to staring fondly at little Marie. "They know not that the dancers have taken my heart... sewn it into a purse of pink, faded satin."

Again I risked being thrown out of his house. "And the predominance of prostitutes in your work? They say yours is an unhealthy obsession."

His look turned fierce. Before I could apologize, his expression softened. A glint of knowing came into his eyes. "Our Suzanne, who can be nothing but guileless, spilled some beans about Mademoiselle and... ***her** obsession with the obsessions of others.*"

"I stand rightly accused."

He went to the door. "Come this way, Mademoiselle Forette."

Unsure, I followed, led back through the paintings I had studied.

"Have you enjoyed my private collection?" A sardonic question as his hand opened for the stolen key. Contrite, I returned it. He nodded, "Apparently your passion for art makes you reckless."

"So it seems."

"Then you shall see Degas's more personal collection."

Led into an unnoticed passageway, I was speechless. The walls on both sides were lined with monotypes, more accurately, a long enfilade of etchings. Slowly Degas escorted me. All of the etchings were of nudes, each unmistakably a prostitute. I felt I was being given a tour of Edgar Degas's hidden seraglio. I could not deny the thrill of privilege. The women on the walls were drawn in pen and the blackest of ink. Some images were harshly stained, some splattered with ink. Yet Degas had astonishingly, with a minimum of rapid strokes, conjured each prostitute's worn-out body, and with a few lines brought their ribald gestures achingly to life.

I was enthralled. "Monsieur Degas, such economy! And yet their exhausted bodies are graphically expressed. Very Japanese."

"Without the grace of the geishas you most likely saw above my bed." A welcoming lightheartedness limned the remark.

"I suppose our Paris whores," I replied in kind, "have been more roughly raised."

"You would be astounded, Mademoiselle Forette, how many of these rough whores behave like little girls when their clients have departed the premises and I am left alone with them. They sometimes invite me to their rooms, and I see what many have brought with them from the provinces, more often their childhood dolls. Naively, they cling to their precious childhood which, for some, was not so long ago."

A feminine voice suddenly floated down the corridor—

"Am I interrupting?"

Suzanne stood inquiringly at the entrance. Degas walked business-like toward her, plainly not wanting to share his seraglio with a third person. He took the drawing she held. I joined them as he examined her work. Eagerly Suzanne and I listened to his critique while he took us out of his private rooms.

"Sometimes you must do the same subject again and again, but under every conceivable condition and angle. Draw it ten, a hundred times if necessary."

"When do you stop?" Suzanne called out as he led us down the stairs.

He spoke over his shoulder. "Until your hand moves without premeditation, until your subject cries out to you, stop Mademoiselle Artiste! You have pinned me down as I am."

We were at the front door. Suzanne spoke. "I tried to do as you said, Monsieur Degas, to reproduce only what particularly struck me."

"Yes, yes, hone into the essentials." He looked at me then the drawing. "Some aspects of Mademoiselle Forette are here. "You hint of her resolute air. Commendable, commendable. But don't overwork your contours."

"But when you met Ingres, he told you 'Draw lines, young man, draw lines!'"

Degas met Ingres. I was surprised. Degas laughed. "Form cannot be achieved solely through the contour line."

The "resolute" jawline she captured had been emphasized with heavy, black conte crayon. More unflattering was the stare Suzanne bestowed upon me—very daunting, as if I were demanding too much of something from someone.

"What of my shadowing?" she asked him.

Her bold shadowing I liked. The pockmarks I owned were wonderfully subsumed in them. But Degas counselled otherwise: "Be respectful, circumspect, and shrewd with the power of light and shadow. It is not to be considered a superfluous addition. The modelling of light and shadow will be thought out—not to obscure but to reveal." He opened the front door. "Now your first lesson is over, off you ladies go."

Before he shooed us out, I asked, "Did she ever achieve her dream?"

"Who?" He looked baffled.

"Little Marie."

Surprise lit up his eyes. One could tell he was pleased that the student ballerina still occupied a place in my mind. "As a matter of fact, Mademoiselle Forette, our Marie did gain a position with the Opera."

I nodded. "I thought so. You showed her spunk."

Degas returned his attention to Suzanne: "I'm keeping this drawing, a keepsake to remind me: you are one of us, an artist."

Before we even had a moment to absorb the significance of the comment, he muttered that when she had drawn something new and to her satisfaction, to come back for another lesson, and then he retreated into his apartment and closed the door.

Suzanne took my hand and we walked briskly down the rue Fontaine, the smile she wore was, for want of a better word, blissful. I, admittedly, felt new confidence bubbling inside me.

After conversing with Degas, I was a little more certain about my path toward art. Above us the sky no longer held the debatable clouds. Now, just faultlessly blue. Suzanne, stretching out her arms, announced to anyone within earshot—"Today I have wings!"

Chapter 32

for appetizers, Garçon

i shall gobble tasty vowels

Entrée, Mademoiselle?

Oh Garcon, s'il vous plait,

a plate of heaping paragraphs

Does Mademoiselle dare dessert?

Garçon, Garçon

a semi-colon or two

shall do

Sabrine

Sabrine and Anna O

Sigmund and I now addressed each other by our first names. We met regularly at a café called the Tambourine, situated on the boulevard Clichy, in the heart of Montmartre. He and I had claimed a corner nook in the Bohemian haunt, noted for its easy acceptance of all manner of clients and eccentric behaviour. Those who frequented the café were a curious mix of Apache gangsters, penurious artists, and off-duty prostitutes. The only rules of conduct, set by the proprietress, Agostina Segatori, were: no knife-fights, no hair-pulling, and above all else, no damage to her tambourines or the student art decorating the walls.

I now laugh when recalling the night she first sauntered over to our table. La Segatori—which was how patrons respectfully addressed the formidable lady who once upon a time had been a model, an Italian beauty. She posed more often as a slave girl in Oriental harems or a kerchiefed peasant maiden waiting for love beside a village well. When we met la Segatori she was in her mid-forties, dressing in colourful gypsy skirts, with a figure somewhat thickened, and always carrying in her eyes a bit of melancholy.

Catching sight of Sigmund measuring eye drops of cocaine solution into the glasses of wine we ordered, she came to investigate. A cigarette dangled from the melancholy corner of her mouth and the many gold bracelets she wore jangled when she picked up the small, blue cobalt bottle. Unscrewing the eyedropper, she let a tiny drop fall on the tambourine table.

"*Mes amis.*" Her dark, wonderfully heavy eyebrows arched. "What have we here?"

"Cocaine hydrochloride." Sigmund took back the bottle and the eye dropper. "Which sharpens the mind, lifts the spirit, and makes one bold enough to shake a tambourine. Care to partake?"

"*Chacun aux goût.*" She spoke French with a strong Italian accent, gave his thick beard a roguish twist, and walked away. *Each to their own taste.* She returned to her personal tambourine table to hold sway over the evening crowd. Sigmund and I were free to seek our pleasures as we wished, la Segatori satisfied we would behave ourselves.

Under cocaine's influence, the two of us were loquacious companions. Our interests—passions really—had converged to where we talked only about dreams, hysteria, and Sabrine.

"Hats!" I granted myself a smile, hurriedly sitting down, the evening glass of cocaine wine in wait, ready to inundate Sigmund with the insights I had gained into Cezanne's dream. I particularly relished the first sip and instant stimulation.

He took a much deeper drink "Muriatic acid, an experimental solvent. Adds tartness, I'd say."

Uninterested in discerning differences in taste, I announced proudly, "The hats lead inexorably to Cezanne's father."

"Certainly the plethora of hats, as I recall everywhere and anywhere, must denote significance." He held the cobalt blue vial close to the table candle. "A rather viscous mixture, somewhat opalescent." He uncorked the eye stopper and sniffed. "Yields a unique aromatic smell. Another drop must go into your glass."

Not protesting although a bracing wind was sweeping through my head. "His father was once a hat maker. Hats, the secret of the old man's success."

Effortlessly he caught up—"The son conjures a surfeit of bowler hats as the collective symbol of his father's riches."

The competitive flag dropped, our race to analyse began. I had no trouble extrapolating. "Acutely dependent on his father's allowance, resentment built up; the hats are stark reminders of his demoralizing situation."

Sigmund quickly recalled the dream's outcome. "Hence, the son bludgeons the father to death with a hat." He took a self-congratulatory sip. "A dream of sweet revenge! But the question remains, why a hat made of iron?"

"His father started out as an ironmonger, buying and selling various metal objects."

"Most ingenious! A synthesis of two elements from his father's businesses—hats and iron. The murder weapon an iron hat. He who profits by such, shall die by such. The hat's symbology has been deciphered."

"Aren't you going to ask about another oddity in the dream?"

"The fourteen years to complete a painting—yes, I brought that to your attention."

"Paul Cezanne, I just learned, has a fourteen-year-old son, a secret he kept from his father. But then it might be just a coincidence."

"There is no such thing as a coincidence," he countered. "The painting he brings into the pawn shop, a bowl of fruit, stands in for his son."

Excited, I picked up on the idea. "So in the dream, Paul can covertly reveal the identity of his fourteen-year-old son without fear of losing his father's monthly allowance."

He raised his glass and voiced admiration. "You have taken a dream awash in absurdity and given it coherence. Well done!"

"It's just a step—you know that."

"Julie Forette is not one to rest on her laurels."

"The dream may still yield more meaning."

He lit up a cigar, reflecting. I was certain he would extract more meaning. "I'm inclined to think your painter friend possesses a deeply hidden rage for someone other than his father."

"For whom?"

He aroused my full attention, puffing like a locomotive at full speed. "His own son."

Unconvinced, I asked for evidence.

"What does he do with the fourteen-year-old painting? He rams it into a hat peg. A still-life, which he stills, demolishes, destroys."

His logic satisfactorily demonstrated, he signalled for more wine.

The waitresses were plentiful at the Tambourine, mostly buxom women who served the tables costumed in dirndls with low cut blouses. La Segatori wanted them to resemble charming Alpine milkmaids from her native Italy. We enjoyed watching them carry impossible numbers of beer, swishing and sashaying in full skirts, gladly offering flirtatious winks to any customer who showed special interest.

Our peasant waitress promptly arrived, out of breath, as if she had just ran down from a mountain top village; she smelled of pine and set down a straw-covered bottle of Chianti—"Compliments of la Segatori."

The benefits of cocaine took me into the milkmaid's eyes, aware that she was at the Tambourine to sell her affections. I saw the same availability in all of la Segatori's girls. I nodded to the milkmaid with my cocaine wisdom, she nodding back to say, *Yes, Mademoiselle, it is the way of the world, love for sale.* I watched her leave with a swish of her skirts and smelled the earthen fragrance of pine.

I turned to Sigmund in my heightened state of awareness, "We have mined much from the dream, but I know you know there's more to understand."

"What more does Julie Forette expect from this painter's dream?"

"Some further clue that might lead me to understand his phobia of touch."

"Yes," he murmured. "Phobias... compulsive behaviour."

He said no more, our dream analysis exhausted for the evening. And so I waited until his thoughts turned to his sessions with Sabrine. Never the first to breathe her name, I kept patient, not wanting to show too much curiosity for his experimental talking technique, not wanting him to feel vulnerable to judgement.

When the café began to thin to the hardened regulars, the effects of cocaine waning, he toyed with the blue cobalt vial, idly sliding it around the tambourine table, no longer interested in taking any more. "Yesterday, she asked if I had come to Salpêtrière to amputate her. Not an auspicious beginning for our session, eh?"

"I suppose not."

I spoke with an unhurried voice while my knees under the tambourine table were bouncing away nervous energy.

"'What would be my reason for amputating you?' I asked. She replied, 'When doctors, accustomed to cutting things, come upon a gangrene limb, they amputate before the infection spreads.' 'Which of your limbs would you suppose I amputate?' I asked. 'With a sharp and proper instrument,' she answered, 'you could very easily slice off the top of my head.'"

The mind-altering effect of cocaine still at work in me, a macabre vision came, the four most popular hysterics at Salpêtrière (I knew them all): Sabrine Weiss, Genevieve Legrand, Augustine Gleizes and Louise Latour, dancing in a graceful roundelay, hands entwined, swaying, like Renaissance muses, the tops of their heads cleanly sliced away. Outside the ring, Sigmund and I are frantic, jumping up and down, trying to peek inside their heads.

His voice disintegrated the hallucination: "I asked Sabrine, 'What would be the purpose for slicing off the crown of her head? 'With a soup ladle, 'she responded, 'you could scoop out all the words, the question marks and those unruly exclamation points.'"

"She speaks in metaphors," I said.

"Well, it still remains a jumble to me. What I do know is that she is damnably intelligent and... she writes poems. When we had our first session, she wanted to write a poem, but failed to complete it."

"Because of her hysterical attack."

"Yes. Then when I had the opportunity to read her case file, there was a marginal note about her writing poems. Charcot confirmed the fact... seems to think composing poems only exacerbates her hysterical condition." Sigmund stopped to refresh our glasses with la Segatori's

Chianti. He took a long drink before saying anymore. "Julie, I risked asking Sabrine about her poetry."

"Yes?" Now, along with my knees bouncing, came my heart pounding.

"She composes one poem a day."

"How encouraging!" I became wildly optimistic. "This is her means of communication."

He showed no enthusiasm. "Subsequently, she chews and swallows each poem, so she claims."

Feeling the rise of despair, I thought of adding more drops of cocaine into my glass.

He took out a piece a paper. "But I do have this poem which she left me."

I was excited. "Then she doesn't destroy every poem! And it doesn't necessarily provoke an attack."

"Do you have a pocket mirror?" he asked.

"Really, you think I would carry a vanity mirror?"

"We need a mirror to read the poem."

I jumped up, went directly to la Segatori's table to ask for a mirror. The ubiquitous cigarette, which dangled from the side of her mouth, seemed to be smoking itself. "Why would I have a mirror?" she asked. "To remind me of my faded beauty?" But she signalled one of her dirndl dressed girls who came over and from a pocket in her pretty peasant apron produced a small mirror.

I hurried back to read Sabrine's verse in the mirror:

would you ask from my mouth

yet one more word of regret?

would you take from my head

one more dream of loss?

then might you ask

ask and ask

why?

are mermaids made into fishcakes?

"It took her less than a minute to compose it," he added, "with her left hand. Mirror writing. Rather remarkable and strange."

"Sigmund, she has devised a method to distance herself from the words."

"I thought as much, a clever way to avoid the trauma of meaning. And certainly this..." he took the poem from my hand and placed it back in his side pocket, "argues for deeper meaning."

"I would not push Sabrine into explaining her poems."

"No-no, that's not my intent," he replied. "To inadvertently provoke another attack might prompt Charcot to forbid further sessions. I must proceed with extreme caution."

I put my hand over his. "No, proceed with risk."

He lit another cigar, looked at me deeply. "Very well, then you should know about a patient being treated in Vienna."

And so I learned about Anna O.

II

He gave more history about his friend, colleague and mentor in Austria, Dr. Josef Breuer. "I shall tell you, Breuer has always taken a fatherly interest in me. When I began my practice before coming to Paris, it was Breuer who sent patients to keep me financially afloat, Josef Breuer who encouraged me to study with Charcot, to learn about hypnotism."

I nodded. "I know that Charcot was impressed by the letter of recommendation he sent on your behalf."

"And without his recent three hundred francs I would be hard put to survive the coming month."

I waited, anticipating something more important about Dr. Josef Breuer.

"Presently, he has an interesting case. A young woman of uncommon intelligence who suffers from many strange symptoms which are dominating her life."

"Hysterical symptoms?"

He nodded. "A veritable cornucopia: paralysis of limbs; anaesthesias affecting various parts of her body; disturbances of vision and especially speech. Sometimes she will lose the ability to speak or remember German, her native tongue. Breuer believes, like Charcot, that trauma is the origin of hysterical symptoms, but Breuer attempts to alleviate the symptoms by placing her in a mild hypnoid state. He then spends hours upon hours listening to her thoughts which she first relates in English, but when more relaxed, she switches to Italian. Breuer's goal is to explore any possible connection between her physical symptoms and past trauma. But here's the important difference, Breuer's emphasis is on emotional trauma."

"Which sharply contrasts with Charcot' anatomical-clinical method." I was fascinated. His friend took into serious account, unlike Salpêtrière, the emotions.

"Anna O is a complex patient. She has been under his care for more than a year. Anna O's father has been seriously ill for some time and Breuer suspects a connection. When in her hypnoid state, she will often go to a place in her mind she calls her 'private theatre.' Here she invents stories, usually centered around a little girl who attends to a sick person. After the conclusion of each story—which are strikingly similar to Hans Christian fairy tales—a particular symptom disappears."

"Thought provoking," I murmured.

"Yet more symptoms develop, most recently her extreme aversion to liquids."

"Hydrophobia?"

"She positively panics at the sight of water, loathes drinking it, and only vomits what she does manage to swallow. And now the young woman is positively terrified to fall asleep because of nightmares."

"Poor girl, so many symptoms, one after another." I felt compassion for Anna O. Sabrine's symptoms came to mind, the amnesia, abdominal pains, frozen contractures.

"Anna O's insomnia has become quite serious. Her family and friends are extremely worried. Actually, Anna O is a friend of my fiancée," he admitted.

"Marty." I remembered her photograph… the 'abstain in case of doubt' crochet panel. I picked up the straw-laced bottle of Chianti, empty. Looking over at la Segatori, she nodded. A new bottle was on its way.

"Breuer knows to prescribe a sedative, chloral hydrate, which at least gives her some rest."

What I administered to Zola a lifetime ago.

"Sigmund, I will be much interested in Dr. Breuer's progress with Anna O. You will keep me informed, won't you?" I worried he wouldn't. "I know there's the matter of privacy."

"Anna O is not her real name," he said.

Chapter 33

Most extraordinary, how in a single race (Semite) their enormous intellectual strengths mingle with mental aberrancies.

Jean-Martin Charcot

THE SLIPPERINESS OF EELS

Poker in hand, Charcot manoeuvred a faltering, sputtering log farther into the blaze. "There is an alternative therapy I am exploring… for Sabrine." He spoke to Sigmund without losing focus, stabbing repeatedly at the recalcitrant log until it ignited. "Go to the bottom drawer of the étagère."

What possible therapy can be inside a drawer? wondered Sigmund.

He took out what at first appeared to be a lady's corset. Puzzled, he held it up to the moonlight gleaming through the French doors. It was a composite of leather, wood, and iron attachments, a closer resemblance to a harness…

Charcot came over. "Here, let me show you, it fastens rather like a saddle." He fitted the apparatus around Sigmund's waist, buckling straps, tightening screws, and turning a knob. Sigmund's earlier dose of cocaine still in his system, he caught the reflection in the French doors, his image eerily doubled, leading him to wild imaginings. Out in the night were twin trollops, wearing perverse undergarments, waiting for clients.

"What you now wear is my invention, forged in the Salpêtrière workshop."

The source of the Professor's pride was a mechanical brace of some sort. The device encompassed Sigmund's waist and abdomen area. It felt cumbersome and rather heavy. An assortment of bolts and nuts supported the principal mechanism—a knobular, wooden rod which Charcot busily adjusted by means of a key-lug, the rod pressing into the abdomen, causing Sigmund to wince. "Yes, the more one twists the key lug, the more compression."

Sigmund smiled lamely. "I do feel the pressure. Hmmm, rather uncomfortable."

"As I tighten the key, it moves the rod or, if you will, pestle into the designated pressure point until the hysteric's abdominal paroxysm is subdued. Then, making minor modifications, locking the mechanism into the precise site, the pain is controlled." Charcot looked at him with interest. "What is your present experience?"

"A certain degree of pain."

"Yes, plainly the discomfort shows in your face." He stopped turning. "However, the device will have a palliative effect upon an ovarian hysteric —which obviously you are not. Now, I confide—at this very moment she is enclosed in a similar apparatus, offering Sabrine relief from the pain which has plagued her for far too long. This device"—he ran his fingers fondly over the bolts—"has even reduced the frequency of her hallucinations. She finds some solace at last." Charcot's hand rested on the turning rod and Sigmund hoped he would not give it another twist. "I'm still pondering a name for my invention, something appropriate. Maybe Hystero-Compressor? What do you think?"

The only name coming to mind included the word, 'harness.' He said nothing while Charcot returned to the fire, sat on the sofa and heaved a weary sigh. "I will be the first to emphasize that the compression belt you wear is nothing but a temporary measure. Not a cure. The goal is to give our Ovarians at least a modicum of peace. The device cannot be worn forever, can it?" The question had him gazing mournfully into the flames as Sigmund concentrated on finding the way to extricate himself, "But then," added Charcot, "if Sabrine removes it prematurely, she risks a resumption of her hysterical spells."

Managing to unbuckle himself, he held out the device to Charcot who, strangely, refused to take it. The harness dangled uselessly from his hand. He wondered, *Is now the time to put forth my idea? But better prepare him. Set the stage*: "I keep recalling Sabrine's claim that Satanic creatures torturously assail her during an attack."

"Yes-yes, I'm more than familiar with her hallucinatory complaints, the serpents, the vipers, the whatever." He shook his head. "Such wearisome delusions."

Seize the moment! "Dr. Charcot, what if, instead of dismissing her belief in these creatures, we encourage Sabrine to talk freely about her hallucinations?" The doctor's wrinkling brow prompted him to add, "As an experiment."

"What would one hope to gain by such a nonsensical approach?" queried a baffled Charcot.

"Making the beasts more familiar to her, more..."

"Digestible, eh?"

The satiric remark best ignored, he struggled to articulate what remained an elusive idea: "Giving these creatures a temporary reality, as a possible way of... taming them."

Charcot shook his head, clearly disapproving. "Young man, long ago I came to a realization that to listen to a hysteric's utterances only exacerbates a morbid sense of their self-importance and perpetuates their illness."

Sigmund continued cautiously, "Dr. Breuer, my mentor... and colleague, has a certain female patient under his care in Vienna. This woman–her pseudonym Anna O—exhibits a virtual museum of hysterical symptoms: paralyses, contractures, anaesthesias, a nervous cough, the inability to take food... even a curious alternating of personalities."

"A suitable lady for the Salpêtrière, it would seem." He rose and took back the compression device. "Does Dr. Breuer desire a consultation?" The invention was carefully replaced in the drawer, Sigmund wishing it would never again see the light of day.

"Dr. Breuer, actually, has had some success. A given symptom disappears the moment she finishes telling the story of its first appearance."

"Obviously, his Anna is an enigmatic hysteric, like our Sabrine."

Venturing farther on the limb. "Breuer's method of allowing the patient to talk through pains and fears seems to affect a catharsis."

"It's inconceivable to me," his irritation growing, "that you would further arouse a hysteric's overactive imagination by inviting her to give more descriptive life to some beast—a dragon perhaps, which you shall lure out of the lair of her mind, to tame, yes? Having Sabrine place a leash around her dragon's neck and leading the hallucination through the streets and gardens of the Salpêtrière."

Charcot's mockery swept over him like a cold wind. "I am aware," he conceded, "that this talking cure does not appear very scientific."

"Ha! If I'm not mistaken, quite unscientific! No, we shall not risk inciting more grievous attacks by giving the child license to paint polka dots on her dragon. We shall stay focused on the somatic!" He marched to a corner of the library and pulled down a chart. Slapping a hand against the female torsos displayed, the chart shimmied. "Front and back, nine hysterogenic zones. And we may find more! Mapping these nerve routes is our fundamental task. Through them," he slapped the chart again, "we will reach the ultimate source of Grand Hysteria. Why, even the Orientals have been exploring similar meridian points of nerve stimulation. I enjoin you, enough!" His hand sliced the air. "Abandon this sudden fancy for a patient's chimeras. No, no, no! Let us look for the real lesions and not the debris of dreams."

The displeasure clouding Charcot's face was worrisome, a warning: *Sigmund, defer. Arouse no more ire from your mentor with fledgling ideas, meagrely conceived, too weak to stand up to his years of medical exper-*

ience and clinical observations. Defer.

The doctor approached with a softened look, took his arm. *His fondness for me returns.* He was led to a chart which Charcot rolled down. "Young man, more important things are in store for you. I have a plan. A proposition of the most profound nature. Before you, an exquisite diagram of a Semitic tree, the Isaacson family, the connecting boxes contain the neurological diseases which, through generations, have infected family members." Charcot smiled at him. "At some point in your medical studies, you surely recognized that Semites possess a strong, unique proclivity toward certain neurological disorders. For example, here is locomotor ataxia." He touched two boxes on the diagram. "Contracted by two of the Isaacson's, Ruth and Martha, twins who began to exhibit the disease in their youth. Now the dears are quite elderly, the disease having reached advanced stages. Both ladies have, in fact, been at the Salpêtrière for decades of observation. Ruth's muscle coordination is beyond repair, a fragile lady, she cannot button her clothing without assistance, is barely able to pick up a spoon; twin sister Martha suffers the same disease but in a different manner, experiencing hysterical seizures almost on a daily basis, sometimes twelve to fifteen attacks. To have the twins under our care, as living case studies, is a stroke of good fortune.

"I have also examined Grandfather Isaacson on an outpatient basis. From him I have gleaned much of the family's degenerative history. Here, as the branches spread, descend," his fingers lightly grazed over the blocks, "the list of neurological and mental aberrancies continue, transmitted from generation to generation." Sigmund's arm gripped again, he is forced to step back with Charcot so as to absorb the full visual impact of the expanding tree. "Who can deny the pattern of hereditary defects among Semites! And let me tell you, Sigmund, not only a remarkably high frequency rate of ataxias are found among the Jewish population, but a surprisingly high percentage of hysterics. And we must not forget their particular affinity for a gamut of arthritic conditions. Such peculiarities are confirmed over and over again in my clinical experience."

Am I to comment? Sigmund wondered. *Does courtesy demand me to respond?* "Certainly thought provoking, Dr. Charcot, your observations."

"These assertions are not made lightly," he added with marked gravity. "I have seen many, many Jewish immigrants in my outpatient clinic, from countries as far away as Russia, where they leave en masse. Apparently, the fluctuations in their emotional temperament produce these cyclical migrations."

What? He knows nothing of Jewish pogroms? Can this be possible?

"Now, do I suggest," Charcot asked, his expression most earnest, "that all Israelites carry the mark of their ancestry? Do I claim that each and every Semite will fall victim to a hereditary nervous disorder? Surely not! Surely not! There are numerous exceptions... case in point," his smile wise and coy, "one Sigmund Freud." He then returned to the chart, gave it a tug and it sprung closed. He paced. "Nonetheless, my clinical observations cannot be disputed, nervous disorders do abound among Jews." He went to his desk, sat, and beckoned Sigmund to a chair. Opening a cigar box, he offered his protégé first choice. "No, I shall not dismiss their proclivity toward a superior intelligence nor their first-rate aptitude in the sciences. Yet... yet the underlying pattern remains in the Semitic trees I have fashioned."

They smoked in silence, puffing and ruminating. *How Jewish do I consider myself*, Sigmund wondered. *How prone am I to degeneration in his eyes? What is his plan for me?*

Charcot emerged from his silence with a sudden reflection. "Most extraordinary, how in a single race such enormous intellectual strengths can mingle with mental aberrancies. Most extraordinary!"

Each puffed away, an agitation of clouds between them.

"To the nub, Sigmund, to the plan!" his voice rang out. "What if some neurologist chose to take on the task of studying this phenomena... no, let me rephrase. What if a neurologist, who is in fact a Jew, chose to investigate, in the deepest detail, the disorders which manifest in his own race... well, that would be of immense interest to me." He leaned back in the chair, pleased that such ideas germinated in his mind. "Such a project will be of great importance in furthering the cause of neurology, to study this peculiar race who from antiquity to the present have played such major roles in the history of mankind."

Sigmund preferred to watch their curling smoke, a welcomed distraction, watching wispy streams rise, drift, higher and higher, wafting around Charcot's stained glass emblem, the indomitable, looming, midnight-blue bear, never tiring of clenching in his taloned paw the hourglass of sand and time. "The Jews," came more reflection, "are a treasure trove for studying comparative pathology." He beamed an inviting smile. "Are you game, my boy?"

The warmth of the hearth fire reached them from across the room, the hearth's ruddy flames reflected on all things glass, the French doors, the glass bear hanging above them—trick of perception, the glowering bear amidst the darting flames, invincible, silently roaring.

Within the awkward silence, Charcot wondered aloud, "Perhaps

Sigmund finds a scientific research project requiring such a large sampling too daunting?" He raised his brows. "Lacking the experience, you hesitate."

"I have the experience." Sigmund puffed. "With eels."

Charcot puffed. "Eels?"

"As a medical student I went to Trieste to research the gonadic structure of male eels." *And spoke to my first prostitute along the Corso Covour. She was dressed quite demurely, save for the candy-cane striped stockings. She was, as I, twenty. My trousers off, so glad was she to see me circumcised, a hygienic relief.*

"Is that so?" Charcot puffed more as he contemplated eels. "Slippery devils, eh?"

"In more ways than one." Sigmund blew up a puff of smoke toward the bear impervious to flames and pain. "I dissected 400 eels, but the male gonads remained elusive. Each and every eel I sliced open was of the tenderer sex."

"Obviously in the eel population males are a minority." Charcot decided. "But with my proposed project, I predict more success, a significantly higher degree of neuropathic finds in the Semitic race."

"The profundity of the project brings me to a loss for words."

Charcot suddenly and inexplicably grew indifferent. "Ah well, it would be a vast undertaking." He checked his pocket watch. "I must soon dress for dinner, sauerbraten and dumplings, I'm told. Come, let me escort you to the gate, by way of the garden."

Through the French doors of flames, the two men went out into the night and walked a gravel path bordered with hawthorn and deep scented flowers. In the darkness just the tips of their cigars flared periodically.

"Dr. Charcot," he wanted his voice to sound contrite, "the project you propose necessitates more time than has been allotted to me in Paris. My travel grant expires in a matter of months. Perhaps upon my return to Vienna, we can outline a plan and work in tandem."

"Yes-yes, there's no need to rush this. We both should give it more thought," came Charcot's quick dismissal of the project.

Sigmund uneasy, the important question had to be asked, "In the short time left to me at the Salpêtrière, may I continue working with Sabrine Weiss?"

Charcot's cigar tip flared extra bright. "Do go forward, Dr. Freud, let your talking sessions run their course. And we should remember that she is, after all, Jewish," he reflected, "at least part Jewish. So maybe part of my proposed plan begins after all."

Exiting the garden, they descended across the sloping lawn toward the front gate. "Have I ever mentioned," said Charcot, "that my first male hysteric was a thirteen-year-old Jew, a Russian lad, who was brought to the outpatient clinic in 1882 by his troubled father?"

At the gate, he flicked the finished cigar between the bars where it rolled on to the street, the tip still glowing.

Sigmund watched Charcot having difficulty with undoing the latch. "What were the Russian boy's symptoms?" he asked.

"Melancholia and sleep walking. Now, what's wrong with this the latch?"

"Looks bent." The memory flashed before him, taking the rock and pounding at the latch. Impulsive, panic driven behaviour which might be interpreted by an insightful doctor as hysterical.

Charcot persevered and opened the gate. "Must have an ironsmith attend to it."

The two men shook hands. Charcot remembered, "The boy's sleep walking had an interesting twist. He always awakened in one of the city's cemeteries, incredible distances from his home, with no recollection of how he got there." Charcot shook his head. "Odd, so young, and so preoccupied with death. But it taught me that hysteria has many faces."

"Like Hydra," interjected Sigmund, "the many-headed serpent in Greek mythology."

"That is quite apt!" Charcot laughingly responded. "Off with the Hydra's head and three more take their place. I might insert that myth in my lectures to emphasize the mutability of hysteria."

"It makes a good metaphor. Good-night, Professor."

Sigmund walked down the street—stopped by Charcot's happy pronouncement: "By Jove! The name has come to me like a thunderbolt!"

He turned. "The name?"

"My device shall be called, Ovarian Compressor! Yes, the Ovarian Compressor!"

"I must say, Dr. Charcot, I think it's an excellent appellation."

"A little more medical history made tonight, eh?"

No appetite for supper, Sigmund decided when he entered his rooms at the Hotel Goff to work on the translation of the third volume of Charcot's Tuesday Lessons, but first he needed a little uplift to relieve the vague discontent bothering him.

Come Sigismund, a small glass of cocaine wine, one tenth of a gram, the best remedy for any ill, even Jewish melancholia.

Chapter 34

**Since now we are all frighted, seeing him—
the vessel's pilot, as 'twere, panic-stricken.**

Oedipus Rex
Sophocles

CADUCEUS

I thought the Zoological Gardens a peculiar place to discuss "a grave matter," yet Jeanne was adamant that we rendezvous, specifically, in the palmarium.

Fretting as to whether this grave matter pertained to Sabrine, I arrived very early at the gardens, having to wait for attendants to uplift bars and unlock latches to the newly designed palmarium. Entering, the first visitor of the day, I felt even more alone amongst a crowded collection of towering plants and spiralling trees. Exploration of exotic flora the last thought in my mind, I sat down on the first stone bench I found, trying to accustom myself to the tropical surroundings. Above me a high domed ceiling, constructed entirely of green tinted glass, gave an eerie, pale glow to everything. Would Jeanne come with dire news regarding Sabrine? Rumours were rampant that radical surgery might be performed on Salpêtrière's favourite patient. I waited, somewhat stiffly and uncomfortable, on the rough stone bench. The palmarium's air, saturated with humidity, was taxing to breathe.

"Julie!" she nearly shouted as she rushed toward me. "I must confide in someone or I will simply go mad!" I took her hand and brought her down to sit next to me in the deserted palmarium. "Oh Julie! The letters posted to my father are unimaginably horrendous!" she cried, squeezing my hand, and suddenly searching into my eyes. "But am I making an awful mistake... asking for your help?" She dropped my hand and turned away. Jeanne Charcot struggled, chagrined and unaccustomed to asking favours.

I seized both her hands, so small and puffy, curiously beautiful, almost identical to her father's—"Jeanne, are we not each other's confidante?"

"The letters are perfidious and, of course, anonymous," she went on, making an effort to speak calmly, only to again lose control of her emotions. "They contain nothing but filth! Vile filth!" Her hands felt extremely hot or were mine just cold? "Each begins with spiteful mockery:

'Dear Emperor of the Salpêtrière Bordello,' 'Dear Maestro of Madwomen', followed by pure hatefulness. The letters arrive, sealed with red wax..." She stopped, a new thought evoked a bitter laugh. "As if their venomous contents contained something official."

Listening to her strange story, I grew more aware of our equally strange surroundings. We sat in the midst of a tropical jungle thick with unknown plants and deep scented flowers, the two of us dwarfed by tall palms, gigantic ferns and vine entangled trees which stretched toward the glass vaulted roof.

"The letters arrive like clockwork," said Jeanne while I tried to ignore how the glass-filtered light turned our clothes greenish and made our faces sickly pale, "precisely on the day which precedes a full moon."

"Celestial clockwork." As soon as the thought escaped, my mind conjured someone cloaked in astronomical garb, holed up in an ancient tower, busily consulting an ephemeris... *the letter writer wears a coned wizard's hat patterned with stars.*

"Julie..." Jeanne's voice intruded, "you must grasp the nightmarish scene—it is I who fetch father's morning mail and bring it to his study, I who observe my father's reaction when his eye catches sight of the red seal, the Caduceus."

"Caduceus?"

"It's like a warning signal... he... father recoils. I've seen..." she struggled. "I've seen the hair rise on the nape of his neck."

A disturbing image to consider—Jean-Martin Charcot stricken with fear.

Jeanne's posture straightened, the Charcot pride seeped into her tone. "It is I who now shoulder the responsibility of breaking the seal, as the task has become near impossible for father."

"And this red seal is embossed with an image of the Caduceus?"

"So it resembles." She rummaged in her purse, handing me an envelope with a broken seal. "How utterly cruel," she declared, "to use the very symbol of medicine itself, my father's noble craft of healing. And this scoundrel makes of it a mockery!" She was beside herself with disgust.

The embossed insignia, though broken, certainly approximated the ancient symbol: twin snakes coiled around a short rod crested with flanking wings. The envelope was empty.

"Father burns all the letters. To read such filth would only sicken you."

"You have no idea who authors these letters?"

"I have my suspicions, someone evil, a doctor so envious of my father's fame that he deliberately misappropriates and denigrates the seal of medical healing."

"The Caduceus has other meanings," I said. "The rod is the magic wand of Hermes."

"Hermes?"

"The Conductor of the Dead."

Jeanne gasped, a hand shot to her mouth. "Oh, no! The letters describe in horrible detail how my father will die!"

"Does your father suspect anyone?"

"Father thinks it may be a disgruntled outpatient with some knowledge of medicine and the workings of the Salpêtrière. But I'm convinced the man moves freely within father's innermost circle of friends. A man privy to an inordinate amount of details regarding my father's private life. He quotes father's favourite writers, Shakespeare, Racine, Dante, the Greek dramatists."

"Have you evidence that it is a man?"

She looked troubled. "What woman could it be?"

"Your father is the Director of the Salpêtrière, home and refuge to more than six thousand females."

"Many demented minds, yes, but these women entrusted to my father's care are either too enfeebled or confused to originate such shrewdness. The letter writer is someone with superior intelligence."

Jeanne guessed my thoughts at the mention of superior intelligence. "Julie, not for an instant could I believe Sabrine writes these poisonous letters."

In recent weeks we both observed how much more rational Sabrine behaved and we took some credit for the improvement. We had won the battle with Charcot to move her out of 'The Ward of Stars' into private quarters—a cosy room a floor above the hysterics' ward which we furnished with modest amenities from the outside world: a hand-mirror, a hairbrush, magazines and books. But it was Sigmund and the talking sessions that seemed to bring her closer to reality. Everything looked so hopeful. I began to envision Sabrine's progress as her ascension toward lucidity.

Jeanne touched my hand which still held the envelope. "Will you help Father and me?"

"What can I do?"

"You spend as much time with my father as anyone at the Salpêtrière, giving you opportunities to observe those who come in contact with him. Perhaps you might detect a telltale sign from someone?"

"But your father is the master of observation. I only record his words."

She had a different opinion. "I see Julie Forette as the master of words who can weigh their worth and judge the character of those who speak them."

I looked longer at the penmanship on the envelope, a forceful hand, letters slanting in different directions, almost deliberately awkward. Jeanne snatched the envelope and returned it to her purse.

How to respond to her plea for help? "Jeanne, you flatter me with too much insight."

"I am certain you will make a perfect police detective."

She was convinced, in her mind the matter settled, I was appointed Salpêtrière's spy. Following her out of the palmarium, tagging behind as she marched and crunched across the sand layered path in her thick-heeled shoes, I was feeling unhappy.

Intuitively Jeanne had determined Julie Forette very capable at spying. My serious character flaw, eavesdropping and rummaging where one shouldn't. The vile letters—I failed to tell her—came as no surprise.

I had observed their impact on Charcot months ago, an evening when I expected to be alone in his library, on the second tier reading and researching what I could find with regard to oophorectomies, the surgical procedure purported to cure hysteria. I had my doubts and among the Salpêtrière staff there were debates as to its effectiveness. Such a procedure, rumours ran, might soon be scheduled for Sabrine.

When hearing the latch on the library door click, I quietly hurried to stoop between the gargoyle posts, observing Charcot enter, sit at his desk, turned up the gas lamp and put down an envelope. I stayed crouched between two gargoyles, he directly beneath me, sitting as still as a stone, his harrowed expression illuminated by the lamp light. I became riveted to the unfolding scene, the gleam of the red smear upon the white envelope, the way he looked at it, as though confronting something ominous, maleficent. Time ticked away until he finally rose, his footsteps heavy, approaching the hearth and faintly glowing fire. There was a moment of hesitation before he tossed in the sealed letter and marched angrily out. When the door slammed behind him, I rushed down the stairwell.

The envelope on top of the flickering embers beginning to smoulder, I grabbed the fire tongs and managed to pinch out the envelope, but it was far too hot to touch. Hurriedly I used the hem of my petticoat to smother the envelope from further scorching. When I saw that the seal was now malleable from the heat, I found Charcot's letter opener on the desk, lifting off the seal with great care to keep the Caduceus emblem intact. The letter inside was readable and horrible, crammed with the vilest imaginings that would shock even the most hardened heart. Its tone was sheer manic, and the last paragraph proof of a darkly damaged mind.

Oh, upon my solemn word, Charcot of the Crooked Eye! When your suffering nears its mortal conclusion, I shall slip in at your beside, disguised (ha, ha!), to assist in your final agonies. Into your ears, to blunt the Greek chorus of your lamenting family, I will carefully insert scoops of rat entrails. For the easement of your burning fever, I will massage your pink flesh with the excrement of

your favourite elephants, Pollux and Castor, which will be thoroughly diseased. Oh, yes I will! And to soothe your laboured breath, I will stuff the passage of your throat with the decapitated paws of your beloved monkey.

Repugnant details surely written by a mind corroded with hate. I took note of the closing sentence:

I remain the sincerest of your betrayed admirers,
> **Thine in death,**
> **M.T.**

Here was a hint of a personal relationship with Charcot, someone who felt betrayed. The only tangible clue to the writer's identity were the initials, **M.T.**

I refolded the letter into the envelope, relieved that I had no difficulty in resealing the Caduceus emblem whole. The winged rod of Mercury, I conjectured, might account for the first letter, M.

I knew the Roman god Mercury carried messages from the other gods of Mount Olympus and delivered them to the human world. Mercury came to be worshipped by ancient Rome as the transmitter of scientific and medical knowledge. It was thought that the god Mercury held the secret formulas to therapeutic drugs.

The Greeks had another view. He was known to them as Hermes. They called him *psychopomp*—the escort of souls through the underworld.

I placed the resealed letter on the desk and left. Why did I leave it? Why rescue a horrible message he meant to destroy?

In the days that followed I sought a rational explanation for my behaviour. The letter was investigative evidence, as such, it should be preserved, analysed, scrutinized, deciphered. Charcot should have a second chance to identify whoever hated him. To catch him. Or her?

Yet, any rationale I came up with after my rash act seemed strained. My conscience nagged. Then I wondered, worried—was there an inherited trait in me that found expression, an imbedded streak of cruelty?

Chapter 35

**Maybe we should live like Goys—modestly
learning the ordinary things without striving or
reaching to the depths.**

Sigmund Freud

A Spoonful of Secrets

A surprise reprieve from weeks of wintery weather gave us the opportunity to saunter along the shoreline of the Seine. We would have—for a change—our 'Congress' outdoors. 'Congress' was the code word Sigmund playfully concocted to indicate a meeting which included cocaine. He smiled and patted his breast pocket to let me know that he had the finely powdered mixture I specifically requested. I wanted to walk for a while before showing him my surprise.

The day was pleasantly mild, the blue sky decorated with small pillowy clouds. On the river, barges of timber, coal and sand occasionally passed north and south. He shared his news.

"Dr. Breuer seems to have cured Anna O of her hydrophobia."

"How?"

"He placed her in a state of mild hypnosis and led her back to the day the hydrophobic symptoms took hold."

"Tell me every detail, Sigmund." I was deeply interested.

So I learned of the day Anna O happened to visit a female friend whose dog was behaving strangely. The dog not only refused to drink water but howled fearfully at its bowl. Then the dog began wobbling around the room, completely disoriented. Anna and her friend were horrified when the dog, frothing at the mouth, raced through an open door to the garden. Running after the dog, they watched it keel over and die.

When Dr. Breuer brought his patient back to normal consciousness, he helped her see how the incident traumatized her, and explained that she was, in fact, mimicking the dog's hydrophobic symptoms.

"And her symptoms went away?" I asked, excited.

"Not instantaneously, but after several more sessions, he was able to help Anna integrate the emotional turmoil she was experiencing to the past event. He calls it 'associative correction.'"

I wasn't sure what Dr. Breuer meant by 'mildly' hypnotizing Anno O, but bringing her to a past trauma and having her describe the event, thereby liberating her from its hysterical effect seemed boldly progressive, a new path in treating hysteria. I stopped. "Sigmund, this is a way to help Sabrine!"

He raised a hand to temper my enthusiasm. "I'm sure that there's more complexity involved in the situation."

"Of course!" I agreed. "More complex."

What better moment to present him with my surprise gift! Then together we can sift through "the complex." I untied my handbag, reaching inside when he unexpectedly declared—

"I view Sabrine, in comparison to the Mademoiselle in Vienna, as a different kettle of fish."

"Fish?" I re-tightened the strings of the handbag.

"Sabrine is hardly inclined to remember events in a linear fashion. Her character has a decidedly unreasonable aspect—as Dr. Charcot points out."

Charcot's hovering shadow, I thought glumly, *blocks daylight.*

"Sabrine possesses a keen intelligence—your own admission," I reminded him.

He looked out at birds swooping along the Seine. "Certainly she has garnered a hodgepodge of knowledge... which she employs in her inimitable, haphazard manner."

"Sabrine is original in her thinking." *He should see her in a favourable light, be made aware of her unique character.* "Someone who possesses great sensitivity to people and her surroundings."

"A puzzling young woman—and damnably exasperating," he confessed. "I often worry that I make no headway with her case."

"In your sessions surely you have formed some opinion of her?"

"As Charcot confirms, everything about Sabrine announces the hysteric, her capriciousness, her coquetry; but what keeps me from quitting is Charcot's dictum: 'Stare at the facts, stare at the hysteric's gestures again and again until they speak to you.'"

Charcot's excessive influence rankled me more and more. Staring at the words coming from Sabrine's mouth was of greater importance; yet how could I fault his rational approach, his effort to maintain a physician's objectivity? I just didn't want him to mimic Charcot's coldness, Charcot's emotional distance.

The moment's arrived, I decided, an uplift from cocaine.

I wanted us to be free-spirited, guided by no one but our unclouded thoughts, uninfluenced by the Napoleon of Neurology—at least an hour out of his shadow. I took the pewter spoon from my handbag. "A gift for you. Forged in England sometime during the late 17th Century, so the antique dealer said."

He seemed unsure of how he should react to the gift I put into his hand. "Quite tiny. I might be able to scoop up a pea, possibly two small peas."

"Once used for inhaling snuff," I explained.

"Julie…" (He looked confused—was he wondering how an engaged man should react to a gift?) "This seems quite expensive."

"Since snuff has fallen from fashion, I practically stole it from the dealer, the price less than a full glass of wine at the Tambourine."

He was quick to remember. "One franc, seven centimes." We both laughed.

"But look at the stem," I urged, "the engraved initial, 'S'—someone forgotten from another century. " I made no mention that the 'S' prompted me to think of him. I would embarrass him no further.

His finger traced the initial, full of admiration for the spoon's delicacy. "And to think, designed specifically for snuff."

"S for snuff," I quipped. "But now in 1886, suitable for a modern use."

"So we simply sniff our cocaine powder?"

"Why not?"

"Why not indeed! Since you have provided the appropriate implement."

As I expected, he was not adverse to any experiment with cocaine. We proceeded to the nearest bridge, underneath the Pont Neuf, to take advantage of the privacy the shadows offered.

Sprinkling a small amount into the pewter spoon, he carefully passed it to me. I inhaled it all in one deep breath. He refilled the bowl, sniffed the powder into one of his nostrils, refilled the bowl and whiffed up more into the other nostril.

Unlike the slow warming, aphrodisiacal effects of sipping cocaine wine, this was an instantaneous shock, a joyous clarity, a sharpness of vision. I'm sure he felt the same way as we stepped out of the shadows into a world of vivid colours and absolute truth. We ran to the shore's edge, cognizant of everything as never before.

My fellow cocainist took a deep breath and exhaled. "Ah, omniscience again. Of course, the illusion of omniscience, but nonetheless, Julie, nonetheless."

I saw the words, or imagined I could see the words leaving his mouth… *nonetheless nonetheless* curling and spiralling upwards, popping whimsically like soap bubbles—gone. Where?

Mildly hallucinating, I accepted the fact with singular happiness. "Your words doth fly to the sky!"

"But do my thoughts remain below?" he retorted, mockingly quoting Hamlet.

Incredibly, all of Shakespeare once shelved in the Pickle Library was at my beck and call. Readily, I finished the quote: "Words without thoughts never to heaven go."

"The spoon might very well have belonged to Shakespeare."

Our erudite exchange made us smile at each other. The cocaine stimulated us equally. We fitted together so well.

An abandoned wine cask, turned over on its side, half buried in the sand, allowed us to sit close together. Sigmund grew immensely interested in the river traffic. I took the spoon from his hand, letting my thoughts swirl around the engraved S.

He pointed out a passing barge stacked with white birch. "She carries timber; fire resides in the wood," he said.

His observation—I was certain—contained a storehouse of wisdom.

My lips kissed the stem, the 'S' of the spoon, and I closed my eyes, reaching for hidden meanings.

Shakespeare, Science, Salpêtrière, Sigmund... and S is Sabrine. A procession of truths.

"Truth embedded in everything we touch." I gave back the spoon, the S, heated with my kiss.

"S is for secret," he said.

"Give me a secret, Sigmund."

He struck a match to his cigar. I found a cigarette in my purse and caught his flame before it died.

"I've become a dream collector," he said.

"When?"

"After encroaching upon your artist friend's dream, I thought in all fairness to Monsieur Cezanne I should undertake an analysis of my own dreams. A deliberative approach must be taken for any serious understanding of the psychic mechanics of dreams." He smilingly brandished a small notebook.

"Your dreams?" I asked, already wanting to covet them.

He flicked the pages. "Empty."

"No dreams?"

"I seek, as you rightly suggest, the most untameable, the most outrageous, the dream which shocks one's psyche, for in that dream may be found the microcosm of one's selfhood."

"The one vivid dream will come," I assured him.

He retorted, "Has not the moment arrived for your secret to spring forward?"

Exhaling a feathery plume, I rose from the wine cask. *Do I want to dance a sea waltz in the wet sand?* But my shoes half-sinking, I walked toward firmer ground.

"Where doth the lady go?"

"I'm following a different path."

With a laugh he scrambled off the wine cask and caught up with me. I looked deeply into his brown eyes, and though extremely dilated, they revealed his inviting intellect. The wonderful frisson between our minds was almost frightening. Now my moment for a secret? But if misconstrued, it might well jeopardize my employment at the Salpêtrière. "I practice hypnotism," I said, spurred by cocaine, "as I need to understand the phenomenon in all of its aspects."

He puffed and puffed some more. "And who are your subjects?"

"Many of the elderly residents who remain at Salpêtrière because they have no place to go... and a few staff members as well."

"I suppose I should be impressed."

"One of several discoveries I've made is..."

"Several discoveries! Not just one! By all means, yes, let me hear them!" He laughed between puffs. "Pride has no boundaries under cocaine's sway."

"And reaching conclusions quite different from Dr. Charcot."

It was apostasy and caused him to raise his eyebrows questioningly, puffing out such clouds of smoke as though to obscure his concern —"What might they be?"

"The dim-witted, slow-minded and mentally impaired are impossible to hypnotize."

"Perhaps you have not sufficiently honed your hypnotic skills," he suggested.

"In point of fact," I soldiered on, "the more strong-willed and intelligent you are, the more susceptible you will be to the hypnoid state." Sigmund pondered, as I knew he would. "Please understand," I added, "Charcot would be furious if he were to learn that I covertly hypnotize at the Salpêtrière, certain to sack me."

He shrugged off any concern for repercussion, as cocaine kept doubt at bay. I walked, following the lodestar of the Notre Dame Cathedral in the distance. "I've been able to gain access to the ward of the incurables," I further revealed. "My repeated attempts to hypnotize the women who are kept shackled or in straitjackets has proven impossible. You do understand that these results are contrary to Charcot's theory that the hypnotic state can be produced only in neurasthenics, hysterics and deranged minds."

"This is preliminary evidence," he countered "a select sampling. Your findings would be better served if you found subjects outside of Salpêtrière."

"Far from the Charcot eye, I suppose."

Arriving at the *Pont Notre Dame*, we climbed the embankment stairs. "Regardless of who can and who cannot be hypnotized, Charcot is on the right track," he suddenly insisted. "Somewhere in the hypnoid state lies the secret or secrets to hysteria."

We stayed on the bridge, leaning over the rail, quietly watching the steady river traffic, collecting our own thoughts. The day grown busy, pedestrians passing, gentlemen and ladies with parasols to shield from the noon day sun, everyone heading to either the left or right bank of the city. On the Seine a swiftly gliding coal barge caught our interest, its deck loaded with a mountain of glistening coal, and fascinating us, a little boy of no more than five or six years of age who sat on the very peak, his sweet face smeared with coal dust. He waved and we waved a hello back. He rang the barge bell, a clang, clang, clang, until the boy and barge sailed out of sight. I had experimented with a hand bell on occasion to hypnotize one or two of the Salpêtrière women.

"Why not hypnotize Sabrine," I suddenly challenged him.

His brow furrowed, he took quicker puffs. "Absolutely not."

I couldn't hold back a sense of urgency and pleaded the case. "If anyone can find a cure for Sabrine's Grande Hysteria and stop her attacks, it is you, you!"

My outburst caused passers-by to cast uneasy glances. I dropped my voice an octave: "Hypnotize Sabrine. Suggest that she is cured of each and every symptom. Cured forever."

Tapping the cigar, he watched the ashes sprinkled down on the coursing water. "Charcot would not approve of such a reckless thing."

"Would it really be too reckless, for **you,** Sigmund?"

He tossed the cigar into the river. "An average of a hundred bodies are retrieved from the Seine each year, claims Guinon, mostly suicides, or murders. The corpses are rarely identified, just carted in hospital wagons to the morgue. Somehow, Guinon has first pick of the lot."

I remained focused. "Surely you are familiar with Dr. Bernheim's hypnosis clinic at Nancy and his opposing hypothesis that hypnosis is not at all linked to the hysterical condition?"

"Let's put aside the controversy between Drs. Bernheim and Charcot for now. I want to continue with Dr. Breuer's 'talking cure'—what Anna O calls Chimney Sweeping—and concentrate on drawing some semblance of a past life from Sabrine.”

“What have you learned so far?”

“When I raise the question of her parents, she claims to have been hatched.”

“Yes, from a dragon’s egg.”

He eyed me closely. “And I suppose you know that it was from a red-spotted dragon’s egg, in a nest atop St. Louis’s golden dome.”

“She’s fond of dragons,” I volunteered. “Jeanne Charcot and I find out such things when we take her for walks on the hospital grounds.”

“Have you two tried to coax her into revealing a history before Salpêtrière?” he asked.

I shrugged. “With Sabrine it’s difficult to construct a coherent picture of actual events in her life. We’ve learned not to be too... pushy. She can easily withdraw into her own world.”

“In my opinion, she inhabits a kind of fairy tale where all manner of creatures exist... dragons, mermaids, demons. Any of which may camouflage a more potent meaning.”

“Yes,” I agreed.

“Hatched from an egg, for instance, why a red-spotted egg? It’s a symbol, like your artist friend’s iron-brimmed hat.”

“Your *forte*, Doctor, may be decoding symbols. Hopefully, another poem will come your way.”

“And your *forte* may be hypnotism,” he replied. “Keep me informed of your discoveries.”

“Perhaps I’ll manage a visit to Dr. Bernheim’s hypnosis clinic at Nancy.”

“If so, that’s a secret you should keep from Charcot.”

“Yes, neither of us wants to lose his favour, do we?”

His face darkened; I said no more. He had to sense my deepening ambivalence toward Jean-Martin Charcot, my feelings, like a pendulum, swinging strongly for and against him. What I knew was that I would keep practising hypnotism at every opportunity. *But outside the gates of Salpêtrière, for Paris will give me more than enough candidates.*

The city did not disappoint.

Chapter 36

Of a truth dark thoughts, yea dark and fell,
The augur wise doth arouse in me.

Oedipus Rex
Sophocles

FEATHERS AND GLOVES

My ambivalence toward Jean-Martin Charcot, I now realize, began early, took root when I was still the novice transcriber, when finally permitted on the Salpêtrière grounds. It had taken several months of assisting him at his private practice before granted the honour of the Salpêtrière, having to outlast his persistent admonitions that working in a hospital populated with the disease-ridden and addle-minded required unwavering strength.

Repeatedly he asked, "Can Mademoiselle Forette, each and every day inside the walls of Salpêtrière, face the torments of the deranged, demented and diseased without succumbing to needless pity?" And always keen to remind me that there was more than enough emotional distress among six thousand abandoned women without adding a pinch more emotion, be it compassion or commiseration. "I speak without bias to your sex," he liked to claim, "as I know my own son, Jean, has given himself over to such superfluous emotions."

My response never wavered. "I am at your service, Dr. Charcot, to record the truth."

One day, at last, he concluded with a sigh of resignation. "Yes, Mademoiselle Forette, I do suspect that you have the nerves of steel required."

Thus, my stenographic duties inside the Salpêtrière complex began. On mornings Charcot required my services, I entered through the Mazarin gate, flanked by two massive Egyptian pillars which never failed to set my heart racing, as though I were entering an ancient temple, a temple of science. And my religion was science.

To follow the energetic Charcot about Salpêtrière City kept one in a breathless state of anticipation. His teaching style continuously fascinated everyone as he found the most novel ways to make his case for a diagnosis. The tours, especially, were constructed with such mastery that I thought of them as works of art.

The 'three feathers' incident occurred on such a tour, a bright, very warm day in June. Charcot was conducting a rather exhaustive amble through Salpêtrière's maze of streets, extolling to a group of six interns the self-sufficiency of the institution. He showed them the general store, tobacco shop, and café where residents, who were able to work, could spend their earnings. He relished telling the newcomers that Salpêtrière was once a prison. "Erected in the 17th century, at Louis IV's insistence, to house the women of loose and easy virtue, but as you now see—" hurriedly we followed him through the library, the school, the newly converted gymnasium—"all radically changed for the greater benefit of our abandoned women."

Outside the wine shop, I recorded what I thought were his concluding remarks, "Yes, we even have a wine merchant, but to counterbalance such indulgences," he chuckled, pointing his cane toward the distant St. Louis dome, "a Catholic Church and, for further balance, a Protestant chapel nearby. Now, let us climb to..."

The sentence interrupted... his assistant la Tourette silently mouthing, *trop de vent*, too much wind. I watched Charcot study the swaying poplar trees and a sky of fast moving clouds suddenly veiling the sun He nodded to la Tourette. "But first, let's explore our nearby industries."

We entered a low lying building, a series of workshops where women mended sheets, sewed chemises, aprons and nursing bonnets which were largely allocated to other public hospitals in Paris. He explained that some form of work was mandatory for the residents and long-termed patients. "If physically and mentally able. Although, we do give latitude for them to choose their craft and hours, receiving payment for their labor, a nominal sum to be sure, as we don't wish anyone to become extravagant."

He smiled proudly at the workers we passed, many shy but clearly happy with his visit. During the tour of the various workshops, he and la Tourette often stole glances out the windows, seemingly checking weather conditions, until the taciturn Tourette unexpectedly cried, "Professor Charcot! The clouds and winds have dispersed! The sun shines! Not a leaf stirs!"

His a shout of unmistakable joy, sticking his head out a window while Charcot rushed to confirm what seemed to them a miraculous turn of good fortune. "My goodness! Yes, it is quite calm! Perfect!"

To view a turnaround in the weather as some miraculously beneficent event seemed quite unusual, yet naively I fell into believing it a charming response for such eminent doctors, their enthusiasm for the re-emergence of the summer sun.

But what would soon become evident was the near childlike delight Dr. Charcot took in orchestrating neurological surprises for an audience.

And one definitely waited for us.

Our outdoor tour resumed, passing the vegetable gardens and fruit orchards methodically tended by Salpêtrière's women. An elderly, silver-haired worker, surprisingly agile, ran up to Charcot and reverently held out a fresh peach. Gladly he accepted her gift then gave it to Tourette for safekeeping. Charcot seemed eager to continue leading our group toward higher ground; he climbed tirelessly, manoeuvring a steep rise until he stopped at last. We were offered a sweeping view of Salpêtrière, the vast complex, the city. He leaned upon his cane, wanting everyone to absorb the enormity of his domain. "Some choose to call what is out there the shadow city… and Paris the city of light." He reflected, removed the black chimney hat, daubed his forehead with a handkerchief. "The reverse more accurate, for out there..." he waved his top hat, "in the multitude of buildings you see, the laboratories, research centres, clinics, in each, we work under a light different than Paris, ours is the torchlight of science which will not, cannot be extinguished."

Charcot's noble profile transfixed everyone, a strong, handsome countenance having the august bearing of a Napoleon, a Dante, and sculpted into the face his dedication for all the women living and interred at the hospital and asylum. He took out a small comb from his breast pocket to smooth back his unconventionally long hair and replaced his chimney hat.

Then we descended in an unfamiliar direction, trudging single file down a paved walkway, passing several miniature parks which Charcot noted, "serve our more meditative residents." He inexplicably began tapping the paving stones as we walked, as if in secret code to signal his approach to someone. When he stopped in front of an ornamental iron gate, we were all perspiring from the sun's heat. He pushed open the gate.

"Let us find shade here."

Entering, we took in our surroundings, a green carpeted park abundantly shaded with willow trees, their branches bending heavily with leaves. Charcot lapsed into puzzling silence and simply stared at us. His stare was his most dominant feature, a steel greyness in his eyes that few found the courage to confront, and everyone keenly aware of the doctor's reputation as the supreme hypnotist of Paris. The weight of his gaze grew increasingly uncomfortable. What was he seemingly waiting for us to comprehend? Each person looked around.

We were not alone.

Deeper into the park, visible through the drooping willows, three women sat on a stone bench in a grassy clearing. A painter could not have conjured a more pleasing image: all three ladies were magnificently dressed in high-necked, white muslin dresses. And despite the day's torrid heat, the women wore white, elbow-length gloves which matched the gorgeous white cream of their dresses. Farther behind them a grey wall, speckled with mildew, served almost as a painted backdrop.

They were like a sitting-room tableau, three genteel women fashionably adorned with large, single-feathered hats, engaged, so it seemed, in an animated discussion for each of their long, feathered plumes waved rather busily as they chatted.

Catching Charcot's smile turn sly, I guessed we were witnessing a planned event. He gave a showman's sweep of the cane to invite an approach to the ladies on the stone bench. No one budged, no one prepared to be the first to advance. Instead, the interns exchanged uncertain glances. Charcot's response was to shrug and walk a short distance away. He took the peach from Tourette, sat at another bench, and focused on eating, making a grand show of indifference as to what we chose to do.

Eventually, an irresistible urge had the group moving, en masse, slowly toward the women. I joined them, prodded by an almost giddy sense of intrigue.

I think we all thought, *Let's eavesdrop on what these elegantly attired women are discussing.*

Their feathered plumes continued to happily wave, ostrich feathers dyed different colours, one a light blue, another buttery yellow, and the third a delicate rose.

We drew nearer until their features took form, a young intern beside me unable to stifle a gasp of shock. At close range, the gentility we imagined was replaced by a depiction of infirmity. Our group, to a person, struggled with disappointment. The three women were a haggard lot. We saw care-worn faces belonging to the Salpêtrière, women who had spent many sorrowed years at the asylum. We had not come upon a tea party, not ladies conversing about art and literature, but Salpêtrière residents uncontrollably shaking with various palsies.

Charcot came behind us. "What you are witnessing are three distinct manifestations of tremors—three discrete neurological maladies." La Tourette's quick signal told me to move to the side and begin transcribing. "But can anyone of you, my neurologists of the future," Charcot continued with his sly smile, "distinguish one tremor from the other? Can someone here make an accurate diagnosis of each woman's condition? Regard them carefully. Is there, perchance, a measuring device at your disposal?"

He waited. No one ventured a response. The silence lingered

unpleasantly. The women, all far into their sixties, maintained their trembling poses, speaking not a word, probably coaxed to show off their fashionable wardrobes. I could not tolerate the growing awkwardness.

"The feather," I spoke up.

Charcot's aide-de-camp shot me a furious look, a fuming Tourette, his thoughts easy to read: *How dare she, a stenographer, an employee callow to the ways of the Salpêtrière, a woman, have the impertinence to actually respond!*

Charcot folded his arms, amused and curious. "How so, Mademoiselle?"

I felt certain of my observation as the woman with the pale blue feather expressed a certain elegance in her movements "The blue feather exhibits an alternating rhythm, from immobility to undulation, a stop-start cycle occurring approximately every thirty seconds."

"Stomp my cane, excellent! What our recordist just described is one of the tremor conditions attributable to multiple sclerosis." He looked for more information. "And what of the woman with the yellow feather?"

I studied her, a petite woman, surely the oldest of the trio. She sat at the far end of the bench, looking absentmindedly in the distance. The heat was taking its toll on her heavily powdered face, dark rivulets of perspiration coursed down yellowish powdered cheeks.

"The yellow feather exhibits a rapid and continuous fluttering."

"Precisely! A distinct feature of Parkinson's disease! But what can one say with regard to our woman with the reddish feather? Be forewarned, this tremor confounds most students."

I began to realize that someone had made a crude effort to coordinate the colour of the feathers with each woman's make-up. The rose-plumed woman, sitting in the middle, a head taller than the others, had a lantern jaw caked with scarlet rouge, melting with the heat.

"The rose coloured feather flutters rapidly then sometimes subsides," I said.

"Is there a consistent cycle?"

"It appears erratic."

"What!" His hands spread outward in mock bewilderment. "A disease with no rules?"

"Wait, I see!" (Oh, how caught up I was in the excitement of discovery!) "The fluttering begins only when the woman attempts to move her body. If she makes no attempt at movement the tremor is controlled."

"Superb! Mademoiselle has thrown a light on to our demonstration clearer than that of the noon day sun. Our patient with the red feather actually suffers from the same disease as the patient with the yellow feather, Parkinson's, but at a less severe state of degeneration. You are a true observer, Mademoiselle Recordist."

"Our probationary recordist." came la Tourette's sarcastic barb.

Charcot, choosing not to contradict his chief assistant's authority, nodded gravely. "A position sorely in need of being filled. Show us your note taking later," he put out his order gruffly. But I knew he had made his favourable decision long ago.

La Tourette, however, pored over my notes later that afternoon in Charcot's outpatient office while our Director, secretly amused, kept a respectful distance. La Tourette put on his wire-rims to scrutinize every line. Every word.

After completing his careful review, he gave me a very unhappy look. "Your dictation is without error," he acknowledged curtly. "It is verbatim."

Charcot feigned surprise. "Isn't Mademoiselle Forette simply amazing!"

The notepad returned, I felt the depth of Charcot's stare, as he never tired of seeking some place behind my thoughts. "Has the lady sent you to me?" he asked.

Lady??

Charcot savoured my confusion. "Providence," he smiled.

A question I didn't answer.

At day's end, heading home to Madame Dujardin's boarding house, my steps were light, buoyed by pride. I had shown the ability to observe accurately, proved my competence as a verbatim recordist, and engendered admiration from the world's greatest neurologist. I was elated.

What then, when reaching the door, gave me a vague, unsettled feeling? My self-importance had strangely eroded, replaced by a kind of shakiness, disorientation, something amiss. When I took to re-examining my behaviour toward the palsied women, it now seemed reprehensible. My eagerness to participate in Charcot's neurological games and parade my powers of perception came at what cost? Had I not, for a taste of the great man's approval, made myself a complicit partner in the theatrical demonstration? Surrendering scruples, daring to view the feathered plumed ladies as necessary object lessons. I was disgusted with myself.

In an emotional turmoil, I hurried inside to find Madame Dujardin. Would she please have the porter fill my tub for a bath? The only thought was to immerse myself in water, as hot as I could tolerate, a cleansing of the guilt which clung like dirt. The women of Salpêtrière were not playthings.

Slowly, I slipped into the tub top full with water and, as hoped, so hot it felt almost unbearable. I sank down until the water lapped to my chin. Closing my eyes did not help. The ostrich feathers were fluttering to measure the depths of disease. I remembered the ancient Egyptian belief that when dead souls passed into the underworld, their hearts were weighed on the Scales of Judgement and measured against the single feather of truth. The ibis-headed scribe Thoth recorded the results. If the scales fell into balance, the dead kept their hearts and were guided into the Boat of the Sun, forever blessed, conducted across the waters to a heaven called the Elysian Fields. If measured unworthy, the heart was devoured by a beast—the heartless soul condemned to a netherworld, ruled by chaos.

I submerged and held my breath to rid myself of the day's events, to ward away the women and their trembling feathers. When my lungs wanted to burst, I shot up, gasping for air, only to see the three palsied women, side by side under the fierce, noon-day sun. Three kindly women coerced to wear elbow-length gloves, abiding the fate of sweltering heat, the different coloured rouges melting in rivulets down their aged faces. The gloves they wore, sturdy cotton, high-buttoned, in the intolerable heat, white elbow-length gloves.

Chapter 37

...stick up something indecent in full view over your door; then you'll get rid of the respectable people, the most insufferable of God's creatures.

Paul Gauguin

PGo

I

What prompted an omnibus ride and then a long walk to the far edges of Paris was Félix Fénéon's tantalizing remark: 'Julie, I know someone who owns incredible Cezannes.'

Yet when I found myself in front of a dilapidated, four story apartment building on rue Cail, I had second thoughts. The entire neighbourhood reeked of neglect, meanness, and such an awful stink that I considered turning on my heels. What in particular unnerved me was the distinct smell of animal blood rolling down the street from a nearby slaughterhouse.

Had my art advisor written down the address correctly? I looked again on the back of f.f.'s calling card: *22 rue Cail* and the name, *P. Gauguin*. If 'an astute collector' who sometimes parted with a painting for a reasonable price, as f.f. claimed, then *P. Gauguin* cared little for earning a profit and moving to better lodgings.

f.f. cautioned, "Four treacherous flights of stairs must be climbed, but perhaps worth the effort."

Prepared to overcome almost any obstacle to perhaps gain another Cezanne painting, I entered a vestibule overrun with foul smelling trash. Cautiously I climbed the stairs, a few nearly rotted through, and noticed walls mottled with mould and urine stains. Unpleasant odours hung in the air, overcooked cabbage from some apartment, and faeces from the privies on each landing. The higher I climbed the thicker the stench. I had to fight the urge to run back down the stairs.

Persevering to the fourth and final floor, there was but one apartment. Across the centre panel of the door someone had painted in florid, red script, one flagrant word—

PGo

I paused. Often I had heard sailors spit out the offensive epithet on the streets of Marseilles—*peygo*. Prick!

Would a bit of gutter port slang steer me away from the Cezanne treasures? The door was slightly ajar, as if a dare to enter. I pushed, taking a step inside an eerily dark room, made more so by a trembling candle which cast a phantasmagoria of shadows on the walls. I called out a brave hello, keeping very still. No one answered. I tried again: "Hello?"

Again, no response—but I heard breathing... light, raspy. Peering deeper into the darkened room, I made out a small, military cot where someone equally small was sleeping. He or she was covered in a blanket, the face turned toward the wall where the moving shadows played. I hesitated, unsure, in a very uncertain situation. The curled shape under the Tartan blanket suggested someone six or seven years of age.

I tried to take in my surroundings. Above was a skylight draped with a large swath of sail cloth, an artist's device to distribute light evenly, but the sun had set, and the table candle the only means to observe that I had come to a very humble, one room flat, hinting of penury; but became somewhat encouraged when I saw a painter's workspace. Quietly, so as not to awaken the child, I went to the easel, but no painting. On a side table there were paint tubes purposefully laid out in chromatic order and expensive marten hair brushes soaking in clear bottles of turpentine. An artist's alcove, very tidy, I thought, arranged with near feminine care. Pinned on the wall were photographs and prints culled from art magazines. No Cezanne on view anywhere.

I sat on the painter's highchair and began to savour the charm of P. Gauguin's private corner, which seemed a deliberate fight against the grim poverty of the one room flat. His two-penny art collection decorating the wall were mostly females. Renaissance choices: Botticelli's lovely Venus rising naked from the seashell; a print of Fra Angelico's *Annunciation*, the Angel Gabriel and the adolescent Virgin Mary balanced in graceful counterpoise.

A touch of modernity was a photograph of Edouard Manet's infamous *Olympia*, the reclining nude whom an outraged public had called a brazen whore because she dared to stare at them with blasé impudence.

What particularly captured my attention was a sepia photograph of a young, quite beautiful woman who stared mournfully at me with dark, lustrous eyes. She had olive skin, ink black hair and charming spit curls. I unpinned the photograph. Written on the back, in similar script to that on the door, the name, *Aline Tristan Chaza Gauguin*. While pondering her identity, the child across the room gave up a tiny moan, a leg jerked, a spasm kicking away a portion of the blanket to show a boy's leg, and then he relapsed into fitful sleep.

Atop the artist's drawing table were more Botticelli prints of voluptuous maidens, another Virgin Mary visited by the angel Gabriel, and several Japanese block prints of half-naked courtesans.

Caught up in discovering another person's taste in art, I realized that I was also gaining unexpected access into the psychology of a man never met. P. Gauguin's pictorial harem evinced an attraction toward women of grace, be they angelic or whorish.

What more of his personality? Opening the table drawer, I sifted through paraphernalia and I came upon a letter, apparently unfinished.

My dear wife, Mette,

Let me paint a picture, in words, of the dismal existence your son Clovis and I endure in Paris: dry bread, cheap drink, and the occasional sausage. Presently the little fellow is confined to his bed by a fever. Don't worry, Clovis will pull through, as will his father.

In these straightened circumstances I have offered myself as a bill-poster to an advertising company. My respectable appearance made the director laugh, but I explained that I had a sick child and that I wanted work. So now I earn 5 francs a day, pasting posters on back alley walls and playbill columns in the train stations. Your Danish self-esteem will be hurt, I'm sure, at having a bill-poster husband.

As for our future, I have no illusions. Therefore if one day, when my circumstances have improved, I find a woman who may be to me something beside a mother, etc., it ought not to astonish you.

Another alarming moan from the boy made me hurriedly replace the 'psychological' discoveries; I went to P. Gauguin's son, Clovis, sleeping restlessly. The candle lit up his face, the forehead bathed in sweat, and cheeks tainted with the rosy rings of the smallpox fever. I hoped little Clovis might recover, free of the pox scars that marked me.

It was disturbing to think a father would leave his son alone in such a condition, hopefully not posting advertisements in back alleys, but perhaps the father had only slipped out to buy medicine at a nearby apothecary? Certainly someone with medical knowledge had shaved the boy's head to keep infection at bay.

The boy, tossing and turning on the cot, made me want to do something. Might hypnosis alleviate his terrible discomfort? Until now I had only practiced hypnosis on the isolated women at the Salpêtrière Asylum. Would hypnotizing a boy of seven be too reckless?

Too dangerous?

His encrusted eyelids suddenly opened. We stared at each other in silence. Strangely, he seemed not fully awake. An amazing thought came —*what if in his feverish state he approximates the lethargic phase Dr. Charcot induces in his hypnotized subjects?* Then I might, in his semi-conscious state, be whoever I suggested. An airy apparition... a dream figure. He still stared without the least sign of fear. If ever an opportune moment for a bold experiment, it had arrived—Clovis and I shall take a journey!

So I let the words fall gently—"Clovis... you see me, you see... your Guardian Angel..." It was shameful poppycock and I scolded myself, *For heaven sake, what is it you seek to do with this child?* His eyes opened a little wider, the boy's focus sharpened upon me.

Amidst the phantasmagoric shadows, I sat beside him, yearning to map another state of consciousness, needing no persuasion to lure a fever-stricken boy into dream travel, angel guarded.

I offered him the serenity and magic of flight. "My wings are sturdy." I spoke in a calm, even voice. "I can fly you wherever you want."

Touchingly, he asked, "May I just walk with my Papa?"

"Take you father's hand." I gave him mine to hold, becoming his father, accompanying the child in his trance through memories. We took steps down into the bowels of what I soon realized was St. Lazarre Railroad Station. *Cold.* He said he felt, so *cold.* Tenderly, I tucked Clovis in the Tartan blanket, encouraging him to describe where we were.

An hour or less must have passed when his dream journey concluded with a sweet, light laugh that only children can give; but this quickly followed by muffled, timorous sobbing. I became determined to quell the heart-rending sobs, to lift the fever from him. My hypnotic whisperings eventually lulled Clovis into true sleep.

As evening closed in, my presence began to feel like criminal behaviour. I wanted to escape. Spurring my flight, the candle flickered wildly then ominously sputtered out. Grabbing my purse I made my way through the darkness. Once out on the landing, there came the sound of wooden clogs heavily climbing stairs. I panicked. What if it were P. Gauguin?

He mustn't find me here!

Running to the water closet at the other end of the landing, I closed the door behind me—but it had no latch, no lock!

The only method to keep the door shut was to insert two fingers into the hole—where a latch should have been—and pull tight. Crouched on the privy, holding the door, I prayed my protruding fingers would escape notice, and prayed again that he wouldn't have a need to relieve himself. I waited, a thief who had stolen a dream.

All water closets are foul smelling but I was trapped in the foulest. The door I clutched, inches from my face, was smeared with old and new faeces. The only means of moving away from the faeces was to release my grip and let the door swing open. I closed my eyes, choosing to endure the stench. When the footsteps withdrew into the flat, I made an ignoble escape down the stairs.

II

Christening the experiment a Hypno-Dream, certain of having accomplished something extremely new and bold, I transcribed Clovis Gauguin's dream or memory in his childish tone.

The clock's big, said Clovis, like a one-eye monster with a long, stiff neck, and two claws that point to 12; but gosh, it's just a clock, and I shouldn't be scared, and I'm holding Papa's hand real tight, goin' step by step down into the dark, colder and colder, down. Papa says we're going down into a train station named Saint-Lazarre after somebody who came back from the dead. I try to count the steps, but they're just too darn many and I'm not too good with numbers. Gosh, I'm so hungry! All Papa and me seem to eat is mouldy cheese with bread so hard I think it's gonna break my teeth. But Papa says, don't worry, buckaroo, 'cause I got baby teeth and new one's will come back. I guess if this Saint Lazarre can come back from the dead, so can teeth.

It's cold down here in Saint Lazarre's belly! The cold hurts in my chest when I take deep breaths. Wish I had a warmer jacket, but I ain't no complainer. I'm already six and a half.

Lookin' up at Papa, he's so tall, and strong like a giant. Papa carries a bucket sloshin' with poster-glue. He lets me carry the big glue brush. Workin' with Papa makes me feel grown-up. When we put up all the posters in the rucksack, Papa says we'll get lots of money from Papa's boss and then we'll eat lamb cutlets and go to the Wild West show and see Buffalo Bill shoot cigarettes out of a lady's mouth.

Saint Lazarre's train station is bigger and grander than any church I've ever seen in Denmark. The roof, w-a-a-y up, is all smoky glass and black sparrows are sittin' on branches Papa say's are beams made of iron. We march past men sleeping on benches and hugging bottles like Aline hugs her doll. Aline, my sister, had to stay at home in Denmark. The sleeping men are all shivering like me! I think maybe they're cowboys wounded by Indians. Or maybe soldiers who lost the war they were fightin'.

Yikes! A train whistle shrieks something awful and really scares me. Then big steamy clouds start rolling over us. Lost inside the clouds, I hold Papa's hand extra tight. Gee, a pole comes out of the

369

clouds like Jack's beanstalk, only it has lots of coloured papers stuck to it, maybe it's a maypole like the one Aline and me ran around once.

Papa sets down the glue bucket and we look at all the coloured posters showing' just about every fun thing in the world. I like the poster of the clown in a circus ring, he's got three, funny clumps of hair and they're orange! And he's pointing to two elephants standing on little rubber balls and to three striped tigers flying through hoops. Sure lots of writing on the posters, but I can't read well yet. Look! There's a picture of a wavy-hair girl who looks just like my sister Aline. She's holding up a cup for her mommy to pour in hot steamy cocoa. Papa wanted to take Aline to Paris instead of me. But Mommy said, No! Poor Aline, she cried a lot because she wanted to go. Then Mommy and Papa got into another scary fight. Papa says girls and boys both gotta grow up. Mommy says, 'take Clovis, he can grow up first.' I sure wish I could have that cup of hot cocoa right now.

From the rucksack, Papa pulls out one of our posters. "Dip your brush, little buckaroo," he tells me.

I'm good at followin' orders. I dip the brush into the bucket and hand it oozing with glue to Papa who's maybe really Buffalo Bill. Or maybe he's a saint, like Saint Lazarre, the guy who Papa says came back into town after everybody thought he was dead and buried. Taking the gooey brush, Papa slaps and smooths out one of our posters right over another one. Papa's poster shows a black, fat-faced cat smokin' a cigarette. It's so funny it makes me laugh. Gee, I ain't laughed since I left Denmark. I miss my sister Aline, and my brothers too. Most of all, I miss Mommy.

I could almost hear Clovis' quiet sobs again. Best for me to steer clear of P. Gauguin, no matter how many Cezanne's he owned.

Chapter 38

... we have only one weapon, our own judgement.

Camille Pissarro

THE WANDERING WOMB

The Charcot family set off for a brief holiday to Venice at the invitation of Madame and Dr. Richetti. The mansion temporarily mine, I gave the servants an evening off and arranged a rendezvous with Sigmund. He still worked late at the Salpêtrière laboratory with his microscopic studies of children's brains. I waited for him in the library which I kept unlit, relishing the darkness, letting the faraway hearth dwindle to a faint, ember throbbing glow.

The entrance gate was unlocked for him, the front door as well. I planned a special evening. Somewhere in the empty house a cuckoo clock chirruped ten times, the precise moment Sigmund entered the library. He had no idea where I was in the darkness. Purposefully I remained quiet, having chosen a corner seldom visited, amidst glass tables of ancient and gruesome medical instruments. I watched his shadowy figure take tentative steps, allowing him to wander and guess where I might be, wanting to put him in a heightened state, his senses acute, so that what transpired tonight would not be forgotten.

I opened the glass case of the herbarium which ignited Charcot's clever automated lamp, the sharp click sounding like the cocking of a pistol. "Sigmund, over here."

He followed the new glow across the library's dark expanse and came to my side, watching me silently reach into the gas-lit display. "All of this is impressively mysterious," he murmured.

From a bed of plant specimens, I snapped off a sprig of heart-shaped leaves, passing it under his nose. He jerked his head back. "A most peculiar aroma."

"Yes, most do find the smell offensive. Valerian. Ancient Greeks asserted that its odour forced the wandering womb back into its proper place." I inhaled deeply. "Cats, for their own inscrutable reasons, purr in ecstasy when anywhere near valerian."

"Wandering womb? *Qu'est-ce que c'est?*"

"A condition the Greeks called *hysterikos.*"

He nodded. "Hysteria, of course."

"Thus began the administering of valerian, in various modalities, to tame the so-called wandering womb; but wanting, in essence, to keep a woman's emotional nature caged, something akin to Charcot's..." (my presentation carefully planned). "Ovarian Compressor."

Yesterday, brought by Jeanne Charcot to Sabrine's room, I took in the horror of seeing the bulky device strapped around her like crude body armour. My fury yesterday would be channelled tonight, presenting to Sigmund what he most valued, cogent reasoning. "I sense that the primitive and preposterous concept of the wandering womb has been resurrected at Salpêtrière, would you not agree?"

Duty bound to Charcot's ideas, he launched a defence. "The ancient Greeks actually put forth a working construct, namely, Valerian's singular scent, capable of affecting the nervous system. We have realized over time that certain nerve endings respond to olfactory stimulation." His sequential thinking, gathering connections, kept me alert. "And we are moving toward certainty that pressure points, brilliantly mapped by Charcot, affect nerve ganglia. So, why not the ovarian harness suppressing nerve pain?"

"First off," I responded, "the ancients failed to appreciate your olfactory hypothesis and gave up on valerian. The sons of Hippocrates turned toward a more efficacious treatment of the errant womb—removing it. Today in certain cultures, not to be outdone by their predecessors, the total extirpation of the clitoris is deemed appropriate to keep a woman's wildness in check. Now Charcot sees the knife, scalpel and surgery on the horizon."

He was quite aware of the hospital gossip that an oophorectomy might be performed on Sabrine. He took the valerian sprig and put it back into its glass enclosed case. "Your knowledge of medical history never fails to impress."

The automated lamp, lighting our faces, clicked off.

I strolled away, coming to the vast collection of books lining the rosewood shelves. Even in darkness, the gold-lettered spines glittered. "Charcot's library has been at my disposal for quite some time."

He watched me closely. "Certainly a monumental collection, the envy of any scholar or scientist."

"Yes. Each and every morning a cartload of journals, periodicals and monographs arrive. I sort and categorize them for Dr. Charcot."

"Do you find time to read any of them?"

"I read most of them."

Quiet and cautious, he waited for where my remarks would lead.

"The idea," I said, "that the organs of reproductivity are the culprits for hysteria has been astonishingly resistant to change."

I walked over to the French doors for a view of the night sky. A pale, gibbous moon, near full, a reminder that Charcot's anonymous letter would soon arrive, offering another horrid description of his impending death.

Sigmund came over, his patience becoming thin. "Julie, I suppose this preamble will lead somewhere, although I thought you had a Congress in mind. I left my portmanteau on the hall table."

I ignored the portmanteau talk. "You've read Sabrine's case folder, you're aware of Salpêtrière's preoccupation with her menstrual cycles."

"The doctors are certainly determined to record all of the hysterics' menses," he admitted. "I suppose the goal is to seek a correlation to their attacks. "

"Yes, of course." I lit Charcot's desk lamp. "Help me clear off his paraphernalia as I want to show you something in Sabrine's file."

He looked concerned. "Do you have permission to be in possession of her file?"

A question I had no intention of answering. "Just help make space so I can spread out her photographic plates."

Ill-at-ease, he nonetheless removed Charcot's quill and inkstand. I took the hand-painted cigar box and placed it on the floor. A framed photograph of Charcot made us pause. It showed him atop an African elephant and a toucan at rest on his shoulder. He wore a pith helmet and a puckish grin, an image making him less a world-renowned neurologist than an exuberant schoolboy on holiday. The inscription read, 'Pollux I, Zoological Gardens.'

I turned nostalgic. "Before finding the courage to meet Charcot face to face, I used to spy on him at the Zoological Gardens."

"Spy?" He picked up the framed photograph for a closer look, a Charcot who was clearly ecstatic to be sitting upon a huge, leaf-eared elephant.

"To gain a better measure of the man before knocking on his door. I read in the newspaper that his favourite pastime was to spend Tuesday afternoons at the Zoological Gardens."

"A respite after his Morning Lesson." He handed me the bamboo framed photograph.

"Even today the gamekeepers accord him special permission to ride any animals of his choosing. I've watched him happily bouncing upon camels, Tibetan ponies, and his favourite elephant, Pollux II."

"What happened to Pollux I?"

"As with practically all of the zoo animals, Pollux I was butchered for food during the Franco-Prussian War. A starving Paris ate anything available."

He frowned. "That cursed war. Would that it be the last between our countries."

"Whenever he trotted around on his Pollux II, a horde of laughing children would invariably follow."

"Jean-Martin Charcot, a pied piper?" He smiled with disbelief.

"How could children not be entranced by the fantastic scene of an aristocratic gentleman, dressed in top hat and frock coat, bumping about on an exotic animal? Charcot merrily tossed candy to them as they skipped beneath him."

"So you became familiar with a tender-hearted side of Charcot?" he pursued.

I set the photograph face down on the floor, amidst the other personal belongings. "He really cared more about the animals than the children."

I produced Sabrine's folder, taking out the photographic plates to line them up on the desk. "Here, numbered in their sequential order, are nine poses that depict a classical attack of Grand Hysteria."

He showed his irritation. "Charcot has already shared these with me."

"Yes, the maestro is quite proud of Dr. Londe's work in the Photography Department."

Again, his accusing question: "Has either Charcot or Dr. Londe given permission for you to have these?"

Again I ignored his concern, directing him to the nine pictures, the nine postures. "The sequential order of a hystero-epileptic attack, as prescribed by Charcot and photographed by Alfred Londe, yes?"

"Yes," he said wearily. My refusal to answer the question of permission, he knew, was tantamount to an admission of theft.

"Let us see what's on the back of them," I suggested.

The reverse side of each photograph bore the date, written in minuscule, Latin script, as to when it was taken. I began turning the pictures, like playing cards, verse and verso, until it dawned on him that these pictures did not depict one spontaneous attack. None of the dates matched, proof the pictures were taken over a period of several years. Now he could deduce that the postures, even though sequentially numbered on the front, had in fact been carefully culled from many attacks and purposefully chosen.

He looked hard at the pictures. "Then you're saying we don't have a spontaneous attack taken with Alfred Londe's rotating lens camera?"

"Correct! None of these were recorded with the nine-lens apparatus."

I could tell he was sifting through his thoughts, absorbing the significance of these misrepresented chrono-photographs, surely remembering how Charcot would speak often and with great pride of Dr. Londe's cameras that had adapted Muybridge's rotating, multiple lens disc to authenticate a spontaneous attack of hysteria.

"Sequential photographs they are not," I said. "A fraudulent rearrangement, for certain. And doctored."

"Doctored? Isn't that a bit of an exaggeration?" he protested. "What Charcot does is merely choose the pose which best emphasizes the characteristics of each phase of Grand Hysteria."

"Doctored," I repeated, "in more ways than one." Rummaging through the desk drawer, I found a magnifying glass. "Choose any photograph."

"What am I supposed to be looking for?" he asked with increasing dismay.

I guided his hand to magnify the addition of paint pigment: the bed gown Sabrine wore showing it artificially coloured a brighter white. "Sometimes chromium white is used, sometimes white gouache, all for dramatic effect. I suppose to better resemble a Grecian robe."

"So Charcot allows his artistic tendencies to come to the fore," Sigmund reasoned.

"Oh, but how often have I heard and transcribed his mantra that the photograph is the scientific means to objectify our vision, that it secures with unerring accuracy the external phenomena of each passion which the patient lives through, offering tangible evidence of her internal derangement. I can quote him verbatim: 'The photographic plate is the true retina of the scientist.' But these!" I became vehement, "Are not corroborative of visual facts, they are enhancements, they are illusions."

He looked sullen. "Perhaps you think longer and more intensely about such things than they deserve."

"There is more, much more." I gathered the photo-plates and replaced them into the folder, turning stubbornly silent.

"If we are to help Sabrine..." his voice a softened plea, "you must tell me what prompts this investigative work of yours? What do you know about her that I don't."

"I... that is we, Jeanne and I, converse with her."

"Yes, I know," he put in, somewhat exasperated.

"She's becoming increasingly inquisitive of the outside world and asks innumerable questions. Sometimes I speak to her of my life... on one occasion I happened to mention that I posed for an artist. That's when she talked of her own posing for Drs. Londe and Charcot. Isn't that cause for..."

He raised a hand for silence. I worried. *Is he unable to take in the incriminating evidence?* He opened the cigar box and chose a cigar. "Smoking helps me maintain perspective." He found a match to strike. "Please, continue."

I took a deep breath—*Thank goodness for the calmative power of the cigar*—and continued. "Specific requests were made for Sabrine to simulate certain poses experienced during a hystero-epileptic attack. Londe and Charcot persuaded her that the purpose was to secure a more accurate study of her disease. She gladly complied. So the poses in the photo-plates are not only factually out of sequence, they are deliberately staged." I looked for a reaction. He appeared not convinced. "The actions Charcot takes here do not comport with science," I concluded, "but rather, art."

"Julie—" I did not care for his sombre look. "Julie, can we rely on the veracity of what Sabrine says?"

I walked away. The winter cold had crept into the room, and at the hearth only dying embers. I set to piling on thin strips of wood from a kindling bucket.

He approached. "You're aware that she is a fantasist."

"She is imaginative."

I built a triangular mound. Cold mornings in the laundry yard, long ago lighting up kettles for the wash taught me how to ignite a blaze under any circumstance.

"I wonder, Julie, if your emotional involvement with Sabrine needs to be tempered."

I faced him, adamant. "I can discern the truth of what she says."

"Yes... of course." His look softened to compassion. "But perhaps," he began, "perhaps Sabrine and your sister, Alexandria, whom you say is confined at St. Pierre in Marseilles..."

"I cannot talk about her."

"I understand. But perhaps the two have blurred into one person?"

He almost inclined me to smile. "A logical inference to draw, Doctor Freud."

"A psychological conclusion, I think." He looked determined to reach a deeper part of me.

"Putting aside my psychological confusion, if such exists," I countered, "consider this detail: Jeanne says her father and the physician-artist Paul Richer are planning a book, an attempt to demonstrate that the laws of hysteria, formulated at Salpêtrière, apply to the past as well. They intend to present a comparison between the demoniacs depicted in the paintings of Raphael and Carpaccio to the doctored photographs of Sabrine." I stressed 'doctored.'

"Yes, I've heard about the book. The intent is to redefine religious possession in terms of the scientific. A worthy endeavour."

How infuriating, his insistence on viewing all of Charcot's endeavours in a favourable light. My anger rose, poured out—"Sabrine is nothing more than a convenient puppet for Charcot! A woman to harness for his own dreamful theories! He has more feelings for elephants and monkeys than he does for the unfortunate women at the Salpêtrière! You are the only doctor who dares to take a different approach with Sabrine."

"I'm not sure if I can adequately help her..."

"It is precisely because of your efforts at listening," I interrupted, "that she becomes more cogent, more mindful of her past... fragments, I admit."

"And so remain fragments, too disjointed to put together in a coherent fashion. I fear my listening approach will produce nothing of consequence."

"No-no!" I protested, not wanting him to lose confidence. "She really has improved because of you, Sigmund. She enjoys her sessions. Astonishingly, she calls them what you said Anna O sometimes calls them, 'chimney sweeps.'"

"That would be astonishing." He seemed disinclined to believe me.

"Something very similar, 'Dr. Sigmund is a good doctor,' she says, 'he wants to sweep out the soot from my brain.' Surely you gain some picture of her past?"

He shook his head. "Next to nothing. I've suggested that unearthing one's past might be helpful, but... here, listen to her answer." He produced a small notepad, smiled at my surprise. "I've become a recordist, like you."

That her words were important enough for him to transcribe gave me hope—"And her answer?"

"To quote, 'But if I attend the costumed ball with Monsieur Present, should I accept a dance with Monsieur Past who may waltz me off to where? Or being more fickle, should I accept a dance with the Harlequin, Monsieur Future, who will surely sweep me off my feet, but to where? Then might not Monsieur Present entertain doubts as to whose arms in time I belong? And he abandons me altogether.' End of quote."

A sad smile escaped me. Her thoughts were like wise poems. *Yes, where in time does Sabrine rightly belong?*

"Oh Sigmund, I feel if she remains much longer at Salpêtrière her chances to recover will be lost!"

"What is it you fear?"

"An oophorectomy."

Uncomfortable, he exhaled a dark plume of smoke and threw the cigar in the fire.

It was critical that he understand my concern. "If the surgeons here have their way, Sabrine's ovaries will be removed. Those competent with a scalpel are urging the procedure, and Charcot might soon relent."

He chose to equivocate. "Surgeons elsewhere lay claim to certain successes with oophorectomies."

I released my fury. "Would you really countenance such butchery? Answer me!" I demanded.

"I would not advocate it," he was quick to state, "and I'm sure Charcot will remain resistant to such a procedure. He is far too enlightened. Other means are at his disposal to relieve her pains."

I laughed, a guttural laugh, and went directly to the étagère where Charcot kept the prototype. I held aloft the Ovarian Compressor with disdain. "And this is what the great mind of Salpêtrière conceives as a cure?"

"Apparently a useful counter measure," he replied, "since who can rule out Charcot's hysterogenic zones, especially the pelvic zone, as depositories of nerve inflammation."

With disgust I shook the compression device in his face: "Something utterly barbaric as this, made of leather and metal screws, to fasten around a woman's abdomen, to tighten the screws so as to squeeze together her uterus!"

Furious, I turned toward the fire. He saw I had every intention of throwing Charcot's medieval contraption into the flames. He seized my arm.

"I don't like men grabbing me roughly," I said.

Disconcerted, he stepped back.

I pleaded, "Sigmund, now is not the time to stumble, to fall back into the darker centuries of chastity belts and oophorectomies. We need to experiment with what is right under our noses."

"What is that?"

"Hypnosis, as a therapeutic tool for Sabrine."

He showed no enthusiasm, shaking his head. "That would open the door to her hysterical condition, to her psychological frailty. There's too much risk involved."

"It seems not too much risk for Dr. Breuer in Vienna," I challenged.

His look showed troubled thoughts. "Has something untoward happened to Anna O?"

"Breuer's situation with Anna O has taken some strange twists." He found the poker, pushed and fiddled with the fire as though he wished to extinguish it. "Breuer suspects that Anna's hypnoid states are more self-induced. And she begins to divide her personality among the many languages she speaks. After one session, when he awakened her from the hypnoid state, she wrapped her arms around him with undue passion. It took great effort to extricate himself. Fortunately, a servant's knock at the door freed him from an embarrassing discussion with the patient. Extremely upset, Breuer may soon discontinue his hypnosis and discourage any of Anna O's hypnotic states."

I plopped down upon the sofa, feeling demoralized, staring at the dancing flames. He sat beside me. Absent-mindedly, I twisted and untwisted the main lug of the Ovarian Compressor. He noticed. "I have heard, Julie, that several of the hysterics gain much relief from the device and actually beg to wear it."

"It pains me to hear that." I meant no pun, but it brought an idea. "What if certain hysterics at Salpêtrière bear some hidden guilt which instigates their suffering?" I expanded the hypothesis, "What if they willingly welcome pain, in any form, to expiate the guilt."

"Such as a compression belt." He was far too clever not to see the chain of thought.

"Yes, a device which painfully crushes the ovaries."

"Expiation and guilt, Julie, run far afield of neurology."

"They run to psychology!"

"Closer to religion."

I stood up, frustrated. Did Sigmund Freud derive pleasure at crossing swords with me? Angrily I jiggled the contraption in front of his face again, "This, at best, is a miserable metaphor for relieving guilt."

And before he had any chance to intervene, I tossed the Ovarian Compressor into the fire.

"A senseless act," he said. His grim look disappointed me.

"Nothing is senseless," I replied.

The leather was first to succumb to the heat, smouldering and smoking, contorting and melting almost like butter, the iron underpinnings more obstinate, the screws, bolts and clamps took time to give off a slow throbbing glow.

He corrected himself, "I spoke hastily. Julie Forette does nothing without reason. But you will be better served at the Salpêtrière if you act more judiciously."

We watched the Ovarian Compressor deteriorate in the flames, become unrecognizable, a scorched heap of twisted nothing. He cast an uneasy gaze at the desecration of Charcot's palliative for hysterics. "This incipient hostility of yours toward Dr. Charcot perplexes me. His vast experience and profound discoveries should shame us to defer to his judgement."

I tugged at a loose strand of hair. "I am of two minds about him."

"Is that so?" He waited for more.

I heaved a sigh, purposefully melodramatic. "Oh, a sudden fatigue has rendered my mental faculties quite useless. Perhaps the moment to administer a dose of cocaine vigour has arrived."

"Yes, maybe a little more brain power might... bridge our divide. I'll retrieve the portmanteau."

"Yes, do that."

Our time for a subcutaneous injection had arrived.

Chapter 39

**My guide and I came on that hidden road to make our way back...
We climbed, he first and I behind, until though a small
round opening ahead of us, I saw the lovely things the
heavens hold, and we came once more to see the stars.**

Dante's *Inferno*
Canto XXXIV

Together in the Ark

Waiting for Sigmund to return with his portmanteau, I took pleasure in watching Charcot's ovarian harness burn to nothingness. Now I had to convince Sigmund to take the bold step of hypnotizing Sabrine, or at least open his eyes to the other school of thought which reigned at the hypnosis clinic in Nancy.

Dare I confide that I entered into a correspondence with the Director of the Clinic? Show him Dr. Bernheim's letter?

When Sigmund returned with the portmanteau, he took out, of all things, the Burq dynameter, obviously prepared, once we shared the cocaine, for more measurements of strength. Politely, I asked him to set the dynamometer aside. Tests of physical strength no longer held my interest.

"So be it." He brought out the red Moroccan case which Jeanne Charcot and I had bestowed upon him. Its tight hinges opened with a loud snap, inside two syringes topped full with a cocaine solution. He spoke in his business tone, "What you asked for."

Our Cocaine Congress tonight, I hoped, would be very different. Wanting a further alteration of consciousness, I asked for the most extreme method. All the needed accoutrements came out of the portmanteau. He saturated a piece of cotton with methyl alcohol and swiped it across the inside of my waiting arm, predicting a subcutaneous injection would accelerate the effect.

Yes! As the syringe sent the viscous stream into my arm, the jolt, yes, was more immediate and beyond imagining. A tidal wave of euphoric clarity swept over me.

Sigmund removed his jacket, rolled up a sleeve, and steadily injected the contents of his syringe. He joked, or half-joked, "I pray to the Peruvian god Mancao that the cobwebs be swept from my sluggish mind." He leaned back on the sofa and breathed in his own epiphanies.

I became entranced with the shimmering beauty of the coloured flames dancing in the hearth. I believed I knew that the purpose of fire was to burn away life's dross.

The energy, electric like, prompted me to my feet. I walked the room, a new-found joy to be here, in a vast repository of science and literature. I could not stop from touching the spines of the journals I had read, the books I loved. He rose, following at a discreet distance.

Does he know I am ready to sweep away all falsehood?

And so I told him, "Charcot is the reason I came to Paris, to be near his throne, to absorb his ideas. At home in Marseilles, I researched everything about him, read every essay he wrote regarding his neurological discoveries and his experimental work with hysteria. Then I knocked on his door, fully convinced that he would take me as his scribe." I paused, gauged his reaction: Sigmund's open-minded gaze invited the truth. Emboldened, I went to my purse and foraged for the letter. "Sigmund, I no longer wish to be chained to the foot of Charcot's throne. And neither should you."

He read aloud:

Dear Mademoiselle Forette,

Your inquiries into the methods we employ at the Hypnosis Clinic offer me, frankly, some amusement. As you appear to be Dr. Charcot's personal secretary and recordist, I think to myself, "Is she also the doctor's spy?' 'Or defector?' Which part you play matters little. Mademoiselle, you are most welcome to sit in on our lectures. Then perhaps returning to the Salpêtrière to infect the hypnosis staff with our common-sense ideas.

Come. We will discuss further your business offer.

> **Sincerest regards,**
> **Dr. Hippolyte Bernheim**
> **Faculty of Medicine,**
> **University of Nancy**

He handed back the letter. "Business offer?"

"To translate his lectures in English."

He rolled down his shirt sleeve, half-smiled, expressing his admiration. "No one can question Mademoiselle Forette's fortitude, determination and superior intelligence."

I wanted him with me on the journey to Nancy and the new ideas there. "You could translate his lectures into German, learn about his theory that the underlying mechanism in hypnosis is suggestion, and hypnotize Sabrine."

"And then do what?"

"Drive out her demons."

"You go to Bernheim's clinic, learn his methods, come back, and you hypnotize Sabrine."

"I can't."

"Of course, you can't. Not if Sabrine Weiss is your sister."

I couldn't meet his gaze. Looked elsewhere, anywhere. The gargoyles who guarded the balcony were sniggering at deceit discovered.

Subterfuge for so long my shield, I said, "There is much in Sabrine that reminds me of my sister."

"Alexandria." He spoke the name I invented.

"Certainly, in a manner of speaking, I have adopted Sabrine."

"She stands in for your sister."

"I suppose, yes."

"Which accounts for your tenacious crusade to have Sabrine cured."

He was encouraging the facade, I knew, keeping our Cocaine Congress of clever semantics in play even as the pure rush of cocaine was dislodging every lie I harboured.

I approached the books: there the gold glittering of Dante's *Divine Comedy*. A favourite of my father's. Unexpectedly, an ocean of gratitude rose within me, for the father who guided me toward books. A desire emerged, as strong as the cocaine that propelled it, to see him in a forgiving light. Not a bad father, he never punished, never scolded, he only jumped into a boat and rowed away. The dream I had of him: a boat stocked with bottles of rum, he rowing away, warmly waving at us, his good-bye and good-luck.

Sigmund directly behind me, encroaching, as I touched the spines, *Hell, Purgatory, Heaven.* Sigmund reaching toward the truth: "Charcot is quite fond of Dante Alighieri, often quotes him."

"My departed father had a weakness for quoting the Divine Comedy. He preferred the cantos of Purgatory. Charcot finds his inspiring quotes from Hell." I turned to face Sigmund. "Your maestro has one carved on the lintel of his summer home in Neuilly."

"Which says?"

"'No word survives their living season; Mercy and Justice deny them even a name; let us not speak of them; but look and pass on.'"

"Who are them?"

"The suffering souls who in life were indecisive, half-hearted: the gray multitudes who fell short because of doubt, fear, those who were neither hot nor cold, now sentenced to hell, but not the deeper rings—for the devils have no wish to bother with them—instead they live eternally in the vestibule of hell."

Sigmund and I saw each other's interweavings. "Is the vestibule of hell where you would assign me," he asked. "Because I fear making radical suggestions to Sabrine under hypnosis? Which might exacerbate her condition and, more than likely, reaffirm her hysterical pathology?"

"I will take responsibility."

"But the responsibility is not yours to assume."

"You know that Sabrine Weiss is my sister."

He had pried the truth from me.

"And the name, Forette?"

"Conjured to hide my identity."

"Forette, of course! Drop the last two letters and you have *le forêt,* French for forest, where one can hide. A perfect pseudonym, worthy of your unconscious self."

"Word associations serve you well, Sigmund. You are the person uniquely suited to find what lies beneath our conscious selves. Juliette Weiss, *c'est moi.* She no longer hides."

He wasted no time. "Then you can explain how your sister came to Salpêtrière."

I felt I had said what was most important, Sabrine was my sister, a declaration, a badge of honour, but to go back into the murkiness of memories? I walked away, still so much energy inside me that needed to be expended. I opened the French doors to a view of a starless night. He came beside me.

I framed what answer I could. "A collusion of ignorance. The neighbours, the clergy, and the nuns of the Sacred Heart all found Sabrine's behaviour troubling. A petition was crafted and sent to the local magistrate. A medical review by an incompetent board of doctors who decided she would no longer stay with me."

"There's so much more I want to know—the family's history!" He was in a state of wonder, anticipation, excitement.

I thought it served no purpose to bring in my older brother, Justin, who gave his signature of consent to her confinement. "Whatever my memories might be," I said, "will only take you far afield. Sabrine has her own memories of what happened in our lives—extract them, however you can."

"Does she remember you?"

"Yes; and no."

I did not want to confuse him with my intuition. When my presence at Salpêtrière became known to her, she actively sought my attention, became happier and more talkative, but said nothing to hint we might be sisters. But I was convinced, at certain moments, by a deep look in her green eyes, her recognition of me. "Sabrine's silence is purposeful." I gripped his arm. "Take her back through time! Trace the history of the symptoms."

"But you must educate me, did she suffer from hystero-epilepsy? In her file, the diagnosis is only recorded several years after her admission to the asylum."

"Never any attacks such as happen here, never a sign of hystero-epilepsy at home. Never."

"But... other symptoms?

"Because she was pestered by everyone, especially the nuns, she withdrew more into herself. The medical board, composed of dullards pretending to be knowledgeable, decided that she suffered from delusions and hallucinations." I wished for a cigarette. I hid a packet of Black Cats in the upper tier library to accommodate Jeanne Charcot's secret habit. "My sister, amidst the cruelty of others, found a kinder world to inhabit." I headed for the spiral stairs.

His query followed me. "A world where she conversed with unseen spirits?"

I climbed. "She always talked to herself. I talk to myself all the time."

"Let's hope she continues to talk to me," he said.

"Your time in Paris is limited," I reminded him.

He asked, stopping my ascent. "When do you plan to tell Dr. Charcot that Sabrine is your sister?"

"When you cure her."

Reaching the upper tier, where I felt most comfortable, I leaned over the railing of gargoyles. The vastness of the library made it seem as if I were looking down in the bowels of a huge ship. Sigmund looked up wonderingly at me. An ark, we were in an ark, equipped with all the necessary knowledge for the voyage. I wanted him to loudly hear my resolve—"One way or another, I will gain Sabrine's freedom."

PART II

Chapter 40

Feelings being at the bottom of what I'm doing,
I believe I'm impenetrable.
So let the unhappy creature,
you know who I mean (Gauguin),
go on copying me as much as he likes,
there's little danger in that.

Paul Cezanne

GAUGUIN ENTERS

When I entered he was sitting cross-legged on the floor, as if the apartment belonged to him. He sat in a rigid Buddha pose, staring up at the Cezanne painting. Atop his head was an outlandish Afghan hat which resembled a crumbled chimney. Surely aware of my presence, he chose to ignore me, his focus riveted to the painting.

Art lover or not, he had let himself in without permission. I walked over to confront his intrusion. *How dare you!* were the angry words on my lips; but I uttered nothing, strangely sensing that the run from fate had ended for me—finally, he was here, the much imagined Paul Gauguin. Only he did not fit the picture I had made of him. He was broad shouldered, lean but muscular, an athletic sort who might engage in sports. The face, even in profile, struck me as brutish.

The more I observed the man's fixation on the painting, the pretence that he was alone, the more infuriated I became.

Very well, if I'm invisible, I shall knock that damnable astrakhan off your head.

Mid-way in the swing he caught my wrist—and twisted. I was forced, incapable of fighting his strength, to sit beside him on the floor.

His hooded eyes, somewhat sinister, never wavered from the painting, the mosaic view of Mount St. Victoire. "What did it cost you?" was his first question, still holding my wrist.

I managed to remain calm. "I don't know how you were able to sneak in here, but I want you to get out."

"Your dear landlady, Madame Dujardin, is a rarity, a trusting heart. She found no difficulty believing me your brother." Gauguin looked at me, finally. I just knew he was Gauguin. "But you could never pass for a sister of mine," he observed, "there is no dark blood in you." His making an aesthetic judgement of me was unnerving. I remembered the pictures of the women he pinned on his wall, his prototypes of desire. They were nudes, their flesh as smooth as alabaster, who rose from sea shells, danced in Edenic gardens, or splayed themselves whore-like on plush sofas. They were temptresses, beyond blemish, palimpsests of Eve. I felt vulnerable. He turned back to the painting. "In today's market, an astute collector might have gotten it for two hundred francs."

"The monetary value of the painting is of no importance to me."

"Well, you paid something?" he insisted.

"It was given to me freely."

"Ah, Mademoiselle, Mademoiselle," he sighed before resigning himself to educate me, "there are no free gifts in life. At best, exchanges for mutual benefit."

Releasing me, he rose and went to the painting for a closer inspection. I studied him. He was taller than most Parisian men, swarthy, beardless, a strong chin, and a long moustache of the type one saw on Spaniards. He wore a close fitting Breton sweater, showing off a muscular chest and a taste for colour, the sweater alternate bands of heather green and dark crimson. Gauguin was Bohemian elegant, from the untied foulard which hung loosely around his neck to the uniquely carved sabots he strutted in. A poseur.

I stayed stubbornly seated on the floor and complained, "You have bruised my wrist."

I was ignored. "His mysterious reds invariably maintain an astonishing vibrancy! Is he doing it with red madder, red ochre, burnt sienna? But his blues are even more intense! Cobalt blue? Ultramarine? Damn that Mediterranean sphinx! Puts the blues in the back, in the front, links them, creates a composition no one else can, a kind of compression. I must speak with him, that's certain." Gauguin found a chair, sat, and crossed one leg over the other, his checked trousers showed signs of wear at the knees, hard times. He smiled, raised an eyebrow. "So where does he hide out these days?"

"Who knows?" I struck a careless tone. I would stand my ground with him while seated. He kept his smile focused. I added, on a whim, "I'm not at liberty to divulge any information."

He came over, extended his hand. I let him help me to my feet. "Give me an address, a prior address," he urged. "Tell me, at the very least, is he still in Paris?" When I hesitated, he spoke gravely, "I must see his current work—it's imperative to me. He is painting toward compositions undreamed of."

"I can be of no help." I walked to the door and opened it. "Good day, Monsieur Whoever-you-Are," I said, weakly pretending I did not know his identity.

He approached, uncomfortably close, his hand covered mine on the door latch. "Cezanne and I are old friends," he said. I took my turn to smile at what I knew to be a lie. His hand manipulated mine to shut the door. We were very close, Gauguin's lips far too sensual not to notice, the eyes fascinating me more, hooded like a predatory hawk. He leaned toward my ear, a voice gently mocking—"May I speculate that Mademoiselle, as well, has a certain relationship with Cezanne?"

I pushed him back. "What gall! You come here, a sneaking prowler, and expect me to treat you civilly, and respond to your speculations?"

"Surely, **you** of all people can find in your heart a measure of understanding?"

The emphasis on **you** troubled me. "What am I suppose to understand?"

"I am, like you, a collector."

From whom has he received this knowledge? Has Félix Fénéon spoken to him?

"Listen closely, Monsieur Gauguin, the stark, sad, bitter truth is that Paul Cezanne has a black list and I'm almost certain that you are somewhere at the top."

"How can that be?" His air of innocence, so feigned, would have struck anyone as ludicrous.

Giving up the pretence of not knowing his name, I went further. "As a matter of fact, Monsieur Gauguin, I'm positive that you are at the pinnacle of that list." A dark pleasure ran through me. Exposing him to Cezanne's enmity.

"But Cezanne and I share fond memories," he persisted with the charade of deep friendship. "We roamed the hilltops of Pontoise, painting side by side, comrades-in-arms, one might say."

"I believe I've heard about that particular excursion. Many years ago, yes? 1874, I think. And wasn't Camille Pissarro on that trip?"

Surprisingly, my intimate knowledge pleased him. "Yes, Pissarro did accompany us—now that you refresh my memory."

"Monsieur Pissarro told me the story, how he had to persuade Cezanne to let you tag along." Gauguin's surprise that I knew Pissarro was something to savour. "And after your week together," I continued, "Cezanne told Pissarro that under no circumstance would Gauguin be in his company again. Cezanne said that you had no respect for his space, he said that you were constantly peering over his shoulder."

"A falsehood, Mademoiselle. I kept a respectful distance from the man, knowing how fearful he is of human touch."

"I think the space Cezanne implied was psychological in nature."

Gauguin grunted, half-amused. "Yes, Félix Fénéon has mentioned your keen interest in psychology and your connection to Professor Charcot, *hypnotiste extraordinaire*."

So f.f. led Gauguin to my door. Now I needed to get the rogue back out. I spoke bluntly, "Paul Cezanne has it in his head that you want to steal his ideas."

Glowering, he walked away. Strangely, the touch of his hand on mine lingered.

My intruder grew reflective as he took another long look at the mountain landscape, then addressed me, caustically, "I should just laugh at your ignorance." He aimed a thumb at his chest. "Paul Gauguin, me, the first to recognize his talent, crudely tentative back then. Me, Paul Gauguin," pointing again to himself, "who purchased his paintings when no one else would dare get near them." He sighed. "As the Bard aptly said, 'No good deed goes unpunished.' Cezanne distorts reality."

"He has a certain pathology," I found myself admitting.

"I agree, Mademoiselle, the man is neurasthenic."

"Nonetheless, his perception of you will not alter."

"And what of your perception of me?"

"That you do not respect civility." I opened the door again for his hopeful departure. He approached, slowly and deliberatively. "I won't have you," I warned, "manhandling me again."

The depth of his stare was unsettling. "Paintings are not all you collect, is it Mademoiselle Forette?"

"What are you talking about?"

"Clovis, my son, speaks of a lady who came to him when I wasn't there. He said that she stole a dream."

"How does one steal another's dream?" I countered.

"Admittedly, the boy suffered from a fever at the time—but he gave a sufficient description of her." Gauguin fingered several strands of my hair. "Her hair was the colour of cocoa, with an undercurrent of dark crimson."

"Your son is how old?"

"Six."

"I doubt if 'undercurrent', much less 'crimson', are yet in the boy's vocabulary," I haughtily challenged.

"He said the lady's cheeks were kind of funny, sprinkled with tiny marks, like pin pricks."

His fingers skimmed the pock-marks of my face. I chose not to react. I remained still, stoic. Perhaps my hostility toward Gauguin was excessive. His hand fell away, the tingling lingered. "Your son is in possession of an active imagination," I said.

"Clovis has little imagination, he takes after his mother."

The cruel letter to his wife came to mind... *As for our future, I have no illusions. Therefore if one day, when my circumstances have improved, I find a woman who may be to me something more...*

"You really need to leave," I said.

"What if I informed the authorities of your unlawful entrance to my flat?" he suggested.

"You must be joking."

"Or inform Professor Charcot of your unusual antics?" He then shrugged, indifferent, and strolled back to the painting—the holy magnet. It began to seem as if he, not I, deserved the painting. He asked if I had other Cezanne paintings.

I let down my guard. "I'm a novice at collecting, only one so far."

He pondered the remark, looking as if he were making a decision about me.

I bowed my head and walked toward the painting, really to rid myself of a funny feeling in my stomach. "And do you, Monsieur Gauguin, own Cezanne's?"

"Six."

"Impressive."

We had reached what might be considered a truce.

Finally, he went to the door to leave, suggesting that we meet again.

What to say? The funny feeling in my stomach returned. I tried to speak his language. "It might, I suppose, be to our mutual benefit."

"Let that be our measuring stick," he said with the air of a matter settled. Turning toward the stairs, he turned back. "By the way, my son Clovis."

"Yes?"

"He said the angel lady made his fever go away."

Chapter 41

i comforted myself
last night
i went through a door forgotten

antechamber of a different light

where i stood naked to my spirit
my toes curled
upon a carpet of millefleurs
speaking in tongues

unicorns listened

Sabrine

Different Paths

Time collapsed fast. I was running down one, two, three, four paths. My passion for art steadily grew stronger. I interacted more and more with those who had similar feelings.

The artist Camille Pissarro and I becoming close friends, he recruited me in his determined effort to organize another Impressionist Show.

I encouraged Sigmund's 'chimney sweeping' sessions with Sabrine, but stepped back from badgering him to hypnotize her. Hypnotizing the boy, Clovis, gave me pause. I kept the experience hidden until I could better understand the process. I also kept my letter writing from Sigmund, my patient campaign to reintroduce myself to Sabrine through letters. A sympathetic attendant, a man originally from Marseilles, not adverse to receiving a few extra francs, delivered them covertly. She gladly accepted the letters and seemed to understand them as our secret.

Perhaps the most dangerous path, akin to running toward and off a cliff, was getting involved with Paul Gauguin—married with children. My excuses seemed excusable, as we were both Cezanne collectors, our ambitions coincided, he and I, viewed from my newfound vanity, were adepts on the path to connoisseurship. He was proud to show off a part of his collection stored at the apartment of his friend, Émile Schufenecker. I was quite taken with Gauguin's artistic sensibilities. He owned a serenely beautiful pastel by Degas, a dancer adjusting her ballet slipper. It took very little time for the two of us to start sleeping together.

* * *

Dearest Bijou,

Paris! How you will love the city! Someday soon we will promenade along its tree lined avenues and grand boulevards in our pink and cream frocks. We will climb the Butte of Montmartre and view the panoramic skyline: the magnificent Church of Notre Dame, the dome ofles Invalides, gold and sparkling in sunlight, and by the end of the year, watch the erection of the tallest spire in the world! On the Butte are several windmills transformed into restaurants and cafés. My favourite is Moulin de la Galette where we shall eat fruit crepes and watch the dancing couples who waft in from every quarter of the city for the gay music.

I have had the good fortune of interesting, intelligent and fascinating friends who are eager to meet you. f.f. writes for the most avant garde journals which concentrate on literature, poetry and art. (Félix Fénéon, his proper name) I warn you, he rarely laughs, but will bequeath a smile to anyone with wit. I call him the Prince of Irony. f.f. composed the following three line filler in today's newspaper:

Finding his daughter (aged 19) lacking in austerity watchmaker, Jallot of Sainte-Etienne killed her. True, he still has eleven other children.

His satire aside, f.f. believes, firstly, beauty the only worthwhile pursuit. So you two will become fast friends.

And I know my pal, Suzanne Valadon, will adore you. When younger she worked as a trapeze artist for the Cirque Molier. She has the same mischievous streak as you. She will wear corsages of fruit and vegetables just to be different. Once Suzanne caused a sensation when she slid down the Moulin de la Galette dance hall banisters like a tomboy. Now she models for the most modern of artists.

Oh, Bijou, you will meet my artist friends—who call themselves Impressionists—and you shall love their paintings! Monsieur Edgar Degas, a devotee of the opera, paints the most beautiful ballerinas. Perhaps he will loan us his subscription loge for a night at the opera (Suzanne, an accomplished seamstress, will dress us up like princesses).

I'm resisting the urge to describe Impressionist paintings because when you come and live with me, you shall see them for yourself. But let me describe my fondest artist friend, Monsieur Camille Pissarro. He is, foremost, a gentleman who has no need for the gentleman's top hat. He wears a cabbie's cap, dresses carelessly in baggy pants, smokes English cigarettes, believes in homeopathy, socialism, and equal justice for women. He also sports a beard that will remind you of Father Christmas. I, like many others, affectionately call him "Father Pissarro."

At fifty-six he is the oldest of the original Impressionists, but he convinced me right away that in his heart he remains the youngest. He is kind-hearted, laughs easily, and listens attentively to everything you say. He expresses himself slowly, in a deep yet soft, almost musical voice. As you and I are partly of Jewish blood, so is Pissarro, who possesses a strong, Semitic nose which, I dare say, is a nose one would gladly follow across parched deserts to a promised land. The younger artists, especially the Cormon students who hang out at Père Tanguy's, respect him tremendously, follow his counsel and benefit from his innate wisdom.

He now gladly instructs me in the history of Impressionism as Father Pissarro is one of the founders of the school. Oh Bijou, I can't wait for you to see the gorgeous colours the Impressionists make!

And here is gossip fresh from the press. Pissarro thinks that he and his fellow Impressionists should have a major show together, and soon! I so much agreed with his idea and offered my services to help in any way. The Show should surpass in size and quality all previous Impressionist exhibitions.

More details will follow about this grand plan in the making. I do so imagine you and I at the Show's opening, gliding like swans through galleries of Impressionist colour.

Your loving, Egyptian Scribe
Julie

P.S. I confide, sometimes in Pissarro's presence I allow myself to feel that I am his daughter.

P.P.S. Might you share a poem now and then? Our Marseilles mailman will be most willing to deliver them to me.

Chapter 42

**Stray notes without sequence, like dreams,
like life itself, all made up of fragments...**

Notes to Daughter Aline
Paul Gauguin

GAUGUIN IN FRAGMENTS

I

The shameful, shameless truth, Paul Gauguin deeply impressed me the moment I set eyes on him. The dark hair which fell rakishly about his neck, the dark, heavy-lidded eyes with their promise of sensual pleasure, and his strong, hawkish nose which he claimed had been broken in a boxing match. Such were among the features I found attractive. A grace in the way he moved, a lazy elegance to each and every gesture, be it as simple as undoing his scarf, picking up a cognac glass, smoking a clay pipe—all became a secret pleasure to watch. He reminded me of a jungle animal, what I sometimes visualized was a slow, heavy footed panther, svelte and dark as night, a panther in whose sleepy look burned rapt attentiveness. And in every drowsy-lidded glance he gave there was just a hint of menace, a readiness to strike if provoked, such that most men were wary of offending him.

Above all else, he was sensuous. I sometimes mused—as any woman alive to passion might—when he paused to finger the silk of a scarf or relish the smoky taste of a cognac upon his tongue—how would he savour me, my skin, hair, eyelids, my lips?

* * *

On our first outing, an afternoon of bright sunshine, I expected Gauguin might suggest something physical, a stroll in the public gardens, taking out a boat on the lake in the Bois de Boulogne, or watching a fencing match at the Military Academy (he boasted of his fencing skills). Instead he wanted me see the Ethnographical Museum in the Trocadero Palace which housed pre-Columbian art. He spoke of the strong affinity he had for primitive cultures, especially ancient Peruvian artefacts, as his mother was born in Peru, and she had taken him from France to Lima, Peru when he was but a year old. He spent five years of his early childhood, he said, with his mother and sister in South America.

"Deep down, I'm more primitive than civilized," he boasted. This characterization of himself seemed of immense importance to him, and something I should know.

Lecturing, he led me through a deserted and peculiarly dank museum. "There's a vital strength in the primitive arts not found elsewhere," he said as we looked at collections of recently excavated Peruvian pottery, bowls and pitchers with imaginative patterns that were often shaped into strange animals or brutish looking humans—all of which fascinated me. He mentioned his own personal collection of Peruvian and pre-Columbian pottery. "Entrusted to my dear wife in Denmark." Seeing my discomfort, he shrugged. "But Mette's another story." I wanted no involvement with his family or any of his children. Clovis' dream vision bore enough familial sorrow to ponder, and enough uncertainty for me to be wary. Gauguin, thankfully, had no interest in involving me with his personal affairs.

He took my arm, his eyes newly alight with mischievousness, and whispered, "Let me show you something special."

Wondering where I was being led, he took me down a flight of stairs, passing through catacomb-like rooms. The musty smell that initially depressed me when we entered the museum now worsened, deepening to something akin to rot, a nauseous and unhealthy smell that seemed to stick in my throat. *Is this why the museum has no visitors?*

Brought before the gruesome exhibit, I was at first appalled, guessing this was Gauguin's dark joke to test how a woman would react. Couched inside the glass enclosure, as if trying to ward away our gaze, was conceivably a small woman, wrapped in tattered bands of cloth.

"A Peruvian mummy. I visit her often," he said.

The horrific-looking creature sat hunched, her legs drawn-up close and bound with frayed cords of hemp. The dry, withered face stared from large eyes that were nothing but dark hollow sockets. It was difficult to believe that the shrivelled, leathery face confronting us was a human being who once lived.

"You come to visit this?"

But already I saw that the image had a strange grip over him. The mummy's skeletal face seemed locked into a hideous, wide-mouthed, rictal scream.

"I come with questions for her. Did you weep? Did you struggle with the ropes that bind you? Or is that a grin, having chewed the coca leaves stuffed into your mouth, proof that you were prepared for your sacrificial death? And the foetal position, a sign that you were ready to be born again?"

The affixed placard read that she had been expertly mummified in the Inca fashion, then left atop an Andes volcano more than five hundred years ago.

"An extraordinary embalming process," he said. "The skin is cured, like leather, to preserve a Peruvian maiden's pretty looks. But first, all of the internal organs are removed through the anus. Makes me quite proud of my ancestors' ingenuity." Gauguin's dark humour never far away.

I replied in kind, "The ancient Egyptians removed the organs and intestines when embalming. All, that is, except for the heart as they believed it the centre of a person's being and intelligence."

"And not the brain?"

"The brain held little value, so was extracted by carefully inserting special hooked instruments up through the nostrils, to pull out the brain tissue, bit by bit, a delicate operation, perhaps to keep men handsome."

"Touché, Mademoiselle Egyptologist." He then tapped the glass cabinet and peered more closely. "But she is no ordinary mummy, she was specially chosen by her people."

"What do you mean, 'chosen'?"

"A Peruvian maiden, usually twelve to fifteen, was periodically chosen as a sacrifice to gain favour with the gods."

"Why don't old men ever volunteer for sacrificial rituals?" I challenged.

"Who's the better gift, a dozen, decrepit old farts or someone still pure?"

I peered down at the mummy. "The skull appears to have been trepanned." My father once instructed me on the science of trepanation, a hole drilled into the skull to release a build-up of blood from an injury.

"She very well may have been bludgeoned with a sharp instrument," Gauguin replied, "as some chosen ones cannot be sufficiently intoxicated with alcohol and coca leaves to leave life stoically."

"I certainly wouldn't give up my life without a fight."

Folding his arms, he gazed intently at the mummy. In profile, his hawk like nose made him seem an Inca chieftain. He mused, "But to be chosen for sacrifice is the supreme honour, guarantees you an afterlife in their Eden, under the sun's perpetual warmth; that is, if you had obeyed the Inca rule of *ama sua, ama lulla, ama chella*."

"Ama sua, ama lulla, ama chella," I repeated. I knew he wanted me to ask their meaning; but I waited for the peacock in Paul Gauguin to show off and translate.

"Do not steal, do not lie, do not be lazy—simple enough rules."

"Have you, so far, succeeded in following them?"

"No one has ever accused me of being lazy. As for lies, they are sometimes necessary to keep your truth unsullied."

"And, of course, you do not steal," I remarked, well informed of Gauguin's notorious reputation with women, 'The thief of hearts,' said f.f.

"I only steal ideas," he replied.

II

Wisely, Gauguin decided to put the seven-year-old Clovis under the temporary care of his older sister, Fernande Marie, who was married to a prosperous businessman. Wisely again, he arranged for the boy to attend a boarding school to further his education. I was relieved that Clovis was being placed in a more stable environment. Gauguin lived, at best, a precarious life, yet managed to survive with the occasional help from artist friends, and selling off part of his art collection. Before becoming a full time artist, he had worked as a stock broker, earning lucrative commissions that enabled him to buy the art he liked.

His closest and long-time friend was Émile Schufenecker, a fellow artist, who lived in Montparnasse with his wife and two children. The majority of the Schufeneckers' time, however, was spent with rich relatives in Neuilly. The Schufeneckers magnanimously gave up their apartment to Gauguin. It was on rue Boulard, a fourth floor walkup, with a wonderful view of the city and the Seine. Our lovemaking flourished there.

I had moved out of Madame Dujardin's boarding house, wanting more privacy, and settled into to a small flat situated part way up the Butte of Montmartre, but when Gauguin came striding into my life, I rarely slept there. The Montparnasse apartment on rue Boulard became our oasis—for art, music, and sex. Gauguin played many musical instruments, including the guitar and the harmonium, but most enjoyed playing Émile Schufenecker's mandolin. The languorous strumming of his favourite Schumann pieces on the mandolin served as a prelude to our physical intimacies. I grew accustomed to laying on the bed as his Schumann melodies drifted in from the adjoining room. Which set the mood for my surrender to him.

Whenever the music ended, he found me in the bedroom, always naked. He would light candles and set them in places where best the shadows played upon my body. I liked, in the beginning, to keep my eyes closed. Nothing escaped his touch, his hands gifted in making me feel wholly wanted. And every part of his muscled body was free for me to explore, touch, caress. Gauguin's viral strength excited me, yet when he sensed my need, he approached with tenderness. More often we were tempestuous, covetous, devouring each other. We were alike in our intensity.

Our only taboo was never to say the word 'love.'

III

Gauguin had no interest in cocaine. My suggestion that the white powder might enrich our senses only made him laugh. He had cognac, wine, tobacco, and me—there was no need to add another vice.

But soon thereafter he brought me hashish. "If you're so intent on altering your consciousness."

I corrected, "Not just mine alone."

So began the ritual of setting a Cezanne canvas on the easel, smoking hashish, and deconstructing the artist's techniques. The Cezannes' he owned had stayed in Denmark, so we borrowed from the ever generous Père Tanguy. I hazard no guess as to whether hashish aided in a deeper understanding of Cezanne's paintings, but smoking the black, sticky substance invariably led me to contemplate Cezanne's canvases for long stretches of time.

We sat side by side on the living room floor, our backs against the sofa, passing the hashish pipe back and forth, Gauguin goading me to "weave your words around the paintings if you wish to be an art journalist."

Was it a mistake, I sometimes wondered, to have shared the ambition of writing about art and artists? Yet, what brought us closer each day was showing our nakedness in every aspect.

He knew I had an emotionally troubled sister who was more important than anything or anyone in the world. I knew he had no intentions of returning to his wife, that painting was his first and only lasting passion. He knew I collected dreams and, when necessary, stole them. I knew that he was not going to show me any of his own paintings until he found his true style.

Tonight an extremely vivid still-life of Cezanne's sat on the easel. I exhaled a plume of the calming smoke. "Pégo, what you consistently failed to appreciate is..." ('Pégo' was my term of endearment when I felt a competitive mood coming) "is... Cezanne's complexity."

"My good fortune is having *Mademoiselle Journaliste* explicate." He took back the clay pipe. "And educate a simpleton such as myself." He exhaled a plume and returned the pipe. "But if will, first tell me how he makes those apples and everything else on that table more real than reality."

"He devises irrationalities."

"You are starting to sound pedantic. I just want to paint an apple like Cezanne."

"He tips up the table so you must view the fruit from a more immediate vantage point. Then leans the wine bottle at a gravity-defying angle. While the folded napkin drops precariously on the lopsided table but maintains a stiff position. All irregularities."

"Yes, I see, deliberate distortions, and somehow he integrates every misshapen form into a harmonious whole. The man's a rebel in spite of himself."

"His forms are not so much distortions as intensive reorderings to make that harmonious whole."

"I see, I see. There are apples in the basket the same size as apples on the table cloth, so he's destroying naturalistic distance, bringing what should be the illusion of faraway and near on the same visual plane. That brings the entire composition into harmony." He leaped to his feet for a closer look. "The greenish-red apple, so damn exaggerated! Yet more believable than any real apple! How?"

"The brush work is the key." When for day on end, when posing, studying through mirrors Cezanne's brush strokes, I had gained a sense of how he achieved his mysterious luminosity.

Gauguin agreed, "Of course, the brush work, but there's a set formula that I'm determined to discover."

I found myself in no hurry to share everything I gleaned from observing Cezanne's nimble hand. Why exhaust my knowledge? Why? When wanting nights in our Montparnasse hideaway not to ever end. Or not to end too soon.

He sat close to me, puffed, gazed admiringly at the work. "Ah, such a luscious apple could have been the very one Eve offered in the Garden of Eden."

I learned of Gauguin's life mostly in bed, in the dark, in fragments. I had never been so ravenous to understand the psyche of a man. The intense, undeniable physical attraction I had for him spurred me to hope for more. Maybe, just maybe, we could reach a deeper place in our relationship, so I savoured every experience life had thrown his way.

At the age of seventeen he became a sailor. Already too old to enter the naval academy, he settled for the Merchant Marines and spent over seven years at sea, rising to the rank of second lieutenant in the French navy. By the age of twenty-three (when I was still anchored to wash tubs in Marseilles) he had travelled around the world. Perhaps the sea, the desire to travel to faraway lands, was in his blood.

When he finally returned to France, he discovered his mother had died. The photograph pinned on the wall of his flat came to mind, Aline Tristan Chaza Gauguin and her dark beauty. His father, Clovis Gauguin, died when Gauguin was an infant. I realized that he cared enough about his parents to name two of his five children after them. .

I gave him fragments from my own life, cautious not to mention my sister was confined at the Salpêtrière. I told him that my father, once a ship's doctor, also sailed the seas. "He's dead," I said, a lie perhaps; but wherever he fled, my father was dead to me. I spoke of Salpêtrière, Charcot, and the visiting doctor from Vienna who believed, as I, that psychology was the new science.

"Utilizing the phenomena of hypnosis and dreams might heal scars of the psyche," I suggested.

"I expected you would try to hypnotize me by now," he joked as we lay in bed, smoking from the hashish pipe, "and steal a dream of mine."

"I have adopted your Peruvian code, *ama sua*, do not steal, except ideas." I hoped that tonight the large amount of hashish he smoked would yield the one dream that would show the core of him.

The feral warmth of his body curved around me as he whispered, "My psyche is not what you should seek." Crawling onto me, the panther that he was, he asked, "Is the doctor from Vienna more handsome than me?"

"His nose is more straightforward," I managed to answer before the thrust of him unleashed a joy a hundredfold better than any drug.

When we spent our passion, I waited for him to drift into the sound, heavy breathing sleep of a lover satisfied then began my vigil: the half-opened curtain and star-studded night gave enough light to observe, having been educated by Sigmund that men, when dreaming, usually have erections; additionally, dreams remain most vivid to the mind's memory if one is awakened immediately after or during the dream.

Eventually Gauguin's penis hardened and after twenty minutes or so, slackened—I shook him awake. "Your dream?"

His heavy-lidded eyes opened. Gradually, he realized what I was asking. Irritated, he muttered, "This obsession of yours is someday going to put you in a pot of boiling trouble."

"Until then," I gently put my hand on his chest, surprised that his heart was thudding fast, "tell me what you were dreaming."

Angry, he pushed away my hand. I kissed his chest, his heart still beating hard. *Had he a nightmare?* He began fidgeting and propped up a pillow behind him. "Give me my pipe," he grumbled, "and not the hashish pipe."

After he stuffed some tobacco in the bowl, lit up, he reflected. "Damn!" He pressed his head back on the pillow, looking up, perhaps seeing images I worried were already fading.

"Damn!" he repeated. "I always thought the two of them were having a clandestine affair."

"Who"

"Aline and Gustave."

"Your mother and...?"

"Gustave Arosa, a longtime friend of the family." He tossed out a laugh. "My mother, before she died, appointed him my guardian."

"So you dreamt about them?"

His look told me that he was debating whether to answer. "Before being rudely awakened, I dreamt I came to Gustave Arosa's house very early in the morning. The door magically unlocked, I entered, my aim to take a gander at a new painting he recently purchased. Gustave, my guardian, was an astute collector. He owned Corots, Jongkinds, Boudins and Courbet's." Gauguin paused. "You know, without Boudin there would be no Monet. But anyway, the new painting I was interested in seeing was Courbet's "*The Origin of the World.*"" He stopped again, looked at me curiously. "Are you familiar with the painting?"

I shook my head. "I hope you will take me to see all the artists who have inspired the Impressionists."

""*The Origin of the World*' is a whopping close-up of a vagina."

"Aptly titled," I said.

"As hirsute as your own." He smiled. I smiled. "Anyway, Gustav

Arosa never owned the painting. But in the dream, I think it's in his house. I walk through the rooms. It's barely dawn and no one appears to be at home."

"You have come uninvited?"

"Gustave Arosa, my guardian, my mentor in art, always encouraged me to visit his collection, whenever I wished."

"At dawn?"

"Are you going to make a habit of interrupting?"

"Continue, if you would."

"Opening doors throughout the house, opening many doors... until I opened the wrong door, or the right door." He let out a caustic grunt. "There she lay, alone, asleep in Gustave Arosa's four poster bed, my mother, snoring not so delicately, buck naked, displaying the origin of the world; then..." Gauguin sighed, pretending to be exasperated, "you..."

"Rudely interrupted the dream."

"I always suspected the two of them engaged in a very discreet affair," he admitted. "Both were damn clever." He pulled me beside him. "My dream found them out, eh?"

"Perhaps." My head on his chest, accustomed to listening to the steady beating of his heart, only it still pounded terribly loud, betraying him and something amiss.

V

A door to Gauguin's psychology cracked just enough for me to peer inside. The dream, his mother naked, sparked my interest in her. More hashish nights at the Schufeneckers' apartment gave me his portrait of her.

Languidly, through the haze of smoke, he remembered her slaps and their sting. "I guess I was always misbehaving. She had little hands, but they were as flexible as rubber. When she gave out her slaps, I liked showing off my impudence, and turned a cheek for another which came faster and harder. It is true, a few minutes later my mother kissed and caressed me, weeping."

The music, the hashish, our lovemaking continued to wear away his resistance to long-ago memories. "When my father died, her life was not easy. She was cheated out of her inheritance by Peruvian relatives, then forced to become a common seamstress, making dresses for the bourgeoisie. She died too young, only thirty-two, still quite fetching, a Peruvian beauty, dark and sultry, who could turn men's heads on the Parisian boulevards. Aline..." he puffed, "Tristan," he puffed, "Chaza," he puffed, "Gauguin." The sweet scent of hashish filled the bedroom.

"In 1870, when I returned from my service in the navy, I learned of my mother's death. Our house in St. Cloud sacked and ravaged by the Prussians, all of our Peruvian art destroyed by fire. Gustave Arosa read my mother's last will and testament. My sister Fernande Marie received most of the bounty plus Arosa took her into his home as if one of his own daughters."

"What did you receive in the will?"

"A few mementos, my mother's amulet, a parrot's claw."

I later learned from another source that he and his sister received a respectable amount of money, split evenly. Gauguin liked to hide what did not fit into his life story.

"I was especially memorialized in the will," he went on, "her parting words were: "Paul better get on with his life, find a suitable career, as he has made himself so unliked by all of our friends, that one day, for sure, he will find himself very much alone."

His mother's biting prediction, I learned, was a sad truth which Paul Gauguin wore like a badge of honour. He set aside the pipe, closed his eyes, seemingly ready to sleep.

"What path did you then take?" I asked.

412

"I listened to my mother, became a good boy, joined the bourgeoisie, a stock broker making lots of money, married, and learned to be very charming."

"All of which you have abandoned."

"Yes, I'm afraid I returned to being a bad boy."

"But you are still oddly charming." I kissed his lips.

Chapter 43

**This project is very much up in the air, Degas's
cantankerousness makes it almost unfeasible;
in this little group there are conflicts of pride that make
any agreement difficult. It seems to me that I'm just
about the only one without a pettiness of mind,
which is a compensation for my inferiority as a painter.**

Berthe Morisot
Spring, 1886

Almost Fisticuffs

Sitting next to Degas as he calmly poured tea into our cups, I tried not to pay any attention to the frustrated Pissarro who paced in front of us like a caged bear. Degas had no trouble ignoring him.

"Some sweetness?" he held out to me a delicate Japanese bowl piled high with sugar resembling a snow-capped mountain.

I could feel his spindle-like leg pressed close to mine on the 'love sofa', a leg more bone than flesh. Politely I declined, slightly shaking my head and giving a small smile. On this occasion I was determined to remain as quiet as a titmouse. Let the two titans of Impressionism do battle.

Pissarro finally gave up pacing in Degas' cramped sitting room. He cast an unsure glance at the framed drawing above the mantel. I knew he would not recognize the fledgling artist. He turned to Degas to make his plea—

"I am convinced we can persuade Monet and Renoir to join the Show if only you rescind your needless regulation. And possibly we can also get more of the others to reconsider, even Caillebotte, Cezanne and Sisley. What do you say?"

I personally doubted if Cezanne would join the Show under any circumstance since Paris represented me and I was anathema. Degas focused on putting down the sugar bowl in its exact place on the end table. The sugar mound now reminded me of Mt. Fuji.

Degas responded with unmistakable authority, "Our comrades have a clear choice, either in our Show, or someone else's—but not both. The rule remains."

I took to gazing at Suzanne Valadon's red chalk drawing above the mantle. Her naked woman stepping out of the bathtub had replaced the naked Oedipus confronting the Sphinx. How sweetly generous of Degas, I thought, to remove his famous Ingres for the novice Suzanne. He really did support new artists if he thought they had talent.

The long-bearded Pissarro looked mournful. "It won't be the same without Monet and Renoir."

Degas remained adamant. "There are others, willing to abide by the rules, who can fill their wall space."

A hope flashed in Father Pissarro's eyes, his lips, barely visible inside his mammoth beard, turned into a smile. "Why don't we just pick another month? Why need we be bound from May to June?" He knew that Monet and Renoir had contracted to show at Petit's International Exhibition to start in June.

"Spring is a most propitious time for visitors," Degas noted. "We avoid the August Diaspora."

Pissarro countered grimly, "Beside Petit's June show, the Salon is having their exhibition in May. Surely you realize that to accept your dates could very well prove calamitous to our Show."

Degas poured himself another cup of tea. "I have no such realization."

"But if we have the Show in May," Pissarro pointed out, "the other exhibitions will siphon viewers away from ours. Why court disaster?"

"We must make our philosophical point."

Pissarro's eyes narrowed. "What might that be?"

"That we care not a whit for juried shows such as the Salon, that as artists we claim our independence from all state sponsored contests, so our exhibition must run concurrently with theirs."

"Your principles are to be admired." Pissarro barely hid his annoyance.

Degas chose to address me, turning playful. "Don't you think this tea a tad bitter, Mademoiselle Forette? Are you sure you don't want something to sweeten your cup. I can call Zoe to bring honey."

"No, thank-you. I'm accustomed to bitter."

"I, myself, am a devotee of the bitter-sweet," he retorted.

Pissarro leaned down toward Degas and challenged, "Are any of the other, more established artists supportive of your heroic stance?"

"Mary Cassatt and Berthe Morisot."

"Ah-h," came a deep exhale, a knowing nod. "Splendid artists both, and fine women."

I could see him guarding his thoughts, but they were easy to read: 'Who else but Cassatt, Morisot and Degas with their inherited wealth would embrace the idiotic idea of competing against the more popular exhibitions and risk few sales.'

"Mary Cassatt, a forthright, courageous individual," Degas volunteered. "My brother, René, having lived in New Orleans, says that such virtues are typical of Americans. Yes, the Show begins in May," he concluded, "or I withdraw my support."

"So you are prepared to compete with the Salon and Petit's prestigious

International Show, lose the drawing power of Renoir and Monet, and run the risk of selling nothing?" asked Pissarro again, still clutching the belief that Degas must not fully comprehend the situation.

"We, that is, Mary and I, consider it more important to maintain artistic integrity, emphasize our independence, and give proof of our disdain for the inanity of the Salon's juries and the meretriciousness of medals."

"Perhaps Monsieur Degas," I ventured softly, "is not cognizant of the fact that Petit's Gallery, where Renoir and Monet will show, is situated directly across the street from the space you intend to rent."

"May will be a merry month," he joked.

"The Petit gallery is but a stone's throw away," Pissarro put in. "A stone's throw."

The response to Pissarro's anguish was a small, resolute smile. "The more the merrier, my good man."

Pissarro plopped his hefty frame down in a corner chair, his head dropped to his snow-bearded chest as he heaved a sigh. The situation was dismally plain: neither Degas nor his wealthy cohorts had need to ponder where their next meal might come from. Wearily, unable to raise his head, he inquired, "Do you have any other requirements?"

"The word, Impressionism."

"Yes?" Pissarro looked up.

"Not to be written anywhere in the program nor in the advertisements."

Pissarro and I exchanged stares of astonishment.

Degas explained, "The word was always a fluke anyway, pulled out of a hat."

Watching my dear friend sink deeper into despair, I voiced an opinion as temperately as I knew how. "Monsieur Degas, the word defines the meaning of your ground breaking movement—the innovative step to no longer concern yourselves with exacting detail, but rather to capture a fleeing scene, no matter how vague. Your school invites a new generation of viewers to appreciate a deeper reality——the artist's personal impression."

Pissarro hurriedly joined the argument. "Mademoiselle Forette has hit the mark! Impressionism defines our revolution."

"Definitions kill," Degas coldly noted. He rose. Was he finished with us? "As an artist, am I to be pinned to a word, a school, as if a butterfly pinned inside a collector's case?" He opened his hands and made a mock plea: "Will you not let the butterfly and I fly? Will you not let us flutter our wings?"

"I find metaphors more deadly than definitions," grumbled Pissarro.

Degas turned almost defiant. "Do you want me and Mary Cassatt in the Show or not?"

Angry that he continued to couple Cassatt to his own views, I almost said, *I thought American women were independent.*

But Pissarro went on, "Are there any more prohibitions?"

"Our paintings will have no gilded frames. Leave such ornamentation for Petit and the organizers of the Salon."

Pissarro was somewhat relieved—"At last something we can agree upon. We shall have white, wooden frames which allow the paintings to speak for themselves."

"I prefer various pastels."

"White."

For a moment I thought they were on the brink of fisticuffs.

"Why not let the artists," I suggested, "decide for themselves which colour."

Degas nodded his agreement. "A splendid idea, Mademoiselle Forette, plain wooden frames painted any colour the artist desires."

Before the meeting concluded, the two artists decided to draw up a tentative list of candidates for the Show. I was asked to record the names. There were quite a few names I did not recognize which told me that I still had a great deal to learn about the current art scene: Marie Bracquemond, Raffelli, Guillaumin, Zandomeneghi. One name mentioned, however, brought my pencil to a halt.

Father Pissarro must have noted the flush I felt rushed to my cheeks. "Mademoiselle Julie? Are you feeling all right?"

"I'm fine. Have I spelled Gauguin correctly?" I asked, showing them the list.

Degas responded with a chuckle, "Yes, perhaps you could add Gauguin the Fox, for that is what I call him, out of earshot."

"He certainly is as wily as a fox," Pissarro muttered with a frown.

"Do you object to his inclusion?" asked Degas.

"Why should I? He paints reasonably well and has been included in previous Impressionist shows. If I am not mistaken, wasn't I the one who first persuaded you and the other organizers to let Gauguin participate in the 4th Impressionist Exhibition?"

"Ah yes, I recall the prosaic sculpture, of a boy."

"His son."

Degas reflected. "The next year he had that nude seamstress in the

Fifth Show, quite realistic; of course, borrowed from Rembrandt's Bathsheba, how her belly spills over the thighs. Admirable. He just put too much blue shadow in the face."

"So you have forgotten the difficulties of last year at the seashore in Dieppe when you and Gauguin hurled sarcasms at each other?"

"We have made amends," Degas admitted. "The man is too interesting of a character for me to bear a grudge. I'm sure if a jury found him guilty of a heinous crime they would nonetheless grant him a pardon for extenuating circumstances. Besides, the other day he approached me with an apology."

"Heart-felt, I'm sure," grunted Pissarro.

"Well, I've always been an admirer of snake charmers."

"So, he's back in Paris," mused Pissarro. "I thought he went to Denmark to be with his family?"

"Rumour claims he has abandoned his family."

The charitable Pissarro said nothing. I rose and handed Degas the completed list with my lover's name included. Degas rang for his maid Zoe who sullenly escorted us to the door (she would never forgive me for stealing the key to her Master's studio). Degas remained very close behind me as if wanting to confide something, I worrying that he knew of my 'adulterous' affair; he spoke low, in a near whisper: "You, Julie, surely realize that I'm not the despot others would make me. Please tell Suzanne she must visit more often. And surely you noticed that I gave her mantle priority over Ingres. She has gained a certain suppleness of line. Inform the child that I am prepared to teach her engraving and soft-ground etching."

"She will be so happy, Monsieur Degas; she will be overjoyed."

As Zoe took us to the front door, Degas suddenly remembered something, rushing to a secretary and taking out two tickets. He handed them to me. "Good for any matinee performance at the Odeon and I know Oedipus Rex will soon be playing there. Perhaps you and Suzanne might gain more insight into the tragedy of the young king."

After thanking him, Pissarro and I walked down the rue Victor Masse. My companion complained, "In spite of the free tickets, his stubbornness and egotism are beyond compare."

Our next appointment was with Berthe Morisot and her husband Eugene Manet who were potential funders for the Show. As we made our way to the Manet house, I forced myself to speak, to admit that I knew Paul Gauguin, then with more trepidation I told my cherished friend, "Gauguin and I are emotionally involved."

He said nothing. We just continued walking, giving me ample time to fret and worry—*Is he weighing me on the scales of decency? Will my wished-for-father judge me a 'home breaker'?*

What almost came from my mouth was an attempt to mitigate the indiscretion, that the relationship had been spurred by mutual admiration for Cezanne's art, but decided that it would strike Pissarro as a sadly ironic excuse. We finally reached 40 rue de Villejuste and stood in front of the elegant Manet house. It looked so inviting, an expansive wooden porch and white Georgian columns which were gracefully entwined with ivy. The front door was an unblemished white with a green laurel wreath in the centre. Berthe Morisot would prove to be a lovely woman in every way, equally thoughtful, beautiful and open-minded. She had little trouble in convincing her husband, Eugene, brother to Edouard Manet, to lend financial support to the 1886 Show.

But before we entered to learn of the glad tidings, Father Pissarro finally responded, "Gauguin has talent. I would not deny it. He has vitality. And he has endurance. But be wary of him, Julie."

Chapter 44

**... with preponderant frequency... men...
dream mostly of their father's death...**

The Interpretation of Dreams
Sigmund Freud

A Devil's Bargain

I

Caught—his hand heavy on my shoulder. He took the two canvases back to the closet where I found them, not saying a word. I had not expected Gauguin's return until later in the evening. He had gone to Chaplet's kiln factory to observe the ceramist's latest firing techniques.

I had been left in charge of the late night supper which only required that I re-heat Gauguin's prepared coq au vin. Time on my hands, the Schufeneckers' apartment to myself, I decided to search for his art. Curiosity won me over when both Degas and Pissarro praised his talent. I guessed that he kept some of his own work in safekeeping with Émile Schufenecker.

Gauguin never showed me his paintings nor did I ever ask to see them, as though we had made an unspoken covenant to keep his art out of our relationship. Perhaps he worried that the work might disappoint me. Perhaps I had the same fear.

In a back closet I found two canvases which I placed side by side on the easel. I knew instinctively that the first portrait was his Danish wife, Mette. Undeniably elegant, she sat in three-quarter profile, wearing a choker necklace, high gloves, and a gorgeously low-cut evening dress, a cultured woman, who might be ready to attend the opera or a gala ball. The décolletage revealed ample breasts and I imagined her hips wonderful resting places for a man's hands. She possessed enviable voluptuousness.

I lit a cigarette, trying to fathom her, or how Gauguin saw her. There was a haughty air about Mette, a stare of impatience or disdain. She seemed a woman able to handle her own destiny. So I hoped, for her sake.

The second portrait was of Clovis, his son, a large picture book in his lap, looking not quite sad, but not a happy boy. Recently Mette had returned to Paris, unknown to Gauguin, and taken Clovis back to Denmark. He was furious. As to why, I'm not sure. Behind Clovis' portrait, he placed a vase of atrociously muddied flowers. The entire canvas was done with dull mid-tones.

Technically, the two canvases were accomplished works, but disappointing. He had borrowed the earthen, mid-tone colouring of Pissarro's earlier works, but nothing of the Impressionists present intensity. Nothing original.

Our coq au vin dinner was subdued.

"Suffocating, aren't they?" He stared hard at me.

I finished a forkful of chicken, sipped the burgundy, and worried how to frame a reply. "The paintings are admirable. You've learned well from Pissarro and the broken brush strokes of the Impressionists."

He drank, turning sarcastic. "My thievery shall be complete after I assimilate Cezanne, that is, if you divulge his mystic formula."

I veered away from the topic. "It must be difficult to have your family so far away."

"They're all better off in Denmark, living a bourgeois life."

"What prompted you to bring Clovis to Paris?"

"Why shouldn't I? He's my son, I'm his father."

"To live, like you, a hand-to-mouth existence? Keeping him from..."

"His mother?"

"And his siblings." I wasn't then exactly sure how many children Gauguin had. (Five, I learned.) "Clovis must be your favourite."

He pushed away his unfinished plate, poured more wine. "He's far down the totem pole, but I thought an adventurous voyage with his father might put more iron in his spine, we'd become closer, he'd get rid of the Danish mediocrity his mother instilled in him." He finished the glass. "No such luck. My daughter Aline would have been better suited for the adventure."

He left the table and set up another Cezanne painting we had borrowed from Père Tanguy's shop. Putting a nub of hashish in his clay pipe, he sat it on the floor. Leaning comfortably against the sofa, he stared at the canvas, waiting for me to join him for a fresh analysis. I took the dishes to the kitchen, wondering whether to divulge the secret of modulation—might it be his open invitation to remain Cezanne's imitator?

I sat beside him and took the pipe. "Why did you hide the fact that you were in previous Impressionist shows."

"Paul Gauguin was not a particular favourite of the critics." He took back the pipe. "But now if my esteemed Impressionist friends can stop bickering and make this new exhibition happen, I will earn the success I deserve. I'll show never-before-seen paintings and establish a reputation, sell, and bring all my children back."

"Your wife as well."

He blew pipe smoke in the air. "That part of my life is finished."

"What if you don't sell anything?"

"Then I will persuade Julie Forette to come with me to America and start anew."

"I loathe sea voyages. The worst place to get lost is at sea."

"Nonsense, celestial navigation will direct us to any isle we desire."

"Here is our island, we need go no further." I turned, so wanting him to take me into his arms, beginning to fear that each sexual encounter might be our last; I wanted us to tear off each other's clothes, grapple in lust on the floor and take each other fiercely.

But he continued to smoke the hashish, subdued, reflecting... coming up with a surprise proposition: "Give every secret you have of Cezanne's and I will let you hypnotize me." He smiled. "Then take whatever dream you can dredge from my dark heart."

I very much wanted to plummet his psyche and find the untameable dream that can haunt a person's life. In my untameable dream, I was always lost in the most unsavoury parts of an unknown city.

He handed back the pipe. "A fair bargain?"

The temptation too strong to resist, I nodded... a devil's bargain more likely. Together we set to quietly gazing at the landscape: verdant grassland, blue-ish trees, orange-roof houses and clay-stained mountains, all ascending orderly into a cloud-filled sky.

He broke the silence. "Tanguy told me that the painting took Cezanne two years to finish, yet I still see patches of exposed canvas, left un-coloured."

"Deliberate," I said. "Canvas brings its own unique colour."

"Yes, I see that synthesizing the colour and texture of bare canvas into the picture scheme can produce interesting results. We then begin to lose the illusion of looking at a scene from nature... a novel concept to consider."

Of all the people with whom I would come to share the analysis of a painting, none compared to Gauguin. He was intense in his quest to break down the methods and intent of artists, always with an eye as to how he might profit from their ideas.

"Cezanne's best kept secret is in his brushstroke," I said, beginning what amounted to a lecture, until then unaware of how much I had learned from the months of watching Cezanne paint me naked. And now Gauguin hung on every word of my possible wisdom. I can only summarize what mesmerized him that night.

"For Paul Cezanne to be satisfied, his brushstroke must exist as a separate plane of colour, it must hold on to an independent structure, must express an aspect of fundamental geometry, a degree of solidity that will allow it to fit into an overall architecture of coloured forms. He's working logically toward an interlocking colour scheme that will achieve a pictorial harmony."

Gauguin's satiric side never far from an interjection. "You make him seem a god creating a new cosmos."

I told him how Cezanne agonized over each and every brush stroke. The daunting challenge he set for himself was to make a bridge from the last stroke to the one not yet imagined. A false coloured note might demolish the entire structure.

Gauguin was quick to grasp. "So his strokes are building blocks of colour carefully thought-out." He kept his focus on the landscape. "And somehow he ends up with this... masterpiece. Unlike the doomed Lantier in Zola's shit book."

"He calls his brushstrokes modulating planes of colour, his task to find the hues to slide over each other..."

"Modulating the hues and tones in each brushstroke," murmured Gauguin.

"Yes, to evoke a transparent solidity."

I said more, he said more, but gazing at the landscape, we saw the trees, houses, sky, and Cezanne's beloved Mount Saint Victoire Mountain all blend into one unified multi-coloured mosaic. Sheer architectural genius.

Gauguin concluded, "He has found a new way to conquer form, motion, space, light."

"Conquer is your word; I would say that Cezanne is less a conqueror than a philosopher."

He scoffed, "Cezanne, a philosopher?"

"He rethinks dimensions and viewpoints, gives us the hint that in nature there is infinity."

"You render me speechless."

His satiric side again? "I've kept my part of the bargain, given as best as I can figure out, Cezanne's formula."

"So you have. Now it's time to fulfil my part. Hypnotize me. Steal my dream."

II

"Think of it as purposeful sleep," I said, "you pass through a portal in order to reach the subterranean realm of the mind."

Gauguin appeared to be listening attentively to my view of hypnosis. "And you will guide me to this other realm?"

"Yes, it's just another stratum of consciousness."

"My Virgil," he teased, "taking me down the rings."

I arranged our chairs to face each other." If that analogy works for you, yes."

The fiasco began. Nothing worked. No matter how many different techniques I tried—a steadily burning candle, the turning of small mirrors, the pinging pitch of a tuning fork. None had any effect. As a last resort, I dangled the Egyptian Eye pendant in front of him. It too failed. He said the jewelled eye reminded him of a rosy red breast. To make matters worse, with each new method he briefly pretended to be hypnotized until he broke into a roguish smile. I lost patience with his foolery. Giving up.

The next morning, when I awakened, he was gone. I thought nothing of it, for whenever we spent an evening at the Schufenecker apartment, we occasionally left separately, he to his flat to paint, I to the Salpêtrière.

Retrieving my clothes from the bedroom chair, I discovered beneath the dress a note.

The Schufeneckers expect to return at the end of the week. I didn't want either of us to brood about the loss of our oasis (our Eden), so put off mentioning the inevitable. I shall lock myself in my flat, painting furiously so as to produce as many canvases as possible for the Impressionist Show. I now better understand Cezanne's technique, in no small part thanks to Mademoiselle Art Critic.

No mention of when we might see each other again. Or if we were continuing our... affair. I couldn't say, 'love' affair as that word was forbidden in our Eden. For a moment I felt a hollowness inside of me. Then there was a stir of sympathy for his struggle ahead, counting on the Impressionist show as his chance to gain recognition. Perhaps... perhaps this would all lead to a reconciliation with his wife Mette and family. *Should I not prefer him to become a good father again... rather than my good lover.*

More followed on the second page: "Pégo lives up to his part of the bargain; the dream came forth in the night."

* * *

It is Mother's preposterous idea, wrapping me tightly in apothecary bandages. She is deluded by Peruvian superstition, believing if her little one is cocooned like a baby mummy, he will be protected from the hazards of an ocean voyage. So I'm carried, fully bandaged, aboard. Trailing behind, reluctantly climbing the plank, are my sister Fernande Marie and my father, Clovis Gauguin. The ship, a two-masted clinker, called the *Albert*, is bound for Peru, hopefully.

Neither father nor my older sister desire this voyage. It is my young, headstrong mother, Aline Tristan Chaza Gauguin, who has conceived the idea of returning to her Peruvian roots. No one can dissuade her. Father suspects this is female hysteria or possibly madness.

Mother cries out, "My children" as she extracts my little hand from the swaddling bands to place it against her breast, "must taste the blood of their heredity!"

My father, born and bred a gentleman in Orleans, shrugs at her extravagant behaviour, frowns at her Peruvian pride. He follows her aboard the *Albert* with grave misgivings, my pouting sister in tow. Once inside our cabin, my goal is to extricate myself from the ragged mummy strips which constrain me—the hand she freed is her mistake. Industriously, I pick away at my bandages, but quickly she slaps the rogue hand, warning me not to interfere with our ancient Inca custom —"An infant on long journeys shall be bound in swaddling cloth to ward off sailor diseases."

Can she not see I'm almost two years old? A clever fellow who has already figured out how to walk, if the destinations are short.

"Paul, your spine will grow stronger," she explains, undoing her raven hair at the cabin mirror, brushing it out to silken smoothness, watching me in the corner of the mirror, and my father in the other corner. "You do want a strong spine, do you not?"

Who in the mirror does she address?

I play pretend at taking a nap on the top bunk. In short order, I've unwrapped myself and tossed the swaddling bands out the porthole while the ship rushes southward, leaving in its wake white ribbons writhing upon the waves. Discovering my transgression, Mother slaps both my hands before remorse sets her to weeping while kissing each and every tiny finger.

I observe it all, a winter crossing, the weather so severe, our ship pitches and lists like a wildly rocking cradle. Sans tears I endure. I walk the sea-sprayed deck, allowing my father to assist. Such displays of bravery gain me a quick reputation among the crew.

"Un petit matelot bien fort!" I hear more than once from the seasoned crew of the *Albert*. A brave, little sailor am I. While Fernande Marie pukes everywhere on the ship. Rough though our voyage be, we eventually reach Port Famine, the farthest point in Patagonia in the Straits of Magellan, where we disembark to board the *Eva* bound for Lima. The *Eva*, while commodious, is nothing more than a made over whaleboat, ill-suited for long, storm-ridden voyages; but the weather proves favourable, more to my liking, balmy, incandescent skies shot through with pinks and violets. Then while still far from land, a gross indelicacy occurs—my father falls to his knees, mouth agape, and suffers an aneurysm.

Ascertaining that the heart attack has been fatal, our ship's captain orders the deceased wrapped ever so tightly in duck canvas, to be buried at sea, *très vite*, due to the tropical heat of the southern latitude. The sailors who have befriended me—ah, how smart they look in striped jerseys and beribboned berets—join together as a team to tilt the plank upon which my father's body lay. He is tightly shrouded, mummified as I once was, only a larger and heavier bundle, and the crew strains to lift and liberate their burden to the sea. But Clovis Gauguin stubbornly sticks to the plank.

Resourceful is our captain. He signals the Chinaman cook for the kitchen grease bucket. The funeral crew each scoop of handful from the bucket. The Chinaman, noticing I've been excluded, places a lumpful in my hand. Together, as a team, we smear grease onto the plank. Father starts to slide, and with a muffled splash, enters the gently lapping waves. A current snatches him as though he were a mere wisp of sea-grass. I watch the shrouded corpse roll over twice, then sink spiral fashion down into Neptune's domain where I lose sight of him forever.

* * *

I knew straightaway this was either a concocted fable or a distorted memory. Not a true dream. Gauguin preferred to mock my penchant for collecting dreams and to show off his writing skills. Nonetheless, the made-up dream begged for psychological analysis. I thought I might show it to Sigmund.

Chapter 45

When young we went out in pairs, Monet and Renoir, Cezanne and I, taking pleasure in painting the same scene from the same vantage point, learning from each other's gifts and perceptions, gaining courage from each other's daring.

Camille Pissarro

A Day at Giverny

I

When f.f. heard that I would be spending an entire afternoon with Claude Monet at his home in Giverny, he made an amazing offer. "I shall pay for the railway ticket. All you need do is bring back an interview for *La Vogue*."

My mouth fell open in complete surprise. We were having "tea and crumpets" at an English tea room f.f. had discovered near the *place de l'Opera*. I finally managed a whispered response. "Me, interview Monet?"

"Your first, official assignment for *La Vogue*. Our *petite journal* is up and running again thanks to an infusion of new capital. Our journal would benefit from an article to explicate Monet's painting technique... but I want more..." He first took a satisfied sip of his black tea. "I'm convinced," he resumed, "that you can do an analysis of the man himself."

Not quite believing that I was being presented with the opportunity to write an article on the most accomplished Impressionist, Claude Monet, I listened to f.f. elucidate—"While our readers expect interesting details about paintbrushes, palette, etc., I envision an interview that goes deeper, leads to something... psychological."

"Psychological?"

"La Vogue adopts the modern spirit, affirms that the new art can claim kinship to science's newest branch, psychology."

More than eager to accept such an assignment, I remembered Father Pissarro's financial straits. If not for his kind-hearted invitation, I would not be going to Giverny. A reckless gambit, I bartered with f.f.: "I accept only if you include another ticket for Camille Pissarro."

f.f. was quick to point out, "Our *petite journal* does not have unlimited funds."

"Deduct the cost from whatever profit *La Vogue* makes from the publication of an interview with the King of Impressionism."

He reflected. "Yes, I will convince Kahn and the other financiers to agree. We will intrigue them with the title: 'Monet, Impressionism's King, the Psychological Interview.'" He spread a small dab of marmalade on the crumpet with artistic delicacy then thought to add, "As you make mention of Renoir's possible presence, why not unearth what psychology you can about him." f.f. gave the hint of a smile. "Two Impressionists for the price of one, Kahn will like that."

* * *

Days before the impending trip, I began dropping things. At *L'Auberge du Clos*, with Suzanne, I accidentally knocked off the glass water decanter set on the table to dilute her absinthe. The glass decanter smashed upon the tiles into so many pieces, one would have thought I had thrown it. At the bar several regular customers, sipping green absinthes, turned and shook their heads glumly. The Auberge's *l'heure vert* (green hour) began at five p.m.

"Dessert for the Mademoiselles?" the unperturbed Georges asked, our waiter on bended knee, gathering up pieces into his apron.

I declined while Suzanne eagerly ordered a plum tart and another absinthe. She had become very fond of absinthe, the drink of fashion that year. After Georges left with an apron full of broken glass, Suzanne's dark blue eyes gazed at me with sympathy. "Dearest Julie, can you be too nervous to eat a plum tart?"

The possible interviews with Monet and Renoir were causing me anxiety, but I made light of it. "I prefer to be fed an anecdote. Tell me about Renoir since you're his favourite model. I'm hungry for background information." Suzanne was painted into several of Renoir's most erotic paintings.

"I shall share how he decides whether or not to employ you as a model," she said. "First, he has you," she lowered her voice in a mock whisper, "undress."

"Straightaway? Completely?"

"Of course, you silly!"

"Well, then what?" I feigned disinterest, reaching over for a sampling of the remaining absinthe.

"He orders the model to walk, very slowly, across the studio to the opened window."

"You must be shivering cold by this time," I remarked.

"I undress for no artist," she insisted, somewhat haughtily, "who does not have a coal burning stove."

"So, one stands naked by the window," I coaxed, quite curious as to what I would learn about Renoir's behaviour toward women.

"The old boy stares at you for the longest time."

Renoir was forty-five. "What kind of stare?" I took an experimental sip of the anise flavoured drink.

"A thoughtful stare," said Suzanne.

I slid the glass back. "Tastes like poison!"

Georges returned with the plum tart, a glass of absinthe, and the absinthe accoutrements, spoon, sugar cube, and a new decanter of water. "What Renoir looks for," Suzanne continued, "is how your skin takes the light."

"Takes the light," I repeated.

"His words exactly."

Georges put the sugar cube on the absinthe spoon, placed the serrated spoon across the rim of the glass, and gently dripped water over the sugar until the sweetness seeped through, turning the colourless absinthe pale green.

"*Merci*, Georges." Suzanne dipped her little finger into the absinthe and sucked.

"Obviously, you passed Renoir's skin test," I remarked.

"That I did, my skin does not resist the light."

Proud of herself, she finished off the inch of absinthe and proceeded to plunge her spoon into the plum tart. "The painter Puvis de Chavannes, he was the one who introduced me to Renoir. Right off the bat, the old boy put me in a dance picture, had me whirling around his studio with one of his pals."

"Ah, 'The Dance Panels'" I responded admiringly. It was f.f. who had taken me to Durand-Ruel's gallery to see them.

"From that very first moment," Suzanne confided, "Rennie and I... liked each other. He slipped into my affection easier than an eel, that one."

I quickly calculated their age difference when the dance panels were painted, Renoir in 1883 would have been forty-three. "And you, all of sixteen..." I reminded Suzanne.

"The artists preferred me to lie about my age. I was happy to oblige."

"Quite extraordinary," I said, "how you've managed to model for only the most talented artists."

"I believe that's a fact, I do not model for anyone who is not talented —which is my talent."

Suzanne took another greedy mouthful of the plum tart before she made her glum announcement. "Due to very tragic circumstances, I no longer model for Renoir. *Un conte tragique.*"

One waited patiently, knowing Suzanne would soon offer a descriptive and entertaining story; but she deliberately postponed her *conte tragique*.

"I'm posing for a new Montmartre artist, who possesses talent and then some."

"Whom, one presumes, possesses a coal burning stove."

Suzanne overlooked the quip and idly twirled her spoon through the remaining cream. "He's an aristocrat, with banknotes to burn if he chooses."

"Then he is, indeed, a rare bird to nest in Montmartre."

But not to be sidetracked, I fell silent, waiting for the tragic story involving Renoir. "Well, if you must know," Suzanne capitulated, "Renoir's concubine decided I must go."

"Renoir's concubine, how exotic; is she part of a vast harem?" I joked.

"I will not mince words," she brooded. "Renoir's harlot, one Aline Charigot, happened upon us one afternoon while we were in a delicate situation."

I exhaled a deep breath, "*Flagrante delicto?*"

"The whore flew into a witch's rage, screaming her lungs out, throwing pots, plates, what-nots all around the studio. But with all the hullabaloo and cursing, she was smart enough to lay neither hand or finger upon my person." The final spoonful of plum tart glided into Suzanne's mouth. She shrugged with indifference. "So that's my story, safely in port, as they say."

f.f. mentioned, I remembered, Renoir living with a model, named Aline, who recently bore him a son.

Suzanne looked moodily in the distance. "Oh, I can forget the incident, but one thing I cannot forgive," she added bitterly, "when I slammed the door behind me I soon learned that the minx wiped out my face in a painting hanging in the studio at rue d'Orchampt, took a rag soaked in turpentine and poof! My pretty face was no more." Suzanne signalled Georges for another absinthe. "Erased," she muttered.

"Expunged?" I was shocked. "Which painting?"

"One of the dance panels." The absinthe came in time to help her tell me more. Suzanne took hold of my forearm. "And do you know what the wench finally made Renoir do? To paint in her face where my face once glowed. Can you believe such spitefulness? *Le salaud!*"

My mind's eye went to the gorgeous dance panels, deciding it must have been 'Dance in the Country.' Suzanne's recognizable torso coupled to another's face. I sighed and tried to console her. "At least you are still in 'Dance at Bougival'."

She too heaved a sigh. "So far, *ma cherie*, so far."

"Well, I shall certainly be on my guard with Monsieur Renoir," I remarked, "making sure I steer clear of any delicate situations."

She grunted, releasing her grip and now patting my arm. "He will only be your second worry."

"And my first worry?" I asked, concerned.

Suzanne measured me with a steady look. "My Julie, whom you need to be on extra guard with is his friend, Monet."

Stolidly Pissarro sat on the banquette, his jaw clenched with fixed resolve, his billowed beard like hardened snow. Our train trip to Giverny unquestionably held great importance. I worried for him, worried whether his mission would succeed, the task of convincing two Impressionists of no small talent to join the 1886 Show.

f.f. warned that in all likelihood Pissarro would be rebuffed. When I protested that Renoir and Monet were two of his dearest comrades, that together they formed the three musketeers of Impressionism, f.f. sighed, "Ah-h, but one musketeer remains mired in obscurity."

Better to do an article on the musketeer the critics inexplicably dismiss, I thought, gazing fondly at my train companion. His work was probably considered by some to lack the colour bravura of the other Impressionists, but he possessed no less strength of purpose in capturing reality. One could argue that Father Pissarro's compositions showed more solidity. "You can smell the hay and cow dung in his farm scenes," Gauguin once said to me.

Pissarro spoke up, "Julie, I'm glad for them. Monet and Renoir are at last achieving a measure of success. And deservedly so, for they are talented artists."

I nodded, and quietly smiled.

Nerve-wracking to realize our train, in mere hours, would pull into the village of Giverny and I would meet them—the two singular Impressionists. Monet, 'the Eye' so Cezanne admirably called him. And for Cezanne, not one liberal with compliments, to think so highly of Monet only made me more anxious.

Can I possibly generate an intelligent article about him? Will he even grant an interview with a novice? A woman?

Soon I fell into wondering about Monet's fabled eyesight, trying to imagine their colour—*green, like mine? Brown and warm like Pissarro's? Or an otherworldly violet? Might he smell of violets as well? Flowers were his passion, they said.*

The conductor knocked on the glass to interrupt my idle fancies and noisily slid open the compartment door. A huge man in uniform, he wore a grin and showed us a pack of cards.

Is he here to entertain us with card tricks?

"A passenger left this deck behind," he said. "Perhaps Mademoiselle and Monsieur would like them to while away the time?"

Gladly Pissarro accepted the gift, eagerly suggesting he and I play whist. The conductor was happy to bring back a make shift table for us. Although I cared little for card games, I welcomed the distraction.

As Pissarro waited while I clumsily shuffled and dealt out our hands, he grew reflective—"Lives, like cards, are made to be shuffled and reshuffled." He fanned out his hand and played the king of clubs. "In the deck Monet is, as you aptly dubbed him, king, for who in the world of art gives the impression of shimmering water better than Monet? And let's not forget Renoir, for no one paints a woman's bottom better." He lay down the jack of diamonds to play. "That's Renoir, the resilient jack-of-all trades! Do you know, a few years back he had a terrible fall, broke his painting arm in two places. So what did he do? He begins painting with the other arm, and equally well! Julie, you are going to meet two splendid fellows—jack and king." As our game of whist continued, Pissarro began to brood, "But where is Pissarro's card? The one to make a strong bid in the game of life? Why do I trail so far behind my Impressionist comrades in sales? I've held the brush longer, I've contributed equally to the theory of Impressionism."

I was eager to agree, "Cezanne compliments you in no uncertain terms. 'Pissarro is the first Impressionist,' he often said. 'We all come from Pissarro.'"

"But outside of my fellow painters and a dealer or two, who has heard of me?" he declared, agitated. "When a journalist takes the bother to put my name in print, usually its misspelled."

How badly I wanted to reassure him. "Cezanne said, in 1865 you were already cutting out black, bitumen, raw sienna and the ochres from your palette."

"That's a stone fact," he admitted.

"And you told Cezanne, no, exhorted him to paint only with the three primary colours and their immediate derivatives, nothing else! As far back as 1865," I repeated, "before Impressionism existed as a word. You have much to be proud of, Father Pissarro."

Not much caring for praise of his past accomplishments, he glumly gathered the cards and put them back in their box. "My dear wife insists the political views I espouse are what keep me out of the winning deck. 'An anarchist will never gain entry,' she says, 'into the higher echelon of the art market.' Perhaps my Julie is right." His wife and I shared the same name.

I took the box of cards from his hand. "Shall we play a different game?"

His mind elsewhere, Pissarro's jaw again tightened; he sat up straight and the snow-white beard seemed to elongate. "Never!" came the sudden outburst. "Never will I relinquish the belief in the rights of men! We are made to be equal! And to share equally in the fruits of the earth!" As suddenly, he grew embarrassed. "Well, here I am giving my other Julie a belly-full of socialist grumblings." He took to watching the passing countryside.

"Be patient, *Maître*, your time will come," I said.

He turned to me, a look of interest in his eye. "Now, I truly see what lies beneath that reserved, steady, forceful temperament of yours— kindness, a deep reservoir of kindness." Further embarrassed, his gaze returned to the rural land he loved. I watched, as time passed, Pissarro's countenance take on an aspect of serenity—the essence of his nature.

When our friendly conductor again stuck his head into our compartment it was to announce that we would be pulling into the Vernon train station—just several kilometres from the village of Giverny.

Pissarro and I each reached for our hats. Quickly, before we disembarked, I asked him, "Are Messieurs Monet and Renoir close friends?"

"Oh, most assuredly!" he exclaimed. "The two go back a long way. They met as students at Gleyre's studio. I know they shared digs together. Two young pups on the prowl," he chuckled. "But Monet was the one who attracted all the ladies. I remember they barely had enough money for food in those days but Monet somehow always managed to wear fancy lace cuffs."

"So Monet is a ladies' man," I murmured, more to myself.

III

A delivery wagon was waiting to take us the five kilometre ride to Giverny. Monet had been thoughtful to hire a local villager to collect us at the Vernon train station. We shared the front seat with our driver as he jiggled the reins to urge his dappled horse forward. Our dirt road followed the course of the River Ept where occasionally, through a sudden clearing of trees, we caught glimpses of village women, ankle deep in the water, washing clothes and beating them clean upon the river rocks.

A few bumpy kilometres later, we turned on to a roughly hewn country path at the end of which the driver said was Monet's property. Pissarro and I were left in front of a green wooded gate in desperate need of a fresh coat of paint. It took Pissarro much time and effort to uncoil the wire that held the double gate together.

There was no path immediately visible in the thick underbrush so Pissarro suggested we follow a very tall line of yellow hollyhocks he spotted not too far from us. Eventually the yellow flowers relinquished their buttery colouring to deep carmine then in turn to a pleasing line of pink hollyhocks. Monet, we realized, was already presenting his visitors with a cheerful parade of changing colours.

"How does he get them to flourish and bloom so early in the spring?" Pissarro wondered aloud.

Past the hollyhocks, the vista changed to picturesque clusters of weeping willow trees. Through the low hanging willows, to the right, a languid pond became visible. On its grassy bank I noticed a small pile of children's size fishing poles.

Pissarro pointed his walking branch to the far side of the pond, ringed with sumptuously blue dahlias. Everywhere well-planted trees and decorative flowers. "Monet is certainly daft when it comes to flowers," he noted, admiring our surroundings. "Can you believe, the man is only leasing the property!"

When we reached the summit of a rise, the country house revealed itself in the distance. The morning sun had gained in brilliance and lit up the rambling house of many windows and dormers framed by climbing ivy, the walls stuccoed in a lambent pink which matched my dress. Encircling the pink house were radiant beds of multi-coloured flowers.

The rumour was that Monet's "fiancée" Alice Hoschedé had brought to their liaison sufficient money affording them a comfortable house situated on a sizeable amount of land. f.f mentioned that the engagement between Monet and Alice Hoschedé had a slight peculiarity, in that Alice still had a husband.

Before catching sight of anyone, we heard the gay, raucous shouts of children. Soon their darting shapes came into view, boys and girls busily chasing one another around the perimeter of the house. Walking forward, still some distance away, we made out adults, two men lounging in chairs upon a terrace adjacent to the house. Then two women came from the side door of the house, the taller woman carrying a bowl of fruit and plates which she set on the terrace table; the shorter, stouter woman went to a large basket or crib, sitting at the feet of one of men. The woman who hovered over the basket or crib wore a mob cap. The taller woman was hatless, her hair in a chignon with one long pendulous curl falling in front of a shoulder. Somewhere a barking dog caused the women to look around and settled their gaze in our direction. While unable to properly distinguish faces, I watched the taller woman behave with a new sense of urgency, grabbing the other woman's elbow and marching resolutely back into the house. Were they annoyed—so it seemed—by our presence? Was the woman with the long, pendulous curl the lady of the house, Alice Hoschedé?

A brown and white dog trotted happily toward us, yapping a greeting and wagging its tail. In short order the dog was following on our heels, obviously designating himself our escort.

The men were still too far away to see clearly. One man, wearing a green, bell-shaped hat, hailed us a friendly wave. The other man, wearing a light grey hat whose loopy, felt brim was twice as wide as mine, had a paintbrush in hand, in the act of painting the face of a little girl. When Pissarro and I grew nearer, the hodgepodge of children ran wildly around us. The rambunctious brood turned out to be part of the Hoschedé-Monet clan and several neighbouring children, all wondrously painted, each resembling an animal.

Both men rose courteously to greet us. I was acutely aware of the importance of our mission and struggled to think of something smart to say. The man who wore the green suede hat with a turned-up brim and bell-shaped crown was Claude Monet. Quickly he poured steaming coffee into bowls for us as we sat down. He was handsome beyond expectation, a richly dark beard, and peeking from his hat a spread of dark curls lay lightly on his forehead... well, one could see why the lady of the house might give a menacing eye to an unknown woman such as myself.

And there, a breath away from me, was Auguste Renoir, tall, erect, angular, who seemed more bone than flesh, directing his first question to me, "What do you think of our new pussy cat?" He showed off the little girl whose face he had just finished painting. She now had splayed whiskers and curling eyelashes. I smiled approvingly which seemed all the criticism Renoir wanted. "Now Lisette," he gently ordered, "give us a meow and off you scat. Go join the rest of the menagerie."

The girl meowed, curtsied shyly, and ran off to join the other children, farm creatures all, their faces transformed into foxes, squirrels and mice.

Pissarro, uncomfortably seated in a chair too small for him, leaned down to look into the crib near Renoir. An infant slept peacefully.

"How does it feel being a Papa?" he asked Renoir.

Renoir looked fondly down at his baby's cherubic face. "Ah, my petite Pierre, a soft but heavy bundle——born eight and a half pounds, now twice the weight!"

"Your first child?" I inquired.

"Yes, truly yes. An old man's dream," he confided, watching me closely. *Does he see a potential model?* so I vainly imagined.

I settled my attention upon the dog, lying motionless beside Monet's leg.

Renoir followed my line of sight. "The dog insists on staying as near as possible to Claude, rather like paste to a stamp."

"What is your dog's name?" became my first, inane question of Claude Monet. I dared not look at him, but kept my focus on the dog, sleeping, his hind and forelegs stretched, as if he might be dreaming of flight.

"*Le Petit Pistolet,*" he replied.

Little pistol. *A name only a man would confer,* I thought.

He dressed smartly, Monsieur Claude Monet, well-fitted in an amber-checked vest and matching jacket, while peeking from his jacket sleeves were lace cuffs. Politely, he asked if I had brought any cigarettes, regarding me with eyes that had the sharpness of a twenty-year-old even though I knew he was more than twice that age. From my side dress pocket I brought out an unopened box of twelve Black Cats, gifted to me by Suzanne.

Renoir grabbed it. "My word! She smokes Black Cats!" He unsealed the box, took the first cigarette, and handed the box to Monet. "Haven't had one these," he said, "since you brought a boatful back from London... when the war was safely over." The remark about the war seemed to have another layer of meaning. He found a match from a side pocket and with a flick of a long thumbnail ignited the cigarette. The Franco-Prussian War was a sore point among the artists, some had stayed to serve, others had gone to England or elsewhere to wait it out. "Of course," Renoir felt compelled to add, "I never left France, having to settle for Egyptian cigarettes." He looked at me. "I served with the cuirassiers."

Monet spoke to the table in general, something shrewd and playful in his manner. "Our gallant Renoir, ensconced high up in the Pyrenees, spent the war years training farm horses for the calvary."

Renoir fired back, "While you and this other fellow here discovered Constable. And Turner. Turner, dammit." The banter seemed friendly enough. I suspected such exchange of barbs was commonplace and acceptable. Renoir, puffing with pleasure, sighed, "The Virginian tobacco, that makes the difference."

We all settled comfortably in our chairs on the terrace, inhaling Black Cats, when Pissarro startled everyone by jumping to his feet. He looked at the two artists with a solemn intensity. "I'm going to ask you both, point blank, to participate in the Show." Silence descended. I gently tugged at Pissarro's sleeve and brought him back to his seat. "I make this request not for myself," he started gruffly, wanting no misunderstanding, "but for the young painters, our descendants, who have great need of our support."

Renoir, ignoring Pissarro, having preferred to maintain his gaze upon me, gently inquired, "Mademoiselle, the apricot coloured dress you wear strikes a memory chord... especially the blue zig-zag stitching about the side pockets and about your waist... although the white papier mache chrysanthemum is missing, which I remember well as it was as big as a cabbage." He pondered a few more minutes. "Doesn't that dress belong to Suzanne Valadon?"

"I have been caught in something borrowed."

"You know my Suzanne?"

"We are friends."

He drew deeply on his cigarette, considering the implication of the information. Finally: "May I ask a small favour of Mademoiselle?" came Renoir's surprising request.

"Yes?"

"My wife... the mother of my child..." He looked down into the crib to ensure that his little Pierre slept well... "My wife Aline," he went on in a distracted manner. "Aline... whose tender breasts are, as we speak, flowing with the milk of human kindness... my wife..."

Pissarro became exasperated, "Speak up, man!"

Renoir looked with the hope that I was reading between the lines. "If, perchance, you should inadvertently mention in her presence the name of

Suzanne Valadon... Well..."

"The milk could turn sour," I said.

"Ha! I need say no more." Relieved, he leaned back in his chair, resumed smoking, letting the blue sky, the rolling clouds, the pleasant spring day capture his interest.

Pissarro had no intention of being discouraged. He locked his gaze upon Monet. "Imagine the significance, if we Impressionists joined together again, as in days of old."

Again no one spoke. In the awkward silence I could hear two birds chirping to one another in some distant tree, sounding like penny whistles.

My dear friend persevered, "Gentlemen, hear me out, another Show! This time more successful than the others combined."

"I should think seven shows enough," snapped Renoir. "Hardly made a sou from any of them."

"But now," argued Pissarro, "haven't we three deepened in talent?"

Conveniently, Monet picked up his sketch pad and occupied his time with drawing my profile, in respectful silence.

"The show will be suitably advertised," I put in, "having the financial support of Berthe Morisot and her husband Eugene Manet."

Alice Hoschedé appeared, marching toward us to take away bowls and saucers, steadfastly refusing to meet my smile. Monet received a stern glance which seemed to have no effect. "Claude, I will be in the kitchen with Aline preparing supper."

Feminine jealousy bored me. I opened the cigarette box to Monet who took another. His wife-to-be banged the screen door shut. I stayed focused, "The 8th Impressionist Show could be the watershed event to truly solidify your movement."

"Impressionists!" Renoir tore off a piece of bread, full of indignation, vigorously smearing blueberry jam on the bread. "How I loathe that word! It's nothing more than a sugared confection!"

"I can't believe my ears!" Pissarro had grown past patience. "Must I remind Renoir that he, more than the rest of us, welcomed the epithet when Leroy coined it in *Le Charivari*."

"I did?"

"You did," put in Monet without taking his eyes off his sketch.

I asked him, "How, exactly, did the name 'Impressionism' come about?"

"If I recall correctly, the birth of the word came from everyone's dissatisfaction with the monotonous titles of my paintings." He pointed his crayon stick at Renoir. "In particular, your brother Edmond complained that I had too many bland 'Mornings' and 'Evenings in a Village' 'Mornings and Evenings in a Harbor' so I changed one of the views of Le Havre to '*Sunrise, An Impression,*' The critics hated my paintings, mere impressions they said, that painting especially, so the word Impressionist stuck to me."

"And stuck to the rest of us," sighed Renoir.

"In the misty harbour the masted boats lay like vague shadows upon the water," I spoke up. "The sky a lilac haze, and the sun an orange disc casting a swath of fire across a harbour sea."

Monet stopped drawing me for a moment. "Yes, that was the painting, the one I did from my window at Le Havre, which inspired Leroy's ridicule."

"I saw it on special display at Durand-Ruel's gallery."

"Thank you, Mademoiselle Forette, for refreshing our memories with such an apt description."

"Mademoiselle Forette has a way with words," said Pissarro, proudly.

"Well, the fact remains." Renoir took another of my cigarettes. "I'm an artist, not an Impressionist. Degas agrees. We started out as the Society of Anonymous Painters to show our disdain for the Salon and should have stayed that way."

"Thank you again, Mademoiselle Forette." Monet smiled, a glimmer of playful intrigue in his eye.

"Mademoiselle Forette is a scholar, steeped in the history of art," Pissarro announced. "She will add gravitas to our endeavour with an article or two." I tried to hide my amazement that he could indulge in such fabrication. "She, as well as other astute critics, Félix Fénéon for example, are convinced not only of the historical importance of this Show but of its commercial value. Mademoiselle Forette, give us a title for the article you shall write to promote the show."

"Perhaps the input of others is necessary."

"Come!" he persisted. "Something that will catch the imagination of the public!"

My mind struggled for a title. Monet tried to rescue me, "You're putting Mademoiselle Forette in a corner."

"I tell you she has a way with words," insisted Pissarro.

"The Impressionists—Final Victory," I blurted.

The impromptu title was greeted, deservedly, with censorious silence —it was, without doubt, most inane. But, but... *I could do better, just give me ample time.*

A quiet Monet resumed sketching; a quiet Pissarro patted and stroked the dog with new found affection; Renoir spread more jam on another crust of bread then showed little patience for silence.

"I ask, `Why should Monet and I, who have worked damn hard to climb and scale the walls of the art market, why should we scuttle back down to join those who are only just storming the gates? It makes," he ended, his anger rising, "damn little sense!"

Monet turned his sketch pad ever to slightly, not wanting the others to notice his charcoal written request: 'May I show you more of Giverny?'

How am I to respond?

The other two artists grew more argumentative. Renoir said to Pissarro, "Candidly speaking, these shows have become too socialistic for my taste."

"Is that a reference to me? Come, speak your mind!"

"Well..." Renoir regained his calm by looking down in the crib at his child, "isn't being in a show which includes Gauguin, Guillaumin and Pissarro similar to participating in a socialist rally?"

"That's a stretch!" huffed Pissarro.

"In these particular times," came the whispered caution, "the public doesn't like anything that even hints of revolution." When Pissarro shook his head in dismay, Renoir grew indignant. "At this stage of my life I have no wish to be seen as a revolutionary or, for that matter, an atheist."

My white-bearded friend looked at me: "Why do Christians have amnesia when it comes to remembering that Christ was a revolutionary." He turned back to Renoir. "And a Jew as well."

"Obviously you have more in common with Jesus Christ than I." Renoir reached for another of my cigarettes, shrugged. "Jewish, gladly I'm not."

Monet grew uneasy. He rose, and so did I. A whiff of anti-Semitism was in the air. A reason why, I began to think, it might be advantageous to remain Julie Forette and not return to my given name.

"Where are you two going?" Pissarro asked us, suspicious.

"I want to show Mademoiselle Forette the flowers."

"I need you both here," demanded Pissarro. "We need to discuss the Impressionist Show."

"Renoir speaks for me," said Monet. "Except in politics and religion."

I wondered, as he led me away, how this day would end?

Here I strolled—almost unbelievable—a companion to Claude Monet. Of course, *Petit Pistolet* accompanied us, trotting loyally at his master's heels. I soon noticed that everything interested Monet. He stopped before the most unlikely subjects, a silvery cobweb in sunlight, the lichen patches of an ageing beech, the mottled pattern upon a single mushroom, pointing out how unexpected nature is.

"Even this still day has no feeling of fixedness: clouds inch across the sky, leaves tremble."

"They say your eye even sees the grass growing." The hyperbolic comment only made him smile. I went on, out of nervousness. "Some have postulated that you possess ultraviolet vision." He laughed. I persisted, "Monet, I recently read, is one of those rare people in the world who have the ability to see ultraviolet light, the farthest range of the solar spectrum, which the artist can reproduce on canvas."

"I have no scientific expertise, except perhaps in horticulture, but isn't ultraviolet light invisible to the optic nerves?"

"For the majority of human beings, yes, but recent experiments by the respected scientist, Chardonet, prove that some people respond strongly to this invisible part of the spectrum. I would venture to say that you belong to this exclusive number."

He merely shook his head, amused and somewhat baffled at my train of thought. In the quest for an interview, I was perhaps advancing too aggressively. He turned his attention to the dog. When he picked up a stick along our path, Little Pistol's cream-dipped tail began to wag excitedly. "I do believe someone wishes to perform for Mademoiselle." Monet flung the stick skyward into a high arc, the signal for the dog to shoot off in rapid pursuit. As the stick descended, Little Pistol leaped and amazingly made a full somersault in the air before catching the stick in his mouth and landing safely. To prove the feat was no accident, Monet repeatedly threw the stick in the air and each time the dog leaped, performing the dexterous somersault and landing on all four paws, trotting happily back to Monet with the prize stick in his mouth.

"Was the dog in a circus?" I asked.

"I cannot say, he simply arrived one day at my studio door and decided to adopt me. *Pistolet's* background is a mystery."

He then threw very high and far away, the dog running after the stick until both disappeared over a rise. As we waited for Little Pistol to return, Monet asked, "Is it true that you work for a renowned neurologist."

"Dr. Jean-Martin Charcot is my employer," I said simply.

"They say that Charcot will soon solve the riddle of hysteria and cure all the women in France who are afflicted with the strange disease."

"The disorder is not confined to women, I can assure you."

"Really?"

"A demonstrable fact proven by Charcot himself. You should attend one of his demonstrations."

"I keep my visits to Paris to a bare minimum."

I gazed at the tranquil countryside around us. "I well understand your reluctance to leave such beauty."

We resumed walking. *Pistolet* had not returned. When we reached the rise, I turned back to take in the full charm of Monet's pink stucco house in the distance.

"We rent," he volunteered, "but some day I hope to create a home here in Giverny for my family."

"You have quite a brood of children." I watched several now masquerading as wild Indians with feather bonnets, running and whooping about the house and gardens.

"I can only take credit for fathering two. My someday-to-be wife, Alice, brings six from her previous marriage."

"Her first husband died?"

"No, Ernest Hoschedé is very much alive." He said no more.

But I had learned from Pissarro on our morning train ride at least part of the curious story. Ernest Hoschedé, a wealthy businessman, had been an early collector of Monet's work. He and his wife Alice became close friends to the Monet family.

When Camille Monet was stricken with a serious illness, Ernest Hoschedé arranged for his wife and six children to stay with the Monets who lived in Vetheuil. The following year, 1878, Monet's wife died and Alice Hoschedé never left. She abandoned her husband and stayed with the artist, taking charge of raising both families.

Monet stared at me with curiosity. "But tell me, Mademoiselle Forette, why have you come to Giverny?"

"I think Father Pissarro needs an ally in his mission to persuade two of the three most famous Impressionists to join him in an 1886 show."

"Ah, then this mission makes of you Sancho Panza to his Don Quixote."

"Is Father Pissarro chasing after windmills? Is his fervent desire to reunite with his comrades a fruitless pursuit?"

Embarrassed, Monet looked away. "Where has our *Petit Pistolet* gone, I wonder? On occasions, he will pick up the scent of a rabbit and embark on a hunting expedition, but always outwitted by the rabbit. Today, however, may be different. Perhaps we will have our first rabbit stew *a la Pistolet*." We resumed walking. "I now know your chief purpose in coming, yet might there be another reason?"

I hesitated. "*La Vogue* has a preposterous notion that I might snare an interview from you."

"Maybe not too preposterous."

My fickle heart which had sunk when he showed little inclination to join Pissarro in a show now leaped at the prospect of an interview. Looking straight into his mythic eyes—not violet, but blue, clear, trusting: "To grant me an interview would be the deepest honour."

"But will Mademoiselle grant me a favour as well?

I said, "Yes" too quickly, and wished I had added, *within reason.*

"My studio is not far," he said.

Posing nude was out the question.

He offered his hand and we left the path. Soon it seemed we were just meandering through a dense wooded area of moss-racked pine. Light barely penetrated and each turn we took resembled the last. Monet led me doggedly, stepping over rotted trees which seemed to have fallen aeons ago, the pine-scented twilight discomfiting.

I grew alarmed. "Monsieur Monet, I have lost all sense of direction!" He could see the panic in my eyes. "I simply cannot take another step forward!"

"I am your compass, Mademoiselle Forette." He held my clammy hand firmly. "I know this area leaf by leaf."

Minutes later we passed through a hedge of hawthorn, climbed a hillock and found ourselves in open land, under reassuring sunlight. Embarrassed, I let go of his hand.

Knowingly, he looked at me. "Was that a phobic episode?"

"You're the first to see it," I admitted.

Saying no more, Monet proceeded toward a large, red barn, disappearing through wide open doors. I followed.

I am not posing nude.

The spacious interior, like a barn, had a hard earth covering, and several bales of hay stacked in a far corner. There were two immensely wide bay windows along one of the walls. The roof, redone entirely in glass, transformed the barn into a cathedral of light. I focused greedily on the paintings, some hung, but most leaned in bunches against the walls.

He gently tapped my shoulder. "May I scrounge another Black Cat?"

Giving him the packet, I went to the paintings and began sifting through an array of gorgeous landscapes. He kept his distance, allowing me time to savour them. I especially lingered over one particular portrait, a woman wrapped in a long flowing kimono who clearly was not Japanese. She wore her reddish blonde hair piled high in a fashion similar to mine and offered the viewer a provocative smile, but the magnificent, silk kimono was the true centre of attention, fiery red, decorated with a sword-wielding, white-faced Samurai.

I turned to Monet who leaned against a saw horse. "Your canvases, Pissarro says, not too far in the future, will be worth their weight in gold."

"He is most generous with his praise."

I gazed back at the painting. "Such a beautiful model."

"She's wearing a wig, but nonetheless, yes, beautiful."

He drew deeply on the cigarette then he cast a worried look out the window. "The weather may not remain favourable."

"Am I here to pose for you?"

He remained silent. I watched in captive fascination as he gained a final drag from the stub of the cigarette and let it fall into the dirt, grinding it under his boot. Seemingly having made up his mind, he walked to me, put his hand under my chin, turned my face into profile.

"Are you admiring the painterly effects of small pox?" I spoke breezily, wanting to be nonchalant.

"You saw how my Alice looked at you."

"Yes, with daggers."

"Jealousy." He was blunt.

"What is there to be jealous of? My looks?" I seemed unable to forget my marred complexion.

He shrugged then chose to answer a previous question. "I would very much like you to pose for me. Only that dress will not do."

"What do you have in mind?"

Here comes the request... maybe I will be amenable.

"A different dress." He went over to one of the bay window alcoves. A very large chest sat on the earthen floor. My imagination took flight as he creaked open the chest—he will pull out a brightly coloured kimono as in the painting. Julie Forette, *une Japonaise*, hair up in Geisha bundles, neck bent as graceful as a swan, an invitation for the touch of his lips. What thrill might that dispatch to my loins!

Instead he pulled out a dress nearly a decade out of fashion, what a

Parisian women would now consider quaint, soft linen and muslin thread, pure white.

Monet sat on the chest, reflective, the dress draped over his lap. "I want you to wear this." I heard a touch of melancholy in his voice. "You can dress behind the divider." He indicated another corner of the barn.

The dress fit perfectly and when I stepped out, Monet startled me by squashing a flat, straw hat upon my head. "We must hurry for the light changes so quickly, and the location is some distance away!"

"You have already decided on a motif?"

"Yes, a certain hill."

And to find it we were nearly running. He had me carrying props, an ivory handled parasol, and one of four, blank canvases. *Pistolet* almost magically reappeared, yapping excitedly, leading the way, and knowing exactly where his master needed to go.

Where I was eventually placed offered a panorama of lushly green, rolling meadows, and cascading down Monet's chosen hilltop decorative swaths of orange and red poppies

Partway down the hill, he set up an easel, told me to open up my parasol, and began sketching in quick slashes of charcoal outlines.

"Can my formal interview begin now?" I asked.

Already he was brushing in blocks of colour. "Only if I can interview you as well. Your Science in exchange for my Art."

I shrugged a puzzled consent, unsure of what he wanted to learn.

"You begin first," he said. "Fire away." He painted with an assurance that Cezanne never possessed.

Nervously I began spinning the parasol while little *Pistolet* ran in excited circles trying to catch it. What first question for my first *La Vogue* interview? "What made you a painter?"

He paused. "May I address you as Julie?"

"Please do." *May I address you as Claude? Ha!*

Abandoning his easel, he walked toward me. *Why?* Stooping, he plucked a single red poppy and approached; he took hold of my ribbon ceinture, standing so close I could smell him, his particular mixture of paint, tobacco, and what reminded me of cocoa. "What made me a painter," he began softly, my heart beating faster, anticipating some amorous advance, feeling both confused and thrilled. "Flowers," he said, placing the poppy's stem into my ceinture.

Flowers, I repeated silently in my head, imagining it as the first word in my article.

"Their beauty made me want to paint them."

"Not beautiful women?"

"I see women as particular flowers. You, for instance, are the long-stemmed iris, blue petalled, with swirls of gold delicately tinted at your edges.

That will not go into my article, I thought, as he returned to his easel.

Painting, applying more fluid strokes, his interview began. "What, pray tell, is hypnosis? Pissarro claims you are an authority on the subject."

"It is a phenomena I study, but one could hardly consider me an authority."

"Surely you have formed some kind of opinion."

"Tentative theories."

"But you yourself have hypnotized people. Pissarro has warned me, he says, 'Mademoiselle Julie Forette can turn people into mindless automatons so mind your manners!'"

I laughed, enjoying the gentle teasing. "Quite the opposite of mindless," I said. "Those who I have hypnotized utilize more faculties of the mind, bring to bear increased concentration."

"How do you begin?"

"Do you want to be hypnotized?"

"Do you think I should be hypnotized?"

"It's not a frivolous game."

"What is hypnotism then? An Art or a Science?"

"I cannot say," I answered with a shrug, unhappy that he had gained control of the conversation.

"Well, whatever it is," he continued, painting rapidly. "I'm quite serious about understanding the mechanics of hypnotism, as you are serious with grasping my painting methods."

A gentle rebuke that our interviews were give and take. My hope now was to bore him. "How I hypnotize is to have the subject focus his or her attention upon a narrow range of stimuli or even one stimulus. Perhaps just my voice, or a visual point, the glint of a turning mirror, the sparkle of a chosen star, a feeling in some part of the body. Sometimes I bring them quickly to imagine a scene."

Monet took the canvas off the easel and replaced it with another. He seemed perturbed.

"You are displeased with the scene... with your model?"

"No-no, the changing light requires another set of colour arrangements."

"So you paint sequentially, one canvas is not sufficient for the motif."

"Nature keeps changing, seduces me with new conditions of light and colour, and so I play catch-up."

"So I can never be one Julie Forette for you?"

"Your appearance changes at every moment by the atmosphere which surrounds you."

The verse came, unsought. "Light manipulates her, manhandles her..."

"What is that you recite?"

"A snippet of a poem my sister recently composed."

"She sounds gifted. Does she count herself among the new school of symbolists? Mallarmé, Rimbaud, and the like?"

"She is her own school."

Monet grew interested. "Can you recite the entire poem?"

"No, I've forgotten the rest." A lie. The poem troubled me. I knew not why.

Light

manipulates her

man-handles her

takes her

upon a chromium bed

where

awash in mercury red

she melts

"What actually happens inside the mind of the hypnotized person?" Monet pursued.

"What I can aver is that hypnosis is a state of altered awareness. More than this would be conjecture."

As the day wore on, the light predictably changed and Monet changed canvases accordingly. He said he would know by the end of the day which canvas to finish, which aspect of nature best suited the subject—me.

While working on the fourth canvas, the ominous sound of a distant thunderclap caused us to look westward. The light around us turned eerily pale. Moments later a terrific rushing of wind blew off my straw hat, knocked over Monet's easel, and aroused *Pistolet* to howl. As the raindrops began to fall, sporadic at first, large and heavy, I rushed down from my earthen pedestal to Claude Monet who seemed strangely unconcerned by the gathering tumult in the heavens. It must have seemed comic to raise the fragile, green parasol over him for the wind's fury turned the parasol inside out and useless. Silver lightening cracked directly overhead, the sky darkened with elephantine clouds and Monet did nothing. The canvases lay on the ground. I couldn't understand why he was not picking them up. The wind was wildly blowing my hair. Little *Pistolet* put his paws on Monet's legs and whimpered. The wind sent Monet's hat sailing then scattered the easel into several pieces. The dog raced after the fleeing hat. I threw away the battered parasol and grabbed at Monet's sleeve, shouting above the wind's roar, "Let's grab the paintings and run for cover!"

Stubbornly he remained moored, the rain striking us like lead pellets.

"I cannot see," he said a matter-of-factly.

I looked in disbelief—his eyes were vacant. I pushed a painting under his arm, another under mine, determined to escape the havoc of the storm. The wind suddenly exhausted itself, but the rain poured down in torrents.

Already drenched, he asked, "Can you can get us safely to the barn?" There was a shortcut, he said, through a dense grouping of birch trees. "Tough going, but if we don't stray we will reach the barn."

I waved my hand across his eyes. "Can you see anything—light, shadow?"

"Blankness, that's all I see."

I took his free hand and through the downpour we reached the cropping of birch he described. There was a path, but narrow, forcing us to march single file. He held on to the back of my ribbon ceinture and in frightened haste I kept stumbling, falling to my knees, the white muslin dress turning into a muddy mess, weighing on me like heavy paste. Monet's face soon became scratched and bloody as we wended through terribly thick bramble, and the relentless thorns clawing at us. Then my worst dread, with the rain pounding down mercilessly, I lost sight of the footpath.

"It's disappeared! We're lost!" I cried out in panic.

"I can smell the damn barn!" he shouted above the deafening rain. "We're getting close, turn left!"

"A thick wall of thorn bushes are over there!" I protested.

"Go!" he commanded. "Use the canvas as a shield!"

I could feel him pressing against my back, urging me straight through. Still, he held on to the other painting as we scrambled upwards, stumbling, ignoring the pricks and stabs until, mercifully, the barn!

Near exhaustion I somehow managed to lift the barn latch, pull open the door, and help the badly scratched Monet inside. We were soaked, pools of water gathering at our feet.

Leading him to a chair, I was very alarmed by the eerie blankness in his eyes.

He asked angrily, "What has happened to my eyesight?"

I found a clean, dry cloth and tended to his facial wounds. Wiping away the blood, I searched his eyes. There were no signs of inflammation, occlusions or cataracts.

He pushed away my hand, exasperated. "Is it some neurological disease?"

I tried to sort in my mind what might have provoked his blindness. The concussive sound of the thunder, the blinding flash of lightning? Charcot often postulated, in the lectures I recorded, that traumatic events could trigger a neurologic disease, especially if one were genetically predisposed. I asked, "Has anyone in your family experienced a similar affliction?"

"No."

I kept searching for an explanation. "Perhaps the sudden storm, the thunder, the lightning bolts provoked..."

He interrupted, "I revel in the sound of thunder, in extremes of nature."

Hesitant, I suggested, "There are other precipitating influences which Dr. Charcot mentions... such as syphilis."

He managed an ironic laugh. "Are then all the men in France predestined to go blind?" He and I fell silent. "Besides," he added, somewhat petulantly, "I have been faithful to Alice Hoschedé."

"Charcot mentions extreme cold and humidity as provoking agents. You're shivering now in your wet clothes," I pointed out.

"Julie," he gently explained, "I tremble because I'm in a state of terror."

I realized his terror, the thought that he would never be able to paint again. "What if," I revealed my suspicion, "your blindness is not somatic at all, but something emotional?" I knelt in front of him, took hold of his hands. "Will you let me find out?"

"How?" he asked, still staring at nothingness.

"Hypnosis," I said.

"How does one hypnotize a blind man?" He sounded both exasperated and despondent.

"There are ways."

Monet reached out, touched my shoulder. "Your dress is sopping wet. Put on dry clothes, now!"

"But you're wet as well."

"Do as I say." He pushed me gently away. I went to change. He called out when I reached the bamboo partition, "I promise not to look."

I removed the dress and my wet undergarments in plain sight, hung them over the partition to dry. He showed no sign of seeing. "Is there anything else to wear until my things dry?" I asked.

"Plenty of dresses in the treasure chest," he said.

Rummaging, I found a kimono in the chest which seemed the very one depicted in the painting, except a deeper red. Delighted, I wrapped myself in its luxuriant silk, coming back to stand before him, an alluring geisha, and Monet was oblivious. I brought over a chair, sat, and faced him.

He expressed doubt again, "Hypnotizing a blind man will be quite a feat."

"It's more a matter of inner sight. So let's experiment."

Unlike Paul Gauguin, I had little difficulty in hypnotizing Monet. He responded to imagery so I guided him through the day's events, focusing on the paintings he made of me, keeping a steady, soft, commanding voice. He easily described what he was trying to capture, the play of coloured light on his subject, the kind of brush work he used.

"You are outside of yourself... observing your own eyes...looking, looking very closely."

"This is most unnerving," he grew agitated.

"You are calm... calmness pervades your being which nothing can disturb."

"My eyes," he responded, in trance, "have no pupils, no irises... milk white, like blank canvases."

I spoke sharply, "You are a painter, paint upon them.... paint the subject that pleases you most; proceed, put delight on the blank canvas."

I thought, possibly such suggestions might be the way reclaim his vision.

"I cannot paint! Those eyes are blind!"

Nonetheless, he was now outside of himself. "Paint into them," I instructed. "Seek the memory of the painting which brought you the most peace..."

He stared, a certain focus came into his eyes... might a stored image from his subconscious emerge? Hurriedly I decided to set the stage: "The palette is upon your knee, your five favourite colours are there, raw and unmixed, the sable brush in your hand; a favourable light enters."

He held the unseen brush—now in a deep trance—daubed from an imaginary palette and stroked lightly at the air in front of him. He worked diligently, patiently, his blindness forgotten.

To facilitate the completion of the hypnoid painting, I offered vague encouragement. "The figures are forming nicely."

"Just you wait!" he smiled. "But first, I want to capture him in a gentle haze as the light filters through the muslin fabric over the crib. Both baby and mother will be bathed in a blue translucence."

What to do but pretend. "Oh yes, I see."

"It costs me difficulty, choosing what to settle upon."

"Yes, the light changes from moment to moment."

"How right you are! Each moment brings its appointed colour scheme."

Are his eyes open to a recent memory? "Where are you?" I asked.

"I've come back to be with them, with Camille and our baby, Jean."

"You have been on a journey?"

"In Honfleur, with Bazille, painting together, trying to run away."

"Run away?"

"From marriage… fatherhood. But I shall now take care of them," he replied firmly and brushed more quickly at the invisible painting. "It is done!" he soon announced, putting the invisible brush and palette on the floor.

Confident that I was close to succeeding, I instructed him to close his eyes and listen to the count of 10 to 1. At 1 he would open his eyes and see. Counting, I told him he would remember nothing disturbing, nothing to cause him guilt. "4, 3... you remember nothing save your last favourite brush stroke on the hillside... 2, 1!"

His eyes opened to me, enveloped in the red kimono. His look of shock made me realize that he was experiencing yet another trauma. Instinctively, to keep him from returning to blindness, my hands grabbed hold of his face and buried it into my lap; I whispered, "Keep your eyes closed, remember where you are, in the barn, your vision has returned."

His voice muffled in my lap, he worried, "Are you sure?"

I reassured him, but suggested we should just talk for a little while, keeping his eyes closed.

Monet explained, "Dressed in the Japanese robe, I thought you were her."

"Ah, the woman in the painting. Who is she?"

"My deceased wife, Camille." He started to raise his head from my lap, but I kept him still, placed my hand over his eyes.

"Tell me about her."

He did. She was the model for many of his early paintings. They fell in love. She became pregnant. "I was twenty-seven, Camille was eighteen. My father disapproved of the whole affair. Three years after Jean was born, I found the courage to marry Camille. Then two months later, the war broke out and I took off for London, leaving her to fend for herself. I wasn't much of a husband or father in those days," he admitted ruefully.

"I'm sure you loved her dearly."

"Yes. Yes."

"What flower was she?" I needed to keep him talking.

"My favourite, the lily."

Encouraged, he began talking fondly of Camille. Gradually, he grew calm and held on to his eyesight.

The storm passed. We heard birds chirping and shafts of sunlight came through the windows. I redressed then carefully folded the red kimono that Camille once wore, placing it back in the chest.

Of the two canvases carried through the rain storm, only one seemed salvageable—there I stood on a hill swathed in red poppies and batches of lavender, the lady with a green parasol.

"You have hidden me well behind the chiffon veil." I said.

He carefully set it aside. "A shadow can evoke a presence."

Sufficiently dry, Monet and I decided to make our return trip, an easier path that skirted the woodland. We remained subdued. The setting sun began to spread a spectacle of pink and scarlet colours across the horizon. "The colour scheme will last only a moment," he remarked, "before the deeper violets touch every tree, every leaf with its melancholy glow."

"Which you will see more intensely with your ultra-violet vision," I said, only half-joking.

"Well, whatever vision I now possess, it's thanks to you." He then stopped with a questioning look. "Julie, what happened in the barn?"

"Some call it 'chimney sweeping,'" I said.

He took my arm and we resumed walking. Suddenly he laughed, clearly glad he had weathered his personal storm, "Hurrah for Mademoiselle Chimney Sweeper!"

"I was not the chimney sweeper," I said. "You were."

Approaching the Giverny house, we could make out in the distance the two artists we had left behind a lifetime ago, still squabbling, still waving arms in the air, still fencing in the purple twilight.

I asked Monet matter-of-factly, "You will join the Show, won't you?"

"I cannot... will not."

The certitude of his reply was hard to take. Still, I persevered. "Father Pissarro is fast sinking into debt."

"Julie, if Renoir and I exhibit at Petit's prestigious gallery we will do more to legitimize Impressionism, thereby benefiting everyone. But Pissarro participating in this hodgepodge of a show will only keep the public laughing."

At that moment we watched Pissarro hurrying comically toward us, his enormous belly leading the way. I was too out of sorts to stay and left the artists to untangle their differences, if at all possible.I took a chair on the stone terrace next to Renoir, uncharacteristically quiet, musing upon I knew not what, until he spoke, softly. "Pissarro and I go back a long way. We have a history of shared hardships. We used to be so poor that he and I began painting blinds for people's homes. A petite bourgeoise business that I crazily dreamed up."

"I'm sure, thanks to you, it put food on the table. He calls you a jack-of-all trades, resourceful at every turn, and in the deck of cards, Monet the king, Renoir the jack."

Relinquishing a small smile, he thought for a moment. "Have you a deck of cards?"

I quickly found the pack the train conductor gave as a parting gift. Renoir sifted through the cards. "Here is Pissarro." He placed the card on the table. The Ace of Hearts.

He rose, regained his stern demeanour. "Mark my words, Mademoiselle Forette, soon enough our deeply talented Pissarro will abandon the pointillist technique he borrows from Seurat. I know he attains more compositional structure, but the dot is not for him, the dots are too limiting, the technique too premeditated. He will drop the dots and use a broader stroke, but don't dare tell him I said so," Renoir warned. "My intelligent prediction will only make him dig in his heels longer than necessary. To reinforce his design and structure, he should follow my new direction: bring back the classical, bring back the line." He sat back down and lowered his voice. "Now don't you breathe a word to Monet of what I have just confided, for he will think I, too, have abandoned Impressionism."

I raised a hand to pledge secrecy. He smiled and directed me closer to the crib. "See Mademoiselle Forette," he said proudly, staring down at his son. "See how well his skin takes the light?"

* * *

At day's end, all that I heard convinced me that each of the three Impressionists wore a mantle of greatness, each would never stop developing their craft, never stop experimenting.

Which made their bickering seem so petty, so wasteful.

Monet insisted on taking us in the supply wagon to the train station. I stayed silent and despondent, our mission having failed. Yet during the entire ride the two artists conversed amiably. Men of character, they were, maintaining the highest respect for each other.

At the Vernon station, when our train arrived with a terrific clanking of iron and hissing of steam, Monet took advantage of the commotion to force a tightly rolled wad of bills into my hand. "For Father Pissarro," he said softly.

What could I say? I said nothing.

As we boarded, Monet cheerfully wished us "a pleasant journey back to Paris!" I waved mechanically. He voiced a parting thought— "Why do you suppose they call it the city of light?"

Pissarro shrugged. "More light can certainly be found in the country."

"Perhaps 'light' is a metaphor," I volunteered to the man who I would never see again.

"Ah, yes!" He smiled with his beautiful, ultra-blue eyes. "The inner light—for you Parisians are very much enlightened."

The light-hearted remark, supposedly his satire, yet I received the message, his deep gratitude for our talking session in the barn. Only more pieces to the Monet puzzle needed to fit into place; more to be found, if I were to reach the root cause of his hysterical blindness.

During the train ride to Paris, I gave my dear companion Monet's benevolent gift.

"Goodness! Four thousand francs!" For the briefest of moments, tears welled in Pissarro's eyes. "This is not the first time he has bailed me out."

Chapter 46

The possessed of the past were, I assert, hysterics.

Jean-Martin Charcot

The Phantom Birth

I

Returning from Giverny I could only think of relating my extraordinary experience to Sigmund. We made arrangements to meet at *le Chalet Suisse*, a popular patisserie always chock full of cheerful, sugar-minded customers. I chose a remote table to escape the general hubbub, the oooh's and aahh's the pastries elicited as waitresses, wearing fanned crinoline headdresses and dainty lace aprons, wheeled their temptations around the rooms on silver carts.

To please and surprise Sigmund, I ordered an assortment of chocolates then kept a keen eye on the entrance, a newly installed revolving glass door which let me watch each customer being whooshed inside.

What would he say to the fact that I had cured Claude Monet of his hysterical blindness through the power of hypnosis? No small accomplishment, I thought, offering evidence that a mental force, operating below the surface of conscious thinking, could alter somatic symptoms.

Suddenly he appeared, slipping into a seat. I had somehow missed his entrance. Flushed and breathless, he apologized, "Ran most of the way so as not to be late. Sorry."

"No matter, you're here!"

He dropped his top hat onto an empty chair. "Had no idea how far the *Gare du Nord* Station was from here."

Not giving any thought as to what business he had at the train station, I poured out the details of curing Monet of blindness, he listening attentively.

"How can we now have any doubt,' I concluded, "that an invisible, potent force operates beneath the conscious mind?"

His handsomely bearded smile showed the admiration I wanted. "You have certainly buttressed my theory."

Excited, I grasped his hand. "The subconscious you talk about exists!"

"The unconscious, my preferred term," he corrected, "since, *de facto*, we are not conscious of its operation."

"Perhaps, perhaps, but let's agree that hypnosis is **the** therapeutic tool to reach its domain."

He shrugged, noncommittal, wanting more information. "Putting aside the instigating trauma of the thunderstorm, what are your thoughts as to what brought on his blindness?"

"A memory escaping from the unconscious. What, precisely," my turn to shrug, "still eludes me."

A lace-aproned waitress took our drink order of two *renversés*. I pushed the tray of chocolates toward him.

"Siren! You set before me strong temptations!" Jokingly he scolded, ferreting out his favourite mints.

I had to confront him once again. "Doesn't Monet's cure signal the moment to hypnotize Sabrine?"

Shaking his head, he arranged the chocolate mints in a separate line. "What brought back your artist friend's sight was not hypnosis. My guess is that his overly excited optic nerves stabilized in the barn as he unburdened whatever thoughts weighed upon him. So with Sabrine, I want to focus on our chimney sweeping."

"Why not take advantage of both?"

He took his turn to confront me, "Julie, when will you surrender some accounting of your family life? Then perhaps I can make some sense out of Sabrine's emotional development."

I stirred three sugar cubes into my *renversé*. "Sabrine has to take you to her own past."

He showed his impatience. "She just tosses out fragments."

Gauguin' philosophy came to mind. "Isn't that what comprises our life, Sigmund, a collection of fragments?"

He tried to persuade, "Please, I will settle for a framework, a chronology."

I had put in too much sugar in the *renversé*. "Relating any details of our life in Marseilles would just amount to my own story-telling."

"Breuer no longer hypnotizes Anna O," came his unpleasant news. "He says, he no longer dares."

"Why?"

"He thinks the relaxation of inhibition stirs up too much of her emotional attachment to him."

"Is that so wrong if it helps rid Anna of her neurasthenic torments."

"Breuer is a married man. He has a wife to consider."

A jealous wife, I thought, dropping the subject.

A pastry waitress paused at our table with her rolling cart, waved away by Sigmund. He had suddenly lost his appetite for more sweets. The idle way he fiddled with his spoon made me suspect. I took to wondering what was behind the vague explanation for his tardiness—"Did you see a colleague off at the train station?"

"Actually, I went to purchase a railway ticket. I shall be leaving Paris and the Salpêtrière in a fortnight."

Stunned, as if physically struck, I managed with a trembling hand to set down my drink. The countless ideas usually generated in his presence flew from my head. He continued to speak but it took great effort to listen.

"At last, I shall see my fiancée again, a visit at Marty's home in Wandsbek, then back to Vienna." He could not escape my look of dismay. "Julie, my travel grant has run its course."

"But Josef Breuer, your mentor and friend," I began to argue. "Does he not still send a monthly stipend?"

"That, too, expires at the end of this month. My funds are depleted," he shrugged at the monetary situation.

Silent and feeling bitter, I fished into my purse for a cigarette. Only two Black Cats left. I lit one, *for this special occasion.*

I wondered. *Were we both to spend the rest our lives chasing after money? If only I had the financial resources, he could stay and attend to Sabrine. If Degas had only let go of the Oedipus painting, I would have Charcot's commission. If, if, if.*

I could barely afford the chocolate bonbons he had finished. I sat, mournful. He leaned forward, unexpectedly taking my hands. I knew his only wish was to console me, but angrily I drew back. Dr. Freud was packing his bags, taking his cocaine, and absconding with an array of intense experiences at Salpêtrière, willing to abandon my sister.

I spoke harshly, reminding him. "Psycho-therapy—**psychotherapy** has been initiated with my sister."

"True."

"Only you have barely ruffled the curtains in her psyche."

"We still have time to delve more deeply."

"Two weeks? Enough time? Two weeks!"

He took a different tact. "Dr. Breuer has made psychological progress with Anna O. To be in Vienna will enable me to learn firsthand from him." His voice sounded nonsensically bright and optimistic and reassuring. "Breuer will be equally eager to learn of my sessions with S. There may well be significant parallels. Anna O's self-induced 'Private Theatre', for example, where in trance she spins out stories, could be similar to the enigmatic poems that S composes."

"S?" A sudden use of the initial bewildered me.

"Her privacy needs to be ensured when I return to Vienna," he calmly explained. "So I need to acclimate myself to using an initial."

I found this new anonymity for my sister insulting. "Now she's S? An alphabetic letter?"

"No doctor wants to inadvertently reveal a patient's identity. And I must consider her, in this new therapeutic endeavour, my first patient."

"Who still needs psychological treatment."

He carefully set the spoon on the saucer. "The reality is... she baffles me at every turn. When I think I'm getting close to something significant, I'm outmanoeuvred or taken down an unfamiliar path. Be mindful, Julie, this talking therapy is still novice work. Unproven." He toyed more with the spoon then dropped it into the cup. I thought of the 'S' spoon, the Sigmund and Sabrine spoon, the spoon used for our mind altering cocaine.

He stirred the dregs of the *renversé*. "What I lack is broader experience, other patients with an array of psycho-neuroses; I plan, upon my return, to establish a private practice." His hand rested upon mine, the touch too gentle to pull away. "Julie, we will correspond, we will conduct our Congresses by proxy. Co-analysts are what we are. And we will succeed in shining the needed light into your sister's unconscious."

Insisting on paying the bill, I hurried through the revolving door, said a curt good-bye on the Avenue de Medicis, and headed straight to the *Gare-de-l'Est* with my own plan. Finding the schedule for trains to Nancy, I intended to travel as soon as possible to Dr. Bernheim's Hypnosis Clinic. It became imperative to discover what he and his staff had learned about the phenomenon of suggestion.

I had scant time, precious little time, before my sister was returned to Charcot, her future cupped in his hands, to be his fragile, wing-torn bird again, placed back in the cage.

II

Two days later, a Mercury Boy came to my door, a gangling adolescent who towered over me, delivering Sigmund's message. Something significant had happened. He could take the noon hour from his work in the pathology laboratory to meet.

I wasted no time. He was waiting in the small garden adjacent to the Metzner Annex where Sabrine now had a private room. He sat on a stone bench, nervously puffing a cigar, and tearing off pieces of a baguette to feed the pigeons at his feet. Catching sight of me, he jumped up, tossed away the bread and stubbed out the cigar on a tree trunk.

His news was almost too startling to believe. He had hypnotized Sabrine. After all of my pushing and prodding, he had taken the risk and successfully placed her in the hypnoid state.

"I was able to regress your sister to the originating memory of her ovarian pain."

Fighting my trembling, I dared not interrupt, wanting to absorb every detail as we meandered through the garden.

I had not seen him so excited. "She gave birth!" he exclaimed and stopped. "It happened when I planted the suggestion that she return to the moment her ovarian pains first occurred."

"She gave... birth?" I struggled to understand.

"That is to say," hurriedly correcting himself, "she simulated the act." He rushed through the events. "To facilitate my hypnosis, I had her lay on the small sofa you and Jeanne Charcot found for my office. When she reached the originating memory of the ovarian pain, she began to scream, grabbing hold of her stomach as though she were experiencing excruciating pain."

I had to interrupt, "Where did she imagine herself to be, did she say?"

"I have no idea. I had no time to ask for the details."

Frustrated, I put aside the fact that he had botched an important step in a guided hypnosis. "How do you know she was simulating the birthing process?"

"Julie, I've seen a sufficient number of deliveries as an intern in Vienna to know." He rifled through pockets to find and light another cigar. "The pains lasted close to a quarter of an hour while she writhed, flailed, and arched her back with each violent contraction."

I argued away the interpretation. "Aren't these particular convulsions

465

you describe just a variation on the rainbow arc she enacts during an hystero-epileptic attack?"

He was quick to rebut, "No, what I witnessed was the birthing process reenacted by your sister with frightening exactitude."

Frightening exactitude? I found the phrase disturbing.

"Her abdomen had extended to an exaggerated degree," he went on, "which one only sees in pregnant women who have come to full term."

"Did you make any attempt to bring her out of trance?"

He took my elbow to resume walking. "I placed a cold compress on her forehead, massaged her shoulders, encouraging her to deliver."

"Deliver what?" My mind was a swirl of confusion and worry. Had he precipitated some grave, unalterable psychosis? And was I to blame for disregarding his repeated warnings that hypnotizing Sabrine might have dire consequences?

Sigmund frowning, silent, puffing out smoke like a fast moving locomotive, escorted me back to the stone bench. "Of course, it was a hallucinatory experience. When her abdomen returned to normal, her breathing relaxed, the delivery obviously achieved, I instructed her to fall asleep. Of course, it was a hallucination," he emphasized again, "but you could say that she delivered a 'phantom child.'"

I had difficulty sorting out different emotions. He had taken Sabrine somewhere farther in her memory than Charcot would have ever dared imagine. Here was the thrill of hope that she would return... to normal. Yet, a dread kept galloping toward me as though a horseman from the apocalypse. I hesitated to ask, "What occurred after this phantom delivery?"

I had the awful fear that my dreamful sister might conjure up a child, make the phantom child real.

He seemed reluctant to continue. "Insistent knocking at the door interrupted the session," he said.

I guessed. "Dr. Babinski."

"Yes, ever-vigilant Babinski. The door was locked and little time left before I had to let him in. His shouts and damnable banging were, I thought, possibly dangerous intrusions into her hypnotic sleep. It was prudent that I awaken your sister quickly. And so I did, in a somewhat disorganized fashion."

He lost the opportunity to take Sabrine further into her phantasy. I said nothing. The mistake made.

"When I awakened her, she gave no indication of remembering what she had undergone. So we are back, in manner of speaking, to nowhere."

He threw away the cigar as if it had suddenly become distasteful. "Perhaps I've only muddied the waters."

"No-no! As of now, the waters are just unchartered; you and she must continue journeying, to make a map. Please promise that you will continue the sessions."

His days at Salpêtrière now numbered, he nonetheless promised, vowed that he would make every effort to reach 'the domain beneath her consciousness'."

Listening to his resolve for more talking sessions, I tried to keep at bay the possibility that Charcot would forbid him any further access to my sister. He now had the same concern. "Barring his interdiction," he murmured as my eyes were drawn to the fourth story window of the Metzner building. A slight movement at the window of her room caught my attention—an object pushed through the bars dropped quickly and fell behind a swath of rose bushes. I said nothing.

When he announced his need to return to the pathology lab, I was left alone. I went to search. Behind the bed of pink roses, I found the discarded object. Sabrine's ovarian compressor, in a mangled heap, the pressure rod had detached, buried halfway into the earth, like a miss-shot arrow.

She had given a sign. She was coming back to me.

Chapter 47

nightly i die in sleep
dissolve
as does the single drop of rain
that sinks into the clotted earth
at dawn's glare
my surly resurrection
to brittle bones and memories

Sabrine

WHO WILL CURE US, WHO WILL RESURRECT US?

I

The hospital staff noted surprise improvement in Sabrine's behaviour. No longer did she express the 'dreaminess' which used to exasperate and confound so many of the Salpêtrière doctors.

I heard Dr. la Tourette remark to a group, "I dare say, Sabrine now speaks with a marked degree of rationality."

Old nurse Botard, who knew Sabrine from the time she entered Salpêtrière, confided to Jeanne Charcot, "Praise St. Anthony, I do believe she's no longer a lost soul and has found the stairway back to our world."

When it became wonderfully obvious that Sabrine no longer experienced hystero-epileptic attacks, I enlisted Jeanne's aid in persuading her father to allow Sabrine a reprieve from the ovarian compressor. She had already thrown several out of her fourth story window. While Charcot tried to point out their proven popularity to his daughter, how the other hystero-epileptics demanded them, he reluctantly acceded to her request.

More freedom! And more inexorably to come! The change in Sabrine gave me immense hope. Sigmund, through hypnosis, had achieved the breakthrough of which I had dreamed. Certainly there were innumerable questions still unanswered, but with Sigmund willing to allow Sabrine to express her unconscious self, I saw the beginning of her cure. The only person who remained stubbornly unconvinced was Jean-Martin Charcot.

Then came the day when Sigmund sought me out in the medical library where I sometimes worked on preparing Charcot's lectures for publication. Sliding into a seat across from me, his look had a granite-like sternness—"I've rid myself of any doubt. Sabrine's hysteria is rooted in traumatic memories."

This seemed where logic led. "Then we can attribute her improvement as a result of reaching a traumatic memory."

He nodded. "Yes, but a traumatic memory that has not been articulated, although I'm certain what it is."

"So tell me then, what memory?"

"She must have given birth to a child before her arrival at the Salpêtrière."

"That is... unbelievable, untenable and patently preposterous." No, he had strayed too far. "No! She-had-no-child." I stressed each word before gathering the work papers. What I wanted was some fresh air. "That line of reasoning is worthless to pursue," I said.

"Can you be so sure?" he persisted. "The pregnancy may have quickly developed into a miscarriage. Or possibly a foetus aborted. Or an infant given away, adopted. Such situations are more than common."

"I think I would have known if my sister had been pregnant."

I walked resolutely toward the exit, he followed. The research interns we passed raised their eyes from books, probably hypothesizing that Sigmund and I were having a lover's quarrel.

The afternoon heat outside was too stifling to walk any distance so I waited at a trolley stop, his chance to pick up the thread to his hypothesis and sew more patterns. "Family skeletons can be cunningly hidden."

Again I insisted, "Sabrine has never borne a child... unless..." A very miserable thought came to me. "Unless it happened here at the Salpêtrière."

He dismissed the idea outright. "Such an egregious incident would have been recorded in her case file."

"Maybe Charcot has another file where Salpêtrière's skeletons are hidden?"

"Unaccountable pregnancies occur all too frequently in asylums, indigent shelters, and orphanages," he admitted, "and not often investigated with any sincerity, but they are certainly not hidden."

"Maybe the time has come for me to take Sabrine out of the Salpêtrière." I threw out the idea, but was I prepared to reveal my identity to Charcot? To end my charade with the Charcot family?

His response was firm. "I would not advise it."

"But everyone agrees that she is behaving rationally. And no more attacks."

"Not precisely," he said. I held my breath. "Sabrine no longer presents the principal stages of hystero-epilepsy, but there is one ancillary contraction which can be provoked, either accidentally or deliberately, when pressure is applied to the spasmogenous zone just below the left breast."

"Which contracture is that?" I spotted the horse trolley in the distance lazily turning the corner in our direction.

"What Charcot labels, 'Crucifixion.'"

My mind raced, trying to reach some reasonable explanation as to why Sabrine, or her subconscious, refused to relinquish this one horrendous pose.

"The contracture can last for a considerable length of time," he noted and proceeded to paint a gruesome picture. "I've seen her stay rigid, arms far apart, for as long as an hour—then, without warning, she wakes up, relaxed and happy. She claims to feel totally refreshed."

"So one can perceive this as some form of catharsis?"

My phantasy interpretation drew a rueful smile. "Julie, I would not construe this phenomenon as therapeutic; nonetheless, the morbid aspect fascinates me, such that I cannot dismiss it from my mind. I very much want to find an explanation."

"But soon you vacate Paris, my sister left with Charcot," I reminded him, not hiding my anger. "Charcot, who will bind her to his nosographical approach, the damnable recordations of her menstrual flow until she becomes yet another withered, decrepit woman, too beaten down to care, wandering the grounds of Salpêtrière, lost in a lost city."

"Your disillusionment in Dr. Charcot and the Salpêtrière is striking… and unjust."

His chastisement signalled me to retreat from expressing the depth of my disillusion. "The date you depart?" I asked. We watched the trolley and the white mare, Aphrodite, slowly clomp closer.

"February twenty-eight."

The empty trolley came to a stop. "Hop aboard, Dear," invited the lady driver who called herself Myrtle. No one knew her real name or her history as she had been at Salpêtrière long before Charcot arrived some twenty-five years ago. Both white haired Myrtle and the white mare Aphrodite had red paper roses tucked behind their ears.

Quietly Sigmund helped me on to the trolley and stepped back. Myrtle, jiggling the reins, whispered encouragement to her equally old horse and off we rumbled, just enough time to hold up nine fingers to him. The precious days left.

I arrived at the Charcot door early evening, a convenient hour as the doctor still worked at the hospital. I hoped to find Jeanne at home. My plan was to enlist her aid in giving Sabrine a gynaecological examination.

My one paramount thought. I must confirm what my heart believed— *Sabrine had not delivered a baby.* I gave the bear several hard, quick raps, not enough time for the hourglass to drop much sand. Madame Charcot came to the door, her frizzed halo of hair flecked with plaster dust, and wearing a surgeon's apron. She showed surprise then confusion. I decided to be humorous. "Have I interrupted a surgical operation?" She put a tiny hand to her cheek, smudging her face with more plaster, and seemingly tried to recognize me.

"Oh, no dear. I've been working secretly in my studio on a new project. My stained-glass period is over; and no more costumed jewellery for me."

"What instead, Madame Charcot?"

"Little people. I make little people out of little bits of dust and clay; I said to myself, 'If God can do it, why not me?" She tittered. "Really, they're only figurines."

I knew not what to say. Her behaviour seemed a little strange.

"You will find Jeanne in the library, busy with her own mysterious project," smiled Madame. "Something to do with words." She then opened her tiny, plaster smeared hands to show me. "I prefer working with these hands. But go, go!" she urged. "My little ones wait impatiently for my hands to beautify them."

Jeanne was engrossed at her father's desk with a myriad of open books and sheets of writing paper around her. My appearance inexplicably embarrassed her, as if she were caught in some indiscreet pursuit.

When I took a seat in an armchair close to her, she asked for a cigarette. Giving her my last Black Cat, she greedily lit up, inhaled, and handed back the cigarette to share. We took turns puffing for a while until I relinquished the rest of the cigarette. Jeanne's father disapproved of her smoking and it amused me that she only gave into the pleasures of tobacco when we two were alone.

"Suzanne Valadon says her source for Black Cats has dried up," I said.

"Well, that stinks."

"But the painter Claude Monet has heard of my plight and promises to send me a packet or two when he receives any from a London friend."

Puffing, blowing smoke across the desk, she said nothing. Jeanne, lately, had lost interest in Impressionist art. I had a feeling that she resented the time I spent helping Pissarro and the other organizers with the upcoming Impressionist Show. She puffed while I tried to steal a glance at the books and scraps of paper spread upon the desk—one large, unwieldy book she deliberately closed and pushed aside. I had only to tilt my head slightly to read the spine: I.F. Pellengahr's *Science of Graphology*. Then I saw that each scrap of paper bore a signature and noticed an opened envelope with the red seal of the caduceus.

I realized, chagrined, that she had taken over my neglected role as detective and writing expert. She was comparing signatures to her father's poison pen letters and wanting to spare me guilt for my failure to seek out the unknown perpetuator.

But I was feeling the guilt. She had taken over, following my suggestion to utilize the science of graphology to compare handwriting samples, beginning with possible suspects at Salpêtrière. I started to recognize several of the handwriting samples. No one, apparently, escaped her suspicion.

Has she a sample of my handwriting? I wondered.

"So, Jeanne!" I put cheerfulness in my voice. "I see you have initiated your own investigation to catch the culprit."

She tapped the ash of the cigarette in Charcot's deformed plaster hand. "I'm perusing all the works on graphology that you cited."

"I apologize, Jeanne. How could I have allowed myself to forget your suffering? I have been remiss in my duties to you and your father."

"I can understand. You have other interests outside of the Charcot family and should."

"Have you made any progress in linking any of the handwriting samples to the perpetrator's venomous letters?"

Among the scatterings on the desk, I was dismayed to see what appeared to be a sheet with Sabrine's handwriting.

"I've only just begun," lamented Jeanne.

"Have you devised a systematic approach?" I asked.

"Just this." She unfolded a large sheet of engineering paper with a schematic diagram of the Brouillet painting. She had outlined every figure and assigned numbers to each person in attendance at Charcot's demonstration. Her faceless doctors, luminaries, staff, totalled twenty-eight, including Sabrine.

"A good start," I remarked. "Anything recent from our villain?"

She hesitated before offering the letter. "Written on the finest vellum, but reeking of foul gutter talk."

Reading, expecting it to be characteristically vile, yet the sheer hatefulness shocked me anew:

Oh! You black, stunted Toad of Infamy!

The salutation set the hysterical pitch, someone who took macabre delight in prophesying the horrors in store for Charcot:

I will be there, Devil Hypnotist, at your deathbed

when the arteries to your heart occlude—doing my duty,

ramming a hundred zoological snakes up your rectum.

However crude the content, the letter revealed a marked degree of familiarity with medical symptoms, especially symptomology associated with a fragile heart condition. The writer depicted death by angina pectoris with chilling precision.

Examining the penmanship very closely, it showed a very laboured hand. I advised Jeanne that the penmanship seemed deliberately falsified.

"To lead us further astray," she remarked bitterly.

"We should concentrate less on handwriting and more on motive."

"A demented mind has no need of a motive!" she spat out her anger, crushing what was left of the cigarette into the clawed hand.

Her distress kept me focused on remaining calm. "He's a physician, I'm almost certain, or a person who has acquired a high degree of medical knowledge."

"I could fit that description, you could fit that description," she concluded with exasperation. "And for that matter, just about anyone else at the Salpêtrière."

Rising, I went to her suspects in the painting. "Who appears sufficiently disgruntled?" I reflected. "Who displays deep unhappiness?"

She joined me to study the expressions of the twenty-eight faces, each painted by André Brouillet with admirable realism. The sober rectitude of Charcot, the caring looks of Babinski and Nurse Botard, my sister in trance, and the amazing detail of her clenched hand. There was only one person in the entire gathering who seemed to carry the scent of hostility. The mouth, as Brouillet might well have observed, was tightly drawn. The young man also had his arms tightly folded. I said nothing to Jeanne. She would have vilified me if I suggested the prime suspect might be her younger brother, Jean, a medical student.

Her deep affection for him stopped me from mentioning my inadvertent encounter with Jean Charcot at the Black Cat Café. Sigmund was with me. I had taken him to the basement denizen of *le Chat Noir* for an introduction to one of the most popular cabarets in Paris, notorious for their satiric shows and general tongue-in-cheek frivolity.

At a certain point that evening, after the entertainment of cabaret singers and shadow puppet plays, the stage was given up to anyone in the audience who had a talent to share, whether to sing, speechify on politics, or recite poetry, as long as the amateur performer mocked the established social milieu of Paris. We were stunned when Jean-Baptiste Charcot staggered to the stage, manifestly drunk, and introduced a poem he called the 'The Song of Salpêtrière.' I recalled how he swayed precariously at the edge of the raised stage, reciting his satiric doggerel. Most of the Black Cat clientele, a sophisticated group, were more than familiar with the young man's famous father.

Laughter rang out heartily that night at the son's bitingly bitter poem. A lengthy piece, I remembered a portion.

We the saddened palsies

We the hysterics perplexed

Ask at our Salpêtrière home

Who will dare curb our moans?

Cure our shakes, crush our snakes?

Only one—the Emperor Great

Only one, the Man's no fake

He stands shortly tall

Portly king above all

Charcot, our Charcot, our Charcot!

Hip-hip hooray! Hip-hip hooray!

Our Pa-pa will save the day!

"The son rebels," Sigmund whispered in the darkness of the café.

"The letters," Jeanne broke into my reverie, "portray someone so cunning and malicious, that I sometimes think it may very well be a woman."

I tried to keep my irritability in check. "Well then, do you have a sample of Sabrine's handwriting so that we might make a comparison?"

"I did not mean to infer..." Jeanne was flustered.

"Come," I left the painting and took her seat at the desk, "let's be quite certain."

Sheepishly, she gave me a sheet of paper. "When I asked Father for a sample of Sabrine's handwriting, he gave this."

A poem! I read quickly and stayed calm. Reopening Pellengahr's graphology volume with which I was familiar, I placed Sabrine's poem and the poison-pen letter side by side.

After pointing out several lettering characteristics displayed in the volume as paradigms, and making careful comparisons, it became apparent to Jeanne that no similarities whatsoever existed.

"And what we can now see," I added, "is that the writer is left-handed, and Sabrine is right-handed."

"I know she is innocent," said Jeanne, blood rising crimson to her cheeks in embarrassment.

I held up the poem. "Do you mind if I keep this?"

She made no objection. "Father says that sometimes Sabrine has been caught trying to eat them. When he gets them in his hands, he burns the poems. Please take it, I think they should be preserved." And again she reiterated that not for a moment could she imagine Sabrine writing the letters. "They are the work of an evil soul, not our dear Sabrine."

Because I had no desire to complicate matters, I withheld the fact that my sister wrote equally well with her right and left hand. Jeanne suddenly came close behind me and, in a most unusual gesture for her, gave me a hug. I felt her cheek warm against mine.

She spoke softly, "I, as you, yearn to see Sabrine completely cured."

Do I tell her now that Sabrine is my sister? That I am Julie Weiss? But I can't. I can't.

To share the truth with Jeanne Charcot was far too dangerous. While she enjoyed making gentle sport of her father, her fierce attachment was crystal clear. And how easily she might run to him with my secret. And what course of action might he take? I feared his power. Whatever decisions came into his head would be incontrovertible law at Salpêtrière.

I put the poem, memorized, safely in my purse. Finally, I asked, "Doesn't Nurse Botard assist the doctors in gynaecological examinations?"

"More often than not. And on not a few occasions I have stood over her shoulder to learn."

I smiled at her boast. "I do believe that Jeanne and not Jean yearns to be a doctor like her father."

"Who for long can keep a secret from you, Julie," she observed, her dry wit returned.

"So you could... by yourself... ascertain a few physical intimacies about a woman's genitalia?"

"I can tell the difference between chlamydia and gonorrhoea."

"And whether someone has been vaginally penetrated or experienced a pregnancy?"

"I'm sure I can."

"And keep such an examination between the two of us?"

"You are my best friend, Julie." She looked quizzically—"Have you gotten yourself into a fix?"

I shook my head. "What did you think of Sabrine's poem?"

"I'm not much for reading poetry. It's not in my purview. I really didn't understand it. Poems can be so vague. Does the poem have a meaning, a point, a message?"

"Yes, I think so. It's about resurrection."

Chapter 48

The aim which I have set before myself is to show that dreams are capable of being interpreted...

The Interpretation of Dreams
Sigmund Freud

FREUD'S DREAM

I

Sigmund wanted to revisit his favourite places before he left Paris, asking for company, only our early morning stroll through the *Pere Lachaise* cemetery seemed an odd choice; yet I sensed an agenda, here might be the place he needed to clarify a thought. Not unlike Salpêtrière, the cemetery seemed a city within a city, an expansive, intricate grid of cobblestone streets which threaded through thousands of grave sites. Chopin and the famous painter Delacroix, I knew, were interred in mausoleums somewhere, although I doubted if he had come to visit them.

The morning was pleasantly mild. We walked a leisurely pace along the broad, Roman-like roads shaded by tall elms, and hearing the trill of morning songbirds high in the leafy boughs. On either side of the road there loomed an endless vista of gravestones, sepulchres and ornate mausoleums, watched over by stone angels and robe-garbed muses, silent guardians all, mourning, weeping, praying. No other living visitors were to be seen. Perhaps he thought such seclusion allowed us opportunity to take cocaine and talk.

"Sabrine, during our talking sessions ..." he spoke her name, gratefully not just an initial, "... never lead to concrete details of her past." So he complained. "And here I walk beside the woman who can open the vault to that past."

He made no attempt to hide dismay and disappointment. I stayed obdurate—she had to relinquish her own memories of the past. I trusted my decision.

If, as his mentor Josef Breuer claimed, all major hysteria took root in a particular trauma, such an event had not been witnessed by me. It felt reasonable, safer, less complicated for everyone if I distanced myself from the chimney sweeping process, letting him guide my sister through her memories. I, far too entangled by love for Sabrine, would be of no true help. But Sigmund Freud could fearlessly accompany my sister into the darker regions of her psyche. He, not me, possessed the fortitude to dredge whatever hurtful memories stayed trapped inside her.

The few suspicions I harboured regarding the difficulties in Marseilles might only mislead Sigmund. I would only resort to finger pointing, to blame, to rail at the vicious nuns of the Sacred Heart for pushing Sabrine further into her own world, the black-robed, barren handmaidens of Christ who set out to rid my sister of every aspect that made her unique. No sooner had she entered their school, falling into their clutches, then they bound her left hand to force her to write with her right. When she began to express herself with "mirror writing" the nuns, gasping in horror, accused her, a mere child, of learning to write backwards in the "devil's workshop," done to deliberately mock Jesus.

"Sigmund, I can promise to corroborate anything she tells you of which I am aware."

That her memories would return in time was the bedrock of hope that sustained me. Sabrine had never really forgotten her sister—I saw it deep in her eyes. When set free from Salpêtrière, she and I would live together in Paris, two sisters again, reigniting all the beautiful shared memories.

"Demonstrably she improves with each passing day," I reminded him. "Plus the fact that she no longer suffers from ovarian pains. Or hystero-epileptic attacks."

"Except for..."

"One pose—instigated only if a specific hystero-zone is touched; and you admit that after an hour in this crucifixion posture, she awakens rejuvenated." Saints and mystics, I thought to myself, had similar experiences, self-induced trances to reach another level of consciousness. "There's much to be learned from the altering of consciousness," I said, then stopped and looked at him quizzically. "Aren't we going to take cocaine?"

"By all means, a morning Congress!" He looked around, an opulent sepulchre farther into the cemetery caught his attention. We left the roadway and found a bench near the sepulchre. Sigmund then realized, delighted, that the stone coffin, resting upon four elevated pillars, belonged to Molière. "His comedies are thoroughly enjoyable. I saw *Tartuffe* the first month I arrived. Ah, I will sorely miss French theatre." He became wistful. "To have seen Sarah Bernhardt and Mounet-Sully, such superb actors, will stay with me always."

Degas' free passes for any matinee at the Odeon, where Mounet-Sully occasionally played, were still unused. Perhaps I might take him, as a parting gift.

First he brought out a packet of finely powdered cocaine then playfully brandished the initialled spoon. " '*S*' for snorting, a little harsh on the nostrils, but most direct."

He scooped the tiny spoon until full with powder; I had to inhale three times to finish it all. Deftly, he snorted his spoonful into each nostril, pondering the initialled stem. "Speak frankly, when you purchased the spoon, did the 'S' make you think of Sigmund or Sabrine?"

"I thought of you both, together, exploring the mind's terrain."

My own consciousness suddenly—no, instantaneously– gained wings! There was, of course, so-called reality, Julie Forette on the stone bench, yet hovering above, my super consciousness, eager to laugh at the ridiculous limitations of reality, now capable of drawing a mental map for all that was essential in my life—

"What plans, Sigmund, for your final sessions with Sabrine?"

Cocaine prompted his answers, handing me a refilled spoon. "I intend to show her photographs of pregnant women to provoke the unconscious, the storehouse of all memories. All memories," he repeated.

"I'm disappointed in such an approach, very disappointed," I responded.

Another observation took him away. "The spoon is very, very tiny."

I whooshed all of the powder deliberately into one nostril for maximum effect. "You pursue a non-existent pregnancy." It was imperative to tell him the truth and apprise him of the investigation. "Jeanne Charcot and I, including Nurse Botard, undertook a gynaecological examination of my sister—there was no physical evidence that she ever gave birth."

Sigmund surprised, then sceptical, "You examined the perineum, the fourchette, and the cervix?"

"Yes."

"And found them unaffected?"

"Yes."

"And the hymen?"

Should I inhale more of the invigorating snow? I rubbed a reflective finger around the concavity of the empty spoon. "The hymen?"

"Yes, the hymen."

"Nurse Botard said it was no longer intact."

We looked steadily at each other. A broken hymen indicated the possibility of intercourse. But not conclusively.

He mulled over the information before taking back the spoon from my indecisive hand. "Well, my working hypothesis has been check-mated. A traumatic pregnancy from Sabrine's past must not be the root cause of her hysterical enactment of childbirth."

"Maybe she was just expelling her demons..."

"Which are?"

"I don't know."

I knew well the demons, devils, centaurs, harpies and sundry torturers who inhabited the rings of hell. Dante's *Divine Comedy* was frequently taken from the library shelf, Father turning the illustrated pages to show us the three headed dog of Hell, Cerberus, the snake headed Medusa, the bat-winged heads of the hideous Dis, and the Minotaur, devourer of human flesh. Father pointed out Lucifer himself while reciting passages in Italian. We were gifted linguists and knew how to evoke demons in many languages. 'my only chance, Juliette,' father once said, 'is a sentence in purgatory... where love is purified.'

Dove l'amore è purificato," I murmured.

Cocaine driving my thoughts in a multitude of directions. Sigmund walked away, another spectre for me to follow. He threaded between sepulchres and tomb stones as if he had a purpose. I followed, keen to be led to something other than my haphazard past.

He came to a marble headstone: *Ludwig Borne, nee:1788 mort:1837.*

He stopped. "More than once I've been here, to pay homage."

"Who is he?" I asked.

"A German journalist who wrote with wit and more insight than most."

The gravesite looked sadly neglected. "Apparently you are the only person in Paris who visits him. What more should I know?"

"His perceptive views of society and humanity guided me through my adolescence. For a period of time, Ludwig Borne's essay on the art of how to become an original writer was my Bible."

"What does Borne recommend?"

"For three days, hide away. Bring along sheets and sheets of paper. Then write what comes into your head. Write about everything and anything, without hypocrisy. Maybe those in authority, the *Tonkin War*, Goethe, *The Last Supper*, or *The Last Judgement*. Write without falsification, your thoughts on these subjects. And write how you view yourself. Borne guarantees after the three days, the amazing novel and startling thoughts will well up in you."

"Which you did?"

"Learning that my random thoughts often linked to deeper thoughts. He influenced me profoundly. Ludwig Borne happens to be a Jew. And like you, like me, he rid himself of his Jewish name to better fit into society."

"Like you?"

"Sigismund Schlomo is my birth name. Which I gave up."

Schlomo and Weiss, both hidden.

"Julie, he can still teach us much. He wrote that true striving in the cause of learning is not a voyage of discovery, as with Columbus, but rather a journey of adventure, like Ulysses."

Joyful, I smiled. "Ours is an adventure, isn't it Sigmund?"

"And it doesn't suffice simply to display one's intellect in the service of truth, Borne said one must show courage as well." Sigmund cast a serious look at me. "Intellectual courage is what you have shown, I will admit, in reaching out to Dr. Bernheim, asking to attend his lectures, offering your translation skills."

I confessed proudly, "Sigmund, he has welcomed me! I shall soon be going to his hypnosis clinic in Nancy."

"As I admire my Jewish compatriot, Loeb Baruch, alias Ludwig Borne, so I admire Julie Weiss, alias Julie Forette."

"To rise from the mire of my own marvellous ignorance is my chief want," I said.

He nodded approvingly. "And do you still want my dream?" he asked. "The one dream the dreamer cannot forget, isn't that how you put it?"

"Yes."

He lit a cigar—soon quick and steady puffs of smoke obscured his face. A voice: "What I shall give you is less a dream and more a nightmare. It shall be my task to find the courage to describe it."

I took the notebook from my handbag, held it questioningly before him.

"Yes, do transcribe; but first a preamble which need not be transcribed." He invited me to sit beside him on Ludwig Borne's grave. "The cursory work I've done in studying my past dreams has brought me to appreciate how day-to-day events can cleverly insinuate their way into a dream's content. So I wish to approach the dream holistically, looking for the daily and workaday connections. We must be scientific."

Sigmund's admirable habit was to marshal his ideas in a deliberate fashion, though yet unformed, untested, uncertain. He had my dutiful commitment: "I shall remain alert to all the connections. To the science." I held up the pencil, the stylus of Thoth. Excitedly, I murmured, "Now the dream, Sigmund, the dream."

"I find myself strolling along the Champs Elysée, in a most affable mood, savouring the most elegant avenue in Paris, rubbing shoulders with the fashionably attired, the debonair gentlemen and ladies who wear wonderfully enormous hats adorned with all manner of bird feathers. Hats are the order of the day and I'm rather proud of my own top hat which gleams handsomely in the afternoon sun. I so enjoy tipping it now and then to the chic ladies who smilingly pass.

"A desire seizes me." Sigmund paused to puff and gauge my reaction. I'm comfortably seated, leaning back against the pillow of Ludwig Borne's headstone, pencil waiting. "A desire quite innocent," clarified Sigmund. "I yearn for a piece of chocolate, preferably infused with mint, which prompts me to seek a patisserie along the grand Elysée. Soon I'm in front of a shop window, admiring the various confections—and my reflection as well. I'm looking splendid with my beard trimmed in the new French cut. I'm feeling so satisfied with myself.

"Then I notice someone else's reflection in the window. He looms over my shoulder, a tall, shadowy figure who begins to obscure my view of the delectables in the window. Even to this day I remember my welcomed struggle between an almond-crusted croissant glistening golden and buttery and a very tempting cream-soufflé puff ready to burst with yellow sweetness; but this shadow reflected in the window irritatingly prevents me from contemplating my choices. Then I observe that the man behind me has a very pointed goatee and wears a cape not unlike the one Dr. Charcot occasionally wears when coming on stage for his Friday lectures. And this stranger has the audacity to scowl at me. I somehow feel that he disapproves of my appearance. I worry if it's the careless way I tie my cravat. But then I think, 'Who is he and what right to censure how I dress?' And why should I care a fig what this mere shadow in a window thinks of me? But his unwavering presence remains very upsetting.

"Then the oddest occurrence. The man wields the ebony walking stick he carries and deliberately knocks off my top hat. Which rolls like a coin into the filth of the gutter. I'm offended by the insult, but I choose to pretend it hasn't happened. I say to myself, 'Why become involved with any further unpleasantness?' The stranger clearly has some neurotic condition even though dressed like a gentleman. I go to fetch my hat—which cost me a pretty pfennig. The once elegant top hat is besmirched in mud and manure from the carriage horses. Bending down to pick up my hat, I realize, much too late, of my vulnerable position.

"With the ebony cane, the man prods my anus. 'Goosey-goose go-o-ose!' he taunts in ludicrous falsetto.

"I am outraged, justifiably outraged, as any man would be. But I pursue gentle reason: 'Monsieur, by all appearances you are a gentleman of means, of education, and so you must be aware that your behaviour is entirely inappropriate.'

"My plea for reason only makes him smirk. With a Prussian-like click of his heels, he gives a mockingly deep bow. *Enough of his foolishness!* I say to myself. Ignoring him, I place my hat, pock-marked with excrement and mud, squarely back on my head. Unbelievably, this tormentor—from I know not where—has the effrontery to knock it off again.

"I rebuke him: 'Absolutely uncalled for, absolutely *pas de rigueur,* Monsieur, Monsieur... whoever you are!'

"He declares himself to be 'Monsieur Mephisto' and proceeds to put on one grey suede glove, and with this gloved fist, he punches me full force in the stomach.

"The blow stoops me over with pain. The dapperly dressed man, who calls himself Mephisto, waits patiently for my recovery. He takes a relaxing moment to smell the red carnation in his lapel. It becomes frighteningly apparent that he has more indignities in mind. Desperately hoping to arouse sympathy, I inform him that I am untutored in the practice of physical combat.

"'"For one of your kind,"' he replies in a derisive tone, 'a duel of honour is out of the question; isn't it, scum?'

"'I warn you, Monsieur!' I shout. 'If you persist in this unseemly manner, I will be compelled to call the police!'

"He smiles. And—incredibly—wrestles me to the pavement where we soon roll together on to the grime and filth of the street. Adding to my humiliation, bystanders begin to form, laughing at our ridiculously awkward grappling.

"I overhear their mockery. 'Imagine! Two apparent gentlemen rolling in the streets like *dummkopfs!*'

"A fear, real and profound, takes hold, that this man may be who he says he is—Satan. Keeping me clenched in a suffocating bear hug, pressing his goatee chin into my cheek, he maliciously bites down on my earlobe, snarling, 'Damn you, Sigismund Schlomo, you're soiling my cape.'

"He knows my birth name! I'm overwhelmed by confusion, and still we keep rolling over and over in muck and slop. The onlookers howl and bend over with laughter—some discarded piece of trash from the street, some sort of rotten vegetable is mashed onto my forehead, like an insignia of buffoonery.

"I plead with my nemesis: 'Can't you see how foolish we both look!'

Mephisto responds with a high-pitch giggle and another stomach punch.

"Somehow I extricate myself, jump to my feet and wipe away the turnip or whatever it is from my forehead. 'Enough is enough, sir!'

"With as much dignity as I can muster, I walk away while the onlookers jeer, slapping their knees, laughing uncontrollably. How, in the name of goodness and mercy, can these people remain so impervious to a man's injuries? My frock coat is ripped at the sleeve, my new shirt is soiled, and my bitten ear lobe is dripping blood. Not one person on the street cares about my wounded condition.

"Mephisto, remaining relentless in his mission of insult, takes a flying leap onto my back. Riding me like a frenzied jockey, as if I'm his horse, he whacks and whacks with his cane.

"My despair deepens, deepens..." Sigmund stopped.

I looked up from my dictation and saw his doubt as to whether he should continue. I lowered my head to the notebook and hoped I could keep recording every detail of his riveting account. He lit a fresh cigar: "In the dream I despair that I may never escape from his savage abuse. Then a new found rage mounts within me and I shout with all the power of my lungs—'No more, you cur! No more! I will tolerate no more indignity, no more injustice!'

"I rise, twist and shake him off."

Incredibly, Sigmund re-enacted the action, standing on Borne's grave, vigorously pantomiming what happened in the dream.

"When Mephisto falls back, I straddle his chest. Wresting the cane from him, I firmly grip each end and press the shaft against his neck. I press harder and harder, with murderous intent..." Sigmund knelt upon the grave, the imagined cane in his hands.

Transfixed within the scene, I had to rouse myself to keep transcribing.

"I press, push! And suddenly—this man who claims to be Satan, opens his mouth wide, as if to roar. I see the gaping, black, deep, cavernous hole that is his mouth and am overcome with horror. From the depths of his mouth pour an endless profusion of snow-white flowers. A vomiting of white petal flowers, smothering my face.

"I turn catatonic—literally, catatonic..." Sigmund stops, I think there must be more, an ending. I wait. He continues, "Mephisto, back on his feet, stroking his pointed beard, ponders my helpless condition. An unexpected transformation occurs in his behaviour. The man who has tormented me, becomes solicitous... even gentle. He takes me by the sleeve, leading me near the patisserie entrance, managing to sit me on the sidewalk. Carefully he folds my legs, as if I were a Buddha statue. He studies me, like an artist would an unfinished still-life. He hurries to retrieve the excrement spattered hat, a ragged rip at the brim, and turns it upside down beside me.

"Then the dream shifts to a new scene: Mephisto, dressed in the white overalls of a house painter, carries a long ladder upon his shoulder. He marches with mock solemnity down the street to where I sit. He adjusts and rests the ladder against the patisserie window. I'm about to protest, but he puts a finger to his lips to shush me. Climbing, a piece of soap in hand, he scrawls across the shop window:

alms for the blameless

"Summarily, I'm abandoned, soon catching the curiosity of passersby. When someone dares approach, I tell them who I am, a respected pathologist, but my words make no sense. The sounds are gibberish. Nothing I say is in any way intelligible. I can only make guttural noises, almost simian. I try to explain that I must be suffering from Broca's motor aphasia, a severe blow to the frontal lobe which disturbs my function of speech.

"'Please Messieurs, please Mesdames. Please be so kind as to find me medical help.'

"But who can understand the thick-tongue drivel that slathers from my mouth? The cruel only laugh at my speech disorder; the compassionate smile their pity. As the long day passes, an occasional pfennig is dropped in my upturned hat."

The dream finished, he found his handkerchief to wipe the accumulated sweat from the back of his neck and face. The recorded dream dropped into my purse.

We meandered out of the cemetery. He wanted my assistance in analysing the dream. "But not now," he said.

I told him that I would be boarding an early train tomorrow for Bernheim's clinic in Nancy.

"I shall help with your luggage."

"No, I can manage. Stay at the hospital."

"I suppose I should utilize my remaining days wisely."
His priority, I hoped, would be Sabrine.

Chapter 49

**...the possibility always remains that
the dream may have yet another meaning.**

Sigmund Freud

Night Train to Paris

I

Had I noticed a suspicious man roaming the corridor? asked the train conductor.

I lifted my veil. "Should I be alarmed?"

He shrugged a `maybe not'... but `maybe so.' "We figure he stole aboard in Antwerp and, more than likely, he's been hiding in the water closets up and down the cars."

"Then you should be able to detect him from his smell." I lowered my veil.

"Be on guard, Mademoiselle," warned the conductor, departing with a brisk, two-finger salute.

My thoughts were elsewhere. Three days at Dr. Bernheim's congress on the nature of hypnosis had convinced me that the hypnoid state had no correlation whatsoever to hysteria. The demonstrations and lectures I transcribed gave me ample proof. Now, to convince Sigmund that Charcot was wrong. His mentor preached an erroneous hypothesis. The power of suggestion was the chief constituent of the hypnotic process. As such, hypnosis possessed the potential to interact with the deeper workings of the mind.

Turning off the gas lamp, I settled back, savouring the darkness and my renewed hope for Sabrine...

* * *

When the intruder entered the compartment, I held my tongue. Apparently far too exhausted to notice my presence, the man fell fast asleep on the banquette across from me. I must have blended well with the darkness, having dressed for the all-male congress in circumspect black. A travelling companion was not what I wanted, but I resigned myself to the situation. The train sped inexorably through the night, and when a crescent moon occasionally lurched from the night's clouds, I studied him. He

490

seemed nothing more than an eccentric tramp, ensconced in a soldier's greatcoat, worse for wear, too large for him, falling raggedly to his boot heels. Everything he wore looked second-hand, purchased probably pell mell from flea markets. The herdsman's cap of rabbit fur looked especially ridiculous, one ear-flap down, one ear-flap up. An inglorious mouth hung open and the moonlight showed two of his teeth missing, and another darkly rotting. He aroused pity as I took in the wretchedly ravaged countenance, the deep furrows across his brow, crow's feet etched, as if by tiny knives, in the corners of his closed eyelids. Here dozed a grizzled, down-on-his-luck man, a fellow accustomed, I suspected, to poor food, bad drink, and late nights.

It surprised me to see rolled up in the side pocket of his greatcoat the literate, Paris newspaper, *Gil Blas*. I played pickpocket, carefully removing the newspaper. He had it folded to an early instalment of Zola's novel, two lines underscored with a Conté crayon.

What was Art, after all, if not simply

giving out what you had inside you?

I smiled sadly: the stowaway across from me reeked of turpentine and gesso, his tattered military coat spattered with paints, assuring me that he was nothing less than a poor fool of a painter. I found myself keeping an almost tender vigil over his sleep which had turned restless. Often he grimaced and put an unconscious hand to his jaw. More rotting teeth, I guessed, were throbbing with pain. As our train hurtled across the tracks, I could easily imagine the staccato clopping of the steel wheels pounding into his troubled sleep. The painter's eyelids began fluttering like butterfly wings, a signal that he was traveling to a dream portal. For certainty, I reached and, very cautiously, pulled back the flap of his greatcoat...

He dreams, I said to myself, glimpsing his bundled erection, always intrigued by this phenomena which peculiarly verified the dream state in men. *But how badly he dreams.*

He moaned timorously... like a child fearful in the night of disturbing others. It was pitiful to hear. Suddenly, shouting out a man's name, he awakened in sheer panic—his wide eyes fixed upon the black, shrouded apparition I must have been.

Jumping to his feet, he seized the newspaper on my lap and, terror stricken, began slapping at me. "Moth-er! Moth-er!" he shrieked. "You're on fire!"

Harmless newspaper slaps raining down on me, I kept composed, determined to bring him out of his hallucination—"Monsieur, you are on a train, a railway carriage train, to Paris."

"Tongues of white fire, Mother, around you..." he stammered.

To orient him to conscious reality, I repeated, "This is a train, a railway carriage train, third-class compartment."

His arm poised, ready to strike again, I gave a stern order that he should sit down. Dutiful, awake, he complied, too embarrassed to look at me, staring out the window.

"A dream disturbed you, Monsieur?" I lifted my veil, unpinned my hat and set it aside.

"It was nothing," he muttered, giving me a furtive glance.

I relit the gas lamp, noticing how his focus shifted to the flame. *How easy to hypnotize him* came my thought. Bathed in more light, he was of medium height and built very solidly, as if he could have been a bargeman. It was his sunken cheeks and missing teeth that made him look undernourished. "It's not unusual, Monsieur, to awaken after a disturbing dream and be disoriented, especially finding yourself in the dark with someone dressed so lugubriously."

"I thought for a crazy moment that you were on fire. And that you were my mother," he admitted.

"Was that part of your dream?"

"No." A sullen answer. He rested a side of his face against the window. He had the beginning stubble of a reddish beard.

The coldness of the glass distracts him from the pain in his mouth. "You have family or friends in Paris?" I asked.

"I have a brother in Paris."

I shall chance a direct approach. "Presently, you are in a great deal of physical pain."

"What do you mean?"

"This..." I held open a gloved hand to reveal the tooth. "fell from your mouth." I gave him the tooth. "It is thoroughly rotted through."

"My teeth cry out for a proper dentist."

"And the pain is such that at the moment you are not thinking coherently."

"A pounding like you wouldn't believe. I'd smash my head through the window if I thought it would help."

"Perhaps I can be of assistance?"

He laughed dryly. "Sure, if you're a dentist."

"I'm afraid that is not my profession."

"Too bad," he said, taking off the herdsman's cap. The intense colour of his hair startled me. Sheared and cropped short, his red hair seemed strangely similar to Sabrine's, shot through with the same bright blaze.

"You called out the name 'Vincent' in your dream," I said.

"The dream was vague," he replied. "And waking up to find your face hidden, dressed in the same black my mother wears these days."

"In the darkness, I can well understand mistaking me for someone else."

He introduced himself: "My name just happens to be Vincent. Vincent van Gogh."

It took effort to hide my amazement—across from me sat Theo van Gogh's older brother, the artist whom Theo boasted was in the thick of his studies at the Antwerp Academy.

"Your brother, in Paris, is expecting you?" I asked.

He grunted. "I will be a surprise."

I only nodded, removing my gloves. Discreetly, I felt for the amulet around my neck and wondered if he were a suitable subject for hypnosis. He could help me verify Dr. Bernheims's hypothesis that the essential dynamic underlying hypnosis was suggestion.

He began studying my hands, perhaps observing the absence of a wedding ring. Bluntly he asked, "What is it that you do in Paris, Mademoiselle?"

"I am... a student." I decided that was true.

"Studying what?" he asked.

"Hypnosis... you see, Monsieur van Gogh..." I began.

"Call me Vincent," he interrupted. "Dutch names are difficult enough for the Dutch to pronounce."

"Vincent, I'm actually returning from Dr. Hippolyte Bernheim's clinic at Nancy, having attended his symposium on hypnosis. Are you familiar with the science of hypnotism?"

"I once read an article which looked favourably upon it," he said. "It discussed a demonstration by Hansen, the famous magnetist."

"Yes, Carl Hansen, his experiments and methods were discussed at the congress."

I remembered Theo van Gogh had once characterized his brother Vincent as a man who, if convinced of the merits of a project, would not hesitate to take any risk involved. So, keeping my familiarity with Theo a 'small' secret, I made the proposal. "Dr. Bernheim theorizes that the fundamental process underlying hypnosis is the power of suggestion, so perhaps I can suggest, while you're in a different state of consciousness, not to feel your mouth pain. Of course," I cautioned, "you will still need to see a dental surgeon. What I offer is temporal relief."

"Temporal in a temporal world. What more," he shrugged, "can one hope for?"

"To begin, we need to put you in a tranquil and receptive mood by focusing on an object. The flame in the gas lamp shall do."

"The flame from a gas lamp?" His expression changed, a hint that he harboured some melancholy memory. Instinctively he began rubbing a pale, thickened scar on his left palm. Was it the result of a bad burn, I wondered? "A gas flame will not put me at ease," he said.

"Very well."

I unfastened the Eye of Ra pendant from around my neck. The beauty of the amulet would absorb his attention. The single scalloped wing was made of silver, encrusted at the edges were colourful gemstones. Centered in the wing, the Eye, a ruby, telling the curious that it was only a garnet. I dangled the amulet in front of him. Air currents in the compartment gently swayed the winged eye. The Salpêtrière women I hypnotized imagined the amulet in different ways. One longtime resident saw a broken wing carrying an egg. Another woman, sequestered because of stabbing her stepfather during visiting hours, saw an all-seeing eye which peered into sinful souls. The curved beads of green peridot which ran from the corner of the Eye was seen by another as teardrops. Gauguin, whom I was unable to hypnotize, saw a woman's breast.

I murmured to Vincent, "It is just a matter of giving all your attention to the eye. Gaze deeply into the translucence of the stone, the Eye."

"I see starlight inside the eye," he said.

"Watch the twinkling starlight, Vincent," I brought the Egyptian amulet closer. "Relax, Vincent. Let all vexatious thoughts float away, far away. Focus on the burning stars inside the eye. Re-lax." Others whom I successfully hypnotized claimed that my voice seemed to be travelling through vast regions of space and time. "Close your eyes. Relax. You are tired, very tired, extremely tired. You-are-sink-ing---down---into sleep. Deeper, deeper, sink-ing---into---sleep." His eyes closed. "Let the pain, all the burdensome pain float away... away. The pain separates from you, does not belong to you, Vincent. The pain is gone, Vincent. Gone beyond the stars. Repeat after me, the---pain---is---gone."

"The pain is gone." He reached the hypnoid state

"How do you feel, Vincent?"

"I feel... at peace." He smiled blithely, his decayed teeth forgotten.

"Yes, at peace. Say it, 'At peace.' "

"At peace."

The opportune moment had arrived. "Your dream, Vincent. *Dites moi vôtre rêve.*" His dream, above all else, was what I wanted.

"I don't remember."

"You do remember, Vincent. You do remember. You are in the dream, Vincent. Tell me what you see."

"The tall acacia tree; I see the magpie's nest."

"Where are you now?"

"Behind our family's house in Zundert; I'm taking a walk with my brother Theo."

"Describe everything you see, everything that happens."

Vincent laughed heartily.

"Something is amusing?" I asked

"Theo. He's dressed in a blue velvet jacket with yellow trousers and yellow gloves." Vincent laughed again. "He's wearing an enormous Panama hat to shield him from the sun. Yes, like Monticelli, like the painter Monticelli! I can't stop laughing. 'You're quite the grandee!' I tell him. He's carrying a bamboo cane nonchalantly over his shoulder. I'm carrying a shovel."

"Where are you going?"

"We're going to dig a ditch. We're ditch diggers. It's an honourable profession."

"Where you are now?"

"In the Zundert cemetery, in back of Father's church." Vincent laughed again. "My brother is more than annoyed because he's trying to dig our ditch with his fancy cane and he's not having much luck. He wants so badly to prove his strength. 'Stand back, Brother, let me show you how to dig a ditch! And you bet we're going to find a potato or two. I dig and dig. Hey Theo, where are you?' He's gone!" A very worrisome frown creased Vincent's brow.

"Is something amiss, Vincent?"

"Theo has deserted me! I'm all alone." Vincent grew agitated, angry. "That's not the way a brother should behave!"

I guided him. "Look for Theo. He can't be far away."

"Yes, I must find him, but night approaches!" Vincent looked fearful.

"Where are you now, Vincent?"

"I'm running. There are so many ditches. Who dug all these ditches? Maybe my brother has fallen into one! I must help him!" Vincent began to sob. "The gravestone. How sad, how sad! Such a short life." His hand seemed to move toward the gravestone, his fingers tracing the lettering as he kept sobbing.

"You are at peace, Vincent. Nothing can harm you," I calmly assured him. "You are in a dream."

"Yes, a dream, night, so many stars."

"Who is buried there?"

"Vincent."

"Who are you?"

"I am... the ditch digger."

Has he split his self into two?

"Oh, *merde*!" He clenched his fists in rage. "I hear Theo's voice calling, he wants me to look inside the ditch by the acacia tree. What the shit are they doing down there!"

"Who is in the ditch?"

"They've all sat down for dinner. Father, Mother, Theo---all dressed in black. They're quite annoyed that I've arrived late. I'm at the edge, there's no ladder. I'm ready to jump in, but Father shouts angrily, 'Damn you, son. You're not dressed properly for dinner.' Mother, as well, screams, 'You've come too late!' Vincent looked sadly at me. *Does he see me as his mother?* He stammered, "Too late? I don't understand. I'm confused, I'm so confused."

I became alarmed by the extreme anguish which contorted his face. The very same expression of torment I had witnessed when the Salpêtrière hysterics fell into the throes of an attack. He was sobbing and moaning loud enough to attract attention outside our compartment. My confidence was being shaken. *Will I be able to bring him out of the hypno-dream safely?*

Signs of convulsion began, twitching in the face, neck spasms, rapid eye movement. In a panic, I shouted for him to wake up, but he was oblivious to my voice. I frantically unbuttoned the top of his shirt and applied palm pressure to the solar plexus region, a hystero-zone Charcot utilized to interrupt muscle spasms in hysterics. But nothing changed, the spasms continued no matter how hard I pressed.

Bereft of options, at a loss, distressed, I slapped him. He grew still. I slapped his face again. Visibly, he composed himself. He wore an oddly serene expression before his head dropped, falling into a deep sleep.

I was much relieved. Perhaps the slaps were a shock to his nervous system, bringing the convulsions to an end, but I really had no clue. It had been an act of desperation.

I blew out the lamp, pulled down the shade, and kept vigilant watch over him. And as our train sped through what was left of the night, I wondered what particulars in the dream provoked the hysterical attack? Undoubtedly, the thought that his brother had abandoned him caused initial distress. The father's harsh rebuke and the mother's cruel dismissal were certainly emotional calamities. And probably what unnerved him most was the mysterious grave, seemingly his own.

II

Raising the shade, dawn flooded the compartment. We were nearing Paris. I replaced the hat and veil to keep my face hidden.

Soon my accidental travelling companion opened his eyes, rubbing his stubbled jaws in disbelief. "Amazing! I feel no pain."

"Don't be deceived," I cautioned, "a portion of your mouth remains infected, the pain still exists, but it has sunk beneath your consciousness, at least I so conjecture."

"So you really hypnotized me?"

"Yes. Do you remember anything?" I asked.

"Only a vague recollection that..." He gave me a puzzled look. "That... you wanted a dream from me. Could that have possibly happened?"

I feigned innocence. "Is there some particular dream that comes to your memory?"

"No."

The dream remained buried in his subconscious. "We will be arriving in Paris shortly," I said.

"My brother says an incredibly tall, iron spire is soon to be erected."

"Yes, construction is to begin soon. It shall replace America's Washington Monument as the tallest structure in the world."

"Have they completed *Sacre Coeur*?"

"Only the steps." Sigmund and I racing, almost dancing up the stairs, was a pleasant memory. He promised to be at the station.

"When I lived in Paris," said Vincent, "I sometimes sketched the labourers digging the church foundation."

"So, you have been here before?"

"Ten years have passed since I left," he said. I used to work for my brother's firm."

"What does your brother do?" I still pretended.

"He's a picture dealer for Boussod and Valadon, once known as Goupils and Company."

"And you also worked for the firm?" I was genuinely surprised.

"A sales clerk," he said, "at their main gallery."

"Most interesting."

Imagining him in a frock coat and starched collar, politely attending to customers, was impossible.

"We, the management and I, had a falling out," he said.

"I see."

"Fired, one might say."

The clanking of the iron wheels, hissing of steam, signalled that we were slowing down for our arrival at Saint-Lazarre.

"Vincent, I should remind you, the conductor will soon enter, asking for our tickets."

"You think I lack a ticket?"

I did not want to embarrass him. "I know what it's like to be in an impecunious state."

"I have money," he replied, not without a hint of wounded pride, "But it's better spent on canvas, paint and brushes." He donned his rabbit fur hat with the dangling flaps. "I'll jump off before the train makes a complete stop."

"Please, is that necessary? Can't you just hide in a water closet for a while?"

He laughed, taking down his duffle bag from the rack. "No more tiny water closets for me." He slid open the door, paused to give me a final look of suspicion. "Is there a reason you hide behind that veil?"

"Light can be cruel to my complexion," I said.

"You have a dream of mine, don't you?"

The question disarmed me. "Something of that sort came out during hypnosis."

"Dreams might predict the future, yes?"

"Or examine the past."

"Mine never make any sense," he said. "They're all crazy. Maybe I am, too."

"I think logical explanations can be found for the strangest dreams." I rose to reach for my travelling bag, but he quickly took it down for me. "It's a matter of decoding the symbols," I said.

"What have you learned about me, Mademoiselle?"

Death permeated the dream, that I knew. And the ditches he seemed fond of digging could only be graves. "Probably," I ventured, "someone close to you recently died."

He looked stunned. "My father... last March..." the words escaped.

"I offer condolences."

"We were not on speaking terms."

The curtness of the reply left no room for any further inquiry. I put on my coat. Whatever he had sadly read on the tombstone must still linger somewhere in his mind.

"Bad dreams are probably bad memories, best forgotten, eh?" He heaved the dufflebag on to his shoulder.

"It's my conviction that dream material, properly interpreted, might reveal what is vital to the dreamer's psyche, might give clues to the dreamer's future."

His eyes, blue as cornflowers, showed an intelligent interest. He laughed again. "Can you tell me if I will ever sell a painting?"

I smiled. "That I can't do. But from an intense dream, one might learn what a person searches for in life, and what helps or hinders him in that search."

"Was my dream sufficiently intense?"

A chastising mother and father, in an open grave, he, theoretically searching for his own grave, would qualify as intense.

"To flesh out significant indicators," I answered, "would require more time."

"Ah, it's so rejuvenating to be back in Paris," he said happily, "where one is sure to meet other eccentrics such as yourself. Take the dream, Mademoiselle. Decode, decipher, dissect as you wish. A more than fair exchange for the pain you discharged to places unknown."

"The pain still exists, only your subconscious guards and keeps it quiescent," I said. We saw the conductor enter at the far end of the corridor, proceeding to compartments to check tickets. Vincent looked for his escape in the opposite direction. As he hurried away, I called out, "Please remember, the pain and its cause still exist."

He was gone. A rash, reckless man, he did jump from the slow moving train. I guessed he had probably boarded the train at Antwerp in similar fashion.

As the train pulled into Saint-Lazarre, coming to a full stop, I searched among the teeming crowd for Sigmund, only to observe Vincent van Gogh, not difficult to miss in his ragged great coat and rabbit fur cap, manoeuvring through the platform crowd. He passed by a respectfully dressed gentleman who happened to be searching for me. The coincidence gave me an odd thrill, having the dreams of both men.

Chapter 50

at the antique door again
i peek
through a crack of light—
at distant enchantments
that grip my heart
behind me
Moon and Chateau
are melting fast

Sabrine

THE CHATEAU AFLAME

I

When I stepped off the train, Sigmund came forward to take my portmanteau and guided me through the busy station. He looked determined not to ask about my three day seminar at Bernheim's clinic. Once we were settled in a cab, I took out Hippolyte Bernheim's book and deliberately set it between us on the carriage seat.

De la Suggestion et de ses Applications

à la Thérapeutique

He still showed no curiosity, but I was far too excited to hold back the news:"Dr. Bernheim has hired me to do an English translation."

He gave the front cover a perfunctory glance. "How will you translate such a long title for the American audience? They prefer we Europeans cut to the chase."

"'Suggestive Therapeutics' I thought, or perhaps 'Therapy through Suggestion?'"

"What I suggest is for you to keep this Bernheim project under the rug. If Dr. Charcot finds out that you are translating his arch rival's major thesis, he will..."

"Strike me down, like Zeus, with his thunderbolts?"

"He will be... sorely disappointed."

I tapped the book, quite happy about my new financial prospects. "You would do well, Sigmund, to consider translating Bernheim into German. He will pay five francs per page."

"I'm afraid that I remain in Charcot's camp. Bernheim and the Nancy School segregate hypnotism from hysteria simply because the complexity of the interconnections scares them away."

"In his opening lecture, Bernheim emphasized that none of his hysteric patients, which number in the hundreds, are susceptible to an hystero-epileptic attack, that is, with the exception of one woman who fell into a dramatic fit, as she just happened to be Charcot's former patient."

Seemingly unimpressed, Sigmund gazed out the carriage window.

I stuffed Bernheim's book into the portmanteau. "For your edification, Sigmund, I was thoroughly cross-examined by the doctors at the Nancy Clinic as to how Charcot conducts his Tuesday Demonstrations. They found it interesting that Charcot explains beforehand to his audience what will occur before his grand hysterics are hypnotized, doing so in the presence of his hysterics, giving fuel to Bernheim's theory of suggestion as the operating force, not hysteria, for the epileptic contortions his subjects enact." I went on, hoping to convince him, "Our Dr. Charcot, as we both well know, is extremely charismatic. The Salpêtrière women are in awe of him. He exudes great authority. A father figure, so to speak. Now, Sigmund, what girl," raising my eyebrows at him, "or boy, for that matter, doesn't want to please their father?"

He stubbornly resisted the line of thought. "Bear in mind, Julie, the authority he carries has been well earned. Salpêtrière has done more than any existing medical institution in diagnosing neurological disorders. And so that you're aware." He looked at me steadily. "My final meeting with him is scheduled for tomorrow."

Tomorrow? I calculated. *Only four days left, four days before he leaves Paris—and Sabrine.* Any hope for his return was a useless exercise.

"And I will have an important idea to present," he patted his breast pocket, "formulated in a letter. I'm almost certain it will arouse his interest and he will take a new look at Sabrine."

"Through the prism of psychology?"

"Yes."

"You will be wasting time," I said drily. Sigmund could not yet comprehend Charcot's strange disinterest in exploring possible psychological origins in hysteria.

It was easy to imagine the great man, until his dying day, inventing novel devices to meticulously record the tics and the tremors of his patients while patiently waiting for the final dissection. I saw the Maestro's destiny, on stage, basking in the glare of theatre lights, hypnotizing his star hysterics again and again to discover and label new contortions, and not once seriously consider the psychic force that might engender them.

I spoke bluntly. "Charcot has reached a standstill in his research and in his thinking. He will throw your letter and your idea into the fire. Only not in front of you."

Sigmund put an end to the discussion, "Julie, you have temporarily lost sight of his genius."

During the remaining cab ride, I occupied myself with how I might eavesdrop on the final meeting between the two men who held the future of my sister in their hands.

II

The Charcot family had long ago entrusted me with a key to their house. Careful not to awaken a soul, I slipped into the library before dawn and sought a hiding place. Removing my shoes, I climbed the spiral stairwell to the second-floor landing where tiers of books and a banister of leering gargoyles could shield someone from view. I had only to sit quietly on the iron landing and wait stoically for the hours to pass until their ten o'clock meeting.

The floor was far from comfortable, constructed not for sitting but for safe walking, composed of what looked like iron goose bumps, and it felt as though I were sitting on a bed of pebbles. During the long vigil, waiting for the morning light, my thoughts wandered, making odd connections. The pebbled floor, as I ran my hand over it, reminded me of my own pitted complexion, of how pleasing to feel Gauguin's hand lovingly cupping my face, his thumb gliding across my cheek as if he were gently erasing the scars. I grew more and more drowsy on the landing, enjoying the memory of Gauguin leaning into my neck, savouring his warm breath in my ear, never able to stifle the shameless moans that his inserted tongue tore from me—

Be damned! I cursed, rousing myself. *Stop!* Why squander thoughts for irretrievable moments? Before I left for the Bernheim clinic, we had called an end to our affair.

I closed my eyes, curled, pressed my head against my knees, letting the sorrow wash over me. My father deceived and abandoned me, how could Gauguin's exit be a surprise? No, no surprise. At the deepest level of knowing, I expected deception. Only not so cruel, arriving in a moment of sexual abandon, in early morning, when awakening from a dream of lust I crawled on top of him, mounting my Gauguin as he slept with an erection. We copulated in the sleepy delirium of desire, reached the apotheosis, and nadir—when he called out another's name. Our passion spilled and spent, I sank into pity for him.

He dressed, left my flat in silence. Did I want him to stay? Had I the love? The strength to see past his dark impulses? Had I the vigour of mind to sort through the whims and taboos that gestated in his psyche? For how responsible were we for our desires if a goodly proportion were, as Sigmund asserted, unconscious?

505

I rearranged myself on the landing to stay alert, propping my back against a shelf of books, making sure my line of vision through the monstrous profiles of the gargoyles took in the desk below where the farewell between Charcot and Sigmund would most likely be conducted. An opened notebook and pencil squarely upon my lap, I was ready to record the last conversation between the two of them, only my eyes soon closed, the effect of little sleep and worrying about Sabrine's destiny. Drifting in and out of consciousness again, I fell back into erotic reverie. Gauguin could, whenever he wanted, evoke a shuddering in my loins, to make of me a virgin on her first night of love—and as easily, make me want to be his bidding harlot. Then half-hearing a door open and close down below, drawers opening, and paper shuffling, I wanted to wake up, but I fell further into a slipstream of desires... phantasies with Gauguin... gardenia scented candles burning, plaintive music wafting, his mandolin plucking out the melancholy melody of Handel's Reverie. And down below in the library, intruding, muffled voices, brief laughter. We laughed wickedly when Gauguin spoke of the dense, dark forest of my pubic hair. His prescient caution: "In time, our bonds with others loosen, and our memories grow fainter." "No!" I whispered the protest. "Memories, those weighted with worth, settle deeper into our subconscious where they gain a stronghold." I find myself dressing and undressing in the darkness, again and again in the darkness, where Gauguin watches with the luminous eyes of a panther—he says, "To endure you learn how to harden yourself. How else to be a first-rate painter?" *Or first-rate lover,* I think. So he gave up the twenty thousand franc position at the Bourse, the bourgeois house on Rue Carcel, the family." I once murmured sympathy and doubt in the darkness. "My Paul, it could not have been an easy decision for you. But what of the toll on them? The wife, Mette, the children? Them?" "This is the sacrifice. The emotional sacrifice. Art takes precedence over everything." "Everything?" "Everything, yes." The voices down below must belong to Charcot and Sigmund, and I need to record them, but I can't find the willpower to wake up. I remain recumbent upon a bed, my body a sacrifice, illuminated by the tiny fires of a hundred candles alight in the room. Gauguin adjusting his animal gaze to the marvellous scene, the candle-lit seraglio I have created. My eyes opened to possibility, I lay perfectly still, knowing my body is a fierce dance of shadows. When he finds the courage to touch the strange me, he marvels, "Your skin as smooth as the wax of the tapered candles that surround us." "I have stolen the candles from many churches," I say with dark pride. "And my body has been rubbed smooth by the calloused hands of a thousand sailors."

Urgently Gauguin whispers in the flickering darkness, "Who are you?" "I am the ivory whore." He steps out of his sabots, takes off his clothing. I feel deranged. The wicks sputter, going out singly, sometimes winking out in pairs. Soon his organ of pleasure rifles me, again and again...

My head jerked back, striking the books behind, a brutal awakening which left me for a brief moment panic-stricken. I was not at all sure of my surroundings, much less why I was here. So deep my shrouded descent into memories and desire, I gazed around like an amnesiac. The gargoyles with their tortured grimaces and malevolent smirks brought me back to my wretched reality: I was Julie Weiss crouching in the airy regions of Charcot's library, intent on spying upon those who would decide my sister's fate. I looked down, surprised to see the Maestro alone... not quite alone as he was pursing his lips to confide sweet nothings to the sleepy-eyed monkey tucked cosily inside his frock coat. Just then a light knock at the door and Sigmund was invited to enter.

How callous of Charcot to bring his pet to this last meeting. Everyone knew that Sigmund Freud had a near helpless phobia toward the monkey.

"Sit down, sit down!" came the eager invitation. He half-rose from the chair as the monkey swaddled under his coat made it difficult for Charcot to move freely. The creature was barely visible, but certainly Sigmund could see its quivering pink nostrils and dark shining eyes peering attentively. The monkey remained surprisingly docile while Sigmund positioned a chair farther away. I was left with only a profile view of him as the conversation ensued.

III

After preliminary pleasantries, I heard his awkward French, "Chèr Professor, I come with a humble request."

I grabbed my notebook, ready to transcribe.

"And I shall hope to grant it," replied Charcot.

A photograph was produced. "Would you be so kind as to sign this?"

A delighted Charcot examined it briefly, smiled, then put it aside. "I shall give you a much better likeness."

A search began through desk drawers until he found what he must have considered a more attractive image and picking up a pen he autographed it for his prize pupil. From my perch I could discern that the photograph showed him standing in his Napoleonic pose, hand slipped inside the lapel of his frock coat... a much younger Charcot who had just taken over the helm of Salpêtrière. He scribbled an inscription. (Before leaving Paris, Sigmund proudly showed it to me.)

À Monsieur le Docteur Freud,

Souvenir de la Salpêtrière

1886 24 fevrier

"I will treasure this—always," came the heartfelt gratitude.

"But... wait!" A brightness in Charcot voice. "I have another parting gift for you!" He brought out a lithograph print, expensively framed, of the Brouillet painting. The detestable original hung deeper into the room.

Sigmund held the picture in his hands with obvious reverence. After a minute of silent contemplation, he spoke... hesitantly, "I, too, have something for you." From a battered looking envelope he took out the letter, Charcot staring at the dog-eared page with some scepticism. Sigmund, chagrined, hurriedly explained, "Please excuse its tortured condition, I buy the cheapest stationery, and have been carrying it in my breast pocket for days."

Nodding, Charcot placed the wrinkled page aside. "Why not explicate its content, in your own words."

"Two ideas... of mine."

Two ideas? I started transcribing, intent on capturing every word.

The Maestro leaned back in his chair, his fingers pressed together into a steeple. "Proceed."

"A plan for a comparative study of hysterical and organic paralyses. I wish to establish the thesis that in hysteria, paralyses of the various parts of the body are demarcated according to the victims' personal and popular idea, not at all in concordance to anatomical facts."

The Maestro's fingertips raised and lowered the steeple rooftop. "Paralysis, as I recall, was once your bailiwick. A career goal, if I'm not mistaken—the investigation of infantile paralysis. Yes, that was your mission," Charcot ruminated, "as our resourceful Guinon procured not a few infants for your autopsies. But this new proposal... quite a deviation."

"All my original goals, since coming under your tutelage," he wanted Charcot to know, "have been shattered."

"I will concede, this idea of yours has some merit," Charcot spoke somewhat peremptorily. "It is an observable phenomenon, that the paralyses of a few hysterics can appear to defy neuroanatomical pathways."

"And not only paralyses, which is but my beginning point." His voice grew more excited. "I have also observed similar neuro-anatomical discrepancies among certain patients with neuropathies and neuralgias—numbness and pains which have no nexus to neural pathways."

I became more attentive. Were his allusions leading to Sabrine? To the phantom pains she experienced in giving a phantom birth?

Perhaps the Maestro guessed as much with his slightly crooked smile. "Yes-yes, let's relegate them to ambiguous pathways for now." His manner dismissive. "But what of your second idea?" Clearly the first held little significance for him.

I imagined Sigmund's masked disappointment. He bravely offered the second idea: "I suggest we use hypnosis therapeutically, as a method of catharsis." His mentor's face darkened in displeasure. Sigmund hurriedly took a different tack to win him over. "The idea is nothing less than an outgrowth of your own brilliant thesis that hysterical conditions have their origin in trauma."

"Physical trauma," Charcot emphasized, "which plays havoc upon the brain's neural system."

"But perhaps there's a psychological impact as well? If so, doesn't that invite an investigation into a broader aspect of the trauma?"

"Good grief! Are you saying that you want our patients to re-live their trauma through hypnosis?" asked an astounded Charcot. "And this will be curative?"

Sigmund persevered, "My friend and colleague, Josef Breuer, has initiated such experimentation with a neurasthenic patient. Taking fuller advantage of the hypnoid state, he has led the patient back to the moments when various hysterical symptoms first appeared—the intent to bring the unconscious feelings of the event to the surface, to re-live them, to engender a therapeutic catharsis. He calls it abreaction."

"Abreaction sounds similar to abracadabra!" scoffed Charcot.

I listened, as I hoped Sigmund listened, grasping the obvious—the most acclaimed hypnotist in Europe thought the idea to employ hypnotism as a therapeutic tool, preposterous.

"Dear, dear Sigmund..." Charcot's steepled roof now tapping upon his lips, perhaps permitting 'dear Sigmund' time to recant. Finally, he asked, expecting agreement, "If a railway worker falls from a beam and suffers hysterical paralysis of the leg, do we ask him to return to those moments of horror, do we force him to re-live his moment, in mid-air, screaming out his terror as he descends?"

The pupil was careful to keep his voice even: "Such verbal expressions might very well have a purgative effect on the mind."

I watched Charcot struggle to control his increasing exasperation —"Sigmund, Sigmund, the moment of trauma occurs when his leg and perhaps his head strikes St. Lazarre's rails, initiating a shockwave through certain neural pathways."

"But if a false paralysis," his pupil persisted, "can we not have him recount, under hypnosis, every detail of the fall? The moments after the event, the moments preceding, to gain an understanding of his general state of mind."

Charcot attempted humour, "How far back do you wish to take him? To his birth?"

"As far back as is necessary."

Cross-legged on the landing, transcribing the conversation, my pride swelled for his persistence.

"Your first idea, of comparative analysis, perhaps could be investigated, more so through autopsies." Charcot's attempt to be conciliatory. "But this second concoction of yours, no, no, no. I find it completely unscientific."

Looking down, I saw that he considered the matter unworthy of any further discussion. Settled and silent, Charcot's thoughts travelled elsewhere, his steepled roof rose and collapsed. Sigmund seemed defeated, he lost the desire to debate any further. The maestro's fingered roof rose and spread apart, his face lit up—"What if," a new excitement in his voice, "we drilled into the brain and devised a silica window, eh? Specifically, to show us the workings of the cerebral cortex, for that is the neural site where we will find it, by Jove, the lesion which accounts for both the psychic and somatic components of hysteria." His gaze turned distant, as though he saw this most peculiar procedure in the far future. "The lesion will look completely different than any that we have so far discovered... a barely perceptible alteration of tissues, something metabolic or chemical which may even quickly reverse back to normal so that it seems, to the naive eye, nothing is amiss, but not to the trained eye of the Salpêtrière neuropathologist. Ah, watching day and night through our window to the brain, he shall see it!"

So Charcot concluded with an air of triumph as if his fiction would soon become fact. Sigmund was left with little ground to win him over. It was a despairing moment. I wondered what more could be said to effect a change in Charcot's thinking? Had my sister lost her one ally? But then the conversation took an unexpected turn.

"Dr. Charcot, are you aware that I hypnotized Sabrine?"

"Yes, an unfortunate turn of events. Sigmund, what could you have been thinking to do such a thing without my permission?"

"An imprudent act on my part. But I believe that I have relieved her of the ovarian pains." He met Charcot's stern gaze without flinching. "She no longer seems to have need of the compression belt."

Charcot rose, the monkey *Rêve* remained nestled under his coat, asleep, making little snoring sounds. Charcot walked ponderously to the French doors, unmistakably unhappy, gazing out at the garden. "So, Sigmund Freud, you presume to have cured our Sabrine?"

Sigmund's nonresponse prompted Charcot to beckon someone unseen in the garden, then taking a comfortable chair in a different part of the library, he said, "Let us hope what you are about to witness will be instructive."

The French doors swung open and in walked Sabrine. The transcription pad slipped from my lap as I stiffened, clutched the balcony railing and stared dumbstruck. Escorted by Babinski, my sister showed herself radiant, a picture of health, expressing her amusement at being brought before an assembly of men.

To betray little interest in her entrance, Charcot took to examining his fingernails. Such indifference, I knew from experience, was the typical prelude to a grand, dramatic spectacle.

Sigmund, silent and fascinated, was already in the maestro's grip. A cursory nod to Babinski signalled the assistant to take his ward to another, distant part of the room. I moved stealthily, on my knees, to see where they were going. There in a nook loomed an instrument of monstrous proportions, the Charcot tuning fork, a construction more than five feet in height. I had seen him use his special tuning fork to place recalcitrant patients in a particularly deep trance—Sabrine was placed beside it. The unparalleled master of hypnotism now wasted no time, giving Babinski another nod. The mournful assistant picked up a cloth-covered hammer and struck the turning fork with unusual force. A loud, deafening ring vibrated throughout the library where various cabinets, objects and curios trembled. The monkey awakened, leapt from his master's bosom and took fearful flight to a hiding place as the sound deepened and turned strangely sonorous, an attenuated hum that never quite left the air.

Charcot approached Sabrine, encouraging her to listen closely to the ringing sound. "Listen, listen, lis..sen..." With an abrupt snapping of his fingers, Sabrine went limp, held by Babinski. "Sleep, child, sleep..." urged Charcot. Her eyes closed.

The scene below coiled my stomach into a knot—the black-frocked pair had re-entered the Brouillet painting! A merciless replication!

"She has succumbed to the lethargic state," explained Charcot. Now he would induct her into final stage of hypnosis. Two of his fingers pressed between her eyes and she fell into the somnambulic state. Babinski, his assigned tasks well rehearsed, gently laid my sister on the floor. What occurred next shocked me to rise.

"You are with child," Charcot told her. "The foetus slowly, slowly grows." Unhurriedly, he spoke of the passing months, the foetus forming inside her. We all watched, transfixed, as my sister's belly swelled. When the ninth month of the hypnoid pregnancy was reached, no medical doctor could doubt that a baby, or something, lived inside her swollen belly.

What ensued next in the chaos becomes difficult to assemble. I thought, at first, *Is his intent to make a mockery of a religious exorcism?*

"Expel your demon!" commanded Charcot, "And know, he is legion!"

From somewhere inside my sister came a scream I never imagined in a lifetime, to watch her face, so beautiful, violently twitch and contort with increasing pain, her back arcing in repeated spasms. The screams echoed in the cavernous library without end. The monkey crazy with fear then trembling furor took to screeching in a hideous harmony, and he raced toward her as though to attack. Sigmund and Babinski pitifully tried to prevent the maddened creature from reaching my Bijou. He grabbed a hunk of Sabrine's hair, attempting to pull her about as though he found a rag doll.

I shouted down my rage. The monkey, catching sight of me on the balcony, let go of Sabrine's hair. He scrambled at an alarming speed across the library, nearly flying up the stairwell. I his target, our encounter ordained, the black dream I knew I had to defeat. Rushing at me with a deafening screech, the monkey leaped. I was calmly prepared.

Airborne, with his grinning and grinding teeth set to bite, I caught him by the neck. I caught the monkey with one hand and squeezed, certain that I could strangle away his life; he whimpered pitifully and went limp. I brought him, powerless, up to the railing for all to see, prepared to hurl his carcass down with all the force I possessed.

The sight of his snivelling pet held high in the air made Charcot fearful. He pleaded, "Please, don't let him fall!"

"Release my sister from the trance," I shouted down, "or I will break your black dream's neck and toss him dead at your feet!"

He recognized the precarious situation, instructing Babinski to place palm pressure on a hysterogenic zone above Sabrine's distended abdomen. Charcot retrieved the hammer, glanced concerned at his pet, then struck the tuning fork. A deep vibrating sound filled the library. When Babinski's hand pressure brought the screams and agitation to a stop, Charcot leaned over her.

"The demons in your belly are expelled, listen to their demon roar retreat, farther and farther away, and so your fullness shrinks, and your womb once again is hallow." The hypnotic suggestion, veiled in religious gibberish, succeeded. Sabrine's abdomen returned to normal. Another Charcot miracle. The turning fork's hum, the demons' roar, faded.

"Sleep, my child, sleep," he whispered. "And wait for God's hand clap. Now sleep, sleep."

The arrogance of calling Sabrine his child stirred me to descend the stairwell, the monkey helpless in my grip. *God's hand clap? When did "God" join Charcot's pantheon of hypnotic inducements?*

Sigmund advanced, I brushed past, kept the monkey's neck tight and secure in both hands, extending him outward, now my talisman to ward everyone away, although ready to choke out its little life if someone dared interfere. The three men were perplexed as to what I would do next.

IV

The monkey, curled in my arms, his eyes shut tight, breathing gently, perhaps lulled by the tuning fork's hum that passed beyond human hearing, fell peacefully asleep. The three men stayed a safe distance. Sabrine lay unconscious on the floor, dressed as in the Brouillet painting, a full country skirt and white blouse, the alluring neckline revealed the deep heaving of her breasts. I stood uncertain as to the next course of action.

Predictably, Charcot regained composure, he waved an arm around at our ensuing spectacle, and grimly asked, "Shall we risk awakening her to these unsettled circumstances?" My hesitation encouraged him. "Shouldn't we take a few measured moments to sort out our positions?"

Babinski spoke, concerned. "Professor, have I your permission to carry Mademoiselle to the more comfortable sofa? Surely she will remain hypnotized until your clap."

God's clap.

"One cannot predict these things with unerring accuracy," he replied. "She may, if we allow sufficient time to pass, fall into a natural sleep then eventually awaken on her own." He looked inquiringly at Sigmund who seemed reluctant to intrude into the situation. "What say thee, my friend, you the proponent of hypnosis as therapy? How should we proceed?"

"Dr. Babinski's concerns are mine, let her rest undisturbed on the sofa."

"To sleep, perchance to dream..." Charcot murmured his beloved Shakespeare as he resumed his imperial position behind the black mahogany desk.

Sigmund and Babinski lifted Sabrine and placed her on a sofa. (I now considered both men as nothing more than Charcot's underlings). Babinski sought a throw rug to ensure her comfort then stood protectively nearby. Charcot set his questioning gaze upon me. "Reveal yourself, Mademoiselle Forette, for I no longer see you in a familiar light."

Stay calm in this man's aggravating presence. Prudent behaviour from this moment on.

The sleeping monkey still cradled in my arms, I went to my sister. Aware of Charcot's surveillance, I chose not to say anything that might unleash his wrath. Sigmund carried such a worried look, I'm sure he thought me hysterically mute.

"Can it be possible," Charcot began to ponder, tapping a pair a pair of eyeglasses against his chest, "that you are related by blood to her?"

How to fashion a truthful response that might give him a semblance of understanding? And perhaps regain a portion of his trust? But before I could find words, a voice came from the opened door:

"Why, Father! It's plain to see that the two of them have the same green eyes."

Jeanne Charcot, arms folded, had entered our unfolding drama. She observed the entire scene with serene amusement. Charcot, fallen silent, fiddled with his eyeglasses, uncertain as to whether his daughter was an intrusion or a welcomed ally.

She added, "Yes, the same, unruly green."

My surprise was complete. *How long has she known?*

Jeanne's eyes narrowed at what was the improbable sight of her father's monkey cuddled peacefully in my arms. A strange paradox, I realized, had taken place. No longer could I find the least antipathy toward the creature. Jeanne walked confidently into the room.

As Charcot was accustomed to drawing comfort from her presence, he seemed to reconsider her an asset. "Jeanne, please examine him, is *le Rêve* still alive?"

She inspected the monkey in my arms, his eyelashes suddenly fluttered, his eyes opened, as though to give Jeanne proof he lived, only to close again.

"I would say, Father, your *Rêve* is alive and quite content."

I held out the pacified *Rêve* for her to take, but she wrinkled her nose in disgust and waved him away, her animosity toward the monkey unchanged. I was certain he would no longer be a menace to anyone. I placed him curled and asleep at Sabrine's feet. The room's silence begged for a voice to guide us out of a situation too tense and untenable. I gave them the truth—

"I am Sabrine's sister."

While no one spoke, Jeanne appeared satisfied that I had confirmed her suspicions. The others? Babinski looked troubled. Sigmund a rapt observer, no detail was escaping him. Charcot? The corners of his mouth, a slight twitching that might form a smile. I waited. The afternoon light lent false cheerfulness to the room.

I observed Jeanne deliberately distance herself from me, joining her father, stationing herself behind him, a hand on his rounded shoulder. The fierce loyalty to family blood I well understood. His daughter's reassuring hand made him sit more erect, with the words to censure me: "The extent of your deceit… disturbing, Mademoiselle, disturbing."

"I have viewed my identity, at Salpêtrière, as a truth unnecessary to disclose." So was my defence.

Genuinely astounded, he scoffed, "Unnecessary truth? Is this Jesuit logic to mask your wrongdoing? I, placing my trust in Julie Forette have been repaid with betrayal. That is unforgivable."

Jeanne's awkward attempt to lay an envelope in front of her father stole my interest. Apparently she had come to the library with a specific purpose. The envelope blazoned with the red seal of the coiled serpents caught Babinski's attention as well. Charcot calmly rose, as if he had not seen the letter, and approached Sigmund.

"Yes, the questions dance in your eyes," he began rather kindly. 'Why did Dr. Charcot hypnotize Sabrine only to precipitate a horrific spectacle? Why put her through the pains of giving a pseudo-birth and then an exorcism?'"

The questions were mine as well—*What reason to induce my sister to suffer through a phantasized birth?*

He looked around, satisfied that again an audience was in his grip. "Yes, worthwhile inquiries: Why did Charcot command the child to deliver demons? First and foremost," he raised a finger, "to demonstrate that I, too, can be midwife to the birth of phantoms—thus…" he opened his hand to Sigmund, "offering to my esteemed young doctor, unequivocal proof that the hypnoid state is a morbid, pathological condition of consciousness. Placing her in a hypnotic trance only exposes her predisposition toward pathogenia. There is no therapeutic value in hypnotism, none whatsoever."

His young doctor's stony silence made an unfavourable impression. He turned to Babinski. "Inform the surgical staff to make all necessary preparations."

Haltingly, Babinski asked, "To perform an oophorectomy?"

Charcot nodded gravely. "The moment has arrived to stabilize Mademoiselle Sabrine's condition."

My heart froze at the word, *oophorectomy*. Desperate, I searched the other faces for an ally. Jeanne stared mournfully down at the desk, as though alone in the library, her finger idly tracing the caduceus seal, more obsessed with the letter's contents than objecting to the removal of Sabrine's ovaries.

Sigmund shoved his hands in his trouser pockets and walked a few steps closer to the sofa. "Memories…" he began, stopped, cleared his throat as though the word gave him difficulty. "Memories," he repeated, "if sufficiently pernicious, Dr. Charcot, may very well attach themselves in an electrical or chemical fashion to the lesion of hysteria. If we could dislodge those memories... from your predicted lesion, so that the latter loses its combinative power..."

A brave and remarkably clever attempt, I thought, to persuade Charcot to a different view of hysteria. Sigmund was struggling for a feasible hypothesis to unite the psychical with the somatic.

But the renowned professor of neurology was not to be persuaded by an idea not his own. "My dear boy, memories are the mind's debris. What cure can you fashion from debris?" Seemingly in charge again, he approached and hovered over Sabrine asleep on the sofa. "The lesion of Grand Hysteria, I now venture to say, resides in the ovaries..."

His elusive lesion moves from the cerebral cortex to the ovaries! I let loose my scorn, "The learned doctors here need to be educated in the matter of anatomical solutions."

Unable to tolerate Charcot's tired ideas any further, I went directly to the shelves where the medical journals from other countries were catalogued. I pulled out an issue of *American Science* and took it to Jeanne who now sat at her father's desk. Deliberately I placed the journal over the unopened letter to revive her attention. "These periodicals arrive from every corner of the medical world," I announced to everyone. "A medical world, one must add, that thrives independently of Salpêtrière." Hoping Jeanne still had Sabrine's best interests in mind, I asked, "Would you kindly read for us the article, dated August 1884, by B.F. Murdock, M.D."

She stood and walked away. The friendship broken. Sigmund approached to read the article for himself. He said nothing after reading it.

Charcot gave a caustic smile. "Since no one cares to read aloud, why don't we let Mademoiselle Forette, or whatever her name is, offer us a précis?"

"Very well!" I paced nervously amongst them. "In July of 1884 an American doctor, Dr. Murdock, was asked to perform an oophorectomy on a patient who suffered from hystero-epilepsy. The American doctor apparently had grave doubts that an oophorectomy, per se, could cure the patient, so he decided to conduct a covert experiment. Making only a superficial incision in the parieties of the abdomen, he left the young woman's peritoneum and ovaries untouched."

"A sham oophorectomy?" asked Babinski, having reclaimed his guardian post by Sabrine, casting her an anxious look.

"Yes," I said and waited for someone to predict the article's outcome.

Jeanne had no trouble in leaping to a conclusion. "And the patient was cured?"

Encouraged, I nodded. "The woman was re-stitched with her ovaries intact. But... believing that the offending part of her body had been removed, she experienced no more hystero-epileptic attacks."

In the awkward silence that followed, Sigmund re-read the article with greater scrutiny. Perhaps he hoped to find some flaw to disprove my evidence. I went back to replace Babinski at his post.

Charcot wasted no time in disparaging the article. "We know that the power of suggestion, especially a suggestion from a person of great authority, can reach a morbid pitch in a hysterical patient. By now I guarantee your American lady has been institutionalized, suffering even more from the insidious disease they foolishly hoped to suggest away."

I fully realized Charcot's flaw, he would never be able to see the link between hysteria and the psyche. His vision peculiarly clouded, far worse than the tragedy of cataracts, he was Salpêtrière's blind king, prepared to wait for my sister to expend her life in his cloistered palace, then, when her heart stopped and her brain went dead, assign his minions to lay her upon the dissecting bier, scalpels ready, to search for the king's mystery lesion.

Sigmund finally looked up from the article. Soberly, he gave the right word: "Auto-suggestion."

Yes! Bernheim's underlying thesis to explain the hypnoid process—hysterical patients invoked their own symptoms. The hypnotist acted as nothing more than a conduit, he had no real power over his subject.

Charcot took back control of the conversation. "These convolutions and abstractions are worthy of debate, no doubt, especially among the Germans. But I have the concrete to deal with, a human being in my safe keeping."

I watched, very wary, as he returned to my sister. His monkey had now found a safer place, asleep with its little snore, under Sabrine's arm.

Charcot looked grim, his voice mean. "My dubious role of exorcist, calling forth demons, was sheer antic play." He leaned closer over her and in a gesture, suggesting tenderness, brushed away a few moist strands of hair from her cheek. "I am no Christ, I have not driven demons into swine, nor into extinction. She lays before me, the same disturbed patient. What choice but to operate..."

"You will not perform surgery on my sister!" I hissed. "And never again parade Sabrine before an audience!"

"She awakens!" cried Babinski.

Charcot calmly explained, "She emerges from a natural sleep—no longer in the hypnoid state." He attempted to extricate his pet, but the monkey had no intention of leaving his new protectress, hugging on to her arm as she stirred.

Placing the palms of my hands flat against Charcot's chest, I pushed him back as Sabrine opened her eyes. She sat up, again looking radiant, and cast a smile at me. Knowingly. Her eyes shining and lucid with recollection. Every loving moment between us seemed to spring to life, we were sisters again. I knew this.

"We must leave the château," she said, "the holy fire will melt it."

The monkey decided to scamper away as I helped her rise.

Charcot had hurried back to his daughter's side to give his counsel from a distance. "Dear Sabrine, the Salpêtrière offers you curative protection and hope."

"The princess of the hysterics shall find her own cure," she answered.

Irony twisted Charcot's mouth. "And where," he asked, "shall the princess find her cure?"

"In a poem." More deliberative silence until she turned to Sigmund. "I shall miss our chimney sweeps, but Paris awaits, glittering."

While he seemed to search for an appropriate response, I had all the encouragement I needed. "I'm now demanding the immediate release of my sister."

"Under whose care?" Charcot inquired.

"Mine."

"Placing her in your unreliable custody would be an insult to the integrity of Salpêtrière standards."

"If I may opine," Sigmund came forward, "taking Sabrine out of the asylum at this particular juncture may be premature."

His prudent behaviour was a bitter disappointment. I ignored him and stated to everyone, "I will not tolerate her incarceration any longer!"

Sabrine took the initiative, opening the French doors leading to the garden and freedom.

Charcot warned, "You are making a tragic mistake. Mark my words, to bring Sabrine into Paris is to launch her into calamity."

"I'd rather she face life's vicissitudes than have you remove her ovaries and turn her into an automaton."

He stiffened. "It's unpardonable that you would risk irreparable harm to your sister?"

"There are times when one must gamble."

"Your irresponsibility disappoints me gravely," he concluded.

Sabrine took a few steps outside, I followed. Babinski looked confused. "Professor, shall I restrain Sabrine?"

"Don't bother." Charcot then addressed me, he pronounced the words slowly, imperiously, as if law. "Be forewarned, as Director of Salpêtrière, I shall exert all my power to have her promptly returned."

I looked at a very reserved Sigmund Freud. He knew my question—*Am I to fight Charcot entirely alone?*

"What if," suggested Sigmund, "she were released temporarily? A probationary period."

"Out of the question!"

Sabrine, unafraid, prepared to leave, took my hand.

"Oh, but do wait one moment." At the desk, Charcot broke open the serpent sealed envelope, scanned the letter, and gave me an ugly smile. Crushing the letter into a ball, flushed with a rage I had never seen, he threw the ball of paper which struck the side of my face, a light, harmless sensation.

"Perhaps now," came his malicious accusation, "your insane letters shall stop arriving each month, at the full moon, when Sabrine bleeds." Sabrine walked away from his noise, into the garden. "She will not get far," he said. "As soon as I notify the proper authorities, the child will be returned."

Jeanne stood closely beside him. "Father is right, Salpêtrière is Sabrine's home."

I smiled a farewell and followed my sister. She walked leisurely, not a worry in her head. I knew and expected future troubles. Charcot would not easily relinquish his power. But I had formulated a plan. I would present my situation to the newspapers, two sisters from Marseilles, orphans, having caused harm to no one, are separated because of the ignorance of neighbours, who deceitfully convince authorities that a fifteen-year-old girl poses a threat. Two sisters cruelly torn apart. A fifteen-year-old imprisoned in an asylum for nothing more than being a gentle dreamer. Now, after nearly five years of unjust separation, the sisters fight to reunite. Their sole happiness is to stay together and support themselves in honest work. What sympathy will Charcot garner in the court of public opinion? To protect his reputation and keep his lofty goals unsullied, he will let us be. So I believed.

The garden path serpentined. We steadfastly walked amidst the scent of many flowers. Hints of spring. I watched her become playful, spinning to see her skirt swirl, behaving like a very young girl. It was so evident, we were no longer apart.

I waited for her to speak.

"We will come to look at our love in a new way," she said, her eyes unfailingly green.

"What do you remember?"

"I remember everything, and nothing."

"The letters?" I had been sending them to her ever since my employment at the Salpêtrière, surreptitiously.

"Oh, you describe the paintings beautifully."

"You shall see much more. And meet my friends."

"And they will become my friends."

"Yes, everyone will adore you."

"I shall meet Father Christmas and Monsieur not-so-grumpy Degas and the lady who rode bareback on white horses and swung on the trapeze."

She phantasized Father Pissarro and Suzanne Valadon. All of art and the artists of Paris were waiting for us. Our chance had come.

And so she dancingly preceded me, reaching the garden's end where several early blooming crape myrtles were matching the colour of her hair, the flames so stunning.

EPILOGUE

**Paris is simply one long confused dream,
and I shall be very glad to wake up.**

Sigmund Freud

OEDIPUS REX

I

Sigmund and I sat on a park bench in the Tuileries Gardens, a bag of chestnuts between us. The warm and smoky scent of the chestnuts helped to ward off the morning chill. This would be our last day together. His train left at nightfall, arriving in Wandsbek, Germany where he would reunite with his fiancée.

He took a moment to light a cigar, drawing in a few puffs before asking, "Are you still determined to take Sabrine out of Salpêtrière?"

"Certain legal documents wait to be signed and duly witnessed, then we will be together."

"I suppose there's no point in debating the issue any further."

"No." I broke open a chestnut, plopped it in my mouth. He tilted back his head to exhale a stream of smoke. I knew that this was my last opportunity to be with this remarkable man. He possessed such a fertile mind that in what time was left I should draw out all the ideas he might have to keep my sister free. And I felt that our exploration into dreams had only begun. Now, in the precious hours remaining, I wished him under the influence of cocaine, to explore further; but knew to be circumspect, to wait until he, not I, proposed his magic elixir.

Suddenly he asked, "Have you brought your recordation of my dream?" I hurriedly opened my purse to bring out the dream book, but he stopped me. "Undoubtedly your transcription is unerring. What I prefer is to interpret what rises to our consciousness."

I was ready for the challenge. "Your dream is weighted with meaning," I said.

After a few moments of silence, he remarked with much gloom, "The dream's conclusion—me, a babbling beggar whose words emerge mangled from my mouth, that's what comes hellishly to mind."

"To be incapable of articulating one's thoughts is disturbing," I said.

Farther into the park, there was a pleasant view of a spinning carousel where exuberant children were carried by gently bobbing animals.

"Your sister said something very similar when we first met," he said.

I was taken aback. "You told her your Mephisto dream?"

"No, no—her remark came from a discussion we were having about aphasia."

"An unusual topic for your first encounter."

"To gain her trust I admitted to my worst fear, a stroke resulting in aphasia. The Mephisto Dream came a few days later. Apparently, the idea of Broca's aphasia stayed lodged in my mind and found an outlet."

"Do you think our primary fears take command in the dream world?" I asked. "Do they demand to be expressed?"

"I doubt if that's the operating force in dreams. If it were so, then all our dreams would be nightmares. Which, of course, they are not."

Dare I speak of my recurring nightmare? Where I wander lost, in despair, always lost.

"I have many pleasant dreams," he added, "quite pleasant."

We both were drawn to watching a little girl leading a very corpulent man to the carousel. She held his hand because he was blind. He carried a folding chair and strapped around his neck was an accordion. The little girl unfolded the chair for him near the revolving carousel and the blind man sat down.

Sigmund asked, "What in the Mephisto Dream rises to your consciousness?"

"The image I find most haunting is an enraged Mephistopheles spewing from his mouth, like vomit you said, a deluge of white flowers. Were they camellias?"

I wondered if perhaps the flower Alexander Dumas made infamous in his novel, *Lady of the Camellias*, held some important place in his subconscious. There was the flirtation incident, the minor jealousy between him and the author.

"Camellias, chrysanthemums, carnations, I'm not sure," he answered somewhat dismissively. "But they seemed to exude plant sap sticking to my face. I feared them to be poisonous.' His hand tapped nervously against a side pocket to where the cocaine vial might be waiting. He drew hard upon the cigar, now hardly more than a burning nub, and unhappily tossed it away. "We should set upon dissecting the dream, logically."

"Since a connection to aphasia was found, shouldn't we seek to establish other causal connections from events during the preceding day or days?" I suggested.

"Excellent reasoning! I'm inclined to believe dreams incorporate the recent experiences in waking life." His hand slipped into another pocket, searching for the blue vial, withdrawing empty-handed.

Is he unaware of his desire for cocaine? "Did you not have several meetings with Charcot during this period?"

"Yes, there was a project he proposed for me, too grandiose to be practical." He answered in a tone of someone who cared to go no further.

I persisted, "Would not any proposal by Charcot make an impression?"

He was weighing what to reveal. "Certainly his new invention, the ovarian compressor, made an impression, designed with Sabrine in mind." Again he felt for the bottle of liquid cocaine which seemed to be hiding from him.

Calmly, I removed a glove. "An archaic device we know Sabrine will never wear again." I reached into his side pocket where the cocaine bottle bulged—this would dispel the resistance he seemed to be developing to any further dream analysis. I handed him the bottle.

"Is this your usual mixture of burgundy and hydrochloride cocaine?"

"Yes, what Merck purports to be its purest pharmaceutical grade."

He unscrewed the bottle's top which also served as an eyedropper. There we were, facing each other on the park bench, like baby birds, mouths open wide, taking turns measuring out viscous drops onto our tongues. As always, the initial bitter taste.

"The tongue accrues a furriness," I noted. We enjoyed sharing our observations.

"Yes, cocaine's peculiar numbing effect on any area of direct contact."

Cocaine scientists we deemed ourselves.

Then came the delicious warmth passing down my throat, meandering like ticklish tentacles through my diaphragm. A spreading web of warmth, like melting sugar. And soon my pulse increased—a great heat emanating from my head, exhilaration sweeping me upward to a realm where euphoria and omniscience promised to be a constant.

"Relate every detail of your meeting with Charcot," I invited, "leave nothing out."

With new loquacity he recounted Charcot's astounding proposal for a comprehensive study of hysteria and neurological diseases in the Semitic race. I listened although unable to take my eyes from the blind man seated by the carousel. He had begun to play his accordion, a jaunty tune, as children sailed gleefully round and round. Astride their chosen animals, their sweet laughter washed over me like light rain.

"This particular effect could last longer than usual," I heard him say.

The big, broad-shouldered accordion man, serene in white milk blindness, rocked side to side, Sigmund foot-tapping the pebbled ground, bravely keeping time to the music.

The carousel revolving faster, the little boys shouting out brave and happy cries, the smiling faces of little girls flushed rubicund, their pretty coloured dresses and white lace pantalettes a continuous swirl, and I wondered which painter could best capture the swift blend of iridescent colour. *Renoir. Renoir will weave it all together.*

How marvellous that I could synthesize sights and sounds into ever changing harmonies and harness my intellect toward a dissection of Charcot's proposal to study Jewish degeneracy.

I asked, "Do you think him an anti-Semite?"

"No, not at all." *Not at all.*

"Are you certain?" *Are you certain?*

He answered. "Truly, he wants the hypothesis explored and thinks me worthy of the task."

I arched my eyebrows to where I expected the exact height of scepticism should be. "And not a scintilla of anti-Semitism when he suggests a need to ferret out the aberrancy in the Jewish race?"

Whatever amount of Jewishness flowed through me, I suddenly felt a mountain tiger fierceness to defend the blood and wished to stir a just anger in Sigmund.

Calmly he replied, "Dr. Charcot is quite fond of me. The proposal was made with the utmost sincerity."

I raised a finger. "Fondness." I raised another finger. "Counterpoint, sincerity. Making the prejudice more pernicious."

I tore open another chestnut and nibbled on it. He puffed smoke from a fresh cigar. I directed him back to the dream. "Might not Mephistopheles, dressed with cape, be a stand-in for Charcot?"

His irritation showed in the deeper glowing of the cigar tip. His foot-tapping had lost all synchronicity to the music. "It is Julie Weiss who wishes to see Charcot as the devil, not I."

As he dared not chip even a piece from the great man's pedestal, I took a renewed interest in the spinning carousel, the rising and descending horses, giraffes and lions, the blind accordion man swaying to his music, glazed eyes rolled up inside the huge, shaggy-haired head, smiling like a saint transfigured.

Sigmund jumped to his feet. "I put up a damn good fight!" he shouted out over the accordion music and the children's squeals of pleasure.

Startled, I asked, "Fight with whom?"

"Mephistopheles. I took away his cane."

Thankfully, we re-entered the Mephisto dream with cocaine insight.

"His modern pitchfork," I added.

"And I almost choked him to death with it."

"You and the devil rolling on the ground, vying for dominance," I kept going. "Two disparate forces."

"You've hit upon something!" he broke out excitedly. "Perhaps these forces represent ideas, eh?"

"Apparently your idea lost," I had to say. "And you were severely punished with the loss of the power to communicate."

How intellectually aroused we were, how keen we felt, every word colluding with another. He strode back and forth, his shoes crunching into the gravel. "Yes, at dream's end the passersby think me imbecilic," he muttered crossly. "A denouement not at all to my liking."

"A dream of defeat," I had to say again. "The devil wins."

He paced and pondered. I found unique pleasure in the crunch and stamp of his shoes into the gravel... into meaning. "We're talking—I think mistakenly—as if the devil and I are separate entities."

"The dreamer and every dream particle are one and the same." I was feeling wonderfully erudite, certain we would weave a pattern of meaning, deciphered before our day ended.

"You should be collecting more dreams," he declared. "To establish patterns."

I eagerly promised, "Yes, I shall." Our ideas overlapping while two squirrels ran wildly after each other through a leafless tree. I tossed out a chestnut, put off guard by the next question.

"Have you collected a dream from Sabrine?"

The chestnut drew the squirrels to scurry down the tree where a quarrel quickly ensued for the prize. Each made high pitch, cracking squeals while snapping their tails at each other.

"I have no dream from Sabrine," I said on a note that made it clear that the matter need not be pursued.

The shabbier grey-tailed squirrel chased off the other and took possession of the chestnut. Cupping the nut in its tiny hands, the squirrel chewed and devoured it in a fiendish like frenzy. Poised on hind legs, the squirrel watched me, the eyes disturbingly black and glistening, its appetite unsatisfied.

"Desire," I said. "A dream must fulfil a desire." As soon as the idea escaped, it felt inadequate.

Pensive for a moment, Sigmund asked, "Paralysis of speech, how could that be my desire?"

He was dubious. I stood and tossed the entire bag of chestnuts to my waiting friend. As vicious as a street rat, the squirrel ripped the paper bag to shreds with its tiny hands, devouring all the chestnuts before I could blink twice.

"Interesting how cocaine instantaneously stems my appetite," noted Sigmund.

"Oh, we're hungry," I said, "but not for food. Come Sigmund, let's walk."

We strolled down the wide gravelled path of the Tuileries. "Julie, there very well might be some validity to your notion that desire prompts the creation of a dream. We should not rule out the hypothesis too quickly." He stopped. "Let's think this through—before coming to Paris, what life's work had I had planned for myself?"

"As I remember, to find a cure for infantile paralysis."

"Exactly!" He resumed walking, I beside him. "Seeking the cause of paralysis, my burning desire for years." His thoughts quickened, so his pace. "However, after certain experiences at Salpêtrière, I give serious consideration to pursuing another career."

I ran to catch up with him and his thoughts. "Meaning your experience with my sister?"

"Yes, I feel the profound importance of understanding the psychology of hysteria because of Sabrine. Another new door of science opens. But what of my original desire? Which career do I pursue? This places me in an unsettled state of ambiguity." He stopped. "What does this wavering between desires do to my psyche, tell me?"

Our thoughts were igniting like electrical sparks. "Causes conflict," I said.

"There you have it! Conflicting desires!" He resumed his speed walk to better absorb the idea we hatched, only to stop again. "And how does my original desire maintain its hold upon me?" I was caught up in the daring of his exploration. "By taking revenge in the dream, by inflicting me with my worst fear."

Two desires in conflict. A brilliant construct, I thought, for interpreting unruly dreams. Yet it seemed too tidy of an explanation.

We kept walking the gardens, fuelled by cocaine, walking tirelessly. Every urinal we approached lured him inside, an obvious micturating effect of the drug. I waited and watched his black polished shoes beneath the iron partitions, and the spread of his legs, envious of men and their convenient outdoor water closets.

The Tuileries Gardens soon lead to the *Place de la Concord* where we stopped to admire the stone Obelisk from Luxor. He pulled from his side pocket a small pair of opera glasses and we took turns scanning the Egyptian tower. Chiselled into the stone, from top to bottom, were strangely beautiful animals. He wondered about the little men seated on stools who were interspersed within the swirl and wave of hieroglyphs.

"Scribes," I informed him.

"Like yourself."

"In Egypt," I said, never forgetting that my introduction to Egyptology came from Sabrine, "scribes were held in the highest esteem, for the scribe recorded the wisdom of the king."

"Your job, precisely!" he noted, offering me the opera glasses.

"No longer," I reminded him.

He had no desire to discuss my lost favour with the king of neurology —a painful subject for both of us. Finally came his sad realization. "This truly will be our last day together."

"At least we have until midnight," I said to brighten the situation.

"And as I adore Paris, I shall take you to my most favourite places!" His chemical euphoria had resurged.

I followed, a little less euphoric, trying to push away the thought of his imminent departure.

We did whirlwind tours of the Cluny and the Louvre. His special fondness was for ancient statuary from the Mediterranean and the Near East. (I could never spark his interest in Impressionism, much less for the upcoming show which had me so excited.) He took particular delight in taking me to the Assyrian room at the Louvre, pointing out the various sphinxes, the winged bulls and Assyrian kings who hovered over us, as tall as trees, holding lions in their arms like lap dogs. "Surely all of this is more a dream world than real," he noted in wonderment.

Our next 'must-visit' was the Cathedral of Notre Dame. Single file, we briskly climbed the tower stairs to test our cocaine strength, neither of us the least fatigued when reaching the top. The city Paris spread out before us. The days strong light gave the buildings and monuments the rich look of ivory. I was able to see the steel-coloured Seine wending out of the city as far away as Issy.

"It still begs a fuller interpretation," I said.

Gay-heartedly, he asked, "Do you mean the city?"

"That, too. But your Mephisto dream mustn't escape us without a thorough analysis."

"I'm the first to admit," he said, "that this dream analysis is a complex business!"

We were leaning over the tower ledge as far as we dared for a better look at Paris, holding on to our hats as the wind gained strength.

"I do believe we go to great lengths to hide the deeper meaning of our dreams." I was finding immense pleasure in taking deep breaths, filling my lungs with the freshness of the air, and ideas. "But clues are planted by the dreamer, don't you think? It's just a matter of finding them to allow the dream's true story to assemble."

"I bet a persistent investigator, such as yourself, can find such clues in my dream."

I relished him prodding me forward. "Well, what stands out for me are the flowers and, of course, the hat," I said, as I held on to my own.

"My guess," he removed his hat to contemplate it, the idea of it, "the hat functions as a symbol for my dignity."

I shot back, "At dream's end it functions as a receptacle... for coins."

"The dream hat is upturned," he argued, "so too my dignity."

I looked elsewhere for clues. "Didn't you mentioned the coins as being pfennigs?"

He reflected. "So I did."

"But if the dream takes place in Paris, why aren't the coins centimes?"

"That is an inconsistency."

"Maybe the essence of your dream experience is not taking place in Paris," I ventured, but unsure where I was going.

"Let's give the Mephisto dream a rest," he suddenly said, "and go look for more trouble elsewhere. Come, let's descend back into perdition," he laughed, taking the lead down the tower stairs, listing the performers he had seen in Paris, including the actress Sarah Bernhardt and how he particularly admired the acting skills of Mounet-Sully.

At a shop near the cathedral I purchased a penny postcard of Notre Dame. "A parting souvenir," I said.

"I will treasure the photograph," he said.

"Shall I autograph it, like Charcot?"

My quip fell flat. He looked perturbed. I was about to blame my loose and sardonic tongue on cocaine—but thought better of it.

II

The time had come to offer a final present. I showed the two theatre passes Degas had given me. "For any matinee at the Orphium Theatre."

Sigmund was greatly pleased. "Splendid! And this my last day in Paris, maybe lady fortune will smilingly bestow upon me Molière."

The billboard outside the Orphium announced a production of *Oedipus Rex*, the antique play by Sophocles. And the principal actor happened to be Mounet-Sully. We looked at each other in astonishment. He checked his pocket watch. There would still be ample time to reach *Gare de l'Est* for the night train. He beamed a smile at me. "My dear Julie, one must always be on the lookout for coincidence!"

I exchanged the passes for matinee tickets, but soon apologized when we were taken to the theatre's cheapest, farthest seats in the upper balcony.

He joked, "I assure you that the power of Mounet-Sully's acting voice can reach even the heavens!"

The theatre, as it turned out, was not full and the usher graciously allowed us two seats closer. From the moment the curtain rose we watched King Oedipus spellbound. Actor Mounet-Sully, full-bearded as the king, fitted in a gold brocade robe, descended the palace steps in measured mournfulness, addressing the plague-ridden citizens of Thebes:

> **Ah, my poor children,**
>
> **what you come to seek**
>
> **is not unknown to me,**
>
> **you are sick**
>
> **and in your sickness**
>
> **there is not one so sick as I**

At the play's conclusion we were both stricken by a gloomy silence which lingered after we left the theatre. The uplift gained from cocaine had worn away to something akin to melancholy. I suggested a cheerful café as an antidote. We were in Montmartre, not far from the popular windmill cafés along the road leading up the Butte.

"At the Moulin de la Galette," I said, "there's music and outside dancing."

"I don't dance," he said.

"We can watch the dancers, and drink, and eat their delicious galettes." I locked my arm into his and we proceeded down Avenue Clichy, only to be intercepted by a flower vendor. The kindly, white-haired lady stepped forward, thrusting a small bouquet of white carnations in front of Sigmund. "Three centimes, Monsieur," she smiled, "Smell, Monsieur, such a sweet scent, not to be found even in a rose."

His reaction was like nothing I had ever seen. When the flower lady held up the bouquet closer to his face, he recoiled, his look one of sheer horror. I was as bewildered as the flower vendor. He looked pleadingly at me. Had the Oedipus tragedy left him vulnerable to some form of hysteria? He tottered, close to fainting as I kept him steady. The flower lady, utterly frightened, rushed away. Sigmund seemed unable to speak. I could only think that he slipped into his Mephisto dream, afflicted by the same neurological disorder.

"I must have a dose!" he managed to demand. I found the cobalt blue vial in his pocket, placed a drop on his tongue, then several more until I watched him regain his cocaine confidence. He now relished the opportunity to hike the winding Butte, so we did, but nearing the windmill entrance of the Moulin de la Galette, he hesitated at the sound of music and laughter.

"Perhaps we should go elsewhere more suitable for deep reflection, for I must sort out my feelings about the play. I feel somewhat unmoored."

"But... where shall we go?"

"The Montmartre cemetery is farther up the hill, isn't it?"

I was astounded. "You want to go to another cemetery?"

"Heinrich Heine, the German poet, Jewish, is buried there."

A terrible poet, I thought to myself. Taking his arm, I directed him into the café. "No cemeteries today, Dr. Freud."

The weather had warmed considerably and the outdoor garden was densely crowded with customers. We luckily found an empty table. "I'm quite thirsty," he said, signalling the waiter for a bottle of wine. I was glad to see his anxiety attack had been subdued by the cocaine. I had ingested enough of the drug for one day.

On a makeshift wood floor, taking up a large part of the garden, couples danced sprightly by us. The men pressed their partners close, quick stepping in carefree circles to lively gypsy music. Two guitarists and an accordionist, wearing gypsy head scarves, played under the bower of a large willow.

Sigmund gulped down his glass and poured out another. I had not seen him so thirsty. Was he going to talk about his anxiety attack? Surely the shuddering terror which overwhelmed him had been provoked by the white flowers thrust into his face, a parallel to the Mephisto Dream.

But he wished to talk about Sophocles' *Oedipus Rex.* "The play stirs my thinking, as if I should probe deeper."

I volunteered my impressions. "What worse tragedy to befall a man or woman than to unknowingly sleep with a parent? Mounet-Sully's performance as Oedipus was intensely moving, the palpable agony he showed when discovering his transgression was unforgettable. I can still see the moment when he tore the gold brooch from his dead mother's dress and gouged out his eyes."

"And his equal torture in having murdered his father," added Sigmund. "The twining of parricide and incest into Sophocles' drama cannot fail to shock."

We continued drinking, smoking, discussing the morbid aspects of the play. I imagined we were the only couple who looked out of place in a café of fun and music.

"Patricide... I wonder. Do you think it is a universal urge among mortals?" he asked.

"I've never given any thought to killing my father—that is, not consciously," I thought it smart to add.

He gave a small smile, as we both had long ago agreed that a division existed in the mind between knowing consciously and knowing unconsciously.

Unexpectedly, he brought up Paul Cezanne. "Patricide—not unlike the tragic component of Oedipus Rex—may well play a part in your painter friend's dream."

I argued for Cezanne. "I don't believe patricide was the unconscious wish in his dream. What he wanted was to reveal his true self to his father, his talent, and his son out of wedlock."

"How about competing wishes? Conflicting desires?" Brilliantly he returned to the cornerstone of what seemed his new theory for nightmarish dreams. "In any case," he went on, "the proof will come when enough dreams are collected so that we can establish patterns."

I remembered. *Gauguin's father, in the dream-fable, was buried at sea. Baby Paul had helped grease the plank.*

Dusk, without notice, had descended. Two waiters emerged and hoisted ladders to light the Japanese lanterns which hung on cords crisscrossing the tree branches and over the dance floor. A ladder, I recalled, a prop in Sigmund's dream play. The couples dancing were now softly bathed in the lambent glow of the paper lanterns. The coming night and first stars had them pressing their bodies closer together, the two guitars strumming slowed-down rhythms, and the accordion moaning sweetly. Romance was in the air. Our gaze followed the couples as they slow-glided past.

"I feel out of place here," he said, "and the time is late, Julie." He dropped down coins for our drinks. "I wouldn't want to miss my train."

Yes, I thought, we don't belong here.

III

We followed the curved road down the Butte. I debated whether to ask for more cocaine. There was little time left and I wanted to try and make a final interpretation of his dream.

I stopped him. "A drop on my tongue."

"Certainly." He produced the cobalt blue vial, placed a drop on my waiting tongue and one on his. We were both enlivened in a moment, continuing down the slope.

"Is it presumptuous of me," I asked, "to want to reach a deeper analysis of the Mephisto Dream?"

"Please proceed as far as you can."

"Monsieur Mephisto addressed you by your Jewish birth name, Sigismund Schlomo, correct?"

He nodded. "You have my undivided attention."

"Consider, the other day your wish was to visit a cemetery to honour the grave of a Jewish writer whom you greatly admire. Today, after what I can only label a panic attack, your first desire was to visit the grave of yet another Jewish writer of distinction who, as I recall, converted to Protestantism. Putting aside their literary talents, what do both men have in common? Jews, expatriates who figured out how to succeed in a European culture not particularly hospitable to the Jewish race. All of this following on the heels of Charcot's proposal to study Jewish degeneracy." I looked hard at him. "Did you not find your mentor's proposal, if not anti-Semitic, demeaning? Were you not placed in an awkward position?"

At this veritable speech of mine, he gave an approving nod. "I see where you're heading."

We resumed walking. "You earlier alluded to the probable conflict of desires in your dream, rooted in your choice of careers. But could there be a deeper conflict?"

"Multi-layers of conflict..." he murmured, "that's conceivable. Now spell out this conflict."

"You want to be accepted in a world of anti-Semitism. Charcot's world. You find encouragement in Ludwig Borne and Heinrich Heine who have successfully sloughed off their Jewishness. Switching religions, changing names. But you, Sigmund, still want to retain your Jewish identity."

He then surprised me. "Perhaps the devil does represent Charcot."

535

"A Charcot disguised allows you to express your anger toward him."

"So, it comes back to my conflict of desires!" He was now intent on making this idea fit. "I want to both hate Charcot for his whiff of anti-Semitism and love him for guiding me toward the challenges of hysteria. So the two desires are achieved by fighting him and succumbing to his greater power. Julie, you have given me much to ponder."

I breathed in my exhilaration. It seemed I had assisted in buttressing his new psychological construct of conflicting desires. But the foundation we built for the dream's purpose also held firm—a dream, no matter how unpleasant, concealed a wish. And I couldn't shake the feeling that in his dream he hid a deeper, more primary wish.

We found the *Gare de l'Est* almost deserted. He had to rouse a dozing attendant to find his checked suitcase in the baggage cage. Out on the station platform, we had our choice of empty benches. We sat and for a while seemed satisfied to follow our own private thoughts—mine went to the white flowers, to his horrific reaction to them, both in the Mephisto dream and today when the flower vendor offered her harmless bouquet.

I put forth the clue to him. "White flowers must lead to a memory."

I waited, taking out a cigarette from my purse. He lit the cigarette for me, replying, "Stored in the unconscious are memories, I believe, more numerous than stars in the sky."

"White carnations," I prodded. "Specifically, white carnations."

His look told me a memory had emerged, but Sigmund took time to light yet another cigar. "In Austria and Germany it is customary for those who wish to quietly profess their anti-Semitic inclinations to do so by wearing a white carnation in their lapel." He shrugged. "But yet, inserted into the devil's lapel, or Charcot's lapel, was a red carnation, the very colour our Viennese citizens wear who want to reveal their sympathies for Jews."

I waited, I smoked, but he seemed unprepared to say any more. Did he still think the deepest meaning of the dream had little to do with anti-Semitism? Only now I was convinced that the compass of his dream pointed toward his native Austria. There were the pfennigs, the coin of Austria. I had a hunch that such dream oddities stored the greatest content. I pulled out my dream book, scanned the Mephisto Dream and quoted, "'I go to fetch my hat—which cost me a pretty pfennig.'" I quoted again, "'As the long day passes, an occasional pfennig is dropped in my upturned hat.'"

I raised my eyebrows questioningly. He gave a smile unfamiliar, perhaps bitter. Taking off his hat, he strangely set it upside down on the ground. I waited, knowing we were going to the crux. "You were shrewd, Julie, to question the hat and the pfennigs." From his pocket he took out a coin, an Austrian pfennig, and tossed it into the hat. "Before my train arrives, there's time to tell a story... or call it a fable.

"In Freiberg, where I was born, a boy and his father took a Sunday morning walk through the town centre. They passed people dressed in their Sunday best, most heading for Church, many wearing white carnations in their lapels. The father and son, wearing red carnations, were Jewish. The father, during their idle walk, was stirred to share a memory: On a similar Sunday stroll, when the father was a young man, he found himself in front of a stranger who blocked his way. On this particular day, the father then a young man, proudly wore his new hat, quite impressive, made of minx fur. The stranger, a white carnation in his lapel, who might have been going to Church, came right up to the father's face, and with a single blow, he knocked off the fur hat, which went into the muddy street. The stranger shouted, 'Jew! Get off the pavement!'" Sigmund paused for a few reflective puffs before resuming. "The boy, but ten years old, naively expected his father's story to have an epic ending, surely a heroic response from his father. He asked, 'What did you then do, Father?' 'I went into the street,' the father answered, 'picked up the hat, and went on my way.' Sigmund picked up his own hat, took out the coin, and put the hat beside him on the bench. "I tried," he switched to first person, "to detect in my father's voice some hint of his feelings. Anger, bitterness, regret? The insult engendered nothing in him but placid acceptance. I thought to myself, 'Is the purpose of this degrading incident to inspire me to similar docility?'"

The faraway sound of a train whistle seemed to give Sigmund a reason to end the story. I stated the obvious, "I guess you were gravely disappointed in your father's behaviour."

"I was left to live with two facts," he answered. "My father's conduct, from any imagined view, would never reach the level of heroic and Jews were a distinctly different people, to be judged by some as less worthy than a dog." He gave the cigar a few more puffs. "Yes, lessons learned, but the incident of the knocked off hat and the sting it caused to a ten-year-old boy obviously burrowed deep beneath my conscious memory for all these years—buried, but alive."

"Undisturbed," I said, "until Charcot's proposal to study the neuropathology of Jews."

"Yes, yes! And the long-ago memory disguised!" He puffed. "The dream's subterfuge."

We both marvelled at the sophistication of the dream process. He excitedly concluded, "The subconscious asserts its existence through the dream, demands its desires or cross desires be expressed by exhibiting appropriate scenes."

"Your long-ago memory rearranged, why?" I asked.

A whistle shriek from the unseen train startled us to rise. Farther down the tracks two railway men waved warning lanterns. Sigmund picked up his suitcase. I followed him to the platform's edge, wanting his brilliant mind to answer my question and innumerable others. The meaning of the soaped message on the window? A wish for Sigmund to be blameless? Then for what transgression? But paramount to understand, what was the underlying desire in his dream?

The station attendant, blowing a whistle, ordered us to stay clear of the tracks. The train, with sounds of grinding steel and hissing steam, slowly pulled in.

"Julie..." he looked at me with such affection that I wanted to cry, "you mustn't stop collecting dreams. We have more work to do together." A conductor from inside the train assisted with the suitcase. Before stepping up, he gave me one last fond look. The train seemed to be making impatient clanking noises. "We shall correspond!" Sigmund Freud promised. "We will be fearless in our exploration, *n'est-ce pas?*"

I eagerly nodded and he was gone.

Preview of
The Dream Collector
Book II

NEW BEGINNINGS

I

In spite of Charcot's dire warnings, I took Sabrine out of Salpêtrière. She was released to me carrying a portmanteau which contained little more than an extra petticoat, several hair ribbons and a tortoise comb. The morning was dismally grey, a dank chill hung in the air as we stood in the central courtyard, hand in hand, staring at the Mazarin gate, unlocked and wide open. We were quite alone, except for scatterings of plump pigeons pecking for things between the damp stones.

We took the first steps toward the opened gate, only to hesitantly stop at the sound of harsh shouting. From the fifth story windows of the Pinel Building we saw indistinct faces peering through the bars. The top floor housed *les isolees*, the isolated ones, those women considered irrevocably insane. They were now greatly agitated, shouting down at us with a desperate plea—"Take us! Take us with you! Take us, too!"

I was familiar with the isolated ward, on occasions visiting them. Some of the more unmanageable had to be straight-jacketed, a few chained, but I found that whenever I approached even the worst of the raging women, just to loosen the straitjacket and patiently hold a hand made their rage in time vanish; though unable to recognize who I might be, each and every woman soon turned trustingly docile.

Now I watched them crowded at the bars; their plight appeared more hopeless than ever. A clamorous chant arose from every window —"Sabrine! Sabrine! Sabrine!"

Word had spread, even among *les isolees*, that Sabrine was gaining her freedom. My sister listened, not at all perturbed, to the chorus of troubled minds calling out to her. Behind their bars did they think her name alone was a talisman to set them free? "Sabrine, Sabrine!"

And she let go of my hand. Anonymous faces pressed against the bars of the windows and a myriad of disembodied hands reached through, grasping at nothing but air. Sabrine directed her gaze toward them, her look one of utter serenity. When she closed her eyes, I tried not to panic, but feared that she might be on the verge of a hystero-epileptic attack. She dropped the portmanteau to the ground, outstretched her arms to the ward above. (I will swear, to this day, my sister embraced in that moment every broken heart.)

The tumult incredulously died, the plaintive cries and pleas ceased. The morning stillness reigned again. Her outstretched arms had a quieting effect on everyone. But I remained anxious.

Are her outstretched arms a preamble to the crucifixion pose? Has she lapsed into a standing trance? Has the hysteria of Salpêtrière lured her back?

I spoke evenly, "Bijou, I see our hired carriage just outside the gate."

Opening her eyes, she had the most natural look, as if nothing had happened. She dropped her arms, picked up the portmanteau and smiled. "Paris awaits."

Not wishing to endure one moment more inside the city of the misbegotten, I escorted her as quickly as possible out the gate. On the other side of *Boulevard de l'Hopital*, the carriage and the coachman waited, he bundled ear to toe in a ragged coat and thick scarf, the reins ready in his hands, the two roans exhaling white feathery plumes of mist.

She eagerly climbed into the back cab while I gave the driver the written address. But I instructed him to first taxi leisurely through the *Bois du Boulogne*. We now had time to do as we wished.

The horses fell into a rhythmic trot, our carriage car rocking us gently as Sabrine stayed intently interested in the passing scenery. She took to humming cheerfully, occasionally turning with a reassuring smile. I thought her smile expressed new happiness of being liberated, of the fact that we were once more together to share the adventure of life. No one under the sun, moon or stars would separate us again.

After a pleasant ride through the park, I signalled the driver, tapping the little window, and he steered the horses toward Montmartre. The moment seemed appropriate to hand her the present I had saved for weeks. "A diary to write down your thoughts, and..." I so hoped, "your poems, but only if you wish." My sister did not disappoint me. When we reached our destination, her new home, she showed me the poem she had composed.

> **you are vellum to me**
> **crisp at the edges**
> **i want to slow-turn**
> **your slim-paged ivory self**
> **and peruse you voraciously!**

We fell into an embrace. So much was waiting to make our lives whole again.

The Dream Collector: Book II

Sabrine & Vincent van Gogh

coming early 2024

ACKNOWLEDGEMENTS

My thanks and unwavering appreciation to Kathleen (Kt) Brannigan who astutely read and critiqued a very rough novel-in-progress. Kt saw promise.

I'm especially indebted to Hazel Smith Adamczyk who dared to give a most thorough interpretive reading of *The Dream Collector* and understood what I was trying to say. She gave me hope that there might be other perceptive readers in the world at large.

Thank-you, Hazel.

ABOUT THE AUTHOR

R.w. Meek has a Master's degree in Art History from the American University in Washington, D.C., his areas of expertise are Impressionism and Post-Impressionism, with a particular interest in Vincent van Gogh. He has interned and conducted tours at the National Museum of American and the National Gallery of Art. In 2022 and 2023 five of his chapter excerpts from his novel *The Dream Collector* were either finalists or published in various literary journals. The author has also won the Palm Beach Book Festival Competition for "Best Writer in Palm Beach' his manuscript judged by a panel of NYT Best Selling authors. *The Dream Collector* also received gold and silver medals in the Historical Fiction Company literary contest and earned runner-up for the "Best Historical Fiction' of 2022.

Visit the author's website at

www.ronmeekauthor.com

www.historiumpress.com

www.ingramcontent.com/pod-product-compliance
Lightning Source LLC
Chambersburg PA
CBHW032100310726
48972CB00001B/39